Prisoner

By Andrew S. Ball
Copyright 2020 Andrew S. Ball
Cover by Gareth Otton

License Notes
All rights reserved. No part of this book may be used or reproduced in any manner whatsoever without written permission except in the case of brief quotations embodied in critical articles and reviews, or for similar purposes guided by fair use.

ISBN: 9798646950056

Table of Contents

Prologue: Wheeling and Dealing
Chapter 1: Down the Rabbit Hole
Chapter 2: Running with the Devils
Chapter 3: Ten Percent
Chapter 4: Purgatory
Chapter 5: Rules of Engagement
Chapter 6: Power Play
Chapter 7: Schism
Chapter 8: State of the Union
Chapter 9: The Prince of Wallachia
Chapter 10: Go Browns
Chapter 11: Smith and Wesson
Chapter 12: Teaming Up
Chapter 13: Games in the Dark
Chapter 14: Beyond Thunderdome
Chapter 15: Double Play
Chapter 16: Behind the Scenes
Chapter 17: Pregame
Chapter 18: Fight Night
Chapter 19: Monsters
Chapter 20: Crypt Keepers
Chapter 21: The Contractor Program
Chapter 22: End of the Line
Epilogue

####

Acknowledgements
About the Author
Novels by Andrew S. Ball

####

For my grandmother, who taught me to appreciate the finer things in life.

####

PRISONER

Prologue
Wheeling and Dealing

Two individuals stood inside an office overlooking Dis, the capital of the Demon Empire.

The first was the Emperor, Beelzebub. Although humanoid in form, his skin was the color of fresh blood. Two ivory horns protruded from his forehead, and where there would be a nose on a man's face, there was only a stretch of unbroken skin on the devil's. He wore a plain black shirt that stretched tight across broad shoulders—even with the top three buttons undone—and crisp black slacks. It was professional but comfort-first attire.

The second was an ambassador of the Klide, Xikanthus. Xik's appearance was that of a man stretched thin by a funhouse mirror. His torso was a tiny cereal box perched on spindly legs. A fat frog's head rested on his odd silhouette, bulbous cheeks projecting over narrow shoulders and wide red eyes atop his forehead. He was dressed in a black pinstripe suit, but the details were wrong—too many buttons, two breast pockets, as if the tailor understood the general style of the clothing but not the function of the various parts. He held a wooden cane in white-gloved fingers, looking like a bit player in a vaudeville act.

Xik stared at Beelzebub's beady black eyes, blinking occasionally.

Beelzebub did not blink.

Xik held all the cards, and had all the advantages, but he couldn't help but feel the slightest bit nervous under that ceaseless stare. Beelzebub was—for now—the most powerful magical being that existed in the twin human and demon worlds. His magical aura couldn't affect Xik, but iron-fisted tyrants had a different aura that had nothing to do with magic.

The office itself was far more mundane than either of its occupants. The work desk and the chairs facing it were a dark wood. The upholstery was a matching deep forest green. If not for the wall of windows revealing a sprawling view of the bustling spaceport, it might have been any other office.

In the distance, the docks bustled with activity. Ships landed and took off in gouts of flame and chemical exhaust. It formed a permanent smog that drifted around the port. Cargo was rapidly loaded and unloaded, shuttled to and from the base of the ships by container-hauling cruisers that hovered above the ground, each one easily five times the size of the 18-wheelers that performed a similar function on the human world.

The spaceport was the beating heart of the capital, a soaring construct of steel and light. It loomed high over an already towering cityscape, a twisted and tangled network of buildings built higher and closer to that centerpiece like metal piranhas leaping to get their piece of flesh. The twin demon suns radiated with a blue-white glow, but the ash and soot scattered the light into a sickly grey haze.

After entering the room—and somewhat surprising its occupant—Xik kept himself very still. Negotiations had only just commenced, and he was not entirely sure Beelzebub wouldn't attack him. If he did, it was unlikely he could harm Xik, but it would certainly harm the prospect of polite conversation.

And in the *unlikely*—but theoretically possible—case that Beelzebub could harm him directly, the desk and chairs between them would provide about as much protection as tissue paper.

"I'm not the ignorant fool you suppose me to be," Beelzebub said. His voice crackled like hot coals, as though a fire was about to ignite. "Only those without magical talent can become a contractor. At least give me the credit of having eyes and ears on Earth."

"I apologize if I offended," Xik said. "Perhaps we got off on the wrong foot. Allow me to introduce myself properly." His words came slowly, each one carefully selected as if drawn from his hat one-by-one. "I am Xikanthus Vol'mund Dovian pom'Nafalstra, Klide representative to both Earth, and the Empire. If it pleases you, I am happy to be addressed as Xik." The frog cleared his throat. "I am here, your Excellency, with an offer of allegiance. The same offer given to the humans."

"You are here to attempt to use me in your games."

"This isn't a game."

"Don't patronize me," Beelzebub said.

"Do you suppose to know everything about contractors?" Xik asked.

"I know enough."

Xik glanced at a chair on his side of the desk. "Might I sit?"

Beelzebub gestured with a finger. The chair quietly slid across the carpet and stopped behind Xik. Xik took the offered seat, folding his stick-legs over one another. He waved his own hand, and a cup of tea filled with a steaming purple ink appeared in his fingers. He lifted the cup and took a long slurp.

Beelzebub remained standing, keeping his gaze on Xik. His expression remained a flat stare.

"I have, perhaps, manipulated some humans," Xik said. "Left some things unsaid, if only for their own good. With you, I would seek a more open partnership, though not exactly in the sense you mentioned earlier."

"I'm listening."

"That I am a diplomat is only part of the truth," Xik said. "Ambassador is a loose term. An accidental mistranslation, shall we say. I am a member of the Anti-Vorid Bureau, Department of Node World Defense and Development. My job is to halt the spread of the Vorid. We seek to encircle the Vorid through the multiverse, creating a net through which they cannot spread."

Beelzebub's eyes held a fleck of curiosity. "And Earth is one of these node worlds, I assume?"

"And so is the demon world, since it tied itself together with Earth way back when," Xik said. "A world possessing many connections to other worlds is inherently more valuable when traveling through the multiverse. Such travel takes time and energy. Longer routes become prohibitive. Key connectors are pivotal on the scale of the greater conflict.

"More specifically, nodes are worlds positioned at intersections that have been deemed strategically vital by our prediction algorithms. These worlds are given higher priority ratios and assigned a development agent. In this case," Xik said, tipping his hat, "myself."

"And contractors are your weapon of choice to accomplish this task?"

"They are the tip of the spear, you might say," Xik said. "Making worlds aware of their invasion and giving them the means to fight back—that is my job.

"The ability of the Vorid to spread quickly, and thereby accrue the blunt force upon which they rely, depends on ease of movement and consumption of worlds without being discovered. They do this by replacing the consumed with soul-shells, and these buffer a greater magical reaction in which the society as a whole forgets that the consumed individual ever existed." Xik poked a finger up; this left his teacup behind, floating in front of him. "Of course, this punches holes in a society. People cannot justify their existence if they forget their own parents. The following pervasive discord and perceived madness leads to widespread collapse, accelerating the ease of total absorption.

"What the Vorid cannot afford is to get bogged down. They want the maximum output from minimum input. That is the weakness of their system of warfare—and capitalizing upon this is how the Klide are building the foundation for a counterattack. A direct assault is untenable. We want to stretch them thin, bait them into overcommitting their resources, then cut them off at the knees, so to speak."

Beelzebub listened to Xik without much interruption. Xik felt the tension leave the devil's expression; he was less to think his time wasted if he was getting valuable perspective, regardless of the deal offered. That was Xik's foot in the proverbial door.

"It would seem," Beelzebub said, "that the humans have bogged them down and driven them away. That doesn't explain why you're sitting in my office."

"You think this is bogged down?" Xik took another sip from his ink tea, then set it back down in the air. "The siege launched a few days ago on New York was a minor probe, the lord sent to lead it the lowliest of scouts in their warrior class. His death is nothing. Stimulated by the setback, other, greater minds will turn toward Earth. They will recognize our hand at work. They will move quickly, before the seeds I have planted can grow into trees and provide the shade that Earth and your empire so desperately need. Or, perhaps they won't. We don't have a complete understanding of how they prioritize targets. Their zealotry tends to fog up our logic."

"You speak of the demons and the humans as a single unit," Beelzebub said.

Xik peered at Beelzebub from behind his cup. He'd expected more interest, more energy. The fact that Beelzebub was showing neither meant that he was content to let Xik talk. Maybe he was waiting to hear something he didn't already know.

"The Demon Empire and Earth universes have been classified as two parts of a single whole due to their interlocked nature. Any human or demon that could become weapon enough—backed by their society—would suffice to complete my mission. And that is where you, Your Excellency, have an advantage."

Beelzebub's shark teeth revealed themselves again. "I already have my entire society behind me," he said. "Whereas this Daniel is a pariah."

"Precisely." Xik released his emptied cup; it vanished. He swung his legs back open and set one hand on each knee, facing where Beelzebub stood. "You are in a position of great leverage to take on the Vorid, given the tools to do so. The humans are paranoid regarding the contractor magic to the point of embracing suicide. Daniel was the largest, strongest tree, by far. They have pulled him up by the roots."

"He was idiotic to let them," Beelzebub said. "But then, he was only human."

"You are an emperor," Xik said. "Your society will not question you. And Daniel is in Hell—in your prison."

Beelzebub folded his arms, considering. "Alright, Xik. Make me a contractor. I'll kill the boy and fight your war."

"I thought as much myself, but then I had a better idea," Xik said, spreading his hands. "Ripen the fruit, first. Let Daniel work his way through Hell. Inevitably, he'll kill plenty of inmates. While he's linked to the prison, his magic will remain restricted, even if his power grows stronger. When the time is right, you waltz in and pluck it for yourself."

"What if I don't like your plan?" Beelzebub asked.

"I like my plan," Xik said, "and you'll have to go along with it if you want to be a contractor."

Beelzebub's eyes narrowed to pinpricks. "It sounds to me like you're trying to protect your original investment."

"I am trying to create a weapon in the most efficient manner possible, while simultaneously ensuring that Earth remains out of Vorid hands," Xik said. "The inmates of Hell represent a collection of some of the most powerful demons and humans from both worlds. Let Daniel…process them, on your behalf."

"I can slaughter and absorb the inmates with or without your magic," Beelzebub said. "It won't be hard to convince the humans to let me kill their inmates as well during these times of war. One less worry."

"You would have already done so if it would do you any good," Xik said. "You've hit your ceiling, haven't you? You did that a long time ago."

Beelzebub remained silent, but his face grew stony.

"What's the recovery rate of your spell? Five percent? Ten, at most." Xik chuckled. "Your growth has stagnated. Your magic reserves are already so large that harvesting more souls is a waste of your time—like adding raindrops into an ocean. And as your empire grows larger, it will be harder and harder for you to keep a grip on things by the threat of your power alone. Like a child trying to hold a ball too big for small hands." Xik brushed a hand across his knee, wiping a speck of dust from his pant leg. "I can change that, but I require cooperation on your end to demonstrate that you're worthy of trust. I have a plan, and it ends with you at the top. You have the qualifications."

A soft, faint rumble filled the room. Xik could see a huge transport ship lifting off the ground in the distance, propelled by rockets and a black haze of gravitational magic. Once it reached a safe height, the magic expanded, wrapping the entire ship up the sides and around the top.

"The recovery rate is somewhat over seven percent," Beelzebub admitted.

"Crude," Xik said. "By your standards, it's the most potent of magic, but by mine"—Xik gestured toward the spaceship out the window—"you're trying to build a spacecraft with scrap iron and spit."

"Get," Beelzebub said, "to the point."

Xik cleared his throat. "The contractor enchantment has an initial 87 percent recovery rate, and it immediately stabilizes the new soul's energy—you don't have to refine anything yourself. This is why it's so potent, why they grow so fast—no escaped energy after the transfer."

Beelzebub's hands clenched tight. His black needle-nails retracted, saving him from gouging his own palms. His eyes were wide. "That isn't possible. Souls fade too quickly, it would have to—"

"It was reverse engineered from Vorid enchantments," Xik said, "but it's still not as good as the original. If you want to know the theory, you'll have to ask them. We have our own specialties, but when it comes to energy extraction from living beings, the Vorid are the foremost experts we have encountered in the multiverse."

"What do the Klide specialize in?" Beelzebub said.

"A few things. Speed of travel, efficiency, obfuscation." Xik met the devil's gaze. "Destruction."

For the first time, Beelzebub looked away. He followed the departing freighter as it left the field of view of the window. "I understand," he said, "that only those without developed magical talent can become contractors."

"Anyone with some magic, no matter how tiny the spark, can become a contractor."

"You lied, then," Beelzebub said.

"I left some things unsaid. It's not my fault everyone else filled in the blanks with their own assumptions."

"Why did you lie," Beelzebub said, pressing his point, "about who can become a contractor?"

The quiet extended out an uncomfortably long time. Beelzebub's nails clicked against one another. Xik let the question hang without a response, determined to outlast him. He'd given the devil plenty enough as it was.

Beelzebub broke the silence. "What do you want in exchange for the spell?"

"Daniel will gather the souls in Hell. In the meantime, I want you to aid Earth with your military forces. The Vorid aren't done."

"It is as you said—I am still emperor in name, but my power grows weaker over time. Mounting concerted efforts can be...challenging. Especially amongst such varied species."

"Then you had best get started," Xik said. "Besides, I can assist your efforts. A little nudge here, a flick there. They'll have motivation to meet with you when you call for them. The war effort might even serve to strengthen your authority."

"We don't go to Earth without summoning rituals," Beelzebub said. "Demons have always followed that aspect of the treaty."

"The humans have already come to you to renegotiate that, haven't they? They're beginning to understand the risks after New York was destroyed. Their treaty holders didn't meet up solely to banish Daniel, after all."

Beelzebub squinted. Xik could practically see the gears working in his head. This was the fact that Beelzebub could not escape. He didn't have to accept Xik's offer of power, but he absolutely needed the humans and their world to survive. He needed Earth, and he needed it intact, with all its billions of lives. It was time to push him.

"The prison is threatened," Xik said.

Beelzebub turned away and stepped up to the wall of windows. Another ship had landed, replacing the last in the same docking bay, this time a mining vessel. The steam of coolant roiled around the bulky, space-scarred hull, clouding over the smaller ships darting around it.

"The prison is fine," Beelzebub said.

"It's creaking a bit, then," Xik said. "An engine running low on oil. I suspect that your chief inmate will want a bit of violent remuneration."

Beelzebub turned on his heel. "You would threaten me, here? Can you feel the enchantments in this room? I could kill you in eight different ways, *ambassador*, and all of them are excruciatingly painful."

Xik knew, in fact, that Beelzebub had fourteen different such methods at his disposal, but he decided not to bring that up. "I'm not threatening you," Xik said. "I'm stating facts. As the situation stands, the Vorid will consume humanity. When that happens, the soul stream flowing between your worlds will grind to a halt. The prison will fail. How could it not? There won't be any more souls. You can't amend that portion of the treaty, or you would have already done it."

"Now I understand," Beelzebub said. "If the prison opens after the Vorid have finished with Earth, you're worried they'll eat it for dessert, aren't you?"

"My understanding is that it would be problematic."

"Problematic does not describe what would happen if the prison breaks," Beelzebub snapped. "You don't understand what you're tampering with." His eyes burned with anger. "You probably think that even if the worst comes to pass, you'll simply walk away, move on to your next *diplomatic* mission. You won't be able to save yourself from what is inside of Hell, I assure you. You'll be eaten alive, along with everything else in its path."

Xik was taken aback. Beelzebub's outburst could be construed as frustration with Xik's ignorance, but that seemed unlikely. He was truly frightened at the idea of the prison failing.

That fear only solidified Xik's strategy.

He decided to change the subject. "Daniel made himself the focal point of my plans, and now he's in your control. That makes you the focal point of my plans." Xik placed his fingertips together. "It's ironic. He was so apathetic, at first, so detached. Maybe that's precisely why he performed better—he wasn't as invested. Those with the power of contractors can be...unstable. Maybe it's the experience. Power tends to change people."

"You really enjoy wasting my time, don't you?" Beelzebub asked.

"I wouldn't have wasted it if I could wrench him straight out of Hell," Xik said, "but I need your help to alter the seal."

Beelzebub inhaled sharply between his teeth. "You tampered with the spell?"

"It was the first thing I tried," Xik said, "but it's quite a monstrosity. Linked to you, linked to several humans on Earth, linked between universes...we don't use such magic. I couldn't touch the important bits without the whole thing imploding in on itself."

Beelzebub became still—very still. Too still, as if he were trying not to show a reaction. He was holding his breath.

Ah, Xik thought. *Not so confident now, are you?*

"Of course," Xik said, "I have a third option on this meandering road of consolidation. Neither you nor Daniel. The prisoner of Hell." Xik smiled. "But if half your records are true, then we don't want to go there all willy-nilly, do we?"

"Records." Beelzebub snorted a cloud of smoke. "I lived it. I know what information you think you've gleaned. I didn't put the real knowledge somewhere anyone else could access." Beelzebub gestured at himself. "I'm the only record of that incident. I'll tell you this: you can't control that power, and you can't destroy it. That's why we had to seal it away. If there are still more powerful Vorid, I imagine it would be something like them."

"A disturbing prospect." Xik put his hands on the arms of his chair and stood. He was tall himself, in his own spindly way—enough to match the emperor's height—though it was rather like a twig facing off against a redwood. "So let's not go there. Better the devil I know, than the devil I don't, as the humans say."

Beelzebub made a displeased grunt.

"You are my primary means of moving the development of your twin universes forward," Xik said. "Another link in the fence holding back the Vorid."

"Another link in the fence." Beelzebub looked at him. "It's really quite something."

"It is," Xik said, tipping his head to the side, "but I get the feeling you're referring to something else."

"This was planned from the beginning," Beelzebub said, "wasn't it? Why bet on a lone toss of the die when you can throw a fistful of them? You created foot soldiers designed to collect and funnel power to one source—the sole individual that would absorb all the others. All under your watch."

"And that so happens to be you. It was almost Daniel." Xik's tone gained a distant melancholy, as if he was recalling a car accident that happened to the friend of a friend in the next town over. "He's a nice young man, once you get to know him. He never liked power. But power doesn't like him, either."

Light flickered in through the windows. A hovercar was passing near the office tower. The shadows of the furniture flashed to the left, then rotated right across the room as the vehicle flew by. Beelzebub's skin shifted from maroon to bright red. Xik's top hat cast his eyes in a line of darkness.

"How did the magicians capture him?" Beelzebub asked.

"He gave himself up to prove he was on their side," Xik said.

Beelzebub made a disparaging noise in the back of his throat. "When is he arriving in Hell?"

"Right about..." Xik looked up at the ceiling in thought. "Now."

Beelzebub growled a sigh. A cloud of smoke escaped from between his fangs. "Are you enjoying yourself, Xik?"

"No, Your Excellency. I don't enjoy any part of this."

"I don't think I believe that." Beelzebub clasped his hands behind his back. "Alright, ambassador. I'll convince Daniel to take care of business down below, and I will gather my forces to assist Earth. In exchange, you'll grant me this enchantment."

Xik nodded. "I'll pay half now, and half later," he said.

"Clarify."

"I'll enable you to absorb the power of the souls you slay—except for humans, and my contractors," Xik said. "None of that until the Vorid are taken care of. They're the real threat."

"All these restrictions," Beelzebub said. His smile could have sharpened knives. "Certainly you don't think I'm that untrustworthy?"

"I trust you to act in your own best interest," Xik said.

"Fair enough, Xikanthus," Beelzebub said. "And when Daniel's side is done, and Earth is secured..."

"I'll complete your enchantment, and he and the rest are fair game," Xik said. "He'd be a sitting duck in your prison. What you do after that is your business, so long as you stand a vigil against future Vorid incursions."

"I can come up with something to keep the boy motivated," Beelzebub said. "Keep him killing."

"That would do nicely," Xik said. "The stronger he becomes, the stronger, in turn, you will be."

"When will I receive the first half of the enchantment?"

"As soon as I've determined your army has in fact arrived to reinforce Earth's magicians," Xik said.

"Then we have an accord," Beelzebub said. "Now get out of my office. You've made a wreck of my schedule."

Xik was prepared to transport himself away, but a vibration under his left sleeve stopped him. He walked out the mundane way, closing the office door behind him. Probably best to keep Beelzebub's observation of Klide magic to a minimum, in any case.

As he turned, one of Beelzebub's aides—another red-skinned devil—swept around the corner of the hallway, his walk hurried and anxious. Xik stepped out of the way. The devil passed the Klide ambassador without so much as looking at him, then rapped on the door. Beelzebub's voice called for entry, and Xik darted around the corner; he didn't want to be caught lingering.

All the hallways in the imperial capital building looked the same. The walls were covered with yellowed paint that might have once been off-white. The carpet was tan. Sterile white light shone from scattered track lighting. The place was intense in its plainness.

Xik had studied Beelzebub carefully; he studied everyone he met with on his missions before speaking to them. The emperor's financial and political empire was garish on the outside, complete with publicity stunts, show trials, and the crown jewel, PrisonWatch. Inside—like the interior of the office, and the decor of the halls—it was strictly functional, worn down to the most efficient minimum possible. He hid a highly functional machine underneath an outer shield of bravado and intimidation. The thousands of years of stable rule, give or take a few recent rebellions, informed Xik that the strategy was effective.

Outside a small zone of quiet that surrounded Beelzebub's central office, bureaucrats, officials, and military personnel scurried about in a dance of uniforms and clearance badges. Between the demons zipped small drones powered by a combination of physical principles and magical sigils. Most of them carried private messages between parts of the building; this reduced the risk of outside interception. If the need arose, they would swarm and eliminate any intruder. Xik observed them with the same casual interest modern humans might consider a carrier pigeon.

Xik passed the drones and the demons of all shapes and sizes without raising a glance, let alone an alarm—though he did have to duck a few times for passing robots. They would have passed through him, but at that distance, even their weak sensors might detect his magic.

Once he found an intersection that was relatively isolated, he reached into his sleeve and withdrew a small metal disc. A point of purple light glowed in its center. He pressed it.

The disc beeped. Blue lettering was flung up onto the wall in front of him.

Xikanthus Vol'mund Dovian pom'Nafalstra,

Universes KDY.234skz943.gamma 21.67-A and 21.67-B and Special Class World 21.67-C have passed your requested awareness review. Their collective Import Class has been raised accordingly from C-5 to B-2. Your allotted energy conduit has been increased to reflect this. Specific requests for temporary injections into your conduit may now be presented to the Board for review. Please allow several hours before requisition is necessary and submit detailed action plans to help streamline the review process. Contact your direct supervisor with questions or concerns.

Thank you for your continued work,

Anti-Vorid Bureau Review Board, KDY Sector

Assistant Board Member Gravan Kal'Seckt Tremb pom'Kash

Xik dragged his finger across the disc, scrolling down the message. Underneath the formal letter was an attached note from his supervisor.

Xikanthus,

You got your approval. If that's not enough to help with your little master plan, then tough luck, you're stuck with the fallback strategy. So don't screw up.

And don't get yourself directly involved in the combat again. We don't need another BYT.alpha. The press eviscerated us last time, and if heads have to roll, yours is hitting the floor before mine.

I mean it.

— Libannon

Import Class B-2. That was better than he'd hoped for; more than a full letter grade.

Xik tapped the purple dot, and the blue projection on the wall vanished. The disc flew from his palm and reattached itself to the inside of his sleeve. He started off down the hall.

Beelzebub was a dangerous element—more unpredictable and capable than Xik initially estimated, and not to be trusted. But in the grand scale of this conflict, the threat he posed simply didn't matter. In front of a black hole, what difference did it make if the star was red or yellow? Everything was sucked in and crushed down just the same.

Xik began to vanish into midair, starting at his shoes, then working up his legs; and then his arms and torso began to vaporize. The last thing to go was his broad grin, a wide smile that pulled his skin tight like green plastic wrap stretched around bone.

Chapter 1
Down the Rabbit Hole

Daniel stood in darkness.

The doors of Hell had shut behind him. He was cut off from his magic. The magicians on Earth were fine with letting the theater burn down as long as they had the best seat in the house. Xik hadn't bailed him out. The frog had only confirmed the worst.

Rachel was dead.

There were wails around him, screams cutting through the air. He stood where he was, unmoving, head down. He couldn't see his feet. He imagined things creeping toward him, ready to grab him and drag him into the dark.

Daniel's jaw ached. His face felt clenched and twisted, his features crushed between anger and fear. He felt a cold chill on his back and shivered.

White lights slammed on. Daniel winced and blinked rapidly. His wrists were still bound by the stone bracers placed on him back on Earth, so all he could do was raise his arms and try to shield his eyes as best he could.

"Great take everybody! Wrap it up and get it ready for the evening broadcast. These contractor guys always give the ratings a kick."

Daniel was baffled. His eyes began to adjust, and the scene in front of him came into focus.

Several white floodlights lined one wall, illuminating the inside of the entrance to the prison. The stone around Daniel ended only a few feet away, transforming from medieval balustrades and gothic carvings into plain grey concrete—as if he was standing on the business end of a photoshoot, and the industrial backdrop was now plain to see.

People were moving around the lights—demons.

A gnome ran under a wooden sawhorse, clutching a glowing blue sphere in his tiny hands. Stomping in the opposite direction was a hulking minotaur, a humanoid monstrosity with a head like a bull and hooves for feet. A stone column the size of a telephone pole was hefted over one of its shoulders. An ink-black creature hovering at the minotaur's opposite shoulder made Daniel flinch—that was a nightmare, a skeletal beast that could phase through solid objects. They'd hounded Daniel for days back in New York, trying to catch him off guard and rip his guts out. And now one was angrily jabbing a claw in consternation and demanding the column be adjusted a few inches to the right. The minotaur made frustrated noises as it shifted the burden.

Daniel turned, and his mind spun faster than his gaze as he watched several of them help themselves to food laid out on a table behind the production equipment. A tall, crow-headed harpy was picking at finger sandwiches with its beak, tossing them into the air, then gulping them down. Surrounding the harpy were imps, little green-skinned goblins dotted with warts across their noses and foreheads. Next to the imps was what looked like a woman with sky blue skin and deep, electric-blue hair, though she was facing away from him. The fins protruding from above her ears made her inhuman enough that he didn't want to see her face.

Daniel almost felt relief when he saw a normal person near the gaggle of imps—and then he saw the scales going up the back of its shoulders and neck, and the raptor claw jutting from its ankles and clacking on the ground.

"Clear the set! We've got the brothers coming up in two minutes!"

"I thought you told them to space the sendings out at least five minutes."

"It wasn't them. Humans screwed it up."

"Why am I not surprised?"

"Hey kid, move it! Get out from in front of the gate!"

Daniel froze up. He was pretty sure they meant him, though he wasn't sure who was speaking to him. He took a hesitant step forward. His eyes darted around, trying to take in something that made sense.

"Everyone relax. He doesn't know any better."

Daniel turned his head toward the voice. A red-skinned horror stalking toward him was the voice of reason in question. It looked like a normal man wearing a relatively normal white shirt, except the man was dipped in firetruck red paint, had black marbles for eyes, grew rows of teeth like white razorblades, and had its nose ripped off and sealed up with more paint.

Holy shit.

It offered a hand that ended in black needle-nails, then drew it back, frowning. "You've still got the handcuffs? I don't know who's sending you people down here, but they really don't get the procedure right. Alright, follow me. I'll explain."

The red thing turned and started walking away. Daniel hesitated, glanced at the heavy stone keeping his wrists clamped in front of him, then started after it. "Wait, wait! What the hell is happening?"

"You're *in* Hell," the thing said, not slowing its pace. "We'll walk and talk, okay? You've got places to be."

They quickly left the noisy circus of a set behind and entered a uniform concrete hallway that led straight into the complex. Pipes and cables ran along the ceiling, some of it bunched together, other pieces hanging loose and haphazard. Green lights glowed above the tangle of factory-like exposure, giving it the feeling of a crammed hallway at the bottom of a dilapidated submarine. The light stained the demon's white shirt the same color green.

Sounds from deeper inside churned around them, sometimes vibrating and rumbling under their feet, as if they were headed into the belly of the great machine behind the scenes of Alice in Wonderland. It smelled like a tire factory. Daniel swapped between frowns of confusion and quick, paranoid glances over his shoulder.

"I'm getting pretty good at the whole two-minute explanations thing," the creature said. "Here, let me do this first."

The demon turned on him, a claw raised high. Daniel recoiled, feet churning backward. With his hands bound in front of him, he quickly lost his balance; his back thunked into the side of the passageway. He leaned against it, breathing, eyes locked on the claw.

"You on drugs or something?" the creature said. Smoke wisped out of its mouth. "Yeah, I get it. I'm pretty freaky looking, huh? You're a gruesome bastard yourself with that nob of skin hanging off your face."

Daniel's jackhammering heart started to settle. He straightened off the wall. "At the risk of sounding like a total asshole," Daniel said, "the thought had crossed my mind."

"Hey, he has a sense of humor," it said. "Good laugh gets you through anything, right?"

Daniel was entirely uncomfortable hearing those words hissing from between its shark teeth, but he decided that it would be best to agree, so he nodded. "Yeah."

"Right," the creature said. "I'm...you know what, I'll skip my full name. Your tongues don't really handle it, even with the spell doing the translating. You can call me Nip. I'm a devil."

Daniel's heart hopped back into his throat. "Devil?"

"Not *the* devil, or whatever the hell you monkeys are calling it now," it said. "*A* devil. You're a human, I'm a devil. It's my race. Get it?"

"Uh...yeah. Okay."

"There you go," Nip said. "Now, you want me to take those things off so you don't fall on your face?" Daniel looked at the stone handcuffs, then back up at the devil. "Come on," Nip said. "If I wanted to hurt you, I'd have already done it. Get a grip."

Daniel couldn't argue with that logic. Slowly, he raised his arms up. The devil raised its hand—and with a nasty shiiick, the needle on its index finger extended another few inches. Daniel tensed, but kept still.

He'd almost expected the sharp nail to cut right through the stone, but the devil merely gave it a tap. Daniel felt a surge of magic. The bottom of the bracers snapped open. Nip removed them and tossed them away down the hall, back toward the set; a dull thud echoed back as it struck the floor. "Somebody collect those!" it shouted.

The bracers were gone. The thing blocking his powers had been removed, simple as that.

Daniel immediately reached for his magic.

It wasn't there.

No, that wasn't right. It was there. Unlike when he was wearing the cuffs, he could sense his power, the humming ball of energy inside of himself. He just couldn't get at it. It was as if it was shielded in a thick sphere of glass. He could sense it, feel it; he could even touch the barrier. But try as he might, his mental scraping and scrabbling was useless. The brief spark of hope burned out, leaving an even darker frustration behind.

"Judging from the look on your face," Nip said, "you're catching on to the score. Trouble with your magic?"

Daniel's eyes shot to the demon. "How did you know?"

"Because that's what the last seven did too, more or less," Nip said. "Calm down and walk. No one's going to do anything to you unless you try something stupid. We aren't paid to rough you up." Nip gestured down the hall and started off, carrying all the air of a competent but somewhat harried stage manager. "We're walking and talking."

Daniel kept up at Nip's shoulder. He glanced at the hall as they clamped across the concrete, examining the few doors they passed. "So, you're a devil. Not a demon?"

"No," Nip said, "we're all demons, just like you're all humans. But you've got, I don't know, what are they called? Amercans?"

"Americans?"

"That's the one," Nip said. "And Asians and Yourpoorans."

"Europeans," Daniel corrected. "But that's more where they're from, not their—"

"Close enough," Nip said. "So, I'm a demon, but more specifically, I'm a devil. You probably saw some harpies, dwarves—imps, of course, they breed like mucoids—dragons were the ones that look like humans with scales, the black floating thing was a nightmare, and the big guy with hooves was a minotaur. Did I miss any?"

"Uh...the blue chick."

"An undine. And that was a male, by the way."

"Wait a minute," Daniel said. "I've seen a dragon. They were huge lizard things with wings. Not like that."

They rounded a corner, then pressed themselves flat against a wall. A dragon and a minotaur were headed the opposite way, and there wasn't enough room for them to walk side-by-side. They both nodded to Nip, who waved a hand in greeting. Once they were by, Nip started walking again.

"Dragons can transform," Nip said. "Normally they don't stay as big as a house—little inconvenient for day-to-day living. But let me warn you, don't piss off any dragons. Most of them are very proud, and they don't let grudges go easily."

"So how come there are so many types of demons?"

"Magic is stronger on our home planet than it is on Earth," Nip said. "Well...more common would be a better way to put it.

Denser. If you internalize it constantly, over several generations, it can act as a mutagen. Bet you didn't know that."

"Yeah," Daniel said, "they left that tidbit out in the school of hard knocks."

"You contractors definitely have it hard, I'll grant you that," Nip said. Between the smoke leaking from between its teeth and its heavy, raspy voice, Daniel almost thought he detected a note of sympathy. "Anyway. Long term separation between very tribal populations, magical specialization in various clans, maybe a little intentional remodeling here and there—you get some pretty varied stuff. Used to be more clans, but genocides weeded out a good third of the variety over the course of history."

"Okay," Daniel said. "So what is all this? What about the fire and brimstone, the torture? Eternal punishment?"

"I really can't believe what you humans come up with," Nip said. "Do you think we have nothing better to do than sit around in this place and torture you people all day as punishment for hacking each other apart? It's like we're supposed to be an entire race of sadists or something."

"Demons don't have a very good reputation where I'm from."

"That's because the only ones that want anything to do with you are the users, the idiots, and the lowlifes," Nip said. "If all I saw of humans were the dumb or the criminal, I'd have a bad opinion of you, too."

"I figured that's all you would've seen," Daniel said, "considering this is Hell and everything."

Nip tapped at his throat several times, producing a hollow, guttural sound. Daniel understood that this was supposed to be an amused snort. He wasn't sure how he knew that, but he did; the knowledge popped into his brain.

"What, did they tell you they've only sent the mean ones down here?" Nip said. "You seem like you're pretty smart.

Adaptable. I mean, half the others I had to carry over my shoulder while they were kicking and screaming for five minutes. You were a little jumpy, but you got over it."

"Uh, thanks," Daniel said.

"So use that head of yours," Nip said. "If you want to get rid of someone, you kill them and you're done with it. If you want to humiliate, punish, or otherwise destroy someone's reputation, make a big show of it, you send them into exile. That goes mostly for the demons, but not every human here is guilty of a crime, either. That doesn't mean they're the kind of people you'd rely on for a kind word, but it's not like an army of raving lunatics or anything. Well, mostly not."

"I think I understand."

"Getting back on topic," Nip said, "I—oh. Hang on." Nip withdrew a slim metal object from the pocket of his pants. Daniel noticed that the demons all wore different types of clothes, but the devil, oddly enough, was dressed more or less like what Daniel would expect a human to wear.

The device Nip held was silver and rectangular. Lights glowed on its surface; not the sharp lines of high-definition electricity, but the diffused haze of magic power. The devil manipulated it with its black nails, then raised it near its ear. "Yes?" Nip's eyes moved to Daniel. "Yes. Yeah, he's right here."

Nip listened at his phone. His jaw fell open. He clutched the device closer to his head. "He's here personally?!" Nip turned and stared at the wall. "I swear on the Third God, Ved, if you're screwing around with me, I'll..."

There was a pause. Daniel could hear the voice on the other end, raised to cut Nip off, but he couldn't make out any words. "Okay. Okay. Yeah, I got it." Nip lowered the device, and, clicking it off, slipped it back in his pocket.

"Don't tell me," Daniel said. "The torture's been reinstated."

"You wish, kid."

****

Nip and Daniel passed through a few more hallways without further conversation. Daniel tried to ask a few more questions, but all he got were grunts, and eventually a dismissing hand wave. He gave up asking.

Daniel was bothered by the change in behavior. Nip had been moving and speaking with a purpose, but none of it too hurried. Now he was scurrying like a mouse worried about a cat.

Deep in the nest of maintenance halls, Nip ushered Daniel through a door labeled *Contestant Preparation 006*, told him to wait, then left without another word. The door clicked shut behind him.

The room was plain and industrial—concrete for the floor, the walls unpainted cinderblock. Daniel sat himself on a steel chair pulled up to a burnished steel desk. Two more chairs were against one wall. Past them was something that looked like a water cooler holding a brackish green liquid instead of water. A flat sheet of steel was hanging on the wall above the table, though it didn't seem to serve any purpose other than to break up the monotony.

Daniel's eyes fell on the far corner opposite the cooler, where an ankle-high cylindrical disk was set in the floor. Its surface was carved with runes. The obscure symbols and figures were crowded together on the stone, but there was a pattern to it that he couldn't quite place. It was more a feeling than the way it looked, as if it was almost-but-not-quite neatly symmetrical. It looked very old compared to the surroundings, like an ancient Roman statue under the glass and fluorescent lights of a modern museum. Steel bars and a hinged gate walled it off from the rest of the room.

Daniel sat, and waited.

And waited.

The unreality of his situation started to fade. Daniel had seen enough strange things lately that normal and abnormal had switched places. If a rabbit came along and declared it was late for a very important date, he'd probably offer it directions. *I wonder if there are rabbit demons.*

As the confusion of the moment faded, and the adrenaline sank back down, other things creeped back up into his head. Daniel leaned forward onto the table. He rubbed at his eyes with the heel of his hand.

Rachel was dead, and he'd been the one to kill her.

It hadn't been intentional, but the knowledge didn't make him feel better. He should have been more cautious. He should have thought things through more carefully. There hadn't been any time. They were cornered by the Vorid lord. Daniel had to recover so he could keep fighting.

He held his forehead in his palms, a thumb resting on each temple, trying to banish the ache that sat inside of him. His hands tightened, pressing in. It didn't help. His teeth ground together in the back of his mouth.

Daniel heaved a sigh, sat back in the chair, and tried to blink his eyes clear. He would have killed for something to do, someone to talk to, anything to keep himself distracted.

None of this would have happened if the Vorid hadn't invaded Earth. Maybe Rachel and he wouldn't have had the exact same relationship, but they might still have met. They may have shared something special, even if Daniel never had magic.

He would trade all his powers away in a second if he could see her—see her smile one more time. Hear her laugh at him for being a moron. Make fun of his pessimism. Make his day a little brighter.

The tears welled up again. He sucked a breath through his teeth and shut his eyes tight, holding it back.

Daniel ran his hands over his face and propped his elbows on the table. He went over the fight against the lord in his head, over and over again, analyzing every part of it, trying to think of what he could have done differently.

It was a wasted effort. He'd already done it a thousand times back when he was locked up in Eleanor's mansion. He felt like he'd made the best choices he could with the information he had at the time.

It wasn't good enough to save her. His best effort simply wasn't enough.

No.

It might have been enough.

Daniel's eyes slowly opened; he stared down at his lap. His brow furrowed, and his mouth bent into a frown, and then into a scowl, and then his whole face clenched up so hard his head shook.

It wasn't the lord. It wasn't his choices. It wasn't that he lacked power or underestimated himself.

He'd pinned the Vorid lord early in the fight. He'd pinned it, held it down with an attack, and the mages didn't back him up. They didn't take the shot—not until later, after he'd been forced to go it alone and gotten himself hurt, after Rachel had died. If they'd attacked when they said they would, instead of looking for an opportunity to stab him in the back, things could have turned out differently.

He saw their faces again, drifting in his mind's eye, the tribunal that had pronounced his guilt. Matthew Aiken and his ugly, self-satisfied smirk; the old witch and her laundry list of excuses and justifications; the cold and silent representative of the Wu.

Lenhard Rothschild. That face stood out the most—the calculating eyes, sharp features, all the arrogant proclamations. Rothschild had been on the ground in New York. He had been the one that wielded the knife. If Daniel was Caesar, then Rothschild was Cassius.

And that cast Henry Astor nicely as Brutus—blaming Daniel for Rachel's death instead of the Vorid, instead of his own unreliable allies, watching on as Eleanor bawled her eyes out and Daniel was sent to Hell. Daniel wouldn't have thought the president of the Ivory Dawn capable of it, but you probably didn't get to the top of the wizard world without any ruthless bones in your body.

Rachel was dead, and the blood was on their hands, no matter how loud Henry shouted or how much he wanted to blame someone else. If they'd accepted him to begin with, instead of trying to hunt him down, the situation never would have happened in the first place. Those same people were now responsible for saving Earth, and they exiled him—the one person able to fight the Vorid off—to ensure that they'd maintain their grip on power when the fight was over.

Daniel tried to do the right thing. He wanted to preserve his relationship with Eleanor, and especially with Rachel; he wanted to be accepted by the magicians, working with instead of hiding from them. He submitted himself to their custody against his better judgement. He felt the facts were on his side, that his contributions were obvious.

He'd tried to be a better person because of Rachel. He wanted to make the kind of choice she'd make, because she was someone he admired—because she wasn't a bitter, cynical asshole like him.

The irony was, if he'd ignored that and trusted his instincts, she wouldn't be dead. He'd known better than to believe those people in the first place. How many millions, how many billions of people would be consumed by the Vorid until the magicians admitted they were wrong? Probably not until it was their turn to be erased and absorbed.

Daniel felt his anger settle down and start to simmer, boiling like sludge somewhere in the base of his neck and bubbling up through his head. The feeling demanded that he do something about it. He reached for his powers, his magic.

He got nothing.

His state of mind wouldn't let it go that easily. He tried to push his core energy out where it belonged, press it up to his skin and feet and hands, the familiar mental ritual that enhanced him beyond normal human limits. He'd done that more times than he could count. It was an instinct for him, easy as walking, like drawing a sword he'd drawn a thousand times.

It was like trying to push a bar of soap, underwater, with mittens made of more soap. No matter what angle he came at it, the magic slid away from him. He couldn't push it where it needed to be.

His anger collapsed into pieces, washed away by a wave of helplessness. He was in Hell. He couldn't touch his magic. He couldn't do anything.

He kept seeing Rachel's face in that last moment—skin pale and clammy, eyes sunken into her head, shivering from the cold. She felt cold because he'd sucked all the life out of her and her body still needed a few seconds to catch up and realize it was dead.

It might not be his fault, but the deeds sat heavy at his doorstep.

Daniel tried to take a breath. It came through rattling and wet with mucus. The second breath was a little easier. He sniffed hard, then focused on the rise and fall of his chest, on breathing. *One step at a time. Don't get inside your own head.*

Daniel took another deep breath and tried to focus on the room around him, reorienting himself. He needed to get a handle on his new situation. His problems seemed big because he was making them big. He had to break them down into smaller bits he could digest.

He wasn't dead yet. If there was a way in, there had to be a way out. Maybe the stone disk on the other side of the room was important.

He was about to get up and take a closer look when the door opened.

Another devil entered, and with him entered a gust of too-warm air—not the comfort of a fireplace, but a searing, dry-hot blast of volcanic ash.

The figure that stepped through was not like the devil Daniel had met a few minutes ago. He was bigger, in every sense. The heat radiated from him so palpably that Daniel could almost see the ripples in the air rising off his skin. His eyes glinted like black stars. They swept across the concrete to fix themselves on Daniel.

Daniel could only stare back briefly before averting his eyes. His head was forced down by some kind of unnatural pressure.

The devil kept him trapped under its gaze a moment longer, then moved across the room. Though he only took a single step, he crossed to the opposite wall easily, as if everything had bent around and rearranged itself to suit the direction he was traveling.

He grabbed one of the steel chairs and dragged it back to the table. The room was filled with the uncomfortable grating of steel-on-stone as the chair slid over the floor, echoing off the cinderblock and back again. He deposited it in front of the table, then sat opposite Daniel. The chair creaked as it took his weight.

The devil exhaled. Thick smoke wafted out his mouth and drifted into the room. It smelled like a furnace. Daniel felt sweat bead on his forehead.

"You are Daniel Fitzgerald?" the devil said. His voice was a roar and a hiss together, like gravel pouring downhill, about to cause a landslide.

"Who wants to know?" Daniel said.

The devil tapped a single finger to his throat, a tiny snort. "My name is Beelzebub. I am the Ruler of Dis, Emperor of the Demon World. I have an offer for you."

Daniel tried to glance up at his face again, but his eyes never quite made it. Meeting the devil's eyes was like trying to stare into an open oven, hot air rushing out and over his face.

He'd felt this kind of pressure before, when he'd fought the Vorid lord. He hadn't made much out of it, but he had his own sort of pressure, then, pushing back. Now he had nothing.

Beelzebub wasn't even doing anything—simply sitting there, looking at him—but it would have taken a huge effort for Daniel to stand up from his chair. It felt like lead weights were resting on his skin, all heated right to the verge of being so hot they burned.

"You're...Beelzebub." Daniel swallowed a few times, trying to get his throat in working order. "*The* Beelzebub?"

"I am," Beelzebub said. "You are about to be sent into the prison proper. I have a task for you. If you complete this task, I will set you free."

Daniel raised his head, not to Beelzebub's eyes, but to a safe zone somewhere around his chest. He wasn't sure his ears were working correctly. He was pretty sure that *the* devil had just walked in and offered him a deal to get out of Hell.

"I'll take your silence as interest." Beelzebub leaned forward. Daniel leaned away almost on reflex, avoiding the pressure. "Did you know? In Hell, you can't die."

"I don't understand," Daniel said.

"You have no context," Beelzebub said. "I will supply it. Hell is a prison, constructed to hold the worst criminals of both the human and the demon worlds. It is an artificial space that exists between where our worlds touch one another. It is maintained by a flow of souls from your world toward mine, and souls from my world toward yours.

"When people die, their soul—their *self*—dissipates into the aether. The prison was constructed using this primal force. It's a little more complicated than that...but I'm sure you get the idea."

Daniel nodded. He'd worked his eyes up to Beelzebub's neck, now. He watched the blood red skin flexing out of the top of Beelzebub's shirt.

"Because of the flow of souls, the life energy in Hell is so rich that the inmates never die. Even the most horrifying injuries heal, given enough time. I've seen a man's body—a human—piece itself back together after having the head removed and the arms and legs severed. A rather painful process, as you might imagine." Beelzelbub's needle-nails clacked the table. "If the body is destroyed beyond recomposition, a new body is made, and the soul inserted into that."

What a cheery idea. "So if you go to Hell, you get to live forever?" Daniel said aloud. "You'd think everyone would start robbing banks with black magic."

The devil raised his eyebrows at that. "You're young. Naive." Beelzebub leaned back. Daniel slumped in his chair, grateful for the slight relief the small distance gave him. "In a certain sense, you're right. But some circumstances might make you wish you could die. The vast majority of prisoners are sentenced to hard labor. Very hard labor."

Who wants to live forever? Daniel thought.

"In thousands of years," Beelzebub said, "no one who has entered Hell has ever been able to leave. Ever."

"Interdimensional Alcatraz," Daniel said. "Got it."

"So, tell me," Beelzebub said. "What do you think will happen when millions of souls that should be drifting into the prison and maintaining it are sucked away by the Vorid?"

Daniel squinted. "Then the prison doesn't work?"

"Correct," Beelzebub said. "Imagine that the prison fails. Imagine thousands of years' worth of human and demon criminals, the absolute worst of all the worst, released back into the wild."

"That sounds pretty bad." Daniel inched his gaze a bit higher. Some stubborn part of him was determined to look the devil in the eye at least one more time, even under the pressure he was exuding. "I guess that gives you a reason to fight the Vorid. Don't want those nasty demons getting out on your end. So you want me back on Earth."

"Xikanthus said you were a smart young man," Beelzebub said. Daniel blinked at the mention of Xik, but Beelzebub kept going before he could ask about it. "I'm going to help you out, as part of our deal. Give you an edge, so to speak. If someone enchanted with an ability such as your own murders another, you'll forcibly suck out their soul—a process you've experienced many times. Plenty of people similar to you, with similar magics, have been imprisoned."

"Are you telling me other people like that are still alive?" Daniel said. "Wizards with black magic that were banished? I thought that happened hundreds of years ago."

"They're in perfectly good health," Beelzebub said. "Physically, anyway. I'm glad you're familiar with the subject. Saves me having to explain it. But they can't kill anyone permanently in Hell. Only you can do that."

"Why only me?"

"Your version of the spell is much more powerful than anything they have. Theirs can't overpower the magic keeping all the souls locked in the prison. Yours, however, can. If I allow it. I have a certain level of...control, over the enchantment."

"Why..." Daniel's throat caught and he coughed. His mouth felt parched, dried by the heat in the room.

"Why you?" Beelzebub said. "The Klide enchantment is special. As are you."

Daniel squinted. It was the same reason Rachel died. His powers had gotten strong enough that he killed her—took too much from her—even if it was indirectly, through one of her spells. It made sense, in a sick sort of way. Daniel might be unique in that aspect, even amongst other contractors. It wasn't every day someone killed a Vorid lord.

"You said something about a proposal?" Daniel said.

"I want you to kill one of those prisoners for me," Beelzebub said. "A woman named Elizabeth Bathory."

Daniel had to let that sink in briefly to fully appreciate it. He'd heard that name before, and not just in history class. After Rachel and Daniel had found out about each other's secret lives, Rachel had told him exactly why contractors were so feared by magicians.

The ability of a contractor to absorb power and grow stronger was a modern replica of ancient vampiric magic. Magicians used it to bolster their powers and extend their lifespan by sacrificing the lives of others. Following its rediscovery, Elizabeth Bathory's rise to power in medieval Europe was only just barely stopped by Rachel and Eleanor's ancestors. Afterward, Bathory was banished to Hell, along with anyone else that practiced the magic—where they were to this day playing the jailhouse rock.

"Okay." Daniel cleared his throat along with his thoughts. "Sure. After fighting insane crusader aliens alongside the magic illuminati, why not go to Hell and murder vampires?"

Beelzebub leaned forward, further than he had last time. Daniel was pinned to his chair by Beelzebub's aura like an ant pinned by a five-year-old under a magnifying glass. "You're funny, Daniel," Beelzebub said, smoke curling out around his teeth. "Very funny." He leaned back again. Daniel shuddered.

"But you should be careful with that tongue. You might run into someone that doesn't have a sense of humor."

"Won't..." Daniel's tongue failed him. He swallowed again, but his mouth felt stuffed with cotton.

"Won't, what?"

"Won't she be way stronger than me at this point? Why not release her and let her fight the Vorid?"

"Really?" Beelzebub said. "Release the vampire back onto Earth?"

"I'm an evil monster according to some people," Daniel said. "The claims against her could be total bull for all I know."

Beelzebub tapped his throat a few times, making that fleshy, hollow-sounding snort. "How considerate. I'm coming to you for two reasons. First, Xikanthus asked for you. We're allies opposed to the Vorid. One human or another—it really makes no difference to me. His preference is acceptable."

"What's the second reason?" Daniel asked.

"You and I have something in common," Beelzebub said. "We both hate the wizards on Earth and their cozy little oligarchy."

Daniel stiffened. "Alright. You've got my attention."

"I thought I might," Beelzebub said. "You are a contractor. We need individuals like you to win this war. They don't want to do what is necessary because it represents a threat to their position. Now that magic is in the open—they've finally grown a spine and announced themselves—Earth will shortly experience dramatic changes in leadership. The mages will stop influencing things from the shadows and step into the light, using the wartime emergency as a convenient political shield. And then, when they've won, they'll stay where they are, ever vigilant as untouchable guardian magnates. A permanent ruling class, or so they imagine." Beelzebub shrugged. "But you understand. They're ignorant fools, jockeying for kingship over what will be a lifeless wasteland."

"Couldn't have put it better myself," Daniel said.

"And, of course," Beelzebub said, "you happen to have good references. I have my choice of ally: an old vampire with her own grudges and ambitions, or a young man that wants to protect his family and dispose of the corrupt and the selfish. I think I know who I'd trust."

"I'm not sure if that's a compliment, coming from you," Daniel said. "Especially as you want to make me into a murderer."

"The term I'd select would be executioner."

"Well goodness me," Daniel said, "that changes everything."

"I want you to dispense justice to a woman that bathed in the blood of innocent virgins to absorb their souls," Beelzebub said, "and thereby gain enough power to rule over the Earth forever. I suppose, technically, that's murder. But you've already killed hundreds of Vorid, haven't you?"

"Technically," Daniel said, "they're combatants in a war. They're the aggressors. Bathory had her day in court. She's already been sentenced. It's a little different."

"You also had your day in court," Beelzebub said. "How did that work out for you?"

Daniel didn't have a comeback for that one.

"Your sense of justice is admirable." Beelzebub folded his arms. "It's why you wanted to be a prosecutor, isn't it? To impose justice."

"How did you know I—"

"Come, now," Beelzebub said. "I am *the* devil. Isn't that right?" He shifted in his chair, causing it to creak sharply. "You're not stupid, Daniel. Bathory is not some falsely accused noble lady, suffering under the weight of her chains. With the recommendation of Xikanthus, you are the superior choice. In any case, it isn't so easy to work with the humans. They banished the so-called vampires themselves, and they don't care for demons much, either. There's a reason our worlds are separate."

Daniel supposed that being called *not stupid* was probably as good as compliments got around here. But if he was trying to get someone to do something for him, he might play things the same way. Use what he knew would get the other person's blood pumping—like the mage council back home. Play along with his jokes. Appeal to his sense of practicality.

Daniel's awareness that he was being used didn't help him much. He had about as many options as a pawn on a chessboard, except it wasn't even chess and he didn't know the rules. He didn't understand what he was being used for, and that was dangerous. Really dangerous.

"Why don't you just kill her yourself?" Daniel asked. "You're…" It struck him, suddenly. "You must be as old as them. Older." Daniel waited. He got nothing, but the devil's silence confirmed his suspicion. "Why do I have to be the one to do it?" Daniel asked, more confident. "If you're worried about the prison failing, get rid of them. Isn't it supposed to be a fate worse than death anyway?"

"Xikanthus asked for you," Beelzebub said. "Perhaps he wants to test whether you're worth more of his time. Certain points of my treaty with the humans prevent me from doing it myself."

Something clicked in the back of Daniel's head. He thought back to when he was purging the Vorid from his hometown of Aplington, night after night, when he'd systematically been measuring his powers. Over time, weaker creatures—the Vorid spawn, to be precise—didn't do much for him. At first, they'd bolstered his powers in leaps and bounds, but each one he killed represented a relatively smaller gain in strength over time. His overall strength leveled out until he was able to defeat extractors.

No matter what magic he was using, Beelzebub should have reached a similar point a long time ago. Killing the prisoners—if he could, who knew if he was lying or not about the whole treaty thing—wouldn't do him any good. That's why they were sending in Daniel, who actually stood to benefit.

But why was Beelzebub cooperating with Xik? He definitely wasn't the sort to do something out of the kindness of his heart. But on such short notice, Daniel couldn't think of an answer.

"Let's say," Daniel said, switching his point of focus to the table, "I agree to this offer. What's happens, exactly?"

"Xikanthus has enlisted me to reinforce Earth," Beelzebub said. "I will hold off the Vorid where the mages cannot. In the meantime, you work on Bathory. She used her enchantment to absorb no small number of souls, mundane and magical. Killing her will provide a significant boost to your magical powers. You then become the cavalry." Beelzebub tapped his throat several times, making strange, hollow chuckling sounds. Smoke drifted into the room. Daniel winced at a sudden rush of warmth. Sweat trickled down his back. "Of course, you don't have to limit yourself to her. But she's your main goal. After that, I'll personally return you to Earth."

"What about the magicians?" Daniel said. "The...oligarchy?"

"Do you think they'll be able to stand up to you if you get much stronger?"

Daniel thought about it. "I'm not sure. Maybe not. But they probably have more up their sleeves than brute force."

"You're right, but together, they won't be able to stop us." Beelzebub folded his arms. "Long ago, I made a pact with the humans, part of the spell that constructed the prison itself. Hell is the greatest magic ever woven by man or demon. However, the humans of the time, and of modern times, failed to uphold their end of our bargain, as I interpret it."

Daniel decided not to mention that, given the chance, he would probably try to wiggle out of a pact with the devil. "Alright," Daniel said, "so you've got your own beef with them."

"Yes," Beelzebub said. "I'm not interested in your world, your resources, or in humans at all, for that matter. The demon world has long since surpassed Earth in magic and technology. But there's something there which belongs to me, something I took a huge risk to acquire. They never delivered."

"What is it?"

"It doesn't matter," Beelzebub said. "I'm only telling you this so you realize we're on the same side. Together, we can extract whatever concessions we want from them. I'll get what I want, and you can get freedom for yourself and other contractors, should you wish. Then I'll go my way, and you can go yours—once we've dispatched the Vorid."

"Why don't you let me out right now?" Daniel asked. "The Vorid are the biggest threat. You need me."

"Right now, you aren't strong enough to fight the wizards, if and when it comes to that," Beelzebub said. "You're right about them having more means that you imagine. You saw only a fraction of what they were capable of in New York; they've been holding back because they're afraid of overcommitting in any one location. You need to get stronger. That means going inside the prison."

Daniel felt like nodding along, but he stopped himself. The devil was asking him to kill someone to get himself out of Hell. The same devil that built an interdimensional prison, who had lived for thousands of years himself, definitely understood how the vampiric enchantment worked. Daniel already suspected he used some form of it himself.

But he wasn't killing Daniel to increase his own powers.

There was no reason for the devil to come to him, aside from commiserating about the wizards. That wasn't a good enough reason by itself. Xik was the one forcing him to work like this. Xik had some leverage over Beelzebub that Daniel didn't understand.

But what, exactly, was the real game? What could Xik be dangling out as a carrot for the devil himself? He didn't have enough information to piece it together. Beelzebub made it clear he didn't plan on handing out too many details. Just enough to make the deal sound good, but not enough for Daniel to appreciate what he was getting himself into. Whatever Beelzebub wanted from Earth probably wasn't in mankind's interest for him to obtain.

Daniel wasn't exactly rolling in options, and he couldn't trust either side. If this is what Xik wanted, then for now, he had to go along with it—make a deal with the devil. Again. He couldn't help but imagine the frog-man floating next to him, wearing that thin smirk, pleased with himself for poking and prodding Daniel into something he really didn't want to do.

"What will stop Bathory from killing me instead?" Daniel asked. "Are you sure she can't do it?"

"Your contractor magic is different in this respect. It's also different because they need to prepare their rituals or formations"—Beelzebub noted Daniel's puzzled look—"that is, the preparatory steps required to absorb life force. It takes too long and they don't have the resources. I make sure of that. Your own enchantment is more...efficient."

Daniel wasn't sure how to feel about being told his method of killing was efficient.

Beelzebub folded his arms. "Moreover...there are punishments for breaking the rules in Hell." Black smoke wafted around Beelzebub's head, drifting around the table. It smelled like acid and cheap cigarettes. "No one breaks the rules."

Daniel absorbed that for a while. He didn't know what solitary confinement looked like in Hell, and he really didn't want to find out. "You've got to give me something to surprise her with. I haven't even fought a wizard before. Not really."

"My time is precious. You'll have to dive from your cliff on your own."

Daniel wasn't familiar with the saying, but he got the gist of it. Sink or swim. "Is there at least something to watch out for? Does she have any weaknesses?"

Beelzebub planted his forearms on the edge of the table and stared Daniel down. "I've given you my terms. You can work within them, or you can rot in Hell forever. There are other contractors. Xikanthus will get over you and move on. Make a decision. Now."

Daniel didn't like anything about this situation. He felt backed into a corner.

Not that it was anything new. His entire life as a contractor was fighting from one big corner, first to protect Felix, and then Boston, and eventually the whole planet. He'd survived all the fights so far. He just had to survive one more.

"Alright," Daniel said. "I'll do it."

"Very good," Beelzebub said. "I will manipulate the seal. When you fight on the first level of Hell—Purgatory—you'll be able to absorb the souls of those you kill."

"Why only there?"

"It's the only place where it will matter," Beelzebub said. "It's where the strong have gathered. The rest are worthless. And if you can't keep your spot there, the same goes for you." He stood. "I have my own preparations to make. The screen there will tell you what happens next." He gestured at the steel square hanging on the wall. "After it's finished, stand on the pedestal."

"Seriously?" Daniel said. "That's it?"

"Yes," Beelzebub said, almost growling the words. "Or do you want me to wish you good luck?"

"You're kinda throwing me down there without much to go on."

Beelzebub tapped his throat. The hollow sound clicked through the room. "Yes, I am. But if I were prone to gambling, I'd say things are about to get very interesting once you start fighting down there."

"I always thought the devil loved to gamble."

"If the odds are stacked in your favor," Beelzebub said, "would you still call it gambling?"

Daniel forced his head up to watch the devil go, but he only caught sight of black claws wrapping around the edge of the door. Beelzebub slammed it shut, iron striking concrete with a sharp clang of finality.

Daniel heaved a sigh as the pressure on his chest faded. The back of his shirt stuck to his chair from all the sweat. His hands were shaking. He pressed them flat to the table to keep them still.

Beelzebub wasn't the devil he imagined, exactly, but he was definitely powerful. Maybe stronger than the Vorid lord. It was hard to tell without being able to scry him, but even if he could, Daniel wasn't sure he'd want to.

The metal panel flickered to life, revealing itself to be a television. A sweeping red and white logo flashed across a black field before settling in its center. *PrisonWatch.* The word flew toward the viewer, growing larger before disappearing entirely.

"Welcome new inmate!" said an extremely enthusiastic, girlish voice. Daniel hated it and everything about it immediately. "I'm your host, Kylylthorxakl, but you can call me Ky!"

A devil popped onto the screen, seemingly floating in space. She looked like the devils he'd seen so far—white horns, blood red skin—but the clothing was stranger than anything he'd seen yet. It was as if someone had taken three paint brushes, one yellow, one red, and one orange, and swept them across a white jumpsuit. It wasn't baggy, though, tailored to form and stopping on her ankles well above bright orange high heels.

Ky twirled her fingers at him. "I'm here to tell you what you can expect next!"

"Obviously," Daniel said at the screen, "I will not be expecting the fashion police."

"Now, I know how you feel," she said. Her eyes went wide, and she made a sad smile that was faker than a 3-dollar bill. "Things for you are bad. But you've got to pep up and think of the bright side. Life can only get better from here, right?"

At that, Daniel withheld comment. *No reason to tempt fate.*

The devil pointed a needle-claw, and what looked like the blueprint of a 9-layer cake appeared on screen. An asterisk next to the map was elaborated by a small line at the bottom: *Not to Scale.*

"This map is the general layout of Hell. There are nine levels, with numerous sub-levels connecting each that aren't shown here. The levels are larger from the bottom up, which generally corresponds to their population."

The hyperactively cheery devil faced Daniel. "Within Hell are a variety of competitions, collectively referred to as games. Depending on your success in the games, you can earn points, prizes, and various other privileges!" The devil winked at him. "Who said eternity had to be boring?"

Daniel felt sick to his stomach.

"Over the years, many contestants realized the benefit of working together and formed teams. Games were made to cater to them, matching multiple teams against one another. The strongest teams live on top, top, top!" She did a little hop of excitement. "Level 1, Purgatory! Where the views are forever and the luxuries are plenty. The most popular teams of different levels often gain sponsorship, enhancing their lives until many live even better than they did on the outside. You could even get lucky enough to make it to level zero!

"But those that can't compete have to live down low, low, low..." Ky crouched slightly, and put a palm out as if petting a dog. "...where you've got to scrape up ice to earn your daily bread!"

Daniel glanced over his shoulder, half-expecting to see Xik standing there, ready to clap him on the back, play a laughtrack, and tell him it was all a big joke. He was disappointed.

"But don't worry. No matter what happens, you've got all the time in the world, so fight hard, win big, and live large!" The devil wagged a finger at Daniel and smirked. "Now I bet you're wondering where you fit in to all this, hmm?"

"How did you guess?" Daniel said.

"All new entrants compete against one another in their first game, and that includes you! If you win, you earn a special reward limited solely to this contest! You'll also be appealing to potential teams that will want you on their side"—the devil flashed her black needle-nails, palms out—"so get out there and hustle! What seems like bad news right now could really be the start of a new chapter in your life. It's time to shine as rising star of PrisonWatch, a new hero of the systems!" She gestured to herself and put a hand on her hip. "And who knows—you could even be lucky enough to meet me, Ky, in person!"

Ky would almost be cute—in an extremely annoying kind of way—if it wasn't for the two nub-like horns growing out of her skull and the fact that her face looked like her nose had been ripped off and it healed up ugly. Daniel was not enthused at the prospect of meeting her.

"Let's get you ready for your first fight!" Ky said. "The name of the game is..." She paused, leaning in. "Pamba Race!"

Daniel lifted an eyebrow. *What the hell is a pamba?* "Here's a brief preview of the battle arena!"

The screen flickered again. It displayed a panorama of what looked vaguely like an obstacle course. The camera zoomed in.

The close-up view was deeply unsettling.

Chapter 2
Running with the Devils

For a human, Jack Killiney was a small person. He barely topped five-foot-three. He was skin and bones, and not from lack of trying. Even his hair was buzzed short, if only because he hated the way it looked when it grew out.

But Jack was more than human. He was a contractor.

Every contract with the Klide granted a unique ability. His was the power to transform himself into a massive, silver-haired ape. On his command, his arms, legs, or even his entire body would surge with muscle. While the stamina of his soul held out, he could run for miles and leap over houses. He was strong enough to flip cars like toys and punch holes through brick walls. The real power, though, was the shaggy fur that grew from his skin when he transformed. It was imbued with a magic of its own, and formed a barrier that protected him from all but the most concentrated magical attacks, turning him into a living tank.

His power—his status as a contractor—made him different. It made him better. He didn't have to be small. He could be big, in every sense of the word; larger than the life he was assigned when he was born, an escapee from the prison of destiny that was set by who your parents were and where you grew up.

Sometimes, though, he could see the appeal of the whole boring destiny thing. Hell was always exciting, and not in a good way.

The men and women locked there didn't simply commit crimes. That was commonplace depravity; that got you a trial, an extended stay on death row. The people sent down to Hell either never acknowledged a greater sense of humanity in the first place—or they were sent there to be gotten rid of by people even worse than they were. And forget humans—for demons, that was saying something.

The room he occupied was packed shoulder-to-shoulder with observers. The vast majority were not human; humans were a tiny minority of Hell's population. There were thick-chested minotaur; freakish crow-people, the harpies; six-legged, spidery grazul; green, leathery-skinned imps; bright-red devils; blue-haired undines; and even dragons, reduced to their humanoid forms, distinguished by the chromatic scales emerging from their necks and temples. A single nightmare, a small, ink-black weasel of a demon, floated above the heads of the crowd, but Jack knew there were more nearby; they usually liked to stay out of sight. There was one ogre, too. They were uncommon on the top level. Too dumb.

The floor and walls were solid black steel. It was the same uniform, riveted metal that everything in Hell was made of, when it wasn't made of exhaust or soot-stained concrete. Purgatory was nicer than most, too, relatively clean and comfortable. If you owned a piece of it, you could change it around, assuming you had the money. But the bedrock was always artificial.

He couldn't imagine what it was like living at the bottom.

He faced a thick plate window that stretched from floor to ceiling. The room sloped up toward the back, giving everyone a clear view of the arena below; viewing screens in the corners offered close-ups of the action. Along the curved wall of the coliseum, Jack could see other window-rooms, just as packed as his. At first, he'd thought he was looking out an actual window, but then he learned it was a virtual display. The arena wasn't large enough to accommodate every prisoner.

The games for new detainees were mandatory viewing for the top few levels—not that they needed to be. They were subject to betting, like all the games, so they naturally drew inmates in. There were plenty of people looking to make it rich quick without competing in the arenas.

Bookies worked the crowd at the back of the box, taking wagers and tracking odds with pads of metal that flickered with magic. The only information to go on was whatever crime each inmate committed that landed them a ticket to Hell, as well as their name and race. Jack didn't bother looking at the list—he preferred safer bets. Rent was coming up, and he hadn't participated in any games the past month.

Dracula had already told him about the only important person coming, the only one of the bunch Jack cared anything about to begin with.

Aside from the betting, everyone wanted to see the fresh meat fall all over themselves, take a gander at the new talent. It was part sadistic curiosity—like watching a train wreck—and part scouting out the newcomers. Ambitious teams always wanted to pad the ranks.

Even if Jack didn't want to go to the matches, he wouldn't have considered skipping. Not after he found out what happened if you broke the rules. He decided to try his best to never break the rules.

When Jack accepted Xik's offer and became a contractor, he thought he'd finally be somebody. He thought he'd finally become a big fish. Instead of putting his head down and getting pushed around by the rules, he'd be the one writing them.

In a sense, he was right. It just so happened the game was a lot bigger than he first imagined.

It didn't help his sense of self-confidence that he was squashed between two infamous giants of human history.

"You look out of your depth, Jack."

Jack looked to the giant on his right.

Rasputin's heavy nose sat on his face like a beetle. His scraggly beard was long, and his wide ears were long, and his hair was long—and his head, while small, was distended by all the longness. He was uglier than some of the imps.

His voice was different. His voice coated the air with butter and warmth, wrapped you tight in a blanket that smelled like mother's cookies. When he spoke, you hardly seemed to notice all that stuff about his face. The man could insult you, and you'd be all smiles, patiently waiting to hear more about how stupid you were.

Jack made it a habit to take a good look at Rasputin's ugly face as often as possible. It helped shake him out of it.

"Why is this one even here?" Rasputin asked. "He can easily view it from the fort."

"Because being a man of the modern era," the giant on Jack's left said, "he may be a better judge of modern men than us."

Jack glanced at the other man. His name was Wladislaus Dragwlya III, formerly the Prince of Wallachia.

His much more frequently used nickname was the one that Jack recognized. Dracula.

Lord Dracula's profile was jagged and elegant, as if he was cut rough from black marble but polished to a high shine. His chin was narrow. A mustache flared out on either side of his face. His eyes were always squinting, analyzing. For now, he was squinting out the window, inspecting the arena below the ring of windowed rooms.

Rasputin's voice lost a bit of its smoothness. "I think myself a better judge of character than some fresh fool of a boy, no matter the era."

"Perspective, Rasputin," Dracula said, tone measured. "Perspective."

"I have eyes, you know," Rasputin said. "Believe it or not, they give me a shocking amount of perspective."

"Jack," Dracula said.

Jack responded immediately. "Lord Dracula?"

Dracula gestured to the arena. "You've been through this; now you have a chance to see it from the other side. Pay attention, learn what you can."

Jack turned back to the screen showing the arena. They had a good view, even if it was virtual, about half field and raised slightly above ground level. Less expensive boxes, or the cheap seats, didn't get the same consideration.

The entrance game he'd participated in was a lot tamer than what he saw spread out below him. It didn't have the suspended steel catwalks, the rope climbs, or the whizzing metal discs that looked like they would slice right through you if you looked at them funny. And it definitely hadn't been floating above a pit filled with seething hot magma. Plumes of the stuff erupted at random, spraying the lower passes with flecks of superheated rock. Jack felt nervous just looking at it.

On one end of the maze was a long steel stage with several pedestals. On the opposite side, about 200 or 300 yards distant and a few floors higher than the starting position, was the goal, a small platform a few yards square. It shone with a bright blue light that cut through the red-orange haze coming off the lava pit.

"Devils and dwarves, imps and dragons, demons of every triiiibe!!" Ky carried out the last syllable, as if welcoming them to a three-ring circus rather than a vicious deathtrap. It was the same too-happy voice the other rooms would be hearing, the same voice broadcast over PrisonWatch—Beelzebub's revenue-generating reality television station that cashed in on cold, hard, guilt-free brutality. After all, everyone in Hell deserved what happened to them.

"Grab your drinks and plop a seat, because the games are about to begin! Today's arena is inspired by the Mining facilities on Omicron-8! A quick thanks to today's sponsor, Omicron Mining Corporation! OMC: Constructing a better future!"

Jack winced away from the room's loudspeaker. Ky could've given Billy Mays a run for his money. "I really hate her voice," he said.

Rasputin sighed. "Something we all agree on, I think."

"Don't refer to it as *her*," Dracula said. He squinted toward Jack. "It. Don't humanize them. They aren't human."

"And now...today's unlucky new inmates!"

A blue spotlight—similar in color to the goal platform—alighted on the stage with the pedestals. A sprinkle of white light heralded the teleportation spell. A body warped into existence, standing in front of the first podium; a devil. Its blood-red skin was made purple by the lighting.

"Today's first inmate is Zelunix! Zelunix's main crime was serial decapitation, followed by removing and consuming the brains of his victims! You may remember him from our earlier courtside specials—Zelunix was infamously unrepentant, telling the judge 'don't knock it till you've tried it!' His innate lack of smell gave him away, as his neighbors couldn't stand the scent of the rotting corpses still decorating the inside of his house!"

Several flying drone cameras, propelled by magic, soared in and hovered around the devil, catching him from different angles. Zelunix played along enthusiastically, raising his arms to greet the viewers. If Jack hadn't been down there before, he might have thought it was almost cartoonish.

One by one, new inmates were warped in, one for each pedestal. Their arrival was followed by a brief summary of their deeds. Most were more of the same—vicious, often shameless, criminals. Some used forbidden magic with which Jack wasn't familiar; their acts ranged from Zelunix's cannibalism to mind-control enslavement to plain old terrorism. They were all demons, of various species.

Their reactions came in two main flavors. About half of them looked almost happy to be in attendance. Others were more subdued, standing in place with distant, blank gazes, as if it hadn't sunk in yet.

Jack decided to risk speaking. "Lord Dracula?"

"Yes?"

"That last one didn't seem so bad," he said, pointing at the platform. The latest criminal, a stout dwarf, had been announced as a thief, but without any specifics. "Why is he here?"

"*It* stole from the wrong person," Dracula said.

"So...it got sent to Hell?" Jack asked."

"Use your head, boy," Rasputin said. "This is an exile. Humanity uses a sentence here as a message. Demons use it as a tool."

"To do what?"

"To control," Dracula said. "Who knows if he really is a thief? Who knows if any of these creatures committed the acts that were announced? The only thing we really know is that someone wanted them gone badly enough to have them sent here." Dracula looked at him. "It was the same for you. As it was for all of us."

Jack could only nod.

"And now!" the announcer shouted, "today's last inmate! We've got a human today, folks, and we all know how feisty those can be! Give the young man a helping hand, won't you?"

Light flickered and sparked at the end of the platform. A new person warped into view. It was a young man, as advertised.

Jack knew him instantly. His hair was somewhere between brown and blonde, and fairly messy. A thick lock of it drooped down over the middle of his forehead. His eyes faced forward, and his mouth was turned down in a semi-permanent pessimistic scowl.

Jack was surprised—not to see him, but at the look on his face. When Jack had first met the guy that would become his best friend, he had that same expression. It was a look that said he'd seen the world, and after giving it all several honest tries, he was still disappointed.

But that attitude went away. The bitterness fell off Daniel's face as they'd gotten to know each other, and then, with time, vanished altogether.

Jack didn't know what he expected to see, but it wasn't that. The old expression was back. Something must have happened. Something bad.

Jack immediately felt stupid. Of course something had happened; he'd been sentenced to Hell. It didn't get much worse than that.

Jack tried to warn him about the magicians, but he knew it would go ignored. Daniel wasn't that great at taking advice. And now he was here.

"Back on Earth," the announcer continued, "he was found guilty of using the vampiric enchantment, and we all know what that means! A life sentence in Hell! Who knows—maybe this one will be the extra boost a new team needs to make it big! Let's all welcome Danieeeel Fitzgeraaaald!"

"Another one like you," Rasputin said. "A contractor."

Jack shook his head. "No. Not like me."

"Yes, he does look quite a bit tougher than you," Rasputin said. "My mistake."

"You know what," Jack said, "you—you just—"

"What?" Rasputin said. "Did I go too far? Touch a nerve?"

"Yeah," Jack said. "He's my best friend."

"I think that tells us all we need to know."

"Rasputin," Dracula said. "That's enough."

"They're sending down children, Dracula," Rasputin said. "Immature little brats that stumbled onto powers they don't understand. Half were so mad, so self-absorbed, we had to put them down. No wonder the world is falling apart." Rasputin brushed his hand against Jack, catching him across the shoulder. "The wizards today are so incompetent they have to rely on trash like this."

"I am not trash, and neither is he," Jack said.

"Rubbish then, or garbage, take your pick."

Ky's voice cut into their conversation. "One more round of applause, for all our contestants! A warm welcome to our new inmates! Or should I say, a hot welcome, with all this lava? Ha!"

As Ky tittered over her own wit, everyone in the booths mechanically started clapping, every human and every demon. Even Lord Dracula lightly tapped his palms together. You had to clap for the cameras, because the rules said you had to clap for the cameras when you were instructed to do so. And everyone followed the rules.

Jack smirked at Rasputin. "Fine, we can be trash. Since you're such an expert in the subject and everything."

Rasputin's eyes flashed, and the trace of warmth in his voice vanished, replaced by a dry, raspy anger. "Don't speak to me that way again, boy, or I will instruct you as to why I help lead this team. I came from nothing, but I had noblemen quivering that I'd sic their own rulers on them and ruin their lives. I could easily do the same to you, and you should keep that in mind when you open your mouth."

"You're a dirty old has-been," Jack said, "and you don't know what you're talking about."

Rasputin opened his mouth to deliver a retort, but Dracula cut him off. "Jack, you will respect your seniors. Cull your tongue."

"I'm sorry," Jack said, "but I'm not going to stand here and listen to him insult my friend." He looked at Rasputin. "You can make fun of me if you want, but don't talk shit about people you don't know."

"I said." Dracula's voice had an extra degree of sharpness. "Cull your tongue."

"...sorry."

Rasputin loomed over Jack, finger raised, picking out the words for another wave of insults. But he exchanged a glance with Dracula, lowered his hand, and said nothing. When Jack looked, Dracula's eyes were on the arena, hard and focused.

Jack celebrated a bit inside his head. He felt like he'd channeled a bit of Daniel, there.

The contestants all stood at their pedestals, looking over the obstacle course and stealing glances at each other. Jack watched Daniel scan the arena.

"What's taking so long?" Rasputin muttered. "Usually they've started by now."

Jack thought about not answering, but decided to fill him in. He had to at least pretend they were on the same side. "Extra commercials, probably," Jack said. "Ratings are higher with all the humans coming through."

"Who would have thought," Rasputin said, "that the time people spend watching entertainment would be sold as a commodity. The demons must be obsessed with their televisions."

"So are we," Jack said.

"Modernity is a strange thing," Dracula said.

"I guess it must be weird for you two," Jack said, trying to make conversation. "I've heard about people that lived a long time, and saw a lot of changes. But for you..."

"Longer lives. More changes." Rasputin shrugged. "It's simple, really. Everyone that couldn't adapt is dead."

"Jack," Dracula said. "You're the first I've heard that knew another contractor personally while still on Earth. What can you tell me about Daniel?"

Jack, for the most part, had kept the exact circumstances of his sentencing under wraps. When they questioned him, he simply said he was caught one night, and left it at that. The explanation was accepted without qualm.

At the time, Jack hadn't wanted to talk about it. He still didn't want to talk about it. The way Daniel looked at him when he found out about everything was burned into the back of his skull. He'd been doing his best to forget it.

Seeing Daniel in the flesh brought everything back to the surface, all the tender, raw memories that had barely started to scab over. It was a strange mix of emotions—he was happy to see Daniel, sad to see him in Hell. Mostly, he was nervous. What would Daniel say to him, when they met face-to-face? And what would he say to Daniel? What could he say? The last time they were together, they'd been trying to kill each other. Maybe it would be better to avoid him. But Dracula and Rasputin—the whole human team—were all interested. Avoiding him was a pipe dream.

"Lord Dracula asked you a question," Rasputin said.

"Daniel..." Jack cleared his throat. "He's, well—he's a good person, once you get to know him."

"He could be screwing goats in his spare time for all I care," Rasputin said. "What are his abilities? What can he do?"

"Something with speed," Jack said. "He's really fast."

"Is he stronger than you?" Dracula asked.

"Yeah." Jack gave a nod. "He was a little stronger than me when I got caught. He's probably a lot stronger now."

"Did you work together back on Earth, fighting those things, the Vorid?" Rasputin said. "How did you know him?"

"I...I don't—"

Ky's voice blasted back into their faces, saving Jack from an explanation. "Welcome back to PrisonWatch! It's time to select the lucky person who'll start off with the Pamba!"

****

Daniel stood on the platform at one end of the arena. The obstacle course opened up ahead of him. It was a nest of chain-link walks, ramps, climbable rope walls, and razor sharp blades held by rotor arms, slicing back and forward in regular patterns like traps from a very sadistic Indiana Jones movie. The heat from the lava sat on his skin; he was already sweating under his clothes.

The arena itself was huge. The entire structure he and his fellow contestants stood on was floating in midair, surrounded by massive walls that stretched up higher than a football stadium. Black windows were set in the walls at regular intervals from eye-level to the roof far overhead. It had the feel of a colosseum, in both the way it was built and in what they were about to do.

"Staaaaart the roulette!" Ky shouted.

The same white light that teleported Daniel to the arena suddenly lit up the pedestal in front of the first competitor, to Daniel's far left. The light vanished, then reappeared two pedestals down. It vanished again, skipped five spots, and lit up right in front of him. The steel glowed like one giant fluorescent light.

The light hopped and jumped and skipped, first slowly, then faster, a strobe flickering in their faces. Perky gameshow music played in the background, as trite and over-the-top as Ky herself. Daniel stared at his pedestal, watching as it occasionally lit up. It all felt just strange enough to make him believe it was a delusion concocted by his brain and that the torture would begin any second.

Here he was again, questioning his sanity. But if everything that had happened to him was all some crazy mind trip, and he was lying in a hospital outside Aplington in a coma, he was probably too far gone to have any hope of recovery. Might as well run with it. *Big bucks, no whammies.*

The music stopped. Daniel's pedestal pulsed blue. Cheery victory horns blared out in front of him.

"It looks like we've got our first runner." Ky's voice reverberated around the steel colosseum. "Seems like the human...has the luck of a devil!"

Daniel might not have murdered anyone before, but Ky was making an honest effort to climb to the top of his list.

He took a steadying breath and glanced to the side. All the other contestants were staring down at him. Some had expressions of pity; others didn't have much of an expression at all. A handful looked like they'd start licking their lips any second. In spite of everything, Daniel felt rather pleased with himself.

"A round of applause for Mr. Fitzgerald!" Suddenly, Ky appeared at Daniel's side, floating in midair. He blinked a few times—this close, he could tell she was see-through. *Some kind of magical hologram?* She jabbed a metal rod into his face. "Any words from our lucky contestant?"

Daniel stared at the mic, then at Ky, then at the faces of his rivals. "God," Daniel said, "if you're listening, I'm really sorry for doing whatever I did to earn this. Go Browns!"

Ky laughed, which was to say she somehow giggled and cackled at the same time from the base of her throat, tapping at it with her free hand. "He's got a sense of humor, folks! I like him already. Make sure you follow this one, I think he'll go far!"

Ky's figure soared up into the air. "Let's do a quick review of the rules! Pamba Race is king of the hill all jumbled up with a good old-fashioned obstacle course. To win, a contestant must bring the pamba to the victory platform." Ky pointed to a tiny blue platform that looked very, very far away from where Daniel was standing. "Of course, Daniel's competitors won't simply let him get there without a fight!"

Daniel felt like a hard lead weight had dropped in somewhere around his liver.

"The magic base percentage is set to zero for all contestants, so look out for powerups. They'll be scattered throughout the course at random intervals, and they could give you the advantage you need to snatch away the pamba for yourself!" Ky pointed down at Daniel's pedestal. "Daniel will have time to get a grip on our furry friend, and the race will begin at the sound of the horn."

Another spark of blue light made Daniel's eyes water. On his pedestal appeared a round lump of white fuzz about the size of a softball. It almost looked like a curled-up puppy, without any legs protruding. He reached forward.

A set of jaws as large as the creature opened up as if the whole thing was on a hinge. Daniel saw a flash of red innards and huge white molars before it clamped down on his hand.

Daniel shouted and lurched back. The pamba's teeth ground down over three of his fingers, as hard as if he'd slammed them in a car door. He waved his arm wildly, trying to throw it off. It didn't budge an inch.

After flailing around for a few painful seconds, he put his hand on the ground and grabbed it from the back, getting his fingers into the thick strands of fuzz. Using his foot, he pinned it to the steel and tried to work its jaws open with the toe of his sneakers. Tears formed in his eyes as he wedged his hand out, working it back and forward out of the thing's teeth. "Ow, ow, ow, fuck, you little fucker!"

Daniel freed his hand, then held it out in front of himself. Blood was pouring down his palm; the fuzzball had stripped the skin off his knuckles. It didn't cut through much—he was pretty sure it had flat teeth. He'd done most of the damage wrenching his fingers out.

The pamba lurched in his other hand, biting at the air. Daniel channeled the pain into his grip on the pamba's backside, holding it still. It kept shaking somewhat, but it couldn't get free.

"Always a good time when a contestant hasn't seen pamba race before!" Ky said.

"Screw off!" Daniel shouted back.

"My, Mr. Fitzgerald, temper!" Ky wagged a finger at him. "Don't worry, your hand will be back to normal soon."

Daniel actually felt his hand starting to numb up—he'd been hoping that was the adrenaline kicking in. But when he looked at his hand, the air was rippling around it. It looked like heat waves rising above a bonfire. He felt a familiar itching, crawling sensation on his knuckles—the same kind that healed his injuries when the contractor magic went to work on him. He rubbed some of the blood away from his fingers. Sure enough, they were rapidly scabbing over. And then the scabs crumbled away, as if days of healing were taking place in the span of seconds—and, smeared blood aside, his hand was back to normal, as if it had never happened.

"See?" Ky said. "Never better! But I think it's time we get started. Leeet's pambaaaa!"

An air horn echoed through the colosseum. Daniel glanced to the side again. A small army of demons was running for him.

He jumped off the stage. The catwalk banged underneath him as he started into his own run. He automatically grasped for his magic, trying to push it out into his legs for speed. His power slipped away from him. The harder he tried to grab it, the more trouble he had holding on.

The catwalk behind Daniel rattled like gunshots under the legs of his pursuers. He had to shake them off. Coming up on his right was a rope climbing wall, about two people wide; on the left was a ramp.

Some of those demons hadn't looked like the best climbers in the universe. Daniel jumped up onto the wall, hooking his arms into the loops of rope and pulling himself up. A few steps up, he realized it was really hard to climb netting when one of your hands was holding an irritated set of fuzzy jaws. Demons were crowded around the bottom of the climb in seconds, shoving at each other in a contest to see who could pull him down first.

A sharp pain ran up his ankle. Daniel hissed through his teeth. One of the devils had gotten a foothold and slashed his claw at Daniel's leg. When the devil tried to get a grip on his foot, Daniel dropped half a step and jammed the sole of his shoe into its face. The devil grunted and fell from the climb, tumbling down onto the others.

Daniel hoisted himself up a few more handholds. The temporary pileup he'd created gave him a little breathing room. He looked out between the loops of rope, trying to get his bearings as he climbed. The rope ladder only went up one floor, and then he had two paths, both leading into the meat of the course. He couldn't quite see where they ended.

"Looks like Daniel's off to a good start!" Ky's voice wrapped around Daniel, as if transmitted straight to his ears, dashing his hopes that she'd finally shut up. "Human ingenuity at work! But it looks like trouble's on the way. Zelunix picked up a beam sword!"

Daniel decided he did not want to find out what a beam sword was. He focused on climbing, putting most of the work into his legs so he could keep his grip firm on the pamba. It nipped and shook in his hand somewhat, but the fuzzball had otherwise accepted its state of captivity.

Daniel checked below. He was keeping pace with the demons climbing up behind him. In a few seconds he'd be at the top—then he could make a break for it and escape the mob.

Daniel glanced back at his destination. His hand seized up on the rope. A devil loomed over the top of the rope ladder, holding what looked like a pink lightsaber. He flashed Daniel a toothy grin, then lowered the humming blade to cut the two ropes connecting the ladder to the walkway and drop him twenty feet straight down.

Daniel chucked the pamba at him.

The white fuzzball flew through the air. As if on cue, its jaws opened up, clamping down on Zelunix's sword hand. The demon roared and stumbled backward, waving his hand around in a panicked mimicry of Daniel's earlier performance. The sword clattered to the floor.

Daniel dragged himself off the climb and onto the walk. He carefully picked up the pink laser by the hilt and inched toward Zelunix from behind.

The demon spun on a dime and swiped his free hand at him—along with its extended, razor-sharp claws. Daniel stepped back and held the business end of the beam sword out to ward him off.

Maybe it was the pain from having his other hand crunched in the pamba's jaws, or maybe he didn't see it, but Zelunix kept swinging. His wrist passed through the beam sword's blade, severing it neatly from his arm. The hand thunked onto the walkway.

Zelunix howled, clutching the stump of his arm to his chest. Daniel stepped in and drew his sword across the demon's other arm. That arm—with the pamba still latched onto it—fell to the ground. Daniel gave Zelunix a stiff kick in the stomach, sending the wailing murderer to the side of the walkway.

Zelunix curled up around his injuries. He bit back his cries of pain and stared up at Daniel. "I'll kill you for that, human!" he screamed. "I'll carve you up!"

"You're welcome to try," Daniel said. "But you'll probably need a hand."

"What a move by Daniel Fitzgerald!" Ky said. "He sacrificed the pamba to create a distraction, only to grab it right back! I guess Zelunix isn't much of a *hand* at swordplay!"

Daniel grimaced, unsure of what disgusted him more—Ky's pun, or the white blood oozing out of Zelunix's arm. He supposed he wasn't one to talk.

He gingerly picked up the severed limb. The pamba was still latched on one side, happy to have something to bite onto. *Better him than me, I guess.*

"But Daniel better get moving, because he's got company. It's a long way to the finish!"

Ky's hint made Daniel check back. The first demon—an imp—was about to get off the rope climb. Meanwhile, Zelunix's wails transformed into angry growls. Daniel gave him a second glance to make sure the madman wasn't getting the drop on him.

His eyes bulged out of their sockets.

The ripples of air that had surrounded Daniel's hand when the pamba used it as a snack were undulating around Zelunix's entire body. Veins and muscle and skin twisted out from the base of his severed stumps, steadily reforming into the rough shape of an arm. Bone cricked and cracked as it restored itself in the midst of the soft tissues, like trees roots pushing through soil. Daniel had recovered from some bad injuries before thanks to the contractor magic, but he'd never had to regrow an entire limb.

Daniel picked a path and took off running, beam sword in one hand, Zelunix's old arm in the other. On a whim, he tested the tip of his beam sword, dragging it on a steel wall. It sent sparks up and left a scorch mark, but the iron repelled the blade. *Okay. Good for people, not for metal.*

Daniel quickly found himself in the heart of the maze. The layers of fencing and walkways made it difficult to tell his exact position, but he could pick out the blue light of the goal flickering through the gaps here and there. The path he chose started in the right direction, but he felt it was starting to curve away. *I guess it would be too easy if I could run straight from one end to the other.*

"Daniel's making his way forward!" shouted Ky. "It looks like most are choosing different paths to cut him off or going for other powerups first. Gearing up might be the right strategy—Daniel looks to be a tough nut to crack!"

He reached a fork in the road. On his left was a flat path that looped wide around other obstacles. It was long, and it didn't have any railing, so it was a straight shot into the lava if he tripped—but otherwise safe. To the right was a path covered with swinging sawblades. It took a more direct path to the finish, aside from the risk of being diced into bite-size pieces. Daniel stared at it, trying to see if there was a pattern to the way they moved. If the blades had a blind spot, it might not be as dangerous as it appeared.

As Daniel thought he might have found just that gap, a gout of fire erupted from a hidden flamethrower in the ceiling, covering the space between the blades for a few seconds. The fire struck the floor and spread out in all directions, licking around the edges of the walkway. When the flames retreated, there was a red glow where it had touched the metal. Deciding he didn't want to risk being cooked alive while waiting for the blades to swing the other way, Daniel firmly faced the outside path.

A crash sounded behind him, and the catwalk rocked under his feet. Daniel spun. A demon was picking itself up off the ground, having dropped from a higher level. Daniel did a double-take, thinking it was another person, but then he saw the orange scales shimmering on its shoulders and the back of its arms. The raptor claws protruding from its ankles clinked as they tapped the floor. Snake-like slit pupils stared at him. It held a gray, triangular shield with a rune carved in the center—more or less a letter P in a fancy font.

"It looks like Sarfazen is the first one to reach Daniel!" Ky's announcement sounded far too excited for Daniel's liking. "Let's see how the human handles a heater shield!"

Daniel faced the dragon and brought the pink beam of his sword between them, keeping the tip high. The dragon marched forward, shield centered. When it was close, Daniel lunged, leading with the sword tip.

The point of contact sparked and cracked, but the shield held. The dragon pushed the shield against his sword to knock it away, but Daniel was already dropping back, keeping his grip on the weapon steady. He hadn't expected that to work, but it was worth a shot.

Daniel backed his way down the path behind him. Sarfazen followed him, shield held out. The dragon's eyes flicked to the pamba, still clamped onto Zelnuix's severed arm, then back to him. Daniel checked over his shoulder—the path was clear.

His opponent didn't try to close the gap, but he had to think of a new strategy. The shield was big enough that stabbing around it would be tough without risking his weapon. Maybe making a run for it would be best, but he didn't know how fast dragons could move. Couldn't be much faster than a person.

Daniel's beam sword fizzed, flickered, then vanished. He was left holding a steel hilt with no blade attached.

"Looks like Daniel's beam sword ran out of power!" Ky said. "They don't last forever!"

It was only with that hint that Daniel noticed the small button under the sword's handle. He'd been burning the thing's battery without even realizing it. *How am I supposed to play this game when I don't know half the rules?*

The letter P in the center of the dragon's shield flashed red. Daniel hunched low, ready to react.

A wave of red force in the shape of the shield shot out. Sarfazen sprinted in behind it. Daniel moved backward and chucked the useless sword hilt at the magic; it didn't stop it from moving forward, but it deflected the stuff slightly. He skipped back the other way. The skin on the side of his face felt the heat as it passed by, but he got away without a hit.

Sarfazen arrived right after. Daniel prepared to grab the shield with the idea of shoving it back toward the dragon—and then the whole thing lit up red again. He felt a wave of hot air roll off its surface.

Sarfazen was already in his face; he didn't have time to turn and run. He kept his arms up and braced himself.

When the shield struck, Daniel felt as if he'd plunged his forearms into a fire. He shouted and shoved back, but Sarfazen had the momentum and a red-hot steel brand the size of Daniel's torso.

Daniel stepped backwards, trying to keep pressure off his arms. He whipped Zelunix's arm around the edge of the shield, but Sarfazen edged it upwards. The arm slipped out of Daniel's hands and fell to the catwalk, taking the pamba along with it.

Sarfazen gripped the shield with both hands and swung. Daniel threw himself sideways to avoid it—only to realize there was nowhere to land. The lower half of his body flew out into space. He scrambled with his arms to catch himself, and ended up hanging over the lava, his arms up on the walk, fingers tangled in the chain-links.

"Looks like all bets are off for Daniel Fitzgerald!" Ky's voice shrieked happily as Daniel scrabbled for purchase. "Uh-oh! Sarfazen isn't done with him yet!"

The dragon wasn't satisfied with taking away the pamba—he wanted to permanently remove Daniel from contention. He bent over and pressed the shield into Daniel's hands. Daniel screamed as the iron seared its way through his clothes and into his skin.

Daniel turned his scream into a roar and pushed all his focus on keeping his grip steady. He had to hold on. The only thing below him was lava. It was either his arms, or his life.

Sarfazen frowned and withdrew the shield. Daniel shivered at the release from the heat. The pain from the burn lingered in his bones. *Hang on. It'll heal. Just hang on.*

The dragon started kicking at his burned skin. Daniel hung on through the sharp bursts of pain, legs kicking as he tried to throw a foot up onto the walk.

Sarfazen drew his leg back again when Daniel still didn't budge, then stomped down with his raptor-claw flexed out. Daniel tried to shift his arms out of the way, but they were half-fried and dysfunctional. One of his hands came out of the chain links, but when he tried to flex his fingers and renew his hold, all he felt was pain. He wasn't even sure if he was grabbing anything.

Sarfazen's claw stabbed through his other palm. Daniel screamed as his burned hand was torn open. The dragon lifted his foot, wrenching Daniel's hand free, then kicked, throwing him out from the walk and over the lava.

Daniel flipped through the air like a dead fish, spinning head over heels. The lava pit flashed in his vision, then the obstacle course—rapidly shrinking—and then the lava pit again—rapidly growing.

The superheated air buffeted his face. He heard shouting. He was pretty sure it was him. And then he inhaled air that was too hot, and his chest felt like it was on fire, and he couldn't scream anymore.

Daniel closed his eyes. With the last bit of himself that wasn't buried under the pain and the fear, he tried to picture Rachel's face.

Chapter 3
Ten Percent

Jack pressed up against the window as he watched Daniel fall. The lava was so hot that Daniel's hair and shirt had already caught fire, far before he hit the surface. He tumbled toward the pit like a human meteorite.

Rasputin's voice was warm and nasally behind Jack's head. "That can't be good for his health."

Jack pounded the window with his fist. "How long are they gonna let this go on?"

"About as long as it takes him to hit the bottom, I expect," Rasputin said. "That's the money shot."

"Would you shut up!?"

Jack felt a hand on his shoulder. He whipped around, ready to punch Rasputin in his big fat nose. But it wasn't him—it was Dracula.

"Discipline, Jack," he said. His voice was quiet, firm. "His soul isn't going anywhere. Control yourself."

Jack shut his mouth. He turned back to the window right as Daniel's body struck the lava.

In the movies, things melted in lava, as if it was superhot water. In real life, lava was melted rock—it was a lot denser than water. And so when Daniel came down, he struck the lava with a resounding smack that echoed through the speakers and across the room. Many flinched at the sound—Jack included. Daniel's entire body was on fire, now, sitting in a deep impression in the lava made by the force of his fall. Gouts of fire and bits of rock gurgled under his corpse.

Ky's floating projection winced visibly as her cheery voice shot over the crowd. "That looked like it hurt! I hope the spell kicks in soon! Oh—there we go!"

Purple light flashed and flickered around Daniel's body. It formed into lines, like the tangled bars of an ancient cage. The bars of light collected him up, holding him suspended. It all pulsed once, then vanished.

Daniel reappeared back at the starting platform, in front of his pedestal. His body—what was left of it—was surrounded by the purple light, and it rapidly went to work on him. The air rippled as his skin healed, turning from charred black into the normal healthy pink. The burned-away part of his face cracked and regrew—first the bone, wrapped up by muscle, then skin. Jack felt his stomach turn—it was like watching a model skeleton be reconstructed in all its gruesome layers.

It was relatively slow, considering the amount of damage, but steady. Daniel was, mercifully, long since unconscious. What was left of his shirt was crumbling into strips of ash, but with such short exposure time, the thicker jeans and shoes were holding together admirably well. At least, enough to cover the important bits.

"Daniel's out of commission for at least a minute," Ky said. "He'll be hard pressed to get back in the game at this point!" She flew back across the arena to where Sarfazen was making his way across a rope bridge, narrating his impending confrontation with two other demons that joined up to stop his progress.

"The boy's quick on his feet," Rasputin said, "but he's like you. Every other demon in this god-forsaken world has been watching PrisonWatch since they had eyes to see. He doesn't know how to use the tools he's been given."

Jack snapped his fingers. "That's it!"

"Of course *that's it*," Rasputin said.

Jack tapped his armlet—the tracking device that was latched onto every prisoner. It doubled as a limited amount of storage space and a way to keep track of his points and his PrisonWatch ranking. It also let him spend those points. A small screen blipped into existence over his arm.

"Jack," Dracula said. "What are you doing?"

"I'm spending points to contact Daniel directly," Jack said. He tapped through the menus, poking at the hologram with his finger. It took a little bit to get used to the interface, but he'd had a few months practice. "He doesn't have his armlet yet, but it should still work, he's an inmate. I'll help him from here. Like that other game, Tactician."

"You're spending on someone who isn't on the team?" Rasputin said. "Some might call that unorthodox. Others would call it an idiotic waste of perfectly good resources."

"Jack," Dracula said. "Can you guarantee you'll be able to pull him in?"

Jack hesitated. Technically, only a percentage of his points were his own—the rest belonged to the team. Jack had leeway for personal expenses, but only minor authority to spend more on what he needed, and he was required to justify it later. That said, Dracula couldn't stop Jack from pushing the button, but enforcement of the team's rules was simple. If you broke them, you'd be fleeced of everything you had and kicked out—which, in Hell terms, made you a sitting duck. They'd put out a kill order if the person did something really bad, or if Rasputin was feeling particularly vindictive that day.

"I can convince him," Jack said. "Even more easily, if I help him now." *I hope.*

Dracula nodded. "I expect you both to make it up later."

Jack tapped the button. A list of contestants in the arena popped up. The price was a lot steeper than usual—probably because they were new inmates. He hadn't heard of anyone talking people through the introductory event before, and this was obviously why. Jack grit his teeth against the loss of points and tapped Daniel's name.

****

Daniel opened his eyes.

He felt like someone had ripped his heart out of his chest, played hacky-sack with it, then shoved it back in. His lungs felt like they'd been burned through by stomach acid. His stomach wasn't doing so hot, either.

How am I alive right now?

He tested an arm. It hurt like hell, so he stopped moving it. It felt like his tendons were being drawn into place under his skin, except the person doing the reattaching was a kindergartener pretending to be a surgeon. Daniel groaned in protest.

He blinked a few times. The air was hazy, wavering. It made everything look blurry and unfocused, but at least it was familiar—he was healing. He was healing after falling into a pit of lava. *I guess Beelzebub wasn't kidding.*

He tried his hand again. The pain was still there, but receding fast. He'd been out for the worst bits. He could feel metal underneath him—some part of the catwalk. Was he back on the obstacle course?

"Sarfazen fought off one of his rivals, but his shield is a little low on heat!" Ky's voice—as bouncy as usual. "Can he hold on against Boska's hammer?!"

Daniel sat up, wincing as his back and hips cracked. He rested there as the magic patched him up and took a look around, wincing when a spike of pain lanced up his neck. He was back at the start, in front of his pedestal—albeit dressed in the bare, burned remains of his clothes. He watched the scars and burns on his arm slip away under the magic.

Daniel was starting to understand why eternal life was not as great as it was cracked up to be, because that had really sucked.

"Daniel, can you hear me?"

Daniel frowned. He recognized that voice.

"Daniel, this is Jack. Can you hear me?"

"*Jack?*"

"No time for details," Jack said. "Basically, I can pay a price to get in touch with you, like radio. I'm watching you from the prison. Can you move?"

"Yeah." Daniel got to his feet. He still ached in quite a few places—the left side of his face felt totally numb—but he could walk, at least. "How screwed am I, exactly?"

"Not as bad as you think," Jack said. Daniel could hear the smirk in his words. "There's a powerup that just dropped in on the top level. You've absolutely got to get it if you're gonna win."

"Okay," Daniel said. "Where to?"

"Go straight, then take the ramp on the right instead of the rope climb. It'll spiral up two levels."

Daniel followed the instructions. He jogged up at first, increasing his speed as his arms and legs came back online from the magic. He inhaled through his nose a few times. It smelled like the inside of a fireplace, but it could smell again. "What next?"

"The path splits in three," Jack said. "Take the center walkway and climb up the rope at the end."

Daniel reached the intersection. He saw a lone rope a couple of yards ahead, tied with knots along its length to make it easier to climb. It went all the way to the top of the arena.

"Looks like we've entered the finale of the race!" Ky shouted. "Things are getting hectic! Boska's hammer only has a few more swings, but it hits hard, and he's already taken out three others!"

Daniel looked out over the catwalks. He was virtually alone at the starting section. Everyone had bunched up near the finish, gunning for the pamba with whatever weapon they'd scraped up along the way. There were a lot of buzzsaws and narrow bridges near the finish line, forcing everyone to slow down. Right now, that was working in Daniel's favor.

"Hit the deck, now!" Jack shouted. "DUCK!"

Daniel flung himself onto the walk. A buzzsaw whipped over his head.

Jack sighed. "Come on, Daniel. Pay attention."

"I've done more than enough dying today, don't worry." Daniel caught his breath, then started up the rope. He wedged a knot between his feet and hoisted himself upward.

"Daniel, how strong are you? Magically? More than before?"

"A lot more," Daniel said, huffing as he pulled himself up the knots. "Why?"

"The stronger the better," Jack said. "It's—wait, hurry, get up the rope!"

"What is it?"

"Someone else is going for it! Go!" Daniel redoubled his efforts and hauled himself the rest of the way up. Jack kept talking as he finished the climb. "Whatever you do, touch the powerup first! Anything else doesn't matter! When you get to the top, it's straight ahead!"

Daniel arrived at a flat expanse of chain-link walk about 30 yards across; it curved like an awning above the entire starting platform. The rest of the obstacle course stretched off below him.

To his left, in the center of the roof, was a spinning purple icon shaped like a giant *10%* symbol. On the other side of the roof, moving toward the powerup, was Zelunix.

Daniel sprinted forward. Zelunix matched him, going in long, loping strides.

"Run!" Jack's voice shouted in his ear. "Dive for it, just touch it!"

Daniel was a half-step behind the devil. His eyes flickered for advantage. It was a flat roof. There wasn't anything he could do.

As Daniel focused in, a strange sensation wrapped his mind. He felt like the world had slowed slightly, somehow closed in around him. He could see the reflection of the lava on the fencing, smell the ash in his hair, hear his heart pound in his ears. Ky's high-pitched voice was mixed in, somewhere, but it was distorted and drowned out, as if he was listening to it underwater. It was unimportant and pushed aside.

Daniel's eyes caught a glimmer set at a different angle than the rest. There was a thick beam of metal running across the roof, linking two sections of the chain fencing they were standing on. He took a shorter step so his next foot forward would land on its edge.

Daniel planted, then pushed off, as if he was starting from the edge of the bag in a baseball game. He threw the front of his body forward, leveling out in a full dive and stretching out his arms. Zelunix's face contorted in slow motion. The devil's black claws swiped for the icon.

Daniel's hand got there first. The icon exploded into shards of violet light that swept around Daniel.

He'd gotten whatever the hell it was—but now he was fully extended, and his face was wide open for Zelunix's claws. Seeing the blow coming, Daniel reacted on instinct, pushing magic up to protect his skin—magic that, a moment later, he remembered could no longer use.

White light flared around Daniel's head. The claws slammed into him and bounced off. They flew past each other, Daniel rolling to one knee, while Zelunix came to a halt still on his feet.

Daniel's eyes popped like a champagne cork.

He could feel his magic. He could touch it. He could use it.

"I was a little worried for a second there," Jack said.

"What's going on?!" Daniel shouted back.

"You've got ten percent of your magic. I hope you killed a lot of Vorid while I was gone."

Daniel stood straight. "You have no idea."

****

Jack settled back on his heels. His grin stretched from ear to ear. A few demons around them were leaning in to listen to the ongoing conversation. Dracula's glares kept them all at a respectful distance.

Jack was watching Daniel from the viewing screen of his armlet. The main TVs followed whatever action Ky was focused on, but there were multiple cameras on every contestant. Jack had tapped into one that had focused on Daniel.

"That was close," he said to Daniel. "Make sure you take advantage, the powerup only lasts two minutes."

"Will do," said Daniel's voice. "Thanks, Jack."

"Yeah," Jack said. "Got your back."

"Yes, well," Rasputin said, "Let's see what he can do. That devil isn't a pushover. I don't expect that—"

A blast of sound echoed through Jack's connection to Daniel. It was matched by a flash of white light in the arena; power pulsed out in a wave, the magic residue from Daniel's strike. In the distance, they saw a red blur fly off the upper perch of the obstacle course.

Jack brought up a second screen, hovering in place over his wristband. Zelunix was already thrown beyond the edge of the arena. Jack whistled when he saw where Daniel hit him. The devil's chest cavity was crushed in by a fist-shaped imprint.

"Nice one," Jack said. "That'll be in the highlights for days."

Daniel snorted through the connection. "What is this, ESPN?"

"You don't even know, man," Jack said. "Stuff is messed up down here. But seriously, get going, you don't want to lose."

There was another flash of light, and Daniel jumped, flying over the arena like a kangaroo on steroids. Jack split his screen between three cameras—two close on Daniel from opposite sides, and one zoomed out slightly. Daniel hopped across the top of the obstacle course, leaping dozens of yards at a time, landing with a crash on the metal walkways, then leaping again. In a few seconds, he'd reached the other side.

The big group of fighters had been whittled down to three. The rest were returned to the start after falling, or they were so torn up they were temporarily down while the magic worked on them. A stout dwarf holding the pamba faced off against a devil and a grazul. The dwarf carried a huge hammer that was nearly as tall as he was. The grazul's spidery body was covered in steel plates—a defensive powerup—while the devil had a set of blue wings strapped to his back, lending him temporary flight.

The only access to the finish platform was a thin steel bridge—or, a wide walkway covered in buzzsaws. If the dwarf went for the bridge, the devil would swoop in with his wings and pick him off easily. If he tried the other path, he'd lose the advantage of his hammer in the close-quarters chaos created by the saws. But neither the grazul nor the devil wanted to attack the dwarf first, afraid that their *partner* would stab them in the back.

"We're reaching the end of the battle!" Ky said. "Our final contestants are facing off—this could definitely decide the outcome. That hammer has been absolutely unstoppable so far, but—what?" Ky sounded surprised. She put a hand to her ear, as if listening to someone talking to her. Everyone was suddenly paying attention. She glanced up. "Daniel Fitzgerald is back in this! He's fought off Zelunix with a 10 percent magical powerup and is on his way to the fight!"

Daniel landed above the three demons, peering down from the nearest ledge. "Okay," Jack said. "The dwarf has a heavy hammer. Slow, but if it hits you, your grandmother will feel it. The armor on the grazul is—"

"It's cool," Daniel said. "I've got this."

"Uh—"

Daniel leapt down from his ledge and landed right between all three demons. They paused, unsure of how to interpret his arrival in the midst of their standoff. Daniel approached the dwarf. "Daniel is ready for action!" Ky shouted. "He's going right for the pamba, no questions asked!"

The dwarf hefted his hammer and swung. Black light trailed the weapon like a comet's tail.

Daniel jumped over the swing of the hammer and landed straight in front of the dwarf. He planted one foot behind him to brace himself. His hands flashed. Jack couldn't see what happened, exactly, but the dwarf was gone, the hammer was flying away, and Daniel was holding the pamba.

The pamba nipped and snapped its jaws. Daniel cocked an eyebrow at the ball of fuzz. "You shut up," he said. His hand clenched, hard. The pamba whimpered and stopped moving.

"Unbelievable!" Ky said. "Daniel wasted him! Let's get that on instant replay!"

Everyone in the entire viewing booth, Dracula and Rasputin included, rotated as one to look at the corner TV.

It showed Daniel planting his feet after the jump, then proceeded in slow motion. The dwarf was still following through on his swing, inch-by-inch. Daniel reached out, grabbed the dwarf's wrist, twisted it straight, and punched the locked joint back the other way. The dwarf's arm broke, and the pamba fell free of his hand. Daniel grabbed it while it was still in midair.

He stepped up to the dwarf, and punched its chest once, twice, then a third time. It all happened in a flash, before the demon could even start to swing his hammer back the other way. The force of the blows sent spittle flying from the dwarf's mouth, and the hammer fell from its loosened grip. Daniel snapped out a kick the next instant hard enough to send the poor guy off his feet. His expression morphed into a wide-mouthed grunt of pain and shock. The slow motion segment ended, and the dwarf zoomed off-screen.

Meanwhile, the devil and grazul had surrounded Daniel. The TV skipped back to the action. Daniel stood there, waiting for them.

The two demons exchanged a glance, then attacked from both sides at once. The grazul brought up its forelegs, balancing back on its four hind legs, and came in like an angry crab, whipping its claws back and forward. The devil used its wings to levitate, then flew toward Daniel, leaving both arms free to swing at his face.

Daniel's body flickered, dodging each strike one at a time in a burst of magic. It appeared as if he was moving under a strobe light—first he was in one spot, then in another, changing position almost faster than Jack's eyes could catch.

Daniel's face was neutral, even bored. He wasn't even trying.

There was a series of white blasts; it came in through the radio connection like a machinegun. The devil was tossed into the rotating sawblades; one of them caught it across the waist, cutting its legs clean off. White innards spilled across the path. The grazul stumbled backwards, stabilizing on its four back legs—but both its armored forelimbs were crushed up like an accordion.

"Incredible!" Ky said. "This kid has the best physical sigil I've seen in years! Feast your eyes on raw talent!"

Daniel powered through another leap, completely avoiding the buzzsaws whizzing around the path. He stuck the landing on the finish platform with the grace of a practiced gymnast. The platform flashed, and the pamba vanished. Horns blared everywhere.

"We have our winnerrrr!" Ky said. "Daniel Fitzgerald!" Ky twirled and winked at the camera. "Hah! My instincts are never wrong!"

Rasputin gave Ky the evil eye. "I really want to kill that demon."

"That," Jack said, "is something we can agree on."

Chapter 4
Purgatory

Daniel was only on the podium a bit longer before magic transported him once again. The room he arrived in had familiar burnished steel furniture and a concrete floor. He frowned at the door opposite himself, unsure if he should go through it or not.

He decided to test his magic first. His mental effort brushed the fringes of his power; he could almost taste the stuff. When he tried to push it up and out to where it could be useful, the power slipped away, as evasive as it was before. "Dammit," Daniel said.

The door burst open. A storm of demons trooped into the room, imps, dwarves, devils. A minotaur shouldered in behind them, holding something that looked like a telescope in its arms. It pointed the device at Daniel's face while the dwarves worked on setting up a tripod. Daniel decided the oversized scope was either a camera or a very unusual torture device.

A harpy came in behind them, plastic case dangling under one arm. Flying at its shoulder was what looked like the telescope, except smaller. It flitted up toward the ceiling, propelled by a green glow underneath it. It swiftly came back down and started circling around him. The lens inside of the flying camera shrank, then expanded again, adjusting focus as it snapped pictures. It reminded him uncomfortably of the Vorid bird-robots.

"Hello there!" the harpy said. The voice was high-pitched, but not as squawking as Daniel thought it might sound, considering it had the head of a crow. "Good work in the arena, Fitzgerald, you'll have a great initial following for sure. A lot of advertisers are going to be eyeing you for promotions. Normally we'd give you your armlet now and send you off, but they'll be wanting photos."

"Uh." Daniel blinked, eyes still following the camera that was buzzing around him like a mosquito. "What?"

"Don't worry, we'll handle the equipment." The harpy snapped its beak at the minotaur. "Hurry up with that, we don't have all day."

The minotaur made an annoyed grunt. The dwarves were busy screwing pieces into the tripod while the devil held it up at the right height. The harpy gestured behind itself with a claw, and yet another guest arrived—a blue-skinned undine. Its face was narrow, flat on the sides, fish-like, but surprisingly human compared to some of the other demons. Its eyes were its most alien quality, a shiny, solid dark green, no pupils or whites. Its ears merged into high fins that wavered gently over its head.

"Take a breath and hold it," the harpy said. The undine raised a hand. Daniel was about to ask why when a spray of water erupted from the undine's palm like a high-pressure hose. Daniel coughed and spluttered and shielded his face with his hands. The undine was merciless; he was drenched in seconds. Daniel turned away to catch his breath, but the water pounding on his back didn't help the effort much.

Eventually, it ended. Daniel faced the demons in time to receive a blast of air from the harpy's wings. It felt like he was standing in an overclocked wind tunnel. His lips rippled as he tried to inhale and shout for them to stop.

Finally, it did stop. Daniel hunched over slightly, breathing. The water had all been sucked away; even his clothes hung dry. "I'm really starting to get tired of this shit," Daniel said.

"Patience, Mr. Fitzgerald," the harpy said. "All standard procedure." The harpy threw some clothes at him—from where, Daniel couldn't tell—and he fumbled to hold onto them. It gestured with one of the three claws at the end of its wing. A yellow pulse flew from the harpy's hand to the wall. An iron privacy screen promptly drew itself across half the room.

"Change your clothes. Plenty of pictures of you in those rags already."

Daniel was somewhat grateful—his outfit had been torn up and burned beyond recognition. He switched into the new clothes—black slacks and a red shirt that fit surprisingly well. The harpy tossed some socks and dress shoes over the screen wall. Daniel had to struggle for a good minute to get the half-melted remains of his sneakers off his feet. The new shoes were stiff but more comfortable than they looked.

Feeling surprisingly refreshed, Daniel stepped out from the privacy screen. Most of the demons had left, except for the harpy, minotaur, and one dwarf. An elaborate set had been constructed in his absence, complete with big lights and shiny umbrella heads. Daniel cocked an eyebrow. "Guess I'm ready for my close up."

The harpy set its case on the table, then opened it up. It withdrew a small paint brush with one claw, dabbed it in something, then approached Daniel. Daniel raised a hand. "Whoa, whoa. What's that?"

"Makeup," the harpy said. "For the photos."

"I'm all set," Daniel said. "Thanks."

"You'll look a lot better if you let me—"

"Dude, I'm doing the best I can to put up with this right now when I have no idea what's going on," Daniel said. "But if you try to put makeup on me I swear to God I'll tear your wings off."

The harpy huffed and ruffled its feathers. "No need to go that far. Suit yourself."

Then began one of the strangest experiences of Daniel's life—a photoshoot. The dwarf busied itself adjusting the light fixtures. The minotaur unraveled a backdrop behind him showing part of the obstacle course he'd been racing on. The harpy shouted directions at Daniel, telling him to raise his arms, lift his chin, and generally look angrier and more vicious.

"Give me some energy!" the harpy said, waving its wings around. "I feel like I'm shooting a librarian!" It drew its claws inward, holding them close to its chest. "You just won your first game going in blind. Give me victory! I want to see your passion for victory!"

If Daniel's eyes rolled any harder they'd jump off his head. He continued to pose in lackluster fashion.

After a while, the harpy was fed up. It inspected the back of the camera, combing through the twenty dozen photos they'd taken. "Most of these are garbage, but there's a few that'll do. Kovach, give him his armlet."

"Mmm," the minotaur grunted. The hulking bull stomped up toward Daniel. It held a plain white bracelet, about three inches long. "Wrist out, human."

Daniel hesitated. Kovach jingled the wristband impatiently. Daniel put his arm out, and Kovach snapped it in place. At first, it dangled loose—but then it flashed with light and resized itself, pulling snug around Daniel's wrist.

"Everything you need in one place," Kovach grumbled. "Track your points, rank, inventory, followers, so on."

Daniel considered recent experiences. "What happens if my arm gets cut off?"

"It'll come back. Depending." A monster of few words, he clomped away and began collecting the equipment.

"Depending on what?" Daniel asked.

The minotaur, busy with its work, ignored him. Daniel twisted the bracelet around his wrist with his other hand. It was secure, but not uncomfortable. He realized that they all had one—the minotaur, the dwarf, and the harpy, too, all the same red-black color. Daniel's was just plain white.

"Your inventory size is more than triple the normal starting quantity for winning the game," the harpy said. "And you get 50,000 points to start."

Daniel looked at him. "Can we maybe pretend for five seconds that I don't know what any of that means?"

"Points," the harpy said. It clacked its claws at Daniel's face in the way someone would snap their fingers at a moron, impatient to get them on the same page. "Prison money. Anyway, I've got to make a call." The harpy produced a flat steel panel. Like the clothes, he conjured it from nowhere, as if he were a cartoon reaching behind his back and pulling out a giant monkey wrench. The harpy manipulated the device with a claw; magic runes flashed across its surface, and it made a call in the same way Nip had earlier. "Yes, we're done." A pause. "Yes. Send him off."

"Wait, wait, wait," Daniel said, raising his hands. "You didn't even explain anything."

The harpy cawed at him. "Not my problem. You'll figure it out."

Daniel opened his mouth and took in the breath he needed to curse the demon into next week—but his body locked up. His breath caught in his chest. The shining lights of teleportation magic flashed around his feet. His vision swam; his stomach flopped over. The world went black.

And then, it swirled back into place.

His body unfroze; he caught himself. He was on a wide stone dais in the center of what appeared to be a city square. The place was packed with demons. They milled and roved about, some in groups, others alone. All the varieties Daniel had seen so far were represented, all in various states of dress.

Daniel sighed. No harpy to yell at now. And no idea what to do next.

A second look confirmed something for him—all the demons he could see all had a wristband. They came in a variety of thicknesses and colors, but the fashion was universal. There was a pattern to it all—groups with identically colored wristbands were milling about the center of the square, looking over the contestants. Daniel could feel a lot of gazes.

The square itself was concrete, surrounded by tall buildings with flashing signboards and neon lights. The air was warm, and a slight smoke filled the air—smoke coming from a fried food stand parked halfway across the square. A grazul manned the grill, using its spidery arms to expertly flip patties of fried meat, while an imp shouted for customers and took orders. Daniel smirked to himself. *Not exactly the lake of fire.*

He took in the skyline. The buildings were packed tight, shoulder-to-shoulder. Narrow, winding streets ran away from the square in random directions. Everything was asymmetrical; the buildings themselves didn't match. Some were traditional square blocks with parallel windows; others were domed, or had more elaborate pillars or crenellations, as if they'd been transplanted out of ancient Greece or medieval Europe. A much weirder structure looked like a gnarled potato perched high on thick stilts; holes in the side of the thing provided entrances for flying harpies to land and take off. Another building looked like a merge between a skyscraper and a pyramid; the top glowed with a piercing blue light. More of the flying cameras were zipping around the sky, coming and going in various directions. Others hovered in place over the square, keeping an eye on the activity.

Daniel looked up. The colorful neon lights played with the smoke in the air, creating a weave of pinks, blues and greens amidst dark shadows. Stalactites hung from a ceiling that was far, far above. The entire thing was inside of a giant cave.

A twenty foot tall statue of someone Daniel recognized stood opposite him, dominating the other half of the square. It was Beelzebub, holding a very large and threatening spear in his left hand.

Three other contestants from the arena stood on the dais with Daniel. One was having a conversation with a nearby group of demons, all wearing the same colored armlet. Daniel figured they had to be the teams mentioned in his introductory video, here for recruitment.

As he took in the surroundings, the haze of teleportation magic started up not far from him. Another demon materialized.

It was Zelunix. Daniel made a face. *Just what I needed.*

Zelunix got his bearings, then spotted Daniel. The devil did a double-take, then grinned at him. "I hoped I'd run into you again."

Black, razor-like nails extended from Zelunix's fingers with a sharp *shiiick*. He charged across the dais toward Daniel.

Instead of backing away, Daniel broke into a run straight for him. He saw Zelunix's swipe coming and dove low, spreading his arms wide. Daniel wrapped up Zelunix's waist and took him to the ground.

A claw wrenched up under Daniel's armpit. He ignored the flash of pain and clenched his elbow against his chest, trapping Zelunix's hand in place. Daniel slammed the heel of his palm up against Zelunix's chin to daze him, then started beating on the side of his face with hammer blows. Zelunix's free arm came up to drive him back, but Daniel ignored it—he'd had a lot worse. He leaned into his hits, smashing his hand into the devil's face as fast as possible.

Daniel felt his weight shift. Zelunix got his legs under Daniel's hips. He was kicked back a few inches, nearly throwing him off. Daniel locked onto Zelunix's waist with his thighs and kept punching. If he didn't keep the demon pinned down and on the defense, he'd be gutted by those claws.

The sound of steel striking stone crashed into Daniel's ear. A deep metallic voice echoed over them. "Rule infraction: instigating violence in a neutral territory against another inmate."

Daniel was coming down for another strike when his arm was caught by a metal hand. He stopped, staring at it in surprise. The thing had fingers as thick as his wrist. Daniel yelped as he was yanked into the air.

A robot about fifteen feet tall held Daniel and Zelunix up apart from each other. A glowing red slit lay across its square head; its arms were articulated in a dozen places. It had a cylindrical torso, and below that, eight supporting legs. Runes and lights ran down its body, starting at its head and traveling out to its hands and feet like pulsating magical circuitry. It reminded Daniel of an oversized, boxy-looking extractor.

The robot lowered Daniel to the ground. He worked his wrist a little where the robot had held him, rubbing the ache away, then checked his armpit. He was bleeding, but a hazy swirl of air told him it was healing up. He rolled his shoulder a few times, testing the motion; everything worked fine. His brand new shirt, however, was torn under the arm to the waist. *At least the red covers for the blood.*

"Inmate Zelunix, you are sentenced with ten days of isolation in room B354," the robot intoned. "Exception: you have arrived within the last 28 days. Sentence mitigated to 2 days isolation."

"He fought back!" Zelunix shouted. The devil pointed an accusatory finger at Daniel. "Anyone that fights is sentenced!"

"No judgement can be overturned," the robot said. It started off, holding the struggling devil high above the crowd.

Zelunix tried to free his arm, but the robot's grip didn't budge. He turned to look at Daniel; his face was twisted and ravenous. "I'll find you, you little piece of shit. I'll slice off your head and dig your brain out of your skull! And when Hell grows you another one, I'll do it again!"

"Sentence increased to 4 days due to use of profanity while in enforcer custody," the robot said. "Inmate, remain silent."

"I'll do the same to you, damn hunk of metal!" Zelunix kicked his foot against the robot's arm.

"Sentence doubled to 8 days due to use of violence against an enforcer. Inmate, remain silent." The robot raised its other hand. An arc of red lightning leapt from the robot's palm to Zelunix. The demon screamed. His body twitched and flailed, then fell limp, sparks still dancing over his head. The enforcer walked off into the distance, holding the devil swinging in its grip.

Daniel sighed and rubbed his forehead. He could feel a serious headache setting in. It had been one thing after another for what felt like hours: his hearing with the mages back on earth; the unreality of his arrival; Beelzebub hiring him as a hitman; fighting in the arena with Zelunix; falling into a lava pit; a bird-headed photographer that wanted to put makeup on him; and then Zelunix a second time, because apparently once wasn't enough in the psychopath department. If that enforcer thing hadn't showed up, he might have been sliced open like a tuna fish.

He put his hands on his hips and looked around. There were a lot of lights, a lot of sounds, and far too many smells for his liking. He wasn't exactly sure what to do next, but he had to get away from the babble of the crowd—and all the people staring at him—before he plotted out his next move.

But if he wandered off, he might end up in a repeat of his most recent situation. It was pretty clear that this was the arrival spot for everyone from the arena, and a sort of crossroads for the whole city. He could see some of the others still in the crowd, talking to groups of demons. It was a lot safer here—under the watchful eyes of several more enforcers, Daniel noted, standing at key points around the square—than in a random back alley.

Daniel frowned, rubbing the wristband. He did have one thing going for him—Jack. Jack had been down here for months, and he had to know where Daniel arrived. Hopefully he'd get in touch again.

Daniel's frown deepened. He had absolutely no idea what to say to Jack. Memories of their fight floated back up. Then memories of Rachel.

Daniel squeezed his eyes shut and squashed it away. He couldn't go there. Not right now.

A gruff voice rose over the bustle of his surroundings. "Are you Daniel Fitzgerald?"

There was a group of demons off the dais to his right, all wearing sky blue wristbands with a black stripe running through the center. The one in front, a dragon with dark, almost black scales on his forearms and golden eyes was the one who'd spoken. "Yeah, that's me," Daniel said. He figured there was no point in hiding his identity—he was the only human in the whole group of new inmates. In fact, he was the only human he'd seen so far. The thought wasn't a very comforting one.

"My name is Kavarssian," the dragon said, nodding to him. "I'm a member of the Sky Runners." Daniel cocked a curious eyebrow. "We're one of the teams here on this level," Kavarssian added. "As a matter of fact, we're ranked third overall."

Daniel didn't feel like being physically assaulted again, so he nodded back to the demon and kept his words polite. "I don't really know much about the ranking system or the teams, but that sounds pretty good."

The dragon smiled at him. "It's more than pretty good. There are about 200 teams in Purgatory alone. So in this whole city, the highest level of Hell, only one group is ranked higher than us."

"Wait," Daniel said, "if you're ranked third, doesn't that mean there's two groups above you?"

"True," Kavarssian said. "I forget new humans don't know how things work down here. The number one ranked team is the only team on their floor, which is the last one above Purgatory, level zero."

"Uh, so are we on level one, or in Purgatory?"

"Purgatory *is* the name of the city," Kavarssian said. "The whole place, including the outskirts, is level one. There are ten levels in total, level nine at the bottom, zero on top."

"That makes more sense," Daniel said. It also agreed with the bits of info he'd gotten from Ky. "Appreciate the explanation."

"Certainly," Kavarssian said. "I'm sure much of this is confusing for you. That's something we might be able to help you with, going forward."

Daniel made to ask another question, but paused, because he noticed a few other groups orbiting Kavarssian's team. They were paying careful attention to the conversation and throwing each other really ugly looks at the same time. They were eyeing Daniel, too, but in an appraising sort of way.

"So," Daniel said, looking at Kavarssian, "what can I do for you?"

"Simple," Kavarssian said. "Join us."

Daniel drew back slightly. "Your team? Why? I mean—why me?"

Kavarssian folded his arms across his chest. He almost looked human in the lighting, even with the snake-eyes, but the black scales glimmered a bit across his arms, reminding Daniel that he was anything but. "I'm in charge of recruitment for the Sky Runners. I watched you in the arena just now. When a good potential talent comes through, we make an effort to get them on board." He gestured to the buildings beyond the square. "We can offer you a firm footing in terms of resources, finances, and personal development. As part of our alliance, you'll have our backing and support if you run into any conflicts. In exchange, you fight with us in the games and help us keep our rank and earn points."

Daniel kept his expression neutral, but his thoughts moved rapidly. The bottom line was that he'd impressed them, and they were trying to rope him in. Kavarssian was, to his credit, being pretty straightforward about it. That explained the other groups—they were there to snatch Daniel up if things fell through with the Sky Runners, but they didn't want to speak before the higher ranked team gave up on him.

That meant Kavarssian's claim about their ranking was probably on the level. In fact, if he'd been exaggerating their status, one of the other groups might have said something to try to get Daniel on their side instead.

Daniel suppressed a smirk. Always nice to be in demand.

"That all sounds like a really good offer," Daniel said. "And thanks for being straight with me. But I'm waiting for a friend, and I want to hear what he has to say first. I can't give you an answer right now."

Kavarssian's smile faded slightly. "I see. Who's your friend? Maybe I know him."

"Jack Killiney," Daniel said. "He's a contractor, like me."

"I'm extremely aware," Kavarssian said. His smile dimmed even further, until it was a bare curl of his lips. "Whatever terms they offer, we'll beat them. We can give you a full suite and courtyard, servants, concubines, and a full monthly stipend in addition to covering your rent."

"Whoa, whoa, back up," Daniel said. "Concubines?"

"Absolutely!" Kavarssian said. "We could dredge up a few human women from the lower levels, if you have narrower tastes. We'll even pay for a virtual reality system—custom scenarios, or plain old memory reconstruction, if you prefer something cleaner. Can't tell the difference these days."

"Let me stop you right there," Daniel said. "I'm not interested in whores. Or virtual sex."

Kavarssian blinked. A dwarf standing next to him whispered in his ear. Kavarssian cleared his throat and rapidly waved a hand. "I'm sorry if I offended you. Dragons take a less...*committal* view to intimate relationships than some other tribes, or humans."

"Right," Daniel said. "I appreciate the interest, but...as a human, I need to take some time and settle in before I commit to anything." When Kavarssian frowned, Daniel hurried to soften the rejection. "Once I figure things out, I promise that I'll give the Sky Runners their due consideration. It's nothing personal, I just don't have my head wrapped around all this yet." Daniel glanced at the skyline. *Maybe a caveline, considering we're underground.*

"Daniel," Kavarssian said, "reconsider. If you accept my offer right now in good faith, the position and benefits you'll get will be far greater than what you could barter for later."

The guy wasn't giving up. Daniel nodded his head once more. "I understand, but I can't say yes right now."

"I'm trying to help you, my friend," Kavarssian said. "There are other teams that aren't as nice as we are. The Sky Runners aim high, but we also have moral standards other teams don't." He made a face at the teams around them. A few of them met his disdainful gaze, but none of them held it very long. Eventually, he looked back at Daniel. "You're making a mistake if you walk away. Not only in terms of your prospects, but your own wellbeing."

Daniel had to work very hard to keep the smirk off his face. The guy had hopped from offering him an apartment suite full of concubines at his beck and call to going on about moral standards. Maybe it was a dragon thing. "This all is really flattering," Daniel said, still trying to ease away from it gently. "But I can't accept."

"What can I do to make you change your mind?"

"Nothing, right now," Daniel said. "The answer is no."

A screeching alarm erupted over the entire square. All the street lamps and neon signs that kept the cave lit went dark. Daniel flinched; his heart fluttered. It was beyond pitch black; he couldn't see his hands in front of his face.

Emergency lights slammed on, glowing in strips that lined most of the buildings. The city was stained in blood red light and shadows; he felt as though he was looking through night vision goggles. The siren pulsed again, winding up and then back down as if a nuclear warhead was about to strike. Daniel's wristband flashed red and white—as if he needed any extra warning that something was going down.

Red neon lettering appeared above the square. It had a countdown—already on 59 seconds and dropping. As Daniel watched the number tick lower, the siren wound down, and a stern robotic voice took its place, resounding from every direction.

"All inmates, prepare for territory battle. All inmates, prepare for territory battle."

The square burst into a flurry of chaotic motion. Demons were running everywhere; groups stayed hunched together, quickly making their way through the press and down one of the winding streets. The food stalls folded up in a snap of magic and sliding steel. The flying cameras multiplied, groups of them following each one of the teams or flocking to other destinations elsewhere in the city. Daniel thought he could see more of them zipping from spaces up in the stalactites.

"Confused?" Daniel snapped his head back to Kavarssian. The dragon looked more like a devil in the red glow. His face was dark. "Territory is important in Purgatory. It's why everyone here is in a team. Controlling territory nodes grants a weekly income of points, and down here, points often equal power." The dragon gestured to the dais. "You're only protected by the enforcers in two places: neutral zones, and your own territory. But they deactivate during a territory war."

Daniel didn't like the look on Kavarssian's face one bit, and he definitely didn't like this situation. The more he thought about what the dragon said, the less it sounded like informative advice and the more it sounded like a threat.

Kavarssian kept an eye on Daniel's changing expressions. The dragon smiled at him. "I see that you understand. I pegged you for a smart one when I saw you in the arena. That's why you should join us."

"I already said no," Daniel said. "That's not changing."

The dragon's smile curled up higher, but it didn't make him look any more friendly. "If you won't join us, you won't join anyone."

Daniel felt a sense of tension creeping up his shoulders. His eyes went to the countdown. 25 seconds. "You can't threaten me," Daniel said. "This is Hell. I can't die."

Kavarssian snorted, then chuckled. The demons around him started laughing.

The dragon waved for quiet. "Daniel. Not being able to die...it doesn't mean you can't feel pain, does it?"

Daniel's spine shivered at the way they were all looking at him. The red light made it all look like shadows and blood. The eyes kept staring at him from the dark, like a pack of wolves getting ready to pounce.

Or a pack of demons.

Daniel checked the clock. Ten seconds, and he was free game.

He turned, broke into a flat out sprint, and jumped off the dais. "Get him!" Kavarssian growled. The demons were after him even as their leader shouted the words, circling the stone platform to get to him.

Daniel took off across the square. The place had already emptied out. He ran past the statue of Beelzebub, picked one of the side streets at random, and ducked in.

The siren sounded again; it bounced off the tall walls on either side of him, shouting in his ears. The battle was on. Almost immediately, the ground shook under his feet; the roar of a distant explosion followed after. More sounds, stuff that sounded like gunfire, magical blasts—it all came in one tremendous rush.

His breath came fast as he pumped his legs. His dress shoes slapped the pavement hard—not the ideal choice for running from a dragon. A quick check over his shoulder told him the entire troop was right behind him—and the lights that were coming off their wristbands warned him they had tricks up their sleeves. He cut a hard right at the next intersection.

The scenery didn't change; he felt like he was running down a canyon of buildings. All the doors he met were sealed shut. He didn't bother stopping to try them. He saw another intersection coming up and got ready to make a left turn.

Daniel banked tight, then skipped to a halt as fast as he could, throwing his arms out for balance.

He was at the edge of a stone courtyard, and the entire place was complete pandemonium. Explosions of magic ripped through the air. Shadowy figures with bright wristbands darted around, clashing in hand-to-hand combat, holding up blue shields made of light, or firing projectiles at the opposing side. A building on his left was covered in ice. Green flames burned nearby, mixing with the ice magic to produce waves of fog that covered most of the courtyard. The green fire danced against the red emergency lights, as if a rebel group of Santa's elves had instigated civil war.

Daniel heard shouts behind him. He was trapped between the madhouse in front and dragon out for his blood behind.

"Sky Runners incoming, northwest alley!" someone shouted.

"Block the entrance!"

Daniel glanced at the rooftops in time to see a ball of the green fire whistling in his direction. He jumped toward the center of the square as the stuff exploded behind him.

Daniel was blown away by the force of the explosion and landed hard on his stomach. He rolled over a few times, then came to a stop on his back. His chest spasmed; he coughed hard. Something wet splattered his hands. He glanced down. The flickering light showed him what it was—blood.

The square spun around him, lights and screaming and magic. His ears rung and whined; his insides felt like they'd been put through a blender. He tried to scream, but all that came out was a dribble of spit and a weak whimper.

The healing magic wavered around him in force, trying to patch him up. He pushed his legs down and shoved himself across the stone, trying to get away from the center of the fight. Pain wracked its way across his chest, and he coughed again—more blood splattered the stone in front of him.

He bumped up against something—some kind of retaining wall. The main battle was on the other side. It wasn't much in the way of cover, but it was better than nothing. He pushed himself upright, back against the stone.

The way he'd come was a sea of blackened rubble and green fire. The fire clung to the surfaces it touched like some kind of magical napalm. Whoever cast that spell drove the Sky Runners into retreat, but Daniel had one less route of escape.

Daniel coughed again, and then fell into a hacking fit. Blood—and bits of other stuff Daniel hoped wasn't important—fell down his shirt and into his lap. Oddly enough, he felt a lot better after coughing that up, and the pain was going away. Maybe his lungs had cleared out the damaged bits. The whining in his ears died back, replaced by the sounds of battle.

He needed to find another way out of the courtyard before he got himself killed in the crossfire. He tucked his white wristband under his sleeve, then lifted his eyes just above the retaining wall.

What probably started as a surprise attack had turned into a more organized battle. Half the courtyard was occupied by figures with white wristbands with a red symbol; the others were orange-red. A group of them were fighting close-in with clubs, swords, and spears. Others stood behind their front lines, crouching behind cover and exchanging long-range blasts of ice and fire. The red-white group had the advantage of blue energy shields, small ones for their front-line warriors, and tall, mobile tower shield versions for their ranged attackers.

Daniel saw a harpy edge out from behind a more mundane iron emplacement and point a metal rod. A tendril of purple lightning lashed out from its tip and twisted toward a spearman. The lightning moved fast, but the man saw the magic coming and blocked with his shield. On impact, the shield fizzled and vanished, absorbing the spell but leaving the man defenseless, holding only the metal handle. He produced a blue crystal in his hand and fumbled to slot it into his shield, probably to recharge it. Before he could do so, his undine opponent ran him through with a sword, straight through the heart, and kicked him away.

Instead of healing, the slain warrior vanished before his body hit the ground. The swordsman rushed back into the fray. The harpy ducked behind his cover as a spray of suppressive blue energy blasted where he'd been standing. Ice cracked and spread over the metal where the spell struck, and the metal cracked, then shattered, destroying the cover and exposing the harpy. A series of follow-up blasts blew away a hastily deployed second barrier, then vaporized him.

Daniel sat there, staring at the people trying to gut each other and watching the magic raining down over their heads—and then he realized. The team with the red-white wristbands and blue shields not only had humans, but they were *exclusively* humans. He couldn't spot a demon amongst them.

Someone emerged from an alley behind the demon forces. Daniel couldn't see them too clearly through the haze of fog and shadows, but it looked like a human had flanked them. He gripped the stone wall with both hands, bracing himself for explosions.

The magician—a woman—stepped into the open. A demon behind her cast a spell forward, shooting a hunk of ice shaped like a spear toward the human shield wall. She'd walked right into the line of fire.

The ice passed through her. No flashy magic, no spell, no ripples of energy. It was as if she wasn't there.

The ice shard continued on and slammed into the ground across the square. It shattered and expanded into a roiling frozen fog, sending the defenders scrambling to ward it off as it billowed around their defenses. But Daniel wasn't paying attention to that.

The woman paused slightly at the disturbance, then continued forward. The demons around her did nothing to stop her progress. In fact, they didn't even seem to see her. They kept fighting as if she wasn't even there.

A few paces later, she stepped out of the shadow of the building. She wore a white gown that hugged her chest and billowed out around bare feet. Her skin was nearly as white as the dress, though it was hard to tell in the uneven light. Her hair was white; it fell straight all the way to her waist. She was there—but not there—in a way Daniel could feel, more than see.

She reminded him of Eleanor—not because they looked similar, but because they moved the same way; the same confident, gliding strides. Her face was set in an imperious mask, one that said nothing she saw was living up to her expectations. Her eyes took in the fighting as if judging a mediocre painting and trying to find something nice to say to the artist.

An explosion of fire detonated at her feet, blowing away a few surrounding swordsmen. The heat wave washed over Daniel, ripping at his hair. Her clothes didn't even so much as ruffle; she didn't wince, or even blink. Her feet brought her around the edge of the remaining flames, but Daniel had no doubt that she could have gone right through them if she'd wanted.

The woman stopped in the center of the courtyard, not ten yards from where Daniel was hidden. She started to turn in his direction, as steady and silent as a ghost. Daniel felt a strange crawling chill climb up the back of his head.

A rumbling crash ripped Daniel's attention away from the woman. The building behind the demons was covered in a cloud of debris and dust because a hole had been smashed open in the first-floor wall. A hulking, silver-haired beast came charging out of the gap, a blue tower shield hoisted in each hand. A white-red wristband was wrapped all the way around its wrist, which was easily as big around as Daniel's thigh.

Voices came up from the demons, all shouting one word in warning. "It's Killiney! Killiney's here!"

"Retreat! Front line, get back!"

"Change targets! Ice magic!"

A flurry of magic targeted Jack. He held up the two shields like a boxer taking cover behind his fists. The shields blocked most of the barrage, but they weren't big enough to cover his entire body. Ice shattered and cracked over the exposed bits of his arms and legs, but Jack shrugged it off. The silver fur repelled the magic like oil repelled water.

Jack barreled his way into the rear ranks of spellcasters. Daniel expected him to use the shields like battering rams, but he dropped them once he reached the magicians, instead using his huge arms to piledrive his way through the mess. His opponents scattered wildly, some forcibly sent flying by Jack's fists, others fleeing in panic.

Without backup, the frontline fighters in the center of the square were quickly overrun by the combination of human swordsmen and their own magicians. They pressed their way forward and swept across the square in lethal flurries of teamwork. Spells harassed foes, either hurting them or disrupting their balance; swords, spears, and axes quickly closed in, slicing, stabbing, and hacking to finish the job. Daniel didn't understand how they were making the enemy team members vanish, but they definitely weren't healing back up.

Jack raged and flailed around the entrance to one of the alleyways, preventing the enemy from falling back and regrouping. An imp hacked at the back of Jack's leg, trying to hamstring him. The sword made contact, but all it did was get tangled in the shaggy fur, leaving Jack unharmed.

Jack growled and whipped an arm around, and his hand came in like a wrecking ball, picking the imp up clean off his feet and sending him sailing up across the square, over Daniel's head, and into the alley behind him. Daniel saw the imp's leg twitch once, and then it vanished, too.

When he looked back, Jack's flank was protected by his friends. They raised their shields high, covering his back from a few rays of magic still peppering him from the rooftops. The repeated showers of ice didn't seem to hurt Jack much, but the sheer bulk of it was slowing him down, the ice collecting on his fur and building up around his feet and ankles.

With their front line hacked apart and their magical forces beaten and bruised by Jack, the remaining demons and their magicians on the rooftops withdrew. Jack, now looking somewhat like the abominable snowman after the magic blizzard, didn't bother trying to chase them down. He slapped his fists and arms against the side of a building, scraping the ice away in hunks.

With the battle reaching a sudden conclusion, Daniel glanced around the courtyard. The woman was gone. She'd been standing right there. Where could she go?

"There's one behind the wall!"

Daniel flinched. Sweat rolled down his back. He braced himself for the receiving end of friendly fire, then raised his arms and stood straight. "Don't shoot! Don't shoot! I'm an ally!"

The whole troop of humans turned to face him, Jack included. Spells of various colors of magic glowed on the fingertips and staves of every magician—blue ice, green fire, reds, yellows, violets. Daniel had never felt threatened by a rainbow before, but this one looked on edge and ready to take a piece out of him. He kept his hands very open and in plain sight.

"You're not showing up that way," one of the men said. He stepped forward, sword raised. "Who are you?"

"Jack, it's me!" Daniel waved at Jack's hulking silverback form. "Daniel!"

"Stand down," Jack said. "He's who we came for."

The magicians lowered their weapons in a collective rustle of metal and cloth. They collected in the back while Jack approached. Some of them exchanged glances and eyed Daniel up and down. Others muttered between themselves. Daniel didn't mind. Judging looks were a lot less painful than explosions.

As Jack walked forward, his form shifted and warped; muscles rippled and shrank. His fur retreated into his skin. Soon he was standing in front of Daniel, wearing only a pair of black skintight shorts.

Jack still looked the same. Buzz cut, thin, on the short side. He skin was pale, but it might have been the bad lighting. Or living underground for months on end. He watched quietly as Daniel hopped over the wall and walked forward.

Daniel stopped a few feet out. Their eyes met, and then they both looked away. Jack stared at his feet. Daniel found a sudden interest in the windows across the courtyard.

It was quiet.

The awkwardness grew thicker and heavier on Daniel's head the longer it went on. Jack was his best friend—a friend he'd fought with. A friend that tried to kill Rachel. A friend that murdered innocent people. The last time he'd seen the guy, he'd been raving like a lunatic.

Daniel had thought long and hard about that night. He still didn't understand it. It was almost as if Jack had transformed into a gorilla in his head as much as his body. He had no idea what to say to the guy to make it better, to gloss it over. He hadn't prepared any words of wisdom.

So Daniel did the only thing he was good at.

"Nice spandex," Daniel said.

Jack looked at him. "Huh?"

"Did you pick those shorts yourself," Daniel said, "or is that some kind of uniform for contractors? I didn't get the memo. At least you didn't go full Superman"—Daniel gestured around his crotch—"with the underwear on the outside. I dunno though, maybe you could pull it off."

"The first time you see me in—how long?" Jack said. His lips went flat. "We've both been sent to Hell. I just saved your ass. And you make fun of my clothes."

"Do they make you say *it's clobbering time* when you transform?" Daniel said.

"Fuck you," Jack said. "Everything else I wear gets torn up, and I don't exactly have a lot of choices." Daniel cocked his head at him, smirking. "I mean, I do, but they're expensive and you can't really waste money down here. You can't even talk. You look like you tried to make a move on Ky and she threw you in a lava pit." Jack snapped his fingers. "Oh, that's *right*. That *is* what happened. I almost forgot."

"You don't even know the half of it," Daniel said. "There was a two-for-one special on psychopathic assaults today. If the friendly neighborhood robot buddy hadn't shown up, I'd be worse than this."

"Enforcer?" Jack said. Daniel nodded. "I'm surprised it didn't haul you off, too. But seriously, we need to get you fixed up."

Daniel looked down at his torn up, singed, blood-soaked clothes. "Between this and your shorts, I think I was accidentally sent to fashion hell. Do you think Beelzebub really wears Prada?"

Jack smiled, then started laughing. Daniel laughed at his laugh. Jack buckled over and tucked his arms into his stomach. Somewhere in-between, the laughs were less about Daniel's lame joke, less at laughing at each other, and more about the sheer volume of stress pushing them into accepting whatever leftover scraps of humor they could find.

"You have no idea," Jack said. He got his breath back. "No idea how good it is to see someone. See you." His face firmed up; the mirth died away. "There's a lot you need to know really, really fast."

"Tell me about it," Daniel said. He waved at the troops behind Jack. "So are you guys all one team? All human?"

Jack nodded. "All human. There are a few other teams with people...most of them are pretty low ranked, or totally scattered. A lot down below on the lowest level. We'll save that stuff for later though, the territory battle—"

Jack's wristband flashed. He did something to it with his hand, and a floating screen appeared, hovering over his arm. Daniel watched as Jack navigated a menu and opened up an overhead map of the city. Purgatory was shaped like a rough circle; near the center was the big square Daniel had first arrived. The cityscape took up most of the land, but there was some open terrain on the east side, across what looked like a river.

The map was washed over in two colors: a green zone, that took up a chunk of the city's northwest corner, and a red zone that spread over the remainder. Jack's position was represented by a blue dot. The cluster of green dots nearby were probably their allies. Daniel was a grey dot; neither an ally nor an enemy.

Part of the green zone extended out into the red, forming a small peninsula of territory. About half of it was flashing.

"Crap," Jack said. "We need to get back now."

"What's going on?"

"Trouble," Jack said.

"That doesn't answer my question."

"We'll walk and talk."

"No one can hold still in this place," Daniel mumbled.

"Everyone, regroup at zone 22," Jack said, "prepare to reinforce 23! Double time, burn your points! I'll escort Daniel myself, tell Rasputin I'll be there soon!"

The men and women snapped to attention. Someone called out a loud "yes sir!" and they were off, sprinting through the alleys or leaping back to the rooftops. The light of magic glowed around most of them. A flock of cameras followed swiftly behind, tracking their progress—and that was when Daniel noticed that he and Jack had nearly ten of their own cameras, hovering over their heads, examining them from every angle.

"This way," Jack said. He ran down one of the alleys, taking a route that branched away from the direction the troops had gone. "No one likes to mess with me, so we should be safe on our own. Probably."

Daniel kept pace behind his shoulder, glancing up at the tall, winding buildings. The glint of every window in the dark lighting made him flinch. "Probably?"

"They'll either try to cut off me or the rest of the squad," Jack said. "Can't afford everyone getting bogged down together again. Splitting up is best for now." Jack pointed at his map; it was still floating over his wrist, following alongside them. "See this?" Jack said. "The green is our territory. Since I've gotten here we've pushed out into a new space. More territory—"

"Is more points," Daniel said. "The welcoming committee told me."

"Who?"

"The Sky Runners tried to recruit me," Daniel said. "I told them I wanted to wait for you, but when the alarms started going off they decided they didn't want to take no for an answer."

"Damn," Jack said. "Lucky you didn't get kidnapped. Left here!" Jack cut to the side, avoiding a broad intersection. "We can't go in the open, just the two of us. That's like asking someone to attack you."

Daniel could hear the sounds of battle and see a few flashes of magic over to the right side. He skidded slightly when Jack suddenly changed direction, then poured on the gas to catch back up. Exhaustion was starting to wear on him; it felt like weights were attached to his feet.

"Territory gives you income," Jack said, "but it also gives you some rent-free living space. Super important, no one can afford monthly rent for an entire team indefinitely. You have to hold territory if you want to stay solvent."

"Right," Daniel said between breaths. "So. Psychos. Psychos everywhere."

"Sorry about that," Jack said. He didn't even seem winded yet. "We were trying to get to you when it happened, we were all the way across town. The territory battles are random—usually once or twice a week, but you can't predict when."

"What the hell?" Daniel said. "Why?"

"What the hell is exactly right."

An explosion resounded ahead of them. Jack grabbed Daniel and pulled him down. A shockwave of wind sliced above their heads, leaving gashes in the stone walls on either side of them. Flecks of rock nicked at Daniel's cheeks.

"What was that?!"

"Looked like wind magic," Jack said. He was already on his feet and tugging Daniel off the pavement. "Come on, come on! If we stay in one place too long they'll think we're setting up an incursion."

"Incursion?" Daniel stumbled into a run as Jack's hand let go.

"When you assault and take the territory of another team. It's happening to our territory right now!"

"Why is this happening?" Daniel said. "What's the point?!"

Jack threw the words over his shoulder as he ran. "Short version—imagine a prison filled with the worst dicks of a whole entire interstellar empire."

Another blast shook the street. Daniel and Jack were thrown against the wall. They shielded their heads from the dust and cinders as a roar of hot wind rushed through the alley. Smoke rose above the roof behind them.

"I don't have to work very hard to imagine this!" Daniel shouted over the noise.

The explosion died down. They slipped into a side alley, away from the immediate sounds of conflict. Jack checked his map, then clicked it shut and tucked his wristband under his sleeve. Daniel did the same—the less light they had to reveal their location, the better.

"Can they see us on their maps?" Daniel said.

"Only if we're in line-of-sight or they're using special tracking tools," Jack said. "No one here is looking for us specifically, so as long as we stay down we should be okay."

"Right," Daniel said. They slinked around another corner. "This is not exactly the maximum-security prison experience I was expecting."

"Take the prison," Jack said. "Now make it into a gameshow broadcasted live to the citizens of the empire."

Daniel hadn't missed the clues pointing toward that state of affairs. In fact, he'd been told as much by several different people, now, in a number of different ways—but he hadn't believed it until he heard it from Jack's mouth. "That's completely insane. The kind of stuff they make sci-fi movies with, insane."

"It's bread and circuses for the unwashed masses," Jack said. "We're the circus."

"This isn't a circus," Daniel said. "There aren't even any clowns."

"They ran out of clowns right before you got here," Jack said. "Sorry."

"But seriously," Daniel said. "The demons. They seem...civilized? Rational? They sit back and let this happen?"

"The Romans were civilized," Jack said flatly. "Didn't stop them."

"That was 2000 years ago," Daniel said.

"The demons like war," Jack said. "It's embedded in their culture. We fight wars over land, religion. They do it as a matter of course. It's pride for some of them. Don't try too hard to understand it, you won't. They're not humans dressed up in fun costumes. Totally different perspective, different frame of experience. If you want respect, you have to be the strongest guy in the room. Otherwise, you're nothing, you don't matter, you don't get to speak. Some demons are more human than others, but that's the most reliable way to figure them out."

Jack tugged his shoulder and gestured forward. "We need to go."

Daniel nodded his head and let himself be steered in whatever direction they were going. He'd lost track of the turns, and they took a lot more turns, winding between shadowy buildings, ducking under ledges and awnings and stone projections.

The decor of city around them had shifted. The roofs nearby had steeples with pointed ridges. Gargoyles peered over them from the top of the alley, each one wearing a unique expression of pain, anger, or both. The brick became great slabs of stone, sitting tight together without mortar.

Jack slowed down and put a finger to his lips to signal for quiet. Daniel inched along behind him. He had to stop himself from jumping at shadows. The cracks and clangs of the city's residents trying to kill each other reached their alley after echoing through a hundred other alleys, creating a slow symphony of war that hovered over their shoulders. The sounds shifted in tempo and volume; it was impossible to pick out direction or distance. Sometimes it descended into eerie silence—to be abruptly punctuated by screams or clashes of metal before rumbling back up into full force.

It reminded him of New York. The constant waiting. The paranoia. The suddenness of the fights, the slaughter. Smashing through extractors, the little silver birds, crushing and killing the overseers as fast as possible. The dark green blood that stained his clothes after he beat them to death.

In war, life was cheap. Cheap in the way useless plastic junk was cheap. Rolls under the bed, forget about it. Falls in the trash, don't bother digging it out. Broken? Buy a new one, easier than fixing it.

The blood never came out of his jeans, even after he tried scrubbing them down in the river. Eventually he'd stolen new clothes from a department store. Rachel would have appreciated the humor in that.

She was in his mind's eye. He'd tried to keep her at bay, but the habit was ingrained in him. Thinking of her motivated him, back when he could barely sleep, when he'd been on edge for days, wondering what the hell he was doing and why he was killing so much for people that wanted to capture or kill him in return. Her red hair. Her smile. The way her face lit up when he'd hit the nail on the head, tickled her funny bone just the right way—and the sound of her laughing. The softness when she hugged him and held him.

"Daniel?"

She'd become his center so quickly. And he'd left her there, pale, sickly, and drained. She'd already been dying at that moment. He'd already killed her.

"Earth to Daniel!" Jack hissed. He waved his arm in a frantic circle, trying to get him to move up. Daniel had fallen behind, still hunched down behind a stoop leading to the front doors of a building. Jack marched back, but stopped when he saw Daniel's face. "Are you okay?"

"I'm fine," Daniel said. He rubbed at his face with the heel of his hand. "I'm good."

Jack dropped into a worried whisper. "We're in the territory of a really nasty faction right now and we don't have time for this. Whatever you need taken care of, I can handle it later. I've got resources, I've built up a little influence."

"Money?" Daniel hacked a wet, broken laugh. "That's great. We'll bribe Beelzebub with his own prison points. That'll work."

Jack's eyes darted around the alley. "Keep your voice down," he said. "What's wrong with you?"

"Rachel's dead," Daniel blurted. "She got killed. I killed her."

Jack drew a breath through his teeth. His face shifted as he grappled with what Daniel said. Daniel kept rubbing his face, as if trying to push the tears back in. All he did was rub his eyes raw. They started to throb in time with his headache.

"Everything's gone to shit," Daniel said. "I don't know what to do. I'm trying to survive in a madhouse, for what? What's even the point?"

"Daniel." Jack knelt and grabbed him, shaking him. Daniel pushed him away, but the effort was halfhearted; Jack didn't budge. "Daniel! Calm down for a second. Look at me. Dan, look at me." Daniel forced himself to look up. "We're going to get back to where it's safe, and then we'll figure this out. Do you understand?" Daniel didn't respond. Jack's grip tightened. "Do you understand me?"

"Yeah," Daniel said.

"Alright." He grabbed Daniel under the shoulder and hauled him to his feet. "The Daniel I know doesn't curl up in a corner when things get tough. He laughs at it and comes back harder."

"I don't feel like that Daniel is doing so hot."

"He'll get over it."

Daniel's eyes were unfocused. He shook his head. "Not so sure about that."

Jack looked away for a second, checking the alley, then gave Daniel a brief half-hug. "When I was down here, alone...I got by because I tried to think like you. 'What would Daniel do?' I said that to myself a million times. It's how I survived."

"Seriously?" Daniel asked.

"Yeah man," Jack said. "Seriously."

Daniel's face screwed up. "That's like...embarrassing? Or something."

"Don't make it weird," Jack said. "Just take the compliment."

"That's me," Daniel said. "Greatest man who ever lived."

Jack gave Daniel's back a hard pat. "Careful your head doesn't swell up again. You might not fit in the door when we get there."

"Shows what you know. No door can withstand my huge noggin."

"Now we're talking." Jack smiled and patted him again. "One step at a time." He appraised Daniel, trying to gauge his mood. "How about it? You good to keep going?"

One step at a time. Hadn't he told himself that earlier?

Rachel wouldn't want this. She wouldn't want to see him like this, giving up. He was better than that. She believed that he was better than that.

Daniel sniffed in hard, as if sucking back the emotion that had dumped out of him. "I'm good. Good enough."

"Alright." Jack turned to face the way they were heading. "A bit further and we'll be out of the real danger zone. The problem is we're near the—"

The double doors above the stoop exploded.

Daniel saw it in a series of images. Light, flashing behind the door. Jack, raising his arms to shield himself from a wave of stone and wood shrapnel. And then both of them flying backward, Jack's arm somehow under his leg—while the rest of Jack was above him, missing an arm.

Then he was lying on the ground, staring up at the flashing red lights. His vision blurred.

Daniel tried to move. He couldn't feel his arms and legs. He couldn't feel anything. A whining buzz rolled in his ears.

He saw a shadow; there was a figure in a mask looming over him, holding a blade. It fell toward his neck.

Chapter 5
Rules of Engagement

Daniel dropped on his rear, hands and feet scrabbling across cobblestone. His heart pounded in his chest. His mouth tasted like sand.

He felt at his neck. Head still attached. *I'm alive.*

"Do you know how many points we had to spend to revive both of you in the middle of a territory war?!" someone shouted. "We've already lost half the new territory, and the other half is under siege from three sides! Your *friend* isn't even on our team. That's double points, and his rating is the highest I've ever seen for fresh meat!"

Daniel glanced around. He was in a courtyard, surrounded by men and women wearing white wristbands. This close, he could see the symbol on them—a big red cross, with little yellow frills stuck on each of the four ends. It was his first time seeing it up close.

Jack was already on his feet at Daniel's side, facing a tall man with a beard that could have been mistaken for a mane of pubic hair. He also had the biggest, ugliest nose Daniel had ever seen. A thick black robe hung off his body. From the way the other people were looking at him, he was obviously someone important. At least Jack's team didn't promote people based on looks.

"Buy us enough for magic upgrades and we'll take it back," Jack said. "Between the two of us—"

"The answer is no," the man said. "I've done enough bringing that one here." He waved a hand dismissively. "Get to the main courtyard. Lord Dracula will want to see you." He glanced at Daniel. "You, too. *Go with Jack.*"

An undeniable certainty filled Daniel's brain. The words made perfect sense. He just had to go with Jack. Go, with Jack. Go see the lord...

Dracula?

The absurdity of it snapped Daniel out of his daze, and it was only then he realized something wasn't right. The warm numbness that settled over him vanished, like a blanket being thrown off on a cold morning. His skin prickled down his neck and between his shoulders. *The hell was that?*

"We can still take back the territory," Jack said. He stepped half in front of Daniel, shielding him somewhat from the freak show. "I'd really rather talk to Lord Dracula after correcting the problem."

"You've done enough damage today," the man said.

"Take the points out of my pay if we don't take the node back," Jack said. "Buy me 25 percent. Daniel only needs 10. Ten minutes for me, five minutes for him. You know how strong he is."

The long-faced man brought a hand to his chin, sternness fading for consideration. "You'll repay the team twice what you're borrowing now."

"That's ridiculous!" Jack said. "The team rules say—"

"Twice what you're borrowing," the man said, "or you can go talk to Dracula with failure weighing on your back after lending points to a non-member on his dime."

Jack forced the words out between his teeth. "Fine."

The man nodded, then tapped his wristband a few times. "It's yours. I hope your faith in your friend is well-placed. You're going to need the capture reward." The man glanced up. "Units 1 and 2, with me. We'll loop around to the western side and attack 24. Units 3 and 4, reinforce the front lines, do not let us lose zone 23. Jack and...Daniel, is it? Are you listening?"

Daniel looked at the man. His eyes were like wrinkled pits, sunk back deep behind the nose. Daniel felt the same creeping buzz slip up on him—slithering across his forehead, then working along somewhere behind the bridge of his nose. Daniel watched it in his mind's eye, wary. The sensation stopped, then started to tighten, squeezing down on an enwrapped prey.

Daniel reacted automatically.

Whenever Daniel grasped his magic, he imagined it like a floating, ethereal inner hand, touching a core where his power sat. He wasn't sure if that's how normal mages did it, or if it was a contractor thing. It was what helped him visualize things when he was first learning from Xik, so that was what he did. That same hand slapped against the oncoming tangle of power, not at Daniel's direction, but as a reaction, like someone flinching away from a baseball headed toward their face.

Daniel felt the contact—unpleasant, as if someone had grabbed his hand and scraped his nails across a chalkboard—and then it was gone. He blinked rapidly, his attention back in front of him.

The man cocked his head at him. "Jack, take Daniel and hold out near zone 24. Once we strike, you two move in to take the node. That should take more pressure off us, regardless of what happens."

"Wait," Jack said. "Just us on the node? Alone?"

"Yes, *just you*," the man said. "Unless you think two contractors can't handle it alone?" Rasputin tapped his chin. "I suppose I could ask Lord Dracula to send one of the reserve units, but I don't imagine he'd appreciate the request."

"We'll be fine, thanks," Daniel said. "Come on, Jack. Let's kick some ass."

Jack and the robed man both looked surprised at Daniel's sudden contribution, but there wasn't anything else to say. The man nodded. "I hope you won't disappoint. The rest of you, with me!" The team members flooded away in a flurry of armor, cloaks, swords, staves of various shapes and sizes, shields, and other strange metallic accoutrements for which Daniel had no description.

"Come on," Jack said. "Let's move it."

Daniel rolled his shoulders. "Great. More running. That's really what I wanted. Yep, definitely more running."

Jack snorted and picked their path after a quick check at his bracelet-map. Daniel glanced around, taking in the relative safety of the courtyard before he followed Jack back into the red-lit alleyways of the city at war.

The crenellations and gargoyles were gone; this part of town was all brick. Daniel suspected the trim was a different kind of stone, but the red emergency lights made it all look like brick anyway. "I'm surprised you spoke up back there," Jack said.

"I just wanted out of that conversation," Daniel said. "That guy was being a dick."

Jack snorted. "He's a walking bag of dicks. But I mean...you bounced back fast."

Daniel gave his head a little shake, then picked up his feet, keeping pace with Jack. "I was...this is a little overwhelming," Daniel said. "Everything is. It's easier when I've got something to hit. Something to focus on. I'm sorry, about before. I don't know what happened."

"It's fine," Jack said. "I've been there."

"By the way, do we still have to be quiet?"

"It's okay to talk for a few minutes," Jack said. "We're in friendly territory for a while. Mostly friendly. I'll get alerts if we've got incoming."

"Okay. So." Daniel paused, composing himself. "Who the hell was that guy, what was he doing inside my head, and how are we alive right now?"

"Jeeze, one thing at a time," Jack said.

"Things seem to happen all at once in this place," Daniel said. "We just got blown up. I saw your arm. It wasn't attached."

"You get used to it," Jack said. "Okay, so that guy was Rasputin. He was trying to mess with your head, get you to go along with what he was saying. He does that. I'm surprised you could tell. It took me a while to tune it out."

Daniel thought about elaborating on his experience, but decided it was a conversation for another time, because another, more ridiculous fact desperately required clarification. "Hold the phone right there bud. Rasputin? Rasputin, as in, the one from Russia when they had czars? And what's up with Dracula?"

"Yeah," Jack said. "That's exactly who they are. History is a little different then what we learned in school. Magic and stuff."

"Oh, great, that explains everything," Daniel said. "Actually, on second thought, I think I need a little more info than magic and stuff, because I don't know the first thing that's—"

They turned a corner, and Daniel nearly tripped over himself when he saw what was waiting for them at the next intersection. A robot loomed over them like a tombstone. He threw himself against the brick and held his breath.

"Whoa. Chill pill," Jack said. "It's deactivated. And if it wasn't, it'd be on our side anyway." Jack walked up to the enforcer and knocked on its leg, producing a hollow, metallic sound. "See?"

Daniel stared at the giant robot another second, then peeled himself off the wall. He'd thought it was a Vorid extractor. His heart hammered a mile per minute. "I'm reaching the end of my rope, man."

"Here, tap your armlet. Select the map."

Daniel tapped on it with a finger. A little screen came up like Jack's—a small holographic panel, floating in midair above his wrist. He raised his arm to his face to bring it closer. There were several menus displayed, as if he was on the home screen of a cell phone: *Contact List, Media, Scoreboards,*

Shopping, and a button that said *Inventory: 1/10*. "How do I get the map?"

"Touch the map icon," Jack said, jabbing his finger at Daniel's screen. In the corner was an icon that looked like a globe, only the continents were all messed up. He touched it with his finger, and a map of the city filled the screen.

"That's you," Jack said, indicating where a blue dot marked Daniel's position. "Let me set you as an ally...here."

Jack touched his wristband against Daniel's, then went through a few buttons on his screen. A prompt came up on Daniel's display, asking him if he wanted to be registered as an ally to Jack Killiney's faction. Daniel accepted it, and his map washed over in new colors, red for enemy territory, green for their own. Most territory was grey—neutral? A few were blue, which he assumed were friends of his friends. He could see dozens of green dots moving around, preparing for an attack along the red borders.

"That doesn't put you officially in the guild," Jack said, "but now you won't get attacked accidentally."

"Thanks."

"The others are going to attack from this side and this side." Jack indicated the east and west sides of the peninsula of territory that Daniel noticed earlier. Half of it was still flashing green; the other half had long since gone red. "That will draw their defenses away from the center. Then we go up the middle and do the job of actually taking the territory back."

"What happens if we get surrounded?"

"It's almost guaranteed we'll be surrounded," Jack said. "The point is we'll be surrounded by less people than we would have been. When we get there, I'm going to wade in and get their attention."

"So you're the distraction." Daniel said. "I can live with that."

"I prefer being called the *vanguard*."

"You're a big, fat distraction," Daniel said. "You'll do a great job."

Jack shrugged. "I can take a few hits, unlike some people."

"Yeah, sure, whatever. So where do I come in?"

"You're pretty fast, right?" Jack said. "You wait until they're focused on me, then sweep in from behind and take them out."

"Seems straightforward enough," Daniel said. "But how do we get to use our magic? Last time I checked, it's not working."

"Rasputin sent us each a special item that will give us access to our magic," Jack said. "Got to wait for them to get in position because there's a time limit on it."

"That's what the bartering was about," Daniel said, realizing. "Is it pricey to do that?"

"Very," Jack said. "The higher a percentage you buy, and the longer the time period, the more it costs."

"Makes sense."

"The rest of the team—most people, really—all carry a bunch of equipment with them because it's cheaper, and about as effective as getting temp access to your own powers if you're a magician." Jack met Daniel's gaze. "We're different."

Daniel felt himself nodding. "I get it. Your average magician does as well with a lightning stick as he does with casting his own lightning. So it's cheaper to buy the stick."

"Right," Jack said. "The weapon is less flexible. The stick always does the same thing. But, you save money and get the same result. For us, it's the opposite. A lightning stick would make us the same as everyone else. If we buy a percentage of our own magic to use, then for a limited time we're really strong, which is more than worth the price."

"Like how I was in the obstacle course," Daniel said.

"Exactly." Jack rubbed the back of his head. "The problem is I'm borrowing money from the team treasury to cover the cost. If we capture the node, it'll pay for itself with the bonus we get. Otherwise...we're gonna be on a diet of microwave ramen for a while. Metaphorically speaking. It'll be just like school."

Remembering the scent of whatever mystery meat was being cooked back in the main square, Daniel thought ramen didn't sound too bad. "I can live with that," he said. "Back on topic. What's the deal with the vampire and the Russian shaman?"

"They got sent down here a long time ago," Jack said. "Dracula, a long, long time ago. He was one of the first humans who arrived in Hell for several hundred years before that. Rasputin was a lot more recent. Basically, when they dropped out of history, they didn't actually die the way they did. They were banished here."

"And now they're running around slaying demons," Daniel said. "I guess that explains the crosses."

"Dracula formed an all-human team as others were banished," Jack said. "Rasputin joined later. I don't know all the details, but Dracula had a hard time with the demons when he arrived, being the only human. Saying he's a devout Christian would be putting it mildly, so he already didn't like the idea of being stuck in Hell. He's...complicated."

"I'm not surprised he's complicated. If he's been down here since what...the middle ages? Guy is like 700 years old."

"I think he's just under 600," Jack said.

Daniel scowled. "This has gone past ridiculous. We're working for Dracula. You know he was a prince, right?"

"I think they were called voivodes."

"He can be god-emperor of my puckered asshole at this point," Daniel said. He glanced up at the deactivated enforcer. The machine took up half the small intersection they were standing in. "That thing gives me the willies."

"The willies?" Jack said, deadpan. "Shiver me timbers, Captain Fitzgerald."

"You know what?" Daniel said. "You sure as hell wouldn't be laughing if you..." Daniel trailed off, then stopped.

"If I what?" Jack said.

"It can wait," Daniel said. He had too much being spooned onto his plate already to bring up the Vorid right this instant. "If the history books on Dracula are a bunch of bull, what's the real story?"

"I don't know all the details," Jack said. "He isn't exactly chatty."

"Funny," Daniel said. "I always imagined Dracula as a fun, life-of-the-party type."

Jack gave Daniel a look, then started again. "He rediscovered vampiric magic when he was away from home, when he was young. I think he was held hostage as a kid by a neighboring kingdom to force his father to behave himself. Eventually he made his way back home, fought the Turks for a while, chopped people's heads off, kept the Ottoman Empire out of Europe by himself, basically. The magic probably helped with all that stuff."

Daniel was about to comment, but his thoughts started churning. Contractors gained power, in most part, from killing other living beings. The contractor magic was blind; it didn't care whether you killed Vorid, or whether you killed other people, it would suck it all down the same. Daniel accepted the reality of it, because if he didn't, his brother and probably his entire hometown would have been consumed by the Vorid. The counterbalance to the grim method of growing stronger was that he kept his activities focused strictly on the Vorid—on the foreign invaders. They were the ones instigating conflict, not him. His actions were a defense of Earth and the people around him. It was grisly, but it was war.

Vampiric magic was Earth's version of contractor magic. Back in Elizabeth Bathory's day, she almost grew strong enough to take over the magic world, but an alliance of all the factions of wizards and magicians was able to stop her and banish her to Hell. After that, any use of vampiric magic, or even association with it, was enough to get you banished. And that's exactly what happened to Daniel, because he was stupid enough to let it happen. And it was what happened to Jack.

The problem was, Jack had been okay with killing people to gain power faster than fighting the Vorid. He killed people he didn't like and took an aggressive position against the wizards. Maybe Jack had been right that the wizards couldn't be trusted, but he wasn't right in abusing his powers.

In the end—after discovering that he was a contractor, too—Daniel had been forced to fight Jack to protect Rachel. After exhausting each other, they both ended up captured by magicians. At the last second—and even after Daniel had beat the snot out of him—Jack used the remaining bit of energy he had to free Daniel from the trap. Daniel escaped. Jack got left behind.

And here Jack was, working with Vlad the Impaler. He wasn't called The Impaler because he stuck toothpicks through picnic sandwiches. He must have done the same thing Jack did—kill other people to increase his power. But, from what Daniel knew of European history—which was not really all that much—the Turks were invading Europe at the time.

So was Vlad defending himself and his home, and things got out of hand? Or was it more than that? How similar was he to Jack? Or was Daniel working from too many false assumptions? The version of history he knew could be a total crock cooked up by the magicians. After all, one huge thing was false already—Dracula wasn't dead, he was in Hell. In fact, even that was small potatoes compared to the fact that magic actually existed, and wasn't just a figment of human imagination. How many other lies were out there?

"Hey, Daniel. You listening?"

"Huh?" Daniel glanced up to see a miffed expression on Jack's face. "Sorry. A lot to take in."

Jack sighed. "What's the last thing you heard?"

"Dracula became what we call a vampire, and was fighting against the Turks, I guess."

"Right," Jack said. "You missed details about the fighting, but it doesn't matter. The point is, eventually, he was betrayed. I don't know by exactly who. I think he was getting overwhelmed—he was only one guy—so he shared the magic with a few people. They turned traitor and banished him. It all spread from there, and eventually was passed down to one Elizabeth Bathory. Bet you've heard of her, huh?"

Daniel tensed up when he heard the name. He considered interrupting to tell Jack about his deal with Beelzebub, but decided to hear the whole story first. "She was the big serial killer. Bathed in the blood of virgins."

"That's not even half of it," Jack said. "Things got real bad in the magician world, but they managed to pull themselves together and banish her down here. Then they started hunting the remnants of vampiric magic. Everyone that was caught was sent here too."

Daniel nodded. That matched up with the version of history he already knew. "So where's Bathory now?"

"She's the leader of the top team in Hell," Jack said. "A mix of humans and demons. Dracula hates her guts, obviously, because she's a descendent of the guy that betrayed him. Blood-feud. These medieval people take that stuff really, really seriously."

"And she's okay partnering with demons," Daniel said.

"Demons are definitely weird," Jack said. "They have their own way of doing things, and sometimes they think in really strange ways. Like, things that would bother humans don't annoy them at all, but things we'd brush off make them want to rip your guts out."

"You're gonna have to fill me in on that part later," Daniel said.

"Honestly," Jack said, "it's not really so complicated. There are good ones and bad ones, like people. Even considering where we are. They have the same general morals. Murder, bad. Crime, bad. Truth and love, good. But they also believe in the rule of the strong. Democracy is a foreign concept to them."

Daniel thought back. "They haven't been all bad so far. Mostly bad, but not all bad."

Jack checked his map again. The dots were starting to look a bit more organized, but more green was still trickling in. Daniel noticed red dots here and there marking active skirmishes between groups. "Most humans that aren't at rock bottom are divided into two camps," Jack said. "Dracula sees himself as the good guy, and Bathory a rightfully punished criminal. He can't stand the fact that she's number one. It's like she's not even being punished, just on a permanent vacation."

This was all good news as far as Daniel was concerned. The enemy of his enemy was his friend. Crazy legends about sucking blood and being afraid of garlic aside, he was probably an alright dude compared to Bathory. He fought to protect his country—albeit in a very vicious manner—but on the surface, it was a good fundamental goal that Daniel could relate to. By comparison, Bathory was an irredeemable psychopath.

Daniel wasn't quite sure if he was being honest with himself, or if he was perfectly willing to make Bathory the villain to ease himself through the process of murder. Dracula sounded like the one who got burned, but Rasputin was high up in Dracula's team, and he didn't have a shining personal history. Daniel found himself wondering if the animated version of *Anastasia* was more accurate than he realized.

"So how did we get in that courtyard with Rasputin anyway?" Daniel said.

"We died," Jack said. "They revived us there. I was on auto-revive, more or less. I had to get you in manually."

Daniel started. He lifted his hands, then clenched and unclenched his fingers. "I'm trying to keep up with this, Jack. Really. Doing my best here."

Jack grinned. "I've died seven times since I got down here, counting today. You get used to it."

"I got hit by an explosion before," Daniel said. "I didn't die then."

"You're considered dead if your heart stops or your head is cut off," Jack said. "Or something else really bad that would basically instantly kill you. Otherwise, given enough time, you heal back up. So always check your kills, or you could have people coming back at you."

"Ooh-kaay," Daniel said. "So what happens when you're *really* dead, as opposed to mostly dead?"

"Then the healing magic stops working and you have to be manually revived by someone else," Jack said. "It's expensive even in normal times, and majorly so during an active territory war."

"Hence our sudden debt issue."

"Right," Jack said. "Stops people endlessly sending reinforcements so nothing ever gets accomplished." Jack's face went solemn. "When you die here...basically, you don't die. Hell's sealing spell doesn't let your soul go. We're all linked to it."

Daniel looked down at his ruined clothes. They were worse than the last time he checked, if that was even possible; scorched and shredded, especially around his legs. It seemed like they were a package deal with his revival. "I don't see any magic."

"It's there," Jack said. "It doesn't show up, usually. It's really, really strong."

"How strong are we talking?" Daniel said. "I've seen some pretty brutal magic."

"Hell's sealing spell is supposed to be the most powerful known spell, ever."

Daniel shrugged and nodded. "Sounds legit. Not that I would know."

"It's the thing stopping you from accessing your magic," Jack said. "It keeps us anchored to this reality. It hangs on us like chains, all the time. Invisible, unless you try to escape."

"It sounds like a Christmas Carol," Daniel said. "The part where Marley comes in and he's wearing all the chains and stuff." Daniel raised his arms and pantomimed a ghostly Jacob Marley. "I wear the chains I forged in life! Link by link and yard by yard!" Daniel eyeballed Jack's flat expression. "What? You haven't seen the movies?"

"This is serious," Jack said.

"I am serious," Daniel said, "and don't call me Shirley." Jack made a sound somewhere between a groan and a sigh. Daniel glanced around at the buildings. His eyes followed the pattern of the brick. "Where is here, exactly?" he asked. "Is this the demon world?"

"Nope," Jack said. "Hell is its own world, sorta. It's an artificial bubble of space locked between the human world and the demon world. The same spell governs it. Everything hooked to the spell is kept here. Permanently."

"Wow. Seems like a lot of effort just for us."

"It's not for us," Jack said.

"What do you mean?"

"Hell was created for one specific prisoner," Jack said. "Everyone else got added after."

Daniel had a moment of realization. "Of course. Hell. The devil. Like, *the* devil, not *a* devil. Satan."

Jack nodded. "I haven't been there, but supposedly, way down below, it gets really cold. All covered in ice. The prisoners that live down there are the ones that lost in the games or couldn't find a team. Maybe they're not any good at fighting, or got unlucky. Made the wrong enemies. But points are everything. If you take on debt you can't handle, lose on bets or in competitions, you drop through the levels until you end up there because it's the only place you can afford. Most of the population of Hell is actually down there—they chip the ice away to make a living, buy food. It's like being camped outside in Antarctica."

"That's messed up," Daniel said. "Wouldn't they run out of ice eventually?"

There's always more growing back," Jack said. "Rasputin told me it's Satan's power, leaking out of the seal. And past that point..." Jack leaned in, voice lowered. "That's where Satan is held. That's what everyone thinks, anyway. Everyone who's gone too deep has never come back."

Even though they were inside a cavern, Daniel could have sworn a cold wind blew across them. "Sounds like a ghost story," he said.

"Except the ghosts are real," Jack said, "and you're standing in the haunted house. Satan is what this place is for. We're tacked on the sealing spell as extras. Beelzebub was using this place as punishment for demons several hundred years before the first humans came in, and he'd been using it to make money. Control of the prison gives him more influence to rule the demon world. It grew up into this giant mess we're in now—PrisonWatch."

"Must be a *hell* of a lot of magic energy powering this place."

"Please don't," Jack said. "I've heard all the Hell-jokes a thousand times since I've gotten here. Some of the other team members think it's great to tell them all to the new guy. I'm sick of it."

"Really? Sounds like a *hell*uva good time."

"It isn't," Jack said.

"Right—I'd imagine those crazy *hell*ions would get old."

"Daniel, I swear to God."

"Alright, alright," Daniel said, raising his hands. "No more bad puns. So how does this bubble reality keep itself from popping?"

"Energy from death," Jack said.

"Ah, yes," Daniel said. He slapped his forehead dramatically. "Of course. The energy from death. Death-energy. Deathergy. Makes perfect sense now."

"Basically, when people die," Jack said, ignoring his sarcasm, "their life force dissipates back into the aether. The aether is the chaotic space between dimensions." Jack waved his hand. "Or something like that. They don't really know. But the energy goes unused. Dust to dust."

"Following you so far."

"So all this energy going back to the aether is sort of like a river, flowing along," Jack said. "And someone had the bright idea—hey, we need to keep this really powerful Satan guy in prison forever. So let's stick a waterwheel into the river of souls moving back to the aether so it powers the prison's seal. That generates power, like electric turbines in a dam. Get it?"

"That makes a lot more sense than I thought it would," Daniel said. He knew some of this from what Beelzebub had told him, but it was definitely better to double check the knowledge with Jack. Daniel didn't take anything that devil told him on faith. "Is that why no one dies down here?"

Jack nodded. "There's more energy than the seal needs. The excess bleeds out around us. We're bathed in it right now. So we don't age, and we heal from injuries really fast. If your body gets...uh...damaged beyond repair, the seal takes your soul away and makes a new body for you at the crypt."

"The crypt?"

"That's what they call it," Jack said. "Basically you get dumped in a crowded pit of people that just died. Not a pleasant place to be. If you still have points, or if someone who's your friend can transfer you some points, you can buy back in to whatever level you can afford at the cost of a month's rent. I had you revived to our position before you made it there, so we got off easy. It's way more expensive to do that during a territory war...which is why we really need to not screw this up." Jack brought his hands together. "So, there you go. That's how we died, how we came back, and why we're here."

"All in a nutshell," Daniel said. "What happens if you die and you can't buy back in?"

"The same thing happens in every level, if you can't pay your rent," Jack said. "You drop to the level below."

"There's a place lower than the crypt?"

"Yeah," Jack said. "Rent is about every 26 days—that's a demon month. But in the crypt, you only have a short time to buy back in, or you hit rock bottom. Ice-land."

"You know," Daniel said, "the Vikings named Iceland because it was beautiful and fertile, and they wanted to make others think it was a lifeless rock so they could have it for themselves."

"Your ability to recall useless information never ceases to amaze me," Jack said. "In Hell, Iceland is an ice land and Purgatory is where you want to stay."

"You want to stay in Purgatory," Daniel repeated. "Bet you never imagined yourself saying that."

Jack sighed and rubbed his forehead. "Any other questions?"

"Tons more," Daniel said. "When you guys were fighting earlier, I saw someone get stabbed, and he didn't heal. He vanished. I guess his heart stopped, so he was considered dead?"

"Right," Jack said. "Makes death a bigger consequence during a territory war. Oh." Jack snapped his fingers. "When you kill someone, you automatically steal half their points. So you lost half of yours earlier."

"Can't say I'm torn up about it. I have no idea what points are worth."

"You started with 50,000 points," Jack said. "That's a whole month's worth of rent up here, it's a ton. But yeah, the team pools points in our stash, and you get paid piecemeal. That way no one risks losing a lot at once."

"Stash? Is that like a bank?"

"It's called a vault," Jack said. "Basically a big safe a team can buy so they can hoard points and items. In theory, another team could bust in and raid our vault, because PrisonWatch doesn't allow anything that's 100% secure. But it would take a hell of a lot of doing, to the point of being impossible as things stand. Fighting in the city is unusual because of the enforcers. You can only legally attack intruders in your own territory."

"So normally, there's no fighting at all?" Daniel said.

"You can still fight, you just don't want to get caught," Jack said. "And if they spot you, enforcers are super hard to escape. They'll give up after a while, actually, as a reward for avoiding them long enough, but it's only been done a few times. In peacetime there aren't many fights in Purgatory, just the usual scheduled games. Other levels of Hell are a lot more chaotic, because they only have enforcers in a few areas."

"I guess I have really bad timing," Daniel said. He sat on that thought. Was it really bad timing? Pure bad luck? It seemed like too much of a coincidence that this war thing started as soon as he dropped in.

"Wait," Daniel said. "What happens if you lose your wristband? Your arm gets cut off, or it's stolen somehow?"

"Nothing much. If you get sent to the crypt, it makes a new one for you. Otherwise, you have to buy a new one."

Daniel paused. "How do you buy a new one if you don't have your wristband to buy stuff with?"

Jack gave him a meaningful look. "Big problem, right? That's the biggest reason teams formed early on in this place. Otherwise you could cut off someone's arm and keep them captive indefinitely. No access to any resources. No access to the system. You could be the richest man in the world but you don't have your credit card." Jack's voice lowered. "That's what they do down below. They take away the armlets—the wristbands. Lets them control people easier. Enslave them."

Daniel decided he did not like the idea of being a helpless captive. He rubbed his armlet possessively. "That's really screwed up. This is all screwed up beyond belief. Who even came up with all this?"

"What's really screwed up," Jack said, "is that it's all televised."

Even Daniel didn't have a snippy response for that. Morbid was not enough to describe the possibilities. He cleared his throat, loudly, trying to dispel some of the bad air. "Where's Bathory and her special snowflake team?"

"They don't have to do territory wars because they're number one," Jack said. "They basically live in the rooftop penthouse suite. Level zero. They only do the scheduled games, or challenge battles. And they do lose on occasion, but not enough to come close to being unseated."

Daniel felt a wave of hope wash through him. He thought he'd have to search up and down to find her, but lo and behold, she was already arch-enemies with Jack's boss and within striking distance. *Now I just have to fight her. If I can survive long enough.*

Jack's wristband beeped. "It's almost time to move," he said.

"Okay," Daniel said. "What's the plan, aside from you go first and get them while they're distracted?"

"The plan," Jack said, "is to hit them hard enough they don't stand up again."

Daniel rolled his eyes. "Wow, we got Sun-Tzu over here. General in 99 battles, victor in 100."

"But seriously," Jack said. "We're gonna roll in and attack them. They'll probably send a lot of backup, because they've been trying to take this node back for weeks. Now that they got it, they won't give it up again easy." He glanced at Daniel. "In order to take a node, we have to hold the capture point against attacks for five minutes. We're gonna have to attack people. Kill people."

"I figured that part out already."

Jack put a hand on Daniel's shoulder. Daniel wasn't sure if he liked it there or not. "Dan, you gonna be okay in there?"

Daniel met Jack's eyes and nodded. "I had a moment, before. I'm sorry I got us blown up."

"It happens," Jack said. "Sometimes, it's almost like a real-life video game. Kinda. It makes it easier to accept if you think of it that way."

"This isn't a game," Daniel said. "You don't know what's going on, back on Earth. It's beyond bad. Shit has hit the fan, big time."

Jack took his hand back. "Let's get a drink after this. Several drinks."

"We can do that?"

"No one's carded me yet," Jack said.

"I have to admit," Daniel said, "the lack of an age limit improves my outlook on Hell substantially."

Jack's wristband beeped again. "Alright," he said. "Let's do this."

Chapter 6
Power Play

Daniel was crouched on a rooftop—a familiar position. Back in Boston, it had always been rooftops, all the time. The city was old, and the winding roads were crammed with buildings. The best way to make up time while staying out of sight was staying up high.

Purgatory was even more packed, if that was possible. Every available space was taken by a structure of some kind, aside from the open squares that marked intersections. The vast majority of buildings had a uniform height, dotted only by vents or chimneys. Maybe it was expensive to build higher? Or maybe the rules didn't allow for it. Either way, there was still a long way to the roof of the cavern.

The flat roofs did make for easy going, but also easy sniping. Daniel didn't have a ranged weapon, but others would. They'd been afraid he would meet with some kind of resistance, but the roofs were devoid of activity. He kept as close to cover as possible, ducking from spot to spot. Further ahead was a long mall that stretched between the buildings—the location of the territory node.

Daniel managed to get an angle on one of the alleys in the direction Jack was coming from. He raised his wristband. "Jack, you there? I can't see you."

"Almost there." Jack's voice came through in a faint hiss. "I'm on your map, but they won't be. Remember, if they have line of sight on you, you'll appear on their map. This team is well organized, they'll have someone watching their map the whole time, waiting for a red dot to pop up. Stay low."

Daniel shrunk lower, pressing himself up against the ledge that ran the length of the roof. Luckily, there wasn't anyone standing guard. Maybe he was the only one stupid enough to be out in the open. He raised his head to peer into the courtyard.

There was a water fountain in the center, about 20 yards from where he was squatting. The fountain was a fancy three-tiered affair with a little statue on top holding a bow and arrow. It might have looked nice if the statue wasn't a wart-covered goblin. The water gleamed blood red in the emergency lighting.

The rest of the courtyard around the fountain was open stone. The left side turned to grass, bordered by several benches. A few scattered trees about the same height as the roofs offered the only cover. Between two trees was a metal pedestal with a round cylindrical top that was as Jack had described—the capture point.

A lighted strip running around the column gave off a cool blue glow that cut a purple swatch through the red lights. They needed to tap and hold their bracelet against the pedestal for 10 seconds in order to begin the capture process. They then had to prevent the other team from recapturing it for 5 minutes to take it as their own territory.

If they won, the enemy team would be immediately teleported out of the captured territory and back to their designated headquarters. If Jack and Daniel let them get their hands on the node again before the 5 minutes were up, they'd lock the territory down, preventing any other capture attempts for an hour. In addition, any remaining enemy forces in the territory would be highlighted on their maps, without the line of sight restriction. At that point, Daniel and Jack would be sitting ducks with no backup.

Normally, teams would fight until they'd actually secured the space around the node. Then, having won the battle, they'd set up a perimeter and wait out the 5 minutes. Trying to take the node earlier was a risk, as if the other team managed to make it through, they'd lock the territory back under their control and leave the attackers stranded and exposed.

Jack was feeling lucky.

The faint trickle of water from the fountain reached Daniel's ears. No other sounds.

There was a tension in the air; the sense he'd picked up in New York was crackling back to life. He could practically smell the battle that was about to happen. It felt like a stone sitting in his stomach. At this rate, he'd get ulcers.

"It's a beautiful day in the neighborhood," Daniel muttered, half-singing the words.

Jack's voice snapped across the radio. "What?"

"Sorry, forgot to turn this off." Daniel fumbled through the menus. "Where is it again?"

"I'm almost there. Be quiet."

"Sorry."

A flash of silver caught Daniel's eye. Jack was coming out of the southwestern entrance to the courtyard—diagonally across from him, on the other side of the fountain.

Fully transformed, he was a hell of a monster. His muscles rippled as he walked; the fur waved to-and-fro like long strands of grass. When Daniel focused, he could almost see the air shiver around the fur; magic rolled off the barrier like water off a duck's back.

Daniel checked the courtyard as Jack lumbered forward. He was in the open now, making his way around the fountain. Daniel saw something, a flicker in the corner of his eye. It was in a window of a building, on the tree side. "Movement, up in the building. Near the tree close to the wall."

"They're hiding inside," Jack said. Transformed, his voice had become deep, grating. "Gonna wait for me to step into the trap, then blast me to pieces. But they don't know you're here."

"How do I get them if they're inside the buildings?"

"They have to come out to get to the node," Jack said. "I can take the magic hits. I'll lay down over the node and you knock them out if they poke their heads out."

Daniel turned his club in his hands. It was a simple rod, really, made out of some kind of alloy. The description hadn't said much. It had been cheap, so he bought it. He was used to it, anyway; he'd been using an aluminum baseball bat back in New York.

Jack reached the grass when the first barrage came—from a direction neither of them expected.

A massive tongue of green fire roared from below where Daniel was sitting. It burst out like a stream from a flamethrower, rolling over Jack. Daniel flinched—he'd be roasted if that hit him dead on.

Jack's ape form barreled out of the flames, forearms raised up to protect his head. He switched to all fours when he cleared the heat and galloped for the node.

Daniel opened his inventory—the pocket space that came with his wristband. It was an advanced kind of space-time magic that was a tiny, self-contained dimension. The wristband allowed him to access this space and instantly store and retrieve up to ten different objects. Most new prisoners started with only three spaces, but he earned a full ten for winning the new inmate competition.

Purchasing and upgrading inventory slots was extremely expensive, so expensive that Jack only had four slots—one more than he'd started with. It was a huge advantage to be able to pull out weapons and devices essentially from thin air, ala Bugs Bunny—and Daniel had more than three times the advantage.

He only had one item stored—a small magic orb that, when crushed, gave the user access to 10% of their magic power for 5 minutes. After tapping the menu on his wristband, the glowing purple orb appeared in Daniel's hand. He clutched it tight, ready to activate it. He could only use it after Jack hit the node—after the 5-minute countdown started. Any earlier, and he'd run out of steam before they took the territory.

Meanwhile, Jack beat it past the fountain and leapt over the benches. A wall of golden lightning exploded from under the second bench—some kind of trap activating. Anyone else would be electrocuted on the spot; Jack was blasted up ten feet in the air, flipped over and over. He landed hard on his back, but rolled up and kept running.

Jack brushed passed the first cluster of trees. Enemy magicians were pouring out of the buildings around him, heavily armed. They didn't head toward the node—they spread out around the trees, taking up spots around the center. Why wouldn't they head toward the middle?

"Jack!" Daniel shouted. "Hold up!"

"I'm almost there!" Jack said. Even as he said the words, he launched himself into the air, avoiding a volley of fireballs from a group of demons. A scorched crater was left behind in the middle of the park.

"It's a trap!"

Metal protrusions unfurled themselves from the surrounding trees and pointed themselves at Jack. A geyser of mist shot out from each one, coating him in a fog of magic. Ice crystals began to collect on his fur, crunching and cracking as they expanded over his body.

"Cold, cold, cold!" Jack gathered his arms in as he plowed through the mist. "I hate ice. They always use ice on me!"

Jack made it to the node. He swung his arm down, mashing his armlet—which had somehow enlarged to fit around his huge forearm—against the cylinder. The blue glow flashed red, and a countdown of light started on its surface.

Jack shifted and stomped while keeping his arm on the pedestal, using his other arm to sweep the ice off his fur. The magicians surrounding him joined in—they all used ice magic. Some shot in shards of ice; others used handheld versions of the mist guns that had been tucked onto the trees. A huge cloud of freezing magic rose into the air, so cold that Daniel could feel his nose start to numb even from where he was sitting.

"I'm going in!" Daniel shouted.

"Not yet!" Jack's voice was muffled in the radio. Daniel could hear his breath coming in heaving, static-rushed gasps. "Wait til the countdown's done!"

Daniel couldn't even see him properly anymore, only bits of silver in a huge cloud of frost. "You're gonna freeze to death!"

"I can hang on!" Jack's voice was hoarse. "I'll start the capture. You defend it!"

"We're defending it together!"

"We knew I'd get screwed from the start," Jack said. "This is part of the plan!"

Daniel's hand twitched on the power-orb. It was a difference of seconds, but could be all the difference.

He couldn't help but think about when they'd both been captured by Eleanor's ice magic. Daniel hadn't been able to escape alone. It was only thanks to Jack creating an opening that he was able to run away. After they'd honestly fought trying to kill each other, Jack used the last bit of energy he had to get Daniel free.

Daniel raised the orb to smash it.

"Don't do it, Daniel!" Jack shouted. Daniel stopped. His hand shook in the air. "Don't even think about it!"

The freezing mist coming from the traps subsided. The magicians ceased fire. There was a long quiet as the frost magic dissipated and the fog cleared. Daniel could see his breath in front of his face from the cold. It felt like the longest ten seconds of his entire life.

The pedestal flashed green. The pulsing lights stopped. Daniel's map beeped an update at him from his wristband. The territory capture had started.

Jack's voice stuttered in chilly through the radio. "O-okay. G-g-go!"

Daniel crushed the orb.

Purple light blossomed around him. Runes and shapes and esoteric symbols flashed across Daniel's face. He didn't understand any of it—he didn't understand how magic worked in the first place. He only knew that it worked, and now he could use it.

As the mist cleared, Jack was exposed. He looked only half-alive, hunched over the pedestal, curled up to protect himself from the cold. His arms and legs were entrapped; he looked like a yeti half-buried in an icy tomb. A squadron of close-combat fighters was closing in from three sides, armed with swords, knives, and staves glowing with elemental magics and intent on hacking him to pieces and prying what was left off the capture point.

Daniel squeezed out his magic as hard as he could, ramming it through his body. It filled him in an instant and soaked through his senses. The world slowed down as his mind accelerated. The fighters running over the grass now looked like they were trying to jog through water.

Daniel jumped over the courtyard, then stopped himself in midair using the one magic spell he was able to pick up—a simple sigil, projected under his feet. The hazy white platform was strong enough for him to stand on and push off. He couldn't exactly fly, but if he put a sigil under his feet, he could jump off it, and then again, stepping his way into the air.

But this time, Daniel rebounded straight down. He landed on the ground in the middle of one of the squads, crouching to absorb the momentum. He gripped his club and swung as he stood straight, pushing his magic out his arms and into the weapon. The club flashed as Daniel's magic reached it, as if someone pulled it white-hot from a furnace.

Daniel's blow smashed through the helm of the first swordsman. The demon's body fell backward, skull caved in.

Before his first kill hit the ground, Daniel was moving again, taking down a second victim. He pivoted off that swing and back the other way, nailing a third, pivot back, number four. Caught in a sprint toward Jack, their own momentum was turned against them.

Daniel lined up the fifth blow, winding up his swung and smashing the imp in the stomach. The former attacker shot back like a missile and plowed through a group of mages before being stopped cold by a brick wall.

The warriors reacted sluggishly—no, not slow, just slow compared to Daniel. They all turned toward him, bringing up weapons and shields. The mages were starting to react too, but if they started shooting now, they'd end up hurting their own men.

Daniel could see something else, too—the haze of energy rising from the bodies of the demons he'd killed.

Beelzebub hadn't lied. He'd grow stronger if he killed demons in Purgatory.

As the energy reached Daniel, he felt the core of his magic twitch slightly. After killing the Vorid lord, Daniel had enough magic under his command that the small fry didn't add much to the total. But Daniel didn't mind. He'd gotten strong in the first place by killing tons of small fry. Every little bit helped.

The immediate benefit was that he was refreshed—wounds healed, powers reenergized. Mental exhaustion was still a problem, but as long as he could keep killing, Daniel could fight indefinitely, absorbing fresh energy straight from the corpses he created. He'd never exhaust his magic stores.

That was exactly what he was counting on.

Daniel was powerful, but his magic worked best in short bursts, applied to weapons or armor when he needed it, especially when he was facing a long fight. When he used it how he was using it now—pushing it all the way through every last toe and finger—he could speed up his entire body and attack faster than his opponents could react. The effort burned through his reserves just as fast—he couldn't maintain that state for too long.

Unless, of course, he had plenty of things to kill.

Daniel sent another wave of power out through his body and zipped away as several blasts of lightning destroyed the spot he'd been standing on. The wave of energy knocked away some of the warriors that were too slow to protect themselves. Apparently they didn't care about killing their own troops after all. Then again, in Hell, death was temporary. *Unless I'm the one attacking.*

Daniel plunged into another group of assailants as they reached Jack's fur. He whipped his club around, smashing them backward. Some didn't die outright, but that was fine. He only had to keep them off the capture node. His efforts produced a hail of bodies.

Eventually, attackers stopped coming. Daniel took stock. He was still surrounded, standing by a frozen Jack. The swordsmen had drawn back when they saw they couldn't keep up, instead protecting the magicians responsible for the ranged attacks.

"Jack," Daniel said, "can you move?"

Daniel didn't get a response. He checked his map. Jack was still on it, a little green dot next to him. He wasn't officially dead yet, so he should be healing.

If the magicians all fired magic toward the center again, he might get dead real fast. Daniel bent his knees, crouching, then jumped. He didn't move at full speed—he wanted his enemies to track him. Sure enough, a hail of lightning and fire struck down on his position. Half the building behind him collapsed as Daniel leapt away, boosted along by the shockwave of the explosion. Protected by his magic, he didn't suffer internal injuries from the blast like he had before.

Daniel stopped himself with a sigil and immediately rebounded in another direction. He landed in front of a group of magicians—a harpy was leading them. He swung, crushing the creature's beak into its face and sending it flying. The magicians tried to scatter, but Daniel was too fast.

As soon as he'd finished them off, a gust buffeted his shirt. Daniel turned—and saw a miniature tornado practically on top of him. A tree that was ripped up by the wind magic spun at him and smashed him in the ribs, knocking the air from his lungs.

He was tossed around in the air like a ragdoll, spinning head over heels as the tornado carried him around. Razor lines of magic sliced at him constantly, nicking at his skin. His grip on his magic was the only thing saving him. If he dropped his power for an instant, he'd be torn to pieces.

Daniel tried to fight the tornado, but the pull was too strong. Every time he got a sigil formed and put a foot down, he got tugged in a new direction. With no footing, all his speed was useless. He only had ten percent of his magic—he couldn't last forever.

Daniel resisted against the wind again, only for it to whip his neck back the opposite way. He was slammed into the ground—he was on the stone side of the courtyard, now—and then smashed bodily against another tree before being carried back into the air.

Daniel stopped again, slamming against something stretched across his path. Pain lashed through his stomach. He tried to get a breath, but some kind of fuzz was jammed up his nostrils—*fuzz?*

"Gotcha!" Jack's voice was a faint rumble in the wind. He brought Daniel down low, close to the ground. Jack's fur shielded them both from the winds. Daniel hunched against the pedestal; Jack was stopping himself from being ripped away by holding onto the capture node.

"Jack!" Daniel shouted. He could barely hear himself over the wind tearing at his ears. "What is this thing?!"

"I heard about this spell but I haven't seen it before. Their leader uses wind magic! He's here personally!"

"How do we get rid of it!?"

"I dunno!" Jack said. He shifted slightly, getting a better grip on the node. "We can wait it out!"

"How much longer?" Daniel asked.

"Two or three minutes!"

The tornado vanished. Daniel's sliding feet went flat on the ground. He relaxed into Jack's arm and finally caught his breath.

The sudden silence was broken by a torrential downpour of magic cast by the enemy team's magicians. Lightning thundered and fire flashed, shooting down on them from every angle like an oncoming apocalypse.

"Hold on!" Jack shouted. He shoved Daniel under him and crouched over the pedestal. Jack screamed as the magic struck his back, pounding into him and ripping through his fur. Daniel saw blood scatter up, only to be vaporized by the heat.

The instant after the magic stopped, the tornado slammed back on top of them. Jack's grip on the pedestal slackened until he was dangling out by one hand. Daniel wrapped his own arms around the node, holding on for dear life as the wind tried to eat them alive.

Daniel glanced up and winced at what he saw. Jack's back was completely torn open; the fur was shredded. The wind was slicing into the open wounds. "Jack!" Daniel screamed. "Can you hear me?!"

Jack wrenched his other arm around, hooking a paw onto the node near Daniel's head. He couldn't pull himself closer—the wind and his injuries were holding him back—but at least he wasn't flying into the air. "This hurts like a bitch!"

"Looks like it!" Daniel shouted back. Their eyes met briefly. Daniel would not describe Jack's expression as hopeful. "I don't think we have a lot of time, they're probably reloading!" Daniel said. "Or whatever magicians do!"

"If they fire on me again, I'm screwed!" Jack said. "I used too much magic stopping the ice."

"How do we get out there and stop them when we're stuck in here?"

"I think that's the point." Jack glanced up at the wall of wind. "I didn't think they'd spend this much to defend. This was set up just to counter me."

Daniel's grip was slipping off the node. Without Jack's shielding, the wind was tearing his fingers raw. He sent more magic out to his skin, but he wasn't any good at protecting himself with pure magic. It was why he used armor—he could put the magic into that, and it did the protecting for him. The spell was too strong for him to fend it off for long.

Wait. He couldn't fight the tornado. So why not try to go along with it?

"Jack, I'm gonna try something!" Daniel said. "Maybe I can bust out!"

"Be careful!"

Daniel nodded, then let go of the node. Immediately the cyclone tore him away from the center of the spell and whipped him around the outside.

Daniel started to form a sigil, holding it ready. When the winds were clawing against his back, he materialized it and leapt forward, speeding in the direction of the wind instead of against it. He shot out like a bullet, but as soon as he reached the border of the swirling winds, it started dragging back against him. Daniel made another sigil, bouncing in the new direction, and then another, and another. He followed the curved border of the storm, letting the wind push him faster without trying to fight it.

After a few more turns, he was sprinting at breakneck speed. He had to make sigils so fast it was as if he was running on a path of gold light, spinning around the tornado faster than the winds could catch up to him. The speed forced him to bank the sigils at a harder and harder angle until he was running horizontal, keeping himself suspended with sheer momentum.

With one more burst of effort, Daniel shielded his head with his hands, planted his feet, and rammed himself through the outer wall of the cyclone. The wind whipped and cut at him; it was like needles jamming themselves through his knuckles and forearms. And then, he was out, busting through the wall of the spell and back into the courtyard.

Daniel forced his power back together again, scraping up the last of his reserves, and slammed it through his system. The world slowed to a crawl, and he used the extra time to look around.

The magicians had retreated to the rooftops; some were posted in the building. All of them were preparing another blast of magic. Heads were just starting to turn toward where he'd escaped the cyclone.

There. Up on the roof, there was an undine, one of the blue fish-like people. It was holding a bright green orb swirling with wind magic; it felt exactly the same as the storm he'd been beaten up by.

Daniel jackhammered his feet, planting a new sigil with each step. He accelerated through the air, shooting straight toward the bastard with the orb like a human missile. Daniel already lost his club somewhere in the cyclone, but he didn't need it for this. He body slammed the undine at top speed, leading with his elbow and nailing it in the neck. A sharp snap shook his arm, and the magician was sent sailing over the roof and rolling across the stone until he smashed into the ledge on the other side.

Daniel felt a rush of energy seep into his arms and hands, healing his injuries; his magic stores topped out. The leader of whatever team Jack's people were fighting was probably not a small fry.

Daniel grabbed the green orb and used his wristband to stick it into his inventory. The wind magic promptly cut out.

Daniel stomped his foot, launching himself into the air. The spells thrown by the undine's guards detonated under him, blowing a hole in the roof of their building. He rebounded back to their level, then sent them over to join their boss with a few high-speed punches and kicks. *Not really my strong suit, but it works.*

Trusting that Jack could hold the fort, Daniel decided to mount an attack and keep them off balance. Everyone he killed was only less member of the enemy team they had to deal with, and were permanently dead to boot. He took up one of the lightning rods dropped by the mages. It was about 3 feet long—good enough as a club.

He jumped into the hole, dropping into the top floor of the building below. He landed right in the middle of a gaggle of magicians, all looking up at their new skylight. Daniel paused awkwardly. "Uh..."

Spells flew at him. Daniel brandished the rod on instinct, pouring magic into it.

Then the rod blew up.

****

Jack peeled himself off the grass as the wind cut out. His ears rung; his back felt like it was on fire. He groaned, then stood straight, blinking.

Daniel's antics had peeled off the majority of the fighters arrayed against them. The soldiers scrambled to surround him and cut him off, and the mages were running for it, trying to get distance between themselves and a vengeful Daniel. Jack could feel Hell's magic working on his fire-scarred backside, steadily stitching his skin back together.

Jack only had a few seconds to catch his breath. Another wave of soldiers was headed straight toward him—all spidery grazul, decked out in thick red plate armor. "Great. The shock troops."

Jack produced a black vial from his inventory and downed the contents. The crawling sensation on his back worsened into a burning itch as his body started to regenerate even faster. He scrunched his mouth against the taste, like coppery licorice. It was worse than the itch by a long shot.

Jack could practically feel his wallet shrink from the expenditure, but the mana vial was worth it. His body greedily soaked up the energy; in addition to his back healing in double-time, his depleted magic reserves were restored in moments. It felt like a gulp of fresh air after holding his breath a bit too long underwater.

A few potshots of magic came from the building behind the oncoming grazul. Jack raised his forearms and sidestepped the fireballs and blasts of ice. Whatever he couldn't dodge, he deflected away with his fur. Stopping a spell cold used more magic, but if he could push it away, divert the force, he could last a lot longer.

When the salvo of energy blasts ended, the grazul were on top of him. They activated their plate armor, and the red color visibly darkened under a magical haze. The first one jumped in the air and came down on top of him, leading with two armored fists. Jack met the blow with his own single fist.

The weight pushed Jack back a step. The grazul's armor took a dent, but it landed in front of him without problem. Two others came at him around it, attacking from both sides with weapons.

Jack dived left to avoid the sword slash from the grazul on his right. He put up and arm to block the other's hammer before it could fall, then used his other hand to grab the grazul's outstretched arm by the wrist. He hoisted it off the ground and threw it into its comrade behind him. The two spiders smashed together like bowling pins.

Their armor clanged as they bounced off one another, sending them tumbling back across the grass, but they scrambled to their feet with an unnatural dexterity. With more limbs came a lot of extra coordination. Jack gave ground, falling back toward the node as the squad of spiders closed in again.

The three grazul swiped and stabbed at him, using their many limbs to harass him, keeping him off balance. Jack fended them off with big swings of his arms. When the one using the sword overextended, Jack sent a piledrive of a fist into its skull, flattening it to the ground. But as he turned to deal with the others, it shook off the blow and stood up again, forcing him to step back.

Jack could hold them off—he only had to keep them from recapturing the node, which needed the ten second contact with one of their wristbands. The problem was their enchanted armor, tough enough to withstand his strength. In the meantime, he was half-distracted by the threat of magical snipers, waiting for their shot from the windows.

It was a battle of attrition, and it was one they knew he'd lose. His magic was exhausted by the storm. The vial he used helped, but it was a temporary shot in the arm. The energy it gave him wouldn't last a prolonged fight.

A flash of purple caught Jack's eye. And then the building behind the grazul blew up.

Jack ducked behind the capture node and covered his ears as a wall of superheated air rolled past him. The heat charred the exposed ends of his fur. Man-sized chunks of stone flew past him, some smashing through the branches of the trees. The grazul, caught without any cover, were buried in a tsunami of debris and violet lightning. The ground rumbled under him.

When the shaking stopped, Jack slowly got to his feet. His legs felt like jelly, even if he was bigger than a gorilla. Rubble sat high on both sides of him, parted by the capture pedestal he'd hidden behind. Half the courtyard was buried; the other half was scoured by the blast wave, clear of any warriors or mages. As the smoke cleared, Jack could see that the building was blasted completely in half. All six stories were exposed across the middle, as if a bomb had gone off at the front door.

Nothing moved in the remains. Jack jogged over to the house. "Daniel!" He raised his wristband up, opening their radio link. "Daniel, you there? Daniel!"

Nothing came through. Jack started digging. He tore away chunks of stone and drywall. There were a lot of bodies. All the magicians that retreated inside to target them from cover had been crushed.

Some of the stone shifted; debris poured away like sand, and a familiar face popped out of the rubble. "Daniel! Oh, man. Oh man."

Jack pulled Daniel free of the rubble. Half of one of his arms was gone, scorched off straight from his body. That side of him was black and pockmarked, from his feet all the way to his face. The skin there was burned through down to the muscle and bone. What was left of his clothes were practically baked onto him.

Jack sighed. At least he wasn't alive to feel the pain. The explosion probably took him out in the first instant.

Daniel's body coughed. A hoarse groan came out of his lips.

"Unbelievable. You survived that? You bastard." Jack drew out his second mana potion. "You are so paying me back for this." He lifted the vial up to Daniel's throat and poured it down, slowly. Daniel managed to swallow most of it, though about half ended up spluttered down the front of what was left of his shirt.

Daniel's condition improved rapidly. The mana vial wasn't enough to heal the arm, but it would mend most of the skin up and let Daniel walk; he'd also have some magic to spare if there was an emergency. The natural healing from Hell itself would kick in and do the rest.

Jack carried Daniel back to the capture point and laid him up against the pedestal. No more enemies had arrived. Jack was fairly certain none of them survived. Or the ones that had ran off.

"Jack." Daniel's voice was grunted with the minimal amount of effort. "We win?"

"Yeah," Jack said. "I think we won. What the hell happened?"

"Hurts." Daniel felt at the grass with his good hand. "Can't feel my right arm."

"You don't have a right arm."

"Wha...?" Daniel pried his eyes open. Jack thought they'd pop out of his head when they landed on what was left. "Fuck me."

"Yeah, fuck you."

"Hey, that's..." Daniel fell into a hacking cough. Something black got spit up on the ground. "Ugh. Not very sporting."

"You seem to have a strange affinity for explosions," Jack said.

"Tell me about it," Daniel said. His voice was starting to come back a bit. "I lifted one of those purple...lightning thingies. I tried to use it as a club. I think I pushed my magic into it."

"Yeah, they don't work that way."

"Gee," Daniel said. "Thanks for the advice."

The pedestal flashed. Jack's map updated, showing the territory now solid green. Notifications of the money he'd won for his efforts popped up. They'd finished the capture. "It's official," Jack said.

The air around Daniel's arm wavered and shifted, like heat rising off asphalt. His flesh started to knit itself back together in front of them, one hunk of bone and sinew at a time.

"This is disgusting," Daniel said. He winced as his new bones cracked into their former position. "And it kills. Ugh."

"You get used to it."

"I don't want to get used to it." Daniel sat up straighter. His skin was improving, too; black, burned skin was sloughing off, replaced by fresh pink. "At least it doesn't hurt as much as last time."

"You're probably in shock. Adrenaline. Something like that."

Daniel nodded vaguely. "Yeah." He lifted his head in Jack's direction. "Question."

"Answer."

"Is it like this every day down here?"

"We don't have days. We live in a cave." Daniel stared at him. Jack chuckled at his own joke. "But nah. It's not usually like this. Everyone set this up special for you."

Daniel snorted. "You don't even know, man."

****

High above the ruins of Jack and Daniel's battlefield, there was a single observer. She floated in the air, silent, invisible to the cameras darting about like so many hummingbirds. She watched the two of them make their way over the crumbled remains of the square.

She almost smiled at the sight, at the glow of victory that hung unspoken in their banter. But the urge to grin failed halfway to her face, as if her muscles had forgotten how to make the expression.

Chapter 7
Schism

Eleanor hesitated at the entrance to her father's office. Twin oak doors barred the way, each about three inches thick and several hundred pounds apiece. They sat within a stone arch that touched the ceiling of the hallway.

The arch was carved with spell runes that followed along its curve, linked together stone-by-stone in a circuit. The runes proofed against magical espionage. The entire house was warded against spying, but the office had that extra layer of protection, the final keep nestled within fortress walls. What happened in Henry's study stayed in Henry's study.

The great doors themselves were etched in detail with four images from modern magical history. On the upper left was the triumph of the alliance over Elizabeth Bathory's dark empire; magicians in robes stood over the crumbled castle of their foe. The second quadrant alluded to the schism that separated the Order of True Flame from the Ivory Dawn, showing mages with different styles of dress standing apart, arms folded, cross expressions on their faces. One of them was her ancestor, a previous patriarch of the Astor family, though they didn't lead the whole organization at that time.

The third panel was the journey of the Ivory Dawn to the United States, where they stood atop a hill, a large sun stretching behind them. America's first generation of magicians solidified the new country's place in the world; the Dawn later came into their full power during the Civil War. The bottom right section of the door captured the most recent scene from history; the Dawn and the Flame uniting once again to fight back against Aleister Crowley and the Nazi cultists during World War II.

The faces and backgrounds in each image were cut deep in the wood, taking advantage of the door's thick material. The left edges of the carvings were painted bright gold; the right edges, a subdued blue. The interplay of colors and depth of the material gave it a vivid sensation of presence. In the right lighting, it seemed as if the figures could step right out of the door and into the hallway, all flowing with colors that matched the rest of the manor—the blues, the golds, and the whites of the Ivory Dawn.

When she was a child, Eleanor used to run her fingers along the etchings and imagine herself standing in the middle of those grand moments. She enjoyed playing with the doors themselves, too; they were big, but well-balanced on the hinges. The momentum made a fun toy as she swung in and out of her father's office, usually as he, seated behind his desk, conducted globe-shifting business on the telephone, keeping one eye on her.

She used to run with Rachel up and down the long hall in front of the office, storming around the chairs and tapestries in a 1-on-1 game of tag. Sometimes they'd play pretend; Rachel would take on the role of Bathory so Eleanor could lead the champions in her defeat. Rachel always complained about that. Eleanor relented once or twice, but she usually quit halfway whenever she was pushed into the villain role. Eventually, Rachel stopped complaining and started going along with what Eleanor wanted.

Eleanor never saw what she did to Rachel. She never saw how oppressed her friend—her sister—truly was. There wasn't anyone to ever tell Eleanor to stop, to point out her entitled and selfish behavior.

Not until they met Daniel. He was the only person that ever made Eleanor feel ashamed of herself.

She wished she had the human decency to be ashamed years earlier.

Eleanor wasted most of her life treating Rachel badly. How many times did Rachel swallow her pride for the sake of keeping the peace? Just go along with what precious Elly wanted, *again*, afraid to speak up, take any kind of stand. Eleanor merrily trotted along, ignoring Rachel's mute melancholy because she was satisfied with the outcomes and her self-centered methods never failed.

But things were going to be different. Eleanor had come to terms with how little she appreciated Rachel, but more importantly, how much joy there was in their relationship that was waiting to be unleashed. Eleanor had crossed a desert in her heart, one she didn't know was there until it was shown to her. And still she had to be dragged halfway, unwilling, before getting to her own feet and trudging across the sand. She finally reached the oasis at the center of that desert. But when she reached out to take a drink, it vanished, like a cruel mirage. Her heart was left cracked, and dry, and barren.

Rachel was gone.

Eleanor took a long, shuddering breath. She put her hand up to her eyes. She couldn't start crying again, not after spending the last two hours composing herself. She focused on the floor under her feet. The carpet swam into view as she blinked water back from her eyes.

How many times had she walked down that carpet to see her father? How many times did she see his frowns melt into smiles when she walked in? He always took her when she came to him, no matter what. He put important meetings on hold; he made dignitaries wait. He casually tossed out schedules that were meticulously crafted by his aides, packed sunup to sundown with vital business, to comfort her when she was upset over things like broken toys or a magic spell that didn't work the way she wanted. He always made time for her.

Those moments were gone, too.

The hall was quiet. It was stuffed with as many decorations as ever, but it felt terribly empty. The carpets, wallpaper, tapestries, suits of armor, chandeliers; they didn't matter.

Useless, absolutely useless pieces of pretension—she used to be proud of them, proud of colors and symbols, as if she was made more important and special by their presence. They weren't important. What was important was dead, and she was too stupid to realize it until after the fact.

She used to be so confident, so filled with answers. Now she was filled with questions that would never be answered. With no outlet, the unsaid apologies, the unspoken words of love were trapped inside her.

Eleanor dragged herself back from her thoughts before she spiraled into a place she didn't want to visit again. She'd done enough crying the past few days.

She briefly eyed the few chairs set near the door. She'd never considered sitting in them. She'd never waited this long before. And she shouldn't wait. She should knock on the door, march in, and tell her father how things were going to be.

Eleanor had raised her fist to knock—but the doors opened. A few attendants were leading the way in front of Matthew and Gerald Aiken. She made to move aside, hoping they would just be on their way with a simple greeting, but the whole entourage paused in front of her.

Gerald Aiken was a squarish, stout man with brown eyes and a thick beard. His son was built in the same way, square, though slightly taller and with less flab. Matthew's crop of brown hair was slicked up in waves, a contrast to Gerald's fading hairline. Dressed in suits and ties, they looked the part of a high-power father-and-son business team. Eleanor had an equally high-power distaste of them both.

Gerald was the CEO of Medusa Entertainment, a major telecommunications conglomerate that got its start in video games, eventually leveraging into social media. He also owned a controlling stake in and sat on the board of directors of several other prominent tech companies. If Eleanor's family was the old money of the United States, the Aiken family would define the Silicon Valley nouveau riche.

"Miss Astor," Gerald said.

Eleanor did her best to politely return the greeting. It was a half-hearted murmur, but it got the job done.

Matthew smiled, but it didn't reach his eyes, them being busy running her up and down. He wasn't even trying to hide it. "Hello Eleanor. It's good to see you."

Eleanor looked past him and at the doors. They were only half-shut, but the runes prevented sound from coming out of the room. She caught a glimpse of Rothschild standing near her father's desk. Anger flashed in her gut.

"Your father mentioned he'd be speaking with you shortly," Gerald said. "I'll go ahead. A lot to manage with the war out in public now." He glanced at Matthew. "Meet me at the car in a few minutes."

The retinue followed Gerald away, leaving Eleanor and Matthew in the hall. Matthew waited until his father was out of earshot before speaking. "I heard about Rachel. I'm sorry. I understand she was like a sister to you."

Rachel was in fact her adopted sister—something Matthew should have well known—but Eleanor kept her tone neutral, falling back on years of social training. "I appreciate your sympathy. She will be missed, by me and all of us."

"I never liked that Daniel character," Matthew said. "He must have known who you were, used Rachel to get close to you. What he did was disgusting."

Eleanor fought to keep the loathing from seeping into her voice. "Is that what my father told you happened?"

"It was his best guess," Matthew said. He picked up on her tension, but interpreted it entirely the wrong way. "I know that when someone takes advantage of you like that, it can be hard to admit when things finally come back around. I wanted to say that there's no hard feelings on my end. I've made my own mistakes...maybe I jumped to conclusions too quickly, even if my instincts were right."

Eleanor ground her teeth. The insufferable prick couldn't stop congratulating himself on his *instincts* even during a half-assed attempt at apologizing for being a boor. "Everyone makes mistakes," she managed.

"I realize that now more than ever," he said. "Whatever lapses in judgement either of us have had, my affections for you are unchanged."

"As is my lack of affection," Eleanor said. "I believe I've made that clear."

"I know," Matthew said, "but I'm not giving up on you."

"Matthew," Eleanor said, "leave it at that. I'm not interested in your advances."

He stepped closer. "I won't let you down, Eleanor. The Dawn—our families—we're the most powerful group of mages on Earth. We can defeat the Vorid. I know I can prove myself to you. Maybe not right now, not soon, but by the end of this, I'll show you what I'm made of."

Eleanor tried to muster up a polite response, but she couldn't form the words. And then, it struck her—the arrogance that wouldn't take no for an answer, the insistent verbal self-righteousness despite all action to the contrary—it was the worst of herself that she saw in him. The worst bits of her character she'd been so desperate to scrape away were alive and living in Matthew Aiken.

When she didn't say anything, Matthew continued. "Together, we can accomplish anything. I really believe that."

"How odd," Eleanor said. "I seem to remember you didn't accomplish much back in New York, other than spending time schmoozing around the command post." Matthew's shoulders tensed. Eleanor tapped her chin in mock thought. "Strangely enough, Daniel Fitzgerald was out there, risking his life to fight with us even though half the alliance was trying to kill him.

Despite his selfless bravery, I've heard him described as disgusting." She looked him in the eye. "What does that make someone who barely showed up?"

Matthew's lips churned. He started to speak, stopped himself, then started again. "I'm not going to take that to heart. You're grieving, and you're confused."

"I'm not confused at all," Eleanor said. "I've seen exactly what you're made of, and it's sad and worthless."

"That was uncalled for," Matthew said. "Just because you're emotional doesn't mean you should take it out on me."

"Emotional." Eleanor was so clenched up her nails were biting into her palms. "My sister is dead. My friend was sent to Hell after putting himself in mortal danger for the sake of people that wanted to get rid of him. My own father has slandered his accomplishments, no doubt in coordination with the illustrious Rothschild—the same Rothschild that wouldn't have gotten Rachel killed if he had simply followed the plan he agreed to in the first place. And the only thing you can think to do is remind me of how stupid we were for associating with him!" Eleanor jabbed a finger into his chest, forcing him to step back. "*You* disgust *me*. I wouldn't return your affections if you were the last man on Earth."

Matthew stared at her, totally taken aback. "You—you can't—I don't—"

"You were right about one thing," Eleanor said. "I'm emotional. Now get out of my house and take your *disgusting* mouth with you before I throw you out!"

Matthew was shaken by her outburst, but his expression settled. He stood straight. "Remember, later, I was the one that tried to make peace. I'll see you again soon."

"Get. Out," Eleanor growled. Something in her voice must have made it through his skull, because Matthew walked away fast. Eleanor kept an eye on him until he turned down the next hall.

When she faced the door again, Rothschild was there.

His blonde hair was cropped close at the sides; his eyes were as sharp as his chin. He didn't look pleased, or compromising. "Miss Astor. We couldn't help but overhear the conversation between you and Mr. Aiken."

"I beg your pardon," Eleanor said. "My *emotions* seem to have gotten the better of me in this time of grieving."

"Daniel needed to be banished," Rothschild said. "He was a threat to the mundanes and to us. To Earth."

"I'm not in the mood for a lecture, Mr. Rothschild."

"That's Lord Rothschild, if you please."

"We don't have Lords in America."

They stared at each other in silence.

"You're an ignorant youth that doesn't understand how the world works," Rothschild said. "That misunderstanding will be corrected by the reality of the situation, no matter how much you try to ignore it. That, or it will kill you. Whichever comes first."

"Are you threatening me?" Eleanor asked.

"Only stating the facts," Rothschild said, "as I stated them to Mr. Fitzgerald. Shame things didn't work out for him. Perhaps you ought to note his experience."

"Unbelievable," Eleanor said. "You got my sister killed and blackmailed the Ivory Dawn into banishing the one solid hope we had of fighting back against the Vorid, and then you have the temerity to stand here and pontificate right to my face. If fewer people were like you, maybe the world wouldn't be the way it is."

"If fewer people were like me," Rothschild said, "there wouldn't be a world forgiving enough to allow for a spoiled child such as yourself."

Eleanor rolled her eyes and brushed passed him. "Good day, Mr. Rothschild."

"Clearly," Rothschild said, his voice fading as he walked away, "I'll have to leave the discipline to your father."

Eleanor entered the office. The runes on the outside of the archway flashed suddenly, scanned over her, then deactivated upon confirming her identity. She raised a hand, summoning her magic—though, as worked up as she was, it was virtually bursting out of her skin already. A physical sigil formed on either side of the doors. Lines of blue light coiled like a spring and slammed them shut behind her, then faded back into nonexistence as she released the grip on her power.

Her father didn't react to her spell, or the slam of the doors. His arms were folded behind his back; he stood at the window overlooking the garden. A dusting of snow covered over the grass and the hedges; the fountain was turned off for the winter.

Eleanor didn't bother to wait for him to speak. Seeing him standing there, at peace with the world, was the last straw she could handle. "You threw Daniel to the wolves! Why?!"

Henry didn't turn. He kept on staring out the window, eyes traveling over the clouds. "You heard what I said to Daniel when we banished him. His actions lead directly to Rachel's death. That was more than enough."

"Rothschild held our forces back when it was time to strike," Eleanor said. "That pushed Daniel to keep fighting until he was weakened. It was only after then Rachel broke ranks to go to him. How many times do I have to tell you that before you believe me?"

"Who should I believe?" Henry said. He rotated away from the window until he was facing her. He had the same ice-blonde hair she did—greying at the temples, now—and the same blue eyes. He was tall and barrel-chested; his frame dominated whatever space he stood in, and that was nowhere more apparent than in his own office.

"Hopefully," Eleanor said, "you believe your own daughter before the self-interested parade of buffoons I withstood out in the hall."

"Even if it's true," he said, "I would have banished him anyway."

"What?!"

Henry slammed a hand down on the corner of his desk. "Eleanor! I didn't raise a fool!" Eleanor blinked in surprise. "It's obvious that Daniel was trying to get close to you," Henry said. "Your first instinct about him was correct—he should have never been involved with Rachel. It is our law to banish those who take up black magic—and Daniel wasn't some rogue magician, he was an aberration created by a foreign power trying to interfere in Earth's affairs. If he really was all that noble, and he had good intentions, then he should have known better than to start a relationship with someone—anyone—and especially Rachel!"

"Daniel didn't know who we were," Eleanor said. "Who she was."

"Do you expect me to believe that it was total coincidence that the strongest known contractor just so happened to become the lover of the adopted daughter of the leader of the Ivory Dawn?" Henry said. He crossed the gap to Eleanor. "We—you—all of us, are being manipulated!"

"Rachel is dead, and the murderer walked past me down the hallway!" Eleanor shouted. "What is wrong with you?!"

Henry's voice dropped. "Xikanthus knew he couldn't change my mind, so he used Daniel to get to you and Rachel, to get to me. This was all orchestrated from the beginning as a ploy to force humanity to accept contractors. The only thing Xik accomplished is making me even more certain I made the right choice in refusing him."

"Will it still be the right choice if we're all dead?" Eleanor said. "Why aren't we working with Xikanthus? Why don't we trust the Klide? The Vorid are at our doorstep and knocking down the gates, and here you are insisting that everything's fine and the house isn't on fire!"

"We defeated them in New York, and we can do it again."

"We defeated them because I brokered a compromise between Daniel and Rothschild. A compromise you couldn't make even if you wanted to, because you were unconscious from injuries—injuries that would have killed you if Daniel didn't intervene and save your life!" Eleanor said. "What happens when they come back with their full forces and Daniel isn't here to fill in the gaps? The Klide are at least offering a dialogue."

"We cannot allow ourselves to become puppets of greater warring powers," Henry said. "The only thing we know about the Klide is what Xikanthus told us. The only things we know about the *Vorid* is what Xikanthus told us."

"The Klide," Eleanor said, "are not actively trying to harvest humanity!"

"For all we know, Xikanthus could be one of their agents trying to undermine us!" Henry said. "He's claimed that the Vorid are incredibly powerful—we're almost comically impotent compared to their true might. But what if he's lying? We have absolutely no knowledge of his supposed contractor magic, and he refused to explain the spell. Even after trying to study it, first with that girl, and then with Daniel, we couldn't learn anything useful, but we do know that kind of power doesn't come easy. An interdimensional stranger wants to create a group of elite warriors to fight the Vorid—but what comes after that, even if he's being honest? The Klide occupation? They could easily control us through the contractors they create. How do we know the Klide have good intentions? How do we know they mean what they say about being our allies? Why aren't they helping us fight? Why insist that contractors are the only way, the only means through which they'll provide aid?" Henry gestured sharply. "We don't have time for romantic ideals of justice and friendship. This is not a storybook tale, this is real, and we have to grapple with real questions. If we accept Klide aid, not only are we ignoring the hard lessons our own history has repeatedly taught us, we are effectively ceding human sovereignty over planet Earth. I won't stop a bulldozer from demolishing our house only to owe a debt we can never pay off to a loan shark!" Henry pressed the tips of his fingers to his head. "Think, Eleanor. Think. You have been used!"

"I am thinking," Eleanor said, "and I know absolutely that Daniel Fitzgerald is not our enemy."

Henry leaned back and sighed heavily. "I thought that would get through. Heaven above, what will I do with you?"

"Everything you've said is based on supposition," Eleanor said. "You don't have any actual proof of any of this. Besides, if Xikanthus is a Vorid agent, why would he work to fight and kill his own forces with contractors?"

"The point is to insert the contractors past our defenses so that we can be destroyed in one fell swoop from the inside. If that costs them some cheap extractors, then so be it." Henry rubbed his eyes. "Xikanthus thought I would break because of Rachel. He thought she would convince me to accept Daniel. She might very well have done so. But he didn't predict her dying. In a way, that saved me. Us."

"All you're doing is justifying an opinion you already had, after the fact," Eleanor said.

"Everything I've said is perfectly rational."

"It's completely irrational!" Eleanor said. "It's all based on fear of what might be. It's suspicions and paranoia all stacked on top of one another. If the Klide were so powerful, or wanted to take advantage of us, what's the point of helping us in the first place? They'd leave us be until we were even weaker, then step in when we no longer had a choice. Instead, they came forward before the war really ramped up, before that many humans had died. And now you're holding Rachel out as a sacrificial pawn that stopped you from giving in? I'd rather owe a thousand of your loans to the Klide before I started betraying the people I cared about!"

"And there's the rub." Henry eyed her. "You care about him, too."

"He was my friend! Of course I—"

"Don't even think about dodging this," Henry said. He studied her. "I saw it at that ball on your birthday. I can see it right now. You have feelings for him."

Eleanor's heart lurched in her chest. "No, that's...father. He was Rachel's boyfriend."

"I knew it." Henry sighed again, seeing something that confirmed his idea. "You're blinded. Your personal feelings interfered with your judgement during the battle. Rothschild made the right call. I was injured, and he saw what I couldn't see."

"No," Eleanor said. Her eyes were welling up. "Don't say that. It wasn't like that!"

"It was," Henry said. "Wasn't it?"

Eleanor shook her head, but she couldn't find the words. Her throat was jammed up in a knot; her heart was doing twists and turns faster than she could keep up with. She didn't expect this from him, the accusations, the finger-pointing. Especially not about Rachel.

Worst of all was the anxiety that some part of what he said was true.

"Whatever your feelings," Henry said, "erase them. This isn't a time for personal indulgences. It's war. We have to prepare for the Vorid counterattack. You're right about one thing—this isn't over, not yet."

Eleanor said nothing. She was afraid her voice would break. Whatever argument she expected, that topic wasn't on her mental agenda.

"I've discussed the consolidation of the Ivory Dawn with George," Henry said. "The Aikens and Astors have grown apart with the emergence of the technology industry. It's time to reunify the branches. You're playing a major role in that."

"Does what I want," Eleanor said, "factor into the equation?"

"What you want has already put enough people in danger."

"I want to go to Cleveland."

"Cleveland?" Henry said. "Ah. The Fitzgeralds."

"I promised Daniel I'd take care of his family," Eleanor said, "and I intend to follow through."

"I'll assign a detail to keep an eye on them. That will suffice."

"I have to do this myself. It's important."

"They're his relatives, Eleanor," Henry said. "You need to eliminate your attachment, not secure it."

"Weren't you the one lecturing me not to look down on mundanes?" Eleanor said. "If I want to bring his brother under my protection, it's my business."

"I've spoiled you rotten," Henry said. "I've given you everything you've wanted, and now, when push comes to shove, you have no sense of discipline."

Discipline. The same word Rothschild used. Eleanor tasted a sour bitterness in the back of her mouth. "I intend to keep a promise," Eleanor said. "If you think that represents a weakness in the daughter you've raised, then you truly are being irrational. If it wasn't for my discipline, we would have lost New York."

"You won't have the time for a personal trip," Henry said. "You need to prepare for your wedding."

Eleanor's spine froze over. "I won't—you...what?"

"Aiken and Astor, together."

Eleanor stepped backward. Her hands felt out for balance; she grabbed the back of a chair near the desk. Her knees almost buckled in, but she caught herself. "No. Absolutely not."

"Eleanor—"

"No! You are not going to attach me to that piece of slime! I won't have it!"

"Calm down," Henry said. "You've known and I've told you for years that your marriage would be political. It's come sooner than we intended. It's not the match either of us would prefer, but I never expected a war like this."

"What about me?" Eleanor said. "Do I even matter? Do my feelings matter? Oh, silly me—I'm a spoiled brat! Clearly the cure is to marry me to an unbearable, pretentious little fuck of a human being!"

Henry looked shocked. "Elly!"

Even Eleanor was surprised at herself. She couldn't remember the last time she swore. She didn't care. "I guess Daniel fucking rubbed off on me exactly like you thought!" Eleanor shouted. "First you fucking banish my friend, and then you tell me my stupid fucking judgement got Rachel killed—"

"Eleanor, I don't—"

"And then you tell me to marry that little fuck Aiken, of all people! Well fuck him, fuck that, and fuck *you!*"

Eleanor blasted the doors back open with another sigil and stormed down the hall. Henry called after her, but she didn't stop.

****

Henry stood in the office, his gaze lingering on the open doors. He felt a little shellshocked.

Nickolas emerged from his hiding spot. His camouflage enchantment dropped from his body as he stepped forward.

The silence lingered for a long time.

"That," Henry said eventually, "went as poorly as I feared."

Nickolas raised an eyebrow. "Did you expect anything else?"

"Not really."

"She needed to hear it," Nickolas said. "There was no right way to go about it. She'll accept it in time."

"I'm afraid, Nickolas," Henry said quietly. "This war is destroying whatever innocence she had left. Did you see the way she looked at me when I brought up the wedding?"

"Do you really trust Rothschild?" Nickolas said.

"No," Henry said. "He's young, ambitious. Too ambitious. I almost expected *him* to ask for Eleanor's hand, but he didn't."

"The Aikens are going to have to start contributing to the war effort," Nickolas said. "Maybe Rothschild has designs on them yet. If something happens to Matthew—something that appears to be the fault of the Vorid..."

"Then Gerald is already committed to the cause, by that point," Henry said, "and he'll want revenge for his heir, locking him in as our support. Rothschild takes Matthew's place with Eleanor, effectively reuniting the Flame and the Dawn. When the war ends, he'll be in charge of the greatest faction of magicians since the Renaissance. And his first order of business will be making sure the Astor branch doesn't have any ideas about who's charge." He looked at Nickolas. "The wedding with Matthew needs to happen. Sooner, rather than later. We need to have our own house in order if we're going to survive whatever is left after this is over."

"Rachel's funeral?"

"We don't have..." Henry's face lowered. Shadows ran down his eyes and under his chin. "I was about to say that I don't have time for my daughter's funeral. God. It almost makes me feel like Daniel had a point about us." He sighed. "We'll make time. Tomorrow morning."

"A burial, or...?"

"The Ashworth crypt. Full enchanted internment, for as long as our home stands. It's the least she deserves." Henry's eyes misted. "The last of her line. She upheld their honor to the very end."

Nickolas nodded. "I'll make the arrangements. You focus on what needs doing." He put a hand on Henry's shoulder, then started down the hall. "I'll try to talk to Eleanor. I get the distinct feeling she's going to do something stupid."

Henry privately agreed, but he let Nickolas go without further comment and sat back at his desk. A mound of paperwork regarding the supply distribution to the refugee camps awaited him. He reached for his pen, but paused, thinking.

Am I playing into his hands?

He could only do what he believed was right. Henry gave his head a shake and reached for the first packet he needed to sign. Self-doubt could wait its turn at the bottom of the stack.

****

There was a knock on the door. A stern voice followed, muffled by the wood. "Eleanor. It's Nickolas."

Eleanor ignored him. She grabbed another fistful of clothes from the second drawer of her dresser—a random clump socks, some underwear—and jammed it into her suitcase.

She was usually mindful when she packed, folding everything so as to avoid wrinkles. Everything tucked in exactly the right place.

She couldn't do that right now. The only way she could stop her hands from shaking was to keep them moving.

More knocks rapped across the room. "Eleanor, I know you're in there."

"It's Miss Astor to you!" Eleanor said. Her voice cracked. "I don't want to see anyone right now!"

"It's about Daniel's family."

Eleanor paused, arm halfway into her dresser. She looked over her shoulder.

Her suitcase lay on her bed; its thick shell pushed a depression into the blue and gold comforter. The carpet was the same colors, blue lines weaving between gold diamonds. The wallpaper was white, with little gold suns embossed upon it in a repeating pattern. Even her dresser was white pine, edged in gold leaf. It all shone down at her, the cheery confidence of power and security heralded by the Ivory Dawn.

She never loathed it like she did then. She stared down the suns on the walls. They didn't budge.

"Eleanor," Nickolas said. He sounded more subdued, less the body man and more himself. "Please. He's trying to compromise."

Eleanor's eyes flicked to the door. "I'm listening."

"I've located the camp in Cleveland with his father and brother. Our agents are keeping an eye on them."

"Does my father," Eleanor said, "mean to pretend that this relieves me of my responsibility?"

"I'd be happy to give you the details," he said, a certain dryness seeping into his tone, "but I'd really prefer not to talk to you through a door."

Eleanor sighed, tossed the clothes she was holding in the general direction of her suitcase, and crossed the room to open the door. Nickolas stood there, tall and stiff in a white suit and gold vest, his black hair tied back tight behind his head. Anyone else might look like they were planning on going to a high-fashion gala; Nickolas somehow made the outfit look solemn and studious.

"May I come in?" he asked.

"I didn't open the door to slam it in your face, Nickolas," Eleanor said. She returned to the task of stuffing her suitcase.

Nickolas's eyes automatically scanned the room; Eleanor saw his gaze unfocus slightly as he scryed, hunting for magical danger. He was born and raised a servant of their family, a bodyguard, not unlike Rachel.

Eleanor's throat tightened. She tried to swallow, but the knot clenched up tighter, almost as if her own body was trying to choke her. Her hands crushed the blouse she was holding.

Eleanor saw Nickolas looking at her, and she put on her face, her mask. She took a breath and tried to put the scrunched-up blouse in the suitcase. The attempt ended in an awkward chucking motion, her arm caught between the half of her brain that wanted to ram the thing down as hard as possible and the half working to keep the anxiety at bay. The blouse caught the air, drifted, and fell to the floor next to the bed.

A spike of frustration raged in her head. She knelt down, grabbed the blouse—now wondrously wrinkled from her manhandling, *perfect*—then started to stand.

She saw the stitching on the front. A sun, again—but softer, better than the angular globes that were up on the walls of her bedroom. It was one Rachel had sewn for her.

Eleanor fell to a knee. She drew the blouse in, clutching it to her chest. She put out a hand to balance herself against the carpet. Water filled her eyes. She breathed in through her teeth, then out. *I will not cry. I will not.*

Suddenly, Nickolas was behind her, kneeling next to her. His hand touched her shoulder. "Elly..."

The sadness burst like a popped balloon. Her body went out of control, forced to clench in and down as if to protect itself—but the pain was inside. All she could do was wrap herself tighter. Her tears stained the blouse in her arms.

Nickolas was a silent support at her back. He kept his hand on her shoulder as the sobs wracked through her. It was already too much.

"Please." Eleanor drew herself up slightly. Her diaphragm ached. "It's fine."

"It clearly," Nickolas said, "is not fine."

"It has to be," Eleanor said. She picked herself up, shrugging off Nickolas's arm. Her jaw worked a few times; she cleared her throat, then went for her dresser again.

"What are you packing for?" Nickolas asked.

"I'm going to Cleveland whether he likes it or not," Eleanor said. "I promised Daniel I'd take care of his family."

"Henry won't be happy."

Eleanor rounded on him. "Did my father," she said, voice rising, "ask about whether it would make me happy when he sent Daniel to Hell? Did he even listen when I told him Rachel would have been fine if it wasn't for that Rothschild bastard intentionally holding back the plan!? Daniel had the Vorid lord on the defensive. He had him pinned down! We could have taken him out in the first few minutes!"

Nickolas raised his hands, a gesture of peace. "I'm not here to debate what should have been done. It isn't my place. I'm here to tell you that if you want to go to Cleveland, then you're going to have to cut a deal. One way or another, you're promised to Aiken."

"What does that have to do with this?" Eleanor asked.

"Trade your willingness for a trip to Cleveland," Nickolas said. "Wartime marriages used to be common, back when we fought each other. It was a guarantee between families that they'd share magical secrets and grow together after—"

"I don't need a history lesson, thank you."

Nickolas paused and let the strain from Eleanor's words fade a bit before he continued. "Promise Mr. Astor you'll go along with the wedding. In exchange, you want to personally ensure the safety of Daniel's brother."

"Trade," Eleanor said. "With him. My father. Did you see the way he looked, back in there?!" She threw her hands up. "I don't even know who he is!"

"He lost one of his daughters."

"AND I LOST MY SISTER!" Eleanor shrieked. The temperature in the room dropped a few degrees. Frost grew at Eleanor's fingertips, at the corners of her eyes. Threads of ice snaked through her hair as her magic fluctuated, tearing out from under her control.

Nickolas's face was still, but he took a step back. Eleanor let the magic roil through her, let the iced-over anger seethe in her core, and then she pushed it down, locking it in place. The ice withered away, but the air stayed chill.

"Listen," Nickolas said. "We all say the president of the Ivory Dawn isn't elected. Almost like a family joke, sometimes." His lips drew thin. "But it's not a joke. I was there, the last time there was a fight over the succession. The Astors have stayed on top for good reason. He's shielded you from family conflicts your whole life, but he can't afford to do that now." When he saw Eleanor's face change, he raised his hands. "I'm not saying he made the right decision. I'm just—"

"You're *just* trying to excuse his self-righteous bullshit!" Eleanor said. "As if he's the only one sad that Rachel is gone. He gets to be angry and act like an idiot, and everyone else has to bow and obey. Daniel was right! They're all a bunch of fools positioning themselves to be king of the ashes! Oh, how wonderful it will be when the Earth is a blasted rock sucked dry of every last fucking ounce of life, but the Astors are yet the leaders of the Ivory Dawn!" Eleanor's chest heaved with her anger; her eyes blazed with it; her throat was sore from it. Her magic swelled again, banging about for an outlet. "I swear, Nickolas, I..." She trailed off when she saw the look on

Nickolas's face. She glanced over her shoulder, then back. "What? What is it?"

He blinked a bit. "I don't think I can get used to you swearing."

Eleanor huffed. "You'd better start. It isn't going away."

His surprise settled back into stern formality. "You can't run off on your own right now. First, it's too dangerous. And even if I helped you, you wouldn't make it fifty feet from the property."

"You'd help me?" Eleanor asked.

Nickolas was quiet. He glanced at the corner of the room, checking the clock on Eleanor's nightstand. "It isn't my place," he said, "to question Mr. Astor's decisions. But I'm a servant, not a robot. I don't think Mr. Astor made the right choice with Daniel. His family should be protected." He looked back to Eleanor. "He listens to me in matters of security. Daniel's father and brother might be targeted by the Vorid. He gave them a serious blow."

"And all I have to do to leave the house," she said, her nose wrinkling up, "is sell myself to Matthew Aiken like a very expensive 18th century whore."

"Imagine the fun you'll have," Nickolas said, "making him miserable for the rest of his life."

Eleanor snorted. "Unfortunately, it would also be for the rest of *my* life."

"It's the only way your father will give you any flexibility right now," Nickolas said. "He knows how you feel about...the Daniel issue."

Eleanor stiffened slightly; her lips squashed in an ugly line. "He's a person," she said. "Not an issue."

"It was poor wording."

Eleanor waved off the apology. "I have to think this through. We need to get out of this house and get to Daniel's family. My father is stopping me." She folded her hands behind her back. "How else can we leave? You know the security runes as well as anyone alive."

"I don't think there's a way through," Nickolas said. "Even when I move through them, my subordinates will know. They'll inform your father if it's unauthorized. Doubly so if you're with me at the time."

"Can't we hide from the sensors?" Eleanor asked.

"Not with any magic I know," Nickolas said. "Maybe a Wu assassin would have something, but I doubt it. We'd have noticed eventually."

"That doesn't do us much good," Eleanor said.

"You could easily do it," said a voice—somehow slithering and stately at the same time—"with magic I know."

Eleanor and Nickolas whirled on the spot, each one calling their magic up on reflex. Green flames erupted from Nickolas's hands; ice crusted on Eleanor's fingertips. The air wavered between them, like a mirage, caught between the two opposing sources of temperature.

Their concentration stuttered when they saw the figure seated on the stuffed chair next to the door. Even described generously, the Klide ambassador was lopsided, like a children's cartoon reflected in a funhouse mirror. A frog's head was perched on top of his small square torso. His legs were long, too long, so that seated, his knees came up almost to his chest. "Terribly sorry," Xik said. "Didn't mean to startle."

"You?" Nickolas said.

"Xikanthus," Eleanor said. She cut off her magic, tamping it back into her core with her mind; Nickolas did the same. "How did you get in here?"

"Well, you see." Xikanthus took a noisy slurp from a steaming cup that Eleanor was fairly certain wasn't there a moment ago. "I rather let myself in."

Nickolas's magic was suppressed, but he still had his hands raised, ready to channel energy out from his palms. "How did you get past my runes?"

"Is that what you call them?" Xik said. "Hmph. You might as well be…" Xik's red eyes met Eleanor's. "Finger painting on cave walls."

"These are Miss Astor's private quarters," Nickolas said. "You'll be wanting Mr. Astor."

"I believe I want Miss Astor today," Xik said.

"What for?"

"I can speak for myself, thank you," Eleanor said. "You mentioned being able to leave the building?"

"Oh yes," Xik said. "I can simply teleport you to Cleveland."

"That's impossible," Nickolas said. "That kind of distance would take at least ten magicians. And you can't teleport in or out within ten miles of this building."

"And yet here I sit," Xik said, "in defiance of the laws of nature."

Nickolas's answer was to edge in front of Eleanor, placing himself between her and the frog-man. "What do you have to gain from this?"

Xik's red eyes focused on Nickolas, and his gaze wasn't pleasant. "Unlike you, I don't have an ulterior motive in approaching Miss Astor."

Eleanor didn't miss the flicker of surprise that crossed Nickolas's face. He collected himself so quickly she might have missed it if she wasn't paying attention. Nickolas wasn't particularly expressive, but he was a bodyguard, not a professional liar. Her father might have sheltered her from the rough side of things, but she'd been involved in the elite-level politicking of her family since she was a debutante.

Eleanor turned to her guest. "Xikanthus. Please continue."

"Eleanor, you can't trust him," Nickolas said. "Who knows what he—"

"I'm at least going to hear him out," Eleanor said. She looked at the Klide ambassador and gestured for him to go on.

Xik steepled his long fingers. "Daniel got involved in this because of me," he said. "And now he's in quite the situation. The least I can do is make sure his loved ones are given adequate protection."

"Why don't you do it yourself?" Nickolas said. "Why come here?"

"I have got a lot on my plate, so you humans say." Xik's voice softened. "And I believe Miss Astor has her heart in the right place, and can be trusted to take care of things on my behalf."

"That's very sweet," Nickolas said, "but I don't believe you."

"As far as I can tell, Miss Astor, you have two options," Xik said. "First, allow me to teleport you to Cleveland, where you can handle matters as you see fit. Or, second, go quietly to your father, agree to a marriage you don't want—to a person you hate—and then be transported to Cleveland several days later...after consummating the union, presumably."

Eleanor mentally lurched in revulsion at the latter idea. Nickolas was less surprised, and more alarmed. "How do you know all this?"

Xik leaned back in his chair, continuing to ignore Nickolas, and took another sip of his drink. "I'd advise you to consider who is helping you further *your* goals, and who is ushering you toward your father for the sake of his own."

Eleanor and Nickolas glanced at each other at the same time.

"Eleanor, don't!" Nickolas grabbed for her, but she danced out of reach—and he collapsed to the ground, his feet iced down into the carpet. She'd already frozen them while he was paying attention to Xik.

"Father sent you to lure me back, didn't he?" Eleanor said. The warmth she'd felt toward Nickolas for comforting her crumbled. The anger came in like a glacier, slow, but crushing. "I don't hate you, but I know you're my father's man when it counts. You said it yourself. You helped him win the succession."

A flash of green fire melted Nickolas's shoes free from the ice. He lunged forward—only to smack into a translucent purple barrier that sprang up across the room. Nickolas stumbled back, a hand on his forehead.

He gave himself a shake, then tested the barrier with his fist. When that did nothing, he extended his palms. A beam of green-white fire leapt out. The flames rolled and sparked against the wall, but didn't leave so much as a mark.

Eleanor glanced at Xik, cocking an eyebrow. "Relax," Xik said. "I won't hurt him."

"Eleanor!" Nickolas's voice could still be heard; it sounded like he was behind a thick pane of glass. "I won't apologize for pushing you in the right direction!"

"So you admit it?" Eleanor said.

"I want you to be safe!" Nickolas stepped up to the purple wall. His features settled to their normal seriousness. "You don't understand the politics right now. Your father hasn't told you about the alliance between the southeast and the west coast. The main household took too many casualties in New York. The Dawn is on the verge of falling apart. Unless we secure your marriage—"

"If the Ivory Dawn can't come together without using me like a piece of meat," Eleanor said, "then it deserves the consequences."

Nickolas was stunned. "Elly...this is our people. Our way of life."

"And what good has our way of life done me lately?!" Eleanor said. Her voice rose higher. "I was so blinded by my own arrogance I almost lost my sister. And before I had a chance to start over with her, she died! Rachel is dead, and not because of the Vorid—she died because of a weak, flimsy alliance between magicians that were blinded by the same arrogance I was! Another alliance isn't going to save us. Daniel was right. He was totally right about us. If the Vorid invasion has a silver lining, it'll be that the old elite that think they can steer the world from the shadows—people like my father—are going to receive serious instruction in hard life lessons!"

Nickolas shook his head. "You can't think like this. You've got to talk to Mr. Astor, at least. He's your father."

"He blamed Daniel because he couldn't accept the real explanation," Eleanor said. "Because he hasn't dared take a look in the mirror. He was a party to Rothschild's plan!"

"Eleanor, that's too much," Nickolas said. "He was injured, he wasn't even there!"

The dark thought Eleanor had been hiding bubbled to the surface of her head. She'd been too afraid to bring it up to her father. She'd been too afraid she'd see the truth of it on his face. She hadn't imagined he was capable—but now it seemed she was being naïve.

"If they hadn't delayed the strike on the lord," Eleanor said, "Rachel wouldn't have had to intervene. Tell me my father didn't know. Say he didn't know about the plan to use Daniel and throw him away like a piece of trash! Maybe they even planned to kill him if he succeeded anyway, if he didn't let himself be taken in. End him there before he could be some kind of *threat* to their power."

Nickolas's lips crimped. "It wasn't—Eleanor. You—"

"Nickolas!" Eleanor's voice hitched. "Tell me he—he didn't know. He didn't know!"

In the end, Nickolas said nothing.

"I knew it," Eleanor hissed. "As soon as he started talking about Rachel like she was some kind of sacrifice, I knew it. All my life he lectured me about duty. Where is his duty now? In a toilet, next to the rest of his crap! At least you have the damn decency to be honest with me."

"And I'm being honest now," Nickolas said. "You can't do this."

Xik loudly, and slowly, cleared his throat.

"What?" Eleanor snapped.

"Sorry to interrupt," Xik said. "He's been activating the house's security runes to contact your father, and I can't block him any longer. They're on the way."

Eleanor's face was a mask of rage as she whipped back to face Nickolas. "You were buying time?"

"Our lives hinge on the Astors staying in power," Nickolas said. "Don't blame me, Elly."

"Don't call me that," Eleanor said. She turned back to Xik. "I'm sorry for my tone, Xikanthus. I'm in a mood."

"Understandable," Xik said.

"I'd be happy if you'd send me to Cleveland."

"One thing," the frog said. "Call me Xik. Xikanthus is too...formal."

"Xik it is." She stepped next to him, ignoring more plaintiff shouts from Nickolas. "What about Daniel? Is there anything we can do?"

"My options there are more limited," Xik said.

The sadness rolled back in. Eleanor clenched her face tight to hold it back. There was no escaping from Hell—not without outside approval from every holder of the treaty, as far as she knew. The leader of the Ivory Dawn, Order of True Flame, the Witch Coven, and the Wu's Thundering Heavens Sect—and Beelzebub—all had to agree. At least, in theory. The politics was even more complicated than that, often relying on the influence of dozens of other magical organizations on top of the few dominant ones. There was always someone with an axe to grind. As a result, imprisonment in Hell had never been reversed once in history—at least, not for a human. Beelzebub managed the demons on his own, so they didn't really know how that end of it worked.

The door burst open; Henry barged into the room. Another servant followed right on his heels. They saw Nickolas across the room, first, pinned behind the purple-tint wall—and then Xik, sitting next to Eleanor.

"Time's up," Xik said. "This may make you a bit dizzy."

Xik waved a hand. Green-purple lights flashed under Eleanor's feet in a complex pattern. There was clap of sound that rattled the walls and shook the floor, and she was gone.

"NO!" Henry launched himself forward, leading with his magic, but he could already see he was too late. He lashed out at Xik with the spell. Shards of ice whipped forward, but they simply passed through him as if he wasn't even there. The chair he was seated on was pulverized into strips of frozen leather and bits of stuffing; the wallpaper behind it crumbled and cracked as it froze solid.

Xik was gone.

"That was rather impolite," Xik said. Henry jumped—the frog had somehow appeared at his shoulder. A blow caught Henry in the gut, and he and his guard were sent barreling toward the purple wall. They passed through it and landed in a heap on Eleanor's bed.

After getting their wind back, and realizing they were trapped alongside Nickolas, Henry spoke. "What is the meaning of this? Where did you send Eleanor?!"

"Nickolas can fill you in on the details," Xik said. "The barrier will only last for another half hour or so." Xik made a face. "If you combined your strength, you could probably break it, but you'd also break your house."

"I don't have time for your games!"

"You do today, Mr. Astor," Xik said. He stepped up to the wall, facing the leader of the Ivory Dawn. "You've forced a tremendous detour in my plans. I'm burning energy that is far more precious to me than your life is on this effort, so you are going to very well listen to what I have to say."

Xik's tone didn't change. He spoke the same way he always spoke—steadily, carefully. But that only made the coldblooded words that much more chilling.

Henry, to his credit, was unruffled. "The true colors finally show."

"You're certainly one to talk."

"Get on with it," Henry said.

"I've recently been able to extend my detection capabilities. The Vorid are going to attack again, soon."

"Where?"

Xik looked at him the way an adult looked at a particularly ugly baby. "Everywhere, first. They'll isolate you, destroy your ability to communicate, hamper long-range magic. Once you're reeling, they'll easily harvest those giant mobs of people you've gathered together in evacuation camps. Their typical weapons platform is indomitable, but slow, so it's quite convenient from their perspective that you've put them all in one place."

"That's the only way we could protect everyone," Henry said. "There aren't enough magicians to do anything else!"

"You ignored my counsel, and now many, many people are going to die," Xik said. "The Vorid aren't interested in the planet or your resources. There's an entire solar system to harvest if they want any of that. They want you." Xik pointed at Henry's chest. "Your souls. They want the extra-dimensional, connective potential energy contained within sentient beings. And you've bunched mankind together like clusters of ripe fruit waiting to be plucked because you persisted in your ignorance."

"Do you have a better plan?" Henry asked.

"Yes," Xik said. "All mages should band together and take up a heavily fortified position. Normal humans should scatter."

"That's ridiculous," Henry said. "Normal people can't protect themselves against this."

"You have this wild, persistent idea," Xik said, making a circle with one hand, "that you actually *can* protect yourselves. You think you're going to be able to defend yourselves when the Vorid get serious. Less people will die if the Vorid collection effort is slowed because of how spread out they are. This is the simple fact of the matter." Xik's red frog eyes squinted tight. "Ideally, at this point, a contractor would be strong enough to fight them head on while you offered support, thus reducing the now inevitable human casualty. I tried to give you one, but you rejected him in no uncertain terms. The Vorid are already constructing a more stable access point to this universe. I've told you this before, but I'll say it again. A contractor is the only—"

"I don't need to hear the all-too-convenient explanation for why we should give over to you," Henry said. "Is that all you have to offer? Tell people to go home? Remove any semblance of protection? There'll be total panic if we do that."

"I suspect you're right," Xik said. "Maybe you should lie to them. You seem to be fairly proficient at it."

"I've heard enough from you about lies," Henry shouted. "You tear my only surviving family out of my arms, then tell me the only way we can protect the rest of humanity has doomed them to death? We can beat the Vorid without your corrupted puppet warriors! The Ivory Dawn will not be the ally of the Klide while I am its leader! I will not compromise our principles! Do you hear me?!"

"I do indeed." Xik tipped his hat. "Good day, Mr. Astor." Xik walked forward and vanished straight through the wall of the room, leaving them sealed where they stood.

Chapter 8
State of the Union

Daniel was hovering in darkness, but around him was a storm of colors. He was at the center of a whirlpool of light, greens, blues, yellows, purples, reds, all swirling and warping around him. The shifting colors were shaded dark by the shadow behind it. The reds were muted, like dried blood; the blues came from an ocean abyss; the green evoked the twilight of a jungle.

Daniel floated in this maelstrom of lights and energy. It revolved around him; he was seated, stationary, at its center. He didn't understand what this place was, or what the lights were, but for some reason, it felt close and familiar. The sensation pressed on him, snug and comfortable, like a favorite pair of shoes he'd worn into the shape of his feet. Like driving past a house he used to live in, a glimpse of memory and time gone by.

Something in the storm caught his eye. Daniel looked closer, and panic broke through his calm mood like water through a dam. Limbs—tendrils—were reaching out for him, the slimy muck of Vorid spawn, the things that merged into a person's body. He could see patterns of light reminiscent of extractors; not their robotic shells, but the enchantments, etched on the metal, that drove them forward. And here and there, screaming through the lights, the alien faces of Vorid overseers, ink black skin and green or white tattoos.

Daniel knew they were the same overseers he had killed and absorbed.

A larger disturbance formed in the storm of energy. A new face, marked from the others. Its gaze locked on him. It drew closer, and its eyes were sharp and vengeful.

The Vorid lord.

It pulled itself out of the light, and a body formed around it as it did, limbs wrapped in a ghost of the robe it had worn when it fought him. Daniel wanted to cringe away, but he couldn't move. He was stuck in place, his being as much a fixture as the deep dark that rested underneath it all.

The lord stopped in front of him. It was a wraith, half-there, half-not, foggy and indistinct. The colored energy whipping around them stole at its form like wind blowing away tendrils of smoke, but it was able to hold its shape against the force trying to grind it down. It raised a hand. A claw reached for him, grasping.

Another figure, blazing red, stepped in front of the Vorid lord. Her hand caught the lord across the face in an open-palm slap. The lord reeled backward, caught by surprise, and its form was sucked into the storm of energy. It pawed out at Daniel and the woman, but it was caught in the current of light, and the self it had managed to pull together was washed away.

The blazing red woman stood there, back to Daniel. Her own form was quickly losing consistency, blown away bit by bit by the storm-force of the colored winds, but Daniel would've recognized her anywhere.

Rachel. He tried to say her name, but he had no mouth to speak. *Rachel.* The words resounded somewhere, but not out loud. *Hey! Rachel! I'm here! Rachel!!*

Her head cocked to the side. She turned, slowly, facing him. Like the lord, she was a ghost made of light, wispy at the edges. The storm threatened to suck her back in. But she stood there, looking at him—through him. Her eyes searched, and her head moved back and forward, as if she couldn't see him, couldn't tell where his voice was coming from.

I love you! Daniel said. *Can you hear me?! I love you!!*

Rachel's eyes widened. She raised a hand, as if in greeting, then formed a heart with her fingers. The movements were hesitant, as if she was unsure if she could be seen, but there was a small, half-smile on her face. All the while, her form was rapidly melting, disintegrating back into the wind.

Rachel, what's happening?! Don't go!

Rachel's mouth moved, but Daniel couldn't hear the words. And then she was gone, turned to a bright red streak of energy that melded back into the dark storm. Daniel was left alone.

It all stretched on, the loneliness, the memory of her, standing tall in front of the Vorid lord when he'd been on his last legs. Even here, in whatever place this was, this half-reality, she protected him. She haunted his waking thoughts, and now, she haunted his dreams.

For a moment, he wanted it all to go away, for everything to have never happened. Daniel didn't like who he used to be before college, before he met her; bitter, defensive, suspicious. But at least it wasn't as painful as this, whatever this was—a lesser life, lived in the ruins of beautiful memories that only served to remind him of what he'd lost.

Things moved in the darkness beyond the light. He could hear the screeching of the Vorid spawn, see their tendrils again. He caught the dark chatter of the overseers, somehow projected into his thoughts, like when the lord had spoken to him. The limbs of the extractors projected into the center of his space, now, metallic outlines around the light of the enchantments.

The lord was in the center of it all, emerging once again, the ghastly general of a small army of spirits. They converged in on him, faster and faster, pulling out against the streams of energy.

Rachel was nowhere to be seen.

Daniel was almost glad. He couldn't bear it, seeing her come to his defense, only to disappear afterward. Maybe he should disappear, too. Follow her to wherever she'd gone.

And then, it all stopped.

The storm of winds froze. The spiteful spirits of the creatures Daniel had slain halted in place, still as sculptures. The murmurs of the dead and the wind of light fell silent.

Another woman stepped from beyond the dark haze, crossing the boundary of the storm. She walked straight through the wall of spirits. She was made from white light, the opposite of the shadow that constructed the boundaries of this strange world; her form was sharp and distinct, harsh against the dark.

She looked toward him, and unlike Rachel, she was looking straight at him. Despite that fact that he couldn't see her face, or her eyes, Daniel could feel her gaze piercing through him.

"Stand up, Daniel," the woman said. Her voice was light as a springtime sun. Her radiance slashed across the darkness as she spoke, vanquishing the spirits back to where they'd come. "I will not see you fall this day."

The frozen world shattered, and the light and dark crumbled around him, sucking him down. He fell away from her, into a void, until she was a tiny, starry pinprick in the black. And then she was gone.

****

Daniel blinked his eyes awake. An unfamiliar ceiling swam into view. He rubbed at his face, trying to mentally collect himself.

He bolted upright.

Panic raced down his spine. He'd fallen asleep. Those things could be anywhere—he couldn't believe he'd dozed off. He leapt to his feet—or tried to. His feet caught in the blanket, twisting him sideways, and he plummeted to the floor.

At this point, momentum dictated that the average human would faceplant into the carpet—but Daniel wasn't average. Even without his magic, his body had changed, adapted to having his energy pushed through it again and again. He reacted automatically, placing a hand on the ground and springing into a flip. He landed on the balls of his feet, knees bent.

Daniel whipped his head around to get his bearings, a little surprised with himself that he was still standing.

Jack's apartment greeted him. Quiet, unmoving. He could hear water running. The shower was on.

Everything rushed back. He wasn't in New York. He wasn't being hunted. He wasn't in some crazy dreamscape, about to be food for ghosts.

Daniel heaved a sigh and flopped back onto the couch. Sleep. He'd actually fallen asleep. How long had he been out?

One of the side benefits of the Contractor magic was that it took away the need to sleep. Daniel required about a half-hour nap every day. He could even skip that without much trouble for two or three days straight. Regardless, he had to lie down and really try in order to sleep.

To be fair, it had been a pretty long day.

His eyes scanned the apartment. It was pretty plain; tan carpet, black wood furniture. The walls were white, and too bare, the way they'd be if a bachelor moved into a new place and didn't have the time or the inclination to spruce things up. In Jack's case, probably the latter. He wasn't big on posters and pin-ups. Jack was the type to have a dozen little knick-knacks on a shelf, something you could pick up and touch, the sort of things that had little stories to go along with them. Otherwise, he wouldn't bother.

A small table with two chairs formed a border between the kitchen and the living room. A big steel panel stretched across the wall in front of where Daniel was sitting; the television. Probably. Or whatever demons called television. *Magi-vision?*

His thoughts wandered back to his dream. It swam back to him in bits and pieces, washed out and broken by the sharp reality of wakefulness. Rachel was there, holding back the Vorid; he wasn't surprised by that. She was on his mind too often, these days.

But he clearly remembered what had saved him the second time. That woman—he knew her. He'd seen her before, in the streets of Purgatory, back in the territory war. She was the same person who'd walked through the magic, that no one else could see.

Who was she? How did she know who he was?

Daniel leaned his head back. He shut his eyes again, embracing the quiet, the stillness of the room. He didn't think about much of anything; he let his mind decompress, let some of the long-running tension finally escape out a release valve.

He couldn't remember the last time he was sitting in a place he felt safe. A week ago, before New York? Back in his dorm, before the Vorid brought down the black columns that produced extractors?

No. Not since that first night he gained his powers, when Xik warned him not to go out—or else. He'd curled up in his bed then, and he hadn't slept the entire night. He'd wondered who in town was getting their soul sucked away. Someone in a different neighborhood? A block over? Right next door? He didn't know. He was too afraid to find out.

Xik had been right. If he'd gone out that night, he would have bought the farm for sure. When he finally did confront the extractors a month later, it nearly cost him his life anyway.

That felt like a lifetime ago.

Suddenly, Daniel started, throwing his blankets to the side. His clothes were shredded, ashen, bloodstained, and barely hanging onto him—Jack must have brought him straight from the fight—but he ignored that, patting wildly, searching the ruined remains of his pants.

And, amazingly, he found what he shouldn't have. He pulled out a green stone, the same one given to him by Xik during those first strange days back home. Somehow it had survived his sentence to Hell, multiple changes of clothing, and several life-or-death moments. He smoothed the surface with his thumb, eyeing it with mixed emotions.

On impulse, Daniel reached back for his pocket. The bottom was nonexistent, the battle having reduced it to a mere strip of cloth hanging from the side of his slacks. The stone should have been long gone. But when he thought of it—his one contact point to the Klide—it was there.

Huh. Daniel peered at the stone again, then set it on the cheap-looking coffee table in front of the couch.

The shower sounds stopped. Daniel could hear Jack puttering around in the bathroom—the rustle of a towel, a cabinet opening and closing, opening again.

Daniel headed for the kitchen. He wasn't sure about the appliances, but there was a sink, same as an Earth kitchen, and what was probably a stove. He couldn't remember associating the word *probably* with household appliances before, but repeated physical bludgeoning had taught him not to take anything at face value down here.

He rummaged through the cabinets for a glass and tried the tap. Thankfully, there was normal running water. He drained the cup, then went to refill it, as if the first drink had only reinforced how thirsty he was.

Jack wandered out of the bathroom, dressed in shorts and a t-shirt. "Well hey there, sleepyhead. I hope you were all snuggled up warm and cozy."

"The blanket tried to kill me," Daniel said.

"Paranoia setting in already?"

Daniel finished the water and slapped the empty cup on the counter. "How long was I asleep?"

"About three hours."

"Wow," Daniel said. "I guess I *was* pretty wiped."

Jack rubbed his chin. "Speaking of, remember that time in school you told me you had insomnia?"

Daniel cleared his throat. "Yeah, about that...I might have been going out and killing Vorid."

"That's what I thought."

"I mean, technically I did have insomnia. Magically induced insomnia." Daniel frowned. "Hey, speaking of, you didn't?"

"Not to that level," Jack said, "but I felt like it got worse the stronger my powers got. Maybe that's why it hit you harder."

There was a pause. Jack took a sudden interest in the back of the couch. Daniel worked his hands on the edge of the counter, tapping out an awkward rhythm to fill the quiet. He felt like they both realized they were getting uncomfortably close to talking about Boston.

"So," Daniel said, changing the subject, "what's happening exactly with the territory?"

"This was a short one," Jack said. "We locked everything down. And—get this—because we took out the meat of their team, and their strongest fighter, we were able to take two of their other territories in the places Rasputin was fighting, all without breaking a sweat. Looks like they planned to reinforce them after dealing with us." Jack smirked. "Too bad they never made it."

"So what you're saying is, we're the badass heroes that saved the day."

"Pretty much," Jack said. "I thought we were screwed back in that tornado spell."

"I hope Dracula won't be too over-the-moon about how well we did," Daniel said. "Werewolves and all that."

Jack's smile fell flat. "Hardy-har-har. Do it again without blowing yourself up, and then I'll be impressed."

Daniel thought. "It didn't happen until I pushed my power into it. I was trying to make it fire, but I think that's what set it off."

"Contractor magic and enchantments doesn't mix well," Jack said. "I've never seen that happen before, but my powers are a lot different than yours. I can't really push magic *into* something."

"Okay," Daniel said. "No using white light on enchanted magic tools. By the way, I have the green orb thingy that the guy was using to make the tornado."

"Hang on to it," Jack said. "It was a pretty powerful piece of work, so we could save it for an emergency or auction it off later."

"By the way," Daniel said, "is there anything I can't put in my inventory?"

Jack thought. "You can't store other prisoners. I think that's it. Anything that needs air won't survive very long, so I wouldn't recommend pets."

"They have pets down here?"

Jack nodded. "It's all weird demon creatures, but a few of them look like variations of hamsters or porcupines or something. There's another that looks a bit like a basset hound," he added hopefully. "With some horns, and a few scales. And two heads."

Daniel made a face. "Twice the howling to keep me up at night. Eeesh."

"Hey," Jack said. "I was thinking about getting one."

"Don't let me stop you, it's your apartment." Daniel glanced around. "Nice digs, by the way. A bit modern for my taste."

"Nothing fancy, but it's mine. Most of the furniture came with it." Jack gestured down the hall. "Want to clean up? You can probably fit into a baggy pair of shorts and a shirt I've got. We can go get some food and I'll show you around."

Daniel glanced down at himself, suddenly conscious of the ashy grime at the nooks and crannies of his body. He felt a strange combination of satisfaction and guilt that his nap might have permanently soiled Jack's couch. "Yeah. Sounds good."

Jack indicated with his head down the hall. "Bathroom's the second door on the right. I'll throw the clothes outside the door."

"Cool." Daniel headed down to the bathroom and shut the door behind himself. It was a standard affair: sink, mirror doubling as a bathroom cabinet, shower with a white liner and a green outer curtain—Jack's favorite color. It was a surreal moment, as if there was a little island of college life hidden in the depths of Hell. He glanced up at the mirror.

Jack had been generous—he looked like a wreck. His sand-colored hair, which he usually kept a tidy mess, was matted against his head by blood and dotted with bits and pieces of *stuff* he didn't want to look at too closely. His eyes looked more green than grey today, though it might have been the light off the shower curtain. The bags under them screamed stress. Ash was smeared across his cheek. He rubbed it away from his eye.

Daniel reached into the remains of his pocket, thinking of trying to contact Xik—and it was almost as if the green stone fell into his palm. He lifted it up, turned it over in his hand. Then he stopped.

The stone had no reflection.

The hairs on the back of his neck stood up.

Daniel set it down on the sink, then started up the shower. He glanced back at the stone, thinking about contacting the alien again. All he had to do was squeeze it in his palm.

But the last time he'd seen Xik, the alien had all but waved goodbye before he was sentenced—after confirming that Rachel's death, inadvertent or not, was all his fault. The idea quickly soured on him. Even if Xik could somehow come into Hell, Daniel didn't want to see him, not then.

He climbed into the shower, determined to wash the blood away.

****

Daniel and Jack sat outside a café, eating a few sandwiches that Jack had promised him multiple times were fit for human consumption. They'd both finished their first beers and were starting on their second round. The demons of Hell didn't bother carding them.

They'd shared the last minute in silence. Daniel had finished more or less a full explanation of what had happened after Jack was captured—the Vorid attack on Boston, the open invasion, the siege of New York, the fight against the Vorid lord. Rachel dying. And then, finally, Daniel turning himself in, only to be promptly handed over to the demons.

Daniel took another sip of his beer. "I have to admit," he said to Jack, "demons know how to brew." He frowned. "Do they even have a drinking age?"

"Old enough to be sent to Hell, old enough to drink," Jack said, "that's what I always say."

"I don't recall you saying that before."

"This is why our relationship is so difficult," Jack said. "You never listen to me."

"That's because nothing you say is interesting."

"That's it," Jack said, "I'm filing for divorce."

"You can have the two-headed basset hound, but I'll be damned if you take my house," Daniel said.

Jack snorted, then took a long swig of his drink. "The whole Vorid thing is turning into some heavy stuff. I can see why you're a little edgy."

Daniel sighed. "I guess edgy is better than PTSD-ridden slab of cynicism."

"Hey," Jack said. "This isn't your fault. It's those bastards that're the problem."

Daniel sighed again, shook his head. "I should have known better."

"It's not your fault," Jack repeated. "I can't believe they told you that you'd turn into some power-hungry dictator if they didn't send you to Hell. That was *after* you turned yourself in? As in, after you proved them wrong with your actions, only for them to ignore it and exile you anyway?"

"Yep," Daniel said. "That's about the size of it."

"Sounds like they were projecting if you ask me," Jack said. "The world would probably be better off if you were in charge anyway. They sure fucked it up nice and good. You can't trust magicians as far as you can throw them."

"They're not all bad," Daniel said. "Most of them can't be that bad. Just the ones in charge."

"Yeah, because they don't want anyone else to get close to being in charge. Then they won't be." Jack tapped his glass with a nail. "Wake up and smell the coffee, Dan. The whole time you were trying to help, they were trying to hunt you down using nightmare assassins. And then at the end, you kill the bad guy, ignore the fact that the True Flame dude—"

"Rothschild," Daniel said.

"Whatever," Jack said. "He stabbed you in the back when you were fighting the Vorid lord, but you brushed it off and still turned yourself in. And they disregard everything and stick you down here to rot. Sounds like they only wanted to use you and lose you in the first place."

Daniel could feel his hands clench up as it was all laid out in front of him. "I know."

"You shouldn't have trusted Duchess," Jack said. "Once a massive bitch, always a massive bitch."

Daniel shrugged. He remembered Eleanor crying as he was sentenced, but she didn't do much other than sit in the back and let it happen. Then again, if she tried to interfere, it would be going against her father and the leaders of the most powerful magical organizations on Earth all at the same time, so he didn't blame her that much…unless the tears were all an act.

He wasn't sure what to believe, in her case. He'd had so many ups-and-downs with Eleanor Astor that he truly couldn't say for sure either way. He was leaning strongly toward her being on his side, though. She was honestly warming to him as things were winding down. *Especially considering she kissed me. That was weird.*

Daniel and Jack nursed their beers. Jack's face darkened. "Daniel," he said, staring into his mug, "if I get out of here, I'm gonna kill them. I swear I'll kill every single one I can get my hands on."

"Okay," Daniel said. "Kinda harsh there man?"

"I'm serious," Jack said. "They're psychopaths."

"You can't mean every single magician."

"Fine," Jack said, "I don't mean every single magician. But the top leadership—they're hypocrites of the worst kind. They're almost always the most magically powerful; that's true now, and it was true in Dracula's day. They pretend to be all high and noble, but the strong rule in the end. The winning side wrote the history books."

All things considered, Daniel couldn't help feeling sympathetic to the sentiment, but he shook himself free of the thoughts. He couldn't afford to get caught up in it the way Jack was.

Maybe he wanted to get back at them, sure, spit in their eye once or twice. But before this was all said and done, Daniel knew he would almost inevitably find himself working with them to defeat the Vorid at some point. No matter how strong he became as an individual, the major magical organizations were the ones with the personnel and infrastructure to actually run a war. Daniel could serve as a nuclear deterrent, but they still needed soldiers.

He needed to keep his head level, think in practicalities—both for himself, and on Jack's behalf. He might be able to escape if he killed Bathory, assuming Beelzebub's deal held up. Jack needed some other method. "These future plots of revenge are based on the idea we can get out of here," Daniel said. "So. How do we do that?"

Jack sighed, glanced away. "We don't."

"What do you mean, we don't? There has to be a way out."

"There is," Jack said. "Here it comes now. It's why I picked this place, to show you." Jack pointed behind him, so Daniel turned in his chair to see.

They were near the edge of Purgatory, where the massive cavern that contained the city finally swooped down and met the floor. Daniel had been under the impression that Hell was one big, cake-shaped facility, and they were on the top, but it was a lot more segregated than he supposed. The entire city of Purgatory was contained in its own separate cavern, with only three entrances to the level below. Most individuals visited via direct teleportation, having been invited by one of the teams occupying a section of the city.

Their café overlooked a circular square that abutted the rock wall. Where the square met the cave's edge, a large half-circle of iron, about twenty feet high, was embedded against the wall, like a gate that had been built into the stone. Daniel peered at it, but there wasn't any door or escape route that he could see—it was a decorative piece, punctuating the stonework on the ground. "What am I looking at, here?" Daniel asked.

"Just wait."

The air began to shift. Daniel could feel magic rising up near the iron archway. A blue light pulsed across the steel. Runes etched themselves across the arch, and in a sudden flash, the stone within its border was gone.

Instead, through the archway, Daniel could see what looked like a huge warehouse. Crates and shipping containers were packed as far as the eye could see. Drones buzzed around in the air above them, many carrying payloads, moving and shifting supplies according to some obscure algorithm. The shelves themselves were moving, too, giving it the appearance of a massive beehive constantly reshuffling itself around the bees. One container flew close to the other side of the gateway; its top was open to the air. Daniel could see piles of green crystals inside of it, glowing with a soft light, and then it was gone, buzzing away to some other part of the facility.

A few goblins and a minotaur walked through the portal, accompanied by a parade of crates hovering over the ground. Daniel stared at it all, caught up in the sheer scale of what he was seeing. "What *is* that?"

"It's a portal to the demon world," Jack said. "It's inventory and logistics for the entire prison. Food, supplies, mana crystals."

The procession made its way to the back side of the café. The drones did the majority of the work; the demons were relegated to light management, occasionally making manual adjustments but otherwise keeping an eye on the bots as they unloaded their shipment. Daniel sat back in his chair. His eyes traveled back to the open portal. "There's no guards," he said. "What's the catch? What's stopping us from walking out?"

"There's always at least one that tries," Jack mumbled. "I need another beer for this." He finished off his current mug, then signaled for the waiter—a devil—to bring another. The arrival of the third drink was prompt. Jack took a sip, then nodded back to the open portal. "Keep watching. Someone will try to—yeah, look down there. Here we go."

A harpy shot out from a nearby alley, using its wings to fly at speed. Daniel followed the harpy's progress across the square. The demons handling the shipping glanced up, but didn't intervene. The crow-like humanoid darted over the open ground, making it to the portal in another instant.

Purple-red light flashed.

It was as if the harpy ran headlong into an electrified fence constructed of pure magic, blocking its passage through arch.

The lines of energy ripped at its feathers, stopped it dead, then dragged it backward. The harder the harpy struggled, the more the magic caged it in a tangle of chains and ropes made from the same fluorescent energy.

The harpy screeched in rage and kept fighting. The light intensified, binding up its prisoner's arms, and then its legs. The spell took the demon off its feet and forced it to the ground, wrapping tighter. Eventually, the harpy couldn't even lift a claw, let alone try to escape; it was pinned to the ground in a cocoon of violet magic. Only after it stopped moving did the spell start to fade.

After about 10 or 15 seconds, the light was gone, leaving the harpy shivering on the ground. Daniel couldn't tear his eyes away. He stared, mouth slightly agape, trying to understand what he was watching.

The harpy lifted its beak up, looking at the portal. It was only a few feet away from the outside world. The harpy stood straight on shaking, spindly legs, then started forward again, shrieking as it did. "Jarkuthaz! JARKUTHAZ!!"

Jack turned his head away. "Man. I feel bad for this guy."

"What does that mean?" Daniel asked.

"I don't know," Jack said. "It didn't translate."

The harpy touched the portal. As if already warmed up from the first attempt, the purple light flashed back into existence at full force. The spell lashed the harpy back to the ground, searing into its skin as it did so. The purple energy bound its target, chaining its limbs and pulling them down, and red bands whipped at it, beating it into submission.

Eventually, the red part of the spell faded, leaving the harpy a sobbing wreck on the stone. The shipping crew watched for a little while, then ignored the whole mess, going about their business as if it wasn't happening. Daniel caught a whiff of something in the air that made his stomach lurch—burning skin, or feathers. As the rest of the spell faded, Daniel saw the harpy's exposed back—skin laid open, blackened from the magic boiling against it.

After a time, the healing force that permeated Hell kicked in and spared it further agony. The violet chains of light unraveled and vanished. It clawed up to its feet, took one last look at the portal, then hobbled back to the city. Daniel couldn't help but feel a pang of pity. The way it shouted...it sounded like a name.

"It hurts," Jack said. "Not like normal. It weighs down on you, and burns, but it's more than that. Like it's tearing you out from the inside at the same time. It has its hooks set in you."

Daniel looked at him. "You've tried it?"

"Yeah," Jack said. "I tried three or four times. But then, working for the Order for a bit, I scraped some money together and bought myself half my magic. A 50% orb for 1 minute of time. Really expensive. As long as you don't attack anyone in the neutral areas, you can basically do what you want, so I used it when I had free time."

Daniel swallowed. Even at half-strength, Jack would be like a human wrecking ball. He'd taken on a small army of magicians by himself at only 25% strength when they fought earlier. "But it didn't work."

"The orb only relaxes the binding that's already there," Jack said. "As soon as I tried to use magic against Hell's seal, it ripped it straight back from me. I turned back to normal and got messed up worse than that guy. Haven't tried since."

"Are there any portals that go to Earth?"

"Nope," Jack said. "Demon world only."

"I know demons can travel to Earth, if magicians help them," Daniel said. "Maybe we could get back if we got there first."

"If there's a way out," Jack said, "that's not it. Dracula's been down here hundreds of years. I'm pretty sure the guy's tried everything."

"Maybe I'm fast enough to get by before it reacts."

"You're not the only one that can move fast," Jack said, "but it doesn't matter." He leaned in over the table. "It's not about where we leave, or how we do it. It's that we can't even try. The spell *knows*. It's already sitting there, waiting for you to even think about it."

"You keep talking like it's alive," Daniel said. "It's just a magic spell."

"Yeah, sure. Just magic." Jack drained his mug of the rest of his beer and smacked his lips. "I didn't think any of this was even possible five or six months ago, Dan. I didn't think magic was real, let alone demons and aliens. So who knows?"

The point rested between them for a minute. Daniel didn't argue it. It was crazy—all of it. But here he was, stuck in Purgatory, the first level of hell, banished by a secret society of magicians for having forbidden magic powers.

That, or he was held up in a psyche ward somewhere, bouncing off the sides of his padded room as he fought off the evil aliens.

"It's not all bad, though," Jack said. "Being stuck down here."

Having offloaded their supplies into the nearby buildings, the demons were walking the empty containers back through the portal. The minotaur was standing at the side, waving the others through. "How is it not all bad, exactly?" Daniel said.

"Honestly," Jack said, "it's a little crazy, pretty brutal. But it's entertaining."

Daniel swiveled back. "Entertaining. You think *this*"—Daniel gestured around—"is entertaining?"

"Hear me out," Jack said.

Daniel folded his arms. "This oughta be good."

"Seriously, listen," Jack said. "Yeah, we're stuck down here. Yes, we can't get out."

"Imprisoned," Daniel said. "For eternity."

"In theory," Jack said. "But also—we're like gladiators. We fight, we win, part of it goes to the team, part of it to us. Then we can do whatever we want. Buy whatever we want. You have to see the list of video games demons have, it's awesome. Their technology is more advanced than ours, they have some virtual reality stuff that plays amazing. And our day job is using our magical powers to fight demons." Jack gestured out with his hands, palms facing the ceiling. "When I realized it was impossible to get out, I started thinking of this as an opportunity instead. And that was when I realized it—this *is* an opportunity. No cubical work. No long boring shifts and paying bills. No worrying about what other people think of you, or people pleasing, or living up to whatever standards society wants. We are the fantasy warriors. We are the heroes from books, from movies. We might be prisoners, but the oldest guy here, Dracula, doesn't look any older than the day he got here. As far as anyone knows, we live forever. It's like Spartacus and Highlander put together. On top of that, we're famous. So are you, probably!"

"Famous?" Daniel screwed his face up. "Jack! Earth to Jack! We're stuck in a cave, inside a pocket dimension, trapped between Earth and the demon world! No one even knows we're here!"

"No, no, seriously." Jack brought his wristband forward and tapped a few screens. "Look. I have a fanclub." Daniel's expression shifted from confused disbelief to alarmed exasperation. On the demon internet—which was a thing— Jack had not one, but multiple fan websites dedicated to his exploits. "See, look at this one. It features an interview I did with Ky a few weeks ago. You know, the demon announcer lady."

"I'm aware," Daniel said.

"I'm considered the big rising rookie," Jack said. "We get a cut when people in the demon world bet on the outcome of our matches. The more popular you are—there's this system we're ranked in—the larger your cut. If you're good enough, you can even get sponsored. I've got a lawyer working out details of multiple contracts for me right now. People on the outside, corporations, can exchange their money for prison points to buy you gear and power orbs. One of my contracts is an advertising deal, should make me a ton money." Jack leaned in a bit. "And if you have the points to spare, you can buy it in Hell. Seriously, anything. Food, clothes, video games, hookers, drugs, whatever you can think of. Aside from not getting out much, it's like we're not even prisoners."

"This is crazy," Daniel said. "I'm supposed to be happy that I can afford demon hookers because I'm a televised gladiator?"

Jack nodded enthusiastically. "You're right, it's crazy. The good kind of crazy. Here, I'll search for you, see what comes up."

Jack typed in Daniel's name into whatever the demons had that substituted for Google and displayed the results across the table. Daniel scrolled through it with a finger. It was as bad as Jack predicted. The top results were footage of them fighting together against the enemy team—the Viridian Gust. The headlines were endless.

The Silverback Killer Jack Killiney Tag-Teams with White Lightning Daniel Fitzgerald

Viridian Gust Scatters to the Wind: Team on Verge of Disbanding

Fitzgerald's Allegiance Remains Unconfirmed

After Decades of Drought, Order of the Dragon Picks Up Two Impressive Human Rookies

Major News Outlets Jockey for Fitzgerald's First Interview: All Requests Remain Unanswered

Footage Feast: Fitzgerald Crushes the Leader of the Viridian Gust

Viridian Gust Leader in Hiding Following Major Loss to the Order of the Dragon

"White Lightning and the Silverback Killer?" Daniel said. "We sound like side characters from a bad episode of WWE."

"Come on," Jack said, "it's kinda cool! We have nicknames! Watch this, watch." Jack tapped a few more screens. "Come on, look!"

Saved in Jack's *favorites* menu was a webpage with the title *Jack Killiney (Human): Live Feed*. The PrisonWatch logo was plastered across the top of the screen. A video buffered, and then Daniel saw a live stream of himself and Jack sitting in the café. There were over 50,000 active viewers.

Daniel looked in the direction of the camera. Sure enough, there it was, a small black dot on the awning of the café. Jack grinned and waved. There was only a slight delay on the video feed.

"This is weirding me out," Daniel said.

Jack closed the screen up. "This is nothing. When I'm fighting, I usually get tens of millions of active viewers. I had several hundred million in one of the arena matches. Back in their world, demons are all about following their favorite prisoners. They'll take an early lunch if something goes down so they can tune in. It's like the World Cup and the World Series every day. Hell has been around so long it's become a part of their culture."

"How do you know all that?"

"I've posted in my fanclub and asked. Searched the web. We don't have access to everything, but most general knowledge is free to read on their version of Wikipedia." Jack smirked. "Don't tell Dracula or Rasputin, though. They aren't exactly big on demon PR."

"So is that the name of your outfit?" Daniel asked. "The Order of the Dragon?"

"That's us." Jack tapped his wristband, showing the red-on-white cross with yellow frills. "This is the original symbol of the order of knights Dracula was in. His dad was a famous member, Vlad Dracul. Dracul means dragon, and so then Dracula—son of the dragon. Get it?"

"I don't care how he got his vampire name," Daniel said. "You're suggesting we accept that we're prisoners and sit here and play these stupid games? Kill people for cash and points, then spend it on hookers and blow?"

"If you put it that way, of course it sounds bad," Jack said. "I'm just riding the wave."

"The wave of what? Demonic internet fans?" Daniel said. "Are you kidding me?"

"What's the alternative?"

"Oh, I dunno," Daniel said, voice rising. "How about we figure out a way to get us both back to Earth so we can stop the aliens from sucking the souls out of what's left of humanity?!"

"Why?"

"Why what!?"

"Why save them?" Jack said.

Daniel was incredulous. He spread his hands open. "Why *save* mankind? Does that need an explanation? Am I missing something?"

"No, I'm missing something," Jack said. "Why should we bother? You already tried to help, and look what they did to you. Eternal banishment. Thanks for playing, better luck next time. The *leaders*"—Jack put the word in finger quotes—"of mankind are selfish garbage that don't want us around, and the rest aren't that great either. And you want to go back—which, by the way, you can't do—so you can martyr yourself for people who couldn't care less about what happens to you."

"I'm not trying to bear a cross here, okay," Daniel said. "I don't care about saving every Tom, Dick, and Harry. I don't even know if I can. But Felix is back there. My dad is back there."

Jack gave Daniel an even look. "Rachel is back there, too. Or was."

Daniel's next words stopped halfway in his mouth. He swallowed the sudden lump in his throat and took a long breath. "Let's not go there."

"Nah," Jack said. "Let's. I don't need to avoid it. I'm not gonna sit here and let my best friend be used."

"How the hell am I being used?" Daniel said. "Please, explain to me how I'm being used. I'm all ears."

"You told me that you brought Rachel to safety after you used her magic to heal yourself, and then she died."

"Yeah."

"Did you see her die?"

"No," Daniel said. "I didn't find out until later, when Eleanor told me."

Jack looked at him like he was stupid. "And you trusted the duchess?"

"Xik visited before I was sentenced," Daniel said. "He confirmed what happened."

"Xik. What the hell was his full name? Xikanthus Bumnuts Neverneverland. That guy creeps me out. I don't trust him as far as I could throw him."

"He did make us contractors," Daniel said.

"That makes him more suspicious, not less."

"What's your point?"

"My point is, maybe it's all smoke and mirrors," Jack said. "How do you know any of these people told you the truth? How do you even know Rachel is really dead?"

Daniel shook his head in disbelief. "What could possibly be the motivation for them to lie about that? The only person Eleanor really liked was Rachel. It didn't seem like she was acting when she came in teary eyed and falling all over herself."

"We both know what the duchess is capable of," Jack said. "And Xik...he's a totally different quantity. He's using all the contractors. Maybe he's trying to manipulate you or push you into something. Did you ever feel like it wasn't a coincidence that we—you, me, Rachel, Eleanor—all happened to get into the same school?"

Daniel frowned. "I never thought about it like that."

"I have," Jack said. "I've had plenty of time to think about a lot of things. We weren't only at the same school, we were all assigned to the same freaking dorm hall. Again, by coincidence." Jack shook his head. "We were sent in there to fight each other. We were supposed to come into conflict. Instead, we became friends, and you got together with Rachel."

"But...why try to make us fight?" Daniel asked.

"That's easy," Jack said. "What was Xik always going on about? Making warriors that could fight the Vorid."

Daniel raised his head in sudden realization, staring at Jack. "He was trying to make a stronger contractor."

"Exactly," Jack said. "The last man standing—you or me—would use the others as fodder. Like rats in a cage, only the strongest survives. But it didn't work."

"Have you considered that Xik set you up to dislike Rachel somehow?" Daniel said.

"The thought crossed my mind." Jack frowned, then shook his head. "There's no way. Xik wasn't around when...look, forget Xik. Let me ask you the same thing. How do you know Rachel was on your side?"

Daniel mustered up his most condescending expression. "How do you think? She could have turned me in any time. Instead she taught me some basics about magic and helped me practice."

"Eleanor found out about where we were fighting so quickly that I got captured," Jack said. "How did that happen? The only other person that knew was Rachel."

"Gee, I dunno," Daniel said. "Maybe they detected us pulverizing Fenway with, you know, the army of magicians that happened to be stationed in Boston at the time."

"Or she told Eleanor what was going on."

"I'm not gonna suspect Rachel over that," Daniel said. "We were causing enough of a problem to get noticed with our fighting. And when the magicians didn't back me up in New York, she's the one that broke ranks and came for me. None of them, just her. So I'm pretty damn sure she meant what she said when she told me she loved me!"

Jack didn't let Daniel's rising tone stop him. "Or, she lied," he said, "to keep you on a leash for the rest of the magicians."

"Bull."

"Think about it," Jack said. "She kept you in arm's reach for Henry Astor and his daughter, the duchess. The duchess, of all people. Where do you think Rachel's loyalties lie—her family, or her boyfriend of a couple months? If she didn't help them, how else did they track you when you were in New York?"

"The nightmares followed me!"

"How?"

"By scent!"

Jack raised an eyebrow. "By *scent*. Really?"

"One of them was talkative," Daniel said. "They found a hair or something I left behind. They used that to track me with magic. Rachel had nothing to do with it."

"What is this, CSI?" Jack said. "What makes more sense? They found a hair lying on the ground somewhere in the middle of a war zone, or Rachel helped them track you? How many of your hairs were on her pillow sitting in her dorm room?"

"Then explain why she threw herself in front of the Vorid lord to save my life!" Daniel shouted. "Does your brilliant theory cover her sacrificing herself to save me?! She saved me, and then I sucked the life out of her to heal myself! Was that all an act?!"

"It wasn't an act, it was circumstance," Jack said, plowing ahead with his logic in the face of Daniel's anger. "She was sent in to delay while they brought in the big guns, thinking you were already out of the picture. She probably didn't realize how big the risk was. Even if she did, she had to obey duchess. Besides, neither of you knew at the time what your powers would do to her. You didn't know yourself."

"You're pulling this out of your ass," Daniel said. "This isn't about Rachel or magicians. This is about you and your woman complex."

Jack did a double-take. "My what?"

"You heard me," Daniel said. "Why the hell are you so bent on convincing me that Rachel was out to get me? You don't have anything to justify any of it except wild conspiracy theories. You're the one that murdered girls in our class to make yourself stronger, you told me that yourself. You told me that you were better than them, that they were sacrificial ants on your path to glory. And now here you are going on about being a famous gladiator. You've convinced yourself that this is enough, but it's an illusion you whipped up for yourself so that you don't care you're one of those rats, trapped in a cage and milked for cash by Beelzebub!" Daniel folded his arms. "You murdered three innocent people. That's not you. This gladiator thing—that's not you. It's an excuse to avoid something that you're not telling me."

"You don't know what you're talking about," Jack said.

"Well." Daniel gestured up to the ceiling of the massive cavern that stretched up around them. "We've got plenty of time for you to explain, don't we?"

"All three of those girls weren't the innocent fairies you think they were," Jack said. "Two of them dealt heroin." Daniel frowned and sat back. "What, you didn't read that in the newspaper? Guess what, nobody did. The first girl's dad had political connections so they hushed it up. It would have implicated multiple people in the Massachusetts statehouse she was selling to. I killed him, too." Daniel was taken aback. Jack leaned over the table, building on his momentum. "Yeah, that part didn't get out, did it? I didn't get as strong as I am from killing three girls. They didn't want anyone finding out that the same people sponsoring their stupid opioid bill were running a drug ring out of those new clinics where you can go to shoot up *safely*. It was the sick and evil Boston Smasher, cruelly slaughtering beautiful, wonderful young women! The second one I already knew was bad, so I pretended to be asleep and caught her stealing cash out of my wallet. I followed her back to her dealer. It turned out she bought in bulk and was the biggest outlet for the stuff on campus.

"The last one was the worst," Jack said, leaning in over the table. "A real, honest-to-goodness pair of sickos. She was the niece of a state trooper. She'd get dirt on girls in our school, get them drunk, take pictures, that kind of thing. She'd use those to blackmail them into prostitution. Then they'd force them to do drugs—stuff the uncle stole out of the evidence locker—and get them addicted so they had more control over them for their little sex trafficking ring. The amount of corruption in Boston is ridiculous. Even I didn't know how bad it was."

"So you murdered them?" Daniel said. "They didn't deserve to die. If you had evidence, you should have called the police."

"Call the police?!" Jack threw his hands up. "Were you listening? Call the same police that had a guy on payroll making hookers out of college students? And this—this, coming from the guy who wanted to go to law school for personal reasons," Jack said. "So yeah, I killed them. I took criminals off the streets. They didn't get to cut a deal, not this time. You should be thanking me."

"You think you're great and honorable," Daniel said, "but you can't appoint yourself judge, jury, and executioner. It messes with your mind."

"You know what's messed up?" Jack said. "The mages did this to me. They suppressed the stories about corruption because they knew a contractor was responsible. They wanted to make me a villain, have the public version lopsided so they could get rid of me, like they did to Rasputin and Dracula. The Boston Smasher, ambushing and murdering innocent women." Jack shrugged. "I killed all the men involved too, but strangely that didn't make it into the news. You're a much bigger monster if you only target defenseless women."

"Not every single mage is a bad person, Jack, and not every cop is either," Daniel said. "You can't do this to yourself. You can't get it into your head that you have the right to do it. How many books have you read where the guy takes the law into his own hands and spins out of control?"

"I'm not that guy," Jack said. "This isn't a comic book. It's not a movie, it's real life. I'm not going to make those mistakes."

"That's what they said too," Daniel said. "Everyone in real life says the same thing. They all think they're special, that they can do what others couldn't. You said it yourself, Jack. I wanted to go to law school, not lawless school. I want to do it the right way."

"You know what Daniel?" Jack said. "Fuck the law. We oughta be the ones making things happen, not waiting for this crap to be sorted out 5 years later after an endless investigation and 500 people having their lives screwed up. I—we—are better than that. Earth was being invaded and these wannabe college sluts were dealing drugs and ruining lives, and the police were involved, and so were some of the people making the *laws* you care about so much. So I got close to them. It was easier than I thought it would be—they all had the same attitude, thinking I'd be an easy pushover that they could use like an ATM and dump later. I waited until I caught them in the act, collected evidence on who they were working with, and then I cleaned up the trash and benefited myself at the same time. Problem solved. Lives saved." Jack threw up his hands. "Hell, I was giving back to the community. Isn't that what you're supposed to do when you move up in life? Give something *back*. La-dee-fucking-da." Jack slapped his hands on the table. "The end of the world is here. Society, moral standards, the social contract—all that is invisible bullshit that doesn't exist in the face of actual, physical power. That's what we have. What we say, goes. And that's the end of it. Your family was screwed over by a flawed justice system. I delivered that justice, and now I'm somehow the bad guy."

Daniel leaned back, taking it all in. He tried to keep his toned measured, move away from the passions of the moment. "You're painting with an awfully broad brush, Jack," he started. "Things are more complicated than that. Lives are worth more than that. Being strong doesn't make you better or wiser than other people."

"But all it takes for evil to win is for good men who can make a difference to do nothing," Jack said.

"That's different than deciding what people deserve," Daniel said, "who lives and who dies. That's what we have laws for, that's why we decide together how to punish people. It's because we aren't perfect that we work together on those things, because we have to shore up each other's weaknesses."

"When did you become this wide-eyed idealist?" Jack said.

"It's not idealism, it's reality," Daniel said. "Taking all the power? Writing the rules, so no one can stop you? Getting rid of people you don't like? Sounds like some magicians I know."

"Don't compare me to them," Jack snapped.

"If the shoe fits."

"So, what do you want?" Jack said. "The planet dissolves into chaos because the people that can actually do something sit on their hands?"

"No," Daniel said. "Society decides what society is going to do—not dictated to by people monopolizing magical power. Yeah, that's frustrating. It's tough when people go in a direction you don't agree with. But that's life. Part of life is living with the consequences of your choices, and you don't have a right to decide those choices for others. You don't get that right because you woke up one day with magical powers."

"But then I get dragged along with their bad choices and worse consequences because there are more of them, essentially," Jack said. "Isn't that unfair to me? Why should I suffer under society's stupidity when I disagreed in the first place? I-told-you-so doesn't put things back the way they were."

Daniel shrugged. "If that really happens to the extent you're saying, then maybe it all wasn't worth saving anyway. I guess if people are worth it, things will turn out good. If it isn't worth it, they'll be punished by their own bad choices, eventually."

"My whole point," Jack said, "is that we shouldn't stand around and be dragged in with them."

"You can't use force to carve out everything you don't like in the world and expect it to stand up afterward," Daniel said. "You'd leave everyone cowering in fear of what you might do next, of what the next thing to get carved away would be."

Jack rubbed his forehead. His eyes searched the paved stone beneath the table. "You're held back, Dan. You're holding yourself back, because you're holding yourself to the rules of the old world. If what you told me about the Vorid showing up in force is true, the old world is over."

"What about your mom?" Daniel said, trying to throw him off. "You never told me what happened to her."

Jack paused. His mouth opened, then closed. He looked away. "She's dead. Vorid got her."

Daniel rocked back in his chair. Despite the anger at Jack running around in his chest, he couldn't help but feel a little bit like a piece of crap. "I'm sorry, Jack. I wasn't trying to accuse you of anything."

Jack said nothing.

"How did it happen?"

"It doesn't matter," Jack said. He sighed. "Say we get back to Earth, we beat the Vorid. What happens to me?"

"You have to take responsibility," Daniel said.

"How does that work?"

"I'd start with turning yourself in," Daniel said. "Admit your crimes, plead guilty in court. If you help fight the Vorid, and if the people you attacked were really involved in shady stuff, maybe your sentence will be commuted. Then you do your time and you put it behind you."

Jack snorted. "That doesn't even make any sense. The magicians wouldn't let me."

"I was thinking that would happen later," Daniel said, "when all this is over. Maybe we can cut a deal."

"I'm not doing time for a society that doesn't want us," Jack said. "They deserve it, Daniel. They deserve the Vorid."

"Now it's not just the magicians?" Daniel said. "It's the regular, everyday people too? Where does this end, Jack?"

"You know what?" Jack said. "Most people suck. Most people are idiots that cut you off in traffic. They cut to the front of the line, they shove you out of the way, they're rude, they don't have a sense of empathy. They scream at the person behind the counter because they're having a bad day. They argue with you over 50-cent discount coupons. They either sweat all the small stuff because they're bipolar control freaks, or they sweat none of it because they don't care about anything. They expect everyone around them to have the standards of Jesus Christ, but it's totally fine if they're a self-loathing hypocritical screw-up, and if anyone points it out, they're an irrelevant hater. They don't care about anyone other than themselves. Shit, they don't even care about themselves, only whatever compulsion is running through their head. Make angry Facebook post. Eat ice cream. Check cell phone. Get another dopamine hit. More retweets. More likes on Instagram." Jack rocked back in his chair. "I don't feel this weird pressure to bow down to their arbitrary moral guidelines, like they have some kind of say in what I can and can't do because there's a lot of them. When I was another guy on the street, I didn't have a choice, but now I do. And I'm choosing differently." Jack met Daniel's eyes. "And all this stuff about laws, about following the society's rules—we're contractors. You already broke the rules. You already struck off on your own. Now you want to waltz back in like everything's fine—but it isn't. Society's laws banished you to Hell. You wanting to break out is breaking the law!"

Daniel didn't know how to respond. The conversation had gone beyond off the rails. Being down here, fighting every day—Jack had changed.

Or maybe he'd always been this way, and Daniel never realized. Back in school, they both kept secrets. Neither had known the other was keeping them. Power didn't necessarily change a person—sometimes, it allowed them to be who they really were without any consequences.

And who was to say Jack was being completely honest with him, even now? He claimed the people he killed were committing crimes—but what kind of evidence did he have? It was obvious Jack had some kind of vendetta. Daniel could feel it hanging in the air. Something was being left unsaid. He wasn't even sure if Jack's mom really got killed by the Vorid—but he wasn't about to start digging into that.

Daniel had planned to tell Jack about his deal with Beelzebub to kill Bathory at some point. Now he wasn't sure he could be trusted.

The moment he thought about the deal was the same moment a sour taste entered his mouth. Here he was, preaching morality, and he made a deal with the devil to murder someone.

Daniel took a breath. She was a mass-murdering psychopath sentenced to Hell. If there was any human that deserved to die, it was probably her. If he ran a poll, he was sure at least 99% would agree. In fact, the only reason she wasn't dead was because a sentence in Hell was deemed worse than death. It wasn't until Daniel got down here that he himself knew Hell was a lot different than he thought it would be—and that was putting it mildly. He wasn't even sure if the magicians knew what the prison had morphed into under Beezelbub's control.

All that aside, what Jack was suggesting—the new rule of contractors after the war was over—was a theoretical situation so far off he wasn't sure where to begin. He'd reacted negatively to what Jack was saying on instinct more than careful consideration, and his personal attacks on Rachel didn't help things, either. Maybe the best way forward was somewhere between the two extremes.

Right now, it didn't matter. He didn't have time to debate the philosophy of future earth when present-day earth could be hit by another attack at any time. He'd gotten stronger by killing demons from the Viridian Gust while fighting with Jack. That would have to be strong enough to handle the Vorid.

He also had no idea how Beelzebub was going to hide the fact that everyone Daniel took out in Purgatory was permanently dead. He needed to make a move before he became a target of other teams and life got harder than it already was.

But even if he did kill Bathory and somehow escape Hell as a result, he wasn't sure how things would work out. His thoughts traveled back to Xik—to Jack's suggestion that they were all set up. They all happened to meet in the same city, at the same college. Two contractors, and both daughters of the leader of the Ivory Dawn, Henry Astor. Xik probably wanted something to go down, and it would have ended in either both Jack and Daniel dying, or in one very strong contractor still standing, ready to fight the Vorid.

Daniel found the train of thought disturbing precisely because it rung with an undeniable strain of truth. If Xik was trying to create a weapon to fight the Vorid...then did he actually want Daniel to be in Purgatory so he could keep getting stronger? What did Xik tell Beelzebub in order to set up the deal about Bathory? Had he lied? Maybe they were conspiring all along, and Daniel was playing the role of a hapless pawn, racing headfirst down a road they'd set him on months ago.

And if Xik lied about all of that, did he lie about what happened to Rachel?

There it was—the thing that made him want to believe Jack's theory. The tiny little golden glint at the far bottom of a dark well. If Xik was a dirty rotten bastard, then Rachel might not actually be dead.

Daniel tried to mentally smack the thought out of his head. He couldn't grab onto that only to find out it was wishful thinking. He couldn't handle that.

"Are you gonna sit there and stare at the table, or do you have something else to say?" Jack said.

Daniel pulled himself out of his thoughts. "Lay off Rachel," he said. "If you want to stay here and be some kind of misanthropic gladiator, fine. I'm going back to Earth."

"Whatever. After you're done beating your head against the wall, you can apologize for being a dick."

"Takes one to know one." Daniel stood back from the chair. It scraped over the stone. "I want to talk to Dracula."

"He'll probably call us in soon."

"The sooner the better. Where is he?"

"Whoa," Jack said, "everybody stand back. We got a big shot over here."

"Can you cool it already?" Daniel said. "I'm sick of arguing."

Jack sighed. "He'll probably see us if we go to his office." He stood. "Dan." Daniel looked at him. "Maybe I was harsh, but the truth is harsh. I'm still your friend."

"Since we're being honest," Daniel said, "I have no idea if I'm still your friend. I feel like I didn't really know you in the first place."

Jack's face clenched up. Daniel couldn't help but feel that he'd said something he shouldn't have—shattered something Jack thought was firm.

Jack spoke first, breaking the silence. "We both kept things secret," he said. "But...I'm just me. You're my best friend, Dan. An argument doesn't change that. Not for me, anyway."

Daniel swallowed hard. "I feel the same. I want to meet you halfway, here. I don't want to fight with you."

"Me neither," Jack said.

"I don't know if you've told me everything yet," Daniel said. "I don't feel like you have." Daniel waited, but when Jack didn't say anything, he kept going. "I don't agree with what you're saying, about staying here and living this life. I'm going to try to convince you differently. But if I can't, then I can't. That's all I can do for you, if we really are friends."

"It's the same on my side." Jack closed his eyes. He nodded to himself. "I won't bring up Rachel. I don't like the way she died, if only because it hurt you."

Daniel's lips tightened, but he kept his tone measured. "Her being gone is less important than my feelings?"

"I'm not convinced she's dead in the first place," Jack said.

Daniel gave him a look.

"I'm just being honest with you." Jack rolled his shoulders, as if trying to shrug off the awkwardness. "You got my two cents. If you don't want to talk about it, we won't talk about it."

"Thank you," Daniel said.

"Since you want to see Dracula, let's go see him."

Daniel kept pace as Jack started off. As they left the café square and entered the streets of the city, Daniel looked over at his friend. "Hey, Jack."

"Yeah?"

"That time when Eleanor trapped us. If you didn't hit the ice one more time, I wouldn't have been able to get out. Thanks for that."

"Didn't really do you much good," Jack said. "You still ended up here."

Daniel snorted. "Only because I was stupid enough to trust the mages."

"I mean, come on man," Jack said. "I get it. You didn't want to be the criminal in the shadows. You wanted to stand next to her in the open. Rachel. That's why you went along with it, isn't it."

"Yeah," Daniel said. "You're probably right. No good deed, huh?"

"If you weren't a bitter asshole with a secret heart of gold," Jack said, "I probably wouldn't like you as much."

Daniel shrugged. "Just one of my many charming qualities."

Chapter 9
The Prince of Wallachia

Thanks to the efforts of Jack and Daniel, the Order of the Dragon simultaneously recaptured their territory from the Viridian Gust while expanding gains elsewhere on their borders. Effectively, within the confines of Purgatory, the Order was already considered the strongest and wealthiest team, and this solidified their position as number two in the rankings. The only team more powerful were the reigning champs, the organization headed by Elizabeth Bathory—the Brotherhood of Sinners. Possessing isolated quarters situated above the cavernous city, they didn't have to participate in territory wars and battle for their continued survival. That dark drudgery was only expected of the normal ranking teams.

The Order of the Dragon was also one of the largest teams. Comprised entirely of humans, it tended to absorb new prisoners as soon as they were banished from Earth, if they had any value. Not every human sent down possessed said value; most were scum, and rightly imprisoned in Hell. Others could not be controlled. Dracula arranged that the unworthy were efficiently deposited into the lower tiers of Hell.

Dracula's office was entirely intentional. There were two chairs in front of his desk. Each piece of furniture was hickory, with a deep brown finish. He sat in the remaining chair behind the desk, a high-backed, hand-carved seat that exuded a looming authority.

The walls were bland sepia, but this served to highlight the décor—two paintings, one on each wall to his left and right. A tapestry sewn with the Order's frilled cross hung behind him. There was a small potted rose bush in one corner, finalizing the room's few excesses.

Dracula built the furniture himself. He sewed the tapestry. He'd also painted both paintings.

When one lived several hundred years, one tended to pick up hobbies.

The rose bush, admittedly, was a purchase, but he thought it lent a touch of gravitas. The flowers were elegant, poised, but hardly defenseless. And the color paired well with the cross.

Dracula's appearance was sharp and defined, like a cast pewter figurine come to life. His brow cut a heavy line above his eyes like a stone ledge jutting over twin pits, but a well-groomed mustache softened his face somewhat. Dracula squinted at the screen displayed on his desk, watching unedited footage of the battle that Jack Killiney and Daniel Fitzgerald had fought against the Viridian Gust.

"What do you think?" Rasputin said. The long-faced man was standing in the corner, leaning between the tapestry and the roses.

"Daniel is extremely powerful," Dracula said. "He's also reckless. He barges into all his fights. His tactics are smart, but repetitive. Still...if it works, don't fix it."

"I don't think he understands his own powers very well," Rasputin said. "Like Killiney, in that way. The contractors are wild experiments."

"Mmm." Dracula kept watching as Daniel forced his power into a lightning rod, and it promptly overloaded. Normally it would only be enough to destroy a room, taking the user with it—but Daniel demolished the entire building. Dracula suspected some sort of interaction between the rod and the contractor enchantment was responsible for generating all that force. Daniel survived his foolishness at the cost of an arm, but that he survived at all was impressive.

Dracula swept a hand down, clearing the screen. "No training. No theoretical background. Reliant on bludgeoning his way through his problems. A good tool, quickly made, quickly disposed of." He faced Rasputin. "What did Jack call their foreign masters? The Klide?"

"Yes," Rasputin said. "The race that opposes the Vorid."

"He claims they were selected almost randomly, on the basis of being borderline mundane," Dracula said. "Not quite enough talent to learn magic." He tapped his fingers along the edge of his desk. "I suspect otherwise. It seems ridiculous to suppose that the Klide could develop magic at this level and then be unable to choose whom they'd grant it."

"Jack seems very loyal to Daniel," Rasputin said. "Problematically loyal."

"Do you think we can rein him in?" Rasputin opened his mouth to answer, but a buzz came in across the desk. Dracula pressed his finger on the digital icon that appeared on its surface. "Yes?"

"Lord Dracula, Mr. Killiney and Mr. Fitzgerald are here to see you."

Dracula exchanged glances with Rasputin. "Send them in."

The door to the office opened. Jack and Daniel were strict opposites. Jack was small and wiry; he wore his hair cropped close to his scalp. Daniel was taller; his face was rounder, and his hair was a brown mess. His eyes weren't hesitant, like Jack's. He stared right back at Dracula and stuck his hand out.

"Hi. I'm Daniel Fitzgerald." His voice wasn't deep, but it carried a steady confidence. "Jack told me you're the head honcho around here."

Dracula allowed a small smile. He took Daniel's hand, pumped it once. The boy's hands were soft, but had stiff calluses in odd places. "That's one way of putting it. Please sit."

Jack and Daniel both sat in the chairs. They eyed Rasputin; Jack in distaste, Daniel with a frowned half-interest.

Dracula decided to address the obvious business first. "Jack. You failed to retrieve Daniel from the entrance in a timely fashion. Once you did find him, you failed to escort him back safely. The delay cost us a hard-won territory and no small amount from the treasury."

Jack hung his head. Daniel looked like he was on the verge of speaking up for his friend, so Dracula continued before he could interrupt. "Rather than report back to me, you took a gamble to restore both that territory and the lost capital, relying solely on your personal judgement of a friend rather than objective orders from your superiors. And because of your insight, and a tremendous amount of dumb luck, you were successful."

Jack perked up. "Uh—is that, um, a good thing?"

Dracula raised an eyebrow. "That you were successful? Of course it's a good thing. But you should understand that you were extremely fortunate things worked out the way they did."

Jack nodded. "Yeah."

"Listen to me," Dracula said. "You're a powerful warrior, Jack. I see a bright future for you. But you must be able to separate personal matters from your service in the Order. You made several mistakes today. Reflect, and do not make them again."

Dracula could see Jack fighting with himself, debating on whether or not to say anything. Inevitably, he was too young to take his licks and keep his mouth shut. "But, Lord Dracula," he said, "I did get the territory back. We won!"

"Just because a choice ends in a positive result doesn't mean it was the right choice," Dracula said. "With Daniel being as strong as he is, we could have taken the territory back at any time in the future. It would have been a fight with proper planning and execution, rather than one that risked both your lives a second time."

"I—" Jack sighed. "I'm sorry. I wanted to make up for it."

Dracula smiled. "I know. I will assess appropriate discipline for you later." Dracula looked at Rasputin. "In doing so, I will consider that there were other factors involved at the time."

Jack and Daniel both fought back smiles. Rasputin cleared his throat awkwardly. "Apologies, my lord," Rasputin said. "It should have all been relayed through you first."

Dracula nodded at him, accepting the apology. "We have more important things to talk about. Daniel Fitzgerald." Dracula faced his guest. "You've done the Order of the Dragon a great service. Without you, Jack almost certainly would have been defeated. You have my gratitude."

"Great," Daniel said. "Would it be possible for you to do me a favor?"

"Depending on the favor, yes," Dracula said. "Speak your mind."

"I want you to set me up in a fight against Elizabeth Bathory."

Dozens of thoughts flickered through Dracula's mind. He noted Jack's surprised expression and settled on the most obvious explanation. "Jack must have told you a bit of my personal history. If you're trying to make a good impression, I assure you that the effort is appreciated, but unnecessary."

"I have my own reasons to take Bathory out."

"Interesting," Dracula said. "Do tell."

"This is the deal," Daniel said. "Jack told me about how things work down here. Like you said, he also told me about you and the Order. So I want to kill two birds with one stone." Daniel leaned onto his knees. "First, I'll show you that I'm on your side, for keeps. Second, I'll cement a spot as someone that no one in Hell wants to mess with." Daniel glanced at Jack, then back to Dracula. "This place—this prison—has ugly rules. I don't want to be a target. I want to be the guy that makes people take the long way around when they see me. I'll catapult off my rookie reputation using Bathory as a stepping stone."

Dracula nodded his head. Those were all excellent reasons. What he was suggesting was risky, but he wasn't risking anything permanent.

But it was all too neat, too prepared. Too...presented. Dracula had dealt with people far more conniving than Fitzgerald. He wasn't lying outright, but there was something he wasn't saying.

Dracula shrugged mentally. Whatever the boy was hiding, at this point, didn't matter. For the time being, he would play along. In fact, it might just be the best way to make sure everything was well in hand.

He couldn't appear to give in too easily. "What happens if you lose?" Dracula said.

"I know for sure I can at least put up a fight," Daniel said. "Even if I lose, I lose against the strongest person in Hell. I'm still a badass rookie; maybe I tried to bite off more than I could chew, but nothing changes."

"In other words," Dracula said, "you *have* nothing to lose."

"Basically, yeah."

"There's always something more to lose. You don't know until it's gone." Dracula sighed, and sat back in his chair. "You have potential, but like Jack, you need seasoning. Experience."

"Is that a no?"

"It would be against my better judgement," Dracula said, "to pit you against someone with Bathory's repertoire and magical control."

"No worries," Daniel said. "Rely on my judgement instead."

Dracula and Rasputin chuckled a bit. "Cheeky," Rasputin said. "Jack recently learned that lesson the hard way. Perhaps you ought to *reflect* a bit more before your arrogance gets the better of you."

Dracula threw Rasputin a look. The hook-nosed man sniffed, but stopped further comments short. "I like your enthusiasm, Daniel," Dracula said. "May I call you Daniel?"

"Sure thing, Vlad."

"Lord Dracula will do," Dracula said, smiling. Daniel gave him a cordial nod. "We're now in a position to issue challenges to the top recognized team," Dracula continued. "They have to accept a certain number of them in a given period of time, and win a majority of the challenges, or they forfeit their privileged status. If we push you as our representative in single combat against Bathory, I think it's highly likely she'll take up the challenge. Do you know why?"

"No, but I have a feeling you're gonna tell me," Daniel said.

"It's because she'll be absolutely confident she can defeat you," Dracula said. "I'd agree with her assessment. She'll fulfill part of her quota, and—yet again—stave off judgement."

"Judgement?" Daniel said.

"Let me tell you a story," Dracula said. He settled back in his chair, placing his hands across the armrests. "One day, there was born a prince of a small but proud country called Wallachia. It was the tiny neighbor of a massive empire. The empire followed a different religion, and in their enlightened magnanimity imposed upon Wallachia a yearly tribute. To ensure Wallachia's loyalty—and their timely contributions to the sultan of the empire—the prince and his younger brother were held as hostages in their court.

"Even trapped as he was in distant lands, the prince was given a fine education: lessons in combat and horse riding; dance; language; history and geography. He had well-kept chambers, the respect of his lessers, and a generous stipend. Everything a noble scion might expect as a guest of another house. But he wasn't a guest. He was a prisoner." Dracula met Daniel's eyes. "They made sure he didn't forget that."

Daniel exchanged a glance with Jack. Something passed between them. Dracula already knew what it was, considering he'd been listening in while they were arguing at the café. But he feigned ignorance and continued his story.

"The prince studied the sultanate, learned their ways, customs, and language. He stayed quiet and watched as the royal line and the nobles schemed and played each other against one another, as factions fought other factions. It was a tangle of deceit and shifting allegiances, but ultimately, they were all the same. Murderous and degenerate enemies of his father and his homeland. Tyrants.

"Eventually, by providence more than intention, the prince discovered a great secret buried deep beneath the capital of the empire. The secret gave him tremendous magical power. He used the power to leverage some of the sultan's military forces to invade his own homeland, Wallachia."

Daniel looked surprised. "Why would he do that?"

"Because," Dracula said, "in the meantime, his father and elder brother had been murdered by others that considered his father a traitor."

"A traitor?"

Dracula shook his head at Daniel's naiveté. "They thought he'd turned and become an ally of the sultan because he paid tribute to avoid conflict. The prince's father was forced to break earlier promises to protect his hostage sons. When this was discovered, they removed him, by force. Familial love was a minor unimportance in the grand scheme of things, you see. A political puppet was installed in his place.

"And so the prince first invaded his own homeland, and fought his own blood, winning back his position—only to be deposed months later. He had no local foundation, only meager foreign support. Despite his magic, he wasn't proof against the tides of politics and war. He couldn't force the masses to obey him with strength of will alone. After a lifetime spent in another country, he'd unknowingly become a stranger to his own people.

"True victory was far more complicated." Dracula stared past Daniel, caught up in his own story as the memories flickered in his mind's eye, still fresh, still biting. "It took years," he said. "Years of flitting from city to city, country to country, managing his personal relations between the empire and the nobles of other countries, many of whom were the same that plotted to assassinate his father. He walked a line between allies and enemies, past and present and potential, slowly building his magical power and political influence until eventually he secured his throne once again.

"He strengthened his position, imposing order upon the chaos that had gripped Wallachia since his father's downfall. The traitorous nobles that conspired against his family were purged; those that remained loyal were rewarded. Roads and churches were rebuilt. Criminals and brigands were slaughtered. It was a brutal and dictatorial time, and so it was the times did not tolerate luxuries like hesitation and mercy. Ultimately, the people cheered that their lives were restored to some kind of peace, some sense of normalcy; that their rightful ruler had returned, and that he was just. His enemies labeled him a psychopath and a drinker of blood to slander him, attempted to use the strictness of his methods as propaganda—but the results spoke for themselves, far louder than the rumors. The people and the remaining nobles were staunch in their support for the prince.

"Eventually, the sultan sent envoys to once again assert his authority and request tribute, demanding that the prince attend him in Constantinople. The prince, however, discovered that the sultan's messengers were working with a secret force that planned to capture him once he neared the sultan's territory. He executed the sultan's envoys and gathered his forces to do the thing they would least expect—attack.

"Wallachia could only bloody the nose of the massive empire, but they bloodied it all the same. The attack was like nothing that had been seen in Europe in 100 years. Lead by their prince, Wallachia tore apart the sultan's garrisons despite being outnumbered many times over. Rather than run from the rumors of his bloodthirstiness, the prince wielded them as a weapon to instill fear into his enemies. The corpses of their soldiers were impaled on pikes and staked along the roads for miles around the border cities, a message written in blood that they would never again scrape and bow before the sultan's edicts."

"Vlad the Impaler," Daniel said.

"Yes," Dracula said. "That is what they called me, eventually. Of course...the story doesn't end there."

"I guess if it did," Daniel said, "you wouldn't be down here."

Dracula could only offer a thin smile. "So it is, Daniel. I held them off with everything I had, but everything I had wasn't enough." Dracula gestured to the painting on the wall; it showed a rolling, forested countryside, ending at a broad river. There was a small fort in the distance across the river, standing alone on top of a hill. "Wallachia was a beautiful country. Wild, free. Rich and fierce. But it could not sustain a war against the Ottomans, not alone. My magic was strong, but I was only one man. We were one tiny country facing the oncoming wrath of an empire more than ten times our size. It was at that juncture I made a fatal mistake."

Dracula paused there and turned to get a good look at the boy. Daniel said nothing. Eventually, he looked away.

Dracula didn't expect him to say anything. What could be said to a man that had half his family murdered by those they believed their allies? That spent his whole life working to right those wrongs? That lived for hundreds of years banished in Hell? Whatever was supposed to be said in response was beyond reasonable expectation for a young man that, by the look of it, might not have grown his first full beard.

"I decided to share the secret of my success," Dracula said, "my powers, with others. I considered them friends, allies.

Fellow Christians. Some were former friends of my father that wanted to bring me back to their fold. They agreed to help me in time of need. And when the time came—when the empire's massive armies were on my doorstep—I went to them.

"They ambushed me. It was another betrayal. They knew I was more powerful, but in the meantime, they had schooled themselves in other arcane methods in a secret attempt to undermine me. They did it all with the help of new friends—friends that told them I needed to be dealt with. Friends that ordered me banished to Hell."

Daniel's eyes widened. "Magicians."

"Yes." Dracula slowly nodded. "The same magicians that banished you and Jack. Or rather, their ancestors.

"Once the nature of my powers was revealed, they immediately conspired to get rid of me. Of course, banishing me didn't banish all those to whom I'd passed my powers, and the knowledge kept spreading, first in secret, and then in the open. Things spiraled out of control. The magic I'd mastered to protect my homeland and avenge my family was eventually taken up by a true despot and psychopath—Elizabeth Bathory.

"Today," Dracula said, "all of the men and women that deserve to be punished, following my banishment, are punished. They do not live easy lives, well fed and comfortable, up here in Purgatory. They grind away at the ice, or at some other laboring servitude on a lower level of Hell. I have made sure of it. The Order of the Dragon lives on through this effort. I am trapped in Hell, but in that, I still have purpose."

"All of them except Bathory," Daniel said.

"Precisely," Dracula said. "She alone has escaped my grasp. She taunts me from her quarters above the city, flaunts her relative freedom and privilege.

"My mistake was sharing my powers with outsiders. By doing so, I plunged Europe into a darkness from which it might never have returned. My retribution shall be ensuring that Bathory is punished in the manner intended.

"Each member of the Order has been hand-selected. Those here, with me in Purgatory, are those like you. Like Jack. Rasputin." Dracula nodded to Daniel's side, where Jack was sitting, and then back toward the man standing behind him. "We are those that were sent here not because of crimes committed, but because of politics, or convenience, or by the word of the magicians that wanted to ensure their hold on power and feared the rise of what they called vampiric magic."

"What is vampiric magic, exactly?" Daniel asked. "Where does it come from? Why are they so afraid of it?"

"In the original text I found, the magic was termed inheritance-transfer power," Dracula said. "A rough translation, but sufficient. The sage who developed it envisioned that old wizards, nearing the end of their lifespans, would use the technique to pass on their strength to their descendants or apprentices. In this way, magic lineages would strengthen naturally over time, and their powers would become great enough to end larger problems like hunger and poverty. He never conceived of the use I made of it, bent on revenge as I was in my youth—taking up death as a tool to artificially increase one's own powers in a short amount of time."

Daniel's mouth was open in disbelief. "But—jeeze. I mean, what? That's where this all came from? Some guy that wanted to pass stuff down to his grandkids?"

Dracula bowed his head. "Despite those good intentions—and because of my own actions—the magicians couldn't see the good that could come of the power. Satan was said to have mastered a more encompassing form of the enchantment, and anything that might be derivative of that was unacceptable in totality. At the time, of course, I knew none of this. I wasn't aware there were other magicians until I'd already been captured by them. I was banished, as were many others, their and my reputations smeared, our deeds mischaracterized. My bloody reputation, and the fact that I embraced it, was used against me. I became—I was transformed into—the vampire."

"They did the same to me," Daniel said, nodding along. "Maybe didn't smear me exactly, but they convinced themselves they had to get rid of me. They gave me this pathetic sham trial." He sighed. "It's not much to be happy for, but at least I'm not the only one."

"You aren't," Dracula said. "I became a garlic-fearing, blood-sucking monster, and Rasputin became a corrupt paganist who undermined the Russian royal family."

"You're supposed to be afraid of crosses, too," Daniel said. He smirked at the tapestry behind the desk. "Guess they got that one wrong."

"It is right to fear God," Dracula said, "but not the symbols of His coming. They did indeed make a farce of my life."

Daniel clasped his hands. He stared at the space below the desk, deep in thought. "Can you tell me about the vampiric magic? Or, the version that Jack and I have?"

"Almost every member of the Order has dabbled in it to some extent," Dracula said. "Yourself and Jack are rather unique cases, but similar."

"Does it have any limits?" Daniel asked. "When does it end? Do people get infinitely stronger?"

"The spell has a limit," Dracula said. "Once one grows strong enough, the process becomes increasingly inefficient. Each cycle—each death—fuses less and less magical energy to the soul. Think of it this way." Dracula cupped his hands. "If I placed a marble in my hands, I'd hold it easily. Two marbles, the same. Three, four, five...but what would happen if I tried to hold thirty marbles? Or fifty?"

"It would get harder and harder," Daniel said, as his face lit up in understanding. "Some would start to roll out. Adding more marbles wouldn't do anything."

"Exactly," Dracula said. "There's a limit to the amount of power you can hold. What you truly need are a bigger pair of hands. In other words, a more efficient or powerful spell. Bathory lived a hundred years or so after I did, in a rising age of dark magic. The spell had been modified and improved beyond my original version. That's part of the problem; she's somewhat stronger than I am. Not overwhelmingly so, but enough to be troublesome."

"Uh, since..." Daniel hesitated. "Er, Mr. Rasputin, lived after both of you, is he even stronger?"

Rasputin grimaced. "By my time, there were only scraps of knowledge that had survived repeated inquisitions by the magicians and their allies. What I cobbled together with my own research only barely compares to Lord Dracula."

"But still," Dracula continued, "she has her own limits."

"The limit to personal power is unimportant," Rasputin said. He moved a bit closer, looming over Jack and Daniel from the corner of Dracula's desk. "Most magicians that tap into the secret are after something more enticing. Immortality."

"Immortality?" Daniel asked. "Is that possible outside of Hell?"

"It isn't known," Rasputin said.

"Theoretically," Dracula said, "it could be done, without any additional help. Hell's own enchantment proves that it can be done. Of course, Hell's enchantment involves being permanently bound in this..." Dracula couldn't hide his distaste. "...*place.*"

"I'm surprised more people haven't intentionally gone to Hell to live longer," Daniel said. "There could be a section set up for normal people who want eternal life without all the fun and games."

"I was thinking the same thing before," Jack said.

"To the best of my knowledge," Dracula said, "Beelzebub hasn't allowed it."

"Why not?" Daniel asked.

Rasputin threw Daniel a condescending glance. "As soon as you have insights into the mind of the devil, be sure to let the rest of us know."

"I'll ask the next time I see him," Daniel said.

"You do that."

"I suspect," Dracula said, interrupting, "that even the Hell seal has its limits. Maybe its limits aren't determined at all. Perhaps Beelzebub does not want to aimlessly wander down that particular mountain pass. If something ever happened to Hell, the consequences would be extreme. Perhaps it would destabilize the normal flow of society. Perhaps he does offer such benefits, to those who please him, and we simply don't know about it." Dracula waved a hand dismissively. "But these considerations are academic. Beelzebub practices his own version of the magic, and he's survived at least since Satan's time, and however many years before. He already lives what seems to be an eternal life, and it stands to reason that his foremost allies do as well. Likely everyone that he wants to have those benefits already does, without the side effect of being trapped in Hell. It's probably how he's maintained his grip on power for so long over demonic society."

Daniel mulled it over. "So what you're suggesting," he said, "is that Beelzebub and his cronies rule the demon world because they're all already practicing this form of magic. So they're stronger than anyone else. Undying dictators."

"That seems to be the case," Dracula said. "The other demon lords are, in their own right, extremely powerful. Much of this is pure speculation, of course; we're humans, we're prisoners, and we have only limited information about the demon world's political structure. Beelzebub seems to be the leader of a loose federation of demonic fiefdoms, each with a magically-empowered strongman at its helm. His own capital of Dis is the strongest amongst these. He was the one that overthrew Satan in an alliance with mankind, and he controls the Hell seal, which bolsters his already disproportionate influence."

"In any case," Rasputin said, standing straight, "if we take Lord Dracula's analogy, and your lifeforce is said to be a handful of marbles...it isn't completely useless to keep adding more. Life force decays over time. People grow old."

"Gives a whole new meaning to losing your marbles," Daniel said.

"Quite," Rasputin said, making an ugly beetle-nosed smirk. "So you occasionally replace old, crumbling marbles with fresh, vibrant energy. Voila. Immortality."

"But it isn't proven," Jack said.

Rasputin opened his hands. "No one has lived forever. Still...Beelzebub makes for a strong case study."

"There's also the tiny problem of continually murdering people to stay young," Daniel said. "Other than that, no major issues."

"Thus the mages have a zero-tolerance policy for using the spell," Rasputin said. "Violators are exiled here. And so we all have the wonderful privilege of getting to know each other much better."

"This all applies to us more than you two," Dracula said. "You are decidedly unique."

Jack and Daniel exchanged glances. "We are?" Jack said.

"I developed my powers over many years. Decades. You two seem to have become powerful magicians in months. The rate at which you're growing leads me to believe that your capacity is far greater than ours." Dracula met their eyes, first Jack, then Daniel. "The ancient histories imply that Satan's version of the spell was far more sophisticated than my own. More like contractor magic—a higher potential. That was why it became such a tremendous threat."

"Okay," Daniel said, "in all fairness, I'm starting to see why this stuff has the magicians on edge."

"Some consider it a violation of the natural order of things," Rasputin said, "but magic is just another force of nature, neither good nor bad. Why stop at shooting fire and cursing your foes when so much else could be done?"

"Are magic curses a thing?" Daniel said.

Rasputin's black eyes flashed. "They are. As are *things* far more horrid."

Dracula tapped the desk with his hands. "We've drifted off topic." He focused on Daniel. "It is my hope that, one day, the Order of the Dragon will be able to leave Hell and work for good in the world, the purpose for which it was originally formed. With our power, we can achieve the peace for mankind that God intended. Once we return to Earth, the paused clocks of our souls will be restarted, and perhaps, before our lives finally fade for good, we might seek some redemption."

Daniel processed that for a time. "It's a very noble goal," he said. "I wish things had turned out differently. Maybe Earth wouldn't be having such a hard time against the Vorid."

"We cannot choose what happens to us," Dracula said. "But we can choose how we respond." Dracula placed his elbows on the desk and folded his hands. "The reason I've told you all this, about myself, and about Bathory," he said, "is not to intimidate you, or to pressure you into any given decision. The reason is because I want you to appreciate what you're asking. You want to fight Bathory. I have limited chances to strike at her. Given, with you and Jack reinforcing the Order, those opportunities will probably become more frequent—but none of them can be wasted. She is an extremely formidable opponent. If you fight Bathory, you will lose."

"I've fought with bad odds before," Daniel said. "I've fought losing battles before. I've won every time."

"If that was true," Dracula said, "you wouldn't be down here."

"I turned myself in to the magicians," Daniel said. "I thought that if I openly tried to work with them, tried to show them that I was on their side...things would work out."

"Instead, you were banished." Dracula's expression was a sword's edge. "The magicians are the same today as they were in my time—blindingly arrogant, intolerant of outsiders, and miserly with their authority. And if Jack's tales are accurate, the world falling to pieces in the face of foreign invasion has not adjusted their attitude. If anything would slacken their standards, it would be a horde of creatures from beyond even the demon world that seek to capture our immortal souls to fuel their war machine." Dracula paused, let the tension fall from his shoulders, and heaved the sigh of a man hundreds of years old. "And so history repeats itself. The insignificant frontier country is abandoned time and again as fodder for the empire while the so-called Christian kingdoms fight amongst themselves." Dracula's expression hardened. "Truly, God tests men."

"Lord Dracula," Daniel said, "since Jack was banished, it's only gotten worse. They aren't trying to invade in secret anymore. It's all out in the open. The last fight—"

"You'll have to forgive me," Dracula said. "I took the liberty of listening in on your conversation with Jack."

Daniel sat back in surprise. "You eavesdropped on us?"

"It was only the part at the start," Jack said. "I patched him in so you didn't have to explain a second time. Our...uh, the rest of the conversation was private."

Daniel's body language was obvious—the thought made him uncomfortable, but he didn't want to be forceful about it. Dracula decided to take a step back; he lowered his head. "I apologize. It wasn't my intention to offend."

"I guess it's fine," Daniel said. "It does save me having to say it all again. I'm kinda done with reliving it."

"I know how you feel," Dracula said.

Daniel's hackles visibly lowered. "Yeah. No kidding." They sat there for a moment, Dracula giving him time before he pushed the conversation along. Daniel stared at his desk. Dracula could see the memories play across his eyes, the swirling thoughts.

"I have a question," Daniel said suddenly. "About magic."

"Please," Dracula said, happy for the opportunity to win a few points back.

"Is it possible to raise the dead?"

Jack stiffened and gave Daniel a sideways glance. Rasputin and Dracula exchanged their own look. Daniel's expression was intent, but guarded, the look of a man desperate for an answer but unwilling to get his hopes up.

Dracula sighed. "Are you prepared to hear the answer?"

Daniel nodded.

"It depends on the circumstances," Dracula said. "Upon death, the soul separates from the body within minutes, then begins to dissipate. There are magics that can seize the departing soul and reattach it to the body. Paired with healing magic, this can restore someone to life after being killed, though they often experience memory loss, and, if the time runs long, permanent personality changes. Other, more…unorthodox methods exist. Necromancy." Dracula looked to Rasputin.

"Pulling souls back from the aether is a messy business," Rasputin said. "The undead rarely have much of their memory or personality left. They're husks. I've been witness to experiments in combining multiple soul remnants to build a full human personality, the goal being to eventually restore someone back to a semblance of who they were. That would be its own sort of immortality."

Daniel swallowed. "You've done this sort of thing? Made zombies?"

Rasputin rolled his eyes. "Don't be naïve. Where do you think you are? Most of the Order has dabbled in necromancy. Real magic isn't about shooting rainbows from your fingers. If you can't accept that, the door is located just behind you."

"I didn't mean it like that," Daniel said quickly. "In my case. Would it be possible?"

"If we use the marble analogy," Rasputin said, "in theory, you could reach into your bag—your soulscape—and pull what was left of something out. But that's all you'd get—what was left. And there wouldn't be anything left."

"Why not?" Daniel said. "Couldn't someone…be in there? Still okay, but trapped inside?"

"I suppose I'm in a lecturing mood," Rasputin said. "The problem with what you're suggesting is that you don't want someone to be in there like a princess waiting to be rescued. That would start to affect your personality; your being would become mixed up with theirs, memories, moods, ideas. It's the worst possible of side effect from our magic—absorb enough life energy, and you become a schizophrenic mash of souls and lose your mind in short order. Another reason our type have a bad reputation." He chuckled at the looks on Jack and Daniel's faces. "The intelligent magician refines and breaks down the soul first before absorbing the energy. This creates a tremendous inefficiency, but it's better than going mad." Rasputin fixed Daniel with a steely gaze. "Were I an envious man, I'd have you both laid out on a dissection table. To get the power you have, your contractor spells must crush souls down like a compactor pulverizes tin cans." Rasputin folded his arms. "I can see you've figured it out for yourself from what I've aid. I'm not cruel enough to give you false hope. Your little girlfriend isn't coming back."

Daniel sat back at the words, as if they were a physical blow. His eyes glazed over a bit, unfocused. "Yeah. Kinda picked up on that."

Dracula decided a change in subject was needed. "You've been through much," he said. "More than any young man your age should have to go through. I feel your determination mirrors my own." Dracula stood. He clasped his hands behind his back and faced the tapestry. His eyes ran along the borders of the cross. "I have tried to find a way out of Hell, but the magic is powerful beyond comprehension. The only place I haven't been is the top level above Purgatory—where Bathory resides. The Order must take her place to complete our investigation. I can't imagine that it will bear any fruit...but we have to try. It's the only place we haven't looked."

"I can help," Daniel said. He sat straight again, fighting away the despair of the moment and looking Dracula in the eye "Let me fight her. I'll stick with the Order no matter how it goes. If I mess this up, I'll help you guys keep expanding until we get another shot."

"So you'll guarantee your work," Dracula said. "Are you sure you want to commit yourself that quickly?"

Daniel nodded. "I'm absolutely sure."

Dracula pretended to ponder. The conversation had gone more or less the way he expected, but it wouldn't do to overplay his hand when things were wrapping up. After an appropriately grave pause, he spoke. "Alright, Daniel Fitzgerald. I'll take a chance on you."

Right on time, Rasputin stepped forward, once more playing the stiff-necked officer to Dracula's fatherly leader. "Lord Dracula, I don't think—"

Dracula raised a hand, cutting him off. "Daniel does have raw power. This could be a chance to catch her off-guard. His popularity will increase because of the circumstances of the duel. The Order's position will strengthen, win or lose." Dracula smiled at Daniel. "But make sure you win."

Daniel smiled back. "You got it, Lord Dracula. I'll help the Order get back to Earth, however I can."

"However," Dracula said, "I can only grant so much faith on credit. You've proven that you can handle yourself in a fight, but you'll have to earn the right to take on Bathory."

"Sounds fair," Daniel said. "What do I have to do?"

"We have a battle coming up with another team," Dracula said. "The Sky Runners."

"I know those guys," Daniel said. "They tried to *recruit me*"—he surrounded the words in air quotes—"when I first got down here."

"Help us defeat them, and the Order will be secure in our expanded position," Dracula said. "Then I'll have the leeway to send you against Bathory."

"Sounds good to me."

"I suspected you'd be up to the task," Dracula said. "Rasputin will be in touch with you concerning the details." He turned to Jack. "You've been quiet, Jack."

Jack bobbed his head in acknowledgement. "This is serious stuff."

"Ask God not for lighter burdens, but for broader shoulders," Dracula said. "I feel I'll come to rely upon the both of you in the coming days. I'm glad to have fresh faces to give a little youth back to these old bones. Now, Jack."

"Lord Dracula?"

"Take Daniel to the main floor, have him properly registered," Dracula said. "He'll be needing a cross on his armlet." He looked to Daniel. "When you accept membership, deposit your points and your inventory into the Order's joint treasury. Your contributions are all tracked by item; we won't lose count of what's yours."

"Why don't I keep my stuff?"

"Far too risky," Dracula said. "We have to protect your assets. You can set a deposit order in the treasury that automatically transfers everything back into your armlet after the fights are over. That said, try never to carry too much on you at once—it's a bad habit in this place. Anyone that kills you takes half of whatever points you have on hand and can steal any one item from your inventory."

"*And* steal an item?" Daniel said. "This place is harsh. Sign me up for the nearest lockbox."

"I figured you would come to that conclusion," Dracula said. "Rasputin and I have a few more things to discuss. I'll have Jack see you out."

"Sure," Daniel said. "Actually—there was one other thing I wanted to ask you, if you don't mind."

"What would that be?"

"I..." Daniel squinted in memory. "I saw something. Someone, back in one of the battles. This woman."

Everyone was looking at Daniel now. Dracula furrowed his brow. "A human woman? Where was this, exactly?"

"Yeah. Near the center of the city, where I arrived," Daniel said. "It was the battle Jack fought to reach me. She wasn't part of the Order, or the enemy troops, but she walked into the fight. Through it. Nothing touched her. I saw magic pass through her." Daniel scratched his head. "After the fight, she was gone. I don't know what happened to her."

"What did she look like?" Rasputin asked. "Hell is crowded, but Purgatory is a small world."

"She had a white dress, and white hair," Daniel said. "Almost albino-looking. Too far to get a good look at her face." Daniel looked between them. "Does that sound familiar?"

Dracula and Rasputin shared a skeptical look. Dracula was of the opinion that the boy's senses were confused by the battle. Rasputin's expression told him that his second was of the same mind.

"Magic that can affect perception is not unheard of," Rasputin said. "It's possible that you were seeing an illusory spell, or that you inhaled something toxic in the smoke from the fires. Perhaps your mind was recovering from a blow—Hell's healing power has done stranger things. Were you injured at the time?"

"Yeah," Daniel said. "I was hacking up half my lung because of an explosion."

"There you are," Rasputin said. "A visual hallucination following a concussion. I've seen it before."

"Weird," Daniel said. "It felt real at the time, but there was a lot going on."

"Combat can be like that," Dracula said. "Fragmentation of memory is common. Images and events can rearrange themselves in the heat of trauma. Don't take it to heart."

"I guess you guys would know," Daniel said. Jack elbowed him. "What?" Daniel said. "They've been down here ages, they're experts."

Jack sighed. "He was doing so well."

Dracula chuckled. "I take no offense, Jack. I'm old."

"I guess—I mean...you—er..." Jack's face worked as he tried to find a way to not put too fine a point on Dracula's several hundred years of age.

"Stop trying so hard," Daniel said.

"Someone has to clean up after you," Jack said.

"Please. I'm as clean and pure as the driven snow."

Jack snorted. "Tell that to your side of the dorm room."

"Surely," Rasputin said, turning his nose up, "this conversation can be continued elsewhere?"

Dracula cleared his throat. "Jack."

Jack hopped back to attention. "Lord Dracula?"

"Daniel needs a partner in his upcoming battle," Dracula said. "I assume you would want the spot?"

Jack blinked. He looked at Daniel, then back. "Well...yeah, I mean, absolutely. If Daniel's okay with it."

Daniel smirked. "Someone has to clean up after me." Jack jabbed his heel into Daniel's foot. Daniel skipped away, wincing. "Ow! The hell, man!"

"You're an asshole sometimes."

"Enough of this," Rasputin said. "Off with the both of you. And get him registered!"

Dracula supported the motion with a dismissing wave. The two boys scampered out of the office. The door shut behind them, but Dracula and Rasputin could still hear the muffled bickering all the way out of the office.

"What do you think now?" Rasputin asked.

"He's a very well-intentioned young man," Dracula said. "Resistant and rightly suspicious of authority, yet respectful, knowing that respect is given to him in turn. Perhaps...a little immature, yet."

Rasputin snorted. "A little?"

"It might be possible to make use of him," Dracula said, turning, "knowing that certain things are in order. But if the last was anything to go by, I doubt that they are."

Rasputin shook his head. "I tried to influence him three separate times. I was careful not to let him notice after he repelled my first attempt, but I didn't make any progress."

"Nothing at all?"

Rasputin shook his head. "I ran through every power sphere I had in my inventory. Even without him actively using magic, his talent is too strong to bend. Contractors seem very resistant to my methods, even the weaker ones. Weeks of work and Jack still gives me trouble."

Dracula leaned back in his chair and nodded to himself. "That's a shame, then. He's rich with potential."

"My lord," Rasputin said, "it isn't that he's strong. He's many times more powerful than Killiney. I'm not sure I've taken his full measure."

"He is frighteningly powerful," Dracula said. "Even Bathory might not compare. The contractor magic is matchless."

Rasputin's eyes shined. "If I was able to get a wedge into his mind, build a platform—"

"His power is exactly the reason he should be set aside," Dracula stated. "We cannot allow greed to destabilize the Order. Not now."

"You can't find talent like that anywhere," Rasputin said. He sounded honestly put-out. "He has a fire in him. Same with the girl that came through earlier. If we could rein him in, he'd prove a powerful tool."

"If he was alone, I might be willing to wait and see if you could make headway," Dracula said, "but his relationship with Jack is creating a major liability. I don't want our progress there to go to waste."

"Even when I pushed, Jack wouldn't go on about it," Rasputin said. "I admit that if we want to keep Killiney, we probably have to give up Fitzgerald. If you really want to play it completely safe."

"It's too sensitive a time to take risks," Dracula said. "Using him to fend off the Sky Runners is already pushing it. Once Daniel is out of the picture, you'll need to finish Jack's conversion to the cause. Time is short."

Rasputin circled the desk. "If you're saying that, you've felt it too, I assume," he said. "The seal of Hell is weakening."

"Of course it is," Dracula said. "The Vorid are eating away at humanity. When the bindings established between Earth and the demon world erode, Hell will fall apart, and the Order can return to Earth. If the Vorid can make contractors stronger, they can do the same for us."

"What about Satan?"

"That's Beelzebub's business," Dracula said. "While he pushes all his resources into keeping that thing trapped, we take advantage of the breach and steal away."

"Is it really impossible to bring Daniel in above-board?" Rasputin said. "It's such a waste."

"It's unpleasant business," Dracula said, "but I've been betrayed by men nobler and more idealistic than Daniel Fitzgerald. He's a loose cannon. If it came down to it, he'd follow whatever moral compunction got into his head, not our orders. We wouldn't be able to control him."

"What about the Wind Crystal he has in his inventory? His points?"

Dracula waved a hand dismissively. "They'll be locked in the treasury after he loses. I've already made sure to include that in the fine print of his registration, in the case of his banishment from the team." Dracula looked up at Rasputin. "Make sure he loses."

Rasputin's long face twisted up in a smile. "Of course. It'll be easy."

Dracula tapped at his desk again. "What of this woman Daniel mentioned. White hair?"

"From his description, it sounded like a magical projection," Rasputin said. "But if that's so, why was he the only one that could see her?"

Dracula narrowed his eyes. "Hell is starting to fray at the edges. Greater powers are beginning to observe the situation. Stay vigilant. It's a matter of time before we leave this God-forsaken hole."

****

Daniel set aside all his money and points into the Order's treasury, alongside the green tornado-making crystal. It was simple enough to have it transfer back to him after the battle. It all happened automatically, right through the armlet's internal magic. It was incredible technology—the ability to teleport physical objects, store them in a weightless, invisible backpack. He wondered how it worked—on its own, or in conjunction with Hell's enchantment? Would it be possible to have something like that back on Earth? Being able to pull inanimate objects from thin air would be a big help in a lot of situations.

After wrapping things up, Jack and Daniel made their way back through the Order's compound toward Jack's apartment, which was located elsewhere on the grounds. Their headquarters was an elegantly-arranged nest of neat courtyards and stone terraces, connected by short stairs or arched paths. The stone was grey-blue, but speckled with black and white, the material a fantasy castle would be built of.

They wound between high buildings and adroitly arranged landscaping. The trimmed hedges and flowerbeds created a serene, peaceful atmosphere. It was an island in the architectural chaos that made up the rest of the city.

Besides them, the paths were deserted. Daniel assumed everyone was shut inside and recuperating from the territory war. Not that he was in a huge hurry to make friends and influence people, but it felt empty—like a college campus during spring break. It lacked the throngs of people it was prepared for, and that gave it an odd, out-of-place stillness.

"What did you think of Dracula?" Jack asked.

"I don't trust him," Daniel said quietly.

Jack threw him a look. "Why not?"

"Cause he eavesdropped."

"I only did that to stop you having to go on about everything all over again," Jack said. "I'm sorry."

"You could have at least told me," Daniel snapped. "It was awkward as hell when he came out with that. I tried to let it go, but honestly, it pissed me off. If he can listen in that easily, how do I know anything I say is private?"

Jack waved his hands, shrinking back at Daniel's tone. "Hey, hey, it doesn't work like that, he can't spy on us whenever he wants."

"Regardless," Daniel said, waving a hand. "What the hell, man."

Jack shifted his mouth about on his face, chewing on his words. "I see what you're saying," he said, "I do. I...it was easier. I dunno, I didn't question it. I'm sorry. He didn't hear anything personal, I shut it off before that, I swear."

Daniel rubbed his eyes a bit, but nodded at Jack to accept what seemed to be an honest apology. It was the latest pressure test on a very fragile friendship, but Daniel didn't have the energy to challenge Jack's explanation. The whole situation sharpened Daniel's suspicion of Dracula, and he was now doubly glad he hadn't mentioned his deal with Beelzebub.

He almost wished he hadn't mentioned the strange ghost-woman to them, either, but that one had Daniel so baffled he was compelled to ask. He held a solid conviction that it wasn't an illusion, or some trick of his mind, but that created more questions than answers.

Daniel shelved the matter, refocusing on his conversation with Jack. "Dracula's goal of getting back to Earth doesn't seem to jive with what you want, exactly," he said.

"I don't really believe there's a way out of Hell," Jack said. "Dracula thinks there might be something to check out upstairs, but if there was, why is Bathory still here?"

Daniel shrugged at him; he had to admit that was an excellent point. "Maybe she'd rather rule the roost down here than be hunted back on Earth."

"If it turns out there is a way back," Jack said, "I'll stick with the Order and keep fighting the good fight up there. Here, or there, the world's changed for good."

Jack stopped in the middle of their current courtyard, which was built around a large tree. The tree was huge, towering over the nearby buildings in a spire of twisting white bark. The leaves were stark purple. The stone path squared off around the tree's trunk, creating a plot that separated it from the surrounding garden. Several paths branched in different directions from the tree, designating it a crossroads for the whole complex.

"What's really bothering you?" Jack asked.

"What makes you think there's something else?" Daniel said.

"I dunno," Jack said. "You sound bothered."

"I'm not bothered."

"You totally are."

"Okay," Daniel said, "fine. There's a whole ton of stuff that's bothering me. A massive heap of stuff. Starting with how I shouldn't have even bothered with my stupid questions about magic." He sighed. "I'm too tired to rant about it all."

"Keep it to what's right in front of us, then."

"The whole point of Dracula's story," Daniel said, "is that he got screwed over by people he trusted, again and again. So what the hell is he doing trusting me right off the bat? I was screwed over and sent down here, and I don't feel like trusting *him*. There's something missing."

"Whoa," Jack said. "Back up here. You're way overthinking it."

Daniel hacked a laugh. "You, telling me, that I'm overthinking it. Hello, pot? This is kettle."

"Put it in perspective. All that stuff happened to him hundreds of years ago." Jack folded his arms and leaned against the tree, tucking his feet in against the roots. "I've been down here for months," he said, "and I'll be the first to admit that Rasputin is a passive-aggressive dickbag and I don't get along with him. But Dracula is the man."

"Dracula." Daniel's voice was flat. "Is the man."

"You heard his story," Jack said. "The guy is a badass. A lifetime of struggle and centuries later and he's still trucking."

"It was all pretty impressive," Daniel said.

"He welcomed me in, gave me a place to stay, helped train me," Jack said. "When I didn't know what was going on, or what was gonna happen to me—I mean, when I got banished, I half expected a lake of fire or something."

"Instead we get the freakshow," Daniel muttered.

"Dracula," Jack said, brushing over the comment, "was the one that helped me. He put me in charge of a squad. He wants me to be somebody. Hell, it makes him happy to see me being somebody. It's like he's really personally invested in me doing well. That's the kind of guy I want to go along with. He's got..." Jack spun a hand, thinking of the words. "Vision. Purpose. He's not like people back home. He means what he says and he follows through. Plus, I like the way he does things. He doesn't get angry, he gets even."

"It's real cute, isn't it?" Daniel said. "Vengeance is mine says the lord. But the guy with the big red cross is all about revenge."

"Well pardon me for not holding Dracula's good Christian upbringing against him," Jack said. "The guy was fighting for his life—for his entire life. Can you blame him for being a little rough around the edges?" Jack gestured to his armlet. "You've got the cross, now, bub. Frills and all. I know structure and discipline is not exactly your thing, but you gotta take it seriously. If Dracula was out to get you, why would he bother taking you in? Why would he even let on that he eavesdropped? If he was out to get you, he would've kept that secret."

Daniel glanced up at the tree. The violet leaves were silent, unmoving. There was no wind in Purgatory—in a cave.

"I don't know," Daniel said eventually.

"Yeah," Jack said. "Good question, huh?"

Daniel raised his armlet. He was registered as a team member of the Order of the Dragon; the white and red colors were proof. A golden tuft at the top of the cross flashed at him as he rotated it on his wrist.

It was a very fancy chain, but he was still a prisoner. They all were.

"I tried trusting people," Daniel said. "That landed me here. Now the local strongman wants me to keep the faith. Fool me twice, Jack, shame on me."

"He's different from them," Jack said. "We have a common enemy in the magical establishment."

"I reserve the right to look for reasons not to trust him," Daniel said. "It all went...too well."

"Too well?" Jack said. "For once something goes well, it turns out the boss isn't a total dick and you've got good prospects. Relax. Stop checking for potholes every 5 feet."

"I'm riding on two spare tires here, man."

Jack sighed, then picked himself up off the tree. "Dan."

"Yeah?"

"Do you trust me?"

Daniel frowned at him. "What do you mean?"

"We're gonna fight a battle together," Jack said. "And you just got finished telling me about how everyone's got an agenda and you can't trust them. So, do you trust me?"

Daniel paused. "Yeah," he said. "I do. I really do trust you."

"Even after lecturing me about how my head's on backwards?" Jack said.

Daniel looked at him carefully. Jack studied him in return, waiting for his response.

Maybe he'd been too harsh earlier. Too quick to judge. Jack was still the same guy he ever was—maybe given opportunities he'd never had before. It made sense he'd react in a way he never had before. At the core of the person in front of him was something good, and honest, that sought out honesty and goodness in return. The realization reminded Daniel of something important, something a part of him was afraid had disappeared.

"If I can't trust my best friend," Daniel said, "then who can I trust?"

Jack held his gaze for a moment, then dropped it. Daniel waited for him to respond, but he kept his face turned. Jack started walking without looking back and gestured for him to follow. "Come on. We better...we should get ready."

Daniel caught up and put a hand on his shoulder. "Hey man. You alright?"

Jack wiped a hand across his face and sniffed. "I'm fine." He pushed Daniel's hand away.

"What's wrong?" Daniel said.

Jack's cheeks were wet. He wiped across his eyes again. "It's real lonely down here, sometimes. I'm glad you're here, okay? Don't make it weird."

"I'm glad to see you too, Jack," Daniel said. "Really."

Jack sucked in a breath through his nose and plodded forward. "Alright. I'm good."

Daniel followed behind, feeling better—better than he had since New York.

Daniel thought about bringing up Beelzebub and Bathory, but he decided to keep that card close to his chest because it was the one thing he held over the Order of the Dragon. He did trust Jack, but characters like Dracula and Rasputin couldn't be let in so easily. If he told his friend, it might make it back to them, under the excuse of *friendly* eavesdropping. He didn't want that happening again.

Jack had waved Daniel's concerns off, but the worry stuck in his mind. Rasputin had tried to mind meld him earlier—and Jack waved that off, too, because it didn't affect him. But how many people had it affected? Did he have to worry about mind control magic on top of everything else? On the other hand, Jack had been down here months, and—personal philosophy aside—seemed alright. Jack wouldn't stay with them if their methods strayed into that kind of territory; Daniel had at least that much faith in his friend's moral compass.

Daniel firmly categorized the Order of the Dragon as the enemy of his enemy. He wanted a go at Bathory, and Dracula had a grudge against her; they could work together on that front. But their shared interests stopped there. He'd use them for that, then move on, hopefully keeping relations positive afterward. Dracula didn't seem bad…but the guy was a brutal warlord, no matter how much he papered it over with righteous justifications. Daniel couldn't be sure of what he was capable. Would he be as friendly if he screwed up fighting Bathory? *Doubt it.*

Daniel felt compelled to send out a feeler concerning Rachel, and he got burned. He'd prepared himself for a no, but that didn't make it any easier to hear. Still, he was glad he asked. If nothing else, he got some good perspective on how his magic worked—what was he was doing and what was happening. Hopefully he'd have more chances to pick their brains. Maybe even pick up a few more magic pointers, see if there were other spells he was able to learn. The one sigil Rachel was able to teach him marked a sea change in his combat ability. Another spell like that could be just around the corner.

Rachel floated through his thoughts—but this time, it wasn't so lingering. Not quite so painful. And he thought of his mother, his college dormmates—Eleanor, for some reason—his dad. His brother, Felix.

When Felix came to mind, Daniel suddenly realized his old plan was still in place. He'd filmed himself back in New York on his cellphone. He'd planned on keeping the footage private if the Ivory Dawn asked him to, but it was out of his hands, now. He couldn't exactly send text messages from Hell.

Daniel smiled to himself. Guess they'd have to deal with it. At least they'd be forced to pay attention to Felix. That ought to keep his brother safe.

Chapter 10
Go Browns

Eleanor bent at the waist and held her arms around herself, staring down at the grass at her feet. The world spun around her. Her stomach was spinning the opposite way.

The nausea of long-distance teleportation slowly started to fade. After checking her breathing a few times, she held herself straight. *A little* dizzy, *Xikanthus*?

She was on top of a small hill; sprawled below her was a massive mundane relocation facility. It looked like a concert campground, a trailer park, and a military dugout all mashed together and multiplied several times over. The vast majority of the tents were uniform green-brown, standard issue, but they were frequently interrupted by large octagonal family tents or neon triangles. Further back, near a tree line, were camping vehicles. The left side of the camp was dominated by a row of military trucks and a swath of camouflage netting. Several portable buildings had already been set up, complete with a central nest of antenna and electronics. Between the portables and the main campsite were massive tanks labeled *POTABLE*. It all stretched nearly as far as she could see, out to the trees near behind trailers and then sweeping along the border of the woods.

The sky above the camp was bright, sunny, and dominated by the presence of an Ivory Dawn airship. The core of the huge warcraft was mostly made of wood, the original hull being a ship of the line. It still carried the enchantments that were originally placed on it, modified and reinforced over time. The only visible portion of that old hull were the three masts that stuck out slightly above thick layers of steel plating—also enchanted—creating an aesthetic that was more like a modern naval destroyer than an eighteenth century vessel. Despite the similar appearance, the most important difference between a mundane ship and an airship was that the wooden core of an airship was still alive, and still growing. As it grew, it became more powerful.

Most airships were like that, amalgamations of magic and sequential modification, a living core serving as their foundation. They were impossible to dismantle entirely—that would kill the ship—so instead, new innovations were tacked on over time. This led to a bulky but modular design that represented cutting-edge efforts to merge technology and magic. Often the tree-core would grow into its new modifications, enhancing them in ways that were greater than the sum of its parts.

Increasing size offered diminishing returns when you wanted something to float, but Eleanor knew from experience that it was still roughly half the size of an aircraft carrier. The hull was large enough that the name, printed in bold on the armor plating, could be read from the ground: *IVD Higher Power 059*. The ship drifted in a slow circle high above the camp, patrolling in plain sight—probably for the sake of reassuring the mundanes, because it was easily capable of going invisible.

Apparently they were starting to roll out the big guns. Her father had avoided using them in New York, mostly for political reasons. They didn't want to intimidate their newfound allies in the mundane military, instead working with them to enchant their weaponry. It was doubly advantageous because fighter jets and helicopters were far more expendable guinea pigs to bait out a Vorid response before risking the airships, many of which were the product of hundreds of years of effort and evolution. They were also extremely wary of the huge Vorid fortress, which might have been designed to counter exactly that type of heavy weaponry.

The deciding factor was that Rothschild had refused to pledge any of his own airships in New York. And if the True

Flame wasn't going to have serious skin in the game, the Ivory Dawn's council didn't want to commit too much either. Airships were major magical power pieces; their living component made each one unique and unreplaceable.

The Mantriks, Magi, and Wu had airships that were said to be grown from a sprig of the original sacred fig tree under which Buddha obtained enlightenment. The Japanese supposedly had a Sugi that was over 10,000 years old. The core of the Ivory Dawn's fleet were old oak trees stemming from the 17th and 18th centuries. More numerous and modern ships had been built, making up for the lack of time spent growing with sheer numbers during World War II. Eleanor had read a few research reports involving grafts of ancient bristlecone pine from California into some of the newer Ivory Dawn ships, but whether those studies bore fruit was outside even her clearance level.

In any case, the mages had been winning the battle at large following their first attack, steadily pushing the Vorid back into the center of the city with Daniel's assistance. The Vorid lord warranted more force, but it would have been awkward to attack a single individual using a hulking battleship without catastrophic collateral damage, not only to the city but their own forces.

By the time Eleanor looked back at the camp, a group of five or so uniformed men were already making their way toward her. She had the idea of trying to find the Fitzgeralds without making contact with the local unit, but the scale of the place was so massive that it would take a week to find anyone without outside knowledge. There had to be at least several hundred thousand people down there.

The other problem was that this little excursion of hers was time-sensitive. As soon as her father and the others got out from Xik's barrier in her room, or maybe even sooner, they'd contact Cleveland to see if she'd arrived. Then she'd be taken into custody and shipped right back to New York. She had to get this done quickly.

And so, Eleanor marched straight toward the oncoming patrol.

"Identify yourself!" came a shout. They didn't point their guns at her, but they were holding them.

Thank god I have my wallet. Eleanor unclasped her personal sigil and flipped it open, displaying a gold sun on a blue background. "Eleanor Astor, Ivory Dawn. Is there a magician present?"

The men shuffled around a bit until a mage made her way to the front. Her skin was a deep brown color, and she had black hair and brown eyes. She was small compared to the geared-up infantry surrounding her. She wore an Ivory Dawn tabard—royal blue with gold trim, stamped with the gold sun in the center—tucked into green camouflage pants.

"*The* Eleanor Astor?" The woman—probably in her mid-twenties—peered at Eleanor's ID. To a mundane, it was just a badge, but a trained magician would be able to verify how real the magical seal there was with just a quick brush of their senses. She straightened, then thumped a fist on her chest. "I'm sorry we didn't receive you properly. I'm Tamara Hurley. Third branch family of the Lowells."

Eleanor flicked her badge back in place. "Of course, the Hurleys. Pleased to make your acquaintance." Eleanor nodded her head politely. She wasn't familiar with Tamara, personally, but she had memorized every branch family of the Ivory Dawn when she was 6 years old. The Hurleys stemmed from the Lowells, who originally developed as the head of a Massachusetts textile empire. The Hurley family had since moved to east-central United States, mostly Ohio and Michigan, where they had a controlling stake in heavy industry. "My transport here was short notice. I'm sorry I took you by surprise, normally we'd communicate ahead of time."

She offered a light chuckle. "And I wouldn't be arriving alone on a hill."

"Not at all," Tamara said. "We're happy to have you, Miss Astor. It's an honor." She was obviously in a hurry to not cause any offense. Eleanor thought it was rather cute. "You came alone?"

"I did," Eleanor said. "Teleported direct from New York."

"In one jump?"

Eleanor quickly formulated an excuse to explain Xik teleporting her hundreds of miles with a single spell. "It was a prepared formation."

Tamara whistled. "Must have been costly." She gestured down the hill, toward the military encampment. "Please, let me take you inside. We'll get you settled. What's the emergency?"

They started walking; the patrol fell into step behind them without much ado. Clearly they were getting used to mages popping in and out. "I'm looking for the family of the contractor that fought in New York, Daniel Fitzgerald. I understand they're at this encampment."

Tamara nodded. "I'm aware of their status. Headquarters called in when we confirmed Fitzgerald's identity after his capture."

"Are they alright?"

"Perfectly fine," Tamara said. "I was ordered to place additional personnel near their tent last night. I moved one of the mid-camp troop posts near their position so a mage would be within scrying range at all times. I've kept them unaware of the surveillance so far, in case someone tries to make contact with them."

"Excellent," Eleanor said. "I'll keep your name in mind, Tamara. We need competent people more than ever right now."

Tamara smiled and nodded. "Thank you, ma'am." She paused. "If I can ask, what do you need to see them for?"

"A chat," Eleanor said. "We're worried about them being targeted in the event of another attack and considering moving them to the manor."

"Understood," Tamara said. "Let me see off the patrol and I'll lead you to them myself."

"Very well."

Eleanor picked a spot to wait near the trucks, arms folded under her chest as she watched the activity. A group of men were working on putting up another antennae tower near a portable shed. A supply convoy was ferried in and waved into parking opposite her—another fresh tank of water, along with box after box of MREs—Meals, Ready to Eat. One of the smaller trucks was refrigerated; it continued on to another of the sheds. Soldiers offloaded the cargo right into the building—medical supplies that had to be kept cold. A helicopter buzzed low overhead, pulling Eleanor's attention up to the sky. It came to a stop at the edge of the camp before dropping down for a landing.

Tamara was back in under a minute. "Right this way, ma'am."

Eleanor considered telling her to not be so formal; it wouldn't be bad to have a personal contact in the Hurley family. Unfortunately, wartime was not moment to start blurring lines of authority. Eleanor had her station; Tamara had her own.

Plus, the clock was ticking. There would be time to schmooze with Tamara after Eleanor collected Daniel's family.

They made their way down a large dirt road that split the mundane campsite roughly into two halves. The road was solid, tamped down by army engineers and complete with gravel drainage pits on either side. They'd help keep the path dry if it rained. "We're planning for the long haul," Eleanor stated.

"You'd better believe it, ma'am," Tamara said. "They're going to start installing secondary fencing around the camp today. We estimate another 200,000 or so refugees will be filtering into this location over the next 2 weeks."

"How many are here so far?"

"About five hundred thousand," Tamara said. "Site B has closer to a million. Cleveland was split into 3 camps. Ohio has 19 total."

"No one essential, I assume."

Tamara grunted in the affirmative. "Anyone with a non-agrarian, non-manufacturing job is holed up here."

"What about doctors, nurses?" Eleanor asked.

"They're in the camps and at protected work sites, farms, factories, distributed as needed. Everyone's an employee of the state, now. Congress passed the bill yesterday."

"Everything going smoothly?" Eleanor asked. "Complaints?"

"We've broken up a few fights, but nothing serious," Tamara said. "You crush everyone together in tents for days on end and there's going to be some cabin fever. Most are responding pretty well, especially after we installed a few short-range cell towers. A lot of the tension came off once they could get on the internet and contact friends and family, see that everyone was safe. There's longer lines at the charging stations for tablets and cell phones than there are for water."

Eleanor could only chuckle. "I guess I don't blame them. Information is at a premium."

"We're hoping to repurpose volunteers into useful labor," Tamara said. "Give them something to do, make them feel like they're contributing, and also adding to our capability to produce enchanted armor, weapons, ammunition that can hurt the Vorid. They don't need magic to etch a rune pattern, just a good set of stencils."

"I'm surprised you're expecting so many more," Eleanor said. "700,000 total? Just at this camp?"

"A lot don't want to leave their homes at first," Tamara said. "Tons of conspiracy theories about why they're gathering everyone up, a lot of plain old natural resistance to up and abandoning their lives. Honestly, I'm surprised it's not worse. We've got two dozen temporary holding cells but only half of them occupied. You show someone a picture of that black ship sitting over New York and they come around pretty quick."

Eleanor couldn't help a sense of grim pessimism when she was reminded of the ruined state of New York City. The black columns that produced the extractors were still standing in the many metropolitan areas where they'd touched down. The strange Vorid obelisks were surrounded with mundane defenses, and magicians were working on them with magic, but they hadn't been able to do much other than scratch them up slightly. The structure of the things didn't even make sense—they were too skinny, too tall, and had no foundation. At that height, strong enough winds should cause them to topple, but they defied normal physics in ways that weren't currently understood.

It was possible to replicate similar phenomena with magic, but they couldn't find any magic holding them up. The working theory was that it had something to do with their ability to travel from another dimension—or, that they were only looking at part of the object, and the rest was anchored somewhere else, tied through the walls that sat between the worlds.

The ship was another anomaly. The floating fortress above New York City hadn't moved, even following the death of the Vorid lord. It sat there, suspended in the sky like a black glacier. Was it the empty shell of a defeated foe, or a beachhead established for the next attack?

Attempts to enter the interior were fruitless. It was made of the same black metal as the columns, invulnerable to any attack they could muster. They hadn't used every card up their sleeves, especially concerning larger magical formations, and the mundanes hadn't used the serious ordinance yet. The problem with turning up the heat was, again, collateral damage to the city. Granted, it was already seriously damaged by the battle, but there was no need to take a nuke to the thing before it became absolutely necessary. Manhattan would be irradiated for a thousand years. Rather, it would have been. Magic could clean up the worst of it, assuming—

"Miss magician! Missus magician!" A woman skipped across the drainage ditch and came up to them, beelining for Tamara. Her blue-gold tabard was only worn by members of the Ivory Dawn, so there was no mystery as to who she was. "Please, can you help me? My son cut his leg, I'm worried about how much it's bleeding!"

Tamara looked to Eleanor, and Eleanor nodded. Never miss a chance for good PR. It was only a small detour, and she was curious for perspective from someone down on the ground; the benefits made up for the delay. She might be fighting with her father, but his lessons were still drilled into her head.

"I can take a look," Tamara said. They followed the woman a few yards into the camp, back to her tent. Her son was huddled inside; he had the gangly, slightly awkward proportions of a boy starting to hit puberty full stride. His leg was propped up on a small box. Gauze wrapped repeatedly around his shin was stained red-brown with blood.

Tamara kneeled next to him. "This looks pretty serious. What happened?"

The boy's eyes lit up like flashlights and darted between Eleanor and Tamara. His body language was tense, nervous—maybe a little starstruck. His mother, more concerned with his health than the niceties of conversation, broke the silence. "He was playing with some of our neighbors and cut his leg on a piece of trash. Metal. It was deep."

"Did you ask for a doctor?"

"Two days ago," his mother said. "They told me he'd be here yesterday, and again today, but it's been hours past the time he was supposed to come. I know they've got a lot on their plate, but I'm worried it's infected."

"Let's get the bandage off first," Tamara said. She unraveled the gauze, peeling it off and placing it aside. The boy winced as she tugged the last bit free. The wound didn't quite look infected, but it was a mess of scabs and still moist. "Lord," Tamara said. "What the hell did you cut yourself on?"

"U-um...fence," the boy mumbled. "Near the trucks."

"You were trying to climb the fence surrounding the military convoy?" Tamara said.

"Alex!" his mother said. "That is not what you told me!"

"Sorry." Alex looked away. His face was beat red.

Tamara sighed, then set her hands over his wound. "Anah Allo'nah Atakai." A spring-green sigil flashed under her fingers; the glow lit the tent. Tamara repeated the chant as she guided her hands up the cut, using the words to guide the intent of her power.

After moving her sigil up and down the wound, Tamara let the magic fade. The wet was gone, and the cut was sealed; a faint pink scar line was the only remaining sign of the injury. Eleanor was impressed. The worse a healer, the messier the results. There was more than one magician with a nasty scar from a botched healing. Tamara obviously had plenty of practice; she didn't even look fazed by the effort.

"You'll need to wash that off, but the skin and the cut are fine," Tamara said. She looked up at Alex. "Don't mess around near the where the troops are working. We've got a lot to do and we don't need more problems, so don't make any. I'll forget about it this time, but I don't want to hear more bad news from this tent. Understood?"

Alex jerked his head up and down rapidly. His mother was bordering on teary-eyed. "Thank you, thank you so much! I'm so glad we have you all. Thank you."

"All part of the job, ma'am," she said. She joined Eleanor outside the tent. "Stay out of trouble."

Alex kept nodding. "Um, can—can I ask a question?"

"Sure," Tamara said, leaning back under the tent flap.

"I was watching some of the videos Daniel posted online," he said. "Is he okay with the government and everything? People are really worried because he said the magicians didn't like him."

Eleanor and Tamara froze.

"What?" Eleanor said. She pushed into the tent alongside Tamara. "What did you say?"

Alex frowned, confused. "You know, uh...Daniel Fitzgerald. He helped fight in New York."

"Online videos." Eleanor had a horrifying flashback to when Daniel nearly blackmailed her with his cell phone. Even though they'd moved past it, the thought still raised her hackles. "Show me."

"Uh...s-sure," Alex said. His stammering increased as Eleanor dropped to a knee next to him, face reddening. He rummaged through a backpack and pulled out a tablet. "It came up on YouTube, um...like, uh, night before last."

"Is everything alright?" the mother asked.

"It's fine," Tamara said quickly, "but we'd like to see the video."

"Oh. Alex, go ahead with your computer screen."

Alex unlocked the tablet and rolled his eyes in the way only a son could. "Mom. It's a *tablet*."

"Sure, honey." She turned and half-whispered to Eleanor. "I honestly have no idea how he learned to use that thing."

Eleanor and Tamara hunched over the screen as Alex pulled up YouTube. A brief buffering circle later, a video came up showing Daniel Fitzgerald backing away from the camera. The view was limited to a red couch set against an exposed brick wall. There were several photographs on the wall above the couch—family photos of the apartment's former occupants. "This is the first video," Alex said.

Daniel slumped down onto the couch. He sighed to himself, then looked up at the camera. "Okay," he said. "I wasn't sure if I wanted to bother with this, but I think it's important. I don't know what the magicians and the government are planning, but you should know what's going on—what's really going on.

"Basically, what Henry Astor said about the Vorid in his speech on TV is true. They're coming for us. They want our souls. They want to capture and harvest every human being on the planet. But..." Daniel scratched his temple, as if deciding where to go from there. "...it's not just Earth. The Vorid are from another dimension, another universe. They're a huge collective, and they're attacking other universes, too. Their goal is to absorb everything. It's a religious thing with them. They believe that for the multiverse to be reborn, all the energy, all the souls, have to be gathered back to a single point. This is the justification for their war." Daniel sighed. "I'm not sure if I'm explaining that right, but it's the best I can do. I don't really understand it entirely myself. But they think if they do nothing, then all the universes will slowly run out of energy anyway, until everything is dead, and there is no second chance."

Eleanor felt like her eyes were about to roll out of her skull. Too much was packed into her head—the mixed bitter-sweet happiness of seeing him again, the shock at what he was saying, and the gumption he had to post it straight onto YouTube.

"Too bad for them, the aliens ran into Earth's magicians, who are fighting back. And, another race, the Klide. The Klide are fighting against the Vorid across the multiverse. They think they can find another way to save all the universes that doesn't involve killing basically everything. So, they're on our side.

"The Klide offered to help our magicians, but we turned them down," Daniel said. "It's a little complicated and political, so here goes."

Daniel went on to explain everything, delving right into that most taboo of subjects—the vampiric spell, the history he knew of the magic world. Rachel must have told him more than a few things—there was no other way he could have known. After establishing the basics, he started on the contractors, explaining their position as fugitive vigilantes from the established magical community that were forced to fight the Vorid from the shadows.

"My hope is," Daniel said, "that by helping them in New York, I can show them that I mean well and that I'm not trying to rock the boat, I guess. I don't know if it will work, but I don't have much choice."

A rumble sounded over the camera. The building shook. Daniel flashed up from the couch—one instant sitting, the next, standing, his head cocked to the side. A hazy white light drifted around him, the discharge of excess energy from his power. "Okay," he said, "the rest will have to wait until episode 2, things are getting a little hairy. Oh yeah." Daniel looked at the camera and pumped a fist. "Go Browns!"

The video ended there, about 10 minutes in length. But it was a hell of a 10 minutes. Eleanor and Tamara shared a long look.

"Do you guys want to see the others?" Alex asked.

"Others?" Eleanor said.

"Yeah. He posted more."

"How many videos are there, exactly?" Eleanor asked, trying to keep the strain out of her voice.

"Three," Alex said. "There's one being uploaded every day. They keep getting deleted, but people are mirroring them so much I think they gave up and let them sit there."

"Mirroring?" Eleanor asked.

"They download the video and put it back up on YouTube themselves, or somewhere else on the internet," Alex said. He was more confident talking about a subject in which he was well-versed. "So say there's copyright infringement or something else that gets a video taken down. If people download it before that happens, then post it somewhere else, it has to be found again before it can be deleted. If a thousand people do it, it's almost impossible to delete all the copies. They stopped trying to delete them yesterday. The one I showed you has 300 million views, but it would have over a billion now if you counted from before it was deleted. People are translating all his stuff into different languages too."

"Wait, wait," Eleanor said. "You said there are more being uploaded?"

"Yeah," Alex said, as if it was a simple matter-of-fact. "His main account got banned but then a different account started posting them anyway. Everyone's waiting on the fourth video to come up today."

Eleanor shook her head. "But he can't be putting up the videos himself."

Alex's eyes widened. "Is it true then?"

"Is what true?"

"Mages don't like contractors? Is the magic they're using actually evil?" Alex seemed thoughtful. "Daniel seems like a good guy, but nobody really knows what to think. But if he was all that bad, why would he bother with this in the first place? Well, some people think he might be trying to make himself look good…" Alex trailed off, looking to her.

Eleanor's lips squirmed uncomfortably. She was too busy processing the implications to come up with a clever answer. Daniel couldn't be uploading internet videos *from Hell*. It was physically impossible. They'd confiscated and subsequently destroyed his cell phone to boot.

Tamara broke the awkward silence. "That's his point of view, but it's a little more complicated than what he mentioned," she said.

"Then why were they trying to delete his videos at first?" Alex said. He looked at Eleanor. "There's a rumor he's locked up somewhere and the videos are pre-scheduled releases."

"Alex," his mother said, "you're being rude!"

"It's fine. It's a good question." Eleanor took a breath and composed herself. "I'm sorry, but we can't go into it. The rumors aren't true. Official news will come from the military and the Ivory Dawn." Eleanor stood. "Tamara, let's go."

They left the tent before Alex could pester them with another round of questions. Thankfully, Alex's mother held him back from trying to follow them to the main path. Eleanor doubled her previous pace, anxious to get to her destination. Xik's spell wouldn't last forever, and she needed to see the Fitzgeralds before that.

Tamara gave Eleanor a respectful silence until they were a little bit along. "Miss Astor...are we doing anything about this?"

"Alex said Daniel's YouTube account was banned, but then another account got made and kept posting videos."

"That's right."

Eleanor looked at her. "The videos aren't being released on an automated schedule. That would have been stopped by banning his account. The Ivory Dawn would ban the second account too, but they haven't. That means the person knew to hide themselves and how to upload the videos. Or, they were told how to do it."

"So Fitzgerald set all this up beforehand?" Tamara said. "How did he know he'd be banished to Hell?"

"He didn't," Eleanor said quietly. "He made himself an insurance policy, just in case."

Tamara spat to the side of the road. "Clever little bastard."

If only you knew, Eleanor thought. "I have a feeling I know who's posting the videos."

Tamara's face firmed in understanding. "His family."

"They're the only other people he'd trust to do it," Eleanor said.

Tamara took the lead in walking. "I'll take you straight to them. We'll confiscate their electronics—if nothing else goes up on YouTube, that'll be the proof."

"I want to try to do this delicately," Eleanor said. "I'll talk to them first, and we'll decide how to proceed from there."

"Yes ma'am."

After a few minutes of walking, Tamara and Eleanor checked in at the military post near the Fitzgeralds' tent. There was a mage—one rank under Tamara—who practically beat his chest to a bruise saluting Eleanor. Tamara spoke briefly with the squad leader who arranged for a small detachment of 3 soldiers to follow them. It made for a bit more of a spectacle as they marched off the path and into the tents, but the time for subtlety had ended. People got oddly quiet when they saw Tamara's tabard, watching them pass before continuing their conversations in hushed voices.

The Fitzgeralds' tent—little more than a big grey pyramid—was near the edge of the forest. A fence had been put up to prevent bored camp dwellers from getting themselves lost in the trees. As they approached, the soldiers fanned out, presenting themselves as a barrier for anyone that might intrude on the conversation. As Tamara and Eleanor neared the tent's entrance flap, it opened.

James Fitzgerald—Daniel's father—paused halfway out of the tent, one hand keeping the flap over his head. He gave them a once-over, glanced at the soldiers, then drew himself up and out the rest of the way. He had thinning, light brown hair and a sallow look to his face, like someone finally getting over a long illness. His thick glasses completed a look that, generously, would be described as intellectual.

James cleared his throat. He looked more resigned at their presence than anything else. Clearly he'd expected a visit at some point. "Is this about...we haven't been able to get in touch with Daniel. Is he alright?"

Eleanor closed to a more comfortable speaking distance. Tamara kept at her shoulder. "That's a complicated question," Eleanor said. "Can you tell me what you know about him being a contractor?"

"I didn't know," James said. "He never told me, or Felix. We only found out the other day, along with everyone else. Did he get hurt? Is he safe?"

"He's in one piece," Eleanor said. *Not exactly safe, but alive.* "I won't forget what he did for us in New York."

"Please, you have to tell me what happened," James said. "I don't blame him for not telling me. Things have been difficult for us. Both of us." His words started to come faster. "I need to see him, tell him a few things, especially if he's going to be risking his life like this—I mean, it's crazy. I can't believe half of it. I don't even know what I'm supposed to believe, but hasn't answered any of my calls and—"

"I can explain everything," Eleanor said, raising her hands slightly, "but I need to talk to you about the videos. We know you're posting them."

James's eyes widened, but then, his expression settled. He fixed his glasses on his face. "I guess...it makes sense that I'd be the prime suspect. Daniel was going on about what seemed to be sensitive information."

"So you admit it?" Tamara said.

"No," James said. "I didn't post them. Like I said, Daniel didn't tell me anything—I only found out after the fact."

"That's a little bit of a stretch, given the circumstances," Tamara said.

"We're not here to cast any blame," Eleanor said, giving Tamara a quick look. "We want to stop more information from leaking. What's out there is already out there. The timing of some of that could have been better, and Daniel isn't exactly the most politically correct messenger..."

James snorted. "That's putting it lightly. Just like his mother, that way."

Eleanor smiled. When it came right down to it, she didn't know much about his family. It was nice to hear about him from another angle. "I see. I hope you can understand why it needs to stop."

"I do," James said. "But again, honestly, I'm not responsible."

Tamara was incredulous. "Who could it possibly be if it wasn't you?"

James shrugged. "I have no idea. One of his college friends? He mentioned a Jack a few times, his roommate."

Tamara snorted. "Not likely, buddy. Try again."

James paused at her tone. There was a certain tension in the air, now, and Eleanor wasn't sure how to diffuse it. One of the soldiers stepped closer, closing a gap between himself and the edge of the tent. James suddenly seemed to realize he was surrounded by armed military personnel.

"Look," James said, his eyes going between Tamara, the soldiers, and Eleanor, "I'm happy to cooperate. I'm sure you—mages?—have a way to tell if I'm being honest. I have nothing to hide."

"I think you have a lot to hide," Tamara said. "This all stinks, and the smell is coming from this tent."

"Let's not make unfounded accusations," Eleanor said.

"Unfounded?" Tamara raised her eyebrows. "He's the guy's dad. You said it yourself—he'd only trust his family for something this important."

"Stepfather, to be clear," James said. "I honestly did not post the videos, and I don't know who did."

"I don't believe you," Tamara said firmly.

James shrugged helplessly. "I can't force you to believe me. It's the truth."

"I did it," came a small voice. Felix Fitzgerald—a young boy barely topping 3 feet—emerged from the tent. His hair was somewhere between blonde and brown, a much lighter shade than Daniel or his father. He clutched a tablet in his hands. "It wasn't dad. I put the videos up."

James turned on his son. "Felix," he said, "you're the one doing the videos? You didn't tell me?!"

There were only two pleading words in response. "Daniel said."

James removed his glasses and wiped his forehead with a hand. "What a mess." He looked at Tamara and Eleanor. "Please, he's just a boy. He doesn't understand."

Eleanor stepped forward and crouched to meet Felix at eye level. "Hello Felix. I'm Eleanor. I met Daniel at college."

Felix looked up at that. "Really?"

Eleanor nodded. "I'm...I'm Rachel's sister."

"Oh," Felix said. "I met her when Daniel called one time, and she was on his laptop camera, so I saw her. She was nice. Um...nice to meet you."

Eleanor had to fight back a surge of emotion at hearing even that simple description of Rachel. "Yeah," she croaked. "Nice to meet you, too."

James was much faster to realize the implications. "You were both...magicians. Both of you."

"Yes," Eleanor said, regaining herself. "I'm Eleanor Astor, the daughter of the president of the Ivory Dawn, Henry Astor."

James put a hand on his forehead. "Then Rachel and…Daniel. God."

Eleanor took a long breath, sighed, and nodded. "Exactly. Things are complicated." She looked back to Felix. "Felix, did Daniel tell you how to upload his videos?"

"Yeah," Felix said. "I followed the instructions he sent me. He said to do it unless he told me not to, and that it was really important, and that I had to do it to help him fight the Vorid." Felix looked down. "I couldn't log into Youtube a few days ago, but one of his other friends helped me with some stuff so that they kept going. I just send them to him every day."

Eleanor had to admit that Felix's brotherly loyalty plucked a bit at her heartstrings. She put out a hand. "I need to stop the way the videos are going up. It's important."

Felix held the tablet closer to his chest and shook his head. "But this is really important! Xik told me so too!"

Xik? Eleanor felt herself frown. Why the in the world was the frog paying visits to a little boy?

"Felix," James said, "Eleanor is a very important lady. You need to do as she says."

Felix shook his head again. "I don't want to."

Eleanor considered lying. She could say she was going to bring it back to Daniel. Maybe cook up something about the magicians needing to see the videos sooner, in case there was important information. In the end, she couldn't bring herself to do it. "Felix, I promise, that if none of the information is critical, I'll keep uploading the videos. But I need to take a look at them first. I'm friends with Daniel. I wouldn't do anything that would put him in danger, or that he really wouldn't think was right. Please."

Felix hesitated, but his grip on the tablet slackened. "I want Dan to be okay. That's why I wanted to help him. Is he okay now? Is he going to come here?"

Eleanor was struggling to hold her emotion in check. She'd had one too many shocks today, and she could feel herself fraying at the edges. She drew in a shaky but steadying breath. "Daniel won't be fighting out in the open for a little while, but he's really busy. I'm going to do my best so you can see him. Okay?"

Felix nodded, then lifted the tablet. Eleanor gingerly took it from his hands, as if afraid he'd bolt with it, then handed it off to Tamara, who tucked it into her satchel. "This is my friend Tamara. She's a magician too. She'll help keep the tablet safe in her magic bag."

Tamara couldn't help a smile. She patted her bag. "See? Nice and secure. You can't make a safer bag then the one a magician has."

Felix's eyes were like dinner plates. "Wow. Can I have one?"

Tamara's smile turned into more of a smirk, and she gave the forever-fallback answer of adults to children. "We'll see."

"We can talk about a magic bag after we talk about how you lied to me," James said.

"But Daniel said—"

"I don't care what Daniel said, I'm your father. This isn't a game, Felix. You can't keep things like that to yourself in the future." Felix kept his defiant expression, but he knew better than to keep protesting.

Eleanor cleared her throat. "Mr. Fitzgerald, I want to take you and Felix back home with me. I promised Daniel that I'd ensure your safety. There isn't any place on the planet safer than our headquarters."

"That's very kind of you," James said, "but are you sure that's really..." He stopped, then reworded himself. "I absolutely appreciate the gesture, but we're close to home here. As close as we can get, anyway."

"Under ordinary circumstances, I'd assign you a security detail and consider it under control," Eleanor said, "but these are anything but. You've seen the videos. Daniel really is what he claims to be. We really are fighting this war for our survival."

James sighed and put hand on Felix's shoulder. "Then maybe it's for the best."

"I'm worried you'll be targeted by the Vorid," Eleanor said. "They haven't taken much interest in us as individuals, but that could change quickly. We won the last battle, but we don't know how the next one will be fought."

"I guess I can't really argue with more safety at a time like this. You'd know better than I would, anyway." He peered at her from behind his glasses. "Where is Daniel now, exactly? Will we meet him there? That young man has got a lot more explaining to do than Felix."

Eleanor had to bite back the smirk she felt at the way James said it. Here Daniel was, a powerful contractor fighting for the human race, but come heaven or earth his father was going to have the last word about it. She was looking forward to the argument, if only to see Daniel on the back foot for once—if it ever came to pass. Hopefully, maybe, it would. Eleanor found herself searching for a response to James's question that didn't involve blurting out that his son was locked in Hell.

The ground rumbled under their feet. Eleanor met Tamara's eyes as they felt a wave of magic wash over them, the residue from a distant but powerful spell.

A series of pops snapped in the distance. From so far away, it almost sounded like firecrackers. At least, that's how Eleanor would have described it, before she heard it a thousand times echoing through the streets of New York.

"Gunfire," Tamara said.

And then they heard the screams.

Chapter 11
Smith and Wesson

Eleanor and Tamara broke into a run. The soldiers were right behind them, unslinging their rifles as they went.

"Stay here!" Eleanor shouted over her shoulder. She didn't check to see if the Fitzgeralds followed her instructions, but she hoped James had enough sense to keep himself and Felix in their tent.

The shouts grew louder as they sprinted through the campground. A swarm of people was on them in moments, all running the opposite way. Eleanor fought to push past the wave of civilians until Tamara sent the soldiers forward. They recognized the military fatigues a lot better than her casual clothing, and most went around the long way.

Another wave of magic pulsed in Eleanor's senses. A small gout of what looked like black fire flashed in the sky. A clap of thunder struck her ears. The crowd screamed at the sound. Everyone confused or hesitating at their tents took the hint and joined the retreating panic.

"Out of the way!" Tamara shouted, having taken point in front of the soldiers. She raised a hand, gesturing a few times to channel her mana. The simple spell created an alternating flash of blue and red light in her palm, a rough mimic of police lights. "Clear the way! We need to get through!"

The closer they got, the thicker the shoving match with the crowds became. "We don't have time for this!" Eleanor said. She pushed between the soldiers and stepped up past Tamara while drawing up her power. She thrust her arms forward, then parted them, relying on instinct to guide the force rather than a constructed sigil.

Without strict form, the spell was rough, all power and no finesse. A freezing blast of wind forcibly parted the crowd, sending people tumbling to the left and the right. Eleanor led the charge up the center of a cleared path between the tents. She didn't like using magic that way, but she had a feeling they'd trade a sprained ankle for their lives.

A flicker of black fire passed them on the left, and in its wake was...nothing. Nothing remained, not even ashes. There was no heat. Everything the fire touched was wiped away, like someone took an eraser to the world and rubbed it out of existence. Tents, the grass, and the ground—and a person. Eleanor tore her eyes away as what remained of the body collapsed behind a tent.

Eleanor had only seen that kind of magic from one source. *Vorid.*

A split second later, the air *whumped* together to fill the space left behind, the same thunderous sound as before. This close, Eleanor heard it more in her chest than her ears, but she still clapped her hands to her head on reflex. People closer to where the flame had traveled winced away in pain.

More gunshots pulled Eleanor's attention from the aftermath of the spell. She gripped her magic and channeled the disgust into anger, forcing her mana—the purified energy—out hard into her fingertips. She started drawing neon-blue lines of light in the air as she ran.

The sigil activated as soon as she drew the last line in place. A barrier of ice two feet thick was created in front of their group. It floated in front of them as they went, a shield designed to divert any incoming spell as they closed the gap to the enemy. The crowds were thinning out—they were getting close to the epicenter of the disaster.

As they cleared another line of tents, they reached a battle-scarred clearing filled with half-annihilated dwellings and strips of grass mixed with striped pockmarks of dust and mud. More bodies ringed the clearing—some eaten away by the dark magic, others blasted away by force.

An 8-foot tall humanoid figure stood in the center of the devastation. It was armored from head-to-toe in interlocking steel plates that glowed with black sigils. Eleanor wasn't sure if it was a Vorid, or one of their machines, but it didn't look like any extractor she'd seen before.

The armored Vorid held a sword in one hand; the other hand held an old man suspended in the air. The man was red-faced and struggling wildly, scraping at the arm keeping him trapped while he kicked at the iron-plated torso of his assailant.

The sword was raised to the man's throat.

Eleanor twisted her hands sideways; her fingers twitched in a precise sequence of gestures. The sigils embedded in the wall of ice twisted along with her movements, as if it were a puppet and her fingers had pulled the strings. The wall shimmered, then split into dozens of long, razor-sharp icicles. A final twitch of her index finger sent the barrage flying forward.

The Vorid turned and threw its victim into the path of the oncoming icicles. Eleanor didn't panic; she simply gestured once again, deftly manipulating her spell. The spikes separated around the man, halted in place, and reformed once more into a wall. The wall scooped the man up and drew him to safety while keeping a firm barrier between them and the Vorid.

While Eleanor operated her spell, the soldiers split apart at Tamara's command, some to the left and right. They raised their weapons and fired at the creature. Its armor sparked and rattled as the bullets struck home, but the thing didn't even flinch.

The Vorid pointed its sword at the soldiers on the left. Dark light gathered at the tip. A sigil climbed and twisted along the length of the blade. "Move!" Tamara shouted.

The sword fired before the soldiers could react. A pillar-sized gout of black fire washed over them, leaving not even ash in its trace. Bits and pieces of what remained—parts of a gun, helmet, and severed fingers—fell to the ground. A crack of wind snapped through the air as the vacuum left behind by the spell collapsed.

Tamara stepped out from behind Eleanor's shield, firing a machine-gun like stream of violet bolts from her hands. The first few shots slammed into the Vorid's armor, and this time, the plates near its hip buckled inward with a satisfying crunch. A few of its protective sigils flickered and died.

The Vorid spun to face her and raised its sword again. A shield of black light sprang up around the pommel, deflecting the violet energy away and into the ground. Dust swirled up into the air as Tamara maintained suppressive fire, keeping the Vorid busy.

Eleanor checked the old man. He was heaving his breaths and squinting hard up at the sky, dazed, but alive. She had her spell set him down a safe distance away, then started to make a new set of gestures. The shield emanating from the pommel of the sword was strong, but it didn't seem to cover its whole body. If she could flank it with another attack on the other side, they might be able to take it down.

A deep hum came from Eleanor's immediate left. She glanced over.

The armored Vorid was standing directly in front of her, its sword charged and pointed in her face.

Eleanor dove back and whipped as much ice as possible between herself and the Vorid. Black fire flickered over her. A searing pain raked across her left arm. She hit the dirt hard.

"Miss Astor!" Tamara redirected her magic. A flurry of violet light flashed over her, but the Vorid let its armor take the blows and raised its sword for a direct strike. Eleanor rolled to the side as the blade came down and buried itself in the ground next to her head.

She channeled her magic, no gestures or sigils; cold air blasted her off the ground and thirty feet straight up. Her back would hurt in the morning, but it bought her a precious second of focus. She gestured as she flew up, and a platform of ice coalesced under her feet. She landed in a crouch and peered down.

The Vorid knight was taking hits left and right from Tamara's pulsed shots; its body shook under the blasts. Despite the beating, the Vorid ignored its mounting injuries. Eleanor could feel its gaze boring into her.

Black light gathered on the tip of its sword again, but a new sigil was forming under its feet. The armor around its shins was resonating with a familiar hum.

Eleanor gathered her magic as the Vorid vanished.

She let out a shout as she activated another sigil hidden in her platform. Her magic channeled into it and amplified. Blades of ice exploded out around her in every direction like a porcupine raising its spines. She could feel the resistance directly above her as the Vorid's armor was punctured by her attack.

Eleanor smirked to herself. Its spell was useful, but the sound was a dead giveaway.

There was a crash of steel on ice. A hand reached down, seized Eleanor under her arm, and hauled her out from the center of her defenses.

The Vorid's entire front side was run through with magic-hardened icicles. It had taken even more wounds in smashing through her spell. Green blood oozed out of the remaining shreds of its armor. None of that slowed it down.

Eleanor had no time to think as the creature's sword whipped toward her neck.

There was a gunshot like a cannon—then, a split second later, a metallic pling. The sword tip was pushed up and over Eleanor's head, missing her completely.

Another gunshot sounded, and the Vorid's head exploded back in a smoldering tangle of armor and dark flesh.

Eleanor fell free of its grip and tumbled toward the ground. She flung her hands out in a wild attempt to stop herself, but barely had the sense to gather any magic.

Tamara's quick thinking saved her. A net of purple light was cast out into the air. The net caught Eleanor a few feet above the ground, slowing her momentum, though she still struck the ground hard on her side. She grunted as the wind was knocked out of her.

Eleanor caught her breath and rolled up sitting. Not the most elegant of landings, but better than breaking something.

The Vorid's corpse slammed into the ground next to her, startling her back. She raised her magic in defense, but let it drop when she sensed the lack of life.

Eleanor got to her feet. "Thanks for the catch."

"Miss Astor," Tamara said. "This isn't over."

The old man stood apart from them across the clearing. In his hands, pointed at the ground, was the biggest revolver Eleanor had ever seen. As they watched him, the Vorid's form crumpled somewhat, and a misty white substance floated across the ground and was absorbed by the man. A green sigil flashed under his feet as the creature's energy was absorbed directly into his body.

"Contractor," Tamara hissed.

Tamara and Eleanor didn't move. The two remaining soldiers from their squad kept their rifles trained on the old man. "Drop your weapon!" one of them said.

The man slowly raised his free hand, keeping the revolver pointed at the ground. "I don't want any trouble."

"I said drop it!"

Tamara raised her hands; purple rings of light flashed ominously on her palms, ready to discharge another flurry of energy. "Drop it now! Drop the weapon and get down!"

Eleanor tried to think of a way to calm the situation, but it had gone from zero to sixty, then back to zero, then back to sixty. She gathered her magic, unsure if she'd use it to capture the contractor or stop him from being attacked.

The man looked between them, then sighed and tossed the gun into the center of the clearing. "Dammit all."

"On the ground!" the soldier shouted. "Keep your hands where I can see them!" Tamara and the soldier approached him; Eleanor followed, keeping her magic ready at her fingertips.

"On your knees, hands behind your back!" Tamara said. "Now! Sudden movements will get you shot!"

"Relax, chili pepper. I'm not gonna do anything stupid."

The soldier kept a distance of about ten feet, weapon trained on the man. Tamara placed a boot between his shoulders and shoved him down over his knees as she whipped out a set of zip-ties from somewhere in her satchel.

"Hey, watch it!" the man said. "I've still got rights! I'm an American citizen!"

"You're a prisoner of war," Tamara said, binding him with practiced efficiency. "Do not get up." The man winced as the zip ties dug into his wrists. Tamara left him on his knees, arms secured.

He twisted around to get a look at them; the soldier flinched with his gun. "Come off it, you lughead. I can't shoot lasers from my eyeballs."

"No sudden movements," the soldier repeated.

The old man made scowling an art form; his wrinkles and thick grey eyebrows seemed designed to make the fiercest frown possible. He looked in his late fifties, maybe sixties, and had a paunch that suggested too much beer and too little exercise. "I saved your lives and now I get treated like a terrorist? You know how many people would've died if I kept my head down? Way more than did, I can bet you that."

"Shut up," Tamara said.

The roar of several engines washed over them. Eleanor could see military vehicles meandering through the tents from the road.

"Well gee whiz, I'm sorry chili pepper. God forbid a man gets his say when he gets indefinitely detained by his own damn government."

"You call me that one more time," Tamara said, leaning near him, "and you won't make it to the detention part of this."

The man's scowl somehow grew even fiercer, but a glint of amusement flashed in his eyes. "My, my, you're as spicy as you look."

Tamara's backhand caught the man right on the jaw. He sprawled into the dirt, coughing as he took a mouthful. Tamara was going in for a kick when Eleanor grabbed her shoulder. Tamara took a long breath, then let herself be pulled away.

Eleanor jerked her head to the side, then moved toward the center of the clearing. Tamara looked at the soldiers before following. "If he tries anything, shoot him."

"Jesus, lady," the contractor said. "No good deed, I tell ya. Shoulda minded my own business and let them folks die."

Tamara planted her boot right next to the man's face. "If you don't shut up," she growled, "this *pepper* is going to give you a *kick*."

That time, he just nodded.

Tamara met up with Eleanor a short distance from the squad. "Miss Astor?"

"What the hell was that?" Eleanor said.

Tamara bit her lip; she hung her head. "I'm sorry. I lost control."

"You did," Eleanor said. "If a few half-assed comments like that can set you off, I can't trust you with something this big. You can't be flying off the handle in front of mundanes, let alone soldiers under your command. What exactly is the problem?"

Tamara hesitated over the question, fidgeting with her hands, but she eventually looked up. "A contractor...he killed my cousin a month back, out in San Francisco. There was a big fight against some extractors. The contractor worked with them at first, but then he snuck up on him and stabbed him in the back."

Eleanor nodded. "I understand. Trust me, I do."

"I know. I heard..." Tamara stopped, but, finding some resolve, she faced Eleanor straight. "The rumor is, Daniel Fitzgerald killed Miss Ashworth. But you told the boy back there he was your friend. It didn't sound like you were lying."

Eleanor kept her face steady. "Rumors spread fast these days," she said. "It's a lot more complicated than that. Recent circumstances dictated that I got to know Daniel personally, but we can discuss that later. Right now, I need you to listen."

"I can do that, ma'am," Tamara said.

"We can't let news of this out right now." Eleanor glanced toward the road. The trucks would roll into the clearing shortly. "No one can learn this man is a contractor except for the people that absolutely need to know. I'll report this back to headquarters, you take care of the local people."

"You worried about the thing with Fitzgerald? The videos?"

"Public opinion is at a sensitive juncture," Eleanor said. "We need to put the word out immediately that this was a Vorid attack bravely fended off by the soldiers and magicians working together. It was designed to scare people, to hurt morale. Terrorism tactics. Mundanes are used to processing it in those terms. Get the military to reach out to any families involved in the attack."

"Understood." Tamara looked at her. "Do you think they were targeting the Fitzgeralds? Or did they somehow know the contractor was here?" She took a breath. "It's scary. This guy was hiding right in the middle of camp. I can't believe we didn't detect him when he registered. We could have ticking time bombs all over the country."

"Contractor magic is hard for us to pick up. The Klide are good."

Eleanor paused, thinking about Tamara's first question. The Vorid could have been aiming at the contractor. Or at the Fitzgeralds. Or at her. Maybe they somehow knew where Xik teleported her. Maybe Xik himself was under surveillance.

Or maybe her father was right, and Xik had led her into some kind of trap.

Diesel engines roared into the clearing. The trucks were on top of them. "Keep your story straight until I tell you otherwise," Eleanor said.

"Yes ma'am."

A flurry of troops jumped off the back of the vehicles and surrounded them. Tamara kicked into soldier mode, directing them to take the contractor into custody. He threw Eleanor and Tamara a look as he was loaded into the back of one of the trucks, but he didn't put up any resistance. The bulk of the soldiers fanned out to secure the area around the dead Vorid.

Eleanor moved to inspect the corpse of the creature. The sigils had vanished with its death, but the body remained—meaning it was a truly living being, not a magical construct. If it was magic, the contractor absorption process wouldn't have left as much behind.

She avoided touching it, instead prodding at the sword and the armor with her senses first. It was iron, mixed with other materials she didn't recognize. Probably an alloy designed to conduct magic. Maybe it was related to the black steel that made up the other Vorid structures.

The value of the find struck her. If this armor really was iron, with only a little bit of something else mixed in, maybe they could reproduce it. Research on enchanting mundane armor and weapons was rudimentary. In the first place, magic was kept secret from mundanes, not used to help them—magic and material science had little overlap. Many spells made for better armor on its own than even ballistic plate, and magicians essentially had access to magic gun-like attacks a thousand years before the mundanes invented gunpowder. The airships were a rare exception to the rule, but even they were large, reinforced weapons platforms, not individual-level gear.

If they could recreate a sigil-conducting, bulletproof, spell-resistant steel alloy...that definitely might be something. Something that could turn helpless mundanes into soldiers capable of meeting the Vorid in battle. Eleanor pried a few plates of the stuff free and tucked them into her bag.

"Miss Astor!" Tamara was jogging back toward her. "One of my mages reported in. We're not the only ones who've been hit."

"There's been other attacks?" Eleanor said.

"More than a few. Reports are still coming in."

"Where did they strike?"

Tamara looked at her. "Everywhere. And more contractors are involved."

Eleanor looked down at the creature's body. It didn't stop once it was locked onto a target—once it had seen her. It defended itself to a point, but only so that it could continue attacking. Getting run through by ten icicles didn't even make it flinch. It was a sacrificial pawn designed to do damage as quickly as possible.

"It prioritized me over the contractor, but only after we made ourselves a larger threat," Eleanor said. "It ignored you almost the whole time." She looked at Tamara. "These things are assassins. The Vorid were targeting contractors."

"Why would they do that?" Tamara asked.

"Because they think they're a threat, and they're trying to nip it in the bud." Eleanor nodded to herself. "I'm going to make certain the Fitzgerald family is taken care of. You make sure that man is watched until I get back. Multiple mages, someone with detection capabilities, space-time specialty, if we have one. This might not be the end of it, and we need an early warning if another one of those things shows up."

"All that for a contractor?" Tamara said. "Maybe we should let the Vorid solve the problem for us."

"If the Vorid want the contractors dead," Eleanor said, "then we probably don't."

Eleanor marched back through the tents, accompanied by no less than 5 soldiers at the behest of Tamara. It took her a good ten minutes to retrace her steps—it was further than she remembered running in all the panic, not to mention that every cluster of tents looked the same as the last one. A good number of people brought their own tents, but most were army issue look-alikes. Every retailer in the country sold out of tents days ago, and anything left was appropriated by the government.

It wasn't easy living like this, out in the open and away from the comforts of home. Given enough time, people would start to chafe, even if they didn't have to do much work themselves. There might be long-term plans to make the encamped population useful, like Tamara suggested, but the problem was that this wasn't an enemy unskilled labor would help against. It was the exact opposite—only mages with years of training and deep knowledge of spells useful in combat stood any chance against Vorid attackers. Enough mundane weaponry could take out an extractor, even an overseer, but against their fast-moving strike craft or a massive flock of drone-like 'birds', magic was almost required to fight back.

All those problems—without even mentioning the threat of a Vorid lord. If her father and a few other top mages teamed up—or if a large number of regular mages had plenty of preparation time—they might be able to reliably take one down. The only person that could fight one off at a moment's notice was Daniel Fitzgerald, and he wasn't exactly available on speed dial.

Eleanor reached the tent and caught James coming out from under the entrance flap. He stopped, looked around, then back at her. "Uh, Eleanor, it was?"

"Miss Astor, if you please," she said automatically.

"What happened out there?" James asked. "Is everyone alright?"

"A Vorid attacked the camp."

James let his hand drop; the tent flapped closed behind him as he stood straight, his expression one of soberly processing the news. "Were they the...alive ones? Or was it their machines?"

"I'm fairly certain it was live," Eleanor said. "It can be hard to tell with them." She paused. "There were casualties, but luckily it didn't seem to be targeting civilians specifically."

"Good god," James said. "One of them came all by itself? What for?"

"An investigation to find that out is taking place as we speak," Eleanor said. "We don't know the specifics yet."

It wasn't that she didn't trust James, but he was a mundane, after all. He'd get the details when he needed to know them—or when he demonstrated he was worth being in the know. Maybe she ought to cut Daniel's father some slack, but she'd need all the slack she could get for herself soon enough.

"I was thinking about going along with what you said earlier," James said, "and this pretty much confirms what I already knew. I have Felix packing right now. If you could give us a few minutes to get our things together..."

"Certainly," Eleanor said. She could almost feel a weight lift off her shoulders. *At least I can fulfill one promise.* "The truck will arrive shortly," she added, as James ducked back in his tent.

Eleanor stood in silence, politely ignoring muffled conversation between James and Felix. The soldiers kept a sharp watch on the surroundings. She glanced up at the sky, taking in the clouds. The airship patrolling the camp was now directly overhead, hovering in place to coordinate reinforcements, but the clouds kept on floating by without a care in the world. Eleanor felt a little jealous.

Soon enough, another personnel carrier made it through the tents. James and Felix were ready, everything they had packed into two backpacks and two large suitcases. The truck stopped, and Tamara hopped off the back.

Eleanor blinked. "Hadn't I asked you to—"

And then Eleanor's father stepped down behind her.

Henry Astor slowly approached, like a thundercloud coming up fast enough to turn the sky dark. Eleanor shrank back as he loomed over her.

His eyes flicked over her shoulder. "The Fitzgeralds, I take it?" Eleanor nodded. "I suppose we'll be taking them in."

"Yes."

"That's good."

Eleanor stared at a safe spot near his waist. She was a bit afraid to look at his face. Her father's fists were clenched, and she could feel the cold aura radiating off him. He was working to keep his magic—and his emotions—suppressed. She could count the number of times she'd seen him like that on one hand.

"Eleanor?" he said.

"Yes."

"Get in the truck."

Eleanor clambered up the back of the truck. Nickolas was there already; he raised an eyebrow at her, then patted the section of bench between himself and another mage. Eleanor sat between them, staring pointedly at the floor. Tamara got in after her; she looked shellshocked, uncertain. Eleanor met her gaze, but Tamara quickly glanced away and focused on straightening loose strands of her hair around her ears.

Eleanor had a feeling Xik wasn't going to pop up and teleport her away this time.

****

Eleanor was locked in a cell in a makeshift jail on the other side of the encampment. Thankfully, the space was new enough that it didn't smell like anything unpleasant.

She was wearing a stone bracer on her left wrist—less punishing than the one Daniel allowed to be placed on himself. She could still use magic—a courtesy, given her station, not to mention the danger of another Vorid attack—but if she did, the bracer would set off an alarm aura that would alert every mage in practically a mile radius. Not that it was necessary—she could sense three mages stationed up the hall, one of them Nickolas.

She hung her head between her legs and stared at the packed dirt under the feet of her stool. She'd gotten herself into serious trouble this time, and it looked like her immediate fate would be house arrest followed by a shotgun wedding. Only the shotgun was turned on her, not the groom.

And that was if her father chose not to press on about disobeying direct orders. They were officially in wartime, and she had been insubordinate. She wasn't sure how far he'd go at this point.

While riding in the truck toward camp, packed in along with her father, officials from the Ivory Dawn, Nickolas, and Tamara, she had the strangest mix of emotions—somewhere between having been caught with her hand in the cookie jar and being court marshalled. The ride was a long, painful silence, and she wasn't sure whether to start eating the cookie simply to spite them, or to gently put the jar lid back on and whistle her way out of the kitchen.

But the moment had passed, and now she was a prisoner.

Footsteps made her raise her head. She sat straight on her bench and steadied her nerves. Whatever was going to happen, she would carry through it with her dignity intact.

Her father and Nickolas arrived in front of the room. A wave of magic opened the cell door, and they stepped inside. They had the politeness not to shut it behind themselves, though Nickolas stood firmly between her and the door as Henry approached.

Eleanor swallowed back the nerves and decided to lead, rather than wait for him to talk. "Well," she said, "here I am."

"The long-range magic to sense dimensional shifts is almost optimized," Henry said, shifting to a topic Eleanor didn't expect. "We'll be able to determine where the Vorid are entering if they're close enough to an airship, and we'll have installations on the ground to expand that coverage soon. We didn't expect this many intrusions at once, but we can adjust for that in the future."

Eleanor frowned at him. "What does that have to do with me?"

"You believe as Xik does," Henry said. "That we need contractors to fight this war."

Eleanor's eyes flicked to Nickolas, then back to her father. *Might as well be forward about it.* She nodded. "Yes. I do."

"You don't know what our organizations are truly capable of," Henry said. "There are many things you haven't needed to know yet, things that keep the balance of power between the guilds and orders. We can detect the Vorid, we can fight them, and we can defeat them. Just like you, they underestimate us."

"We almost lost New York."

"We didn't commit everything we had there," Henry said. "I was overconfident thinking that Rothschild and I would be enough to fight the Vorid lord. The next time we fight a major battle, I won't spare our resources."

"We need Klide expertise to fully counter them," Eleanor said. "We need Xik's help, if not for magic, then for information, for strategy. We're flying blind."

"Assuming he is here to help us," Henry said, "and isn't secretly leading the Vorid himself."

"Assuming," Eleanor said, echoing his argument, "that he would bother with the charade in the first place if he could come and go as he pleases—like he already does. He had you both trapped back at the house with a snap of his fingers, but he didn't do you any harm. Why not destroy a few powerful human leaders when he had them right where he wanted, then make it look like a Vorid attack?"

"Temporarily trapping us is one thing," Henry said, "but killing us would have been far more difficult, and you know it." Eleanor opened her mouth to keep arguing, but Henry cut her off. "Enough, Eleanor. I've already made these decisions, and I don't intend to relitigate them. I'm here to tell you the facts."

"They have magic that can cross dimensional boundaries at will," Eleanor said. "They have technology that is at least a half-century beyond ours. Those are the facts."

"And that is exactly the reason I can't waste time chasing you down while you go sauntering around in unsecured locations!" Henry shouted. Eleanor flinched back at his tone. "This is a war, Eleanor! It's not the kind of war the military fights a thousand miles away while you play games on your cellphone. It is not a sect dispute in which our chosen champions duel their chosen champions, and then we shake hands when someone gets a paper cut and all head home until next year. This is the kind of war you have to fight in your backyard, outside your front door, and if we lose, our house will burn down and everyone will die. I will die, you will die.

Our home—this entire planet—will be completely ravaged. The Dawn's leadership would have you stripped of your rank and thrown in holding if you weren't my daughter. You'd be lucky if you saw the light of day again before this was over, if ever!"

Henry finished his rant with a huff. Eleanor shifted herself and sat straight in her chair. She folded her arms and firmly met his gaze. "Then do it and be done with it."

"What do you mean?" Henry said.

"Clearly, I'm not a very good soldier," Eleanor said. "Strip me of my status and disown me, if you feel that strongly about it."

They stared at each other. Eleanor kept her eyes on his. Her father's jaw muscles clenched and unclenched as he tried to wait her out. She willed herself not to budge.

"You will marry Matthew in a few days time," he said eventually.

"I refuse."

"Then you will be kept in holding in New York until you change your mind," Henry said. "That seems to be the safest place for you, since you seem so bent on creating problems if left to your own devices."

Eleanor's gaze fell. "Seems like you're forming a habit of taking problems you don't like," she said, "and locking them away."

"You are not a problem," Henry said quietly. "And I don't want to lock you away." He and Nickolas moved toward the door. "You need time to come to terms with Rachel's death and put Daniel behind you. Once that's done, I know you're strong enough to put pride aside and get on with this." He paused, probably expecting her to respond, but when she didn't say anything, he kept talking. "It isn't as if your marriage can't be strictly political. I'm not asking you to cherish him until the end of days. I'm asking you to do your duty so the Ivory Dawn can move forward as a unified whole."

"If they need something so superficial to stay unified," Eleanor said, still staring fixedly at the ground, "then they deserve the suicide pact you've signed them up for."

"Eleanor."

"What?" she snapped.

"I would never disown you," he said gently. "Ever. You're all I have left."

Eleanor tried to think of something positive to say. A part of her longed to repair the frayed bond she had with him, to restore some of the chipped, childish image of his invincible fatherliness. If she could rebuild those feelings, then she could convince him out of this mental pit he'd climbed into, lift him up like he would lift her up.

But she couldn't find the words that were able to do all that. The words were just air, and they couldn't bear the weight of all those feelings.

"You're all I have left too," Eleanor whispered. "Why are you doing this to me? Do you really want me married to an idiot like that?"

Henry glanced at Nickolas, then gestured. Nickolas took the hint and left the cell. Henry stepped back toward her, closing the gap between them. "In a perfect world," he said, "I'd leave the choice to you. I wouldn't ever want something so harsh and sudden to be put on your shoulders. But I can't control the fact that others in the Ivory Dawn want power and influence. You are who you are; you are my daughter, and with all the magic and power you hold comes a corresponding responsibility. This marriage is the least of it. But even if it was for our family, or the Dawn, I couldn't bring myself to force this on you. Because you're my daughter."

"But here you are, doing it anyway," Eleanor said. "Even though I'm your daughter."

"We don't choose the times we live in."

"What a pleasant-sounding excuse," Eleanor said, bitterness creeping back into her voice. "Did you read that on the back of a postcard?"

"I could have lost you today," Henry said. His voice was hushed—he almost sounded desperate, as if trying one last time to pull her to his side. "Our camp was hit by a single would-be assassin. Another camp in South America had a full dome dropped on it. They lost ten mages and thousands of civilians. If one of our airships wasn't nearby, it would've been worse. That could have happened here. Xik put you in the line of fire on purpose."

"Xik gave me a choice," Eleanor said. "I put myself in the line of fire."

"He knew what you would do if you were offered. He used you against me."

"I don't believe that!" Eleanor took a breath after raising her voice and sat back fully in her chair. "I'm sick of arguing about that. I'm sick of the double-think and the self-doubt."

"There's one thing I don't doubt, ever," Henry said. "And it's that I love you."

"I love you too," Eleanor mumbled.

They went quiet. There was muffled conversation down the hall, too far to make out any details. The distant rumble of a diesel engine filtered in through the cell's small window, grew louder, then passed them by.

"But maybe this is for the best," Henry said, "if that's what it takes to keep you safe. At least think things through." He looked at her. "Tamara told me what you ordered her to do. Even in those moments after the attack, you were protecting the Dawn. Shielding our family's reputation."

Eleanor didn't respond. Henry was satisfied with getting the last word on that note, and after their silence lingered long enough, he left.

And then Eleanor sat there alone, in a dim cell at the back of the camp, head hung between her knees, staring at the bracer on her arm that kept her a prisoner.

Chapter 12
Teaming Up

Jack and Daniel were sitting in a waiting room that bore a striking resemblance to the room Daniel was first taken to in Hell, where he'd spoken with Beelzebub. Instead of a table and chairs, there was a metal bench long enough for the both of them to sit side-by-side. They were dressed in casual but comfortable clothes—jeans all around, though Daniel was in a long-sleeve collarless shirt, and Jack was wearing a form-fitting spandex top. Both their shirts were white, emblazoned by a red cross and yellow frills. *Team colors,* thought Daniel. *Yay.*

Jack also—to Daniel's considerable amusement—had spandex shorts under his jeans—in case a full-body transformation ripped them apart.

They both wore matching black cross trainers—selected to have a bit of extra weight, a strong rubber grip underneath, and extra-long ankle support. Daniel preferred to either go with sneakers or boots, but they could be running, climbing, or fighting. Jack insisted that all-around footwear would pay serious dividends, and Daniel didn't see any reason to argue—Jack was the expert, after all.

Across from where they sat on the bench was a wall of steel slats, slotted floor-to-ceiling like the one-way exit of a subway station. The slats divided their side of the room from a familiar stone pedestal which Jack had informed him was a teleportation circle. When the match was about to start, the gate would open and they would stand on top of that ring, which would magically transport to them to the arena.

"This teleportation stuff makes me feel like my powers aren't all that special," Daniel said.

Jack rolled his eyes. "You want some cheese with that whine?"

Daniel scoffed. "What's the point of running really fast if people can instantly move from place to place?"

"I wouldn't worry about it," Jack said. "Supposedly, teleportation uses a lot of energy, so you can't do it much. Usually you need a lot of mages working together, or an enchanted emplacement like this that was prepared way ahead of time. A single mage could teleport themselves a short distance, but the spell is very complicated and inefficient."

"How complicated?" Daniel asked.

"It takes them a long time to cast it, so I guess that means more complicated," Jack said. "I haven't been able to cast spells aside from the contractor stuff."

"I can do this one physical sigil thing," Daniel said. "Rachel told me it was the simplest possible kind of spell, but it's really useful, lets me get into the air and change directions faster. But that's it."

"I wonder why?" Jack asked. "Something to ask Xik."

"When he conveniently decides to show up again," Daniel muttered. "Hey. Question."

"Yeah?"

"What's with stone and enchantments?" Daniel asked. "My bracers were made of stone, the ones the magicians kept me in. The teleporting ring is made of stone. Is there something to that?"

"I guess you have to have stones big enough to be a magician," Jack said.

"Yup," Daniel said. "No stones about it."

"They never leave any stone unturned," Jack said.

"You think they ever get stoned?"

"I can hardly withstoned my curiosity on the matter."

"Dracula's too stone-faced to ask," Daniel said.

"I wouldn't have the stones," Jack replied.

"That was the first one, already used it," Daniel said. "Try again."

"Come on, that was different enough."

"No way," Daniel said. Jack stuck his tongue out in thought. He started tapping his foot. Daniel began a countdown. "Five. Four. Three. Two. One..."

"Dammit," Jack said.

"You look a little stony," Daniel said.

"You suck."

"Losersayswhat-?"

Jack made a face at him. "Anyway. I don't know if stone is important to enchanting. I mean, stone is cheap, and it doesn't move. Plenty of metal stuff has magic, like our armlets or the floating cameras. I think the main thing is not drawing an enchantment in silly putty."

Daniel nodded at the explanation. "Concerning more immediate problems," he said, "no idea what we're in for?"

"You've asked me that like three times now."

Daniel nodded. "I thought maybe there was a pattern to it or something."

"Not that I know of," Jack said. "Have to wait and see."

They fell quiet again. There wasn't much left to talk about on that front. Jack was right; they'd gone on for hours previous about all the possibilities. It was inevitable that their conversation devolved into shooting the breeze.

Jack and Daniel watched non-stop recordings of their opponents—the Sky Runners—back at Jack's apartment, trying to narrow in on who would most likely be their opponents. They hadn't had enough preparation time to get in-depth with every duo they could face, but Daniel gained a shallow knowledge of the roughest nasties that might pop up.

The battle was a 2-on-2 affair, Daniel and Jack against two members of the other team. The identities of the participants were hidden right up until the moment of truth; the suspense drove viewership of high-level team battles for PrisonWatch. Jack and Daniel had been secretly brought to the waiting area using a tunnel under the city, but Dracula encouraged them to assume the worst and expect to be expected. Daniel's entrance into Hell hadn't exactly been subtle, and—being the only two contractors around—it was a good bet they'd be paired up. The Sky Runners wouldn't be surprised they were chosen, considering that not only was the whole city talking about them, but the whole demon internet, too.

More valuable to Daniel than the exact demons they might fight was learning more about the rules of Hell. It was almost a dark reflection of *The Price is Right*, in the sense that the challenges faced by the teams were a large set of games replayed over and over. Pamba Run was one of them, in which the players competed to get a living pamba to the goal. Its free-for-all nature made it popular for the new inmate contests.

Another game was a miniaturized, short-form version of the Purgatory territory war, in which large groups from each team fought over 3, 5, or 7 pieces of territory in a custom-built arena. Basically, it was a King of the Hill match, with multiple hills. After a set period, the team that had held the most control points for the greatest duration was declared the winner.

Of the more gruesome varieties was a chess-like board game, with the fun twist of game pieces being linked to specific body parts. Lose a pawn, and your kidneys stopped functioning—or maybe you'd get lucky and only lose feeling in one of your hands. Play continued until a contestant either won the game, or someone died. In the version Daniel watched, pain was a significant factor. In order to counteract the healing magic innate to Hell, the game's spells constantly damaged the affected area of the body—so not only couldn't you use your fingers, they felt like they were on fire for the remainder of the match.

The torturous process was, in fact, entirely unnecessary. Jack explained to him that for most games, certain magical formations were erected to keep the excess magic power from leaking into the arena. This stopped Hell's ubiquitous healing properties from 'interfering' with the progress of most battles.

That type of attrition-style board game was a relatively new and wildly popular category, jumping from two basic rulesets into 15 unique games in less than a year. Jack had informed him that it made for very interesting betting, because you could put stakes on a lot of different factors: who would be victorious; what state they'd be in if they survived; and whether or not a contestant's death would be a deciding factor at all.

Daniel sincerely hoped they weren't going to play one of those. He was good at thinking on his feet and playing things outside the box, but long-term, incremental strategy was more Jack's thing.

There were over two hundred distinct events in active rotation, with a historical backlog of thousands more. Some were similar, to be sure, with slight variations evolving over time and occasional revivals of old favorites. New games would naturally be cycled in, and old games put on the shelf, perhaps to make a nostalgic return a few decades later.

The only thing missing was the chummy, dad-joke tossing game show host that somehow got away with kissing all the pretty contestants.

"We were busy earlier," Daniel said, "but something I kept meaning to ask."

"Yeah?"

"What are the stakes in this battle?" Daniel asked. "Is it for ranking, points, or what?"

"Shopping rights," Jack said.

"Shopping?" Daniel looked at him. "Don't tell me this is all so Rasputin can get that Coach handbag he's been nagging me about."

"Please," Jack said. "Rasputin wouldn't be caught with that garbage in a hundred years. He's a Louis Vuitton man to the core."

"You know," Daniel said, "if it's only a hundred years, he may have actually once wore Coach purses."

Jack paused. "That really puts it in a different perspective."

"When did they even invent purses?" Daniel said.

"Coin-purses have been a thing since there was money, right?" Jack said.

"But as fashion pieces."

"Hell if I know," Jack said. "Who cares?"

"This could be important," Daniel said. "We might finally get Rasputin to crack a smile."

Jack lifted his eyebrows. "Do you really want to see that man smile?"

"Every time Rasputin smiles, a puppy dies," Daniel said. Jack made a half-snort through his nose. "So back on topic, what's this secret shopper opportunity we're risking our immortal souls over?"

"So," Jack began—in way that told Daniel he was in for some education—"every piece of land in Purgatory has something built on it. Restaurants, shops, housing. We're fighting to take possession of one of those. They work independent of the territories themselves."

Daniel thought back. "But what about the restocking, back at that gate out of the city? Isn't PrisonWatch doing that?"

"Yeah, they do that, and they're the real owners of the shops," Jack said. "But if you have them marked as your territory, you get everything at-cost, you set the prices for everyone else, and you get a points-converted cut of the proceeds. More importantly, some stuff is only available in certain stores. Armor, weapons, food that doesn't suck, clothing. I wouldn't have an internet connection if we didn't own territory that gives us those services at prices we can afford."

"I had no idea," Daniel said. "Sounds more like outright ownership, honestly. Or maybe Hell-based franchising. Was that restaurant we went to before one of ours?"

"No," Jack said, "but it's owned by a team we...maybe we're not allies, but neutral, I guess. They don't rip me off, and it's a good café."

"Wouldn't you save money by only going to Order-owned places?"

"Sure," Jack said, "but do you want to eat at only one restaurant for the rest of your life?"

"Maybe if it's Olive Garden," Daniel said.

"I can't believe that coming from someone that makes his own homemade lasagna." Jack's face got a faraway look. "You should make that again. Stop bumming around my apartment and make yourself useful for a change."

"Hey," Daniel said, "you can't beat those breadsticks."

Jack's face screwed up. "You sicken me."

"Do the demons even have pasta?" Daniel said. "Or tomatoes? Or any human food?"

"We could probably find some equivalents," Jack said. "I don't think there's a lot of experts in demon-human cuisine running around."

"At long last, I've found my calling," Daniel said. "I will introduce the wonder of human gastronomy to the demon world. Peace through food! The collective ecstasy of our taste buds shall bring us to an everlasting state of harmony!"

They sat there, Jack wearing a flat expression, Daniel gazing up at the concrete ceiling of the waiting room, a fist raised in mock-triumph.

"You done?" Jack asked.

"Yes," Daniel said. "Please continue."

"So, we took territory from the Viridian Gust," Jack said, "which forced them to lose control of a store. The store itself is on the edge of the territory, and you have to own adjacent land to be able to own the shop."

"Makes sense so far," Daniel said.

"We have a new border with the Sky Runners there," Jack said, "so we're qualified to claim ownership. If both teams make a claim—which they usually do—they have to fight for it. At the end of the day it's another way for PrisonWatch to get us to fight each other and keep the show going."

"Makes sense," Daniel said. "So the only good way to buy items is to have some shops."

"Your armlet has a full list of stuff you can buy," Jack said. "Check out the shopping menu. You have access to a basic selection by default. I've heard it changes a bit depending on which level of hell you're living on, but basic shopping is universal for everybody. Stuff like clothes, simple weapons."

"But long story short," Daniel said, "shop good. Other team with shop: bad."

"Unless your allies wanted it, or if you make an agreement not to contest a claim for some side benefits," Jack said. "Purgatory is a massive weave of alliances and under-the-table deals. The Order of the Dragon is really the only team that doesn't have regular allies. Dracula avoids dealing with the demons."

"Why don't the demons team up and run us over?"

"Who's going to volunteer to weaken themselves to take us out?" Jack asked. "There's been a couple tries, and you can imagine that the all-human team makes a politically convenient public enemy, but the Order comes out clean in the end. They can't help but stab each other in the back."

"The plot thickens," Daniel said. "You think they'd be pissed at Bathory for being number one, even though she's a human."

"A lot of them are," Jack said, "but she earned her spot, and she isn't exclusive; her team is almost all demons. So she gets some begrudging respect. It's not like she doesn't fend off attacks periodically. She's a tough nut to crack, like Dracula and Rasputin."

Daniel rubbed his chin. "If we lose the wrong shop, the whole team could get in serious trouble."

"Dracula tries to keep that from happening, but yeah," Jack said. "We're large enough we could take a few blows without problems, but it's life and death for some of the smaller teams. Worse, PrisonWatch has ultimate control over the shops. They can close them, move them, even change their stock, for better or for worse. There's a rumor that when teams get too comfortable, PrisonWatch management will rip a few stores away from them to make them desperate, keep them fighting. If you let that go on, you're forced into a position where you have to buy tools from your enemies."

"At a healthy premium," Daniel said.

"Exactly," Jack said. "Not a good place to be."

Daniel turned it all over in his head—the deathmatches, the slaughter, the constant push to fight other teams. It might be a prison for terrible criminals—mostly—but to make a blood sport of crime and punishment was wrong. He'd gone to Boston with the hope of getting into law school, of pursuing justice the right way. It felt like a lifetime ago, now, but he still believed it was the methods that made the monster.

It was for that very reason he recognized the consequences of becoming a contractor at the time and asked Xik for an actual contract. Daniel wanted to be careful, even if he was forced to acknowledge that it might take a monster to fight other monsters. He didn't have a lot of room for higher moral principles; Felix was gonna die, and he'd made a decision to give his brother a chance.

Fighting fire with fire was a brutal way to live, and the absorptive magic of contractors was a power that could easily be misused. Jack might be an example of that exact thing happening, taking the law into his own hands. So what did that say about their jailors, using people for television entertainment, when they had other, more reasonable options?

"The people that run this place are brutal psychopaths," Daniel said.

"They're not people. They're demons."

"There have to be some good ones," Daniel said. "You can't write off whole races of people, man."

"Dracula doesn't seem to have a problem with it."

"Sounds uncomfortably close to racism if you ask me." Daniel frowned at him. "You told me yourself there were some good ones, that they have similar morals, like we do."

"Okay, say there are some good ones," Jack said. "What makes you think they're down here in Hell?"

"Point taken," Daniel said. "But we're down here, aren't we?"

Jack shrugged his shoulders and nodded a bit. "I feel like we're the exception, but I understand where you're coming from. It's like most things. There's good people everywhere, even if some bad ones are in charge."

Daniel was happy to hear that, especially coming from Jack. It seemed a step back from the *magicians are completely evil* train he'd been riding on. He kicked his legs under the bench they sat on, then sighed. "How much longer, you think?"

"Couple minutes, probably."

"What's this shop we're fighting over for, anyway?"

"Armor," Jack said. "Something we could really use. We have a good supply of energy shields, but..."

"Yeah," Daniel said, "I saw you guys use the shields earlier."

"Armor would make us even tougher," Jack said. "Remember the red armor the grazul shock troops had, from the Gust?"

"Oh yeah," Daniel said, nodding. "Those guys roughed you up."

"Exactly. Imagine me in that stuff."

"Whoa," Daniel said—and he did imagine it, Jack's towering ape form clad head-to-toe in magic-resistant metal plates. "Instant tank mode! Alright. Now I'm actually pumped for this. We're getting you an upgrade."

"Hell yeah," Jack said. They bumped fists.

Light washed over them. Daniel and Jack looked up; the pedestal was glowing with a soft, incandescent haze. The gate opened on its own, inviting them in with a long creak of steel-on-steel.

"Good pep talk," Jack said.

"Gold team rules," Daniel replied.

A voice boomed out over an intercom hidden somewhere in the room, a little too loud to be comfortable. "Inmates, step to the pedestal and prepare to enter the arena. Your match begins shortly."

"Ladies first," Daniel said.

Jack went for the opening. "Bitches last."

Daniel leapt to his feet and tried to beat Jack to the pedestal. Jack was already running, but Daniel had the edge in speed, even without his magic turned on. They hit the gap in the bars together, awkwardly trying to press themselves through a space sized for one person. Jack's shortness worked in his advantage; he squeezed under and in, then jumped onto the pedestal. "Gotcha bitch!"

"Yeah, whatever." Daniel climbed up after him. "How long do we have to wait before—"

Daniel's throat was frozen mid-vocalization. A tug under his stomach made him feel like he'd lose his lunch. The world swirled in mushy, molten colors at his feet, then shimmered back into place.

Suddenly unfrozen, Daniel's sentence ended in an ugly croak as he blinked away the dizziness. Jack jabbed him in the ribs, hard. "Get it together, champ."

Daniel winced, rubbing his side. "Taking advantage of my moment of weakness. You fiend!"

Jack ignored him, turning to look at their surroundings. "Oh joy. It's Dungeon Run."

Daniel faced the direction Jack was looking.

They stood on a stone pedestal matching the one they'd come in from; it rested in the center of an island made of the same rocky material. It was a rough circle, about 30 feet across.

At the edge of their little patch of land was a lightless void. It expanded in every direction, a solid black field that stretched from the sky and wrapped down under their feet.

Daniel inched as close to the edge as he dared go. He put his head out far enough that he could see there was nothing beneath them, and felt a shiver run down his spine. It was worse than the lava pit—at least that was something he could feel and understand. This looked like you would drop off, and fall. Forever.

Stretching away from their island were two stone paths, wide enough for 4 or 5 people across. One parted to the left, the other right. After that initial separation they stayed roughly parallel to one another, climbing and twisting into the distance. They were close enough that a person standing on one side could easily shout across and be heard, but far enough away that Daniel wouldn't even consider trying to jump.

Despite the lack of obvious light sources, Daniel could see it all quite easily. The stone stood out stark and harsh against the solid black background. It was as if someone had taken the entire arena and moved it past the edge of the galaxy, into the dark and lightless space far away from any star.

The lack of reference points was playing with Daniel's sense of distance. He couldn't tell how long the path was; it got smaller at a distance, but it didn't quite seem proportional. It was almost as if he knew he should be able to see more, but it faded away, like a fuzzy object sinking into a dark fog.

Diagonally down from them were two other paths, leading from a very similar-looking island. It was difficult to judge, but from the size of the two individuals standing on the other island, Daniel gauged they were at least 100 yards away. Their paths traveled through the dark, separate, but seemingly headed to the same destination. The darkness obscured his vision too much to tell for sure.

A dozen cameras zipped out of the darkness, tiny drones that buzzed circuits around Jack and Daniel. Daniel almost felt a sense of relief from having something normal show up, even if it was one of the cameras. It was a reminder that they weren't trapped in some freaky dark world for the rest of eternity, that the magic and technology was still working.

Two of the cameras opened into small screens that hovered in front of them; they displayed a video feed of their opponents. One was a demon that Daniel recognized— Kavarssian, the *insistent* dragon that tried to recruit him to the Sky Runners, only to turn on him as soon as things went sour. The other was a towering ogre that looked almost as tall as Jack when he transformed, with an extra hundred pounds of body fat to boot. His lower incisors were so large they protruded out above his lips like miniature tusks, and his skin was a mottled green-brown from head to toe, rougher and thicker on his shoulders and forearms.

Kavarssian was dressed to the nines; with his scales covered, he looked almost human, though Daniel could still spot his hooked talons protruding from his ankles above polished black shoes. The ogre wore lose brown pants, proudly flaunting his hairy chest and feet.

"And here are our contestants!" Ky's announcer voice came in small and tinny through their floating television, making it even more annoying than usual. "From the Order of the Dragon, we have Jack Killiney and Daniel Fitzgerald! Everyone has been dying to see more of this dynamic duo in action, and it looks like the Order isn't going to disappoint! With two of their strongest out front and center, they are in this one to win it!"

"Hear that?" Jack said. He waved at a camera as it swooped in for a close-up. "We're the dynamic duo."

Daniel forced an awkward smile onto his face, trying to follow Jack's lead. He had no idea how to act in front of cameras eager to broadcast his impending death and dismemberment on live television.

"And fighting them for the rights to Argent Armory is Gulthak Fist-Smasher and Kavarssian of the Red, two top contenders from the Sky Runners!" Ky's voice practically squealed the dragon's name. "Kavarssian is as merciless as he is handsome, and Gulthak is old reliable when it comes to muscle-on-muscle slugfests. Between the two, they have over 650 years of Hellish experience under their belts. It's a battle of ages; the powerful newcomers against the old hands! Get your snacks and drinks ready because you aren't going to want to leave your seats!" Ky paused for a breath before rattling into a well-practiced transition. "We'll be right back to watch this action-packed Dungeon Run matchup after these commercial messages. Today's events are brought to you by Planet Express, the fastest business class shipping service for interplanetary deliveries. When you need it now, trust Planet Express!"

The cameras dimmed; small lights on their casings started to blink. Daniel knew that meant the broadcast wasn't live anymore. "Alright Jack," Daniel said. "Start talking."

"Okay, Dungeon Run," Jack said. "The point is to get to finish as quickly as possible. We each take one path." He gestured to the two roads that vanished into the black. "Along the way, you'll hit an obstacle you can't pass. On my side, I have to complete some kind of challenge, and then your path will open up. Eventually I'll hit a roadblock, and you have to complete a challenge to open my side up. We go back and forward like that twice. After you get past your challenge, make sure you hit the switch that opens my path—it'll be easy to spot, big green button. You don't have to sprint the whole way, but always keep moving."

"So, first team to get both people to the end wins," Daniel said.

"It's not that simple," Jack said, "but staying ahead gives you advantages. Our paths intersect with theirs one time. In other words, you'll cross paths with Gulthak and Kavarssian one time each. So will I."

"What happens then?"

"The first person to the intersection usually gets their pick of something good," Jack said. "Could be weapons, powerups, some kind of magic. The exact order of the challenges and the intersections can change, so be prepared for anything to pop up next."

"When I get to that part," Daniel said, "how do I know what to pick?"

"The best thing will be really obvious," Jack said. "Take it and move on."

"What if we get to the intersection at the same time?"

"Can't happen. As soon as one person makes it in, a barrier prevents entry for the other person. It only drops once they leave—you can't fight them there. Eventually, our two paths meet up"—Jack gestured between himself and Daniel—"and we have to complete a final challenge together. If we get past that, we make it to the final arena. And then we fight them."

"Okay." Daniel thought it over. "Worst case scenario they get all the goodies. They still have to beat us at the end."

"Worst case scenario," Jack said, "is that we don't finish the run fast enough, the path drops out from underneath us, and we lose instantly before we even get to the fight."

"Wait, wait, wait," Daniel said, waving his hands. "The whole thing's on a timer?"

"Yeah," Jack said, "but there's nothing to tell you how much time is left. Eventually the path will start collapsing behind you. That's your cue to run faster."

Daniel glanced at the paths. The whole place already gave him the creeps. Now he couldn't even trust the stone under his feet.

Jack gave him a light punch on the shoulder. "Don't sweat it. You can run really fast."

"That won't help me if there's nothing to run on."

"It's not about being the fastest," Jack said. "Yeah, you want to move it, sure. But surviving is more important. If you don't live through the challenges, the obstacles, it doesn't matter how fast you were going. So take it at your own pace."

Daniel nodded. Jack was right—in a straight footrace, Daniel would win every time, but there was more to this than outrunning people.

The lights on the cameras turned red. They blinked once, then again, then a third time. Jack and Daniel straightened. "I'll take the left," Jack said.

Daniel started half-singing his next words. "You take the high road, I'll take the low road!"

"Hilarious," Jack said. "Just don't fall."

Daniel's reply died in his throat. He didn't mind heights that much—he really didn't—but this was different. That pitch-black void was unnatural, almost as if something inside of it was alive and looking back at him.

"And we're at the start of another day in Hell, and another battle in Hell!" Ky's voice said. "Welcome, one and all, to Dungeon Run!" She did the typical announcer spiel—reiterating a bare-bones version of the rules Jack told Daniel, and reintroducing the contestants.

"But for a contest this intense," Ky said, "we need a little something extra, don't you think?"

Daniel and Jack exchanged glances. "What's that supposed to mean?" Daniel said.

"Dunno."

"All contestants will have access to their own magical powers for the duration of the game!" Ky said.

Jack's mouth dropped open. "No way!"

"Hell yeah," Daniel said. "Up high!" Daniel and Jack slapped a high five.

"But..." Ky's voice trickled back through the camera, as if teasing them for their early celebration. "That wouldn't be fair to every contestant, would it? Not everyone has the same talent for magic, so we're going to have to level the playing field! Each contestant will have access to a percentage of their magical power that gives them a similar relative strength. Let's find out how our fighters stack up. Activate the magic balancer!!"

The cameras in front of Jack and Daniel had been displaying panning shots and close-ups of themselves and their opponents, but now they switched to a display of portraits. Headshots of Kavarssian and Gulthak were arranged diagonally across from himself and Jack.

A small number started flickering at the bottom of each portrait. Cheery contest music played in the background, as if a saccharine prize-show wheel was about to be spun to determine someone's reward. A chime sounded, and the number under Kavarssian's portrait ground to a halt.

32.7%

"Interesting!" Ky said. "Kavarssian is well known for his magical skills. That high percentage underlines how strong our other contestants are. Coming up next...Jack Killiney!"

Jack's number chimed out.

21.4%

"Incredible!" Ky shouted. "For those of you out there who are quick on the uptake, like yours truly"—Daniel resisted the urge to groan—"you might realize that Jack is about 50% stronger than Kavarssian. The Order of the Dragon might be ordering up some dragons sooner than we think!"

"I'm surprised she hadn't used that joke already," Jack said.

A chime sounded, and Gulthak's number stopped.

100%

"Oh, and poor old Gulthak had to be granted all his magic to keep up with the others," Ky said. "But that's okay. Magic isn't where he shines anyway. Just look at that smile!"

The cameras changed briefly to display Gulthak. His grin showed rows of blackened gums and worn-down teeth. When he noticed himself in the cameras, he flexed a bicep that popped so large it could have given deck guns on a battleship a run for their money.

"And last but most definitely not least, our newest up-and-comer, Daniel Fitzgerald!"

Daniel peered at the spinning number. He'd never had an opportunity to see his own strength quantified quite so clearly. He wondered where he stacked up in comparison to Jack, or a dragon like Kavarssian.

The chime sounded.

0.6%

There was a brief silence. For an instant, Daniel thought he might have rendered Ky speechless.

She came roaring back the next second. "Absolutely astounding! Mr. Fitzgerald is putting our other contestants to shame! Even compared to the aces of other teams, he's an absolute monster. We'll have to see what happens when the Order really goes to war in Purgatory!"

"Dude," Jack said. His tone was quiet, serious. "How much stronger did you get?"

"I dunno," Daniel said. He was equally stunned. He didn't think there was that much of a difference. "What's 21.4 divided by 0.6?"

Jack looked at him. Daniel looked back.

"What happened, back on Earth?" Jack asked.

"The Vorid happened," Daniel said quietly. "I told you before, back at the café. I got lucky and offed one of the bigshots in New York. But he's still small potatoes compared to the real stuff that's coming. If we don't get back…"

Daniel trailed off, leaving the obvious unsaid. Daniel was probably the strongest contractor at the time of his banishment. He was strong enough to take on a Vorid lord. By himself, he could make a significant difference in the battles ahead; he was a check against other singularly powerful fighters. While he kept them busy, mankind would be able to fight a winning battle.

And he was in exactly the wrong place. The numbers didn't lie. He'd been a little less powerful than the lord during their fight; now, having essentially absorbed it, he was that much stronger. Maybe strong enough to take one down by himself.

"Without further ado, let's get started!" Ky said. "Once you take your places in front of a path, you'll be on your own! Sad to say my commentary might give you hints on what the other team is doing, so you won't be able to hear my wonderful dulcet tones while you're racing!"

Daniel heaved a sigh of relief. He'd almost overdosed on her overblown brand of positivity. Though—as he and Jack took their positions, and he eyeballed the dark road ahead—he wasn't sure what he wanted less—her voice chattering in his ear, or the silence that awaited him.

As Daniel inched forward, he realized there was something blocking the way—a hazy white pane of magic he hadn't noticed against the black background. He pressed a hand to it; it felt like warm glass, vibrating under his touch. This must be the barrier Jack mentioned.

"Once we pass through," Jack said, "you won't be able to see much. No communication until we meet back up. I'm out there, though, so don't die and keep moving."

"Thanks for the advice, champ," Daniel said.

"Our players are on their marks!" Ky said. "Contestants at the ready! Get set!"

Daniel and Jack both looked forward. Daniel bent his knees, feeling out the path under his shoes. The rubber grips felt a bit off, like his feet were a half-inch larger than usual, but it was more than worth it. He did not want to slip off this path.

"Good luck," Jack said.

"See you on the other side," Daniel said.

"Ready!" Ky said. "Three. Two. One. And...go!"

The barrier vanished. Daniel took Jack's advice to heart and resisted the urge to take off at top speed. He was probably the fastest of the bunch; he could make up a little hesitation later on. Caution wouldn't kill him, but barreling headlong into the unknown definitely might.

He stepped onto the path.

As soon as he completely passed the barrier, there was a sound like a rush of wind, the thump of a closed door. The void advanced toward him, roiling in like dark clouds and eating up the path forward. Daniel stepped back in alarm—only for his heel to drop through open air.

The rubber sole of his toe stuck on the edge of road. He tipped back, swaying his arms, then caught his balance and stumbled forward. Daniel fell onto his knees, catching his breath and letting his heart settle before glancing back.

The island he'd left was gone—and so was Jack's path. And the other team's paths. And all the cameras, and any other sign of anything else.

He was alone, and now he could only see roughly twenty feet ahead. Everything else was total and complete darkness, a landscape of lightless ink-black. No horizon, no ground, no sky. Only the sole road forward.

Daniel swallowed back his nerves and started into a jog.

Chapter 13
Games in the Dark

The path was hard beneath Daniel's feet, no dirt, no give. There were pebbles, bits and pieces here and there, but nothing was scattered by his passing, like it was all cast from one huge mold instead of naturally formed.

Everything sounded confined and muffled. His footfalls were heavy and dull; his breaths were hushed; the sound of his jeans brushing together was a bare whisper. Noises traveled out, then went dead, as if the air was so thick they couldn't make it back to be heard. It seemed like the loudest sound was his heartbeat, pumping in time to his arms and legs.

As he moved forward, more of the path showed up, rolling in pace with him out of the darkness. Outcroppings of rock, rough patches, divots, and potholes threatened to trip him up. He kept his steps light and careful, one eye on the darkness. A glance told him that the path vanished into the gloom behind him at the same rate, as if he was the center of a twenty-foot bubble of visible reality. It was almost like running on a treadmill—only the uniqueness of the coming path ahead gave him any hint he was making progress.

Beyond that, a silent void.

Without any obstacles or points of interest to slow him down, Daniel kicked up the pace a little, channeling some magic into his legs. His power felt sluggish, difficult to draw out, like trying to suck a too-thick ice cream shake through a thin straw. But the effort kept him energized, made the feeling of his brisk jog seem as easy as a slow meandering walk. He felt like he could maintain it for hours.

He ground on.

And on.

The slog continued. He built a light sweat; his breathing was harder than at the beginning, but even. At first, he'd been catching the sides of his cross trainers on the rock, but now he was getting a bit more used to the terrain.

Daniel started to notice a change. The path was wide enough for four people at the start, standing shoulder to shoulder. Now three people would have a hard time. And then, after he passed a particularly large boulder on the left side, it noticeably shrank to just three or four feet across.

The void loomed underneath him, empty and waiting. Taunting at him to trip. Just once.

He started to imagine shapes in the dark. Faces, eyes. Swirling shadows. He blinked a few times, trying to chase the visions away.

Daniel realized this was part of the challenge. Staying focused, staying on track, not letting his mind drift. He clenched and unclenched his hands a few times, using the sensation to bring him back to the moment.

It was hard to keep himself on task. Alone in the black, with no reference other than the churning path, the time ticked by slowly. Someone could have told him it had been five minutes, or five hours—he would have believed either explanation.

A barrier emerged ahead of him.

Daniel could see it clearly this time—a swirling, translucent shield expanding out to the edge of the black, barring further progress. He slowed to a halt, and stood there. The path seemed to track forward under his feet—a weird sense of disorientation from being in motion for so long.

When the sensation passed, Daniel put his palm against the barrier. It felt the same as when he tested it previous—solid and glassy, buzzing lightly under his fingers. He tried channeling a bit of his magic into his hand. The vibration increased in intensity, enough to numb his skin. Taking that as a warning sign, he let his magic drop and backed away.

Almost as soon as he thought about sitting down, the barrier vanished. Daniel poked his head about, as if it were a trick, then tested ahead with his foot. *Definitely gone.*

"Alright Jack," Daniel said aloud. "Nice one."

Even his voice sounded deadened in his ears. Daniel squatted down a few times, bending his knees, shooing away the ache of repetitive motion, and then he jumped back into his jog, feeling a little bit more motivated. His own obstacle would be up next, the first of two, and he needed to get it done quick to keep up what had to be an early lead.

Daniel put more grit into his run. He'd probably been a little behind Jack's pace, considering the barrier dropped almost as soon as he got there. Jack reached his obstacle and had time to complete it almost before Daniel even made it to the roadblock. That said, there was no guarantee their paths had the same length or structure, but without anything else to go on it was the safe assumption.

The path kept getting narrower. Daniel kept up his half-run for a while, but when it shrank to barely two feet across, he had to slow down. The terrain flattening out, fewer rocks to trip on—but he couldn't bring himself to go faster. One wrong move and he was gone.

Something that sounded like metal swung through the air.

Daniel didn't think; he reacted. He dove forward, and a whizzing *something* rushed behind his neck.

His chest hit the ground first, knocking the wind out of him. His arms and legs splayed out off the path entirely. Coughing and hacking, he wrapped his limbs around the thin ledge, clinging on for dear life.

After a few seconds, the sound came again—the parting of air before a blade. Steadily, he brought his knees back under him, getting on all fours before craning his head to take a look. It appeared out of the darkness—an axe blade at the end of a mechanical arm, swinging straight for where his neck would have been. It cut past him and vanished back into the deep to repeat its pattern.

He carefully crawled out from under its range of motion, then got back to his feet. The path was even thinner ahead; a single foot across, if that. The axe behind him kept swinging at intervals, a reminder that another machine could take a whack at him out of the darkness at any time.

This was definitely his obstacle.

Daniel smirked. It had given him a scare there for a second, but this was his specialty—reaction time.

Now that he knew what was coming, Daniel marched forward, planting his feet firmly, balance centered, head on a swivel. He could have kept crawling, gripping the stone at the sides to insure he wouldn't fall, but that would be way too slow, and there was no guarantee they hadn't considered that strategy.

Almost as soon as he had the thought, twin blades stabbed out of the darkness below him. Daniel tucked his arms in, and their edges slid by his skin. One of them nicked his right knuckle, sending a sharp sting through his hand and drawing blood—but it wasn't anything major. If he'd been crawling along, it would have cut his arms clean off his body.

Daniel diverted more magic from his legs and into his arms, balancing it out through his body. Normally he'd be able to shove power through himself, but now he needed to conserve it, use it carefully. Balance, that was the key—ready to react from every angle.

A buzzing sawblade jutted out from the ink fog, slicing at his knees. Daniel jumped over it—and two more sword blades spiked in from the left and right, trying to catch him midair. He twisted as he flew, bringing his legs up and his head down, snaking through the gap and falling into a roll. He popped back up to his feet and kept walking, brushing the dust from his shirt.

The blades kept coming. More combinations, more traps to catch him off guard. There was a frequent pattern of a first strike—less intended to kill him than to put him into a compromising position. That was followed with a second, and sometimes, a third trap. Those were the lethal moments where he was tested. But Daniel's magic might have been tailor-made for the challenge; he was faster than every blade; he had the edge on every axe.

The thought struck him that it was intentional. They were about their ratings, about their business. The whole challenge itself might be designed to show him off.

As Daniel kept his magic flowing, he noticed something curious—he could almost hear the blades better. He'd found that his eyesight was noticeably improved by his magical growth—he caught movement and small details easily, and it was as if he could see farther. He'd never considered his hearing before. Experimentally, he pushed extra magic into his ears.

Daniel's vision spun; a wave of nausea gripped his stomach. His legs failed him; he collapsed onto the path. He scrabbled for purchase on the stone, almost rolling off before he hooked his arms around it again, more by feel than anything. He didn't know which way was up, and every sense was telling him something different.

Sounds smashed into his ears like bricks through a storefront. Rustles of clothing sounded like crashing waves. His skin across the stone was nails on a chalkboard. His body hitting the ground was a bass drum pounding through an amp. It was a shrieking symphony, played off-key, out of tune, and as loud as possible.

His magic vanished—not because he consciously withdrew it, but as a result of his lack of control. Without Daniel pushing on it, the power trickled back into his center.

Slowly, the world stopped rotating around him. The headache that had spiked in behind his eyeballs was very much still present, but now a generalized throbbing instead of a peak migraine. He realized he was breathing hard and fast. His heart was beating a mile a minute; he was coated in sweat.

Daniel wrenched himself to his feet. He ran his hands over his face, brushing his hair back a few times. A few gulps of air helped settle his body down.

How could he have been so stupid? He thought it would be straightforward, like his eyes—but now he realized how ignorant he'd been. The ears didn't only govern hearing—he hadn't considered his sense of balance and orientation. It was a system that needed precision and fine tuning, not something he could throw magic at and expect to somehow be *better*.

Shaking his head clear of the last of it, he seized his magic and shoved it outward, pouring it evenly through his body enough to make his skin gain the familiar white haze. He wasn't sure how long he'd been down, and now he had to make up for lost time.

Fully empowered, Daniel took off at partial run, as fast as he dared go to make up for the lost time. The path narrowed to the width of a balance beam, too thin to put his feet under his shoulders. If he wanted to keep pace, he had to go fast enough that his feet could land in a straight line. He doubted the traps would be forgiving.

Alright, you sons of bitches. Let's see what you've got.

Daniel dug deep, pulling up every bit of his restricted powers. He poured the majority into his legs and broke into a full sprint. A trail of white magic followed his path, like an afterimage dragging behind him. He dodged the next three trap setups in a row with sheer speed, gone before they had a chance to fully activate.

His luck ended quickly. Three buzzsaws came in straight at him—one at the ankles, one at his waist, one at head-height. He planted a foot down hard and leapt up. The highest saw shaved the rubber toe of his shoe off, but he cleared all three.

Another obstacle, an axe, came in across the path, swooping low—too low to hit him after his jump. Still in the way, however, was the long mechanical arm on the other end of it—and he was flying forward, unable to change direction.

He didn't have time to twist out of the way. Instead, Daniel reached out and grabbed the metal arm. He flung himself around it, bending like an athlete performing a high-jump, and in the process accelerated. He went up another few feet before his leap finally peaked, and then he was falling, plummeting in slow-motion toward a tiny stone path that now looked no wider than a piece of string.

Another trap activated below him. Five blades instantly speared across the path, three from below and two from the left and right. Daniel was still too high, and he flew over them. Two more buzzsaws swept in, their mechanical arms moving on three joints to offset their pattern of attack, but he passed over those, too.

And then, something he didn't expect happened—the path turned left.

Daniel's little maneuver with the axe had thrown him slightly to the right. He'd been planning on catching the walkway with his arms on the way down. Now there'd be nothing to catch—at his current speed, he was going to land in the pit past the turn.

Daniel tried to create a physical sigil, some kind of platform he could jump off. The spell did its best, but he didn't have the power to generate it properly; a brief buzzing and a faint push was all he got before the magic fizzled out. Not enough.

He was definitely going to overshoot the path. The darkness loomed beyond like an open mouth waiting to swallow him up. His magic sped up his perception enough to give him a few moments to think, but there was nothing to think about. He was out of options.

A glint of metal caught his eye. Below him, the arm from the two buzzsaws was still there. The back end of the joint had lingered behind its attached blades.

Daniel threw himself to the left as hard as he could, arms straight, and kicked out wildly with a foot.

His shoes struck something; it gave slightly, but pushed him back, away from the darkness and toward the thin white stone.

He banged hard into the path on his ribs. His arms caught hold, but gave way with the force of his weight, scraping against his upper arms, then his elbows, then wrists. His fingers found the path, and they curled hard as Daniel jammed his magic into his hands.

He swung violently; his legs flailed in the darkness. His thumbs slipped. The rough stone surface ground against his palms; the sting made his fingers want to let go, but overriding survival instinct caused Daniel to clench them even tighter.

He swung back the other way, then back again. He came to a slow, swaying hang, every fiber of his being focused on not tumbling into the pit below him.

Daniel grunted, strained, and pulled himself up to lean against it on his waist. The path was like a pipe, now, so thin he couldn't really stand on it. He swung a leg over, then straightened, keeping it gripped tight between his thighs. His hands were red and sore from the rough surface; they trembled when he unclenched them.

He worked the feeling back into his fingers and started to shimmy forward, making his way along the pipe of path a few inches at a time. If something tried to hit him now, he wasn't sure how he'd avoid it.

Ironically, it was the harrowing thinness of the rock that had saved him. If it wasn't so small, he couldn't have been able to grip it in the first place.

Following the sharp left turn—he mentally cussed out whoever thought to throw that in at the last minute—the path continued straight. Daniel scooted along, hands ahead of his body, going as fast as he dared into the darkness.

Stone emerged from the fog—a wider path. It rapidly returned to its normal size, a walk several feet wide. Daniel made it off his little pipe of stone and crawled onto it on his knees. He stayed there a long moment, letting the ball in his gut unravel. He had to fight the urge to kiss the ground.

Remembering he was in a race, he got back to his feet and broke into a quick jog. A square block of stone emerged from the dark, sitting to the left of the path; a big green button sat on its face. He pressed it to open Jack's barrier, then, confident the challenge was well and truly over, he fell into a full run.

The path blossomed into a circular island made of the same pale grey rock. This one had four stone pedestals rising to about waist height near the center. He could see three other paths leading away from it—one adjacent to his, and two on the opposite side, splitting off into the dark. It was depressingly similar to where he'd started.

Daniel crossed the threshold onto the island. A chime played around him, the same low-quality showtunes dancing in the background as before. "Congratulations on being the first arrival, Daniel!" Ky's voice said. "You get first pick...and look what we have in store *for youuu!*"

Multicolored lights glowed atop each pedestal, and the tiny image of an object appeared on each one. The three in the back quickly lost their glow; a metal breastplate, a helmet, and a roughly hewn block Daniel thought was some kind of shield. The pedestal in the front and center glimmered with an eye-catching silver light, and it showed the image of a full suit of armor.

Jack had been right. The choice was obvious.

Daniel reached for the armor. The image flashed, and the light ran up his skin, coating over his body not unlike his own magic when he ran it on full charge.

Silver scale-mail grew up his hands and feet like a second skin. It coated his hands close, like gloves, but rode up over his shirt. It reinforced his shoes, sliding right over where his pants cuffed the ankles. The stuff felt a bit cool as it climbed over him, but also weightless, as if it wasn't even there. It road up his neck and came in close over his hair like a skullcap. A clear face shield snapped into place as the armor finished expanding.

"Now we're talking," Daniel said. He eyed his hands and arms. Despite going over his clothes, it was surprisingly comfortable and didn't hinder his movement. He didn't know how much protection it would give, but it filled in one of his worst weaknesses—the fact that, on the other side of his speed and magic, he was still human. He tapped on the visor in front of his eyes, curious. It thudded like metal on hard plastic.

"Unsurprisingly, Daniel uses his advantage to the fullest and picks the elven armor! He'll be a force to be reckoned with later on. Oh, look—he has an unexpected guest! Or, rather, a very expected guest!"

Daniel glanced back—and there was Gulthak, towering above him, but stuck on the other side of a barrier. The ogre stared Daniel down, barring jagged, yellow-black teeth. It growled at him.

Daniel flicked him the bird, then walked to the other side of the island. One of the exits was blocked by another barrier—probably Gulthak's next route. The other was left open. Daniel waved a cheery goodbye to the ogre, ignoring the increasing volume of his growls, then took off down his path at a quick pace. Since Daniel had reached his island first, Jack probably had, too. If they could keep the edge they had going, they'd have this match in the bag.

The darkness swallowed him again, limiting his visibility and soaking up sound. Daniel disliked the feeling of isolation, but he shrugged it off better now that he'd made some progress. It was an intimidation tactic, nothing more.

The path was broad and unremarkable. Daniel fell into his previous quick jog, ears perked and eyes focused, on the lookout for the next trap. He wasn't going to let this place surprise him again.

Despite his best efforts, when Daniel reached his next obstacle, he was certainly surprised.

The path opened up into another round island of rock. At first, he'd thought he'd already made the next intersection—but that didn't make any sense. If that were true, then one team was virtually guaranteed to have first pick both times. As he stepped onto the island, and his vision cleared up, he saw the nest.

The center of the island was pitted, and covered irregularly in a black ichor, like someone had thrown a few buckets of black paint over the rock. The central and darkest portion of the goo held a few bright red eggs. They were shiny, glistening like Jello, and as he watched, they wobbled, vibrated, as if something inside was alive.

There were three wooden signs staked out near the nest. Daniel approached, squinting suspiciously. He could tell the writing was the demon language—because it wasn't like anything he'd ever seen—but as he looked closer, the words shifted into legible English. At least Hell's translation magic still worked in the arenas. He leaned in to read them.

Hello Daniel, and welcome to your next obstacle! I can't talk to you while you're in the middle of your challenge, so this will have to do.

Further along your path is a basket. Take an egg with you and drop it into that basket to clear Jack's next barrier.

Any egg will do—you just need one. But be careful...egg-snatchers aren't well received anywhere!

"Isn't that great," Daniel said. He could practically hear Ky's voice in the words etched on the signs. "What could possibly go wrong?"

Daniel tested a toe on the black goo. It smeared a bit, but otherwise wiped off without problems. He was glad to be wrapped up in the armor; he didn't want that stuff on his bare skin. The eggs sat a few feet into the pit, little jiggling red orbs a bit smaller than his fist.

He crept step-by-step into the nest, pausing periodically to look over his shoulder. That last line about egg-snatchers wasn't Ky being cute; it was a hint. If there were eggs, something had to lay them.

Daniel reached down and touched an egg. His armored fingers gripped it without trouble; it felt somewhat rubbery, almost sticking to his hand. Not exactly pleasant, but far preferable to a pamba.

He stopped there, a few fingers around the first egg, waiting for something to leap out at him.

Nothing happened.

Daniel relaxed slightly, then palmed the egg, raising it up to take a better look at it. Brightly colored and more pink than red up close, like a somewhat creepy Easter egg. He moved to put it in his pocket, then remembered halfway that the armor was covering up his clothes. And yet, even as the thought occurred to him, the armor shimmered near his waistline and parted slightly, revealing the front pocket of his jeans.

"Now that," Daniel said, slipping the egg inside, "is nifty." The scales of metal merged together as he lifted his hand away, almost like a living thing responding to his intentions. He shook his head in wonder, mentally comparing his old homemade armor to the silvery bodysuit. It was like comparing a kindergartener's scribbly clouds to a professional landscape painting. "I gotta get me one of these."

Daniel frowned and glanced back at the nest. The signs said he only needed one egg—but they didn't say he couldn't take more than one. He squatted down again, leaning over the black goo.

A shriek shook the island, a sharp, high-pitched staccato that cut straight into Daniel's ears and right through his bones. He froze, tensing up so hard he could almost feel the knot twist in one of his shoulder blades. The sound came again—from underneath the island—like the dissonant, chopped-up roar of a velociraptor.

Somewhere inside the bottom of Daniel's brain was a primitive monkey, and it cowered in fear at that sound, hands clutched tight over its face.

Daniel shoved his hand into his pocket. And then he bolted.

Magic blasted down into his legs and out through where his shoes hit the ground; he cleared the edge of the island in a flash. His armored feet pounded the path with a machine-gun rattle of metal on stone. His arms churned as he sprinted as fast as he could.

Something heavy beat into the path behind him. He could feel it under his feet, a thumping that was following him, gaining rapidly. Daniel lowered his head and ran even faster, going all-out in a blind race through the darkness ahead.

The terrible roar echoed right behind him. It shocked through his system like ice water down his spine. His legs failed him; he half-tripped, caught himself in a bend, and straightened just in time to avoid hitting the ground face-first. As soon as he had his balance, he chanced a look over his shoulder.

A thing loomed out of the shadows, a creature of living ink that was somehow blacker than the dark fog that obscured its lower half. Its tree-trunk sized limbs slammed into the stone in a long gallop, its talons almost too big for the path. Its head was a twisted maw, barely distinguishable from the ichor that was dripping from the glistening folds of its skin.

That was all Daniel saw before he threw his head back straight and focused every iota of his being on running. His heart was in his throat; he felt like the image of the creature was burned into the back of the eyes.

Daniel ran in a blind panic. He didn't have a plan, and he couldn't think of any clever ideas. His mental functions were sold out to instinct, co-opted in a hostile takeover that screamed *FLEE* into every neuron in his body. It was like the creature was designed to scare him—or that he was hardwired to be scared of it.

Another bone-stabbing shriek came out of the thing behind him. Daniel's arms and legs flailed, suddenly out of sync, as if the roar was a defibrillator attached to his brain.

He got his feet back under him and poured on the speed. A glance back—carefully calibrated to look at the ground, and not directly at it—told him it had gained a step on him. Another few steps and he was lunch.

An island appeared in front of him—at his speed, virtually exploding out of the dark and into his vision as he skidded into the center. Relief flooded through him as he sought the delivery basket, desperate to get rid of the egg and get the hell out of dodge.

The creature stopped behind him, also sliding to a halt. It shrieked its choppy growl at him, practically roaring in his face. Flaps of its oily neck-flesh bucked and wobbled, producing the halting, unearthly howl that resonated out of its body. Daniel recoiled, stamping his feet a bit to keep his balance. It was a little easier to take when he knew it was-

Another howl shrieked out behind him.

Daniel threw himself mentally against the grinding unease, fighting the urge to dive forward, and he stepped to the side instead. It was all he could do not to dash straight into the grasping claws—tendrils—*somethings* of the creature in front of him. The sound seemed to override his control of his body.

Daniel backed himself to the center of the island as he risked a look over his shoulder. He chanted a mantra in his head against his anxiety. *There's only one of them. There's only one of them. Only one of them.*

There was a second creature on the other side of the island, prowling forward out of the dark. Daniel tried to let go of the breath he was holding. It came out in shuddered, wheezing gasps. He withdrew into the very middle of the plot of stone, as far away as possible from both of them.

Surprisingly, they didn't follow. They held their own positions, stalking the entrance and the exit to the island. They were prepared to wait him out. Daniel stayed on his toes, wondering if he'd be able to duck under the legs of the second one. The black fluid dripping from its underside made that a nasty and potentially slippery prospect.

They both roared again. The pulse of sound scraped Daniel's ears from both sides, turning his muscles into paralyzed mush. The creatures lunged in unison, talons and tendrils extended to wrap him up.

Whether his magic was buffering against the worst of it, or he was getting used to the noise, Daniel came back to himself as they closed the gap. He drove a pulse of magic into his legs, skipping back—but he wasn't quite quick enough to dodge a claw from the one on the left.

The talon scraped against his left side, drawing sparks off his armored scales. The force pushed him back; he stumbled, but managed to keep his balance having avoided the brunt of the attack.

He immediately bolted for the exit, trying to get around the second creature. It was ready for him, cutting him off before he could escape. Daniel returned to the middle of the island, and they were right back where they started, each monster keeping a close guard on both ways out.

Daniel watched them carefully, eyes shifting to one, and then the other. They didn't—or perhaps couldn't—roar at him continuously. That would make a swift end of his little resistance. There must be some kind of limit to how often they could produce the sound. Maybe it was magic.

That thought sent a lightbulb into his head. If the roars were magical, they could be affecting his mental state. Maybe *all* the sensations he was feeling were artificial. If that was true, he should be able to fight it.

Daniel rebalanced his magic through the entirety of his body. He could feel his fists relax and his back straighten as the raw fear washed away—not entirely banished, but suppressed. The creatures didn't look quite so terrible—almost as if his own eyesight had betrayed him, built them up to be more monstrous than they really were.

The roars they produced were definitely unnatural—almost like they could shake his grip on his magic a few moments, make him lose control over his body. The only thing keeping him lucid was his pointed control of his magic. He had to figure a way out of this before they got another shot at him.

Daniel wasn't able to slip by after the first confrontation, but he did catch sight of a glimmer of hope—a broad, steel-barred basket, beyond the exit to the island. If he could get by the second creature, he was virtually home free.

If.

Daniel pulled a bright red egg out of his pocket, holding it so it was clearly visible. The two creatures immediately sent out smaller, more communitive chitters at one another. They crept forward a few feet.

Daniel gripped the egg tight; under pressure, the rubbery substance bulged past his fingers. The creatures made series of low-pitched, threatening growls. "Yeah?!" Daniel shouted back. "You want your egg squashed?! Huh? Come on, you freaks, lets see what you got!" Daniel wielded the egg like a caveman with a torch, stepping forward and brandishing it at the animals, more to pump himself up than truly intimidate them. They seemed unsure of how to deal with this latest development, snipping at each other and shrieking at him in turns.

One of the roars was loud enough to shake him. The egg slipped from his fingers, and he bobbed wildly to catch it before it got away from him. Both the creatures creeped in and bent low, as if to pounce.

The egg skipped from his left hand, off his right palm, and back to his left. He snagged it from the air, checked his hold on it, then raised it again. His arm shook from the adrenaline of near-death. "Get the hell back! I said back off, assholes!"

The creatures stopped closing in, but they didn't step away. They were within easy striking distance if they stunned him with their roars. He'd hoped to worry them into moving out of the way by using the egg as a hostage, but it didn't look like they were smart enough to appreciate the nuance of his strategy. Or maybe they weren't dumb enough to fall for it.

Time for plan B.

Daniel raised his hand. The fleshy heads of the monsters followed the path of his arm, necks craning. He wound up, bent his knee in, then hucked the egg like he was trying to skip a stone.

The egg flew toward the edge of the island, skipping over the rock like a bouncy ball. The creatures yelped in alarm, then galloped right after it, throwing themselves over each other in a mad scramble to reach the red orb before it vanished into the void. Daniel broke for the exit, drawing the second egg he'd snatched from the nest out of his other pocket.

By the time he reached the basket, the creatures had recovered from his distraction and were scrambling to turn on him, legs and inky tendrils propelling them in a hunched, lopsided sprint. He dunked the egg into the container, and the cheery gameshow music came back on even as the two beasts charged at him. Daniel ran for his life.

He hadn't gotten far when he heard a walloping THUMP. When he looked back, the two monsters were plastered against a barrier, their ugly shrieks muffled to a dull whine by the magic. They threw themselves against it in a mindless rage. The barrier shuddered and warped, but it held.

Daniel decided to get moving—the farther away he was from those things, the better. He rubbed a hand across his armor's visor as he started down the path again, wishing he could wipe the memories out of his head. Some things you couldn't unsee.

With his second obstacle completed, Daniel knew he was going to hit either an island or a barrier next. He glanced down at his armor, inspecting the damage where the creature had landed a hit. There was a foot-long scratch dug across the silver scales. It didn't seem to affect the armor's flexibility. Daniel wasn't sure if the blow would have been life-threatening without any protection, but his chances of survival would have dropped quite a bit if he was injured. Plus, from the look of the inky freaks, they might have poisoned him—or who knows what else—if they landed a clean blow.

He was doubly glad to have stolen the suit from Gulthak. It would have turned the ogre into a mobile fortress.

After a relatively short time compared to the other distances, Daniel saw an island emerge out of the dark fog. He started to lift his arms in victory—then dropped them. His shoulders slumped; his mouth hung open slightly in disbelief. There were four pedestals in the middle of the island, and they had items floating on them—except the central one, which was completely bare. Three distinctly less-shiny images hovered over the remaining spots.

Daniel trudged in, feeling more than a little deflated. He'd flat-out sprinted the length of the last challenge, spurred on by a combination of fear and magic. He'd only been trapped near the basket for a short time. His backup plan to distract the monsters worked better than he could have hoped.

And he still hadn't made it. Kavarssian or Gulthak must have gone up against something that didn't even phase them. Maybe he'd been running longer than he thought.

"Up-and-comer Daniel Fitzgerald is eating a disappointment sandwich!" Ky shouted. Her tinny voice projected from a camera that swooped down on him from somewhere above. "My lovely Kav-Kav has already come and gone, stealing the show out from under Danny's feet. Let's see what he makes of the slim pickings left behind!"

A small voice in the back of Daniel's head restrained his impulse to swear at her, counseling that it was a very bad idea to piss off the game show host. He grumbled his way to the pedestals, keeping the choicest words carefully under his breath. A look at them showed a series of metal weapons—a sword, a spiked set of brass knuckles, and finally, a mace. The mace had a spherical head complete with sharp rivets and spikes jutting out at regular angles—not unlike what he'd made himself in the past.

Daniel went for the mace without hesitation. He was far more familiar with it than the other two. The sword looked cool, but aside from putting the pointy end in the other guy, he didn't have the first idea of how to use one. The brass knuckles were more useful, and he knew how to throw a punch, but he doubted he'd compete with either Gulthak or Kavarssian if it came down to fists.

His original reason for buying a baton—and then later, making a mace—was that it was easy to learn and use, extended his reach, and was more effective than hitting things with his bare fists. It also made good use of his magic, which he could channel into objects to strengthen them. In this case, maybe it was good luck that he picked up a mundane weapon, rather than something enchanted. The last time he put his magic in an object that already had an enchantment, it blew up. Even since he got his elven armor—including in the midst of his earlier panic—he'd been very careful to only push magic through himself, and not the armor, paranoid he'd get lethally explosive results.

Daniel picked up the mace. The shaft was grey metal, and it was all one solid piece, merging with the head of the weapon without any joints or welds. There was a ribbed grip at the bottom which was stiff, but slightly rubbery, like the stuff they made cell phone cases with. He gave it a few test swings. It was a little heavier than he was used to, weighted too much toward the head, but it would do.

"From that quick pick, it looks like Daniel wasn't totally left out in the cold!" Ky said. "I'm looking forward to see what he can do with that morning star. Daniel's done with his side of the job—after meeting up with Jack, they'll be off to the arena."

At her words, Daniel duly started toward the sole remaining path into the void. The island vanished into the black behind him. Daniel tucked the mace in and picked up into a swift jog. His half of the challenges were over—he should have a straight, easy shot to the finish.

Aside from the barrier that popped out of the dark at him. He sighed at the sight.

It was like the others, a flat, misty field of magic. It stretched out far past the edge of the path and into the dark, spitting on any attempt to circumvent it. Daniel trod to a halt, but he stayed on his toes, expecting Jack to take action for him soon enough.

The seconds ticked by. Eventually, he put his arms on his hips and let himself relax. Hopefully Jack was doing alright on his end.

Daniel glanced at the barrier. There didn't seem to be any rule preventing him from trying to force his way past. Everyone took it as a given that it couldn't be done. Maybe he'd have better luck with a weapon?

Cautiously, he pushed power down his arm, through his fingers, and into his mace. He kept his senses peeled for any unintended side-effects. His armor, thankfully, didn't react. In fact, everything operated as if it wasn't even there. *I really gotta get me one of these.*

The white light typical of his particular brand of magic filled the mace, turning the dull steel into a gleaming pale-gray lava lamp. He pressed the head of his mace against the barrier.

It warped, trembled, then buzzed, harsher and harder than before. His mace rebounded off its surface with enough speed that Daniel was forced to step backward to keep his grip on it. The head of the weapon struck a nearby boulder before he got a handle on the momentum.

He glanced at the boulder—not a scratch. The barrier's wavering power had concentrated at the point he'd struck, but it spread back out into a calm, even haze.

There wasn't any real harm in trying again, but Daniel decided against it. He might exhaust himself for no reason, and he needed to save his strength for the battle ahead. Plus, the feeling he'd gotten was akin to the wall almost grabbing his weapon then throwing it back with similar force. If he hit harder, it would fly back harder—and if he wasn't careful, he would lose his mace to the abyss. He had a feeling that if his weapon fell into the pit, he wasn't getting it back.

And so, without anything else to do, Daniel waited.

And waited.

Time flowed by, but it could have been five minutes, or twenty. In this place, his sense of time had been a frequent frustration. There was no telling minutes from hours here in the void—no sunlight, no reference points.

The barrier buzzed if he touched it, but otherwise, it was quiet. The only sound was his own breathing. He hummed and tapped his feet to break the silence. It came off as forced even to himself.

More than once, Daniel caught himself looking over his own shoulder, back the way he'd come. He was half-afraid one of those things would show up again, lunge in at him without warning and pin him against the barrier with no way out. Sometimes, he could see shapes in the darkness, wavering faces, flecks of light. He rubbed at his visor to chase away the visions, hoping it was just his eyes playing tricks on him.

He came up with a little game to pass the time. The barrier wavered slightly, to and fro, almost like a curtain in a gentle breeze. He timed roughly 6 seconds for it to slowly ripple from one side to another. 10 ripples made for a full minute. That way, he could tell time.

He got sick of it after the first minute.

Daniel stood there, sometimes staring at the darkness, sometimes at the white-grey rock under his feet, quietly contemplating his speck-like existence on a thin path in a silent void. It felt like the final stop, the place where the sidewalk ended. The darkness encircled him, as if all the rest of the world had fallen away and the only thing left was him and this little strip of stone. Everything else had been swept away by the powers that be.

Daniel felt a strange sensation, then, as if the path trembled slightly under his feet. Nothing had moved the path so far; man, beast, and magic had left it all undamaged. The pale surface was even tougher than normal rock, glued in place within the darkness by unnatural forces. He adjusted slightly, thinking his feet were tingling from standing still so long; he tapped the toes of his shoes against the ground. The armored scales that sleeved them plinked against the stone.

More shaking. Stronger this time. Daniel bent his knees, eyes wide. That was definitely not him. He checked the barrier; it hadn't budged.

The path was practically vibrating now. Daniel took a step and threw his arms out wide to get better balance. As the shaking worsened into a full-on earthquake, he crouched low, cautious of being thrown into the pit. *What the hell is going on?*

Something was moving at the end of the path. He lifted his mace up, keeping it between himself and whatever it was.

It looked almost like the edge of the path was moving toward him, out of the dark. Daniel squinted, confused. The path wasn't actually moving—bits and pieces of it were falling away, creating the false perception it was coming toward him.

Jack's warning from the beginning of the match flashed in his mind. If they were running out of time, the path would drop out from under them.

Daniel moved up against the barrier, flattening his back against it. The magical wall buzzed hard against his armor, but otherwise didn't harm him. He wasn't sure, but it seemed like the rate of decay was getting faster.

A chunk the size of his head broke off. The darkness swallowed it a heartbeat later. The unstable, cracking portion of the rock stretched closer. *Yep. Definitely faster.*

"Come on, Jack," Daniel said. The cracks spindled deeper into the path. Larger and larger sections were breaking away. "Come on, you dick. We can't lose like this. Come on!"

The cracks reached Daniel's shoes. Another thick chunk of the path snapped off and vanished into the black. He could feel it shifting under the soles of his feet, threatening to give.

Daniel's jaw worked as he pressed back into the barrier, ignoring the uncomfortable vibration. He worked his toes back, scrounging up every available inch of stability.

The chunk under his shoes gave slightly. Daniel began to lean forward as it tilted, not quite dropping but threatening to slide him into the abyss. He worked his feet hard, as if trying to get purchase on a hill that was a little too steep to climb easily.

Daniel fell. His gut lurched as he experienced the sickly sensation of an unexpected drop. For an instant, he thought the path dropped him—but he slammed into the ground on his back.

The wind rushed out of his lungs. Daniel kept his head and used his elbows to drag himself backward as he coughed the air back into his chest, ignoring the complaints of his wracked shoulders. He pulled his ankles up over where he'd previously stood.

The barrier was gone. It had vanished behind him.

"Jack, you glorious, dickhead sonuvabitch." Daniel was on his feet a half-second later, and he took off at a run. The crumbling path followed him, but the worst of it quickly fell out of sight. The shaking faded somewhat as he distanced himself, confirming that he was out of the danger zone.

Daniel settled into an easy jog; the path was still shaking a bit, and he didn't want to risk his footing. He started laughing as he went, eventually throwing his head back; the relief poured out of every pore of his body. That had been really, really close. "Hey, Jack!" Daniel shouted into the dark. "You seriously had me freaked out there!"

There was no answer, but Daniel didn't expect one. He'd meet up with his friend soon enough. And then he could pummel Jack's shoulder way too hard as punishment for hanging him out to dry too long.

There was a loud snap behind him.

Daniel glanced back, and the smile fell off his face like a sack of bricks. Cracks were rapidly spreading into the path behind him; they popped and cracked under his feet and raced past his position. A random chunk of the path dropped away, vanishing into the pit like a stone dropped into a well.

Daniel threw himself into a sprint.

The cracks were far past him now, signaling total destabilization of the pathway. Bits and pieces were coming off the edges. It wasn't crumbling behind him bit-by-bit anymore; it was falling apart everywhere. The immovable rock was turning into swiss cheese.

Daniel ran, his left fist pumping in time, while his right tucked his mace into his chest. His feet hit the path hard, and every time they did, he felt something gave in more. The path transformed into a deathtrap under his feet, filled with craters and holes that threatened to trip him. Some sections shuddered dangerously when he put weight on them, almost costing him his balance. Ignoring the potential danger, Daniel lifted his feet high and sprinted at top speed. He might trip and fall, but if he slowed down, he was dead anyway.

Daniel turned on his magic. He had a lot more control than he did when he faced off against the monsters—without their howling interference, he was in full command of his powers. He squeezed out everything he had, flying down the path like an Olympic sprinter that refused to tire.

When he hit the tiny limit he was allowed, Daniel pushed harder, trying to forcibly give himself more speed. It felt like trying to pump the ocean through a garden hose. The problem wasn't with the water itself, but he didn't have any other tools. Whatever curse the transfer to Hell had placed on his magic, or his soul, was beyond his ability to influence.

And then, the darkness itself dropped away. Just as it had closed in and cut off his visibility in the beginning, it opened, and he could see into the distance.

The path had hit a long rise—stretching slightly to the left, and then back to the right, before meeting with a huge island holding a square steel structure. Jack was standing on the island's edge, leaning forward over the path. His head snapped up when he saw Daniel emerge from the dark. "DAAAN! RUN!"

Daniel ran—but it was easier said than done. The path leading up to Jack was a trembling, pockmarked mess, actively falling apart at the seams. Fist-sized pieces of rock were raining down into the black pit below, and chunks larger than he was tall were breaking off periodically.

Daniel made it a bit closer, but the rock became too chewed up to run straight across. He hopped more than ran along the broken path, stepping from spot to spot, trying to keep to the sturdiest-looking bits.

His next hop forced him to put weight down on a piece of cracked rock—and his leg crashed through, the rock shattering like ice breaking on a frozen lake. Daniel slammed down into the path; his whole leg was stuck in the hole. Jack shouted encouragement at him as he hoisted himself back up. "Come on, man! Almost there! Go, go, go!"

Daniel hopped as soon as he got up—to a tiny island of rock, still floating in space, all the rest of it fallen. As it started to collapse, he jumped again, catching the next section with his arms and pulling himself up. Like that, he leapt between the last few grains of stone that were hovering in the void, closing the gap to Jack one bit at a time.

"You gotta jump for it!" Jack shouted. "It's gonna fall!"

Daniel glanced at the gap ahead. There were no other footholds between himself and Jack. There was no way he could do it in a single jump. "I won't make it!"

"I've watched this game before, you've got like five seconds!" Jack said. "Jump! Now!"

"I can't make that distance!"

"Just do it!"

Daniel shoved as much power into his legs as possible, bent his knees, and jumped. He bounded into the air; his scant magic still pushed his athletic ability to the human peak, as if he was a professional track star at the height of their career. His scaled elven armor responded to his focused intent and flared out under his arms like miniature wings—not enough to push him forward, but maybe enough to glide an extra inch or two.

Even that wasn't enough. Jack was too high, too out of reach. If only the path was level, instead of uphill at the very end—he might have made it.

Daniel's arms flailed out as he hit the peak of his jump, then began to descend. He was several feet short of the ledge—but it didn't matter how close he got. The jaws of the abyss loomed below him like a waiting predator, eager to swallow him up.

A massive, hairy hand appeared in front of Daniel. He slammed into it, and the fingers of the hand wrapped under his arms like a claw machine hoisting a prize. Daniel's face was buried in a tuft of fur.

Jack, leaned over the edge of the island, had transformed his arms into their ape-form. His left arm anchored him down, scrambling to keep a grip on the smooth stone; the other clenched Daniel tight. Jack grunted, then roared with the effort as he brought Daniel up and deposited him on the island.

The two of them splayed out, arms and legs flopping onto the ground. Jack's arms shrunk back to their normal sizes; the long hairs retreated into his body. Daniel spat to the side and heaved in his breaths. They both lay there, sucking in the tiny reprieve.

Daniel rolled over, raised his hand, and punched Jack in the shoulder.

"Ow!" Jack leaned away, cradling his limb. "The hell, man! I saved your life!"

"Yeah, yeah." Daniel laid onto his back again. "Took you long enough."

Jack snorted. And then he started laughing, and then Daniel laughed at his laugh, and they rolled around on the stone like idiots for almost a minute straight.

Daniel got onto his knees, still wheezing a few chuckles. "Can we not do this again, please?"

"Unfortunately," Jack said, "we're just getting started."

Chapter 14
Beyond Thunderdome

Daniel and Jack turned to face the structure on the island, but a flock of flying cameras zipped down into their faces. "And by a single hair, Jack is able to rescue Daniel from certain disaster! What a dramatic turnaround! This game is going to be running on the highlight reels for a while, folks!" Ky's high-pitched wail continued unabated as Daniel leaned back and grimaced at a particularly aggressive camera. "Meanwhile, Gulthak and Kavarssian have been sitting pretty for over ten minutes! They're well-rested and ready to go. The Sky Runners have the edge going into the second round!"

"What took you so long, anyway?" Daniel asked.

"Long story," Jack said. "I was able to cheese my way past the last challenge, but it took forever."

Ky continued before Jack could get into more detail. "Now our teams must enter...*the chamber*." The last two words were hushed and solemn, as if they were archeologists about to descend into the tomb of an ancient and powerful pharaoh. "Each pair must now together defeat the challenge lying in wait before them. If they can survive the trial within, they'll make it to the final round to duke it out for victory! Hunker down and brace for the action, because the doors are opening momentarily." Ky paused for a breath, then delivered another advertisement in rapid-fire host ramble. "Special thanks to our sponsor, Planet Express. For fast, efficient, and company-guaranteed interplanetary delivery services, accept no substitutes. Use Planet Express today and have your package delivered tomorrow. Planet Express."

As the cameras backed up a few feet, Daniel finally got a good look at the building that dominated the center of the island. It was tall, rectangular, and entirely constructed of shiny grey steel, towering over them like an alien monolith. There were two doors at the bottom, one on either side, and no other features.

"So what's this about?" Daniel asked.

"Dunno," Jack said. "We'll have to work together in some way to beat it. The rest we figure out ourselves."

"Great," Daniel said. "More surprises. You know, I used to like surprises. Remember when they were things like birthday presents or nice dinners? Now all the surprises are trying to kill me."

Jack snorted, shrugged. "Pretty much sums it up. Nice armor, by the way."

"Yeah, this stuff is sweet," Daniel said, admiring the shiny steel scales. "It responds to what I need it to do. Basically doesn't even feel like I'm wearing it, either. Did you get anything?"

"Yep," Jack said. "I beat Kavarssian to the first island. I got this." Jack pulled a round silver plate about the size an open palm out of his pants pocket. It was polished to a mirror shine; Daniel's face winked back at him even in the dim light. "This will reflect one attack back at the attacker. Magic spells, punches, anything—it absorbs the force, doubles it, and shoots it back. But it's only good for one shot, it breaks after."

"Not bad," Daniel said. "Any problems with your magic?"

"I won't last long if I transform my entire body," Jack said, "burns too much energy. But in and of itself, no problems."

"I basically can do everything, too," Daniel said. "I'm just way weaker."

"Right," Jack grumbled, "Mr. zero-point-zero-zero-zero something is weaker."

The doors in the bottom of the construct unlocked, sliding up and into the building; light flooded out of the openings. "One contestant to each door, please!" Ky said. "The challenge begins as soon as you enter the room. Be prepared, but don't linger outside!"

As soon as the words were out of her mouth, a familiar feeling started shifting under Daniel's feet. He glanced back—the edge of the island was already crumbling into the darkness. "Let's go!"

"Let's do this!" Jack shouted. They each ducked into their respective doorways, and the portals slammed shut behind them.

The room in front of Daniel was perfectly square, about 15 or 20 feet on either side. To his left was the outer wall of the building; it gleamed and winked with glare spots like stainless steel. Evenly-spaced lights embedded in the wall made the whole space bright and easily visible. The closed-in sense of security was a welcome change from the oppressive abyss.

The most notable feature of the room was a series of levers lining the wall. Each switch had a bright yellow-black handle, like the main switch of an electrical maintenance panel. Daniel counted 10 switches in total.

On his right side was a barrier—the typical translucent, hazy wall that had dotted the path previously. This one was far larger, stretching up all the way to the ceiling and dividing the space in two. He could see Jack on the other side, in his half of the room. The two sides were essentially symmetrical; Jack had his own set of switches, though his had red and black handles instead.

Jack turned to face him. His mouth moved, but Daniel didn't hear anything. Daniel put a hand up to his ear. Jack spoke again—obviously shouting—but nothing came through. "I can't hear you!" Daniel shouted.

Jack shook his head. He took a big breath, then opened his mouth and screamed as loud as he could. At least, Daniel figured that was what he was doing from his expression. The barrier was completely soundproof.

Daniel made an obvious frown, then shook his head and shrugged. Jack ambled over to a switch, pointed at it, and opened his hands as if to say *should I try it?*

Daniel raised his mace to guard against possible surprises and nodded at him. Jack's body grew a layer of fur; he didn't increase his size, but the fur would protect him from attack. The long grey hairs made him look like a life-sized, stuffed animal version of an abominable snowman.

Jack put his hand on the handle of the first switch and glanced at Daniel. Daniel gave him another firm nod, signaling that he was ready.

Jack threw the switch.

There was the sound of steel moving, like a bar slotting into place. Daniel wasn't quite able to pick out where it came from.

They waited. Daniel was tense, ready to twitch at the slightest sign of movement. They exchanged glances, then turned back to their rooms, expecting the worst to leap out at them as soon as they looked away.

Seconds of anxiety ticked away, but nothing happened. Daniel relaxed slightly.

Jack made a face, then dropped his protective fur coat. Daniel frowned, then cupped his ear again and rotated his head like a radar dish. Jack looked confused, then nodded in realization, pointing a few times in various directions. Daniel was confident he got the meaning, and shortly after, Jack flicked the switch back. This time, they listened closely for the source of the sound.

Steel slid against steel, and there was a muted *clang* as it struck home.

They both looked up at the same time. High above them— three or four stories straight up—was a circular hatch bulging from the ceiling. Half of it was on Daniel's side; the other half was on Jack's side, neatly cut by the barrier. A series of exposed metal bars kept the hatch shut, like reinforced rods holding a bank vault secure. Some of the bars were locked in place; others were slotted away from the hatch.

Daniel imagined that the point of the challenge was to open the door and escape, but even if they opened the hatch, how were they supposed to leave? It wasn't that he hadn't leapt tall buildings in a single bound before, but the tiny trickle of magic he had access to walled that option off. Daniel's magic could be concentrated to focus on power, rather than speed, but the process was inefficient; he didn't have the resources to push himself up the 30 or 40 feet to the ceiling.

Rather than waste energy that way, he used the one spell Rachel had been able to teach him—the most basic physical sigil. It was a small, hazy pad of light, shaped somewhat like a dinner plate, and the only thing it could do was repel things that came near it—that, and give off a little bit of light. Daniel had repurposed the simple magic by forming them directly under his feet. That created a sort of magical *step*, which he could push off in an alternating sequence to propel himself through the air.

But he'd already learned the hard way, back with the axes and buzzsaws, that he didn't have enough magic to keep it stable. Control and finesse was not his thing; traditional magic was beyond him. Maybe he could try to kick off the walls or something, make his way up to the hatch that way? But even if he did, Jack was still stuck.

As Daniel ruminated on the problem, two of the bars shunted into the open position. A different bar on the other side shunted closed. And then they shifted again, and again, switching places. Daniel glanced at Jack—he was testing the switch up and down, confirming their function. He caught Daniel's eyes, then gestured him to try.

Daniel tried his first switch. A single metal bar opened. Two slid shut. One step forward, two steps back.

Jack got Daniel's attention again and waved his hands. Daniel approached the barrier to get a better view. Jack pointed very clearly at the first switch, then held up an index finger. At first, Daniel thought Jack wanted him to wait for something—but then Jack then pointed at the second switch, and held up two fingers. And then the third switch was three fingers.

Realization struck, and Daniel gave him the thumbs up. This was the way they could communicate—every switch could have a number, 1 through 10, starting at the one closest to the door. With that established, it shouldn't be too hard to solve the puzzle and open the hatch. The real issue was getting up to the hatch afterward.

As Daniel started to brainstorm that problem again, four square grates banged open on the walls. Both he and Jack flinched—and Daniel took note that Jack's side of the room had four grates of its own. Daniel looked up at the open holes, squinting against the light. They'd been almost completely flush with the steel of the building, so he hadn't picked up on them.

A gurgling sound rose up through the ground and walls around them, as if someone on another floor had started taking a shower—and jets of water streamed out the grates at high pressure, as if someone opened up four water mains all at once. It splashed down in the center of the room and came back up in a spray that caught Daniel across his legs and chest. The water ran off his armor, saving him from getting drenched. His ears rang with the sound; what had been a quiet, solemn silence was replaced by the roar of streaming liquid.

Well. I guess we can swim to the hatch, eventually.

Since the first switch had been net unproductive, Daniel threw that one back up, and the bars reversed to their original position. He sloshed over to the second switch, trudging through the ankle-deep water. His armor was working another wonder—it kept him dry from head to toe, as if he was wearing a full-body wetsuit. No matter how badly he was splashed, the water rolled right off him. *What the heck is this stuff made of?*

The second switch was a good one—it moved three bars into the open position. They had the hatch close to halfway done, now. Jack tried his next switch. Three bars slotted shut. He visibly winced, then threw it back. They proceeded to the next set; Daniel's switch cost them a bar, so he returned it to its original position, while Jack kept his flipped.

By the time they reached the fourth switch the water was at his thighs. It was pouring in at an incredible rate—perhaps even faster than when it first started. It was churning and buffeting at him, as if he was standing at the base of four waterfalls, making it harder to move. It was coming in so fast he suspected magical forces at work.

Daniel wiped his armor's visor clean with his gauntleted hand as a particularly nasty splash sprayed over him. He glanced up at the hatch. If they didn't get that thing open by the time the water filled the chamber...he shook his head clear. He didn't want his thoughts to go in that direction.

Something jabbed at his leg.

Daniel flinched in surprise, stepping back and windmilling his arms. The *something* was purple and eel-like, fitting about between his feet. Daniel kicked at it, but his legs were sluggish through the water. It ducked away easily, but not before sending him off with a violet spark of what looked like arc lightning. It crackled along the surface of the scale armor, but it felt like pins and needles jammed into his ankle, and his foot numbed up slightly. Daniel tested his foot a few times, and the numbness passed quickly.

Daniel peered into the water. He could see hints of it here and there, approaching, then swimming away, then approaching again, as if waiting for the right moment. A look to the other side of the room treated him to a show of Jack pounding his fists into the water, splashing to try and scare something off—no doubt he had his own friendly guest.

This was starting to get frustrating.

Daniel waited until Jack was done messing around, keeping one eye on the water, which was now up to his waist. Jack finally calmed down and nodded over to him. They tried the next set of switches; Daniel's ended up being the best of the two, and the hatch was down another bar.

Daniel waded toward the next switch; he felt like he was pushing through the water at the ocean, trying to go deeper, and the waves were dragging back. The eel slithered close to his legs again; Daniel kicked out at it, and it vanished into the far corner of the room, out of sight under the frothing water.

Something stabbed at his lower back, pins and needles that made him lurch sideways. Daniel whipped his hand around, chasing the eel away with a spray of water. How had it gotten behind him so fast?

And then he saw them—two eels. Three. They were multiplying.

One of the eels wasn't so bad; a sharp poke, and then his foot felt numb for a few seconds. But if three—or more—of those things all got him at once, they could cause some serious damage. His armor was turning out to be the luckiest thing that happened to him since he got down here. And Jack had his fur—that would probably help too.

Daniel realized that as the water continued to rise—water now at his chest—it would get harder and harder for him and Jack to maneuver, and there would be more and more eels trying to take them out of commission. It wouldn't be long until they were in over their heads, literally. Daniel looked over, and his fears were confirmed—Jack, who was shorter, was practically standing on his toes to keep his head above the rising water level.

The only thing they could do was keep at it. They were at the sixth switch; this time, both of their switches were bad. Daniel's cost them two bars, and Jack's switch closed three bars, and they ended up leaving both where they started. It made sense—the more bars were open, the more likely it was that any given switch would cause some to close, and the harder it became to find the final, correct combination.

Something jabbed into Daniel's feet, shocking it harder than before. It turned his foot numb and prickly. He took a step back—and his foot failed him, slipping on the smooth floor as he lost sensation in his toes. He plunged under the water.

Eels were swarming around him—violet, slimy-looking creatures each a few feet long. Their mouths looked like suckers, lined with teeth, almost as if they were gargantuan leeches. Two protrusions above their mouths crackled with lightning. Daniel felt more jabs at the backs of his legs—they were trying to keep him submerged.

Daniel swatted at the eels with his hand and his mace in underwater slow motion. They swam away, but were back at him when his hand passed; their dexterity in the water outstripped his own by a wide margin. One of the eels went for his knee—and its mouth extended, then widened large enough to wrap around his whole kneecap. The jagged teeth ripped at his armor, and the lightning leapt out to shock him at the same time, chipping away at the silver scales.

The armor held fast, though it gained a series of thin scratches and a small scorch mark for the trouble. If he hadn't been protected, that thing would've swam away with a chunk of him missing.

As it was, Daniel's knee was totally numb; he dropped into an underwater crouch, supporting himself on his other leg. The eels buzzed about like flies, seeking another shot at him now that he appeared weakened.

But Daniel had two advantages the eels wouldn't expect from trapped prey. First, air wasn't an issue—Daniel's armor kept him fully sealed, and he wasn't having any problem breathing normally. Second, he had his own magic.

Daniel's mace lit up white like a glowstick, illuminating the eels slithering around in the dark. His arm, empowered by the magic coursing through it and out to his weapon, whipped through the water at three times its previous speed, catching two of the eels in the side. Daniel couldn't hear anything but the muffled rumbling of the water through his armor, but he could feel the force of his mace impacting—he'd definitely done some damage.

The eels retreated rapidly, driven away by both the light and the threat of his weapon. Feeling returned to Daniel's feet and legs, and he pushed up. His head surfaced, but his eyes were barely above the level of the water. Daniel glanced over at Jack—who was now treading water near the eighth switch. One of his arms was matted with wet, long hair; periodically, he smashed it down into the surf, driving away attackers.

Daniel tiptoed to his seventh switch, and he finally had a stroke of luck—3 bars slammed open. Jack threw him a bigfoot-sized thumbs up. Daniel felt a sense of relief—but the moment's inattention allowed a stiff wave of water to lift him off his feet. He bounced on his toes and stretched his neck to keep his visor clear of the foam. He fought to orient himself back toward the next switch, battling hard against the swirling current in the center of the room.

Just as Daniel cleared the worst of it, the lights in the room shut off, plunging them into near-total darkness.

Flickering specks of purple darted through the water—the lightning conducted by the eels. He counted at least ten; they were moving so fast and so clustered he couldn't get a bead on every single one. As if sensing an opportunity, they swam towards him in a single, balled-up school of electric death.

Daniel sent a pulse of magic into his mace in response. Light washed around him in a pale haze, illuminating a few feet into the water. The violet pinpricks paused at the edge of the dim sphere created by the light, hovering in the dark just out of sight. Daniel caught glimpses of their long bodies and wavering fins as they swam back and forward, as if testing a boundary. Daniel imagined the slithering creatures were the type to seek dark, hidden spaces; the light must be enough to give them pause.

At this point, Daniel couldn't touch the bottom anymore. He started to tread water, kicking his feet to keep his head clear of the bubbling surf. His armor, though incredibly useful, added enough weight to make swimming hard enough to be annoying.

Yet suddenly, Daniel bobbed up, as if springs were added to his feet. His head cleared the water. At first, he thought the current had turned in his favor and pushed him up, but Daniel could feel a strange drag on his boots as he kicked. He peered down into the water, holding his mace so the light illuminated his feet. The armor had extended slightly outward and flattened, transforming into rudimentary pool flippers.

Daniel smiled at his ever-adaptive elven armor. It struck him that, in all his time in Hell, he hadn't met a single elf, or even heard mention of them until now. Maybe they had their own prison.

Daniel kept a bit of magic flowing into the mace to maintain the light. He'd never really tried to focus on the superficial portion of his magic before—the light that accompanied all his spells and powers was a natural part of the package. The energy spilled over, like how an engine growled when it revved up—the point wasn't to make loud sounds, it was to push a car forward, but nothing was 100% efficient. Some of the energy leaked out as sound.

Daniel played with the feeling of his magic, almost as if tuning an instrument. The light flickered brighter, than dimmed. He settled on a happy medium that didn't seem to take up too much of his energy but was reasonably bright. Good enough for the time being.

Since he'd lit up his mace, the eels hadn't gotten more than a few feet close. They had, however, split off from one another, surrounding him to probe at his little sphere of light from all directions. If it went out, they'd get potshots at him from all sides. Thankfully, at this rate of consumption, Daniel had magic to spare.

With his situation stabilized, Daniel realized that Jack was probably not having such an easy go of it. He glanced at the switch he was next to, mentally marking its position, then swam over to the barrier. He stopped just in time to avoid smashing his visor against it; the hazy wall was barely visible in the dark.

He pressed against it, then channeled more power into his mace. He tried to direct the magic forward, having it act like a spotlight as he searched for his friend. While the light around his mace grew brighter, it wasn't so easy to control. The entire time, the sparking, slithering eels followed along, an ever-present threat hovering outside arm's reach.

Jack leapt into Daniel's face, plastering himself against the barrier. He'd come up from directly below Daniel's line of sight, and Daniel was so surprised his light flickered a bit. Daniel checked on his purple friends—he was still wary that the light wouldn't truly keep them at bay—but the eels didn't risk testing him again so soon.

Thankfully, the soundproof barrier that kept them separated was not light-proof. Daniel's light leached into Jack's half of the room, enclosing his friend in its protective bubble. Daniel could see blood welling up from Jack's shoulder—a small injury, but still bleeding.

Jack pointed at himself, then held up nine fingers. Daniel tapped his helmet, then gestured twice with his free hand—a five and a three, indicating he was on his eighth switch. Jack indicated himself again, then thumbed behind himself—back into the dark of the water. Jack then pointed at his eyes with two fingers, pointed at Daniel, then up toward the hatch. Daniel got the meaning—Jack wanted him to keep his eyes peeled while he went for another switch.

Daniel took a look at the ceiling. The shadows confused things, but he could make out the hatch fairly clearly; the metal reflected the light in a pattern of shimmering glare marks. Jack gave him a thumbs up, and then pushed off the barrier, diving back for one of his switches. Daniel pulsed his mace brighter again, giving Jack as much cover as he could while keeping his eyes up.

Daniel knew Jack made it to his switch when two bars shut and one opened. Jack himself made it back to the barrier, but the eels were nipping at his legs like piranhas. He visibly winced and rubbed at his foot; his fur didn't seem to be as effective as Daniel's armor in repelling the electric attacks. Daniel pointed up at the hatch once he had Jack's attention, then gave him a thumbs down.

Jack's lips formed an obvious swear word. He checked the hatch himself, nodded, then visibly gathered himself. He took a big breath, then swam back down. The problem reversed itself—and Jack must have thrown his tenth and final switch, because two bars opened and one went closed. There were now only three bars total that were sealed shut. Jack made his return—but not without another slice across the outside of his elbow, below his already injured shoulder.

The wounds couldn't easily stanch themselves in the water. Jack wasn't bleeding too much, but it was enough to make the eels around him swarm aggressively; they were getting a taste of their prey, and they liked it. If it went on forever, it wouldn't be good for his health, especially with all the effort they were spending to keep afloat.

The water was now well over halfway to the ceiling; with time visibly running low, they had no choice but to continue the slog, no matter the risks. The problem was, now Daniel was going to have to swim to his switches—leaving Jack alone in the dark with the eels. Daniel gestured over his shoulder and gave Jack a questioning look through his visor. Jack shrugged his shoulders, then raised his fists; they visibly bulged larger as he channeled magic into them.

Daniel nodded. He bunched his legs up, planted his feet on the barrier, and pushed off in the vague direction of his switches. The light kept the eels off him; he tried to make it as bright as possible, though after a certain point, it mostly fizzled and sparked erratically. He never really imagined a situation in which he'd use his powers like a flashlight, so it wasn't something he'd ever practiced.

Daniel found the switches. He swam to one side, pushing his way along the wall as if feeling his way across a pool bottom. He hit the final switch, then counted backwards to the eighth one, making absolutely sure he didn't pull the wrong one by mistake. The last thing they needed was to confuse their switches. He threw the lever down, then pushed off the wall and paddled back to the barrier as fast as possible.

Jack was under the water, right in the act of punching an eel in the teeth. His other arm was slack at his side, probably completely numb. Daniel arrived as three more were going after his unprotected flank; they made a sharp U-turn at the oncoming light and swam away. Jack followed Daniel's light back to the surface; he was visibly spluttering and heaving his breaths when they made it. He held up a hand, obviously asking for another few seconds.

Daniel waited until Jack had his breath back; he checked the hatch. Thankfully, with them being pushed closer and closer to the roof by the rising water level, it was easy to see. They'd gained one bar—out of the entire mechanism, only two were left shut. Jack gave him a thumbs up again when he was ready.

Daniel repeated the process again with the ninth switch—which led to three bars being sealed. He had no choice but to swim back and throw it down. The tenth switch was equally unproductive. Two bars closed, and one opened. Daniel went back and flung it up again.

After multiple trips, Jack struggled to keep the eels off him. He'd gained a new gash on the back of his thigh, and this one was nasty—the eel had managed to take off both fur and a good chunk of skin. On top of that, all the switches had been tried, and they were still stuck with two bars. There was nowhere left to go with the brute force method. Now came the hard part—they had to find the right combination of off-and-on to complete the puzzle.

Daniel glanced up at the hatch. There were too many switches and too many distractions—between the water threatening to drown them, the eels, and the loss of their light source, he hadn't really kept track of which bars corresponded to which switch. And even if he had, there were so many it would've been tough to remember. He frowned at Jack and shook his head.

But Jack wasn't looking at him. He was staring up at the hatch; his pained look was replaced by a thoughtful one. He stared so long Daniel was starting to worry about their time when suddenly, he looked back down. He pointed firmly at Daniel and held up three fingers. Then he pointed at himself and held up a five.

Daniel nodded up and down. He didn't have any better ideas, and Jack seemed to have a handle on it. Jack lifted one finger, then two, then three, in rapid succession. *A countdown?* Daniel nodded that he understood.

Jack promptly gathered his legs under himself, putting his feet on the barrier. Daniel did the same. Jack lifted his hand again. *1...2...3!*

Daniel pulsed magic as hard as he could through the entire mace; the light flared, fizzled, and sparked. At the same time, they both launched themselves back toward the opposite walls.

From all the previous trips, Daniel had a better idea of how far he needed to travel. He quickly found the very first switch in the far corner, followed the wall to the third switch, threw it, then gathered himself to push off.

As he was about to launch, four of the eels attacked, braving the light to send jolts of violet electricity arcing into his feet and ankles. Daniel's boots slipped off the wall, and he was sent flailing into the water. His light flickered and dimmed with his loss of focus. He paddled hard with his arms as more shocks numbed the rest of his legs; they instantly turned into dead, prickling weights, dragging behind him in the water. With only one arm paddling, his progress slowed to a halt.

Daniel turned as a few of them were opening their mouths to take a bite of his feet. He brandished his mace, driving off most of them, but one eel clamped its grotesque jaws around his entire foot. Daniel tried to kick it off, but it was like trying to move a limb that was asleep. The eel's mouth was latched on firmly; its teeth ground in circles like a rotor as it tried to cut through the armor. The sparking electric light snapped into Daniel's foot again and again, keeping it numb.

Daniel still had feeling near his hips—so instead of trying to kick it off, he pulled his leg in, dragging his target closer. The eel let go of Daniel's foot and dove for his chest—only to crash straight into Daniel's mace. Daniel could feel the impact up his arm as he smashed the thing aside. Its broken form twitched and writhed in the water, then went belly-up. Its brethren descended ravenously, dividing the corpse of their companion amongst themselves. Daniel wrenched back in revulsion and drifted away from the feeding frenzy, kicking his legs to work feeling back into them.

Oh, no. Jack!

Daniel paddled furiously for the barrier. His helmet clunked into it before he could stop himself—a bit jarring, but he was fine. He searched through the water for Jack, but couldn't make him out in the murk.

With the respite from the eels, his legs were functional again. Daniel kicked off the bottom of the room and powered toward the surface. Thrashing movement and violet lights caught his eye—and then a hairy hand, plastered again the barrier like skin against a shower stall. Daniel led with his mace to drive away the eels with the light.

Blood swirled around Jack like red ribbons through the water. There was a slice across his face—one of the eels had almost got him straight on. His grey fur was tattered and chunked out of him in multiple places—but better the fur than the rest of him.

One of the eels was tangled up in the long, tough hairs, trapped under his arm. The eel panicked in the sudden light, but unable to swim away, it lashed out with its teeth. There was a brief scuffle, but Jack managed to pin it to the barrier and smash it flat with his other hand. Daniel made a face as blue-green guts smeared across the 'window' keeping them separated. Thankfully, the current swept the remains away from Jack. The last thing he needed was more visitors trying to pick off a snack.

Daniel and Jack surfaced. Jack was a coughing, spluttering mess, and his wounds weren't healing. Hell's ambient magic wasn't instant, but it should have started by now.

It was then that Daniel remembered Jack's description of the games. Jack wasn't going to get stitched up for free; he had to suffer through. Most games cut off their players from the ambient mana—or magic—that permeated the prison, preventing exactly that healing. Jack hadn't been too clear on the difference between raw magical energy and mana, but his layman's understanding was that it was similar to the difference between crude oil and refined gasoline.

Eventually, Jack coughed it out; he took a couple steadying breaths, met Daniel's gaze, then glanced up at the ceiling. He pumped a fist. Daniel—too concerned with his friend's immediate health—hadn't checked it yet, but he grinned when he saw that there was only a single bar preventing their escape. Jack had it right.

Their time was definitely running low. The bubbling waves had almost sealed them in; with a little effort, Daniel could reach out and touch the ceiling. He wasn't sure exactly how long his armor would let him last underwater, but it was probably a lot longer than Jack holding his breath.

A waving ape hand got Daniel's attention. Jack was smiling excitedly—at least, Daniel thought he was. With the way his face was changed by his powers, it looked like the lopsided grin of an orangutan. Jack pointed at himself, then held up a single finger. He pointed at Daniel and held up both hands, palms open. *Switch 10.*

Daniel nodded. Jack definitely thought he had it—they just had to survive one more round in the water. Daniel brought his knees up and prepared himself. He spared a bit of focus to add power into his legs; he needed to get the light back to Jack's side as quickly as possible once he threw his switch. Jack counted down with his fingers again, and with a rush of water, they both dove into the swirling current.

Daniel's initial push powered him down at speed. The streamlined weight of his armor cut through the water; he kept his body straight and cruised into the corner. He caught himself against the bottom with his arms, stepped over, and threw his switch.

He turned, putting his back to the corner of the room—and the eels were converging on him, a veritable storm of violet, static-charged needles. They'd learned to try and take advantage of the opening created when he changed directions.

This time, he was ready. Daniel braced himself against the corner, using his feet to push his back into the walls. That let him grip his mace with both hands. With the strength of two arms channeling his magic, his radiant weapon cut lines of light through the water, smashing away the first few eels and frightening off the rest. He stayed there for another few breaths, until he was sure they were gone, then pushed off again, swimming full-out with his arms and flippered feet to get back to the hatch.

Daniel arrived at their rendezvous—and almost as soon as he did, a bright ray of yellow light cascaded down around him like a halo promising salvation. The hatch was open; they'd done it! Daniel's head cleared the water; he could easily reach the ledge and pull himself up, but he paused, waiting for Jack to get back.

Seconds ticked by. Daniel glanced into the water, peering this way and that. No movement. No Jack.

A rising panic gripped him. Daniel reached up and clambered out of the water.

Immediately, a cheery, gameshow fanfare blasted into his face. Spotlights danced around him; cameras were buzzing in his ears and around his head. Water dripped off him as he stood up, now on the roof of the building.

"And at the last minute, the Order of the Dragon has opened their escape hatch!" Ky's voice echoed around him. "Kavarssian and Gulthak won't get away without a fight!"

Daniel spared the rooftop a glance—his opponents were opposite, on the other side of yet another magical barrier. Both were sitting, hands on their knees, with lazy, smirking expressions painted on their faces.

"But Jack has been left behind in the water, a feast for the eels!" Ky said. "In an incredible display of solidarity and unselfishness, Jack made the ultimate sacrifice, allowing Daniel to escape relatively unscathed! Anything for the Order of the Dragon—anything for the victory of the team. Truly, Jack Killiney is a contestant to be feared. We can only imagine the thoughts running through Daniel's head, knowing that even though he made it out, he faces the battle ahead alone and—"

Daniel leapt back into the water, this time on Jack's side of the barrier. He blasted magic out to every part of his body, no longer trying to conserve any energy. His arms churned as he paddled down to the depths—and there was Jack, floating lifelessly near the switch he'd barely pulled down. The eels were hacking at him with their teeth, jabbing with their lighting. Jack's body flailed at their strikes; he spasmed in the water, his muscles contracting and twitching under the electric assault. His body was pockmarked with wounds; the water was dyed red around him.

Daniel roared as he swung his mace at the closest eel. With full power coursing through the weapon, the eel was blown in two on contact. Blood and guts burst through the water; Daniel waded into the mess, pushing Jack beneath him and out of the way as several eels broke off for a shot at their chummed ally. Daniel swatted down another two eels, thinning their numbers before they swam out of reach.

One eel's teeth were latched around the side of Jack's abdomen; it wriggled there, gnawing at his flesh. Daniel grabbed it by the middle, but as he pulled, its mouth sucked down, threatening to pull a chunk of Jack away with it. It was too risky—if Daniel forced it off, Jack might bleed out then and there.

Daniel didn't think about his next move as much as he simply reacted. It wasn't something he'd ever tried to do before, but the adrenaline and the desperation drove him to try something, anything, to get the eel to let go. He forced magic down his arm, out the fingertips of his armor, and into the eel he was holding.

The eel's arc lightning flickered, ready to shock Jack yet again—but then, the purple electricity was drawn away from Jack's skin. It traveled down and through the eel's body—which began to flail and spasm itself—and up against Daniel's hand. Even underwater, the eel's skin visibly sizzled and blackened where the lightning moved; its own magic was out of the creature's control. The eel's mouth released Jack, leaving behind only superficial bite marks. Daniel crushed it in his armored grip, then tossed it through the water and toward the other eels as bait.

Daniel wasn't sure what exactly he'd done, but it could wait. He got underneath Jack, positioned him over his shoulder, then pushed off the bottom. Without his armor shaping itself into fins, swimming upward with all that weight would have been extremely difficult. It still took him longer than he would've liked, but between the armor's adaptation and Daniel's magic, he was able to power up to the surface. He threw Jack bodily over the side of the hatch—the water was overflowing right to the brim—then climbed out on his hands and knees, heaving his breath hard enough to fog up his visor.

"And Daniel, incredibly, has made it back with Killiney's corpse!" Ky tutted through the speakers. Daniel hadn't really noticed it before, but her voice wasn't limited to being sent through the cameras anymore—it bounced about, coming from every direction at once. "A noble gesture, but unfortunately, if the blood loss doesn't get him, the fact that he drowned certainly will. It's a shame that—uh...oh my! Hmm. Well. I guess they're, err, closer than we realized."

Daniel had laid Jack flat on the roof. He tilted Jack's head back to open the airway—and, right when he realized his helmet was going to be a problem, the visor portion covering his face snapped open, responding to his intentions without a hitch. *I love elves.*

Daniel pinched Jack's nose, then sealed his mouth with his own, exhaling a pair of rescue breaths. Jack's chest didn't rise; the air wasn't getting in, which was good and bad. Good, because it meant not much water had gotten into Jack's lungs, and bad, because now he needed oxygen. Daniel pressed his hand against Jack's neck, feeling for a pulse.

"Even in the face of death, Daniel refuses to let Jack go!" Ky's voice gained a lilt like buttered frosting. "Daniel was unwilling to let Jack go without one final—uh, a second final kiss as well!"

Daniel finished his second set of breaths and checked Jack's pulse again. Jack's heart was fluttering like crazy; even Daniel's amateur effort could feel how erratic it was. But it was pumping. He didn't need compressions. Daniel created the seal again and exhaled into his friend's lungs, doing his best to ignore Ky. Hopefully the barrier separating them from the other team was going to be there a bit longer, because he could practically feel Kavarssian and Gulthak staring at him. If they attacked, he'd be a sitting duck.

Jack had only been under the water for a minute, two minutes tops. He wasn't dead yet. Daniel waited, then inhaled, and went back in for another two breaths.

It was on the second of that pair that Jack's body heaved. Daniel got a face full of spittle and water as his friend hacked it all up; he rolled over and kept coughing.

"Ugh." Daniel wiped his face clean and spat onto the ground. "You alive over there?"

Daniel's smart remarks came too soon; Jack was still coughing and in no shape for a retort. His entire body trembled with the effort, every part of him bent on making his coughs as loud and vicious-sounding as possible. And then, Jack quieted—shivering in place—before promptly vomiting all over the floor, adding the contents of his stomach to the pooled water and smeared blood.

"Eww!" Ky shouted. "This is—I don't even know what this is! Is Jack going to be okay?!"

Daniel gently patted Jack's back. "Easy, man. I'm right here. Looks like we've got a second. Take your time." Jack was back to coughing again; it sounded like he was trying to get a lung out. "How you doing?"

Jack tried to push up on his hands, but they slipped out from under him as he continued to cough. Daniel grabbed him and moved him away from the nastiness on the floor. Jack's coughs started to settle; he managed to wave a hand at Daniel, signaling that he was being heard, then shaped it into a thumbs up. His arm promptly thumped back to the metal, energy spent.

"Unbelievable!" Ky shouted. "The Silverback Killer lives again! No magic involved! How did Daniel pull that one off?! It's one miracle after another with these two rookies. I don't think I've used the word unbelievable so many times in so few days before, and I definitely *wouldn't* believe it if I hadn't seen it myself, folks!"

Daniel shook his head. "Does she ever shut up?" he mumbled, more to himself than anyone else.

"No," Jack croaked.

"Hey, he lives," Daniel said. Jack was rolled over and looking at him. Daniel cocked an eyebrow. "So, baby, you come here often? What's your sign?"

"I," Jack said, wheezing the words, "am not. Gay."

"I dunno, I think we should roll with it," Daniel said. "Think of the ratings. Your fan club will get a huge boost. All those squealing preteen demons love the guy-on-guy stuff, right?"

"Fuck...you."

"Funny thing to say to the guy that saved your life," Daniel said. His voice dripped with mock-indignation. "See if I bring you back from the dead next time you drown in a pool of magical electric eels."

"I hope...you not...expecting...fight," Jack wheezed.

"You'd better be ready for one," Daniel said. "Jekyll and Hyde don't look happy you lived." Gulthak and Kavarssian were now both on their feet and standing near the barrier. Gulthak looked baffled, but Kavarssian was pure frustration. He looked like a businessman that thought he came away on the better end of a deal, only to find out after the fact he'd been screwed. Daniel flipped them the bird, then turned back to Jack. "Besides, I didn't kiss you so you could sit in the corner while I do all the work. Get over it."

"I almost drowned," Jack said. He started hacking again. Daniel waited until he finished. "You...you're a dick."

"Yeah," Daniel said. "But I'm your dick." He screwed his face up. "Do you think they'll interpret that sexually?"

"Killiney must be feeling pretty good, because he's all about the banter with Daniel!" Ky said. "I've been informed by our resident human-culture expert that Daniel was not, in fact, exchanging a final moment of passion with Jack, but was performing a life-saving technique called CPR, often used in the case humans are cut off from air for an extended period. He literally breathed life back into his teammate! Though often underestimated, humans are incredible creatures in their own right."

"Aw, shucks," Daniel said. "We've been found out." A vengeful smirk rolled onto Daniel's face. "Good thing Rachel dragged me to those CPR classes, huh?"

Jack's chest rose and fell in big, uncertain stutters; he was only able to get his words out on the exhale. "Just. Don't. Even. Okay?"

Daniel laughed. But his laughter quickly died, and the look on his face fell, as the realization welled up on him that Rachel would never drag him to anything again. The feeling was as if he'd turned to the side, about to comment on something on the TV—only to realize the person he expected next to him on the couch wasn't there. The words he prepared died away on his lips, empty and wasted.

And yet, Daniel's smile revived as he remembered that day. It was a good time—them and another, older couple, the only ones signed up for that time slot with the CPR instructor. The old man and woman teased Daniel and Rachel the entire time, asking Daniel if he'd bought a ring, how he was going to propose or when their wedding was. Once the woman started acting out the drama as if they'd have a child out of wedlock, Daniel called her a crotchety old woman—and her husband loudly agreed, saying he'd been trying to convince her of that for a decade. It was constant laughs after that.

"You got lucky, Killiney. But I think we all know how this is gonna go." They both looked up—it was Kavarssian. His voice was growling and dangerous, but his sharp attire was still waterlogged and rumpled, undercutting the threat in his voice. "You're half-dead as it is. I'd concede before you get hurt. And I promise, I'll make it hurt."

Daniel's memory of Rachel—the image of her, caught in his mind's eye—was pushed away at Kavarssian's words. A cold, prickling anger ran down Daniel's spine; his lips thinned as he ground his teeth together. Every muscle in his body felt like a clenched fist. It might be painful to think about her, but even worse was having that brief, happy memory interrupted by this opportunistic bastard.

"You'd better be okay to fight, Jack," Daniel said, "because I need someone to hold him down so I can curbstomp him on the ledge over there."

By this time, Jack had sat up. He heaved out a breath that rattled in his chest from the phlegm and muck still trapped inside. "Don't say"—he coughed slightly—"I never did you any favors."

"Both teams are already at each other's throats!" Ky's voice echoed over them, eager to stoke the rising tension. "It looks like this is going to be a finale that you won't want to miss. The Order of the Dragon vs the Sky Runners, a battle of rookie spunk and age-old experience, the hottest thing going on in Hell right now! Stay tuned—we'll be right back after these messages from our sponsors."

****

Daniel and Jack were given a brief respite while the lights dimmed and the commercials rolled. They needed every spare second, because as the adrenaline faded, Jack started to feel every last one of his injuries. That was without mentioning the ache from his chest and back contracting as hard as possible. Normally, Daniel would tease him relentlessly until he manned up, but he didn't have it in him after Jack backed him up against the dragon.

"Dude," Jack said, "I still feel dizzy. It feels like I got a knife stuck in here." Jack raised his left elbow. There was a particularly nasty slice in his skin where one of the eels had sunk its teeth into the joint; the injury was still oozing a little blood. "I don't know how we're gonna do this. I'm dead weight."

"How's your right arm?" Daniel asked. "Still okay there?"

Jack moved it in a circle, stretching it out. "Not bad, really. I mean, every time I move, something hurts."

"Okay," Daniel said. "We can work with that."

He glanced over his shoulder. Once Jack got his breath back into his lungs, they'd moved near the edge of the roof, as far from Kavarssian and Gulthak's side as possible. This particular barrier, as evidenced from earlier conversation, was not soundproof.

They were now on top of the steel monolith in which they'd been swimming. The roof was completely flat—no obstacles, no bumps or projections, and no railings: a square metal surface. It wasn't shiny and reflective, but dull, like the reverse side of aluminum foil. He had no idea where the light itself came from—as with the stone path back in the darkness, everything was visible on its own despite the lack of external lighting. The translucent barrier cut the building down the middle; it was the only thing keeping the two teams separated.

The abyss was back, and it completely surrounded their little rooftop arena. They were adrift on a tiny grey islet in an all-encompassing darkness. The island that previously supported the structure was gone, crumbled to dust.

It didn't take all of Daniel's brain cells to realize that falling off would be a bad idea. The slick steel didn't promise much grip if you had to hold on. Staying away from the edges was vital—the team that held the center had a huge advantage in simply pushing their foes off.

"It was a good thing you had that light back there," Jack said. "Your powers are pretty useful."

"How situational was that though?" Daniel said. "But I know what you mean. My power really does have a lot of utility outside of moving fast."

Daniel thought back to the eel he shook off Jack. The thing sunk its teeth deep into Jack's skin, and it hadn't let go until Daniel pushed his own magic straight into the creature—something he'd never done before. It almost felt like he *pulled* on the creature's lightning magic, causing it to go haywire, then pushed it back in, stronger, crisping the creature from the inside out.

He pushed his magic all the time; it was how Xik had first taught him, how he visualized it when he used it, pushing energy out from his core. He used that same mental push to place energy and magic into objects all the time—knives, his clubs, his old homemade armor. It reinforced them, made them harder, sharper, better. He pushed his magic through himself all the time, too—it was how he sped up and strengthened his own body.

Pushing it through another living creature had completely different results. He'd simply never considered grabbing on and trying it. Keeping a weapon between himself and the Vorid had been by far the best option at the time, and he wasn't any kind of boxer or wrestler. The only thing he wanted to touch extractors and overseers with was the business end of a club.

Something about the experience nagged at Daniel, and not in a good way. It was like he had something on the tip of his tongue, about to put 2 and 2 together, but his brain wasn't quite spitting it out.

"I feel like I still have a lot to learn about it," Daniel said. "Using it better, or in different ways. I'd never tried focusing on the light. I always thought that was excess energy bleeding off—maybe it is, really—but when I paid attention to it, I could control it. Sort of." Daniel nodded to himself as an explanation came to him. "It's like when you wiggle your ears or flare your nostrils. This little muscle that doesn't quite move the way you want it to."

"Mine's the same," Jack said. "I think I can get a lot better control over my fur, over how my transformation works. I can harden parts of it if I focus magic into some hairs, rather than all of them at once. I can grow them longer, too. I was thinking I could form kind of bubble around myself." Jack gestured in a circle. "I could build up speed and roll toward people, which would probably help deflect magic. I'm thinking I could use that to close the distance to mages, or I could transport other people safely with me."

Daniel screwed up his lips. "All with hair? Sounds a little, uh, grungy."

Jack shrugged, unoffended. "Beggars can't be choosers."

"Sounds like it could be useful," Daniel said. "Are you able to, say, only transform one arm?"

"Yeah," Jack said. "I can do different parts of my body on their own. I don't have to go full-body ape every time."

"Does that help concentrate your power?"

"Kinda," Jack said. "If I focus all my magic on one limb, it does get stronger than if my magic is distributed evenly. But it creates a new problem."

"What's that?" Daniel asked. He was curious about Jack's experience, having experimented with exactly that just recently—and their conversation was giving him a few ideas to deal with the Sky Runners.

"Balance," Jack said. "Try throwing a straight punch when one arm weighs 40 pounds and the other arm weighs 10 pounds—moving around gets real awkward. And try running if your legs are two different sizes. If I'm already punching or need to jump, maybe for a quick burst of speed—there are some times where morphing one arm or leg might help. But then I have to worry about timing. I've been practicing, but I don't think it'd be much good in a fight yet."

"But if you didn't have to move," Daniel said, "and if timing wasn't a big deal, it might help?"

"Sure, in theory," Jack said. He furrowed his brow in thought. "What are you thinking, exactly?"

"We're definitely at a handicap," Daniel said. "You can't fight either of them head on, so we need to take out one of them right off the bat and even the odds, come out swinging. Who do you think we should target?"

Jack glanced over the arena, eyeballing Gulthak and Kavarssian. "Gulthak might be hard to take out fast. Even if we surprised them, he's heavy. We'd have to hit him incredibly hard to kill him, and it would be difficult to knock him off the arena. But he's slower, and a huge target."

"What about Kava—Krava..." Daniel frowned, trying to remember the exact pronunciation. "The dragon guy?"

"*Kavar*ssian," Jack said, "knows fire magic, strong stuff, but he's physically weaker. One solid hit could do him in, if you hit him in the right place. Glass cannon." Jack raised a finger in warning. "Gotta avoid the scales on his skin, they're basically armor patches."

"Dragons can transform, right?" Daniel said. "I'm kinda worried about that."

Jack shook his head. "He has to use all his magic power to switch into his true dragon form, but none of us have that right now."

"So, you're thinking we should take the dragon out," Daniel said.

"Yeah. Even if we hit Gulthak hard like you're saying, I don't think it'll do much good. He's as much of a tank as I am, and he doesn't need magic. We can't get it done fast, and then Kavarssian's going to be standing there throwing fire at us."

"So Kavarssian's an easier target, but if we could take down Gulthak, we'd be in a way better position."

"Basically," Jack said. "But I just don't think we could get rid of Gulthak with a surprise attack. He's the kind of thing you wear down over time."

"And that's exactly the issue," Daniel said. "Now we have to attack Gulthak."

"What do you mean?" Jack said.

"Kavarssian has probably thought out exactly what we did," Daniel said. "He's done this a hundred times, right? He knows what we're capable of, and he knows you're hurt. It doesn't take a genius to figure out we'll try to hit them hard and fast to level the playing field, and from there he can reason out he's the likely target. He'll plan for that, and instead of launching a surprise attack, we're walking into an ambush."

Jack frowned hard, then slowly nodded. "Yeah. You might be right. If he's expecting it, we're screwed."

"So instead," Daniel said, "we attack Gulthak."

"We might as well be attacking a rock," Jack said. "You can outpace him, maybe catch him off guard, but I don't think we'll be able to hit him hard enough to take him out in time. And what do I do, sit over here and twiddle my thumbs? While you run over there and whack at him, Kavarssian will light me up. I'm resistant to magic, but I'm not feeling too great right now." Jack shifted position on the hard floor. Something caught in his chest, and fought off another bout of coughing. He cleared his throat. "Burning is not a good way to go, I hate fire magic."

Daniel squinted into his lap, then looked out over the edge of the building. His eyes wandered across the darkness, searching for an answer. He glanced back at their two opponents; they were holding their own little hushed conference. The hulking, bare-chested ogre comically outsized the humanoid dragon. Gulthak stooped low, nodding his tusked head and grunting loudly, confirming instructions as they were given. Kavarssian was clearly the brains of the operation.

Kavarssian's clothes were prim and proper, now, dried off with what was no doubt a bit of his special blend of magic. Gulthak, Daniel noted, was wearing the helmet he'd left behind at the first island, but also hair a pair of thick, iron gauntlets. The gauntlets looked round, almost like boxing gloves—designed more for crushing than fine finger movement.

"I don't see Kavarssian's item, but what do you think those gauntlets do?" Daniel said. "Are they magical?"

"I actually recognize those," Jack said. "They look kinda dumpy, but they'll concentrate all his punching power on a single point if they hit. If he lands it straight, it would blow a hole right through you." Daniel felt his spine tingle at the sudden mental image of a hole through his stomach. "Your armor might be able to take a hit or two, though," Jack added. "My hair works good against those kinds of attacks, it distributes the force across my body."

"All the force on a single point..." Daniel drifted off for a moment as all the ideas that had piled up through their talk slapped themselves into the shape of a plan. It would depend on if Jack still had enough gas in the tank. He fixed his friend with a sudden stare. "You said your right arm is doing okay?"

"Yeah."

"Is that your throwing arm?"

"Uh...sure, I guess it is," Jack said. "I mean, I haven't thrown a ball since my mom forced me into little league. That was, like, 12 years ago?"

"No worries," Daniel said. "You're not gonna be throwing a ball."

Chapter 15
Double Play

"Welcome back to our live broadcast of the battle between the Order of the Dragon and the Sky Runners!" Ky's voice was as bright as if she was introducing the competitors at a beach volleyball championship. The cameras—there were almost two dozen of them by Daniel's count—were sweeping around in arcs, taking dramatic panning shots of the arena. "The two teams have arrived at the end of this dungeon run after navigating a harrowing darkness, traversing safely past deadly obstacles, and braving the wrath of vicious creatures. And so it all comes down to this—a no-holds barred battle to the death!" The largest camera took a position at the halfway point and steadied itself there. "Our arena today gets right to the point—no more tricks, no more traps. A straight up battle on cold, hard steel!"

The smaller cameras swarmed Daniel and Jack, as well as their competitors. Small screens were on a few of the devices, displaying their own viewpoints back at the contenders so they could see themselves as they appeared on the other end. As Ky announced each of them in turn, multicolored lights blazed from underneath the cameras like a spotlight, casting them in the colors associated with their teams.

"With...the Skyyy Runnneeerrrs!" Ky dragged out the words with all the dramatic flourish she could muster. "Kavarssian of the Red!" A sky-blue spotlight painted Kavarssian from head to toe, causing his deep red scales to glisten purple. A vertical black line cut through the blue down his chest. He stood with his arms folded behind his back, heels together, staring off past the camera into the distance, the picture of refined dignity.

"And...Gulthak Fist-Smasher!" Gulthak's mottled green skin was briefly replaced by the same spotlight of blue and black light. He waved his hands over his head and grunted, then brought his arms down, smashing his fists into the arena floor. Daniel could feel the vibration in his shoes through his armor. *This guy is like the freaking Hulk.*

"I hope you know what you're doing," Jack muttered. "If you screw this up, he's gonna—"

"Not helping," Daniel interrupted.

"And their opponents, from the Oooorrrder of the Dragooooon!" Daniel rolled his eyes at Ky's voice; he half-expected her to shout *let's get ready to rumble* to start the actual match. "The Silverback Killer, Jack Killiney!" Jack was flashed head-to-toe with white lights; a red cross with yellow frills appeared on his chest. Jack mustered up a weak wave for the cameras, smiling through his injuries. "And his up-and-coming partner, White Lightning Daniel Fitzgerald!"

The lights shined straight on Daniel, casting him in the Order's colors. He winced slightly at the light blaring from the camera. Daniel considered waving, but stopped himself and turned his eyes back to the competition. He wasn't here to be a sports star, he was here to win and get out.

Ky went through the motions of a good announcer, summarizing the match thus far and describing the abilities of each contender. Daniel paid attention to that part, trying to glean more details about the extent of kava bean and pig-face's abilities. She didn't add much to what Daniel knew already; it was a shallow overview, designed to get people who were tuning into the show for the main event up to speed. Kavarssian was a dragon and could perform fire magic. Gulthak was about smashing things. Then there was a bit about the recent activities of the Sky Runners, and why they had such a large interest in the armory. Ky went into Daniel and Jack's recent exploits as well, detailing their big victory over the Viridian Gust, as well as rumors that Daniel had kicked their leader's butt so hard he'd gone into permanent hiding and turned over leadership of the team to his former commanders.

Lucky nobody seems to know he's actually dead. I wonder how Beelzebub covered it up. As that thought crossed Daniel's mind, he couldn't help but wonder what would happen if, during the course of battle, he killed the two demons across from them. The contractor magic activated whenever he killed something, seemingly through any means; Daniel didn't know what arcane principle it operated on, but it hadn't failed him yet. Normally, that wouldn't do squat in Hell; Hell was a massive construct designed specifically to keep people, and their souls, locked up, and it was stronger than Daniel. No more absorption for him. But Beelzebub, for his part, adjusted Hell's soul-constraining magic so that the contractor enchantment still worked for Daniel—as long as he was in Purgatory, anyway.

The confusion of the territory war and the fact that he was the only person in Hell that could kill people permanently might have helped disguise Daniel's abilities. But this fight—broadcast live by a flock of drone cameras—would making hiding the true results more difficult. If he killed them for real, then when their team tried to bring them back to Purgatory or contact them in the future, it would be as if they completely vanished. He had to assume big-ticket combatants like them had some sort of following—it would be weird if they didn't, with Ky acting like she had a crush on the guy.

Maybe, technically, they weren't in Purgatory right now. And it wasn't as if camera footage couldn't be edited or stopped, there was always the good old 5-second broadcasting delay.

Daniel tossed aside the worry. Hiding it simply wasn't his problem. Even if he did get found out, it wouldn't be all bad. Bathory would be less likely to fight him, but it might help keep some distance between him and the serious criminals and psychopaths.

"And without further ado, the final battle of this tumultuous Dungeon Run!" Ky said. "Fighters at the ready!"

As Ky's words echoed around them, Kavarssian's hands surged with light; twin red flames grew in his palms. He held them out away from himself, tensed and ready to hurl. Gulthak beat his chest a few times, then pounded his iron mitts into the steel, growling and roaring and building himself into an eye-reddening frenzy.

Jack positioned himself behind Daniel, out of their view. His good arm rippled, twisted, and surged with muscle. Long silver-grey hairs erupted from his arm and curled around it, cupping the skin in a protective sheath, almost like a layer of thick steel wool. He laid his palm up on the ground—his hand was big enough for Daniel to stand on, now. Daniel did just that, stepping onboard below his fingers. The skin of his palm felt hardened; even where there wasn't any hair, it was thick and leathery under his feet.

"That weight okay?" Daniel said.

"Feels like a feather," Jack said. Daniel nodded back to him, then dropped into a crouch.

"When the barrier drops, the fight begins!" Ky said. "In three...two...one!"

A blaring horn sounded, and the translucent barrier vanished.

Gulthak roared, but held his position as Kavarssian's bodyguard—as Daniel expected. Kavarssian, too, held onto his flames, waiting to respond to whatever they had planned.

"Don't miss," Daniel said.

"No pressure!" Jack shouted back. And as he did, he lifted Daniel up, brought him back, then flung his arm forward with a grunt.

Daniel leapt out of his crouch in a blast of magic as Jack's arm threw him. The force was enough that Jack stumbled backward, nearly falling over as he scrambled to steady himself on the steel. Daniel was catapulted through the air, zooming across the arena and straight toward Gulthak, holding his mace out in front of him. A fireball from Kavarssian streaked by him, missing wide underneath.

Daniel was there in a blink. He caught a surprised Gulthak straight across the throat with the handle of his mace, one hand on either end. The momentum flipped Daniel up and above him; the bar dug up and into Gulthak's neck and chin as Daniel rotated, swinging up and then down like an Olympic gymnast on the uneven bars.

Daniel shot magic through his entire body as he hit the peak of his swing. He came down hard behind the ogre, choking the orc with the bar of his mace. His hands strained to keep their grip on the weapon, and his shoulders groaned in protest, but the magic coursing through his body kept his grip firm. Gulthak was bent back by the force dragging on his neck. Daniel completed his swing, falling behind the ogre. As he landed, he could feel the weight and energy of his momentum drive through his hips and down his feet into the hard steel beneath him.

Daniel pulled down on the bar, hefting the huge ogre over his back. There was brief resistance—and then Gulthak's feet came up off the floor, and he flipped into the air, a boulder lifted by the force of a lever. Daniel pulsed his magic again, as hard as he could, pushing everything into the effort. His perception jolted erratically as he tried to force the magic into his muscles and generate more power.

Gulthak's weight finally came off the bar as he flipped into the air, head down, feet whipping above him. Daniel caught a glimpse of his face as Gulthak flew over his shoulder—eyes wide, darting, face twisted in alarm.

Gulthak was in the air, but he was too heavy, and already dropping. The throw wasn't enough to guarantee he'd be flung off the edge.

Daniel was already bringing his mace around, both hands on the end of the handle, grip tight, elbows straight. He took all the magic that was coursing through his body and shoved it up and through the mace. The weapon lit up like a glowstick.

The mace was inches from contact. Daniel pushed harder, forcing the light to concentrate into the tip of his mace until the spiked head glowed like a strip of burning magnesium. As Gulthak fell, Daniel's baseball swing smashed straight into his chest. Gulthak's torso caved in from the blow; spittle blasted out his mouth as his eyes bulged.

His body tumbled backward, slamming hard on the steel and rolling over and over. His hands went out to stop himself, but the heavy, rounded gauntlets prevented him from getting any purchase on the smooth roof. His momentum was too much, and he tumbled straight off the edge, into the abyss. A roar of dismay echoed through the air, growing fainter before it was abruptly cut off.

Heat caught Daniel's attention. He turned—and there was a fireball in his face. He threw himself to the side, avoiding a direct hit, but the flames smashed into his shoulder. The fire rolled off him unnaturally, almost like rainwater off a coat, but he could feel the scorching magic even through his armor. Daniel put some distance between himself and Kavarssian, using his free hand to brush the cinders off himself. *I love this armor so much.*

"Fitzgerald is at it again—blink and you'll miss it!" Ky shouted. "Daniel dealt with Gulthak with some kind of strange wrestling technique. Though Jack has trouble moving with his injuries, they maximized his strengths to ensure a quick catch-up attack. Great strategy from the Order of the Dragon!"

Daniel ignored the commentary, running back toward Jack while keeping an eye on the dragon. Kavarssian definitely looked angry—but he wasn't holding any more fire. He stalked toward them, his hard shoes ringing sharp against the steel.

"How you doing?" Daniel asked.

"Think I tore something open," Jack said. He heaved his breaths. "Here." Jack fished out the silver mirror. "You'll get better use out of it."

"You need that to defend yourself, you can't even—"

Jack pressed it into his hands. "Take it, moron. Use it to win. Dying doesn't matter."

"What a touching moment." Kavarssian's voice crawled over them. Daniel slipped the mirror into a pocket that opened on his armor, tucking it out of sight, then stood, keeping himself between Jack and the dragon. Kavarssian was at the center of the arena now, with Daniel and Jack halfway between him and the edge. "But it doesn't really matter what tricks you think you have left. I don't need Gulthak to win." He pulled out a small red pill from his pants pocket.

"Stop him!" Jack shouted.

Daniel shot forward, but Kavarssian was already swallowing. Daniel was almost there before a wave of magic washed over him. The force pushed him backward, almost taking him off his feet; it felt like the same kind of pressure that Beelzebub could exude, or the Vorid lord. Maybe not on the same scale, but the same free-ranging suppression that came from a huge amount of magic being used all at once.

Within the circle of force, Kavarssian was rapidly growing, tearing through his clothes as scales rippled over the clear parts of his skin. Bat-like, bone-edged wings spread from his back; sharp spikes erupted one by one from his spine, and he fell on all fours as he continued to gain weight and muscle. "Oh my," Ky said, "Kavarssian has used his reward from the earlier challenges—a transmogrification pill! Despite not having access to his full magical stores, the pill allows Kavarssian to return to his true form! And might I say, he looks far more dashing."

Kavarssian was now three times his original size, and still growing, easily dwarfing even Gulthak. Daniel had seen a dragon once before, back in New York, and if this kept going, he'd take up half the arena with his body mass alone. He had to interrupt the process before it finished. Daniel struggled to move forward, fighting the force pressing against him, but it was like trying to push through a wall of molasses. He wasn't getting pushed back, but he couldn't close the distance with any speed.

Daniel's fears were realized as the transformation completed itself. The transforming magic died away, but Kavarssian was now a fully-scaled serpent of terror. His jaw opened, revealing lines of teeth that were the size of butcher knives. A tremendous roar raged over them.

"Hopefully the Order's name isn't for show, because it looks like Jack and Daniel have their work cut out for them!" Ky said. "Let's see what Kavarssian's first move will be."

Daniel skipped back toward Jack, getting a safe distance from Kavarssian's teeth and claws. "What the hell do I do against that?"

Jack managed a shrug. "We're pretty screwed. I thought your armor was a good reward, but his pill is totally rigged."

Kavarssian wasn't letting them talk strategy. He took a lumbering step forward, cutting off another few feet of free territory and boxing them further into a corner. His neck flexed, keeping his massive head cocked slightly, one slit-shaped pupil fixed on them. His wings opened, expanding like ship sails—and then he flapped. And flapped again. And he kept flapping, building up a wind like a gust. Daniel hunkered low and shielded Jack. Kavarssian's wings beat at the air, generating a hurricane-force wind that threatened to throw them into the pit below.

Daniel kept his eyes up, looking Kavarssian up and down. His wings looked thin, but they were high up and out of reach.

The rest of him was covered in inches-thick scales. Wicked bone spurs and points jutted from every joint, keeping them well-protected. His eyes might be a vulnerable spot, but they were high up too, and very close to a lot of very sharp teeth.

"Okay," Daniel shouted over the winds. "I've got a plan!"

"Yeah?"

"This time, I throw you! And then you land on him, grab on to one of those bone spikes, and beat the stuffing out of him!"

Jack's eyes darted away, then back to Daniel. "Are you serious?!"

"While you smack him, I'll try to keep him distracted and find a weak point. He can't be invincible!"

Jack gestured with his hands. "What, am I gonna punch through his scales? I don't even know if I could stand up right now!"

"Go for the eyes or something!"

"This is stupid!"

"Do you have any better ideas?"

Jack and Daniel slid back slightly as the winds continued to build in ferocity. Kavarssian was taking deep, measured breaths—obviously, the effort was winding him—but it was also a zero risk means to send them to their deaths. Daniel jammed the business end of his mace into the roof several times, building up a slight indent on the steel to give them a little grip. It wasn't much, but it was better than nothing.

"He can't keep that up forever," Daniel said. "As soon as he stops, I throw you!"

Kavarssian noticed Daniel's attempt to stabilize them with his weapon. The dragon growled, easily loud enough to hear over the wind. He pumped his wings harder, burning up his stamina for a last-ditch attempt to blow them away. Daniel shifted, trying to reposition his mace to withstand the extra force, but a gale snuck under Daniel's armor and threatened to lift him up.

Jack shoved his hand on Daniel's back, pressing him flat to the steel roof. "Fine!" Jack said. "You owe me a beer! Two beers!"

Daniel barely made out Jack's demands over the wind whipping in his ears. "I owe you what?"

Jack leaned toward Daniel's ear. "Two! Beers!"

"I'll buy you a whole keg if we get out of this alive!"

"What?!"

"I said, I'll get you a whole keg!"

"I'm pretty sure I already broke a leg!"

Daniel decided to cut the small talk and focus on the two-story monster trying to blow a couple ants off its front porch. The wind bit at them like a hungry animal, tearing at their skin and clothes. His hand ached from gripping the handle of the mace; his arm burned from the weight of himself and Jack dragging in the wind. He clenched his teeth and tried to work the weapon into the roof, rocking it back and forward slightly to dig one of the spikes in deeper.

Right as he started making progress, a nasty blast of wind dislodged Daniel's mace from its slot. They immediately started sliding backwards. With the roof being so smooth, the wind was strong enough to push them around like a puck on an air hockey table. Daniel repeatedly struck his mace into the roof, but he only managed to scrape up sparks as they inched toward the abyss.

Jack's hand wrapped around his. Daniel was surprised, but went along with it as Jack's stronger arm lifted his, then slammed the mace home. One of the spikes drove into the steel again, catching them firm and halting their slide.

Daniel and Jack kept a joint grip on the mace as the wind periodically picked them up before their weight slammed them back into the ground. His shoulders and forearms ached with the effort of keeping them anchored. Daniel could hear Ky's voice in the background, but it was muted in the wind. He tuned it out and focused on staying alive.

Kavarssian's wings started to slow. His voice growled out at them, having more pronounced serpentine quality to it, but 3 or 4 octaves lower than it had been. "Ssstubborn little monkeys. Let's sssee how you handle a little heat."

Daniel didn't waste any time. As soon as the wind died, he poured on the magic, grabbed Jack under his shoulders and hauled him from the ground. Daniel grunted as he hurled his friend bodily into the air, tossing him up and over his hip.

Daniel didn't have Jack's raw, locomotive-force strength, but it was enough. Jack's body flipped up through the air toward Kavarssian's back. Silvery hairs spread from Jack's legs, preparing to soften his landing.

To Daniel's horror, Kavarssian took a step back, angled his head up, and opened his mouth. Jack was going to fall straight into his teeth.

"Should've known better than to use the same trick twice!" Ky said.

Daniel charged magic into his legs and shot off in a flash. Jack had reached the peak of his arc and was already descending. By the time Daniel reached the dragon, Jack was only a few feet from Kavarssian's open mouth.

Daniel leapt off the ground and slammed his shoulder into the base of Kavarssian's neck. Daniel felt the collision in his bones—it was as if he'd tried to shoulder a telephone pole. He bounced off and tumbled down onto the steel. The momentum flipped him back, head over heels, but he landed on his feet, arm throbbing as he screeched to a halt.

Daniel didn't think he'd hurt the dragon much, if any, but it was enough to shift his head off to the side—letting Jack land safely midway up Kavarssian's neck.

"Daniel barely secures a safe landing for his friend," Ky called out, "but it remains to be seen if Jack can follow up and dish out the hurt!"

"Ugh. Disgusting little pests!" Kavarssian shook his neck, trying to jostle Jack off, but Jack had an ape-arm firmly hooked around one of the bone-spines. Injured, it was probably all he could do to hold on; he needed a distraction.

Daniel ran up to the feet of the dragon. Kavarssian's knuckles stood out to him, bulging up behind gargantuan claws. He came down hard with his mace, but his weapon bounced back with a metallic ring as it hammered the scaled finger between his mace and the steel floor. Daniel's hands went numb from the vibration traveling back up the handle.

Kavarssian stepped back, wincing, then shook his claw loose—as if he'd done no more than stub a toe. He growled a rolling chuckle. "Oh my. Keep that up and I might develop a hangnail."

Kavarssian opened his mouth in Daniel's direction. The only hint Daniel had that something was wrong was a small orange flicker in the back of Kavarssian's throat.

A geyser of flame erupted from the dragon's mouth, blasting the small section of platform Daniel occupied. Daniel was already sprinting away, but the flames billowed into an explosive cloud of heat as they struck the roof. The burst caught him from behind, enveloping him in white-hot fire and sending him flying forward off his feet. His armor protected him, but he went from a little warm to scalding hot on his skin in an instant, like steam in the shower a few degrees too unbearable.

Daniel broke free of the flames only to realize he was practically out of room. He churned his feet backwards to halt his forward momentum, but he was going so fast on the steel it was like slipping on ice; his armored boots shrieked and skidded against the roof. He slid to a halt at the very edge of the arena and threw his arms out for balance, wobbling as his toes dipped toward the abyss.

Tiny fires were still live on his armor, patches of flame that threatened to burn right through his protection. Daniel patted and scraped at them wildly, and the flames actually fell away, as if he was wiping off magical napalm. His armor was singed black where the bits of fire had stuck on too long.

"Daniel's mace is no match for dragon scales!" Ky called out, "and now he's on the run from dragonfire, no cover in sight!"

Once he spotted where Daniel emerged, Kavarssian redirected his attack, eating away the free space with an unceasing flamethrower spewing from his mouth and along the ground. The dragon stepped forward, following Daniel's retreat to pen him in.

Daniel sprinted up to duck the fire and sneak under the dragon's body, but Kavarssian predicted him. He lowered his chest and tucked his tree-trunk legs closer together, forcing Daniel to stop. The stream of fire finally died away as Kavarssian was forced to draw another breath, but Daniel was left stuck directly under the dragon's head, the only free spot of iron left. A sea of flames surrounded him on all sides. Daniel glanced around for a way out, but despite not having anything to burn, the unnatural flames flickered and sparked as fiercely as when they'd first emerged.

"Daniel has been walled in by dragonfire on all sides!" Ky shouted. Her words came out with a quickened, wide-eyed excitement as she described Daniel's worsening situation. "His armor won't withstand a straight shot, and there's nowhere left to run. Kavarssian has him cornered! Is this the end for our freshman warrior?!"

Kavarssian drew back slightly, another gout of flame ready to roast Daniel where he stood—and then his head jerked. A silvery fist smashed the side of his jaw; the fire went wide, harmlessly arcing into the abyss. Jack's thick fingers clawed forward, digging into Kavarssian's eye.

Kavarssian gave an ugly screeching growl and tossed his head, but the crown-like growth of spikes above Kavarssian's head was working against him. They were sized to protect him against other dragons—not little monkeys—and Jack was lodged in tight, some of his protective hairs snaked around the bony projections. His legs dangled free behind him as he was rocked up and down, but Jack wasn't going anywhere.

"Killiney has managed to climb up Kavarssian's neck and distract him from above!" Ky's tone hit a high-pitched squeal. "Kavarssian can't shake him loose!"

Daniel decided that he wasn't going to do much good from the ground. Luckily, the dragon's body had plenty of handholds. He reached up to the spikes jutting between the scales at its knee—well over head-height—to pull himself up and onto the beast. Daniel went unnoticed as he climbed up onto Kavarssian's shoulder, the dragon preoccupied with stopping Jack from worsening the damage to his wounded eye.

Daniel hunted along the scales for weaknesses. Where the dragon's front arm joined his body, below the joint, was another nest of spikes, but the scales under it were smaller and thinner. It would make sense—a shoulder had to be more flexible than a claw. With Jack running interference, Daniel took his time lining up a shot, pressing the small amount of power he had all the way into the tip of his mace. He pushed it further, trying to concentrate the magic onto the point of a single spike on his weapon.

He couldn't quite cram all his energy into such a small space. It felt like trying to push sand into a pyramid; eventually it was too tall, and the sand slipped back down the sides. Daniel managed that sensation carefully, sinking far deeper into his core than he usually did. His magic was soon trying to squeeze past him and back down as he struggled to jam it in harder. He reached a point of equilibrium, where all his mental effort put in energy at the same rate it fell away.

Realizing that his magic was as concentrated as it could get in the short time he had to spare, Daniel drew himself back to the surface. His eyes refocused. Taking another half-second to line up his shot, he slammed the single radiant spike into the scales. The strike felt different—his weapon didn't bounce off, or shake, or rattle his hands. The spike quietly *thumped* into the scales, shattering them like glass and tearing straight into the muscle.

The magic ripped out in every direction from the point of contact, tearing away in a sphere of destruction that shredded the surface layer of Kavarssian's shoulder and shot rays of white-gold light into the air. It was as if a tiny, quiet bomb of magic had gone off at the end of Daniel's weapon.

Kavarssian roared again, loud and deep enough that Daniel felt the sound in his chest—but there was a distinct note of pain mixed into the anger. Kavarssian raised his claw up, slammed it into the ground, and otherwise shook his shoulder. Daniel learned from Jack and propped himself in tight against the spines with his legs, holding firm.

Now that he'd penetrated the scales, Daniel sacrificed power for speed. He slammed his mace in again, and again, widening the breach with rapid, repetitive strikes. His hits slammed into the exposed muscle with wet, nasty squelching sounds, and the spikes and rivets on his morning star ripped pieces of flesh out every time he drew it back.

"Kavarssian had the upper hand, but persistent harassment is getting the better of him! Daniel's attacks are absolutely brutal on his shoulder. With Jack pestering his eyes, he isn't able to bite Daniel off!"

Flecks of blood splattered the front of Daniel's armor and visor as he laid through layers of muscle—until finally, there was a bit of exposed bone and pale connective tissue. Daniel jammed his mace into the core of the joint and twisted, pushing his weight and his magic into it. His mace fell in, caught, stopped. Daniel kept twisting; there was a loud, sickening crack, and something popped loose.

Kavarssian's arm collapsed. The dragon shrieked as it fell sideways, neck and chest crashing through the fires below. The metal roof distended from the weight striking down so hard in one place. Daniel rode out the fall unscathed, his legs still tight on the spines, one hand dug into the open hole in Kavarssian's shoulder.

Flames licked at Daniel's feet as they settled to a stop, but the dragon's scales repelled the fire, saving his legs from being cooked. The dragon's injured arm splayed sideways, flopping lifelessly as its other three limbs tried to prop it back up. Daniel had the feeling he might have dislocated the joint.

"DAMN YOU HUMANS!" Kavarssian roared. The words shook Daniel's ears like bass reverb at a rock concert. "You dare—YOU *DARE* TO—"

Kavarssian's ego trip was interrupted as Jack's fist hammered into the dragon's bone-spurred ear. His head lurched sideways from the blow, and he spluttered, gouts of flame and smoke coming from between his teeth.

With another roar, Kavarssian's wings started to beat, his whole back rippling in a wave. Daniel was braced in that direction, so he was flung up and out of his perch at the shoulder. He landed on his stomach, higher on Kavarssian's back, and reached out to grab the nearest handhold—one of the long, thick spikes that ran down the dragon's spine.

"Kavarssian's taken some solid hits, and it looks like he's in the mood for a change of scenery," Ky said. "The sky is a dragon's realm! Hope Jack and Daniel are holding on tight!"

Kavarssian's back kept pumping to work his wings. Daniel followed Ky's advice and held on for dear life as he flopped up and down against the scales. They rose into the air above the arena, then left it and Ky's voice behind entirely as Kavarssian flew into open air. They were engulfed by darkness, the only point of reference a rapidly shrinking steel pillar, gleaming alone in the abyss.

The world began to shift around Daniel—and as gravity dragged him to the side, he realized Kavarssian was flipping. He dragged himself closer to the spike of bone and wrapped his arms and legs around it, squeezing tight as the dragon inverted underneath him. Daniel screamed bloody murder as gravity and the pumping back muscles threatened to push him into oblivion.

Kavarssian couldn't fly upside down forever; after losing too much altitude, the pit below grew uncomfortably close, and he righted himself, pumping his wings again to gain altitude. Daniel felt the g-force press him into the dragon's scales they banked a turn.

"Daniel! Back here!"

Daniel looked—and rather than ahead of him, somewhere on Kavarssian's head, Jack was near the joint of the wing. Another nest of spikes defended the point where the wing met the body, and Jack was propped inside. Daniel let himself drop flat against the dragon, then carefully pulled himself down the spines until he reached Jack.

Jack was a mess. His injuries were oozing blood; it ran down his arms and stomach, staining all his clothes. His protective hairs were frayed and torn across most of his body. "You look like you lost a fight with a lawnmower!"

"Is this the time?!" Jack screamed back. Kavarssian flipped again, faster than before. Unprepared, Daniel tumbled sideways. Jack caught him by the wrist and hauled him up between the spines. They huddled there as Kavarssian rolled and tumbled through the air, performing flips and barrel rolls as he tried to end the fight by dropping them into the darkness.

"That's three beers!" Jack shouted.

"What the hell do we do?!"

"I dunno!" Jack said. "I—I'm getting really dizzy. I don't think I can keep going. Lost my grip on his neck, almost fell off. Lucky I landed here."

"We have to force him to land, somehow," Daniel said. "We're sitting ducks out here, one wrong move and we're dead."

"I don't..." Jack shook his head, as if clearing his thoughts. Daniel grimaced, glad his visor was hiding his expression. Jack had to be feeling the blood loss, powers or not. "Wait." Jack looked over Daniel's shoulder. "His wings! Rip the skin with your mace!"

Daniel glanced at the wings. They were huge and lined with bone—reinforced to support and propel the weight of a dragon. But the fleshy interior looked weaker—at least, as weak as hardened leather compared to solid iron. "We all die if he falls!"

"We'll die last," Jack said. "We're on top!"

Despite himself, Daniel snorted a laugh. Here Jack was, almost having drowned, injured and actively bleeding, stuck on the back of a dragon in the middle of an endless abyss—and his genius plan was mutual suicide with their enemy. Albeit with them dying a second or two slower, and maybe, probably, winning on a technicality.

"Here goes!" Daniel said. He poured magic into his mace. It was rougher than his last attack, as he didn't have the time for finesse—but it was more than enough to break the defenses of the wings. The mace ripped a hole near the joint, tearing a flap of skin lose. Wind rushed through the tear, straining the broken skin.

Kavarssian's roar was muted by the abyss, but it was clear that they'd hurt him. Jack reached in; his hands rippled, growing in size, and he seized the torn edges, tearing them up and past his shoulder. The hole ripped wider.

They laid into the wing as much as they could from their position. Jack held Daniel's arm so that he could lean out and punch holes with his mace. After yanking him back, Jack called on his reserves and reached out to the new tears, wrenching the holes wider. Daniel was the can opener, and Jack turned the screw.

Kavarssian banked hard; the force pushed them down into the spines. The tiny dot of the steel arena swung into view in front of them. Kavarssian was heading back toward land.

"It's working!" Jack said. "He's worried he can't keep flying. Down him before we get back!"

"Stay here and keep tearing!" Daniel said. "I'll get the rest!"

Daniel left the safety of the spines near the joint and reached out along the bony arm of the wing. He charged his mace, then jammed it through the flesh of the wing, eliciting a new roar from the dragon. Daniel gripped with his other hand where the mace protruded out the other side. With his hold secure, he crawled up along the edge of the beating wing, hugging tight as he was carried up and down.

Daniel hooked his free arm in tight, then pulled his mace free, widening the hole. He checked his grip on his weapon—losing it now would be terrible—then reached out and punctured a fresh hole. He dragged himself forward, moving up a foot when the wing paused at the end of a flap.

Jack reached behind Daniel and ripped the loose skin free of the bat-like arm. They'd torn away nearly a third of the wing. Wind whipped and whistled through it as it began to lose its ability to keep Kavarssian aloft. With each new punched hole, Kavarssian roared in pain, and Daniel split more flesh off the wing. He could feel the dragon dipping sideways, flapping harder and harder to compensate. Daniel's progress started to slow; the farther along he crawled, toward the wingtip, the more he was thrown up and down.

Daniel was halfway up the wing when he heard Jack screaming, but between the wind and focusing on what he was doing, he couldn't make out the exact words. Daniel looked up to shout at Jack to repeat himself.

The arena was right in front of them, and Kavarssian was barreling in too fast. Kavarssian's ruined wing feebly flapped to stop their forward momentum. It wasn't nearly enough.

They impacted the edge of the roof. Daniel's world turned over; his left leg felt like someone had dipped it in a deep fryer. His left arm was next; he could feel it crunch, then only pain. His sight flickered, black, grey, black, as the rooftop arena turned over in a series of images too fast for his mind to process, as if he was a passenger in a car that was rolling into a ditch.

He was still. Flecks of light and spots dotted the edges of his vision as it swam back to normal. He blinked hard, trying to clear away the daze in his mind.

He was lying on something hard. Steel. The arena. He craned his neck to look.

Kavarssian was next to him, crumpled in a broken heap. The dragon heaved long, halting breaths; three of its ribs were protruding out of its chest. His left wing was shredded to pieces; his right was snapped off entirely from where it had slammed into the edge of the arena, leaving a bony, fleshy stump behind. Blood was everywhere.

"Jack." Daniel's words came out hoarse and feeble. He tried to clear his throat. The small effort made his stomach churn. "Jack. Jack!"

There was no response. Daniel tried to move and immediately regretted it as his left arm and leg sent shooting, stabbing pains up his body. He managed to lift his head enough to examine the damage.

His left leg was torn and twisted backwards; his foot was bent the wrong way. Blood leaked from where the elven armor had ripped at the joint. He stared at it for a second, in a half-disbelieving, muted surprise. His eyes traveled to his arm. He could see white bone poking out from his elbow.

The haze in his head was thickening, rather than dissipating, as if his consciousness was sinking slowly into mud. The black spots at the edge of his vision were turning red-pink. He knew he should be in incredible pain; he should be unconscious. Was he in shock? Or...what? He wasn't sure.

Kavarssian shifted.

Daniel felt a thrill of fear race up his spine as the dragon moved, briefly shooing away his mental cobwebs. Kavarssian's head reared itself from within the folded-up bundle of limbs, his neck pushing aside the remains of his snapped-off wing. His good eye fixated on Daniel.

The dragon dragged himself forward, ignoring his dislocated front leg with seething single-mindedness. Panic rose in Daniel. A surge of adrenaline powered a scoot backward using his good arm. Incredibly, the elven armor responded, closing up around his wounds and helping push him away, but he was dragging half his body. The dragon was too large; the arena was too small. A few seconds later, Kavarssian had pulled himself into a three-legged lean—wounded and shaky—but still strong enough to stand, looming over Daniel.

"Looks like you're out of tricks," the dragon growled.

Daniel looked down, then back up at the dragon's face. "Looks like you have a small penis."

The dragon stood there, baffled—then the light of anger dawned in his eyes as he processed the insult. Kavarssian's jaws opened up, and he emitted a massive roar straight into Daniel's face. Daniel felt his ears shake, felt the vibration in his chest and his bones. A sharp pain stabbed into the right side his head, and the sound level cut in half. His eardrum had burst.

The pain washed out quickly. Daniel's body didn't have the energy to spare on ugly sensations—or the energy to keep him alive, for that matter. The raw survival instinct was a temporary jolt, but there was a hazy, tempting darkness of unconsciousness lingered at the back of his head.

He needed something to turn the tables. Something to protect himself with. He felt something slip into his hand, ejected from a pocket in his armor. Round, smooth. Jack's item.

Kavarssian's words shook him back from his drifting thoughts. "Know your place, insect." He lifted his one good claw slowly, higher, then higher still, until he had to rear back on his hind legs. And then he dropped down, putting his entire weight behind the limb that would no doubt squash Daniel into meat paste.

Daniel lifted his right arm, placing the tiny reflective mirror Jack had given him between himself and the oncoming claw.

Kavarssian struck the mirror, and the world stopped moving, as if someone had hit the pause button on life. Daniel could feel it, almost like how time slowed down when he poured out his magic at full force. They were stuck there, Kavarssian's claw permanently frozen above him, the tip having made only the slightest contact with the mirror. The massive momentum of the dragon's body was stuck still.

The mirror shattered.

Kavarssian's arm snapped straight up and ripped free of the socket. It dangled in the air, held on only by a few tendrils of flesh. Kavarssian was thrown back by the force and the pain, stumbling on his hind legs. On instinct, he threw his other arm out for balance—but that was the one Daniel had already rendered useless.

Kavarssian tripped over the dislocated arm and tumbled head-first over the edge of the arena. His remaining wing—and the stump of the other—flapped up and down in desperation, doing little to help. His neck lashed out, and his jaws clamped onto the steel next to Daniel, hard enough to cut through and bend it inward. But as the rest of his body dragged down behind him, the steel groaned, then snapped away, and the dragon fell into the abyss, roaring in rage, frustration—

Until the roar cut off.

Daniel set his head back onto the roof. Everything was still and silent.

That had been close. Too close. He'd almost forgotten he had the mirror until the armor did some of his thinking for him. He really needed to make some elf friends.

He tried to exhale and let out some of his tension, but his breath wracked out of his body in uneven gasps. The pain was coming on fast, overtaking the shock and adrenaline in worsening waves. His arm and leg were starting to throb. His head throbbed. Everything throbbed. His thoughts were starting to slip again, faster than before, trending back to the elves for some reason. He imagined getting a set of armor as a Christmas gift.

A demoness with skin redder than the blood smeared on his visor materialized from thin air. She was wrapped in a skintight, generously revealing tri-colored dress, exuding the beatific confidence of a prime time anchorette. She held a mic up to her mouth.

"And at the last minute, Daniel pulls out the win! What a show-stopper of a finish!" Ky leaned down to Daniel's crippled body, favoring him with a bright grin of shiny spiked teeth. "Any words from our victorious warrior?!" She thrust the microphone into Daniel's face, gleefully ignoring his crushed limbs and near-comatose state.

Even as bad as he was, the words came to Daniel immediately. "Size isn't everything."

Chapter 16
Behind the Scenes

Beelzebub's claw prodded the air, and the display screen froze, locked on a camera shot of Ky standing over Daniel. The frenetic PrisonWatch hostess had embarked on an immediate play-by-play, on-site review of Daniel's performance, doing her best to keep the viewers engaged and hanging on through another round of commercials for the post-match analysis. The metering for the advertisements on this fight alone far exceeded projections; their average live viewership about quintupled for the fight, drawn in by the prospect of the two contractors teaming up. Ky didn't even realize Daniel had fallen unconscious until she stopped her stream of commentary to ask him a question—but she deftly spun it into a comedic transition, promising a personal interview at a later time for interested viewers. That would be another moneymaker.

Ky was the right choice to take over the host job for Purgatory. She'd held the spot for 27 years, now, longer than her last three predecessors combined. Her overly friendly, over-the-top façade was matched with a subtle swirl of dark humor that, while seen as annoying by more than a few, had endured with the audience longer than anything else Beelzebub had tested this century. She was a character with a defined role, as much a part of the show as the prisoners themselves, and she was a master at acting her part.

Setting aside his calculation of the impending profits, Beelzebub faced the long table opposite the screen. "That," the devil said, opening his claws toward the image hovering behind him, "is a fraction of Daniel's power. He's entirely untrained, and he doesn't use his magic efficiently, but he doesn't have to. He has reserves to burn. That is the kind of power we're talking about—power we might have. Sheer brute force can solve a variety of tricky problems.

"The absorption process is rapid and efficient, and requires no external refinement of the raw soul energy." Beelzebub turned his hand in the air, like a professor indicating figures on a blackboard. "We took measurements of the energy transfer after his conflict with the Viridian Gust. They were even better than Xik's claims. No signs of destabilization in his power, no risk of personality disjointment. The spell activates as soon as the soul energy separates from the physical husk. No messy rituals long after the fact, no storage of the corpse or the soul. Daniel is constantly monitored and he hasn't displayed any of the schizophrenic side-effects that normally result from integrating soul fragments prior to refinement.

"That being said," Beelzebub added, "I prevented Gulthak and Kavarssian from dying when they fell into the abyss. It would be difficult to explain their disappearance on top of the issues with the Viridian Gust; they're too popular to both suddenly go into isolated, private retirement. The wrong people might start asking questions if every top talent that encounters Daniel disappears."

Beelzebub turned again to the council room. The long wooden table stretched out in front of him, lined with mostly-empty seats on either side. The majority of the chairs were designed for a humanoid form, though one was twice the size to fit an orc, and another was almost bench-like in shape, to allow for a grazul's spidery form to relax straight down. Aside from the allowance of the plush seats, the room was stark and utilitarian, aligned in form and function with the rest of his government center in Dis. Decoration—in a government facility—was a waste of time and money.

The other council members usually attended by hologram, the distance between star systems being such that routine live meetings were impractical without the extreme expense of ultra long-distance teleportation. With few physically present, there was little need for physical accommodations. Beelzebub was more than happy to forgo the grand trappings of state receptions; he hated padding egos, especially the egos of fools who threatened to peel off significant sections of his empire.

Today, only two of the council's other seven members were in attendance. Asmodeus, his top military commander, was seated on the first chair to the left. He was covered from neck to toe in opaque black adamantium plate armor. The black was marbled with rose gold where orichalcum, a valuable metal suited for channeling mana, was doped through the metal. In partnership with the adamantium, which boasted surpassing hardness and strength, his armor was one-of-a-kind, designed to amplify his already formidable martial might. Asmodeus dressed for combat as a rule, though he made the usual compromise of taking off his helmet for the meeting—albeit within arm's reach on the table in front of him.

Lilith, chief of domestic affairs, was in the first chair on the right. Her dress was a solid diagonal sweep of blue and black cloth that curled up around her figure, not unlike the style that Ky wore, but her clothes swam up neatly to her neck. The outfit subtly revealed her figure, but contained no hint of bare skin. She'd dressed conservatively for the past several millennia, and Beelzebub expected the trend to continue. She wore orichalcum as well, but kept it hidden and secured within her clothing.

Lilith had more sense for social niceties; she was a talented politician and diplomat that balanced her counterpart Asmodeus. The general was more the straight-laced, results-oriented strategist. He had to be, to manage a military so sprawling and unwieldy, let alone the territories themselves. If Asmodeus was the fist of the empire, Lilith was the velvet, gloved lining.

And Beelzebub was the arm wielding the fist.

The two councilors, along with Beelzebub himself, made up the Devils' Three, a triumvirate that formed the backbone of leadership for the empire. Each other councilor represented an independent imperial interest—one of the several major races—with enough weight to warrant a vote. Less important races were represented, lawfully speaking, by Beelzebub—and for that reason, his vote counted twice. Nominally, each member of the council had one vote in policy decisions, but the devils always voted in unison, typically having hammered out their disagreements in advance. Carrying 4 of 9 total votes usually weighed affairs in their direction; they only needed to convince one other council member to see things their way to effectively steer the empire. Put another way, every other councilor had to vote unanimously to thwart Beelzebub's plans.

This was, in fact, a progressive arrangement. There had been a time when Beelzebub wielded absolute authority as emperor; authority he was forced to dilute with the involvement of Lilith and Asmodeus when the empire became too unmanageable for a single devil, no matter how great his magical talent. As they expanded, and expanded again, exploring star systems and colonizing useful planets, not every action or policy could be managed by the central government or automated via magic or technology. Other races struck out on their own, developing themselves until central control became even more untenable.

The dragons were the first such race. While reasserting authority by force had been an option early on, Beelzebub judged it too costly. He compromised instead, establishing the first semi-autonomous governorship and council seat. The dragons were staunch in maintaining the discipline of the empire, generally allying their interests with the devils. They were also strong, as strong as the devils, in many ways, so compromise with them was not regarded as a dishonor or unusual circumstance. Beelzebub easily spun the arrangement as a natural political development that had long since been in the works.

Still, the dragons had their own will—and worse, the precedent had been set. The other races unexpectedly surged to earn their own council seat in a collective series of cold political conflicts and hot civil wars in which Beelzebub had exterminated more than one upstart government and more than one race entirely to maintain control. At first, the dragons, and then the orcs and imps, in exchange for their own seats, had fought on his side, unwilling to see their own votes diluted further.

As time passed, their perspective changed. True power wasn't found in indefinitely riding the coattails of the empire—it was in achieving independence. It was a big universe, and unsatisfied with the scraps from Beelzebub's table, they wanted their own slice. With internal unity starting to slip, the oppressive wars couldn't be continued indefinitely. No matter how much they loathed bowing their heads, even devils could simply grow tired of conflict. Endless infighting was counterproductive.

Beelzebub had come to accept the bitter reality that he had limits, and the council steadily swelled to its current eight seats, following the addition of the grazul and the undines. While he'd maintained most of his power, it was a crabby and jealous grip on something that was being drawn away from him bit by bit. The dwarves and the harpies, especially, were jockeying fiercely for their own council seats, and he was on the cusp of having to give over to them. At that point, the triumvirate would be only 4 of 11 votes.

As an individual force, Beelzebub was incredibly powerful, acknowledged as the strongest in the empire even by the dragons. But there were a handful of beings in his tier of strength. If they worked together, they could likely defeat him, or at the least force him to withdraw. He controlled the Hell seal, and he had a diplomatic monopoly with the humans on behalf of all demonkin, but even those tools could only reach so far. While the humans had made plenty of progress and could still be counted as a powerful ally—or a threat—they'd grown proportionally weaker compared to the totality of the demon empire.

Beelzebub had lived for a long time. He could see the long game playing out before him, the final end approaching in slow motion. It was only another century or two before he was leader in name only, and perhaps not long after that until the empire fractured into its component pieces.

He looked out over the empty council table. The Goblin Consortium, the Engu Warband—mostly orcs and ogres—the Dragon Hegemony, the Undine Kingdom and the Darkweaver Hive, entirely grazul. These were the rising, would-be independent powers, still under the banner of the empire—for now.

In the past, Beelzebub restructured the two worlds and sealed away the monster with the help of his human allies. Following that, he personally united the various races of the demon world. He wasn't about to let it all slip through his fingers; it simply wasn't in his nature to quietly retire and watch what he'd built crumble to pieces from a safe distance. If he was such a coward, he wouldn't have come to rule it all in the first place.

The long millennia had fused his pride into him, made it part of him; no sooner would he give it up than cut off his own hand. He was a devil. It was in his nature to hold on to what was his, to attempt to grasp even more. His glory would only—*could* only be limited only by the extent of his ambition and imagination, not the mundane trappings of politics and unhappy realities.

His life's work, his pride, his empire—they had no respect for what it meant, no appreciation for the effort taken to forge it in the first place. They weren't there at the beginning. They didn't face the Satan in combat; they didn't rewrite the rules of reality to set in place the current status quo. Beelzebub could feel his jaw clench as the thoughts ran through his head for the thousandth time—hangers-on, parasites, weaklings. It was he who cut the wheat, ground the flour, and baked the bread, but there they were, right at the end, ready to steal their share with smiles on their faces. His pride as a devil was being spat on, thousands of years of history, honor—*his* honor—but unless something changed, atrophy was inevitable.

And something had changed. A wonderful, terrible something. The Vorid had arrived.

Beelzebub heaved a breath in front of himself, part sigh, part huff of resolve. A cloud of smoke emerged from between his fangs, hanging over the end of the table. He gazed at the cloud as the room's ventilation sent it spiraling up toward a corner. His gaze narrowed as his plans solidified in his mind's eye.

Following his explanation of Daniel's contractor magic, Lilith and Asmodeus had fallen into their own thoughtful consideration of the huge implications of contractor magic. Lilith was the first of the three to stir; she examined the paused display screen again, then folded her fingers together and leaned forward onto her elbows, resting her weight on the table. Her movements were careful, perfectly measured to avoid wrinkling her dress. "Xikanthus has promised you contractor powers if you can stabilize the situation on Earth," she said.

"With conditions," Beelzebub said. "If our military mobilizes under my leadership, I receive half the payment—the spell itself. I won't be able to absorb any humans or other contractors. The Vorid, however, should provide plenty of fodder to build strength." Beelzebub smirked. "And he didn't exclude other demons in his little deal."

Asmodeus laughed, low and gruff. "Plenty that might have unfortunate accidents in times of war."

"Are there? My, such a shame that would be."

"Xikanthus holds great sway in this arrangement," Lilith said. "It strikes me that what he gives, he may be able to take away."

"It's possible," Beelzebub said. "Daniel has been and will be the target of his long-term grooming, and I don't blame him. Much easier to manipulate someone that young and impressionable. I'm the stopgap when that fails. He's insane enough to tamper with the seal, but ultimately, he doesn't care who gets the job done, so long as it gets done. I've spoken with him directly, and I believe his sole motivation is stonewalling the Vorid. He isn't interested in the mess he makes along the way."

"Is he sentimental in his relationship with the humans?" Asmodeus asked.

"Somewhat," Beelzebub said, "but not to the point of letting it get in the way."

"You've steered us this far, but we all know what's at stake if you're wrong," Lilith said. "Are you sure you want to put everything on the line?"

"If I'm wrong," Beelzebub said, "then our situation remains the same. Even without Xikanthus's prompting, the Vorid need to be confronted. If they finish with Earth, we'll be next. Besides..." Beelzebub smiled at them both. "We don't need to put that much on the line."

Lilith smiled back. "Now I see where you're going with this."

Beelzebub nodded. "There are plenty of eager upstarts looking to prove themselves and carve out a spot on the council, as well as established militaries that will serve as the vanguard. Many ogres and dragons will be clawing at each other to fight at the front so they can improve their personal political prospects with direct achievement. We offer a token from our own forces to secure a foothold on Earth, let the idiots hack it out amongst themselves, then clean up afterward."

Asmodeus nodded, enthusiastic at the prospect of weakening forces he considered sometime-allies at best. "I like it. I can pull on my contacts with those two races especially, and the undines are still raw, new to the council. They'll fall in line concerning military matters."

"The dwarves and the harpies too," Lilith said. "Simple matter to dangle council seats in front of them in exchange for a full military commitment."

"Precisely," Beelzebub said. "Even if we don't benefit from Xikanthus's magic, we've weakened challengers to imperial authority in the short term." Beelzebub picked at his long, dagger-like nails. "And if I assassinate some of the more *problematic* generals in the process to experiment with the limits of contractor magic, all the better."

"Mmm," Asmodeus mumbled. "I can see the look on Varnifax's face now. I want to be there when you do it." He looked over. "How do we lure them in, exactly? The smart ones will stay out of it unless we have sufficient bait."

"I've been renegotiating the treaty with the humans," Beelzebub said. "I plan on giving portal authority over to the other factions if they aid in the assault on Earth."

Lilith and Asmodeus both sat back. "That's a huge risk," Lilith said. "We've held a monopoly on interdimensional travel for three thousand years."

"And this is exactly the time to take that risk," Beelzebub said. "Xikanthus told me he'll grant the first half of the contract as soon as he sees demons in force on Earth. Once we have it, then by current standards...we become limitless." He stepped closer to the table, looking both his advisors in the eye, the two devils that had stood by his side the longest, who had never betrayed him even in all these long years. "We have two choices before us. Either we slowly waste away until we're deposed from the very empire we founded...or." He opened his palm. "We roll the dice and see what happens."

Asmodeus tapped his throat, producing a hollow snort. "You always were a gambler."

"As long as the dice are loaded," Lilith said. "How do we control this human, Daniel? Xikanthus may move to protect a big investment."

"I expect exactly that," Beelzebub said. "We have to demonstrate to Xik that I gave him a fair chance, but that ultimately, Daniel proved useless. That will earn faith with the Klide and nip a potential problem in the bud. The Order of the Dragon is already planning on getting rid of him; Dracula doesn't think he can be controlled. I'll make sure Bathory accepts the duel and fine-tune the results from a distance. That will ensure his exile to the bottom levels of Hell without any obvious interference on my part, and then he'll be stuck there, unable to grow in strength and fulfill the role that was planned for him.

"Once Xikanthus acknowledges that I'm best positioned to lead the fight against the Vorid," Beelzebub continued, "he'll give me the rest of the magic. And once I unravel its secrets, I can pass the technique to both of you. Once the war is over, we'll have unsurpassed might on the demonic plane of existence, and the fighting will have left the upstart autonomies weakened and vulnerable. Either they acknowledge our return to rulership, or they will be destroyed, council be damned."

"You're banking too much on this outsider," Asmodeus said. "I agree with Lilith on that front."

"There's another problem," Beelzebub said. "The seal itself is failing."

Asmodeus nodded. "It's been a growing issue. The external containment platform we built has helped, but it's only a matter of time."

"Without a flow of human souls in our direction," Beelzebub said, "toward Hell—it will weaken. We can't afford the consequences—not until I'm strong enough to deal with them. The Vorid have to be stopped regardless of anything else we do, and with the contractor magic I can grow stronger and stave them off at the same time.

"So you're right," Beelzebub said. "It's a gamble. Much relies on Xik and his enchantment. Judging from what I've seen, however, he's powerful enough to grant this enchantment, but he hasn't—or perhaps, more accurately, cannot—interfere in other manners. If he was interested in taking over himself, he would be making notable waves in other ways; he wouldn't come to make deals with us or the humans in the first place."

Lilith squinted. Beelzebub could practically see her coming over to his way of thinking. "Even if Xikanthus betrays us, worst-case scenario, it's a win-win," she said. "We can weaken our enemies here at home, end the threat of the Vorid, and simply leave Earth to its own devices after the fighting is over. The humans have no way into our world from theirs; their contractor situation won't impact us."

With Lilith coming around, Asmodeus chose to back up Beelzebub's argument. "I'd rather fight the Vorid in human territory than on our own. Limit collateral damage."

"That may be the most salient point so far," Lilith said. "Not that the concern has stopped you before."

Asmodeus tapped his throat with a finger, snorting at Lilith's comment. "I'm up for another gamble, Emperor. My armor's gotten rusty without a little blood to grease the joints."

They both looked at Lilith. "Are we agreed?" Beelzebub said.

Lilith paused, holding their attention hostage a moment, then nodded. "We need a little chaos to shake up the political situation. The war is coming either way. Better to move proactively."

"No time to waste," Asmodeus said. "When shall I begin?"

"As soon as possible," Beelzebub said. "I'll be in touch when the humans are ready for us; Henry Astor is working on the other treaty holders, and he says he's close. Pull all the strings you have. Leave no stone unturned. If anyone balks, apply force—you'll be the stick, and the potential reward of portal authority or a council seat will be the carrot. Run the communications through Lilith's office."

"Information control?"

"Rumors have been swirling about the Vorid already, especially with our two contractors in Hell commenting on them at length," Beelzebub said. "I'll make an official statement from the palace once our forces begin to move. Coordinate the gathering of forces in the meantime. The portal will be ready for you by the time you've finished."

"By your command." Asmodeus stood, saluted, then fixed his helmet back on his head. His white horns slotted neatly into holes on the top of the helm, a well-worn fit. The general strode out of the council room, shouldering into a crowd of advisors and messenger drones that were hovering outside the door. He shut it behind himself, cutting off the brief burst of voices.

Lilith turned her eyes back to Beelzebub. "What would you have me do?"

"Work your magic," Beelzebub said. "I expect the call to arms will bring in the dragons and the ogres without issue. Asmodeus was correct on another front—the undines are too new to the council to put up much resistance. Promise the Darkweavers and the Consortium whatever they want for their aid."

Lilith raised an eyebrow. "Whatever they want? We're already giving them portal authority."

"Exactly," Beelzebub said. "Don't tell them how willing we are. Tempt them into making the deal. Make them think it's their idea."

Lilith smiled. "That's my specialty."

"I know."

"Even for you," Lilith said, "this is a gamble. Something else is driving you forward."

"Only the fate of the empire."

"Come, Beelzebub," Lilith said, her voice warm and amused. "I know you too well for you to play games with me."

"I suspect Xikanthus will try to break the seal before this is over, regardless of what happens," Beelzebub said, "if only to satisfy his curiosity. He seems to have a penchant for chaos himself; anything to throw the Vorid into disarray, to buy time for whatever he's doing in the background. I don't believe for one second that he's sitting somewhere with his feet up, twiddling his thumbs while letting children like Daniel do the fighting for him."

"And if he does that...?" Lilith let the question hang in the air. Her eyes flicked to the side, then back at him.

Beelzebub paused, then channeled mana, pushing it into a spell that wrapped around them in a buzz of air and a flash of yellow light. Their surroundings fell entirely silent. It was the height of paranoia—yet another spell of secrecy to keep their words from leaking. The core of their government center was already protected by layer after layer of such enchantments. But at their earlier meeting, Xikanthus slipped in and out undetected. They couldn't take the chance.

Beelzebub placed a hand on the council table and leaned toward Lilith. "There are things Xikanthus does not know about our worlds; he has no knowledge of the keys, or he surely would've mentioned them."

"You still want the Longinus? After all this time?" Lilith scoffed. "I should have known you wouldn't give up on it."

"The humans still have the other four keys, but the fifth rests with me."

"What does it matter? The sixth is lost."

"I've located it," Beelzebub said. "It's down below, watched over by her obsessive little guardians at the core of the seal. The last place I thought to look. It was the seal weakening that let me detect it."

Lilith's eyes flickered back and forward with her thoughts. "You're thinking of breaking it yourself, aren't you? You'll die. We can't face them, not even now."

"They had the Longinus at their backs."

Lilith raised a hand. "Even still—"

"I need to grow stronger, to be sure," Beelzebub said, interrupting. "Once Henry Astor opens the path, we can establish a strong enough presence on Earth that the humans will be unable to dislodge us, all in the name of defeating the Vorid. And then, when the opportunity presents itself, I take the other keys by force." Beelzebub couldn't help a grin. "Xik said I wouldn't be able to absorb essence from humans, but he obviously doesn't expect I might kill them anyway."

"Clever," Lilith said. "But what does that get you? Still only 5 of 6 keys."

"In the meantime, I'll have bolstered my strength fighting the Vorid," Beelzebub said. "Holding most of the keys will give me enough influence over the Longinus to approach the core and poach the final key with less risk. If Xikanthus balks at my killing off a few humans, reneges on the deal—or even if he decides to tamper with the seal—he'll only be helping me. Even if Daniel somehow defies all odds and defeats Bathory, having been betrayed by the magicians already, he'll be easily manipulated into helping me defeat the key-holders."

"Do you believe Xikanthus will defend the boy, if it comes to it?" Lilith said.

"No," Beelzebub said. His expression grew pensive. "I believe Xikanthus does have some sympathy for him, but his gaze is set higher than that. I need more time to get a handle on his true motives, which is another reason I want Daniel to lose his battle."

"A delaying action," Lilith said. "Even if Xikanthus is pursuing Daniel's success, that will represent a major setback in time and resources."

"Correct," Beelzebub said. "I don't think it will come to that. Xikanthus wants to create a weapon to beat back the Vorid, and if Daniel fails then he'll take the path of least resistance. That means abandoning him and strengthening me."

"Whichever way the game is played," Lilith said, "it seems you'll be in an advantageous position."

"That's usually how I like to arrange things." Beelzebub's devil teeth shone as he grinned. "The house always wins, as they say."

"Very well," Lilith said, "but you'll still need the prisoner, in the end."

"She's required to activate it," Beelzebub said. "With most of the keys in hand, when the time comes, I can confront her directly."

They fell quiet, imagining what that confrontation might be like. Across the ages, truly powerful magicians often avoided direct conflict. Reducing risk to themselves was how they lived long enough to grow so strong in the first place. When tremendous powers clashed, when pinnacle warriors fought, victory or defeat could be decided by a single slip, an instant of inattention, one single variable out of place.

"Sometimes," Lilith said, her voice subdued, "I imagine that we might run away from it all. Abandon the empire, take a small retinue, escape into deep space. I doubt the Vorid would spend too many resources trying to hunt us down."

"I considered that as a backup plan, in the worst case," Beelzebub said. "But *she* wouldn't ever let us escape. The Vorid might give up hunting, but for her, it's personal."

Lilith nodded. "I suppose you're right. I still remember how she looked when she realized the truth, when she was so close to achieving her little ideal world. No one could ever let that go. I know I couldn't."

"She trusted too much," Beelzebub said. "Such is the fate of fools." His expression firmed. "Lilith. If the choice is between fleeing with my claws retracted, or fighting to the end, I'd rather be remembered as a devil that stood and fought. Immortality, in the end, is only gained through achievement. What use is living forever if no one knows about it? I will not fade into obscurity. I will not lose this battle. Not then, not now."

Lilith sighed, then smiled, her fangs showing in a shark grin. "And if you didn't drag me along for the ride, perhaps I never would've risen so far."

Beelzebub met Lilith's gaze. "Our success in this matter will determine whether or not we survive this encounter of our worlds with the Vorid. Allow no mistakes."

"Wait for the right moment," Lilith said. "Don't show your hand even an instant too early."

"I never do."

Lilith nodded to him, then stood from her chair. Beelzebub let his spell drop, and Lilith left the room, exiting to another burst of voices and sound. Beelzebub turned to the front of the council room and activated a switch behind the display screen. Mana was funneled into a teleportation pedestal hidden beneath the floor, flowing into the runes there like so much electricity.

Beelzebub reached into himself and found the key he'd hidden within his soul. More of a small stone talisman than a true key, it was present in three realities at once, tied to the human world, the demon world, and to Hell, the source of connection between them all. It was a font of raw magical power, diminished from its former state due to its isolation from the other keys, but still potent. It was his physical link to the Hell seal, one of six required to control Longinus—the great machine that was supposed to alter the destiny of their worlds, but that ended up forming the foundation of the prison for its own creator.

Fate, at times, was fickle.

A portal opened over the teleportation pad, and Bathory's room was on the other side. He rarely enjoyed his talks with the psychopath, but he wouldn't allow anything in his plan to be out of place, and that required a more personal touch than he usually preferred. She needed to accept the duel as offered by the Order of the Dragon; no negotiation, no games, no delay. She might be a bloodthirsty savage, but she understood force, properly applied. Everything bowed before brute force. That was the beauty of the contractors.

Beelzebub smirked to himself as he stepped through the opened portal. Interdimensional conflicts aside, the ratings for this fight would be tremendous.

****

"If I wasn't convinced before, you've made a convert out of me," Rasputin said. The beetle-nosed man was seated at Dracula's desk in their main office, idling away the time while they waited for Bathory to either accept or deny their request for a formal duel. More likely, she'd do neither, and instead negotiate terms to her satisfaction.

"I've converted harder men than you," Dracula said. He was half-joking, but his words were muttered; his gaze was fixated on the computer screen.

Rasputin sighed, loudly. Dracula understood he wanted a conversation, but he had little patience for debating the details of the bout Daniel and Jack had fought, especially with something so important on the line. Bathory wouldn't keep them waiting long; she always jumped at the chance to wave her influence in front of them.

Rasputin, unfortunately, was more the impulsive type. That often translated into an inability to wait patiently. "The irony is rather striking, wouldn't you say? Who would imagine the Order of the Dragon, throwing away a man who actually slayed one?"

Dracula snorted. "Daniel was lucky. He had the right tools at the right time."

"You must admit he made good use of them. Resourceful. His armor wouldn't have held against the fire without Jack's distraction, that took some daring. He thinks quickly under pressure."

"Are you trying to convince me to keep him?"

"No," Rasputin said, waving a hand, "just analyzing the particulars. The more we know about him, the easier it will be to keep him under heel in the case of unexpected circumstances."

"I suppose," Dracula said.

Rasputin visibly held back another sigh at the dead-end answer. Dracula ignored him.

The computer beeped. He leaned forward. Rasputin ambled around the desk to look on.

Bathory sent a single message in response. *I accept the duel conditions as written. One day. Details to follow.* After the message was an internal timestamp that proved she'd acknowledged the request through the official PrisonWatch system.

Dracula clenched a fist in victory. "She fully accepted the terms, banishment and all. Daniel will have no wiggle room. You've made the preparations for his reception down below?"

"I've been in touch with the usual," Rasputin said. "No matter where he ends up, the word's been put out amongst those who need to know."

"And the fight itself?"

Rasputin straightened as he reached into his thick woolen robes. He drew out a stuffed doll, haphazardly stitched into the shape of a human. Messy gold-brown hair and grey eyes tinted blue marked the doll as a crude mockup of Daniel Fitzgerald. Rasputin put the doll away, then flashed a vial of blood tucked securely into another pocket. "I collected it in the aftermath of the territory war," Rasputin said. "There was plenty of the stuff after he had a limb blown off, though it took quite a while digging through the rubble. It's only enough for the one use, but that's all we'll need."

"Then everything is arranged," Dracula said. "Very good." He looked up at Rasputin. "Do you think it's suspicious that she accepted so quickly?"

"Perhaps she sees it as an opportunity," Rasputin said. "She likely wants Fitzgerald gone more than we do, and I don't doubt she's confident of winning. The boy is green, but he'd be a threat given time."

"Mmm. Perhaps."

The thought lingered in Dracula's mind as their discussion turned to other matters; managing new resources from their recent gains in Purgatory, examining their new neighbors for potential weaknesses. Despite everything going to plan, he couldn't quite help but feel as though he'd missed something. PrisonWatch itself was unusually silent on the matter. Their influence was heavy-handed when it came to preserving ratings, and that sometimes meant protecting popular fighters, or instigating conflict between them.

Their representatives hadn't sent him any missives or statements of intent. Daniel's popularity couldn't be higher, but it didn't seem they had any interest in shielding him from banishment. Did that mean they wanted to get rid of him, too?

Dracula couldn't imagine that was the case, but very little escaped PrisonWatch's notice, and this was not little. Hopefully, with the Vorid threat, Beelzebub was concerned with matters elsewhere and wouldn't interfere. Considering Daniel's raw strength, Dracula had been worried about outside political concerns getting in the way, but there was nothing to suggest they were. Running through it all several times in his head, Dracula couldn't find any evidence for worry, but his instincts nagged at him.

Ultimately, they were already committed. He would prepare for the worst and be ready when it came.

He did not see the woman standing in the corner of the room, opposite Rasputin.

Her skin was pale; her hair was white. A white dress hung from her shoulders, ending above her ankles. Her face was a delicate mask, as pale as her hands and feet, but her lips were the color of blood.

She stood, silent and invisible, listening to the planners plan the downfall of the young boy named Daniel Fitzgerald. A boy that could see her, even in this place.

****

Daniel sat on Jack's couch and grunted, stretching back to open up room for his stomach. He'd eaten past the point of early warning, and now he was paying for it with a constant, throbbing belly ache.

It was so worth it. He hadn't eaten that good in weeks.

Jack was collapsed next to him, rubbing his own stomach through his shirt. He belched loud enough to rattle the walls, then smacked his lips. "Dude. That was good."

"I'm glad we were able to get mostly human food," Daniel said. "I didn't have to substitute much."

"If you did, I didn't notice," Jack said. "Probably better than last time."

"It'll be even better tomorrow," Daniel said. "When it sits in the fridge, all the flavors mix in together."

"I always wondered why that is."

"Acids from the tomatoes, and the temperature change," Daniel said. "Same thing with chili, beef stew, that kind of thing."

"Huh," Jack said. "The more you know."

Behind them, in the kitchen stemming from the apartment's living room, was a mess of dishes, sauce splatters, and a sink so crammed full the plates and spoon ends were sticking out above the counter. A half-eaten tray of fresh lasagna sat on the small table closer to the fridge.

Daniel burped, then groaned. "Ugh. Too much."

Jack leveraged himself up and walked toward the kitchen. "Want a drink?"

"I'm thirsty," Daniel said. "But I'm too full to drink anything. Life is hard."

"Hah." Daniel heard the sound of a seal cracking open and a hiss of carbonation. Jack returned to the couch with a can of some brand of soda Daniel wasn't familiar with. As he looked at it, the demonic language printed on the can rearranged itself, the words translating in real time so that he could read them: *Snozberry Surprise*.

"What's a snozberry?" Daniel asked.

"Ehh..." Jack took a sip. "Kinda tastes like orange and banana mixed together. Citrusy, but mellowed out."

"The spell that translates for us is amazing," Daniel said. "I wonder how strong you have to be to do something like that."

Jack shrugged. "Magic." He looked at Daniel. "Thanks for saving my life. Back in the water tank."

"I mean, you ended up dying anyway." Daniel looked away. "I owed you for Boston."

"I guess so." Jack frowned. "Actually, that's a good point. I would've revived eventually. You still owe me."

"Don't get greedy."

"Cheap bastard." Jack took a slurp of his soda. "Did you mean what you said? About putting me in jail when we get back?" The question was thrown out there, casually asked, but it hung in the air with all the awkwardness in the world.

Daniel sat back and cleared his throat. "I didn't want to press you earlier," he said. "But you remember what you told me, in Boston? When we met the first time, and we didn't know who the other was?" Jack looked at him, so Daniel kept going. "You told me you would be okay with killing random people to get stronger. You told me it would be worth it in the long run, to murder a few to make yourself more powerful. So you tell me how much of that was true, and I'll tell you if you should go to jail or not."

Jack looked away. "I didn't really believe that crap. I never killed anyone innocent. I was trying to psyche you out. I figured you'd kill me if I didn't kill you first." Jack made a shaky smile. "Honestly, you scared me shitless when I saw you."

"I did?" Daniel said.

"Yeah," Jack said. "You were decked head to toe in that metal armor, going head on against the Vorid. Your helmet made your voice all warped and metallic."

"I always thought I looked kinda junkyard," Daniel said.

"Not from where I was standing," Jack said. "I waited to see what you thought about the magicians, but when we didn't immediately agree, I even thought you might be working with them. That's where my thoughts went, anyway. They were good and ready to go there. I'd almost been captured twice before then. When I saw you with Rachel, after, when everything went down...I thought she was on to you, and you didn't know it. I thought she was tricking you, using you. Why wouldn't she be?"

Daniel sighed. He remembered his own anxieties about fighting, the tense cycle of combat and survival in New York. He hadn't quite come around to completely forgiving everything Jack had done, but he could at least see where he was coming from.

"Honestly, with all the stuff going down on Earth," Daniel said, "I don't think a lot of people will care about what happened in Boston. But that's not really what I was getting at. If you help with the war effort, I figure you can get off with a slap on the wrist. Do you have evidence of the stuff you were talking about? All that corruption?"

"If Boston's still in one piece, should be on my computer," Jack said. "I backed it up to an external drive, it was in my desk."

Daniel squinted. "The police probably grabbed it. If I can get it back, or at least have them take a look at it, I might be able to get Eleanor to help."

"The duchess? I doubt it."

"She's definitely prickly, no doubt about it," Daniel said, "but she has a heart in there somewhere."

"So," Jack said, "assuming she's really on our side, and assuming the magicians even give us the time of day, and assuming they haven't already destroyed my computer or something...maybe I can get off lightly."

Daniel shrugged. "It is what it is. I was strong enough they considered me a threat, so they couldn't walk up and grab us as soon as we got back. Maybe Eleanor can act as a liaison between the two camps."

"That's a nice thought," Jack said, "but even if I was justified, I know they'll say I'm a glorified vigilante at best."

"You did kill people," Daniel said.

"They deserved worse," Jack said. "You didn't see what I saw. The pictures. What they did to those women."

Daniel waved his hand. "Again, not what I want to get at," Daniel said. "I believe you, man. I believe that you're a good person."

"I appreciate you saying so." Jack sat back slightly, and they fell silent. There was the soft sound of fizz from Jack's open soda can; a hum in the background of appliances working. Jack swallowed hard. "I'm not so sure," he said. "That I'm a good person, I mean. Maybe I went too far. But...it's done."

Daniel chose not to drive home on that point, especially considering that was the farthest Jack had come toward the middle. They could debate the moral ramifications and figure out the right thing to do when Earth wasn't in danger of being erased from the universe. Besides, Jack already knew Daniel's stance on the matter; no sense in beating a dead horse. "There are other contractors out there, too," Daniel said. "If we can get people together, we'll have bargaining power. We'll be safer, too; they won't be able to capture people one at a time and throw them into Hell."

"Could be dangerous," Jack said. "I mean...I attacked you, before I knew it was you."

The blunt words struck Daniel hard. His face screwed up as he considered it. After thinking of a few responses, he kept it short. "Why?"

"Well, I...I had it in my head that any other contractor would probably kill me to make themselves stronger—unless I killed them first. It's how our powers work. This is a war. No one would ever know how I died." Jack hands balled fists on his lap. "Maybe I made up a bunch of reasons to pump myself up so I wouldn't be afraid or hesitate. But I was afraid. So, better to take away the source of fear than live wondering if I'd get stabbed in the back one day. Be stronger, more ruthless than anyone else. It really comes down to that." He looked out over the living room, staring into space. "Maybe it's why I killed those people I caught red handed. I was trying hard to build that mindset, kill or be killed. Why wait years for the courts, for a corrupt justice system? Simplify the situation. Make them disappear, problem solved, I get stronger. Two birds with one stone."

Daniel thought back to the girl he'd saved in New York, the contractor with lightning magic, Gabby. She'd returned the favor in the end, allowing him to see the fight with the Vorid lord through to the finish. At first, she'd been dead scared of him, and even after he helped her out of a jam, she hadn't wanted to partner up.

Bringing contractors together might be harder than he thought. Everyone was paranoid at best, looking over their shoulder and jumping at shadows. One bad apple would be all it took to undo any efforts he made.

But the last thing Jack said made Daniel think. Making people disappear to solve problems. It sounded wrong. It sounded like the Vorid. Did they truly have to become monsters to get through this?

Jack sighed and sat back on the couch. "I don't think it hit me, until I saw the numbers," he said. "You're insanely strong after beating that Vorid lord. Was it hard? That fight?"

"It was overwhelming," Daniel said honestly. "I used all my strength just to keep up. The Lord wasn't even winded by the time he had me cornered, I don't even think he did half of what he was capable of. I didn't beat him alone, either. If it wasn't for the magicians actually helping me in the end, and that other contractor I told you about—and Rachel—I'd be dead. I'd say I was maybe a third as strong as he was when I fought him."

"So it was a big boost for you, winning that battle," Jack said.

"Yeah. Definitely." Daniel looked at him. "I have no idea how strong I am now, honestly. I haven't been able to go all out since that fight. Been locked down here."

Jack tapped his chin. "In terms of raw power, you could demolish me, Rasputin, maybe even Dracula. You have an actual shot at beating Bathory. When this is over, you'll be like superman. I wonder if the non-magical government will want to work with you. You could end wars, bring peace to the world and all that jazz."

"Maybe I can do some stuff, but I'm also only one person," Daniel said. "People won't ever stop fighting. I want it all to end and go back to my life, not be an eternal savior. We're just a couple guys that drew winning lottery tickets."

Jack shook his head. "You're fooling yourself if you think it'll be that simple. I respect your principles and everything, but no one will let you go back. You're too powerful, too important."

"Maybe," Daniel said. "I can worry about it after the Vorid give up trying to destroy the planet and I get my family back in one piece."

"Speaking of getting you back." Jack looked at him. "You really want to that bad?"

"I have to," Daniel said. "If I wasn't before, I have to be the strongest contractor so far. I'm the only one that can fight them straight on right now, or even try to fight them straight on in the first place. You might be right about the magicians, or Eleanor, or Xik. It doesn't matter. I have to try, and the contractor magic is the only tool we have. Otherwise...I don't think I can live with myself. I don't think I can stay here and have it all on my mind every day, wondering what I should have done, or could have done, or if anyone up there is still alive."

"You said you don't want to be a hero," Jack said, "but now you're talking about how you can't live with yourself if you don't do something. I don't get it."

"When I first started all this, it was to save my brother. You know Felix." Jack nodded, having seen Daniel's brother in video calls back in school. "He had a Vorid spawn on his back. I saw it when Xik showed me."

"Jeeze," Jack said. "Talk about putting the screws on someone."

"I know. I told Xik to go to hell at first. Actually, at first, I thought I was going crazy. But that pushed me into it, for good or bad.

"After that was taken care of, I wanted to keep myself alive, help my family survive what I knew was coming. I didn't buy into Xik's crap about fighting the Vorid and saving the universe or whatever. I didn't think I had it in me. But Rachel...I don't know how to put this. She saw something in me I didn't see in myself. She gave me something more important to fight for than myself. I want to hold on to that. I want to be the person she saw." Daniel looked at Jack. "I was a lot more cynical before I met you and Rachel. I was a worse person. I didn't give a damn about anything. It was a safe way to live, but now I know I wasn't even living.

"Rachel—Rachel, she—" Daniel's voice stuttered. His lips pressed together as he blinked back the tears that wanted to form. He cleared his throat. "She was fearless. She threw herself in front of the Vorid lord to save me, Jack. And then I took even more from her. I used her to heal myself back up and sucked her magic dry, and she died.

"But I can't sit here and feel bad for myself," Daniel said. "I've got to fight the battle. Yeah, I guess I want to *save the world*"—Daniel waved his hands about at the words—"but it's not only that. It's like I'm fighting who I used to be, too.

Getting to know you changed me, Jack. Rachel too. I'm not going back to the way I was."

"Damn," Jack said. "What do you even say to that?"

Daniel snorted. "Sometimes I feel like I'm so far down inside my own head I'm coming out my ass."

Jack took another sip of his soda, then sat it down on the coffee table. The metal can clinked loudly on the glass. "So what comes after?"

"Hell if I know."

Jack heaved a sigh. "You just had to go and make me feel bad. Fine. If there's a way out, I'll help you take it."

Daniel nodded. "Thanks, Jack."

"I'm sticking with the Order, though," Jack said. "I'm not working with the magicians in any form, and neither should you."

"I'll be more careful in the future," Daniel said. "I learned that lesson the hard way."

"Good," Jack said.

Another silence passed between them, floating over the room; more comfortable this time, the good quiet of matters settled. Daniel was building up the motivation to get off the couch and grab a drink when his armlet beeped at him. He checked it to see he had a new message from Rasputin.

Bathory had accepted the duel.

"The fight is on," Daniel said.

Jack practically jumped half-off the couch. "When?"

"Tomorrow," Daniel said. "That was quick."

Jack shook his head. "You are gonna set a new ratings record, Mr. Popularity."

Jack's jibe was true—Daniel's messaging application on his armlet had been completely flooded with notifications. He'd gotten fan letters, hate mail, advertising partnership offers, more interview requests, even marriage proposals. One particular message offered a bribe in exchange for throwing his next match.

"Hey, Dan," Jack said.

"Yeah?"

"You sure about this?"

"About what?"

"About fighting her," Jack said. "Not in general, I mean, right now. PrisonWatch is known for throwing in things to screw people over, to keep ratings going. They aren't going to want you to succeed too quickly. But you don't know Hell well yet, you don't know the rules, the system."

"What are you trying to say?" Daniel said.

"I'm saying you should get your feet wet, get some experience," Jack said. "Maybe build up your prison points a little while, get a nest egg going for emergencies. Come back at her later."

Daniel shook his head. "I've officially got a shot now, she accepted the fight. This is my best chance."

"She's going to be a tough nut to crack," Jack said. "Are you sure?"

"No, I'm not sure," Daniel said. "But I'm the main line of defense if the Vorid mount another assault. If I don't do it now, it might be put off months. Years even. Earth doesn't have that kind of time." Daniel considered explaining his deal with Beelzebub, but decided against it. Jack was on his side for what counted, but he still didn't trust others not to listen in. "If Bathory's got some super-secret entrance back to Earth," he said, "we have to check it out."

"I figured you'd say something like that," Jack said. "Alright, superman. Maybe if you circle the globe in the opposite direction fast enough, you can turn back time."

"Ha, ha," Daniel said. "That's hilarious."

Jack smirked. "Hey, a day isn't a lot of time. Better start prepping."

"I need to digest this lasagna," Daniel said, patting his belly, "so I think practicing is out of the question. Maybe we'll still have time for those demon video games you wanted to show me."

"No way, man," Jack said, shaking his head. "We gotta get you ready to go." Jack reached for the remote and flicked on the TV.

"By watching television?"

"PrisonWatch reruns," Jack said. "Stuff over 10 years old is free to view. With commercials."

"I guess the demons beat us to streaming services," Daniel said. "So we're going to do some research."

"She has a lot of different spells she likes to use. Hard to predict her." Jack looked at him. "If you ask me, she's certifiably insane."

"Probably has something to do with all that mass murder."

Jack searched for Bathory's name. Her PrisonWatch profile popped onto the screen, along with several subheadings, including *Recent Bouts*, *Fan Favorites*, and *Most Viewed*. Jack clicked on the fan favorites section. "She's got a couple hundred years of publicly accessible combat footage. So that's something in your favor—there's not much known about the extent of your abilities, not as many fights under your belt."

Daniel leaned in as the video started up, a wide-panning shot of a battle arena. The humor left him as they began to watch, and Daniel focused in, determined to scrape out every piece of information he could from the footage.

It became clear to him, a few minutes in, that it was going to be very, very hard to win this battle.

Chapter 17
Pregame

Jack sat in one of the restaurants in the Order of the Dragon's territory.

He sighed, then looked at his half-eaten lunch. The food itself was fine; he wasn't hungry. Incoming events had robbed him of his appetite.

Jack left his apartment with Daniel not long ago, seeing him off at the arena before getting lost in his thoughts on the way back. He didn't feel like returning to his apartment straight away, and he'd come up to the pub in taking the long way home. The place was pretty cleared out, just the barkeep and four or five Order regulars occupying scattered tables; good enough to be left to himself without feeling quite so cooped up. Most of his team would be back at the headquarters building, schmoozing and drinking while watching the duel. That was usually what happened when they had a big match, but he wasn't in the mood for rubbing elbows.

There were TVs in the restaurant, hung up in corners and near the bar, so he could watch the match while he ate. They weren't TVs, really, but the demonic equivalent, relying on mana to function. They knew about and used electricity, but the demon civilization had grown up on magic and physical science together. It resulted in some pretty unique devices—and in the fact that the demons had colonized their solar system, and even beyond that, while mankind was still stuck on Earth.

Jack only had a vague understanding of the relationship between the human world and the demon world. In the past, things used to be closer, more linked and intermingled, like rivers running together. You could sail down and then up the other river without too much trouble. That was the source of most of mankind's myths and legends; the supernatural had once been as real as anything else.

The current regime of worlds was a strict separation. Hell itself was an artificial space inserted between the human and demon worlds, a mini-universe that was basically a big rock, bordered on all sides by nothingness. Or, more precisely, edged by a dimensional wall that would rip you into your component matter and dissolve you into energy if you tried to cross without the right magical protection. Fun stuff.

The walls of Hell created a permanent traffic barrier. Travel between the human and demon universes was now very costly, and Beelzebub's empire had a monopoly on the method needed to make the portals from one universe to another. In other words, it didn't happen much.

Travel was easier if you were *invited*, so to speak—by a mage on the other end. Otherwise, multiversal travel was prohibitively difficult. It explained why the demons hadn't absorbed humans into their empire, which supposedly spanned multiple solar systems—or simply stamped them out—but it made Jack wonder how the Klide and the Vorid did it.

Pre-game talking heads were displayed on the TVs. They were all tuned to the same show—PrisonWatch. The PrisonWatch logo was garishly printed all over the walls, along with photos of notable team leaders of not only Purgatory but the other levels of Hell. They never missed an opportunity to remind everyone that they were being televised at all times.

Jack could see a camera out of the corner of his eye; they dotted the ceiling of the bar. In the eternal, joyful cynicism of PrisonWatch, inmates were allowed to purchase back their own privacy, or make certain moments secret from even the viewers, but that cost money on a scale that would bankrupt smaller teams. All of PrisonWatch had a one-week delay for other inmates, aside from the direct combat footage. That allowed a buffer period so inmates could make short-term plans in secret, even if they couldn't afford private talks. Dracula, for one, always paid to keep his offices a camera-free zone, so the team had a space to discuss strategy without others finding out about their long-reaching plans.

When Jack first arrived, he might have avoided eating while watching a match that could very well involve brutal death and dismemberment, but there wasn't anything you couldn't get used to given enough time. Or maybe he really was messed up in the head by all this—being a contractor, the killing, locked in Hell, treated like a bug under a microscope for entertainment. Maybe Daniel was right, and he was only working hard at justifying it to himself.

Himself. Jack felt less and less like himself lately. The concepts of right and wrong were mixing together, growing grey and vague and hard to hold, like trying to cup water in his fingers.

Dracula wanted Jack to make up any wrongs he felt he'd committed with service to the Order. Daniel said that he should follow society's rules, mostly. The two weren't necessarily in opposition, but if Dracula's rules clashed with what society said was acceptable, Jack had no doubt Dracula would go his own way.

Jack didn't regret what he did in Boston, but what he was so sure about a few days ago had been torn to pieces by the tornado that was Daniel's arrival in Hell. Ideas he'd built up as pillars of purpose were crumbling in the wind. For all the ranting and the arguments over the past few days, Jack felt like it was less like he was trying to convince Daniel of his points and more himself that everything was fine.

His friendship with Daniel had always been like that, in a way. Daniel was someone he trusted; someone he could tell things. But in trusting what Daniel said, it changed how Jack looked at the world, because it opened him up to having holes poked in his excuses.

Daniel had a way about him—sometimes too cocky, or too presumptuous—but there was something about the way he did things that was convincing by itself. He had a kernel of confidence, of self-reliance, that most people lacked. He was someone that could make you see things in a way you'd never considered. He had the ability to ignore the crowd and take his own road, but in a way that made sense. It wasn't rebelling for the sake of rebelling, but because he had a knack for discovering a third path. He lived life outside the box, and he did it without realizing he was doing it. It was who he was.

Jack admired that, because he felt it was exactly that ephemeral quality he himself lacked. It was that state of mind he was trying to reach. And now—in finally having arrived at what he thought was his own version of it as one of Hell's top gladiators, a member of the Order of the Dragon, defying the mundane conventions of society and rewriting the rules—Daniel came along and told him he had it all wrong. Contractors weren't different than other people, they should be held to the same standards and within the same boundaries of law and order. But how could he say that when those very rules had condemned them both to imprisonment?

Maybe Daniel would say it was different with the mages. Jack wasn't certain. Another addition to a long list of uncertainties.

A chipper, high-pitched voice distracted him from ruminating further. Jack looked above the bar. The match was finally about to happen, narrated by everyone's favorite female devil, Ky, dressed as usual in the red-orange-yellow colors of PrisonWatch. For once, he was grateful for her cutting in; he was sick of dwelling on everything.

Jack leaned over his plate, focusing on the screen as the camera did a flyover of the arena. Daniel seemed confident even after watching the reruns of Bathory's fights, though he acknowledged it was gonna be tough. Jack didn't share his opinion—he'd hoped they would convince Daniel to back out for the time being—but he did his best to put up a positive front. Worst case scenario, he lost, and they tried again next time, better prepared. It wouldn't be the first time the Order of the Dragon had been beaten back by Bathory. With two contractors fighting on their side, they would snatch up more territory in the city and get another crack at her sooner or later.

"Hello Jack."

Jack flinched. Rasputin slid into the chair next to him at the table. "Oh," Jack said. "It's you."

"That's no way to great a superior."

"My greetings, vice-captain," Jack said flatly. "How may I be of service?"

Rasputin sighed, drawing a hand along his scraggly beard. "We'll work on it. Has the match started?"

"Not yet. What do you think of his chances?"

An ugly smile crawled its way under Rasputin's nose. His beady little eyes creeped Jack out. "Not a chance in Hell," he said.

Jack felt a flare of annoyance. "I think Daniel will win," Jack said, even though he thought nothing of the sort. "Bathory doesn't know what to expect, and Daniel can hit her hard and fast."

"You would know about that, wouldn't you?"

Jack cocked his head. He'd never explicitly told Rasputin about his personal history with Daniel—especially not about how they'd once fought. "What is that supposed to mean?"

"I think you know what it means." Rasputin tilted his head forward, looking up at Jack from the shadow of his brow. "He's no friend of yours, is he?"

"What?" Jack tried to leave his seat—but his arms and legs felt heavy, like he was waking up after a deep sleep. He couldn't quite bring himself to push his chair back. "What would you know? Of course we're friends."

"We know you fought, Jack." Rasputin still stared at him. Jack couldn't look away from his eyes, glimmering black in the low light of the bar. "We know where your true loyalty lies. With the Order. Not with this fool that pretends to be your friend."

"Pretends to..." Jack felt so tired. He tried to blink it away, shake himself out of it. "He's—it's not pretend. What are you—"

"Look at me, Jack."

Jack found himself drawn back to Rasputin's eyes. There was something there waiting for him, at the edge of his perception, like a hint of movement inside a deep stone well.

"*Look at me, Jack.*" The dark, greasy voice echoed in Jack's ears. Rasputin's beady eyes expanded; their edges swam into the shadows around his face, twisting like oil on water. "He's your enemy. We—the Order—are your friends. I am your friend."

"You're...my friend." Jack heard himself mumble the words. Something was wrong about that. He had to look away.

"Look at me, Jack."

The pools of black that were Rasputin's eyes swirled and shifted. Jack found himself sliding forward, slipping across the table and into the darkness. A voice echoed in his head, and it said his name over and over.

"Jack."

It was comfortable. So comfortable.

"Jack."

The bad thoughts and questions went away. No more confusion.

"Daniel is your enemy," the voice said. "We're on your side. We are your purpose. He's trying to take you away from us."

The Order was his true friend. Daniel was against him. Daniel was trying to confuse him, turn him against the Order. From his purpose.

The darkness came for him, washed over him in warm, steady waves. He didn't need Daniel. All he needed to do was listen to the voice.

"*Jack.*"

Jack's armlet beeped.

A blaring tune sang out, one every gamer on Earth would know in an instant—the main theme from the Mario series. That was ringtone he put in his armlet for when Daniel called him.

Dah-dah-dah dum-*dahdahdah* dum *dahdahdah* dah *dah-dah dahdah*-dum

The whirlpool of darkness shattered like glass. Rasputin's face snapped back into focus.

Jack grabbed at the sides of his chair, stopping himself from toppling out of it. His brain felt like it was swimming in muck. "Wha..." His tongue felt numb. "Whas...wrong with me?" He forced himself upright, working his jaw to get feeling back in his face. "The hell did you do to me?!"

Rasputin clicked his tongue. "Dracula was right. He does have too much influence over you." He looked over Jack's shoulders. "Hold him down."

Jack tried to get out of his chair. Multiple pairs of arms lifted him up and slammed him to the floor. Jack kicked out wildly to free himself, but hands grabbed his legs, pinning them down and stopping his struggles before they could start. Someone grabbed at his armlet and silenced the ringtone.

They all stared down at him—other members of the Order of the Dragon, men and women he knew. Their eyes were gone, replaced by oily swirls of magic that Jack could feel crawling over him like slime. He screamed as the unearthly gazes lingered on his face.

Rasputin stepped through the crowd. "You're a coward at heart, Jack. Only brave when Danny is around to brace your spine."

"What is this?!" Jack shouted. "What the fuck is this?!"

"It's easier for me if I can convince them to let go on their own, but we're a little behind schedule," Rasputin said. "I can do it by force, too, it only takes a little more effort." He knelt next to Jack, who was forced flat on his back, eyes wide and panicked. Rasputin smiled again. "I think I'll enjoy putting an end to your sniveling attitude nonetheless."

Jack tossed and whipped his body to break the grip of his captors. They were forced to shift where they had their hands, but he couldn't break free. He stopped resisting after a moment, hoping to lure them into thinking he was subdued. "When Dracula finds out that you're—"

Rasputin slapped him across the face, cutting off his words. "You truly are an idiot. Dracula ordered this himself."

"Wha—I don't—what?"

"Wha-wha-what?" Rasputin sniggered as he mocked Jack's stutter. "You did a fine job keeping Daniel distracted the past few days—just as you were told. You let us listen in on all your conversations, just as you were told. Like a good little dog."

"What are you talking about?!"

"You've been under our influence for some time, Jack, but you were also told to forget that," Rasputin said. "You've made yourself quite useful in that capacity; there's something to be said for allowing looser patterns of behavior. But Daniel's been creating…problems. Disrupting your thinking. You almost tried convincing him to back out of the fight, rather than walk him into it as you were supposed to. We've decided to tighten your leash and complete your initiation into the Order." Rasputin grinned in twisted satisfaction. "It's about damn time."

Jack squirmed his shoulders, twisted his arms, and bucked his hips. His leg slipped free and he kneed Rasputin in the face, throwing him back into the men at his ankles, freeing his other leg. Jack caught one behind him in the windpipe with his elbow; he shoved past while the man choked from the blow, tripping and falling across the tangle of bodies but breaking free of the encirclement. "Bar the entrance!" Rasputin shouted.

Jack made for the door in a desperate, crawling shuffle, kicking away hands reaching to trap his feet. If he could get outside, get somewhere public, the enforcers would stop them.

Footsteps near his head alerted him to others in the restaurant closing in. He rolled under and out the other side of a table to force them to go the long way around. Using the moment that bought him, he leapt to his feet and ran for the door.

A mug whipped out from around the corner of the bar and smashed into Jack's face. His head slammed into the corner of the counter and he collapsed. His vision rocked and spun; his face felt warm and numb. He pushed himself in the direction of the entrance, driving his hands through shattered bits of glass. He could see the bronze door handle, glinting in the dim pub light.

Hands grabbed his arms and legs. He was pulled back, dragged under the edge of the bar. Stinging pain broke through the numbness in his face, the glass embedded in his skin shifting. This time—not trusting their grip against his strength—they physically sat on his arms and legs.

Rasputin's face loomed over him. He nursed a broken nose, and blood matted his beard. He glared at Jack with a vengeful scowl. And then his eyes began to twist, turning into dark, yawning portals.

Jack kept his head away, tried to shut his eyes—but he couldn't. Hands kept his head from moving, and some other power forced his eyes open. Desperate, he grasped for his magic, but it slipped away from him, stopped by the Hell seal. He couldn't reach his armlet to activate the items he needed to unlock it.

Rasputin's eyes grew larger, and larger. They bored into him, until all Jack could see was the darkness, carving its way deep into the back of his skull until his senses were smothered into silence.

****

Daniel sighed and kicked his legs idly over the bench of the waiting room.

Jack didn't answer his call. Daniel had felt like a last-minute pep talk, but maybe Jack wasn't in the mood. He wasn't too hopeful about the whole thing, though Daniel appreciated his efforts to hide it.

Daniel also wanted to talk because he was in a very poorly designed waiting room, in that it held nothing to take his mind off the fact that he was about to fight quite possibly the most dangerous person he'd encountered in his entire life. Possibly. Considering he'd met the devil in person, he couldn't say for sure that Elizabeth Bathory was *the* most dangerous, but she definitely ranked in the top three. And then there was Dracula, Henry Astor, Lenhard Rothschild. Maybe that witch lady from Scandinavia or whatever, she was uncanny as hell. Well spoken, sure, but creepy, in the ancient witch kind of way.

His social life had really gone down the tubes lately.

Daniel sighed again and shifted on the bench to stop his butt from falling asleep.

The room was somewhat cold, which was a good thing. He felt too warm, jumpy. He didn't know what to do with his hands, so he tapped them along the bench. The real problem was what to do with his eyes—the place was a concrete bunker.

The sole decoration besides the bench and a small table was the teleport pedestal, fenced off by a small gate as usual.

There was nothing to look at, and so his eyes unfocused, and he was stuck in his thoughts—exactly where he didn't want to be.

Despite the tension of the last couple days, Jack and Daniel had somehow settled back into their old rhythm of friendship. Fighting demons in Hell together definitely made that a little easier. It was nice to see his roommate again—to recapture that sense of being fresh friends at an unfamiliar school, feeling their way into college life and bumbling about the vicissitudes of newfound adulthood. Or whatever you called sneaking beer into the dorm. God, that had been a bad idea. The hangover was grisly.

Theirs was a friendship built on a mutual love of meandering conversations, good Italian food, B-movies that were so bad they were good, and video games. And Daniel had to admit, the demons had some pretty damn good video games. He'd gotten a crack at a handful of them after declaring a study break following 4 straight hours of Elizabeth Bathory replays.

And yet, for all their trying, Daniel felt like they couldn't go back to how things used to be. That old companionship was a bit out of reach. Things were slightly uncomfortable, like a new couch that hadn't quite been broken in, that didn't have the comfy spots staked out yet. They were still raw from their arguments about Boston, about Rachel. About what their role as contractors really should be. Jack was so certain with his answers—staying in Hell, living it up as a gladiator—but Daniel couldn't let go of his family that easily, of life back on Earth.

Maybe they just needed time. But it was time they didn't have.

Being spied on by cameras 24/7 didn't help. When Jack told him not even the bathrooms were safe, it set him off for a while. Daniel assumed that PrisonWatch would have to edit the content of their conversations before broadcast; or, then again, maybe not. He didn't know if the demon world's general population knew about the Vorid threat, or if they knew and simply didn't care what happened to the human world.

One thing was for sure, they definitely had 'online' followers. Many had speculated that a confrontation with Bathory was on the horizon, and Hell blew up with the news that the fight was scheduled so quickly. Daniel's crowded inbox only grew more chaotic with requests for photographs, comments, a written statement, anything at all. Bathory maintained public radio silence. At Dracula's advisement, Daniel did the same. At least she'd accepted the matchup without issues.

Daniel watched dozens of videos of Bathory fighting, trying to figure out if there was something he could use to his advantage. She knew a limitless number of spells; she was power combined with flexibility. She could bind up her opponents with tendrils made from shadow. She could shoot fireballs from her hands. She could teleport herself—instantly traveling from one point to another—something she did frequently to escape danger—though it was short range, no more than a few dozen feet or so. She could accelerate healing. She could form ice from thin air and—like Eleanor—shape it at will into dagger-sharp projectiles or protective walls. If those failed, she could produce barriers of pure magic to deflect attacks. He even saw her invert gravity in a small space, sending a squad of attackers up and smashing them against the ceiling of a cavern. There were multiple occasions when she used more than one kind of magic spell at once—something that was considered extremely difficult. If all else failed, she was still able to hold her own in hand-to-hand combat. It wasn't her specialty, but she had hundreds of years to practice, so she was way better at it than Daniel.

That all wasn't even the worst part. The worst part was what she did to people she defeated. She rarely killed or overwhelmed her opponents outright—she enjoyed making them suffer before finishing them off. If there were any doubts Daniel had about her being a bad person, the recordings disabused him of the notion.

He had to kill her to fulfill his deal with Beelzebub. The context of a duel made the perfect excuse. Even though it was another person, another human, Daniel didn't feel trepidation about fighting her, and he wasn't worried about getting squeamish at the last second. He'd killed Vorid overseers; he'd smashed the Vorid lord itself against the pavement. He'd already confronted those feelings in Boston, and he'd cremated them in New York.

It struck him his casual attitude toward bloody confrontation might not be a good thing.

But even if she was guilty, she was already locked away. She'd been tried, and her punishment had been meted out; it wasn't his place to take it further than that. But could this kind of Hell even be considered a punishment? In that sense, it could be taken as a duty for him to take her down, to end her once and for all. That was Dracula's logic talking, the mission of the Order; to ensure human criminals were, in fact, punished as intended.

For all he lectured Jack on right and wrong, Daniel was about to become a hypocrite.

Daniel shook the thoughts out of his head. Running through it over and over wasn't getting him anywhere. He could come to terms when it was over. But suddenly, considering it all, he was glad for the thoughts, for some of the doubts. If he could do this all without any problem, without thinking twice, then maybe he really would become a monster.

In watching Bathory's past fights, Jack and Daniel came to the same conclusion. Daniel's main tactic would be to overwhelm her with speed and power right off the bat, before she had a chance to build any momentum. If Daniel got put on the backfoot, she'd systematically dismantle him.

With that in mind, Daniel had to be able to use his own magic to be a threat. But if the rules of the match stated that he could use magic, then more than likely, so could she. He was bringing with him a single item stored in his bracelet—a purchased powerup that would let him access 25% of his magic for 5 minutes. It was one of two rules of the duel he knew beforehand, aside from the fact that it was a fight to the death: he was allowed to bring one item stored in his inventory. Dracula had splurged on his behalf.

The second rule was the allowance of one mundane weapon. There was a selection of ten different weapons to choose from, including a knife, sword, spear, and hammer. Daniel had chosen the club, it being closest to what he was used to. It was a thick but straight metal rod, weighted at one end, with a wooden handle. The comforting weight sat on his lap even now.

The choice of arena was random, as was the choice of an added extra 'effect'. The effect could be anything; from swarms of killer robots that tried to off both of them while they fought; or, giving both of them access to more items of their choice. It could be an obstacle, a restriction, or a bonus. There could also be more than one effect, or additional effects added in or taken away if the fight went on too long. Daniel was less experienced, so he was hoping for something as plain and boring as possible. In Hell, *exciting* was synonymous with *lethal*.

Daniel's mind turned back to that first fight in the city streets—that had been plenty exciting, by PrisonWatch standards. He thought again of the strange woman he'd seen floating between the swords and the spells, untouched. Dracula and Rasputin were both confident that he was seeing things.

Neither had any idea who she was, to the point of dismissing it outright. Having seen her on video, Daniel already eliminated the possibility of it being Bathory.

It was so real at the time. And the sense that she knew he could see her...he could feel her attention coming to rest on him, almost like a hand sliding up his back. And then, she appeared in that crazy dream he had, with the lights, and the Vorid, and Rachel. She'd known his name; even spoke right to him.

It had been bothering him in-between the hustle and bustle of everything else. If she was real—and he felt that she was—then who the hell was she?

Daniel's armlet beeped. He glanced down. Jack was calling him back. *Thank god.* He tapped the answer button. "Hey man."

"Daniel."

Jack's voice creaked through the line. It sounded like he was hoarse. "Jack?" Daniel asked. "What's wrong?"

"Nothing's wrong with me," Jack said. "Just with you."

"What?" Daniel cocked his head in confusion. He tapped a few buttons on his armlet, bringing up the full video chat option that displayed Jack on the other end.

Daniel's eyes widened. Jack looked like he'd run a marathon then gone through two funerals in the last half hour. His hair was messed up, his face was gaunt; his eyes were rimmed in pale streaks of exhaustion. "Man," Daniel said. "What the hell happened?"

"I wish I'd killed Rachel back in Boston," Jack said. "I wish I could have seen the look on your face when she died."

Daniel's mouth fell open. He tried to process the words.

Jack didn't wait for him to respond. "You've been the thing holding me back," Jack said. "I've finally realized that. All these debates and arguments we've been having—it's all pointless. I could have been a king back on Earth. You got me caught by the magicians and sent to Hell. I could have had everything!"

"Jack..." Daniel stopped, tried to collect himself. "I don't even—"

"Shut up!" Jack shouted. Daniel sat back on the bench. "You're gonna lose to Bathory, you know that?" A smile started on Jack's face, a small smirk that steadily grew into an awful, lopsided grin. "You saw in the videos, what she does when she has them right where she wants them. That's gonna happen to you, and then...then, you're gone." Jack savored the words, as if there was nothing more in the world he wanted. "You're gone. It'll be easy to get you kicked out of the team. We won't bring you back into Purgatory. You'll never get back to Earth. I wanted to let you know, before you hit rock bottom"—Jack pointed at him through the video feed—"because I'm gonna watch it all happen to you on live television. And I wanted you to know it was me."

The video cut out. A blinking red light telling him the call had ended flicked twice, then dimmed.

Daniel stood up from the bench; his club clattered to the ground, forgotten. "What in the fuck?" He redialed Jack. The call rang, rang—then went to voicemail. Daniel hung up and dialed again, but got the same result. Daniel mashed the button a third time. "Pick up the phone, asshole!"

This time, the call didn't go to voicemail. A robotic female voice answered him. "We're sorry, but all messages from you to the selected inmate ID have been blocked. Goodbye."

The call hung up.

Daniel slowly sat back down onto the bench, still staring at his armlet. *Did that just happen?*

Was this how Jack really felt? Was he holding all that in, bottled up inside the whole time?

No. It made no sense. If Jack really felt that way, he wouldn't have bothered helping him join the Order of the

Dragon, or explain anything about Hell. He wouldn't have come to save him during the territory war. He wouldn't have radioed in during his first challenge to give him advice. They might have radically different ideas about the path forward, but they were still friends when all was said and done.

The way he'd looked stuck out—haggard. Exhausted. Like someone had done something to him—forced him into it.

His first thought was to call Dracula—but he didn't have Dracula's contact information. He did, however, have his superior officer's number automatically logged into his armlet during his registration with the Order of the Dragon. Daniel didn't like the idea of having more conversations than absolutely necessary with that slimeball, but desperate times called for desperate measures.

Daniel flicked through the menu, looking for Rasputin's ID number—but before he could get there, a voice blasted in over the intercom, echoing through the empty waiting room. "Inmate, please proceed to the teleportation pad and prepare to enter the arena."

Daniel glanced up at the pedestal—which was now humming and glowing blue—then back to his armlet, then back again. He didn't know what to do.

"Step over to the pad," the intercom said. The voice was metallic and uncompromising. "We're live in 10 seconds. If you create a delay, you will be penalized."

Daniel clenched his teeth, then got up and walked to the pad, barely remembering to take his club with him. A thousand thoughts flickered through his mind as he crossed the scant few feet, but they settled on one thing—he had to defeat Bathory to get himself and Jack out of this mess.

If Jack wants out.

Chapter 18
Fight Night

As soon as Daniel's feet hit pedestal, his vision washed out. He blinked, but everything was white, even if he shut his eyes. He could feel his eyes were closed, but it didn't seem to do anything.

A sensation of weightlessness made his stomach flip. It felt like he was riding on a high-speed elevator that suddenly came to a halt. He swam back into himself again, and his sight returned to normal. It felt different every time he teleported, but at least he barely had any nausea—this time.

He stood at the edge of a flat field of grass. There were a few boulders scattered around, some large enough to duck behind, but other than that, it was empty. Daniel's eyes traveled along the high rock ledges that formed the walls of the arena. The ceiling was metal, reminding him that he was still inside, but bright stadium lights gave the illusion of full daytime. It had the feel and scale of a football field, which was exactly what he wanted—straightforward, no tricks or trip-ups. *At least one thing is going right.*

And then, at the other end, there she was—Elizabeth Bathory.

She was tall, with dark, almost-black brown hair. Her skin was fair, and her face was powdered white, emphasizing the paleness—presumably a medieval fashion statement. He couldn't make out much more detail at this distance, but he'd already seen her up close in the recordings. It made her that much more disturbing—even after Daniel witnessed video footage of what she did to other inmates when she caught them alive, she looked like someone you could pass on the street; another face in the crowd.

"And now!" Ky's voice screeched. "The moment you've all been waiting for!" Her voice was coming from his armlet. He wasn't sure what was worse—an inescapable prison, or her inescapable announcer's voice. "We have for you tonight a one-on-one duel between the champion of Hell, the leader of the Brotherhood of Sinners, possessing the highest win-loss record of any team in history"—she paused dramatically—"Elizabeeeth Bathoryyy! Set against her is a rising challenger, the rookie member of the infamous Order of the Dragon, and—by the numbers—the strongest human inmate, Danieeel Fitzgeraaald!

Daniel cocked an eyebrow. His title was growing in length by the day. Maybe he was the strongest, on paper. Jack had run the numbers from their bout with the Sky Runners through a calculator. Going solely by the amount of magical power, Daniel was about 36 times stronger than him.

Ky continued after an appropriate beat, no doubt allowing for the cameras to get close-ups of their faces. "Today's battle arena has already been selected, but so far, we've kept the stakes of the fight top secret. It's time for the big reveal!"

What looked like a giant slot machine materialized on one side of the arena. A scoreboard was perched above it. The screen flashed with dramatic PrisonWatch graphics that flew around in time to a sports channel-style intro theme. A portrait of Bathory and Daniel were superimposed on either side, backed by their team's colors. Above them, the winner's reward was printed in black, flaming letters, and the loser's punishment outlined in blue.

Winner: 5,235,000 Points

Loser: 10 Year Banishment

Daniel frowned. That last part sounded bad. He assumed Dracula had to offer up something pretty juicy to get Bathory to jump for the duel so quickly. They would probably have to buy him out of whatever it was, on top of putting up money for the pot.

Daniel licked his lips, then rolled his shoulders back, straightening. He didn't plan on losing, so he wasn't going to dwell on it.

"Our top teams are definitely not kidding around this time! The Order of the Dragon is taking a big risk on their powerhouse rookie. We'll see if it pays off for them soon enough. But before that, let's find out exactly what sort of fun our contestants will be having!"

Ky flew up—Daniel only then realizing that she was physically there, and not a magic projection, when he saw the movement. She wrapped both hands around the arm of the slot device, then leaned back and tugged down, a little bit at a time. The size difference made it look like watching Tinker Bell try to operate a machine designed for normal-sized people. After huffing and puffing her way to the ground, she looked back at the camera following her. "I really need to work out more, huh? Here we go!" She released the arm, and it flew back up with a solid ka-chunk. The lights and happy electronic beeps you'd expect from a casino rang out as the slot started spinning.

The overblown antics were like the one-liners a gameshow host would deliver between events with a dash of physical comedy to add some personality for the viewers. A twisted tension built in the pit of Daniel's stomach. It was one thing to tell a joke before someone answered a trivia question, but another entirely to do it before two people tried their best to kill each other. Something was wrong with demon society; very, very wrong.

The display panel rolled too fast for his eyes to follow. Daniel could only wait while his fate was decided.

I wish I could have seen the look on your face when she died.

The words replayed in his mind while Daniel stood there. Jack's face. The way he'd looked. The way he'd grinned. That sick smile floated in his mind's eye.

Daniel rubbed his face. The slot was starting to slow. He had to focus.

The face of the machine turned and whirled and blared with music, eventually trundling to a stop.

50% Magic Power

No Items Allowed

"Well buckle your flight belt, because we're in for a wild showdown tonight!" Ky said. "Both contestants have access to half of their magic power, but aside from their main weapon, they cannot use any items they may have brought with them. Despite being robbed of hours of careful strategizing to select the perfect item to bring in their inventories, they now have a plethora of options they weren't prepared to counter. We can only imagine how our contestants will respond, but it's definitely going to be head to head, mano-a-womano, Daniel's fast and furious versus Bathory's vicious and versatile! Can Daniel's recent momentum carry him through a dramatic upset, or will Bathory crush him underfoot? Before we find out, a brief word from our sponsor—but stay tuned, because this is one fight you do not want to miss!"

The lights dimmed slightly. The slot machine's image flicked onto a number—2:30. It started to count down the seconds. Daniel cocked his head. *A commercial break?*

He immediately reached for his armlet. He had to get in touch with Rasputin before things got any worse. As he tapped back into his contacts screen, his arm buzzed with an incoming call—which was odd, because he'd blocked all external calls from numbers he didn't know after his voicemails filled to the brim.

But it wasn't an outside number. It was an inmate ID.

Daniel's eyes moved to the next line with the inmate's name. *Elizabeth Bathory.* He glanced up across the field; it was plain to see she was looking back at him.

"I don't have time for this right now." Daniel heaved a sigh and tapped the answer button.

Her face greeted him on the communication panel. "Hello," she said gently.

"Uh...hi."

Bathory studied him. She was pretty, in a pleasant, nondescript way, like the young married lady next door with a kid and two dogs. Daniel had trouble connecting her face to that of a psychotic torturer.

"So, I finally meet the most popular man in Hell." Her voice was calm, stately. "What's your game, Daniel Fitzgerald? What do you expect to accomplish here? Don't you see the pit you're throwing yourself into?"

"There's no game," he said. "I'm here to win. And speaking of pits, maybe giving you a little of the Hell you actually deserve, instead of this joke."

"Ah, yes. Dracula still wants his little revenge, sins of the father and all that. How high and noble." She sighed. "Is he really that willing to throw you away?"

"It doesn't matter if I lose," Daniel said, "I'm new. You beat me, things stay the same, maybe I get a little street cred. It's a win-win." He glanced at the clock. *1:43.*

Bathory, surprisingly, took him at his word, nodding seriously. "I can see the logic. If you defeat me—well, that certainly speaks for itself. But aren't you underestimating the consequences of your own defeat?"

"Can we get to the point here? I've kinda got something else on my plate."

Bathory searched his face—and then, realizing something, she broke into a smile. "They didn't tell you. You have no idea what you've gotten yourself into, do you? Playing at schemes against old men far more experienced at scheming than yourself. I almost feel sorry for you."

"What are you talking about?" Daniel asked.

"Oh, I wouldn't want to spoil their fun," she said. "I might as well play along, keep things a surprise. It's a win-win for me, too." She looked straight at him through the camera. "Don't get caught too quickly. After all..." Her lips curled up above her teeth, and her eyes changed, widening until he could see the whites all the way around. "I like my flesh properly tenderized."

The feed cut out. Daniel took a steadying breath. *I really hope the crazy in this place isn't contagious.*

He took another look at the clock. *1:10*. Great. He flicked down to Rasputin's number—wasting a few more precious seconds—and dialed it, thinking about how he was going to explain himself in the shortest possible time.

It rang. Rang again.

And rang again.

Daniel started tapping his foot. "Come on, come on, pick up. What is with my damn phone today?"

The dial tone cut off. A familiar robotic tone came from his armlet. "We apologize, but outgoing communication is blocked 60 seconds prior to an arena event. Good luck!" *Click.*

"Dammit!" Daniel smacked his armlet, stomped his foot. He heaved another breath out, then combed his hair back with both hands.

The past five minutes had been one thing after another. His nerves were already gurgling in his stomach from coming face-to-face with the very moment which would either save or damn him and quite possibly a significant part of the human population. It was a moment which happened to involve a gladiator-style death match with someone that redefined the term crazy eyes. It was a moment now following his still-probably-maybe best friend having some kind of mental breakdown and flipping out in the extreme. To top it all off, he had to settle for contacting Rasputin to figure out what the hell was going on, and his sole remaining window in which to do so was soaked up by the circular taunts of aforementioned crazy-eyed psychopathic killer.

Daniel cupped his face, bending down into a crouch as he tried to get a grip. He took a few breaths, then stood straight, running his hands up over the legs of his pants. *Alright. Get a grip. One thing at a time. First thing's first, beat Bathory.*

As the clock closed in on the start of the match, Daniel looked up at the giant slot machine, still poised high on the rocky wall of the arena. The sight helped the frustration immensely. He'd traded bad luck on one side for good luck on another. No items meant one less wild surprise from Bathory. 50% of his magic was exactly what he wanted, even better than what he was carrying with him as his own item. Half his current strength would be a bit more power than he wielded in New York against the Vorid Lord, and that wasn't counting his gains against the Viridian Gust. That had to be enough to take her down.

The clock flicked to zero. The lights shined at full force. He blinked a bit as his eyes adjusted.

"Welcome back!" Ky shouted. "Thanks for joining us tonight for the main event on PrisonWatch. We know our fighters, we know our terms, and we won't keep you waiting any longer. The fight begins in...10! 9! 8!"

A massive clock replaced the screen on the slot machine. It counted down in time with Ky. She had all her claws raised, letting them drop one by one.

Daniel bent his knees. He hefted his club in one hand, ready to swing. He reached for his power, too. Though unable to get at it directly, he kept his attention there, his mind on the surface around the core of energy inside of him, ready to push out everything he had. He was sure that his chance of winning was highest in the first few seconds.

"3! 2! 1!" Ky raised both her hands. "Go!"

Daniel's power slammed into his grip, chomping at the bit to be unleashed as much as he was pushing on it. All his frustration and nerves were driven into the singular act, opening the floodgate to his magic as wide as possible. The energy blazed out every pore of his skin, flaring with the intensity of a flashbang. Power surged into his muscles; he could feel everything in him tense like a coiled spring. The world around him slowed as his perception accelerated.

Daniel extended his power behind him, forming a flat physical sigil—a simple platform—then pushed off.

He hurtled fast enough that the rock edges of the arena blurred at the corners of his eyes. He was at Bathory's position in an instant, as if he'd crossed the entire field in a single step, club raised, swinging for her stomach.

BAM

Bathory exploded—not into gore, but into a black, particulate mist. Daniel tried to pull up short after blasting through her, but he had too much momentum. He used the short time he had to reinforce his skin with his power, then bounced off the rock wall in front of him before stumbling back to a halt, unharmed.

He coughed. The black mist was everywhere, blocking his sight. He leapt backward, clearing away from the stuff, but a layer of it clung to him—and it burned, the way cold burned when the temperature dropped below what skin could tolerate.

Alarmed, Daniel pushed power to the outside of his body, holding it there like an armor. The black mist sat on top of that shield of light, eating away at his energy at a frightening rate. He pushed a bit of extra power into his club and tried to brush the stuff off his arm. The mist only wavered, reforming as soon as he moved it away, almost like an illusory fire fed by his own magic.

"What the hell...?"

"My, my," came Bathory's voice.

With his heightened perception, Daniel could almost pinpoint where the sound was coming from. Without looking, he leapt in that direction, then came down with his club, smashing at her head.

She vanished before he made contact, and he stumbled through his swing as he caught air. He kept better control of his momentum this time, and he didn't get covered in more of whatever that magic was. Daniel halted near a boulder and quickly put his back up against it as he peered around the arena and tried to find some hint of her passing.

"Over here."

Daniel ran over, but this time, she was gone before he made it, simply disappeared.

"No, no, over here!"

Daniel leapt over. His club smashed into the ground, tossing up a cloud of dirt and gravel, but he didn't make any kind of significant contact with her. Meanwhile, the black mist kept burning away at him; he'd stopped it from doing any harm, but it was chewing through his reserves faster than he could sustain, burning up magic like a brushfire devoured dry prairie grass. The constant effort to hold it off was a huge distraction, slowing down his reaction time and blunting his speed advantage.

Bathory giggled. "I feel like I'm toying with a child."

Daniel looked first instead of leaping this time. His mouth gaped at what he saw.

A total of 7 different Elizabeth Bathorys were idling about the arena, some leaning against boulders, others with their arms folded or standing in place. The one closest to him spoke. "Catch me if you can." They all smiled at him, then spoke simultaneously, the words echoing weirdly in his ears. "I hope you can do that before your magic runs out."

"What an exchange!" Ky said. "Daniel exploded out of the gate, but Lizzy's technique has given her the edge. Now that Daniel's cursed, he needs to make something happen, and fast!"

Daniel could feel the black magic eating into his energy, burning it off him and into useless vapor. At this rate, he had five minutes or so before he was out of gas, and it would start eating him instead of his magic.

If he was a normal magician, he might have a serious problem. Bathory had set the terms—a war of attrition. The longer the fight went on, the worse off he'd be. Casting spells recklessly to try and kill her quickly would only hasten his inevitable demise. That's what this was—a one-two punch designed to get him to panic and waste energy chasing after illusions to no effect.

But Daniel wasn't a magician. He was a contractor. He had no hope he'd be able to outwit her in the arena of magical technique, but he could try to do it the old-fashioned way—overpower her beyond what her spell was able to handle.

Daniel dug his heels into the ground to brace himself. He reached deep into his core—as deep as he could—and dragged out the full extent of his power. He grunted, and then shouted with the effort as the magic welled up inside of him and crushed out through his veins, muscles, and pores. He pushed it out in a flash, revealing his full potential in a nova-like burst of energy.

The black mist on his body stiffened, then contracted, thinning as it attempted to keep up with the sheer amount of energy. It started to vibrate, wavering faster and faster. The mist stilled, solidifying, then shattered off and scattered into the grass like pieces of tinted glass. When they came to rest, the shards burst into smoke, vanishing into the air. Daniel took a long breath, then let his magic fade back down to a half-state of readiness, like a strongman flexing his muscles and looking for another boulder to lift.

"Impressive," Bathory said. "I've never seen anyone able to break that spell by force." Another copy, standing to the right of that one, smirked at him. "But how is that going to work on me?"

"Shut up already," Daniel snapped. He rocketed forward, swiping his club through the first clone of Bathory. She vanished—something he fully expected. He kept running, blasting his way through the one behind, and it vanished too. *Two down.*

He formed a physical sigil in front of himself and bounced off it, launching toward the next target without hesitation and causing it to vanish as well. With the third destroyed, he turned, having already positioned himself with his previous strikes such that next four illusions were in a rough line. He dug his feet in, and a cloud of dirt and grass flew up from where he pushed off. He drove through the next three in a blink.

That left only one Bathory left—the last one in line. He raised his weapon, preparing to put more energy into the strike as he charged forward. At the last moment—spotting the same smirk still plastered on her face—he held back, going with a casual swing. As his club passed through, he knew it was just another illusion.

He stopped with a few quick steps, turning around—only to find that there were already more of her. His enhanced perception helped him quickly count 15 copies. Daniel started up his momentum again, then kept going, feet falling into a rhythm as he flew around the arena.

He struck his way through the illusions as efficiently as possible. She wasn't trying to strike back with magic or traps, so hopefully he was moving too fast for her to easily react. *One of these has to be the real one.*

Despite his speed, Daniel was always one move behind her creation of more copies. When he stepped up his speed, she made more clones, giving herself more time to react. He came close to eliminating them all a few times, but then she started putting effort into it, and eventually he was surrounded by dozens of illusory Elizabeth Bathorys, some smirking, others calling out insults and jeers.

One was even skipping circles at the other end of the arena. That copy gave him a jaunty wave as he erased a half-dozen other illusions nearby. "Come on, Daniel, faster! I can't keep this up forever, right?" She grinned at him as he changed directions, a hint of the crazed murderer flashing over her features. "Hurry up before I kill you." And then that Bathory was gone, vanished like the others.

Daniel wasn't even using his club anymore; it was a waste of energy. They fell apart as soon as he touched them with his magic, even if his only medium was his bare hands, so he kept up the effort on a low burn, trying to think while he ran. Breaking the curse magic had taken a lot more energy out of him than he thought it would, and while he was conserving the rest of his power fairly well, he couldn't keep it up indefinitely.

"Too slow, Daniel," one copy said as he swept through it. It faded away, melting under the pressure of his magic. "Guess it wasn't that one either," said the next one over. He stabbed his hand through her, watching as the spell faded. He wasn't even touching magic—only a product of it, the energy powering it already gone as he eliminated each one in turn. None of them made any pretense of trying to fight back or protect themselves. Clearly she was fine with waiting him out—probably until he let his guard down and got caught in another trap. He was fairly certain she couldn't pull the black mist trick again, or she would have done it by now. Or maybe only her real body could produce that magic, and she didn't want to risk it.

He tried to think like her. Was she really hiding in the forest of copies? He knew she could teleport, so she could be leaving copies behind as she moved—but what if Daniel got lucky and he guessed right? She might not be able to react in time, but only if he moved at maximum speed. He could probably kill ten clones a second if he really pushed it for a minute or two, but he didn't want to use that much energy.

If he could create copies like that, what would he do? The smartest strategy would be to hide somewhere completely different and keep him guessing, create clones from a distance while the real one was totally removed from the conflict. There was no need to cast the spell while standing right next to the person.

But where was there to hide? They were in an open field; she was confined to the space of the arena. Daniel stared at the ground through the vanishing body of his latest illusory victim, thinking, when something caught the corner of his eye—a boulder.

He pushed extra power through his head—a crude but effective way of slowing his perception down a step further. The half-second stretched into ten seconds by his reckoning, giving him time to scan the battlefield without looking suspicious. A small part of him remembered how disoriented he'd been when he'd tried to enhance his hearing; doing everything at once didn't seem to carry the same problems. Maybe it was because of a mismatch between his brain and his ears.

It wasn't time for figuring that one out. Daniel peered at the boulders, examining them one by one. He remembered the one he'd put his back against early, and the few scattered around were mostly small, unremarkable. They were more to break up lines of sight and create little obstacles than true hiding places; he might be able to squat down behind a few of them.

There. A large boulder which he could have sworn wasn't there at the start, noticeably larger than the others—enough to stand up inside comfortably, if, say, it was an illusion.

Daniel let his magic even out again as he worked his way there, cutting through illusory copies until he was close. He feinted as if moving away—then immediately created a sigil in front of himself, spun so his feet were against it, and blasted backwards, slamming his club through the rock.

And there wasn't any rock—but there was a magician inside of it. His club struck Bathory in the shoulder with a satisfying crunch, and her body flew across the arena, tumbling head-over-heels.

Red light jetted from Bathory's hands. The magic stabilized her flight and held her upright, like the twin flames of a jetpack. She landed on her toes, but the momentum from Daniel's strike forced her to slide back across the ground, digging furrows in the dirt with her feet. As she came to a halt, she brought her hands in front of her and snapped her head up, the red light shifting purple and then blue as she switched spells.

Daniel was already winding up behind her, club held hand-over-hand like a baseball bat.

His fully-charged weapon slammed into her midback. There was a resounding snap as her torso bent the wrong way. Her body bounced hard off one of the boulders, and she careened into the ground. A plume of chewed up grass and dirt rose from where she came to rest.

Daniel sighed, then placed the butt of his club to the ground, leaning on it slightly. He got her straight on with his follow-up strike, with an extra moment to concentrate his magic to boot. Even the Vorid lord would have a tough time taking that; he was pretty sure she wasn't getting up.

"Wow!" Ky had been relatively quiet—the fight was speaking for itself. But nothing could keep her down for long, unfortunately. "Daniel fights back with a shocking counterattack! I hope we can get that replay in slow motion, otherwise we won't know what happened!" Daniel glanced to the screen still displayed on the fake slot machine. Even as Ky hinted to whoever was running the live feed, Daniel's movements were replayed in slow motion, his darting back behind Bathory faster than she herself traveled through the air, and then planting his feet on a sigil to stop and ground himself for his back-breaking attack.

"Can Lizzy continue after taking two direct hits?!" Ky shouted. "The healing magic won't kick in until this battle is over, and she might not be able to heal herself in her current state! Is it really all over just like that?!"

The dust cleared from Bathory's landing site—and Daniel gawked. She was gone.

He looked left, right. No extra boulders or new copies. She'd up and vanished for real, this time.

"It looks like she's not done yet folks," Ky said, "as expected from the champ. Daniel looks as confused as everyone else!"

Daniel resisted the urge to flip her the bird. He stayed on his toes and kept his magic on alert, ready to shoot off his feet.

"That was fun," came Bathory's voice.

Daniel swung behind himself, spinning in a circle. His club hummed through the air, but he didn't catch anything, not even a whisper of an illusion. He swirled to a stop, baffled. It had sounded like she was speaking into his ear.

"I wouldn't be stupid enough to stand right next to you," she said. Daniel flinched, but she wasn't anywhere to be found. She must be using some kind of spell to project her voice. "You really helped me work out a sore spot. I appreciate it."

"Do you ever stop talking?" Daniel said. "You're worse than Ky!"

"Hey!" Ky said. "I take offense to that!"

"Simple fights can get so boring," Bathory said. "I much prefer our titillating conversation." He could practically hear the annoying smirk on her face. "You won't find me this time. I guess you'll have to keep burning up magic...otherwise, who knows what I might do to you."

Daniel schooled himself, trying not to reveal anything from his expression, but she was right. He had burned a lot chasing around her ghosts. Maybe she could sense his magic fluctuate.

Seizing on that idea, Daniel tried to feel out for her own magic. He was fairly sensitive to most magic while in touch with his powers—and even sometimes when he wasn't, if it was a strong enough spell. He could feel plenty of magic—a lot of it reinforced the walls of the arena. More of it floated around them, everywhere, really—drifting through the air. Maybe that was Hell's natural state, all the ebb and flow Jack had been talking about. He never had a chance to examine it with his powers constantly being walled off. He could feel the seal on him, even now, blocking the other half of his magic tank. But no Bathory.

"Like a blind pig trying to find a truffle," Bathory sneered. "Have you even been trained?"

"Come out and fight!" Daniel shouted. "Or are you all smoke and mirrors?"

"You're a few centuries too young to bait me, young man," she said, laughing. "I don't have anything to prove. You do."

"It looks like Daniel Fitzgerald is in a pickle!" Ky called. "Bathory might have taken a hit, but she's recovered fast and knows better than to fight Daniel head on. Her concealment magic is powerful, and it's only a matter of time before she strikes from the shadows!"

As annoying as Ky was, she was right. Daniel was stuck. If he dropped his magic to conserve energy, he'd be wide open. If he couldn't find her, he'd run out of power soon enough anyway. What was he supposed to do?

Magic. Sensing magic. That was it!

Daniel stood straight and shut his eyes. He took a breath, staying as still as possible.

"Hmm." Ky's voice came in clear. "It looks like Daniel is up to something!"

Daniel scryed.

It was something Xik had shown him long ago, a Klide technique to detect the Vorid. It was a lot different than the general sense of magic he had; it let him float away from himself, disembodied, to personally investigate at a distance. While it was a useful technique, Daniel hadn't used it too much, his base magical senses usually doing the trick without so many situational limitations—the first of which was to stay motionless. That wasn't usually compatible with Daniel's approach to conflict.

As Daniel's spirit began to scry, the world was rendered in grainy grey-black hues, like the image on an old tube TV. It was much sharper and clearer than he remembered. Xik had mentioned that, as he grew stronger, he would be able to scry more clearly and at greater distances. It looked like that was true.

Bathory stood out from the grey like a lit-up Christmas tree. Daniel opened his eyes; the sense of scrying and the sense of his sight overlapped on one another in a weird sensation of double vision. She was invisible, but she existed, totally vulnerable, in the strange scrying world.

Daniel charged up his powers and dashed toward where she stood. His scrying sense snapped shut as he moved, returning his vision to normal. He swung his club through empty space—and connected with a solid thunk, on something.

Impressions in the field marked where Bathory was rolling across the ground from being struck, but her spell held against his attack, maintaining her invisibility. Daniel followed the signs of her passing, slapping his club wherever he thought she might be. He didn't get lucky enough to hit her a second time, and if his earlier attack hadn't killed her, he doubted that one would.

"Impossible!" It was Bathory's voice—and this time, she sounded less the snide champion and more completely surprised. "How did you do that?"

"A magician never reveals his secrets," Daniel said.

Bathory huffed imperiously. A cold wind picked up around the arena. Daniel squinted. He could feel magic building, prickling the hairs on the back of his neck as the energy concentrated.

Goosebumps ran up his arms as the temperature plunged from chilly to frigid. A swirling column of snow formed at the arena's ceiling, then plunged down over him. Sleet soaked though his clothes. His could feel the magic in the storm weighing on him, as if he was at the center of a blast chiller actively trying to freeze him solid.

Daniel tucked his arms in, trying to stay alert while preserving his warmth. The swirling blizzard layered down harder; the wind howled in his ears. A few seconds later, the icy storm transformed into a total whiteout. His magical senses were reduced to a static haze, dulled by the massive spell moving around him in every direction. The snow coated the grass across the entire arena and piled up over his ankles. The frost nibbled at him as if it was alive, seeking gaps in his clothes and knifing across his skin.

Despite all the effort she was making, Daniel wasn't much bothered by it all. He could tell it was cold, certainly, the same way he could feel the wetness of his clothes plastered on his skin, but it was just *there*. He could as easily ignore it.

Since Daniel couldn't see through the snow, and his other senses were washed out, he shut his eyes to scry instead. If even Elizabeth Bathory didn't know how he'd found her, the Klide detection method must be more unique than he realized.

Bathory showed up clear, like a human-shaped candle glowing through the haze of the storm's energy. The blizzard was driven by magic that leapt up from her outstretched left hand. Interestingly, it was the only thing that appeared in color; blue-white light trailed through the grey-black of the scrying sense, reached the ceiling, and then interacted with—something—to create the blizzard that then descended on Daniel's position. The whole arena, now, was covered in snow and ice.

Daniel launched himself forward. The snow clung to him, slowing him down somewhat; he had to spend more energy to plow through it. Bathory was so focused on her magic that he caught her easily, slamming his club into her stomach.

Daniel caught a hint of her body creating a trench in the snow as she flew backward. He followed the trail, but the whiteout closed in around him, and she was gone, vanished into the storm. He was confident that he was doing damage—if not hurting her directly, at least draining away a defensive shield. She didn't have unlimited reserves, either.

Daniel thought he could catch a word or two of Ky's commentary, but the wind was going so hard he didn't know what she was saying. Ignoring the snow soaking through his pants, Daniel settled in to pinpoint her location again. As soon as he started to focus, Daniel felt an impact catch him in the chest. He took a step to the side, flinching away from the hit.

When he looked, he hadn't been hurt. There was some extra ice on his clothes, and he could feel the remains of a spell, but it hadn't done any damage—too weak. "Is that all you got?" he shouted into the wind. He could barely hear his own voice in his ears.

This time, Bathory didn't answer.

Daniel tried to set his focus again—but as soon as he did, another bit of magic struck his chest. He opened his eyes in time to discover a magically-propelled snowball sliding down his shirt.

A snowball was keeping him from scrying.

"Really?!" Daniel shouted. "Is this what it comes down to?!"

"Whatever works," Bathory said. Despite the storm, he heard her easily.

Daniel kept trying to scry, but Bathory insisted on distracting him with snowballs. After four or five more tries, ducking behind boulders for cover and even once hiding in a snow drift, he gave it up and simply waited. He knew from his earlier scrying that it was taking her a tremendous amount of magic to keep the whole blizzard thing going; now she was the one burning through her reserves.

Almost as soon as Daniel had the thought, the blanket-thick whiteout began to thin. The winds died down; the blizzard faded to a mild squall, and then to flurries. The arena went totally quiet, sounds muffled by the fresh powder that layered over everything a half-foot deep.

Daniel kicked his feet free from the snow and tamped it down under his shoes. He was a little chilly, but otherwise unaffected. His defenses weren't tested nearly as much as they were by her black magic spell. He'd never thought about it before, but maybe he was more resistant to some types of magic than others.

Daniel felt another spell; coolness settled on his skin again, but this time it lingered, more like a fog than a wind. The temperature dropped, more than before, and for the first time it truly felt like uncomfortable cold. The wetness in his jeans and shirt was stiffening—turning to ice.

More ice condensed around him from all sides, erupting from the air without warning. Daniel was encapsulated in a transparent crystal sphere, walled in on all sides, though still free to move in the center. It was a spell he was quite familiar with—it looked exactly like when Eleanor had tried to trap him back in Boston, but the walls were thicker and he was confined in a much smaller space, only about as high as he was tall.

Daniel leaned in to inspect the boundary. Ice cracked and fell off his pants and shirt as he shifted. His breath clouded in front of him, fogging up his side of the ice wall. He didn't feel too bad; despite the obviously freezing temperatures, it was like being a bit exposed on a raw fall day, uncomfortable, but bearable. He wasn't actively using his magic to keep it that way, either; its passive protection was enough.

"Distracted by the blizzard, Daniel looks to be trapped inside an icy prison," Ky called out. "That cuts off his biggest advantage, but I think we've learned that you don't bet against Daniel when the chips are down. Let's see if he has a plan to work his way out of this one!"

Bathory appeared in front of him; her left hand was holding a bright blue light. Her right hand cupped a grey-colored spell, but it was fading—maybe that had been her concealment magic. Scrying briefly informed Daniel that there was a link of magic between the blue light in her left hand and his ice shell.

Another blue light, a lighter shade, appeared to replace the fading grey. He watched it with his enhanced senses as the magic seeped through the icy shell and sank into the air around him. The temperature immediately dropped even further, and kept dropping. If he had a thermometer, he felt like he'd be able to see it plummet in real time.

All Daniel felt was a little chill wash down his spine. He shrugged it off, taking in the spell-casting process as he considered how to break out. Bathory frowned at him. She poured more energy into her effort. Daniel watched with interest, having never really had a chance to see magic work up close with his scrying sense.

Rachel had taught him a little, but he'd never thought of using scrying to observe her; he hadn't needed to. Bathory didn't use the sigils and incantations he'd seen and heard from other magicians to set a 'program' for her mana; a small gesture did the trick. Maybe it was a matter of experience, or familiarity.

Bathory's face scrunched into a scowl as she continued to channel more magic from her right hand. The temperature went from below freezing to sub-arctic, and then even colder, as if he'd been dumped into the vacuum of space. Daniel shifted slightly, finally forced to focus his magic a bit to stay warm, but it was no major effort compared to her forceful exertion.

Daniel smiled at the look on her face—and was surprised when bits of ice fell from his cheeks to the ground. He rubbed at his nose, brushing away a dusting of frozen water that had collected there. "I think I'm gonna catch a cold," Daniel said. Bathory's frustration reached a peak on her face. "What? Not feeling so chatty all the sudden?"

"You should be frozen solid by now," Bathory grunted, all her focus on the spell. "How are you doing this?"

"Like I'm gonna tell you." Daniel picked at his nails, digging tiny bits of ice out from under them. "Maybe you're not as great as you think you are."

"Fine," she spat, "I'll seal you in." Bathory relaxed the energy flowing to the one hand, and the other—which created the prison—grew brighter, two of her fingers twitching left and right, up and down. The direction the energy flow shifted, responding to the gestures. *Weird. Do the movements make it happen, or is it some kind of mental cue?*

It was only when the glare of the stadium lighting shining through the ice started to warp and shift that Daniel realized what was happening. The prison's walls were growing in toward the center. His hand brushed one of the walls, and the ice reached out, trying to wrap up and suck his fingers into its depths. He recoiled, ripping his hand free of the suction with a burst of his magic. He crouched in the center of the prison as the ice closed in from above.

"Daniel doesn't have trouble staying warm, but Bathory can hold him in place," Ky said. "And then she'll go to work on him. Things look bad for Fitzgerald!"

Daniel's mind churned as he tried to figure a way out; he blasted magic up into his head, slowing down his perception, giving himself more precious seconds to think. The ice slowed, inching inward instead of flowing like frozen lava. He might have half a minute before the jaw of the trap snapped shut.

He'd almost broke out of Eleanor's ice shell in Boston. He'd laid into the wall with his mace, smashing it thin in one spot, but the effort exhausted him before he could finish. Jack landed the final blow at the last second, opening a hole through which Daniel escaped.

Chipping away at the barrier might work again, but he didn't have that kind of time to spare. Bathory was a lot stronger than Eleanor; the ice walls were thicker and were actively trying to seal him in. The cold wouldn't do anything, but the solid ice would suffocate him.

He needed a way to break through faster. A thick flat surface like the ice wall made things tough for him. Daniel's mind flashed back to Kavarssian's scales. He'd been able to jam the spiked tip of his morning star in a weak point, then, concentrating his magic, tear a hole in the dragon's armor. The homemade mace he used back in Boston had little bits and spikes he'd added to it, giving his weapon a bite. The morning star had spikes, too. His eyes flicked to his current club. The rounded head definitely wouldn't catch on the ice. It was reliable and easy to use, but that choice was working against him now.

Unless the ice caught it on its own.

Daniel shifted to one knee for stability and raised his club toward the walls closing in around him, pointed at Bathory. He drew in his magic, condensing it, concentrating it the same way he had with Kavarssian. The light emanating from Daniel died away as he cautiously pushed his power down his arms, out his hands, and into his weapon. *Hope this works.*

"Daniel's magic appears to be fading, but he's taken an odd position!" Ky said. "Does he have something up his sleeve?"

"I doubt it," Bathory said, responding to Ky's commentary with a smile. Her fingers began to clench together, signaling the walls to subsume him entirely.

The first thing the ice reached was the end of Daniel's club, held up to the walls. Daniel held on tight as the iron handle grew shock-cold. Crystals of water condensed on the club's surface as it dropped to the same temperature as the ice. The ice wall, reacting to the contact, melded against the club, working down toward his grip like greedy vines trying to bind him up.

Daniel's arms clenched up with the effort of pushing more and more magic into his club. Flickers of light leaked out here and there as the energy threatened to burst out of his control, but between the arena's lights and the way the ice reflected it all back out, he hoped Bathory wouldn't notice. He drove all the energy up into the tip of the weapon and held it there, steadily adding more fuel to his time bomb until it was as concentrated as much as he dared to risk without giving himself away.

The ice wound closer. A thick branch of the stuff covered the end of the club. Icy tendrils stretched toward his hands, questing for his bare skin. Daniel grit his teeth. *Just a bit longer.*

"You're mine," Bathory said.

Daniel detonated the magic at the tip of his club.

There was a *whoomph*, like an explosion heard underwater. The ice screamed in protest as chunks of it blasted outward, sending a hail of frozen shrapnel out from the tip of Daniel's club and directly at Bathory. She flinched back as ice pelted her, hands going to protect her face—which left her stomach open to a particularly nasty shard that clipped her in the side, ripping through her blouse. She toppled backward into the snow.

Daniel gathered his legs beneath himself and leapt into the air, bursting out the hole in his prison with enough force that he traveled to the ceiling. He burned magic as he flipped over midair and planted his feet on the roof of the arena. The world slowed around him as he gathered his feet to push off, eyes searching the snow. Bathory was gone, invisible—but she couldn't hide the imprint she left in the snow where she'd fallen.

He pressed magic into his legs and exploded off the ceiling and toward the ground. Aided by gravity and his own magic, he was there in a blink. He didn't bother trying to time a swing, instead landing with legs extended, pile-driving his feet straight into where she should be. His legs crunched into something that was definitely not the ground.

"What a turnaround!" Ky shouted. "Daniel flipped his impending doom into a killer double-kick. Bathory's on the defense!"

He dropped to a knee, then brought his club down into what felt like a body under him, catching her between his strike and the arena floor. Snow and dirt blasted away in every direction from the force. There was a flash of green where his club struck, burning back against the power of his magic—that had to be whatever shield she was using to keep herself from getting hurt.

Daniel kept at it, smashing at something that definitely felt like it was starting to give way. He slammed his club home with both hands, using the momentum from one strike to lead into another, his knee working to pin her below him.

Daniel's club fell for another strike, but before he hit home, there was a flash of orange light. His club smashed into the dirt, sending up a dust cloud of gravel and snow. He frowned at the sensation—whatever he'd been striking at before was gone.

When Daniel glanced up, there were more illusory copies of Bathory waiting for him, though they looked like they'd been dragged through a washing machine. Her hair was a mess, her powdered face sweating, and ice and dirt clung to the back of her clothes. Despite her bedraggled appearance—he was convinced he had her on the ropes—she was still smiling.

One of the illusions waved at him. It reminded Daniel of the wave Jack gave him before he hung up. "I don't mind a man on top," Bathory said, "but it gets old after a while."

Daniel stood. "Aren't you supposed to be the champion? Is there gonna be any actual fighting, or are you gonna run around and hide the whole time?"

"It looks like Lizzy is messing with Daniel at this point!" Ky said. "So far Daniel's had an answer to all of Bathory's spells, but her bag of tricks is far from empty, and Daniel has yet to land a clean hit through her shield!"

A wave of frustration rolled over Daniel at Ky's commentary, mostly because she was right. As close as he might have gotten, he hadn't actually touched her once, and she didn't seem worried about the possibility. Regardless of how effective they'd been, he'd taken the brunt of all her magical antics; following his first attack, the entire battle had been Bathory acting, and Daniel responding. She was content to lead him around by the nose with illusions rather than confront him head on. Was he going to play ring-around-the-rosie for an hour before burning out?

Daniel turned his head to the floating devil. "Hey, Ky!"

"Huh?" Ky pointed at herself. "Whatever could you want with me?"

"This fight is a load of crap!" Daniel said. "Is this what the viewers want? Me chasing her around while she hides like a coward behind illusions? This is the champion of Hell?"

Ky shrugged. "You have a point, but there isn't anything I can do about it." She looked up in mock thought, before bringing a fist down into her open palm with a slap. "Or is there?! How about another spin on the slot machine to *spice!*" She cocked her hip. "Things! Up!"

Daniel blinked. He didn't actually expect that to work.

The slot machine's spinning dials flicked back into view on the arena's screen, and Ky tugged down on the giant lever. All of Bathory's clones glanced up at the rotating images, as did Daniel, their battle paused in some brief, unspoken truce. He bit his lip as the flashing images slowly came to a stop. This could be good—or it could be extremely bad.

The slot settled into place. Electronic bleeps and bloops rang out from it as Daniel's eyes scanned the displayed text.

Anti-Magic Field

5:00

"Be careful what you wish for, Danny!" Ky said. "Magic is turned off in the arena for five minutes, regardless of any other rules or items! It's a straight-up brawl now!"

A rust-colored red light pulsed out from the slot machine, washing over the arena in a wave. His power vanished, like a cup slipping out of his hands. His magic senses went dead. Bathory warped into view twenty feet ahead of him, standing right in the middle of the field; her clones popped as the wave of light passed through them, vanishing one at a time. Daniel grinned at her.

Bathory smirked back at him. "What are you happy about? All you had going for you was that strange physical enchantment."

"That's what you think."

Daniel had one little ace still up his sleeve—his own natural abilities.

The contractor magic had changed him, physically, beyond giving him his power. He thought it had something to do with the way the magic entered his body over and over. Similar to Jack, he needed a lot less sleep. More uniquely, Jack was a lot stronger than he used to be. Daniel had different advantages—he was definitely stronger himself, but his senses were heightened. His vision was sharper, caught more detail. He was tougher, and most importantly—and why he thought it was a side effect of his powers—his reaction time was virtually superhuman. In a good old bar fight, he'd probably kick ass.

So he hefted his club and charged straight at her.

Daniel brought it up, then down, aiming for her head. Bathory leaned out to the side, letting his swipe pass by. Daniel kept his momentum going and spun all the way around, aiming his next blow about shoulder height.

Bathory ducked it, then stepped in and came up inside his reach faster than he could recover. Her fingers curled in tight, and her fist slammed into his gut.

Daniel stumbled back from the uppercut, feet crunching through the thick snow, and ended up coughing to get his air back. He felt like the wind was almost knocked out of him, but he managed to keep his feet. She was a lot stronger than she looked. *Okay. I might not be the only special one here.*

Bathory stepped in again, following him closely to eliminate the reach advantage of his club. A jab nailed him in the side of his face, and another glanced off his cheek as he reeled back. He managed to react to the third, stepping aside and getting his club up between them.

Bathory seemed to expect exactly that reaction. Her fist opened, and she caught the club with her hand. She leaned back and snapped out a kick as she jerked his arm down, landing a blow on his wrist and forcing the weapon from his hands. She spun it in her grip, then tossed it away over her shoulder.

Daniel cursed in his head. He thought he'd have an advantage, but she hadn't even bothered with her knife yet. He faced forward, raised his guard, and began to sidle around her, trying to work his way back to his weapon. She smiled in a way that told him she knew exactly what he was thinking, then snapped out a spinning high kick aimed at his head.

Daniel blocked it with both arms, but the kick had way more power than he was expecting, knocking him into the snow. He rolled away, staining his clothes with ice and mud, but avoiding a stomp at his head. He scrambled to his feet and set a guard again. She stepped forward, and he stepped back, trying to maintain his spacing—only to bump up against the arena wall. A glance told him she'd pushed him even farther away from his club.

"You're awful at this," Bathory said, closing the gap. "Although you're very quick, I grant you."

She jabbed with her left hand, a sharp punch aimed for his stomach. Daniel parried down with his guard, deflecting her fist away. She jabbed again, probing his defense, but he saw it coming and bobbed. Another—he moved to sidestep, anticipating it before it reached him.

Pain spiked through Daniel's neck as if someone had driven an iron rod through his spine. He screamed, wrenching his hands up to cover himself, half expecting Bathory's knife to be lodged in his throat—only to touch bare, unblemished skin.

Daniel almost slapped at the spot in a wild panic, trying to find something, anything to justify the pain. Repeated spikes of searing agony rammed their way up his neck, starting from his collarbone and twitching their way out his jaw. His hands found nothing wrong, no reason for any of it. His brain sputtered in confusion at the contradictory sensations.

Daniel only realized he'd fallen to his knees when Bathory's foot was in his face. He threw himself backward, sheer alarm momentarily distracting him from his neck. Her foot still connected, but instead of smashing his nose in, her heel glanced off his forehead. The hit stung, but he was able to scramble off to the side, dodging a follow-up kick and getting away from the wall.

The pain was gone by then, vanished as quickly as it had come. Daniel pat at his neck as he ran away, then looked at his hands, expecting blood—but there was nothing. *The hell was that?*

"Who's chasing who now?" Bathory said. She caught up with him near a boulder, one of the only points of reference left in the snow-blanketed arena. Daniel faked left and drew a kick from her. Bathory's boot struck the stone behind him, catching her leg up. Daniel came back in with a sharp uppercut while she was off balance.

Daniel's leg spasmed in pain, as if someone had dipped it in fire. His knee buckled mid-attack, and he collapsed like a wet paper bag, falling bodily into Bathory's waist. He flailed like a fish, part from the pain stabbing behind his knee, partly to get the hell away from her. Luckily, Bathory interpreted his fall as an intentional tackle, and she was just as interested in getting away from him.

Daniel dragged himself up to one foot as they separated, smearing the snow off his face, his other leg still tender—until it wasn't anymore. He frowned, cautiously putting weight on the limb, only to find it completely fine.

"You didn't mean to do that, did you?" Bathory said, squinting at him. "Body acting up without your magic? There had to be some kind of drawback to driving mana through your nervous system like that."

Daniel opened his mouth to respond when his left arm simply went numb. It flopped against his side. Daniel stared at it, willing it up, but he couldn't feel it—not even pins and needles. It was as if it wasn't there at all, existing as a dead piece of flesh sewed onto his shoulder.

"Ah-ha," Bathory said. "So that's what it is."

"What?" Daniel looked up at her, heart pounding in his chest. He could feel a sheen of sweat on his forehead. "What is this? What did you do?"

"I didn't do anything. Someone out there"—she gestured at the wall of the arena—"is getting impatient." Bathory drew her knife. Her eyes widened, and a half-manic grin slipped over her face. Gone was the nice lady next door. With how her hair was mussed from tumbling in the snow and across the ground, she looked like a mad scientist, ready to enact her latest experiment. "Let's see how fast you can run when your legs stop working."

****

Rasputin and Dracula were situated in the spellcasting chamber under their main office, and this time, Rasputin's eyes were also glued to the screen. They watched as Daniel rocketed off to a strong start, trying to catch Bathory early—but she, of course, expected such a move. Her body exploded into a fine black mist that then chewed through Daniel's white-gold energy at a tremendous pace.

"I could hit him now, while her curse is active," Rasputin said, stating it almost as a question. "Two curses would be tough to come back from."

"Too early," Dracula said. "Let's see how he deals with this first and inform ourselves. He might have countermeasures."

Daniel shielded himself from the curse's energy by moving his magic up to cover his skin. It was a tremendous waste—effective, but it would multiply his energy expenditure several times. Still, Dracula had to shake his head in amazement.

Daniel's physical sigil—or whatever the contractor magic had given him—almost operated like 10 or 12 spells at once. Like Jack, he could shift it on whim, dramatically redirecting the function of the mana with no more than a thought; no words, no conduits, no technique whatsoever, as easy as breathing.

It was true that magicians could wield their power intuitively, if it was a branch of magic they were familiar with, but the risk of backlash or unintended effects were correspondingly increased. Some spells were more flexible than others, exchanging raw power for the ability to convert between forms or change purpose entirely. It was also possible to rapidly chain different spells together, and with enough skill and proper timing, this allowed multiple effects to be achieved simultaneously. But nothing like this—this contractor magic. It was less a spell and more raw mana, wielded like a weapon, restricted by only a few vague guidelines. It was, without a doubt, one of the most impressive brands of magic he'd ever seen.

Even with his substantial reserves, Daniel was visibly frustrated with how quickly his energy was being consumed. The boy hunched over, concentrating, and the white light surrounding him flared like a miniature sun. Overwhelmed by brute force, the curse scattered, bursting to pieces. Daniel didn't notice, but Bathory's right hand twitched as her spell collapsed. The backlash whipped back into her body from where she'd channeled the mana, though she brought the chaos under control before it did lasting damage.

"I'm glad we waited," Rasputin said. "If he can shrug off a curse that easily..."

"It has to be at the precise moment," Dracula said, eyeing Daniel's feeble attempt to swipe away all Bathory's clones. The boy was powerful, but he lacked understanding of magical theory. Bathory's illusion simply let him smash through it, only to reform elsewhere with minimal effort. Clearly Bathory planned to bleed him of his mana before moving in for the kill. "Let's wait and see how this develops. She's not going to attack right away." Rasputin nodded back, returning most of his focus to the spell in front of him, though he did keep one eye on their viewing screen.

The underground casting chamber was about 20 feet on a side, lined with grey slate, all enchanted to contain excess magical energy if something went wrong with a larger, pre-planned spell. There were several work lights set up within, electrical leads running back up the sole staircase out of the chamber. A viewing screen had been hung up above the stairwell—the volume turned as low as possible, to spare them Ky's voice while still allowing them to hear. Dracula stood in the corner, eyes on the screen, giving Rasputin his space.

Rasputin sat cross-legged on the floor at the center of a drawn spell circle. Runes and figures sprawled out from his position, all formed using thin lines of fine metallic powder, a unique mix of tin doped with a few measures of gold and Rasputin's blood. The central rune was drawn entirely in blood—Daniel's blood. His straw-stuffed likeness laid at the exact middle of that construct, next to a small silver needle.

The complex, intertwined sigils were designed to ensure absolutely secrecy, slipping under the radar of PrisonWatch's usual precautions to prevent outside interference. A few other men and women stood at strategic points in the wider circle, members of the Order that would serve as living energy conduits to power and reinforce the spell, allowing Rasputin to devote his focus to wielding it. Jack was trussed up to the side, unconscious, a small cut on his arm already healing where they'd taken a sample. Flesh of a betrayer was critical to Rasputin's technique—even if the betrayal had been against Jack's own will, forcibly directed by Rasputin's control of his mind. The convenient synergy of the two magics gave Rasputin much of his power and influence back in his days on Earth.

On-screen, Daniel was standing in the middle of Bathory's blizzard, almost more interested in the spell than the threat to his life. Even when he was imprisoned in ice, he didn't seem fearful.

"Now?" Rasputin asked. "She's got him right where she wants him."

"Look closer. The cold isn't affecting him the way it should." Daniel bent into an awkward kneel, holding his club out, as if offering it to the oncoming ice. "He's got a plan."

"I could stop whatever it is, if I hit him."

"Patience. We've lost the timing."

"But—"

Even with the screen almost muted, the sound of the explosion echoed through their chamber. Daniel had somehow detonated his magic at the end of his club, while it was buried inside Bathory's ice. The meeting of magics caused a sharp backlash to affect Bathory's casting arm, and the shrapnel from her own construct knocked her away. She barely got her defenses back up before Daniel was on her.

Daniel laid into her shortly after, pressing Bathory's magic directly while he had the advantage. Rasputin flung his hand at the screen. "He almost had her because she's not taking this seriously! We need to act before he gets lucky."

"Not yet," Dracula said, more insistently. "He disregarded her curse easily, and we're casting at range, with Hell's ambient mana interfering. He'll ignore your spell too unless we catch him at the right time. We're not desperate enough yet to force him to burn up energy."

Rasputin huffed, but, mollified by the clear reasoning, settled back into position. His desire to take Daniel and his flippant attitude down a few pegs was interfering with his judgment. Dracula appreciated Rasputin's talents, but he wouldn't allow his impatience to create any ripples in their plan.

They kept watching as Daniel shouted at Ky in frustration, only to be shocked as she actually chose to interfere in the fight. It was typical that they changed things up if a fight went long, but those changes were—supposedly—randomized for fairness from a pre-selected list. No one really believed PrisonWatch let fall truly randomly, but allow the audience to control anything inside Hell was unprecedented. "What does this mean?" Rasputin asked. "Have you ever seen this before, this direct interference?"

"No," Dracula said. "The implications are unnerving. Ky wouldn't interfere because she felt like it. This was planned—easy enough to influence mass polling to get the results they want. She's only pretending to act at Daniel's prompting; this would have happened sooner or later."

"Do we abandon ship?" Rasputin asked. "It's still soon enough that I could wipe Jack's memory of the past hour."

Dracula examined the complex lines of the sigil they'd painstakingly created over the past day. It represented not only time and effort, but the resources of the order invested into the material components—not exactly cheap or easily found in Hell. His eyes stopped at the bound form of Jack, still curled up in one corner.

"What could possibly warrant this?" Rasputin asked.

Dracula squinted, his political mind working the angles. "I can come up with an explanation, but I'm not sure I believe it." Rasputin looked to him, so Dracula continued. "PrisonWatch controls everything that happens in Hell, but here they are, obviously reaching to appear transparent. They're trying to convince someone of something. Someone's watching this."

"Who's powerful enough to earn that much consideration?"

"I don't know, and that bothers me," Dracula said. "Perhaps a demon has risen to rival Beelzebub. It could be the Vorid, or the Klide."

"If we interfere," Rasputin said, "they could come down on us hard."

Dracula's eyes traced the lines of the formation. "It's too late. We're already committed. But be on your guard."

Rasputin nodded, and they both returned their attention to the fight. The flickering screen of the slot machine came to a halt. Their television displayed the text in bold in a flashing red chyron. Light washed over the arena as Daniel and Bathory had their magic wrenched away from them.

"Patience rewarded," Dracula said. "Activate the spell."

Rasputin narrowed his eyes, full focus on the screen. "Will it make it through to him? It's as if the energy there has vanished."

"A show trick of PrisonWatch," Dracula said. "And propaganda for Beelzebub's regime. It's a high-level manipulation of the Hell seal; there is no anti-magic, only their ability to grasp it is blocked." Dracula nodded to Rasputin. "Do it."

Rasputin didn't hesitate longer than necessary. First, he squeezed his fist and crushed their most expensive investment—a crystal sphere purchased through a merchant connection on a lower level of Hell. It temporarily relaxed Hell's seal on him and restored the majority of his magical powers. He flattened his hands to the ground, each fingertip carefully touching the metallic lines without nudging them out of place. Each one of the other magicians crushed their own, lesser version of the purchased spheres, enabling them to help Rasputin channel his spell.

Dracula, too, palmed a small, glass-like sphere. Weaker than the others in the set, his purpose wasn't to contribute to the spell, but to stand guard and direct Rasputin's efforts. Though it was extremely unlikely any of their enemies could infiltrate their headquarters outside of a territory war—let alone interfere in their own casting chamber—Dracula suffered nothing left to chance. Still, he didn't crush it immediately, not wanting the added expense if it turned out to be an unneeded precaution. He'd already had to swallow the cost of giving one to Daniel to maintain their deception.

The entire construct hummed with red-gold light in an instant, washing out the white utility lights. Their faces shimmered in the glow, alternating between shadow and a fiery orange as if they stood in the midst of a flickering sunset. The central bloody rune glowed brightest of all, a deep, almost maroon shade in the center of the curse formation. The rune pulsed as mana swirled about the circle and was sucked into its depths, a convulsing heart toward which all the lights and energies were bent.

A similar maroon cast shone around the silver needle, and it rose into the air. The needle hovered there, and the formation grew still and silent. Another pulse of energy turned the needle to action, and it shot down at the propped-up doll of Daniel and stabbed into its neck.

On screen, Daniel reeled and fell to his knees, having moved out of the way of Bathory's punch. He barely managed to escape a kick with a scrape to his forehead, retreating wildly to one side. Eventually, he managed to set himself square against her, ducking her jabs as he waited for a chance to strike back.

"He's going to attack," Dracula said, studying Daniel's feet. He had obvious tells. "Take a leg."

The needle, which had worked itself through the doll's neck, shifted direction. Rasputin grunted with effort as he leveraged the massive spell circle, and the needle jabbed back in, jamming through Daniel's leg. Daniel stumbled in time with the attack, but he'd moved faster than Dracula anticipated; rather than falling flat in front of Bathory, he fell on top of her. After a brief struggle, he managed to slip away again. In sheer arrogance, Bathory hadn't bothered drawing her knife yet, or the fight would already be over. "Damn."

"What happened?" Rasputin said. His focus was entirely on the magic, now, relying on Dracula for direction. Despite the extent of their preparations, at this range, and with the restrictions of Hell, it was all he could do to maintain the beating pulse of the spell. Moving the needle around was the equivalent of suddenly changing directions while hauling a 300-pound backpack.

"He got away," Dracula said. "Forget pain, cut off control to his arm. He's moving too fast to predict the usual way."

Rasputin managed a brief nod. He directed the needle to flip and jam itself into the doll's shoulder. The curse could only perform one function at a time—either cause pain or render a limb useless—but still powerful in that, once cast, it could be maintained indefinitely given energy. The members of the Order hunched over as Rasputin drew power from them directly for that purpose, using them as living batteries to maintain the activated state of the curse and keep Daniel's arm limp.

Bathory, seeing Daniel's state, realized what was happening. Dracula wasn't surprised; after all the long years, they were intimately familiar with one another's capabilities. She drew her knife, then set upon Daniel in a fury, threatening him with it to get him to flinch back, then whipping her legs at him in a series of kicks.

Daniel was pummeled backward, but the arena had ample space to retreat. Still, that only opened him up to more attacks. He held his good arm out to divert what he could as he racked up bruises in rapid succession. Bathory started laughing as she toyed with him, using the lethal threat of the knife to control his movements, jabbing and slicing through the air—only to take more cheap shots at him with punches from her free hand.

Rasputin's eyes occasionally darted to the screen as he held the spell in place. He growled through his teeth. "She has to know what we're doing," he said, more to the display screen than to Dracula. "End it!"

"Her mind has long since warped out of any normal shape," Dracula said. "She might be holding back to spite us, even at risk to herself."

"Psychopath," Rasputin muttered.

Dracula grunted in agreement. "All the more reason to put her down."

A guttural roar sounded from the corner of the room. Dracula looked over his shoulder in time to see Jack throw himself bodily into the spell circle, smearing a path through the sigils and scattering the delicate metallic dust. Even tied up, Jack thrashed on the floor, eyes red, a satisfied grin plastered on his face as he stared up at Dracula.

"What have you done?!" Dracula shouted.

"I trusted you!" Jack screamed. "I believed in your bullshit! Well fuck! Your! Shit!" Jack punctuated his words with his movements, kicking his legs as wildly as he could within the confines of his bindings. "And Fuck! You!"

The light in the room stuttered erratically, the balance of the spell thrown wild as a consequence of the ruined sigil, but Dracula was on him in an instant. He kicked Jack in the gut, hard, throwing him back into the corner. Dracula crushed his sphere, restoring access to his magic, and muttered a pair of command words. Tendrils of yellow light leapt out from his hands, gathered up Jack, and threw him face-first against the wall, pinning him there like a spiderweb.

Dracula worked with the closest magician to realign the sigils of the spell. Most of the material was lost, squeezed into cracks in the stone or stained onto Jack's clothes. Rasputin was silent, his face pale and coated with a sheen of sweat. He fought to keep the spell going as much as to keep the energy from rampaging out of control through his body. The rhythmic throb of the spell stuttered as they fought to save what they could.

They were able to recreate the core lines of the sigil, but the details were lost. The light of the magic stabilized, but Rasputin's heaved breaths were evidence that it wouldn't last long. The spell's heartbeat had taken on a permanent and erratic arrythmia.

Jack cackled in the corner, spitting his words out from where his face was pressed into the stone. "Hope I didn't almost accidentally kill you!"

"That's quite enough from you," Dracula said. The light binding Jack stuffed itself into his mouth, forestalling further interruptions. Dracula twitched a finger. The light wrapped Jack's limbs and forced him into the corner, jerking him forward one step at a time. Dracula was surprised it took some of his focus to do so. Even without his powers, Jack's strength was surprising. That dealt with, he turned back to the room. "Can it be salvaged?"

Rasputin's arms clenched and unclenched as he fought to hold onto his spell. His spread fingers trembled where he still pressed them on the stone. "One more act. Then I let it go or the backlash sends us to the crypt."

"He should've been unconscious for the rest of the day," Dracula said, glancing at Jack. "What happened?"

Rasputin struggled to answer; sweat was dripping down his face. "I don't...not sure. Miscalculated."

Rasputin was too impulsive, leaving things half-done in his eagerness to bring Jack to heel. Dracula should have dealt with it himself. Still, it wasn't all his fault. The contractors resisted his spells in unpredictable ways, as they'd most clearly seen with Daniel. Another strong piece of evidence they were doing the right thing by getting rid of him.

"We have one minute before they regain control of their magic." Dracula glanced up at the screen, eyes on Daniel—who, annoyingly enough, had made somewhat of a comeback, regaining possession of his club and swiping wildly to keep Bathory at bay. Bathory, for her part, was happy to keep toying with him, aiming her attacks at the weak side with his disabled arm. "Rally yourself. The next one needs to count."

****

Beelzebub was seated above the main command center of PrisonWatch.

The studio was located on-site within Hell's pocket dimension. It was situated above the prison proper, near the ice-coated surface. Windows at the top of the studio offered a direct view of the front 'gates' of Hell, including the sweeping backdrop of craggy black cliffs and snow-capped peaks stretching into the horizon.

It was the inside that was the true marvel. The command center wouldn't have been out of place on the bridge of an interstellar starship. Thousands of screens were monitored by hundreds of observers, a flickering kaleidoscope of simultaneous events that dwarfed the scale of human television networks. Dozens of managers directed the 54 main channels and 612 sub-channels, each following multiple, carefully-curated *narratives* active at any given time in various locations in the prison. Supervisors each had additional control of hundreds more popular streams—not official channels, but dedicated followings of individuals or teams popular enough to generate advertising revenue.

Beelzebub leaned back, sitting above it all, feet planted on the control board in front of his swivel chair. The main screen dominating the room was locked on Daniel Fitzgerald's duel with Elizabeth Bathory. A female devil nearby was dressed to distract; she offered him a squirming grub, holding it near his mouth. Without looking away from the fight, he opened his jaws and bit off the front and a good portion of fatty underside of the grub in one shark-toothed chomp, like a child ripping off the head of an animal cracker.

A female undine, another member of his harem, swooped in to dab his chin before any juices could leak down it. He stretched back as the still-twitching corpse of his snack was disposed of by a third servant, quickly replaced with another by the first. He did really prefer the front half of the grubs, and, if he had a choice, why bother choking down the legs? Too gamey.

Bathory was currently taking advantage of Daniel's limp arm. Or, rather, not taking advantage, which was somewhat boring. The young human made a pathetic punching bag.

Beelzebub considered the impact of the lack of magic on the advertising for future reruns of the battle. It was an unusual move, especially when audiences were used to the flash and spectacle of spells, but he was tired of waiting for Dracula to make his move; simple enough to bait him into it by putting Daniel at a disadvantage. The boy had little practical combat skill, but his speed was a small saving grace.

Beelzebub didn't know how far Xik's reach extended, but if he could sneak into and out of the core of Beelzebub's government offices unopposed, he probably had some ability to peer into the inner workings of the prison. With that expectation in mind, Beelzebub allowed for the hands-off approach with Daniel. Events proceeded as he predicted, Dracula conspiring to dump him like the remains of one of his grubs, just like anyone else he felt he couldn't control. Dracula's neurotic inability to accept working equally with strong allies was a chronic downfall. He only tolerated Rasputin because he was weak enough to not feel threatened by him.

Beelzebub tapped the control board with a toe, bringing up some statistics. It was with pleasant surprise he watched the live audience numbers tick up bit by bit. Some mundane fisticuffs might be healthy for the audience after all.

"Now, Beelzebub," a slimy voice said, "this all doesn't seem very sporting."

It took a significant force of will for Beelzebub to maintain his cool. His servants leapt back in surprise. Beelzebub dropped his feet and rotated his chair, facing his guest. "Xikanthus. How could you imply that I, of all devils, would be unfair?"

The frog, dressed in his black pinstripe suit—a pathetic mockery of human business garb—gestured to the screen. "You can't tell me you don't control that slot machine device. Or that you don't know about the curse being cast on Daniel from afar."

Beelzebub waved away his servants. They scrambled to comply, abandoning the office. They'd been informed of Xik's identity previously, but Beelzebub hadn't bothered with the sensitive details, only that he might visit unexpectedly. Xik's appearance, in defiance of introduction, protocol, or any warning whatsoever, was a clear enough message that he was someone they didn't want to be around any longer than necessary.

"The prisoners are fighting," Beelzebub said, shrugging. "I haven't interfered. If they put in the effort to avoid Hell's restrictions, it's allowed. The dramatic tension is great for ratings."

"Hmm." Xik's tone was skeptical. "If you say so. But I'd like you to put a stop to those men muffing up the fight. Daniel should get his fair shake."

"I'm not sure what you mean," Beelzebub said. "Our agreement didn't include protecting the boy. Just using him."

"And so I am." Xik turned to the screen; he watched Daniel being used as a target for Bathory's jabs and kicks for a few seconds. "Daniel is a measurement of human potential. I want to see how he reacts, here at this most important juncture. What will he be willing to do to win?"

"He's barely had any time in the prison to grow, like you planned."

Xik shrugged. "The results won't change our agreement. You'll get your contract, as promised."

Beelzebub flicked his finger against his throat, producing a single, hollow snort. "Alright. I'm happy to demonstrate that I can be flexible. But you'll find it's a waste of time."

Beelzebub tapped into the key to the Longinus. It reacted cheerily, jumping to obey his control, as if it couldn't wait to be used. That always bothered him, as if the *thing*—an inanimate object—had a mood. He wasn't worried about Xik detecting its usage; hidden within his soul, the key might as well not exist. The greatest risk to its secrecy was discussing it openly with Lilith.

Within Hell, the keys had absolute control over space. A portal opened directly next to Beelzebub's chair without spell, artifice, or preamble. It was a swirling gap in reality linked straight to the private spellcasting chamber of the Order of the Dragon.

Beelzebub reached through with an arm, barely glancing up from his chair. He grabbed Rasputin's throat. A pulse of mana disrupted the man's concentration, and Beelzebub lifted. Rasputin's fingertips ripped away from where they were temporarily fused to the spell circle. Beelzebub tossed him into a corner of the room; he slammed into the stone and collapsed in a heap, dead or unconscious. It didn't matter—in Hell, both of those states were temporary.

The red glow of the spell rapidly flickered, spiraling out of control. The room looked like the inside of an overheated furnace about to blow.

Beelzebub looked through the portal and locked eyes with Dracula. To his credit, the man stood firm in the midst of the sudden chaos, holding his gaze. "Your interference in this battle is over," Beelzebub stated.

"Did we offend?" Dracula asked.

"Do humans explain to bugs why they get stomped on?" As Dracula's face twisted in anger, Beelzebub withdrew his arm and waved the portal shut.

Xik chuckled. "He'll remember that."

"That was the limit of human potential, there," Beelzebub said. "It's locked inside my prison. They're too afraid of themselves to amount to anything. Let the Vorid feast on them. No great loss."

"Sadly," Xik said, dryness seeping through his words, "the Klide decided to stop the forward progress of the Vorid, and that involves saving mankind."

"You'll have to save it from itself, first," Beelzebub said. He gestured back to the screen. "And here we have two humans, a young fool who knows nothing and an old woman who's lost her mind. A microcosm if there ever was one."

Xik watched the countdown close out on the so-called anti-magic field. "Let's see what that young fool can do."

****

Daniel poured magic through his arms and legs as the clock on the wall of the arena finally dropped to zero. Power flooded into his limbs, as sweet as the relief he felt in his head. He zipped away from Bathory's next punch—which had turned into a fistful of flames. He skidded to a halt at one end of the arena, pausing to eye his competition.

He didn't trust the arm holding his club, or any part of his body, for that matter. He felt like he'd been thrown into a washing machine with Mike Tyson for a full ten rounds and a rinse cycle. It was hard to feel a part of himself that didn't ache or hadn't taken a blow. Somehow he'd managed to avoid her knife, but he wasn't sure if that was his own ability or if she enjoyed the act of threatening him with it more than actually stabbing him.

He looked at the screen—and annoyingly, there was another countdown clock, this time going down from two and a half minutes. It was half the time of the previous segment; he wasn't sure if that was somehow important.

"Daniel's taken a beating," Ky's voice called out, "but he's not finished yet! What happens after yet another mysterious countdown, we won't yet reveal—stay tuned! Perhaps it will be a…reversal, of fortunes!"

"Well?" Bathory's voice came to him from across the arena, not shouted, but clear as crystal in his ears. "What other tricks do you have?"

"I don't need tricks, unlike some people!" Daniel shouted back.

Bathory chuckled. "Alright. Let's do this the old-fashioned way."

Daniel could have sworn that they had been doing it the old-fashioned way, but he raised his club regardless, ready for whatever she threw at him. Magic flashed in both her hands, twin colors. One was a dark purple, almost black, and the other was stark white.

And then, she was gone.

Daniel's senses screamed that she was directly behind him.

He whipped his club out as he turned to face her. His bruised bones and muscles protested against the sudden movement, but he ignored the pain, following through at full power. His glowing weapon crashed through a dozen shadowy limbs reaching out from Bathory's figure; claws, tendrils, hooks, hands. The hands and arms vanished to smoke on contact with his club, but reformed almost instantly.

The regenerated limbs kept up their attack, swiping, clawing, and slashing. Daniel danced away in time to avoid injury, but not before they opened a few tears on the front of his shirt. One limb transformed into a hammer and smashed down at his head. He sidestepped the attack, and when it struck the ground beside him, he swung his club to cut the tendril in half, and the hammer tip dissolved into smoke.

They fought in a furious, rapid-fire series of blows, Daniel using sheer speed to fend off waves of attacks. He used physical sigils to give him a directional boost or redirect his jumps midair, staying a half-step ahead of the living shadows. Ky called the shots like a boxing announcer, falling into her element as they dueled with their respective magics.

Daniel got caught between a half-dozen shadow arms, three from either side closing in like a vise. On instinct, he blocked half of them using his sigil as a shield. They slammed into it with the force of a car crash; his left arm trembled, throbbing with the effort, but the magic held. He whipped his club in an arc into the remaining batch, smashing them to smoke. Unlike her illusions, Daniel felt a satisfying sense of contact as he destroyed the limbs, which almost helped restore a normal cadence to his blows. Trying to hit *nothing* was an exercise in frustration.

Daniel stepped toward Bathory's position, trying to take advantage of the opening, but the regrowing tendrils clustered together, walling her off. As soon as she was protected, they lashed out wildly, covering the ground in front of her with hard-tipped whips and scratching claws. He retreated, and they didn't follow far; their reach extended about ten or fifteen feet from where she stood.

He shoved power into his legs and bounced off a series of sigils, rapidly darting to her exposed side. He went in for an attack, but the tendrils bent at an unnatural angle, sweeping in to block him. Daniel reversed course, coming to rest outside her range while he tried to think.

Bathory didn't spare him the time. The black light held in her hand flashed brighter, and new bundle of tendrils grew under her feet, extending and articulating on unnatural joints. The legs churned through the snow, propelling her forward like a distorted, shadowy spider. Daniel was forced back as the tendrils began to hone in on him.

Daniel warred with the claws and fangs of her conjured shell, but he couldn't break through in a meaningful way. He was forced to fight on the run, working to stay outside the spell's reach. A few times, he tried to circumvent the tendrils and hit her from behind, but their flexibility and independent movement made that strategy a waste of energy. He couldn't afford risking a serious injury; unlike her, he didn't know any healing magic. If only he had some kind of shield—maybe he could bully his way through to the middle.

The shadow limbs moved quickly, with her protection as their priority. Often they altered their trajectory without her input, making it difficult to bait them out of the way to create a weak point. Destroying them didn't help much, as they started growing right next to her. He was always too late after dispatching them to press through her defense.

He might eventually wear her down, but he was already too worn down himself. He had his magic back, but that didn't help him recover from the beating she'd delivered when they were stuck without it. His legs were so tired and sore they were shaking when he really put weight on them. In fact, she was probably only fighting directly now that she could count on him slipping up at some point.

He churned his feet through the snow as he strategized. Bathory was right on his heels, never giving him an instant of rest. Her shadow-claws had no trouble finding purchase on the ground beneath the ice. He was able to outpace her, but she was always right behind, and their fight was churning the arena into a pit of mud. He used sigils to balance and save himself from tripping in the muck. He kept his eyes on the core of the spell, sometimes catching snatches of Bathory through the forest of shadowy limbs.

Daniel sensed something happening inside—magic was coalescing. It was focusing, tighter and tighter, being gathered to a single point. He frowned as he dodged another salvo of claws; they scraped foot-long furrows in the snow, down through to the mud, but left him untouched.

The hair on the back of his neck was standing up; it was as if he could hear the ratchet of a guillotine being raised above his neck. He caught a glimpse of a red twinkle as he bashed another tendril into smoke, somewhere inside Bathory's shell. As his eyes landed on it, his spine shivered. Acting on that instinct, Daniel made a sigil under one foot and drove himself left, bounding up and away over the snow, even though there weren't any attacks headed his way.

An instant later, a laser-red light flared out from within the shadows. A beam of fire burned a path across the floor of the arena, directly through where Daniel had been standing, all the way to the far wall and across part of the ceiling, leaving behind a charred and smoking trail of ash. The ash detonated, erupting in a conflagration of fire that melted away the snow and scorched the exposed side of the boulders.

Daniel reeled from the sudden destruction. A wave of air rushed over him, and sweat beaded on his forehead from the heat. If it wasn't for that last-minute gut feeling, he would've been charcoal.

"Bathory launches a surprise attack to roast Daniel," Ky shouted, "but misses by a hair! Daniel's so fast, it's like he's got a sixth sense, but he's tiring quickly. If he can't turn this around, it's only a matter of time until he gets himself a high-powered sunburn!"

Daniel felt a rising sense of dismay. Unlike most magicians, Bathory was skilled enough to fight a battle while channeling two different spells at once. Now he not only had to contend with the nest of shape-changing shadow blades, but who knows what else she might launch, still hidden within total cover. He hadn't laid a hand on her since she first cast the spell.

Daniel glanced at the clock above the slot machine up on the wall. It felt like they'd been fighting for an hour, but there was about a minute left—and then something *else* would happen. He checked back. Bathory hovered opposite from him across the short side of the arena, supported by the shadows, but she didn't make a move to close the gap.

"It looks like that spell took a lot out of Bathory—or maybe our contenders are trying to get inside each other's heads," Ky said. "The clock is counting down while the fighters gather their reserves with enough time left for one more big exchange!"

Daniel used the respite to wrack his brain. Maybe he could combine two ideas—first, lure all the limbs to one side. Then, speed back around and go in at maximum force. He might not beat their ability to redirect, but he could have a shot if he went all out—no intention to leave himself a backdoor to retreat. He'd either make it through the shadows or get himself diced into bitesize pieces. But if things kept going the same way, he might not be so lucky the next time she tried to blow him up. Again, he found himself wanting a shield—that would reduce a lot of the risk.

A flash of inspiration struck him. He didn't have a shield, but he did have his sigil. Once he created it, it didn't move—

couldn't move—so he never thought to use it that way. It wouldn't be very flexible, but he'd been able to block her tendrils earlier when she caught him from two sides. It wasn't perfect, but it was better than nothing, and it might catch her off guard long enough to land a hit.

Daniel planted himself, ready to enact his plan, when the snow and mud rolled under his feet. Twin mounds of stone formed from the earth on either side of him, then closed in, trying to snap shut and smash him flat. Daniel jumped, soaring into the air as the stone slammed shut underneath him. A thunderclap of air rustled his hair and clothes.

A pulse of magic made Daniel snap his head up.

Bathory and all her shadowy fury had teleported above him, and she had pushed off the ceiling, falling straight toward him even as he was still rising midair from his jump. Her limbs were stretched out in every direction, enclosing him in a circle intended to prevent another escape. As he landed on the surface of the stone, Daniel raised his free arm and his club and formed two sigils simultaneously, one touching each hand.

Daniel poured energy into his magic as Bathory closed in. The white-gold lines underlying the haze of magical energy surged with light and merged together, like crystal vines growing and supporting one another. The intertwined sigils flashed and sealed shut, and the hazy barrier nearly doubled in size, thickest in the middle.

Bathory's shadow constructs slammed into the barrier. The spell buckled and warped under the repeated hammer blows. The spell held firm, poised above Daniel's body like a gold umbrella.

After a few more failed attempts, the limbs contorted and bent around the edges of the barrier, stretching to go around what they couldn't smash through. Daniel focused on the points of his elbows. Two new sigils appeared there, tangent to his body. The linking effect multiplied as the borders of the new sigils sprang out to meet the two at his hands, stretching the size of his spell out around his body and blocking the progress of the tendrils. Despite attempting to smash, stab, or burrow through with a variety of implements—hammers, axes, claws, and daggers—they couldn't breach the golden haze created by the spell.

The stone below Daniel suddenly began to grow, reaching up to grab at his legs. Daniel created two more sigils at the point of his feet. They flashed into existence as the stone crushed down on him. Daniel grunted and grit his teeth; holding back solid rock was a lot harder than keeping the immaterial shadows at bay.

The rock contorted and wrapped around his barriers almost like thick gel rather than rock, manipulated by stone-shaping magic. They reached halfway, making contact with the shadows, but by that time, Daniel had created two more sigils using his knees as extra points of focus.

Daniel was consumed by the effort, suddenly caught holding a total defense against the oncoming attacks. He felt like a man standing in the jaws of a beast, holding it open as shadows crunched down from above and stone teeth pincered his legs below. The defense was working, but he'd walled himself into a corner. Holding up the sigils like this was like trying to balance a row of spinning plates, and the plates were stacked on his shoulders and weighed a hundred pounds each.

As Daniel poured his tired magical reserves into the sigils, they steadily grew, increasing in size as he reinforced them. When the edges finally touched, the sigils all bound and locked together, enclosing him within solid golden fencing. While it still took more energy to maintain, the amount of focus he needed was cut in half; now, it was as if he was maintaining one solid sigil, rather than multiple individual pieces.

"It looks like Daniel still has a few tricks up his sleeve!" Ky shouted. "Caught off guard against Bathory's three-pronged offensive, he's managed to hold her at bay and draw the fight to another standstill."

The strengthening effect of his sigils was additive. The shadows scraped at his raised arms and hands to no avail. The stone finished entrapping his lower half, but despite how it squeezed, trying to smash him, it couldn't break through. Daniel blinked back sweat from his eyes, trying to ignore the sting. Despite the chaos of the battle, the burning need for victory, the fear of losing, he found himself grinning, smiling stupidly up at the mass of shadows where Bathory was hiding.

He was holding his own. He could do this.

And then he felt Bathory start to gather magic again. The stone stopped moving, but four red points of light gathered above him. They started blazing brighter and brighter as Bathory fed them power, another set of flaming lasers aimed to pierce his shield and turn him into ash.

He was locked in by his own barriers. There was nowhere to run; in order to move, he'd have to drop the sigil first. He was cupped by solid rock up to his thighs, and the shadows would shred him. All he could do was pour power into the shield and hope it could save him from the worst of it.

"With Daniel trapped in her spell, Bathory is pulling out all the stops—but she might not complete it. We're down to the wire—five! Four! Three!"

Daniel grit his teeth as the light of the lasers shined like stars. They grew so bright he winced, shutting his eyes and turning away his head. He poured everything he had into the barriers, trying to focus his strength on the top portion.

"Two! One! Zero!"

A wave of grey light washed over them. The shadows vanished. The burning lights disappeared. Daniel's sigils warped out of existence, and his power was cut away from him, snatched out of his hands. The stone crumbled beneath him, almost instantly shattering into powder. Daniel tumbled to the ground.

It was hardly his first time making midair maneuvers. Daniel kept his head and landed feet first. He hit hard through his heels, bent his knees to absorb the shock, and rolled backward onto his butt. Despite his best efforts, the force jarred through his body, knocking the wind out of him and sending a stinging pain through his hips. The softness of the mud probably saved anything from being broken.

Bathory slammed into the ground after him, having fallen a good ten feet farther. Daniel caught her trying to turn her momentum into a roll, but it didn't matter how good you were—the human body could only take so much. She collapsed into a pile a distance away from him with a sharp cracking sound.

Daniel could move his head, but when he tried to get up, his hand slipped through the ice and mud and he fell back. His chest was emptied of air; he coughed and spluttered, trying to get it back, trying to breathe. The breath didn't come.

He'd pushed himself hard, harder than he knew he could. His magic supported him, let him drive past his limits, and now he was paying for it with an absolute burning exhaustion. His chest heaved as he laid there, lungs fighting for oxygen.

His head fell back into the snow. Icy wet soaked his hair. He brought his feet in, gritting his teeth with the effort, but his shoes slid out through the mud. His legs didn't ache so much as he had trouble feeling them. The cold worked its way from his hair down his neck, seeping in under his shirt.

A memory rose in his mind's eye. He remembered lying on his back on a winter day in Boston, making snow angels with Rachel. He'd hit her twice with snowballs before she came up and stuffed ice under his jacket.

Daniel clenched his jaw and lifted his head. He put his hands on the ground and tried to lift himself up. His palms slid through the mud, but he caught himself on his elbows and held there, refusing to fall all the way back again.

Bathory crawled to her knees. She cradled one arm, which Daniel saw was bent unnaturally at the wrist. She dug through the mud and snow, searching. A wink of a metallic blade caught his eye—she'd find it in seconds as soon as she turned around.

Daniel forced a cough up his throat, and finally, air rushed back into his chest. He turned up and over on his side, beginning his own desperate hunt for his club. He spotted the handle sticking up from a snow drift and hobbled over.

He drew his weapon free from the snow in time to hear Bathory's shriek. She charged at him, broken arm flailing behind her, the knife held tight in her good hand. Her hair was frayed at the edges; mud and damp was smeared across her face and clothes. Her eyes gleamed with a wild light.

Bathory cut and slashed wildly with her knife, technique forgotten in a flurry of blows. She all but ignored her broken limb as Daniel fended her off, his club sometimes smashing against the dagger's edge with a sharp ring of metal on metal. "I had you right where I wanted you!" Bathory screamed the words; her expression was contorted between a manic grin and a mask of frustration. "But I'll kill you all the same and take my time skinning your corpse. So just! Hold! Still!"

Daniel knocked away her swings; his mind worked furiously, but his bruised and exhausted body was a step behind. His eyes flicked over to the wall—it had another countdown, under a minute left for whatever was next. The time intervals were getting shorter—or maybe they'd been down on the ground longer than he thought.

"Don't you look away from me!" Bathory said. She flipped the knife in her hand and cut back the other way, catching Daniel off-guard. She cut him across his forearm, drawing blood, but her knife stopped against bone. He winced back from the pain automatically, it wasn't that bad. He was washed in so much ache he hardly felt it.

Maybe I can use that.

Bathory came in wide with a follow up strike. Daniel raised his other forearm, smashing away the knife blow by taking another slash through the skin on the outside of his forearm and keeping the damage superficial. She was left wide open.

Daniel's club came up and smashed her broken wrist. He felt the crunch as he connected home. Bathory screamed and tumbled backward, rolling through the snow. Daniel pressed forward to finish the job—too quickly. The ground, churned from the fight, proved terrible footing, and as he put all his weight forward he face-planted into the snow.

"It's a life-or-death struggle in the mud!" Ky said. "Both our contestants have taken tough blows, and both are exhausted and nearly out of resources. They're struggling just to stand!"

Daniel hoisted himself to his feet, grunting and groaning like an old man pushing his way up from a chair. Bathory made it back up too, wincing at slight shifts in her wrist. They stood there, panting, their breath misting in the low temperature, staring at each other.

Bathory started laughing. "I've lost my edge. Who knew a cute little greenhorn would give me this much trouble?"

"I've been learning a lot the hard way," Daniel said. "Earth is under attack, in case you hadn't heard."

Bathory straightened, positioning her damaged hand out of Daniel's line of sight. She took in the clock, gauging the time left in the round. "I have heard. Poor little mundanes, harvested for life energy like so much wheat. If I hadn't been sentenced here, my empire with a united humanity behind me might've stood a chance. Let the fools suffer in penance, I say."

"Billions of normal people are blameless."

"Little ants," Bathory said, "squashed underfoot as the giants dance. Such a tragedy."

"That's people you're talking about," Daniel said. "Real people, with real lives."

Bathory shrugged. "Mundanes."

Daniel spat into the snow. "Then you really deserve to be here. You have more in common with the Vorid than humanity."

"Maybe I do. But magicians have always held themselves above the chaff." She cocked her eyebrow. "Do you think Dracula—Rasputin—any of the magicians you know truly relate to or care about the *normal* people? People will use you as long as you make yourself useful, whether they're powerless mundanes or born of the blood. Then they'll get rid of you as soon as the larger threat is gone." She chuckled, holding the back of her good hand up against her mouth. "Oh, rather, excuse me. They were so impatient they've already rid themselves of you."

"What other people do doesn't change what's wrong and what's right," Daniel said.

"So self-sacrificing," Bathory said, mock-breathless. "A true hero of the people—*people* who don't know you exist and don't care what you're doing. You think you have it all figured out, but you can't even see the knife at your back."

Ky started counting down again. Both of them looked up at the clock. There were less than ten seconds left in the round, and probably an equal amount of time left in their temporary standoff—until something shook them up again.

Daniel felt anger turn in his gut. He'd risked too much and worked too hard to be put down by a crazed murderer, but it sounded like she might know something he didn't. "What are you talking about? Do you know something about Jack?"

Bathory laughed again. "You're a blind pawn in someone else's game, Daniel. You aren't truly to blame; such is the fate of many. Far worse is what little independent force you possess is wasted, defending people who will never truly thank you, who have classified you as a wild beast that must be put down. Just like Dracula. Just like me."

Daniel rolled his eyes. "Spare me the psychoanalysis. The pity party never ends with you people."

Bathory ignored him, turning up to the clock. They both watched as the current round came to an end. Daniel had no doubt that their chatty pause would end with it.

Chapter 19
Monsters

"And...time!" Ky said. "As you've seen on your screens, we've spent the last round collecting an at-home audience vote for what happens next. Let's reveal the top four results!"

Ky gestured to the slot machine's screen like a game show model revealing a brand-new car. Four lines were listed with little percentages showing how popular each choice had been.

Full Magical Power
Anti-Magic Field
Klaxyde Swarm
Arena Shift

"Great choices everyone! Now we'll randomly select two of these four to shake things up. Start the roulette!"

Two colored bars began to flicker and flash, one blue, the other red. They jumped from choice to choice at random, humming along with cheery music and matching laser lights. After a few long seconds, they stopped, and the two selected choices zoomed larger to take up the whole screen: Full Magical Power and Klaxyde Swarm.

"Now we're talking!" Ky said. "Contestants, prepare for battle!"

A pulse of energy washed over both of them, removing the seal blocking Daniel from his magic. He reached for it, calling on his powers.

Instantly, that power slammed into his grip—the sum total of all his effort on Earth fighting the Vorid, more power than he'd ever wielded at once. He could feel an electric potential in his hands and feet; his skin glowed with light from holding the stuff. A thunderstorm of magic roiled inside of him; he felt less like himself and more like a barely restrained hurricane of force, condensed into a Daniel-shaped body. The aches and pains; the cuts across his arms; and the heavy weight of exhaustion all faded into the background—not gone, but washed out by the wave of energy surging from his head to his toes.

He'd never been in this state since killing the Vorid lord, and he'd never really used that power. He'd gone almost directly into willing captivity after that fight, magic sealed away, and then he was banished. This was his first time truly coming to grips with the absolute force of his full power.

And it felt good.

Daniel glanced up.

If he was a flaring beacon, then Bathory was a mass of slithering shadows. Her multi-limbed spell bolstered and grew into a heaving ball of tentacles three or four times larger than it had been. It was so dense he couldn't see through it; Bathory was hidden within, protected by layers of shadowy mass. They faced off across what was now an incredibly short distance, a tiny gap either of them could cover in a blink.

Magic pulsed between them. Something was warping into view, teleported into the arena. Daniel gaped at the creature that arrived, suddenly sitting on the mud-churned grass off to the side.

The Klaxyde was a bubbling pile of green ooze. The snow beneath it vanished; the mud below that started sizzling, letting off faint white smoke. Whatever grass was left was eaten away in an instant. The pulsing flesh carried a scent like vinegar mixed with rotting dog food, and it hit Daniel's nose like a hammer. He winced back from it, blinking water from his eyes.

"Human versus human versus Klaxyde!" Ky shouted. "Let's see who eats who in this dramatic finale clash! Bump them up to 5 minutes! If all three contenders are still alive at the end of the time limit, both fighters lose and suffer all penalties together!"

Daniel cursed in his head as he heard that last part. He either had to kill this thing—whatever the hell it was—or kill Bathory.

Both Bathory and Daniel hesitated as the Klaxyde got its bearings. Its body shifted left, seemingly inspecting Bathory's tendrils and tentacles, before shifting right, looming closer to Daniel. He took a few cautious steps back, eyeing it carefully.

Within the ooze, Daniel's enhanced eyesight picked out small purples spheres that glowed with light. He imagined it was a magical source of energy, though he couldn't feel anything distinctly magical about the creature itself. The purple spheres—ribbed, and coated with black dots—swam and shifted through the translucent green flesh as the Klaxyde moved.

Daniel was a little confused—from the name of the creature, he'd assumed there would be more than one of it. Perhaps the purple orbs were the swarm. It was unlike anything Daniel had ever seen or heard of—no head, no organs, no visible appendages or real means of getting around. It was a big pile of ooze, as if a bacterium had grown a million times larger.

The purple spheres gathered into the center of the creature, then burst to the outside edges in a blink, stretching the oozing flesh out like the weighted points of a net. The Klaxyde fell toward Bathory's slithering tendrils, collapsing directly on top of her. Daniel expected her to bat the creature away, but its flesh dissolved the shadow tendrils on contact. Daniel watched its size multiply as it physically ate through the magic, absorbing the energy and converting it to mass. The fleshy net turned into a tidal wave that threatened to completely crush Bathory underneath.

Daniel kept his distance as the Klaxyde closed the noose on its trap. But Bathory had an easy way out—she teleported away, well before it could bring its bulk all the way around her. Her tendrils were far worse for the wear, hacked off at the base in all directions, and they weren't regrowing. The Klaxyde shuddered and grew even larger—Daniel suspected it had absorbed some of the magic from her teleport.

Daniel didn't waste the chance. He poured on his fresh reserves of magic and rebounded off multiple sigils, circumventing the convulsing Klaxyde and blasting toward Bathory. He came in hard with his club, but she teleported again as he arrived, and his swing whiffed air. She teleported again in rapid succession; Daniel's eyes followed her carefully as she blinked in and out of existence, stopping at the far wall of the arena.

The Klaxyde cast itself over Daniel's position, leading with the purple cores. Daniel instinctively threw out a sigil with his hand to block it off; the barrier surged to life instantly, larger and sturdier with his increased rate of magical flow. The ooze slapped against the sigil, and for a moment, it held—and then its flesh began to pour down through the barrier like rainwater through a leaky roof. As the holes widened, the sigil's underlying structure disintegrated, and the entire thing vanished. It felt as if it was ripped out of his hands; the magic went with it, sucked into the oozing monster.

Daniel vacated his spot with lightning speed, easily escaping the entrapment of the Klaxyde. It was dangerous, but with his enhanced agility, it might as well have been crawling along. It definitely had some ability to feed on magic. Normally, he'd keep his distance and avoid it, but he needed to make something happen within the time limit, or he'd lose by default anyway.

Daniel's senses alerted him to Bathory casting a new spell. An incoming fireball was aimed near Daniel's feet, shooting down between him and the ooze. Daniel channeled magic through his body, flooding himself with it to test the limits of his power. As his perception speed multiplied, the fireball seemed to put on the brakes. It trundled gradually through the air like a fastball pitch played back in slow motion. The Klaxyde was even slower by comparison, reaching out toward him at a speed Daniel could walk around and avoid.

He jogged away from the fireball, holding his magic at maximum force. The momentum of his speed was a strange thing; his shoes slipped oddly on the mud, as if he couldn't get good traction. From his view, he was jogging, but from a normal perspective, he must have been taking off as fast as the fireball. Stopping was worse than starting; he slid awkwardly until he made a physical sigil under his feet and bent his knees to come to a halt. His distended sense of time didn't stop the forces involved playing out as they normally would.

Daniel cut the flow of magic off. His maximally enhanced state was powerful, but he didn't want to waste too much experimenting. As time zipped back into its normal rhythm, the fireball exploded behind him, knocking him forward a step and washing him over with a wave of hot air. Scattered debris knocked against his back.

The Klaxyde was scalded with steam—vaporized snow—and globs of magical fire. Superheated bits of mud flung away by the explosion poked holes in the creature, zipping through like thrown rocks. Daniel thought the fire would destroy parts of it too, burn away its watery flesh. Instead, it only fed the creature's endless appetite, increasing its size even further. Daniel observed as the purple orbs steered the body around, gobbling up splatters of the napalm-like flames. As Daniel watched, many of the orbs swelled, then split in two, like cells dividing inside a giant oozing bacterial culture.

"What a disgusting creature," Bathory said. Daniel looked over at her. She glanced back at him, smiled, and shrugged. "Have fun." Light flickered in one of her hands, and she vanished.

Daniel cursed under his breath as Ky laughed, a little too jolly in announcing how Bathory had abandoned him to deal with the Klaxyde on his own. He could ferret her out if he scryed, but he'd have to focus in place, leaving himself open to an attack by the green amoeba.

Daniel wasn't sure if the Klaxyde could sense or locate Bathory with her invisibility spell, but it turned on him anyway, having gathered itself back together following the explosion. Daniel skipped back as a tidal wave of pulsing green crashed down in front of him. The purple spheres led the creature as it stretched after him, surging left and then right as Daniel dodged. Contrary to his expectations, its speed increased with its size—or maybe with the number of control spheres—but it was still unable to touch him. When Daniel ran out of room, he jumped into the air. He sailed over the creature, out of reach of stretching green projections, and landed neatly back on the other side.

"It looks like Daniel can keep this up all day!" Ky shouted. "Too bad he doesn't have all day!" Daniel glanced at the clock at her words—they were already down to three and a half minutes. "He'd better keep his guard up, the swarm is changing hunting patterns!"

Daniel looked back at his foe to find it shrinking. The purple spheres gathered in the center, and it was drawing in on that central point; the green color grew dark, almost opaque, as its flesh condensed. One sphere swam up to the outer skin, and a projection grew around it, lifting it up into the air. The purple sphere was bound in a hard, forest-green shell of glistening ooze, hung above the main mass on a long stalk. The stalk leaned, tensing up as it did, almost like a tree branch being bent back.

The stalk snapped, and the sphere of slime was flung toward Daniel at high speed. Daniel fell onto his butt to dodge the sudden attack; air swished as the sphere passed by. A tendril of green reached out from it, snagging his shirt and tearing a hissing hole in his clothing, but it was moving too fast to hang on.

The sphere continued across the ground as Daniel popped to his feet, maintaining its speed toward the other side of the arena. He glanced at his shoulder. The edges of the hole in his shirt were blackened and smelled awful, as if acid had eaten a portion of it away. *Okay. Definitely don't get touched.*

Daniel glanced over his shoulder in time to see a handful more of the spheres winding up, like an array of spoons about to fling food at him from across the cafeteria.

Daniel poured magic into his legs and shoved off a sigil, not trusting the mud to give him the boost he needed. The hardened spheres, each controlled by a purple orb, blew through where he'd been standing, then continued on, not stopping. The pile of ooze flung itself at him rapid fire, sometimes multiple spheres at a time. Daniel dipped, ducked, dived, and dodged the sudden onslaught.

It was running low on control orbs to fire at him. Daniel started to let his guard down—and so it was only sheer luck that saved him from a direct hit. As he stepped back from the latest attack, another sphere flew in front of his face, horizontally, having bounced back from the other side of the arena. Daniel turned to face a swarm of bouncing green spheres of acid converging on him from all sides.

Daniel fled through a gap in the enclosure. The spheres smacked into each other, but instead of smushing together, they rebounded almost perfectly, scattering away like bouncy balls. The main pile kept firing at him, forcing Daniel to stay on the move, tracking him with the orbs as if they were heat-seeking missiles. *Or magic-seeking missiles.*

Even as the pile finally emptied itself out, Daniel was dealing with a continuous storm of bouncing orbs striking at him from every direction. It wasn't possible for them all to come at him like this with the arena being so large—they'd scatter and spread out eventually. He realized the creature must be controlling the motion somehow, directing the momentum magically. One of the spheres caught his foot, sizzling a section off the heel of his shoes.

"The Klaxyde swarm," Ky said, leading with a voice like an expert on Animal Planet, "is a master hunter and top of the food chain in the underground cave systems of Kalatan 9. They've evolved over millions of years to hunt the flighty and magic-rich Qualxyde, with whom they have a predator-prey relationship in Kalatan's five years of summer, but a commensal relationship during winter, when food is more plentiful. In wintertime, above-ground creatures are driven to seek the warmer climes of the cavern system, thus allowing—"

The rest of the biology lesson was lost on Daniel as he focused on skating through the endless bouncing swarm of hungry slime orbs. He used sigils to twist himself out of the way of coordinated waves of orbs, staying one step ahead of where they were targeting. The creature made a few fumbled attempts to lead him, but when Daniel easily faked it out, it fell back on the general chaos of the barrage to keep him off-balance.

Daniel planted his foot on another sigil—and an orb swept by his leg. A tendril, reaching from the orb, sizzled through his magic, eating away the sigil—and then it started sucking on the source, tugging more magic out from him. Daniel ripped away from the link, saving the energy—but cutting off his spell.

The sigil crumbled under his foot, vanished before it fully formed. Daniel fell backward as his foot lost the platform it had been pushing against. Another orb rebounded off its passing friend and curved straight for him, catching up with his fall faster than he could get out of the way.

Daniel swung his club like a baseball bat, pouring magic into it until it glowed. The strike pushed the orb away, but the ooze sucked the magic flowing through his club right out of it.

As the orb sailed by, Daniel watched it form another purple orb and divide in two, having absorbed enough energy to multiply.

His continued fall moved him out of the path of the rest of the rebounding orbs. He flipped himself upright and started running through the air again, feet making dull drumbeats against the sigils he created. The central flurry of orbs tracked him as he ran laps around the arena, keeping pace a half-step behind him.

As Daniel rounded a corner, four of the orbs—evenly spaced—came at him from the front, arranged like the points of a square. He planned on ducking through the middle, but even as he pushed off, ropes of slime snapped out and connected them to one another, turning it into a deathtrap. He immediately formed another sigil under one of his feet and hauled himself up in a jump, pushing as if taking a stair three at a time. He got his shoe up over the top of the square before they flew by.

"Daniel barely got out of that one!" Ky said. "Even when separated, Klaxyde can communicate over a short range to coordinate their attacks. Looks like they're wising up!"

Daniel rocketed away from a follow-up attack by more groups of ball-nets. A glance at a clock showed he had two minutes left. Bathory was nowhere to be seen—clearly, she'd successfully hidden herself from the Klaxyde. Probably waiting to stab him in the back if the slime monster didn't finish him off.

Daniel tried to think up a way to do damage to it. Magic was a dead end. Neither his contractor powers or any of Bathory's spells had done anything but make it stronger. Even fire hadn't helped. Had anything even hit it yet?

An image flashed in Daniel's mind. He remembered the debris from the explosion—not the fireball, but the hot bits of mud and rock. He was far enough away that they didn't hurt him, but they tore holes through the Klaxyde. They weren't magical.

Daniel glanced at his club, squinting. This was either going to work, or he was going to lose his only weapon.

Daniel banked again, having reached the other side of the arena. He unleashed his full magical might, giving himself the advantage of sped-up awareness. This was going to take some timing. He slowed slightly, allowing one of the orbs to catch up with him.

Despite how fast they were still going, his magically enhanced vision took in the Klaxyde with gruesome, high-resolution detail. The black-flecked purple sphere glowed as it directed the flesh to move and shift around it. He could see it warp as it drew close, reaching a bubbling tendril out for him; the arena lights played across the surface of the flesh as it stretched wider.

As it was about to make contact, Daniel drew his legs in, then formed two sigils underneath his feet, catching himself and pushing off to change direction. The orb flew by his left side, unable to stop its momentum midair.

Daniel was already winding up. He poured magic into his arms and his grip, but avoided letting it travel up into his club. The nuance was harder than he thought it would be; ever since he'd been fighting with weapons, he'd always done the same thing, pushing magic down his arm and out his hand to strengthen his tool of choice. It felt like swinging while keeping his pinky and index fingers raised; everything in his body told him to tighten down his grip. Flares of light flickered around the handle as he fought against the magical equivalent of muscle memory.

But he managed well enough, because his iron club crushed through the ooze like paste and slammed into the purple core. For Daniel, it was like watching a metal bar blasting into a piece of fruit at high speed—played back using a super slo-mo camera. The core dented inward, rippled, and was sent shooting away, disintegrating into bits. It ended up as a wet smear on the far wall.

"And ka-boom!" Ky shouted. "Looks like Daniel's found a way to fight back. Can't use magic to kill a Klaxyde!" She winked at the camera following her.

Daniel fought the urge to roll his eyes and kept moving. He started lining up shots. After pulverizing a few more, the Klaxyde wised up and started bending and shifting out of the way. The spheres started coming at him from bad angles, above and behind. That made straight shots at them with his club awkward and left him open to attacks from other directions. At the current rate, there was no way he'd get them all before the clock ran down.

Daniel increased his speed, channeling most of his magic into his legs. He outstripped the main cloud of Klaxyde orbs and sped to the center of the arena. He used more sigils to stop himself there and pushed away the snow with his landing. He planted his feet and worked his heels into furrows in the mud.

Having built up behind him, the bouncing swarm of Klaxyde turned into a long train of spheres, some connected by tendrils to form flying nets, others going it alone, bouncing off their peers to create unpredictable patterns. They filled the air almost entirely from floor to ceiling, converging in a coordinated attack on a single point—where Daniel stood. As the first wave came in, Daniel reached down into himself and dragged all his magic to the forefront.

Daniel glowed from head to toe, white gold, as if he was a solid piece of metal. The intense shine washed out the arena lights; sharp black shadows formed behind the boulders strewn across the ground. The light pulsed as he smashed away the first orb, causing the shadows to blink and shift as if he was the source of a strobe light.

Another three spheres were on top of him an instant later. Daniel's form flashed three times, each flicker of light a strike from his club. In real time, the orbs were blasted into bits almost simultaneously, sent careening across the arena until they were stopped by the outer wall.

The rain of orbs continued. Tendrils lashed out to wrap Daniel's arms or catch his clothes; none did. The force from the continuous hits drove Daniel's heels back through the mud, out of the furrows in the ground, until he halted his backward momentum with sigils. His stance and the position of his feet changed with each swing, as if he wasn't in motion, but like a series of photographs, appearing one way and then the next too fast to be tracked. Green slime and purple ooze stained the snowbanks in front of him; the waves of force emanating from him sent clods of ice and bits of grass up across the ground.

The last wave of orbs tried to get out of the way, but it was too little too late. Daniel stepped into their midst, taking out the easy targets in a flash. He was forced to chase down a handful that escaped in time, but without their brethren to coordinate with, they were easily isolated and finished off.

"With 17 seconds left to go, Daniel has destroyed the rest of the Klaxyde swarm!" Ky said. "Our newest human inmate has definitely planted a flag for the Order of the Dragon. Watch out, Purgatory, this kid's got some serious moves! Let's give our fighters another few minutes with their magic as a reward, shall we?"

Daniel set down in the center again, heaving his breaths. He put his club down head first, leaning in on it, staring at the ground. He closed his eyes and steadily tightened his grip on his weapon, getting ready to swing. He bent his knees a bit, and quietly created two sigils beneath his shoes—just under the mud, hidden from sight.

Bathory appeared behind him, teleporting from nowhere. Her shadowy construct blossomed around her like a dark version of the Klaxyde, claws and blades and grasping hands swarming Daniel and surrounding him from behind.

But Daniel was already gone.

In the stillness following the defeat of the Klaxyde, he'd been able to scry Bathory out. Rather than move on her, he'd waited—because he could see magic forming at a place she *wasn't*, behind him. He pretended exhaustion, gambling that she was going to teleport herself to that spot.

Daniel sprinted around her at lightning speed, maintaining control with his sigils so he didn't slide in the mud. Her shadows were already reacting, bending back the other way, but his club screamed in, glowing white, aimed at the portion of her body where the limbs and tendrils were thinnest.

Daniel's attack crushed through the shadows. They were able to divert his blow, but not enough to save her entirely. He caught her straight on her shoulder, striking home with a satisfying smash. Her shoulder joint twisted unnaturally from the force, punched out of its socket by his club head. Bathory reeled from the strike, screaming.

Her shadows swarmed to her defense before he could ground himself for another hit, so Daniel backed away—and then kept backing away. With all her magic available, her maximum reach was huge, nearly a third the arena, and the shadows ripped and tore after him like an angry beast. Bathory huddled on the ground in the center of it all, shaking.

Eventually, she stood. Her wrist was healed up—she probably used magic on it while she was hidden—but her arm hung loose, bloody and dislocated. She leaned forward, then looked up at him. The shadows around her flared larger, extending out from her like streamers blown back by the wind.

Her lips curled up around her teeth in a feral snarl. She screamed across the arena at Daniel, a wordless, primal exercise in frustration. The shadows trembled and buckled with the weight of her anger, as if they were fearful pets cringing at the rage of their master.

"Uh-oh," Ky said. "I think you made her angry!"

Bathory warped into the space ten feet on Daniel's left. Thankfully, the majority of her shadows didn't survive teleportation, but the tendrils regenerated almost instantly from their origin points around her body. She was on him just as quickly.

Daniel fled close range. Her shadows dug through the mud and snow to propel her after him. She peppered him with multiple fireballs, trying to shoot him down as he ducked away. The explosions threatened to knock him off course.

When she tried to lead her next fireball, Daniel abruptly turned, diving into a nest of her shadows. He held up his left hand and shoved a sigil straight into them, pouring energy into it to force it to grow. The spell blossomed outward from his hand, cutting off shadows at the edges and smashing the rest. Bathory ran into it headlong, and she scrabbled at it with her bare hands, nails scraping on the golden light. Her face was rabid, a mess of sweat and hair.

Daniel dragged his left hand along the sigil, maintaining contact to keep it in place. With his right fist—still holding his club—he created another sigil. It linked to his first, creating a larger golden fence and cutting off more incoming shadows. Daniel kept his left hand in contact with the shield and created another sigil, and another, and another, sliding along outside her as he increased the size of the wall.

Before he'd been trapped by Bathory, Daniel had the idea to use the sigil as a shield to fend off her shadows and land a hit. When he was trapped, he discovered that multiple sigils would merge together if they touched one another. He wasn't sure if that was always a property they had, or it was his increased power giving them that ability, but it worked.

The weakness of the sigil was that he had to maintain contact. They also couldn't move once he created them, being locked into position in space. But though they couldn't move, he could.

Daniel ran the boundary of his growing barrier. Two sigils on his feet kept him moving; one hand dragged against it all, maintaining it. His other hand formed the new sigils, new links in the chain as he reached the edge. He only had to maintain three sigils at once, well within his capabilities, and his full access to his magic let him hold up the shield against her shadow claws even easier than before.

If he could trap himself inside his own shields, why not trap her instead?

After walling off the ground level, Daniel skidded through the air, slowly expanding a sphere around Bathory to contain her. She smashed and slammed her shadow limbs against his sigils, but it didn't do her any good. His sigil ability trumped her shadow spell; he'd already figured that out earlier. As he penned her in more and more, it became harder to finish the job, with more and more limbs and claws pressed into a smaller and smaller space. Bathory's anger turned to confusion, and then, as she realized what he was doing, panic.

Daniel moved to close the last hole in his defenses. Bathory gathered her shadows beneath her and shot herself toward the final gap. Seeing where she was headed, Daniel beat her there, reached out a hand, and sealed her in. She slammed against the inside of the shield, pounding her shadowy spell—and her fists—against his magic, like a psyche ward inmate banging against the glass.

"Remarkable strategy from Daniel," Ky said. "A lot of commentators have been calling him a one-trick pony, but I think they'll have other ideas when this fight is over." Bathory's next move was predictable. Red laser lights gleamed from within the golden shell. "It looks like Bathory is using her trademarked fire magic to attack a single point. Where will she strike?"

Bathory's attempt to destroy his barrier confirmed his suspicion. If she was able to teleport through his barrier, she would have done so rather than attempt to break out. He'd noticed before, when she teleported, that she never passed through anything—not him, his magic, or even the Klaxyde. She only ever traveled through open space, which is why he decided to try trapping her. It looked like the idea was going to pay off big time.

The lasers fired toward Daniel. He saw it coming from a mile away, and, one hand still on the sphere, neatly stepped aside. The concentrated fire magic shattered a piece of the sigil and ignited the distant wall of the arena.

Daniel grinned at Bathory, then reached in and created a new sigil in place of the broken section. He formed it inside the sphere, cutting off a little more space even as it connected to the rest of the wall. It looked like a deep divot in the shell. Bathory growled—he could hear it, somewhat muffled behind the wall of magic—and began channeling more lasers, this time focused across different sections of the shield.

Daniel didn't wait for her. While she was busy, he let part of the sigil drop open, then ducked his head in, taking a swipe at her shadows. After blasting a nice hole in them, he created a new link, sealing the gap with another divot. He drew back in time for the lasers to cut through several other sections of the sphere.

Daniel pumped magic into the sigil as a whole. The shell began to heal over the broken sections, extending into the holes and sealing them shut. He moved to cover the largest gap himself so she didn't escape, chopping away shadows that were trying to widen it.

Daniel worked on his trap, gliding across the surface of his sphere. As he recreated parts of the sigil he let fall away, and reformed parts that she broke, he steadily closed off her space. Bathory's shadows were forced into a tighter and tighter orbit around her until Daniel couldn't force the shell any smaller. At that point, if she reached her arms out, she'd almost be touching either side of the cage.

Daniel placed both hands on the surface of the sphere. Then, he poured power into the sigil, attempting to thicken the shell. It was slow going, but as the sigil thickened on her side, he let the outer edge thin out and dissipate. In this way, he slowly drew the trap shut.

It was a nasty way to finish the fight—eventually, he'd crush her—but it was by far the safest. He reminded himself of how crazy she was, of the stakes in the fight, even as she beat against his enclosing cage of light. He couldn't go soft when victory was in sight.

"And the walls are closing in on Bathory," Ky said. "Literally! Daniel has her penned in and left her unable to counter effectively. She can't teleport through his physical sigil. What can she do? Is this the end? Is Elizabeth Bathory going to lose a duel to someone less than a week in Hell?!"

Bathory's form emerged from the shadows. Her face peeked through the web of light next to Daniel. Tears were running down her cheeks; mud and blood was smeared across her mouth. She looked up at him and screamed in terror. "Not like this! Please! Don't do this to me!"

Daniel looked away and ignored her. She kept yelling at him, using his name. He clenched his jaw tighter. *She's trying to get to you. You watched the reruns with Jack, she'll say anything to get herself out of a jam. Don't fall for it.*

When Daniel looked back, the fight was gone from her. She hung her head, shaking it from side to side. She'd let her shadows fade; she kneeled alone in the slowly shrinking space of the cage. "I can't believe this. I can't believe it. I can't believe..." She looked up at him. Her face shone with a wide, crazed grin. "...how easy it's going to be to kill you."

Bathory lifted a finger—but it wasn't a finger anymore. A long, black claw had replaced it. It was dark as obsidian, as if all the shadow she'd been wielding was condensed to that single point. She touched it against his sigil.

Daniel felt like a truck ran over his heart while it was still in his chest. He cringed backward, bending double, desperate to keep a hand on his construct, to keep it active. Bathory raised her finger, and he could feel the magic gathered there, ready to spear through his own spell to get to him.

But she'd given up her defenses.

Daniel lifted his hand. The cage vanished, and Bathory's shadow claw was rendered useless. Daniel still had his club in his hand, and he wound up for a direct hit, stepping into the swing.

Her form vanished on contact. Daniel stumbled, caught off guard as he stepped through the swing.

A searing pain tore through his left side. Bathory was there, digging her claw into his abdomen, licking her lips in his face. They fell to the ground, Daniel without his sigils, his magic disrupted by the black energy coursing through him.

They crashed to the grass, and it was the fall that saved him, the force pushing them apart. Daniel got to his feet, wincing and grunting. It felt like someone had jammed a steel rod into his side and left it there. He stepped back from where Bathory was collecting herself.

He pushed magic around the wound, clutching at himself with his free hand. He glanced down; the tear through his shirt exposed his skin and a bloody gash in his side. Blackened, necrotic welts lined where she'd cut him. His magic was staving off further damage, but it was bleeding badly.

He pushed his hand on the wound to stem the blood. It felt like the bar stuck in him had been set on fire. He gasped, then held his breath, everything wound up tight as he fought against the urge to let his hand fall away. He wasn't sure if he could run, or how fast he could even move.

Bathory leaned her head back and laughed. Blood stained her hand—his blood. Otherwise, she was unhurt, somehow healed again. She was worse for the wear—mud, sweat, mess—but in infinitely better shape than him.

"How…you couldn'tve—"

"Daniel, Daniel," Bathory said. "I simply teleported out one of the gaps I made before you closed it. You had the right idea, but any break in your cage large enough for me to fit was a hole I could leave through. You were quick in closing them down, but not fast enough to stop me when I had the spell ready. Your plan was flawed from the start."

"But you cast a spell from the inside," Daniel said. At this point, he was stalling for time, trying to keep her talking while he fought through the pain and gathered his magic back under control. "How could you do that if you'd already left the cage? There's no way that was an illusion!"

"You're right—I cast my next spell from the outside while invisible. Easy enough to time it with the movement of my illusion to make you think I was still trapped. And then…there you were, ripe for the taking." She brought her hand up to her mouth and ran her tongue through the blood.
"Mmm…delicious. The potential of youth." Her eyes went wide. "I think I'd like another taste."

It was then that a wave of grey light washed over them, and all of Daniel's magic vanished from his grasp.

He almost bent double. All the exhaustion he'd suppressed, the bruises, the blood loss, the hits and tears and scrapes came roaring back. His club fell from his hand and thumped to the ground. His wound was on fire; his forearms ached where they'd been cut by Bathory's knife. The black marks on his skin were gone—artifacts of Bathory's magic—but the injury itself was still as bad.

Bathory didn't take the loss well either; she took a step and put out an arm for balance. For Daniel's part, he'd put her through the ringer—but he was in a far worse state.

"What an incredible turnaround!" Ky said. "You heard it there yourself folks. In a few years, Daniel might be unbeatable—but it looks like there's no substitute for experience. His quick-thinking tactics were no match for Bathory's legendary subterfuge!"

Bathory glowed under the praise of the devil, under the lights of the arena. She raised her hands, turning her face up to the cameras that were no doubt fixed on them. She smiled, then looked back down at Daniel. "Fun while it lasted. But I think it's time."

Bathory stalked forward. She raised her knife. Daniel scrambled backwards. Part of him wanted to go for his club, but where it was, down on the ground, felt a million miles away. If he bent to grab it, he was worried he wouldn't be able to stand straight.

Bathory moved closer. Her footsteps pounded in his ears; his blood pounded along with them. His heart was in his throat. Daniel's mind raced, searching for a way out, a way to turn things around.

Bathory's knife, held backward in her hand, stabbed toward him.

Daniel reached up, trying to knock her knife off course before it gutted him. The knife plunged straight through his palm. It drove through to the hilt, and she followed it in, pushing his hand back toward him.

Daniel screamed, in pain, in anger—in pure determination. He brought out everything he had left—every tiny bit of energy in his body, scraped out from places he didn't know he had. And with that distilled willpower he clenched his blooded fingers around the hilt and ripped the knife from her hand. Bathory stumbled forward, not exacting him to pull back.

Daniel took the hand off the wound on his abdomen and clenched it into a fist. "Here's your fucking taste!"

His fist flew for her face. His knuckles smashed into her chin, knocking her off her feet and into the mud. She sprawled there, dazed, the blow ringing through her head.

Daniel's hand fell to his side. It ached from the punch, vaguely, but it was peanuts compared to how the rest of him felt. He swayed slightly, steadied himself.

He looked for his club. It was behind her—not enough time to grab it. He looked at the knife embedded in his other hand.

Daniel grabbed the hilt with his free hand. He screamed even before he started pulling it, just to rev himself up, keep his heart pumping. He dragged the blade out of his palm, bracing it against his body and pulling. It ripped free on the second tug.

He stood there, holding it. The world had started spinning around him. Bathory was stirring. He held the knife in front of him. He thought about kneeling, then stabbing her, but he wasn't sure he would make it. He was so dizzy.

He fixed his grip on the knife. It was slippery, smeared with red. With blood. He saw Bathory moving. He was out of time. He held the knife in front of himself, and fell toward her, trying to push her down with his weight and get her with the knife at the same time.

Bathory's foot came up and slammed him in the ribs. Daniel flipped sideways and landed hard on his back, arms flailing out. He tried to check his good hand, but the knife was gone, fallen away somewhere.

His vision swam black and red at the edges. Pain lanced through his side, down his arm, and out his bad hand. His fingers dug into the grass. He had to get up.

He pushed his elbows down for leverage, but Bathory slammed her body on him, straddling him at the waist and knocking out the little breath he'd gotten back. The knife was in her hands, dark and soaked with blood.

She plunged it down. A searing pain ripped through his stomach. His scream turned into a gargled yell as she dug the blade through his diaphragm and into his torso.

Spots flickered in his eyes. He tried to move—too painful. She was still sitting on him.

He coughed, slightly. Something wet specked onto Bathory's clothes.

"Mmm...there's what I want." She glanced at something. "I usually like to play more, but looks like playtime's over."

The dagger plunged toward Daniel's heart. The burning in his belly was met by a searing, crushing pain from the dagger working into his chest. The sensation overwhelmed his last attempt at gathering himself.

The last thing he saw was Elizabeth Bathory, smearing a red-soaked hand over her mouth, her face cast in a freakish excitement.

****

Beelzebub clapped his hands together. "Not a bad fight." He glanced over at where Xik stood next to him in the command center, suspended above the massive screen that displayed Daniel's failure in real time. "So. What now?"

Xik's eyes lingered on the screen, watching as Bathory did what she wanted with the boy's remains. It was a gruesome sight.

Ky narrated the entire thing, not breaking character for an instant. They watched in silence as Xik considered Beelzebub's question, all the way until Bathory waved her bloodied arms at the camera and kissed goodbye to the audience. The act smeared more of the boy's blood across her face. Ky joked with Bathory before she vanished away on the teleportation pedestal that appeared in the center of the arena. *I have to give that devil a raise. Maybe next quarter.*

Xik sighed, then glanced at Beelzebub. "What are the consequences?"

"According to the terms of the fight, signed independently by the Order and by Bathory," Beelzebub said, "banishment, for a period of 10 years. Without support or funds from his team, Daniel will hit the bottom in no time, and there he will stay."

"I see," Xik said. "At the bottom of the prison, he'll have little chance to grow stronger."

"Precisely." Beelzebub shrugged. "The seal is more powerful nearer the core of Hell—I can't weaken it there. His contractor magic won't help him. Daniel made his gamble. He came up short. I don't want to say I told you so, but…"

Xik smiled; it stretched his jaw wide, too wide, like a bullfrog did when it was about to swallow something larger than itself whole. Beelzebub wondered if he'd pushed a hair too hard—but Xik's words came out as calmly and considered as they always did. "Oh, no, you're quite right. Daniel had his chance, and we simply don't have time for more chances. A terrible shame, considering my time and resources spent." Xik stretched his hand out to the devil. "I've taken note that Asmodeus is ready to move for Earth in force at the head of your army. So, as promised. The first half of your contract."

Beelzebub rose from his chair. His claws retracted, and he took the frog's hand, pumping once.

Lime-green flames flickered across Beelzebub's fingers, then raced up his arm. He stepped away from the handshake and watched with interest as the heatless fire spread across his entire skin, from his neck to his toes. He could feel it there, crawling across him more like the slime from the Klaxyde than a warming fire.

A glowing sigil appeared on the floor. Beelzebub focused as numerals and symbols flashed around him in a multidimensional dance, encapsulating him in a cylinder of complex magical calculations. The light played across the windows of his office; he could see the reflection against the glass, his own red skin gleaming brighter in the red light. He bent all his senses onto spell as it wove and weaved its way into his very being, trying to memorize as much of it as possible. The more he learned now—even if that amounted only to impressions and feelings for the more cryptic portions—the easier it would be to reverse-engineer later.

Beelzebub could feel a connection to a massive energy source start to form. No—less that, and more a fundamental force, as if his body was experiencing gravity for the first time. He shied away from it, alarmed by how familiar it felt—strikingly familiar to the key to the Longinus, on an even more massive and potent scale.

And then, it all froze in place; the spinning symbols and numbers, the lines of light, the world, Beelzebub himself. The light flickered into a strange mirror of itself, blacks becoming greens and reds becoming blues. And then, it was gone. As suddenly as it began, it vanished, as if it had never happened.

"Well then," Xik said. His form was already fading. "A bargain struck, Emperor Beelzebub. Good luck." Xik tossed Beelzebub a small green stone. Beelzebub caught it, holding it up against the light for a better view. Aside from the color, there was nothing remarkable. "If you need to talk, squeeze it in your palm. I may not answer immediately, but I'll come when I can."

Beelzebub nodded at him. "Until our next meeting."

And then, the Klide ambassador was gone.

Beelzebub waited another five minutes before pulling the security footage of the inside of his office. Interestingly, Xik wasn't in it. On screen, Beelzebub reached out and shook hands with nothing, then stood there for a half minute, looking around at a spell that—as far as the camera was concerned—didn't exist. The green stone only appeared in his hand as he moved to catch it. *Fascinating.*

He'd expected as much—there was no way Xik would allow the secrets of Klide magic to slip out easily. He still sighed a puff of smoke in disappointment. It would've been so much easier if he had a recording of the spell. Months of research would be reduced to weeks. It was unlikely he'd be able to pass it to Asmodeus and Lilith before the war was over.

Beelzebub's work screen flashed with an incoming call from an inmate—one of the few that had his direct line. Bathory. Beelzebub rolled his eyes, then accepted the call. "What is it?"

Bathory appeared on the other line. Daniel's blood was smeared across her face and matted on her hair. She glared at him. "When I agreed to the terms of the fight, you happened to forget mentioning banishment. I barely stayed in character. I could've been exiled from my own team! Everything I've earned, my position—everything! I agree to help you and that's the thanks I get? The dossier you gave me didn't tell me half of what that boy was capable of—"

Beelzebub raised a hand. "Be silent."

"—and if you think I'll bow and scrape every time you have some random request, then—"

"Silence!" Bathory went quiet, grinding on her frustration. Beelzebub loomed over the screen, staring her down until she looked away. "You did what I asked. That is all you need to be concerned with. Remember this. All those benefits you mention were given to you by me, and I can take them from you at any time. I don't need the excuse of a fight to do so."

"You wouldn't dare," Bathory said, smirking. "Your precious ratings wouldn't survive me leaving the—"

Beelzebub slammed a fist into the console. "Do not test my patience. You'll do exactly what I tell you, when I tell you to do it. You are a prisoner, and you had best remember that fact before I send you to the frozen pits and rid myself of your insolence permanently."

Beelzebub closed the connection, then leaned back in his chair, huffing away the foul mood the human managed to put him in. And as the moment passed, a smile steadily worked its way up to his face, his mind turning over exactly how he was going to test out his new contractor magic.

Chapter 20
Crypt Keepers

Daniel shivered.

For an instant, he could still feel the knife, slicing around his heart.

He blinked his eyes open, then blinked them again, repeatedly, before realizing that it was that dark—pitch black. He raised his hands up, but he couldn't see them.

Something nearby clicked, and Daniel dropped through the floor. He screamed bloody murder, and flailed with his arms and hands, trying to stop his descent, but his skin burned from the friction. When he realized he was actually sliding down a chute, he kept his hands at his sides and tucked his chin.

He quickly built up speed, rocketing down far faster than was safe, until the wind was ripping at his hair and eyes. The sensation of being pressed to the left or right informed him of turns and banks in the doomsday slide. His back rattled hard over the rivets and bumps that connected segments of the chute, repeatedly knocking the air out of him.

After what felt like miles of travel, the steep incline started to level off, and he slowed along with it. Light filtered in from the distant end of the tunnel.

He came to a stop in a dim cavern. A massive, multilimbed figure—one of the robotic enforcers—stood over him. The robot's head swiveled to examine him.

Daniel tucked himself back into the slide. *What the hell is going on?*

"Inmate." The robot's voice was flat and uncompromising. "Vacate the arrival zone."

Daniel translated that in his head, then clambered out the end of the slide, nearly tripping over himself as he lifted his legs to clear the sides. He held his arms out wide as the world revolved around him, his sense of balance still recovering from the rollercoaster. He immediately noticed he was wearing a plain brown robe—and no undergarments—because it was itchy as hell. Daniel scratched his butt a few times, wincing as the rough cloth scraped over his skin. At least his new sandals were moderately comfortable.

Almost immediately, he could hear the sound of wind rushing through the tunnel behind him. A dwarf arrived at the base of the chute—stubby, short, and fat-nosed. It was dressed in an identical brown robe, sized for its shorter height. It climbed out of the slide swearing and grumbling under its breath, then caught sight of him. "Keep your eyes to yourself, Earth monkey."

The dwarf huffed and moved off down the tunnel. Daniel glanced at the enforcer. "Um...can I ask you a question?"

"Yes," the enforcer intoned. "I am programmed to provide basic information to all inmates, including inmate behavioral expectations, directional guidance, and all pertinent rules and regulations."

"Great," Daniel said. "Where exactly am I?"

"You are on the Body Restoration and Relocation Floor. This floor is colloquially known as the crypt."

The crypt. That rung a bell. Daniel remembered Jack explaining that to him—it was the place you ended up if you died in a territory war, or if you were so blasted to smithereens in a fight that Hell decided making you a new body was less effort than repairs.

Daniel was a little afraid to ask his next question.

Another whistling sound marked the arrival of another inmate—a devil. The red-skinned creature climbed out as ungraciously as the dwarf had. It gave Daniel a look, but walked past him without a word.

Daniel turned back to the enforcer. "How did I get here?" he asked.

"Records indicate that you lost an arena match," the enforcer said. "The losing condition was banishment."

"So it wasn't because I couldn't be healed?" Daniel said. "The only reason I'm here is because of this banishment?"

"That is correct," the enforcer said. "If banished, regardless of your condition following the match, you are forcibly revived in the crypt. This is considered additionally punishing due to the cost of transport back to higher levels of Hell."

Daniel fell into his thoughts—enough that he ignored the next arrival, a goblin that snorted derisively on his way past. No one—including Jack—had mentioned the consequences of banishment to him before the fight. That being said, they probably knew and would buy him back into Purgatory.

It all hit Daniel like a bolt of lightning.

Jack, suddenly turning on him. Bathory saying she felt bad for him, that he didn't know what was going on. His suspicions about Dracula, about things going too well too quickly.

Jack's voice echoed in his head. *You're gone. You're gone.*

Daniel ducked down the tunnel. He had to call the team and figure out what was going on. But he couldn't have a private talk in front of the slide; he had to find a quiet spot first.

It wasn't long before he could hear a babble of conversation in front of him. Daniel emerged from the tunnel and stepped onto a dirty, crowded street. It looked like a shantytown jammed into a long, straight cavern. The street barely deserved the name, being more a beaten rock-and-dirt path. To his left and right, a steady trickle of arrivals were walking out of other pits similar to his own and into the crowd.

"Hey, there he is!"

"Fitzgerald, one and done. Good try though!"

"Hey, I'm a fan!"

"I hope it costs you, demon-hating bastard!"

"Better join the order of the flagon after you got beat down like that!"

"Come on," hissed once voice, "he's a kid!"

"Yeah, even younger than he looks on camera."

Another voice clacked and clicked more than spoke, but somehow translated to garbled English in Daniel's ears. "Foolish to challenge, however, well done as much as could be!"

Daniel looked around. Dozens of inmates milled around him: blood-red devils; fishy undines; dwarves, imps; a few of the spider creatures—he remembered they were called grazul—and some he thought were humans, but flashes of scales or clawed feet marked them as dragons. All of them wore the same plain ugly robes. They must have heard about the fight; a few might have even been watching. Daniel waved at them, eliciting about a 50-50 split of cheers and jeers.

Suddenly, the crowd fell completely silent.

Daniel's hand paused. Everyone started whispering; some were chuckling darkly. He glanced around nervously as more and more turned, and stared. And then he realized they weren't looking at him—they were looking at his wrist.

Daniel followed the collective gaze.

His armlet was plain white. No red cross, no yellow frills. Blank—like it had been when he first arrived, before he joined a team.

A quick look told him that, of the armlets not hidden by the long-sleeved robes, everyone had a color, a flag, some design. Everyone had a team that was going to bail them out.

Daniel did not.

He tucked his arm under his sleeve and pushed his way through the crowd. No one made a move to stop him, but no one really cleared the way, either. The more gazes followed him, the more Daniel felt he needed to get away from prying eyes. He shouldered his way out of the gathering and hurried away from the growing pressure on his back.

He came to an intersection, another thin cavern merging with his own. More inmates were coming in from the left and right out of other slide pits, so he pressed forward, slipping deeper into the crypt.

The clashing architectural glimmer of Purgatory was replaced by ramshackle buildings built from wood or stone and packed with dirt. The crypt looked like a broken down, Western ghost town suffering 50 years of sandstorms without repair, all shoved into a cramped series of caves. He turned at a few intersections, winding deeper and away from the inmates that had seen him with a blank armlet.

He was still drawing some attention. He hadn't seen any other humans yet, and he stood out like a sore thumb. Many of the others moving around him had hoods drawn over their heads; Daniel reached back and discovered that his robe had one as well. He pulled it on and ducked his head low, hoping he could pass for a tall dwarf with his face partly obscured. The closest thing to human here was them, maybe a dragon, but he didn't have any of the scales, or horns. The hood didn't hide as much as he liked, but it kept most of the inmates from giving him a second glance.

The further Daniel went, the more it all looked the same. Inmates were packed in like people at an amusement park, forming a sea of uniform brown robes—apparently standard issue after you'd been chopped to pieces. He wasn't sure how big the crypt was, but it couldn't be endless. With all the people coming in, there had to be some place where they were leaving.

What really struck Daniel was the sheer numbers. It wasn't quite jammed floor-to-ceiling, but it was getting there. That translated to deaths in territory wars, or prisoners getting ripped to pieces beyond repair. Jack had hinted that enforcers weren't as prevalent on most levels, and Purgatory surely accounted for some of the numbers, but the scale of it was tremendous. It hadn't occurred to him previously, or maybe nothing had really hit home, but Hell did have hundreds, maybe thousands of years to accumulate prisoners. If the lower levels were larger than the sprawling city of Purgatory, there was who knew how many people living in this place, this pocket between worlds.

As he moved, Daniel got a general sense that most people were headed in one general direction—the center of the cavern. He found a quiet corner and flicked up a map on his armband. The crypt was a rough circle. A fat central cavern branched off into several longer, thinner caves, and those branched, and branched again, thinning each time until they ended at the actual arrival points. The neat structure was broken and pockmarked by extra caves and passageways in various locations. Without a map, it would be easy to get lost in the maze-like side tunnels.

He'd made it about halfway from the outer portion to the middle, so he decided to make that his goal for the time being. He eyed an alley that fluted between two leaning buildings. His map indicated it would be a shortcut, and it would be nice not to be shoved up against sweaty minotaurs and trolls.

As he left the bustle of the crowd behind, Daniel leaned in, squinting. His eyes had trouble penetrating the scarce light of the alley. A skitter of sound in the dark made him stop. Thinking better of saving a few minutes, he turned back to the main road, settling for being treated like a sardine with the rest of them. A safer and brightly lit sardine.

After a 20 or 30 minute walk, he reached what was marked on the map—a wide square, possibly larger than the main square in Purgatory. Dotting the perimeter, and forming another, inner circle at the center, were rows and rows of what looked like telephone booths. Unlike the cramped, skinny version he'd seen in movies, they were very wide—probably so the wider-set demons like grazul and ogres didn't have to wedge themselves inside. The clean metal structures stood out stark from the dingy town around them.

Instead of a phone, there was a steel plate set against the far wall of each booth, not unlike the televisions he'd seen in the waiting rooms and Jack's apartment. A video screen was displayed on the plate, which could be manipulated by touch. Some appeared to be talking to other demons; others weren't talking at all. Flashes of blue-white light flared frequently from the booths, after which their occupant vanished. It looked suspiciously like teleportation—and Daniel noted round pedestals forming the base of each booth, similar to his earlier experience.

While there were a few enforcers patrolling the square, Daniel thought he'd make his ignorance too obvious if he started asking loud, basic questions. There were long lines leading to each booth, so he joined one and stood quietly, making himself as unobtrusive as possible. He wracked his memory for clues—Jack mentioned that you could buy back in from the crypt. Maybe there was a fee associated with teleporting. *Bad time to be broke.*

It was a long line, but with so many booths, it moved along pretty quickly. It was clear everyone else knew what they were doing, so there wasn't a long delay once they stepped inside. Soon he made it close enough to hear the conversation the inmate was holding in the booth in front of him—mostly because he was yelling.

The minotaur pounded the sides of the booth with meaty, hairy fists. The walls rattled under the force, but didn't budge. "What do you mean you can't bring me back yet?!" Mumbled speech that Daniel couldn't make out came through the other end. "Then get some! The team owes me for taking that hit, I'm not spending another damn second in this shithole longer than I have too. The longer I'm here the more it costs us!"

There was a mollifying tone from the other end. The minotaur smacked his hand on the panel, ending the call, then stormed out through the square. The line parted to let him pass, and the next demon took his place in the booth, an undine with electric-blue hair. It didn't call anyone, just touched its way through the screen for a few moments. The teleportation pad flashed, and the demon was gone.

Daniel frowned as the line moved up. Why was everyone relying on the booth when they could make calls from their armlet? Sure, they needed to teleport, but the minotaur could have found out that his team couldn't bring him back before wasting time standing in line.

Daniel opened his armlet menu, keeping it positioned so the person behind him—an imp—couldn't see what he was doing. He opened his Contact List, but everything was greyed out. He didn't bother calling Jack, remembering how he was blocked, so he clenched his teeth and dialed Rasputin. A message popped up.

Private calls are blocked in the Body Restoration and Relocation Floor. Please use a public facility.

Daniel sighed. *That explains that.* He tried a few other buttons, and the remaining features were working fine.

He had no points—he'd deposited all his cash in the Order's treasury when he first registered—but his inventory still held the item that Dracula gave him, the single-use power orb. Daniel felt a sense of relief wash through him. Worst case scenario, 25% of his magic could get him a long way inside of 5 minutes. With the duel conditions being stipulated ahead of time, Bathory must not have been allowed to pilfer it after beating him. He would confirm that with an enforcer later—he wasn't going to get himself into another duel until he had read the entire rulebook of Hell front to back.

A few flashes of light later, and it was Daniel's turn at the booth. He touched the panel. The top of the screen prompted him for an inmate number to make a call. He put in Rasputin's ID. Another prompt informed him that as he did not have the 50 points required for the call, it would default to calling collect. *Wonderful.*

Daniel pressed the call button.

It rang.

It rang again.

At the fifth ring, Daniel could feel sweat forming on his brow.

beep

"Ah," came an oil-slick voice, "if it isn't Fitzgerald."

The screen flickered up, showing a live feed of Rasputin standing near the central square of the Order's grounds. Daniel had never been so happy to see a man as ugly in his life—and that was saying something, because Rasputin looked even uglier than usual, hair disheveled, robes thrown on in haste. "Hi Mr. Rasputin."

"That's Lord Rasputin to you."

Daniel swallowed back the annoyance, then decided to go in innocent and see how it played. "I think something's wrong with my armband. It doesn't have my team marker on it."

"That tends to happen after you've been banished."

Daniel leaned forward and spoke quietly. "What does that mean? No one mentioned anything like this."

"Banishment means you're banished," Rasputin said. "From our team, and any other team you might think of joining. For the next ten years, if I remember the terms of the fight correctly."

Daniel chewed at his lower lip, trying to keep the creeping panic from overwhelming him. "I can still help out off the books, I guess. Can you send me my points so I can teleport back? They're all still in the treasury."

"We'll be keeping your points," Rasputin said. "Your fight with Bathory conveniently became an easy way to cut you out.

We've put out our own kill order on any teams that might take you under their wing, even if you can't join officially. And for you as an individual, of course. No one will touch you with a ten-foot pole."

And there it was. He couldn't deny the obvious any longer. Rasputin wasn't trying to make a secret out of it—he didn't even look unhappy.

Daniel turned over his next words in his mind. Half of him wanted to start swearing at the guy, but if he said the wrong thing, Rasputin would hang up on him. He leaned in close to the screen. "At least tell me why. I deserve that much."

"There is no longer a place for you in the Order of the Dragon," Rasputin said. "Not after what Jack told us about you."

Daniel seized on the topic of Jack. "That's what I need to talk to you about," he said. "Jack called me before the fight. Something's wrong with him, he wasn't like himself at all. I don't know what he told you, but—"

"He was in tears, you know," Rasputin said. "Telling us about how you betrayed him to the magicians. He was afraid to bring it up at first, because we took an interest in you. You showed such promise." Rasputin squinted his beady eyes. "How could you do that to him, of all people? He looked up to you, Daniel."

"It's not like that!" Daniel said. He took a breath, lowered his voice again. "That isn't what happened. You have to give me a chance to explain myself. Someone or something got to Jack and made him do this. I've done everything the Order asked me to do. Give me a fair hearing."

"I've already wasted 50 points answering your call," Rasputin said, "and the evidence is arrayed against you quite clearly. Despite you knowing one another, Jack arrived here first. You arrived later—but not before you turned on him to stop yourself being sent to Hell. It seems the magicians didn't trust a traitor, and now you're eating your just desserts."

"That's purely circumstantial," Daniel said. "If that's really what Jack said, then he's lying to you!"

"It's evidence enough if Lord Dracula says it is," Rasputin said, "and the timing is suspicious, isn't it? Even reduced to your word against his, Jack is a tried and tested member of the Order. You are an arrogant idiot who honestly thought he had a chance fighting Elizabeth Bathory. Good riddance, I say. And goodbye."

"Wait!" Daniel said. "Please!" Rasputin paused, finger hovering over the button to end the call. A greasy smile was high on his face; the man was reveling in Daniel's desperation, and they both knew it. "Let me go cleanly. Send me enough points so I can get myself out of here. I won't bother any of you again, if that's what you want."

Rasputin's smile grew even wider, but his eyes were cold and unfeeling. "I don't really think that will be necessary. Where you're going, you won't need points."

Daniel slammed his hand into the side of the booth. "You can't do this to me! It isn't fair, you haven't even—"

Rasputin's finger tapped his armlet, and the feed cut out.

Daniel stood there, staring at the blank metal. His hands tightened their grip on the edges of the display until his knuckles were white. His diaphragm clenched up, balling into a knot.

It took all he had not to scream at the top of his lungs.

"Ahem." A tapping foot made Daniel turn. The imp had its arms folded. "Are you done yet?"

Daniel flipped him the bird and turned back to the plate. Touching it again brought up the main screen. There was another choice aside from calling an inmate ID, namely, teleportation. He touched that menu, and the display showed him possible destinations, each a separate level of Hell. The cost associated with them was listed in points.

Level 1	*Purgatory**	50,001
Level 2	*Stormfields*	39,560
Level 3	*Undermire*	33,781
Level 4	*Grimmholm**	25,225
Level 5	*Magma Labyrinth*	20,098
Level 6	*Sanguine Briar*	17,898
Level 7	*Scorched Sands**	9,208
Level 8	*Cavernous Pits*	4,853
Level 9	*Crystal Mines*	200

*Direct transport to indicated levels or higher requires officially registered 3rd, 2nd, or 1st Tier Challenge Completion OR prerequisite accumulated Ranking in addition to access fee.

Please note: In the case of failure to pay rent, the auditing process will transport you to the highest level you can afford. Points will be deducted from a prisoner's account accordingly. Audits resulting in transport to the Crystal Mines do not cost points.

Daniel puzzled over the list, then brought up the help menu on his armlet. That had been his main source of information after Jack got annoyed answering questions every 5 seconds. His main problem was not knowing the right questions to ask, so he hadn't used it much previously, trusting in Jack to steer him away from any pitfalls.

On a monthly basis—27 days in Earth time—every inmate had to pay the system rent to stay on their current level. The higher the level, the higher the cost, but the better the amenities. The lower levels also carried all sorts of environmental dangers that weren't present in Purgatory.

Come collection time, if you couldn't pay the cost, you were bumped down a level, sometimes multiple levels. At any time, you could also move anywhere else you could afford by paying its associated cost, aside from the crypt. You could only get there involuntarily. Everyone in the prison paid rent at the same time; needless to say, attacks skyrocketed in the days prior to rent, out of sight of any enforcers, of course.

Daniel used the help system to answer a few more questions. The information was limited—it wouldn't tell him about other inmates, and it had nothing educational on magic or demons themselves—but it did go over Hell's rules and structure, and it stopped him from having to ask obvious questions out loud. Daniel learned that after the system registered his heart stopped, he was considered dead and teleported down here for healing, with new, itchy brown duds.

On a whim, Daniel looked up the rules for challenging someone to an arena fight. The threat of banishment was not typical, which is why Daniel hadn't heard of it before. It only potentially applied when challenging someone from the top team of each layer of Hell; in his case, Elizabeth Bathory's team, the Brotherhood of Sinners. This was one of the perks of being at the top of a floor's respective rank ladder; no one wanted to mess with you lightly. The threat of banishment was often more useful than the consequences. The number of times the team could invoke it as a potential punishment was limited to prevent the wholesale destruction of entire teams, making it a rarely used, strategically targeted move—the nuclear option, essentially.

Daniel ground his teeth. Jack—Rasputin, Dracula—they must have known this the whole time. They just didn't tell him.

Daniel didn't know what to believe. Did Jack really have some wild change of heart? Or did they push him into it, and Rasputin fed Daniel a line of bull afterward? Maybe someone else got to Jack, another team or person that wanted to get rid of Daniel in a blackmail scheme.

Beelzebub came to mind, but he couldn't puzzle out a motive for the devil. On some level, it made sense—send Daniel to complete an impossible task to ensure his failure. But why bother coming to talk and offer a way out in the first place? Daniel wasn't going anywhere; he was stuck in Hell. Unless there was something specific about getting him out of Purgatory, about having him banished—but Daniel couldn't imagine what.

There was another possibility, one that Daniel had been trying to avoid. It could be the case that Jack had been plotting behind his back the entire time, only humoring Daniel while arranging his removal.

Daniel rubbed his forehead and forced himself to mentally abandon the topic. He couldn't keep turning it all over and over right now. Once he had a place to stay, he could work it all out and rearrange his short-term goals.

The crypt charged rent every few hours, rather than every month; a low-cost fee of 10 points, deducted automatically from every inmate. It was enough of a sting to force prisoners to move elsewhere, quickly. Otherwise, you'd be bled dry and forced into the Crystal Mines.

Daniel was cut off from his only source of points. His only possession was the one item in his inventory that gave him access to his own magic for a short time. That, and a scratchy robe and matching sandals, and if he didn't mind going naked, he wouldn't be able to give those away.

Daniel stepped out from the booth. The imp threw him a nasty glare for taking up so much time, then went in. A flash of light told Daniel that the creature had teleported almost immediately. Daniel sighed, then took a spot on the wall away from the booths and folded his arms to think.

An enforcer stood not far away, and he glanced up at it. The robot towered over him, a creepy cross between a Vorid extractor and a spider. Right now, it offered an umbrella of safety in case anyone recognized him. No one would try to start a fight right under the thing's nose. But just as surely, it would be the thing enforcing the lack of rent on unlucky inmates.

Daniel recalled Rasputin's words—a kill order. That meant they would probably pay well to take Daniel out, and if Daniel was defeated, he would lose the only thing in his inventory. Once he did get some points together, he'd be constantly looking over his shoulder for bounty hunters. The Order of the Dragon wanted him to stay down.

For now, that was academic. The first thing he needed to do was get points.

Maybe he could sell his item? Daniel brought up the inventory screen on his armlet. It was a gold sphere, with text beneath it describing its benefits. He imagined himself hawking it to the crowd, trying to gin up interest and raise the price. It was a valuable weapon, rare outside of Purgatory.

Unless someone thought it was better to try to beat him up and steal it. Could they do that? Probably, if they thought they wouldn't get caught. Daniel eyed the enforcer again. In theory, the robots should stop an unjustified attack.

In theory.

He didn't know how much money the Order of the Dragon was offering on its bounty. It might be worth it to some teams to risk breaking the rules for a big payoff.

Daniel decided on a new strategy. He knew the bottom level—the Crystal Mines—was a bad place to be. Jack had said as much, and the fact that it cost a dirt-cheap 200 points spoke volumes about the quality of the accommodations. For that exact reason, it might be an even better market for his relatively high-quality goods. He couldn't pay the rent right now anyway. He could let himself be shipped off to the mines, then find a private buyer that was willing to make a deal. Once he was out of the poorhouse, he could figure out his next move.

It wasn't much of a plan. From what little he'd heard, the mines were essentially slave pits, and their chief product was despair. Daniel did have one advantage—he was a well-known, recognizable figure. He could parlay that influence to avoid getting caught up by the rough types. Maybe do someone a few favors under the table if he had to, far away from the influence of Dracula and Rasputin. Go in, sell for cash, get out fast. Then try to work his way back up with a team willing to flaunt the kill order in exchange for his allegiance.

"My pardon, human." Daniel looked up. There was an undine standing there—pale skin, electric blue hair, and wide, fish-like eyes. Its fin-shaped ears flapped once it saw it had Daniel's attention. "I couldn't help but overhear some of your discussion"—he pointed toward the booths—"over there."

Daniel pulled on his hood, making sure it was as low as it could go. "What about it?"

"You're in need of points, yes? I could offer a trade, should you have anything to sell."

Daniel let his arms drop. "I might have a few things," he said. "What are you offering, exactly?"

"There's a place in the crypt my team offers trades," the undine said. "Items of value exchanged directly for points, or other items. We have a large building rented out in the marketplace."

Daniel narrowed his eyes. Right after he was thinking he needed to sell his item to make some money, along comes a guy offering to do that. *Is this an opportunity, or a trap?*

"We've got the best rates you'll find," the undine said. Seeing Daniel hesitating, he kept talking. "I bet you're wondering if I'm making a fool of you? Get you out of sight of the enforcers, so that you might be taken advantage of?"

"The thought had crossed my mind," Daniel said.

"Allow me to ease your anxieties," the undine said. "Down here, steady business relies on good reputation. Trickery doesn't win and keep long term customers." The undine raised a hand. Daniel could see the webbed flesh between its long fingers. "Certainly we have an advantage, in negotiation. This is the crypt, and many come to us in need. But by no means is it an uncertain tide, trying to squeeze you between the rocks and the coral."

Daniel hadn't heard that phrase before, but the meaning was clear. "Why should I deal with you when you have me over a barrel?"

"In a way of speaking," the undine said. "But what are your choices? You might risk trying to find someone in the mines?" Daniel couldn't stop his frown. The undine nodded understandingly, the way someone did when they knew they'd confirmed what you were thinking. "It's dangerous down there, my friend. There's no guarantee you'll find buyers, let alone ones that can afford what you're selling. And that's assuming you land somewhere friendly, and not somewhere that ships you straight off into the mines." He gestured behind himself, into the busy street. "You can at least see what they'll offer you. If not to your liking, then so it is, and you can walk away."

"What's in it for you?" Daniel said.

The undine brushed his fin-like ears back against his head. A sudden awareness struck Daniel—this was an undine shrug. It was eerie how even the body language was translated, in a way—how did the knowledge get into his head?

Maybe Jack was right. The Hell enchantment really is everywhere.

"This is something tasked to me, by my team," the undine said. "We specialize in trading items and information. If I haul in profitable trades, my personal standing increases." The undine bowed his head slightly. "My name is Sulashoun."

"What's your team called?" Daniel asked.

"Ocean Pinnacle," Sulashoun said, smiling. "Often just Pinnacle. Perhaps you've heard of us?"

"Can't say I have."

Daniel's flat answer visibly surprised Sulashoun. He cocked his head, peering at Daniel's lowered hood before continuing. "I see. So what do you say?" The undine smiled in an attempt to revive the conversation. Daniel could see that it had no teeth—rather, an irregular, blue-tinged gumline. "Take a chance on Sulashoun?"

Daniel studied the demon from under his hood. He didn't seem particularly shady, but a lot of people who seemed positively wonderful had been stabbing him in the back lately. At the same time, he wasn't exactly rolling in options. Half the work—finding a buyer—had been done for him. There was no guarantee someone in the mines could offer a better deal, especially considering it housed the poorest of the poor in Hell. On top of that, it did represent its own set of risks—transport to yet another place about which he knew next to nothing.

"Alright," Daniel said. "Show me where this place is. If you're messing with me, I walk. Got it?"

"As you please," Sulashoun said. "I'm confident you'll see we deal above board. Right this way."

They walked into the street, turned at an intersection, and then another, onto a smaller side road. Daniel kept his eyes moving amongst the buildings and windows, on the lookout for an ambush—but Sulashoun was on the level. They never took any of the smallest alleys, and for the most part kept to the center of the crowds. There was almost always one enforcer within eyesight. Daniel kept his map out, tracking their progress as they moved to the northeast section of the crypt, roughly opposite of where he'd come in from. The conditions of the shantytown improved as they made progress; most of the packed wood vanished, replaced by solid stone construction and windows that actually looked as though they were cleaned regularly.

Eventually, they reached a square that had to be the marketplace. Daniel immediately noticed a building that stood out from the rest, because it was painted bright blue, with a dark tan trim. He didn't care for the colors much, but the well-kept exterior lent it a sense of legitimacy, like the opulent architecture outside an old bank. Surrounding the square were wooden stalls, packed shoulder-to-shoulder in front of the buildings, many with colorful draperies. People were shouting, talking, and trading, and for the first time, he saw a few individuals not dressed in the brown robes. It was by far the nicest part of the crypt that Daniel had seen.

"What is this place?" Daniel asked.

"First time in the crypt, I knew it when I saw you." Sulashoun smiled again and opened his palms, like a real estate agent proudly displaying the granite countertops of a kitchen. "This is the marketplace. It is run by our team, in the main building, there. Pinnacle is Hell's premier merchant organization. Most stalls are our businesses; the blue awnings. The different colors are merchants from other teams that pay us a small fee to trade in this space in safety."

"It has to be expensive to keep people down here," Daniel said. "10 points is a lot when you start to add it up over time."

"So it is, but so also the crypt forms a crossroads, of sorts," Sulashoun said. "Death leads here, from every floor. Rare items can be found and trades made between factions far distant. Some arrange suicides to intentionally come trade, then return home."

"Are you telling me," Daniel said, "that people kill themselves to come here and trade with you guys?"

"So it is," Sulashoun said. "Humans are rare—I know you must be from Purgatory. And with you, rare items, perhaps?"

Daniel smirked. Unlike him, Sulashoun wasn't new at this. Clearly there was a reason his team was paying the bill for him to stay down here—he had a good eye. Or a good ear, in this case. It might be exactly his strategy to hang out by the teleport booths, looking for this kind of opportunity. "Maybe I do," Daniel said.

"I thought as much," Sulashoun said, chuckling lightly. "If you please?"

Sulashoun led Daniel from the bustle of the trading post and into the main building. The place was packed; most waited in lines in front of a long counter, trading their valuables for points. It again reminded Daniel of a bank—on Friday afternoon, with people lined up to cash their checks. Others were gathered in circles in the lobby, discussing the day's trades or negotiating prices of specific items. Lounge seating offered places to linger in comfort, and two grazul were running a bar on the far side of the room, their many arms helping them quickly serve customers.

Daniel glanced at a series of displays on the wall, opposite the counter. Most of the screens showed pictures of what looked like gemstones, though they varied in color, shape, and size. They updated themselves regularly, flickering through numbers and types on a cycle. Dozens of demons were gathered in front of them, discussing amongst themselves and watching intently, as if it were all a miniature stock exchange. Messengers flittered between groups, sometimes retreating through doors in the back of the hall, sometimes entering again, often with paper notes clutched in their hands, which they would exchange with the groups outside. Daniel realized that, without armbands to make calls, inmates in the crypt must rely on physically exchanging information.

Seeing the technology made Daniel realize he hadn't spotted any of the usual flying cameras. He knew that enforcers had their own cameras that were public viewing—that might be enough for the generally boring circumstances of the crypt. Maybe there were cameras, and he just couldn't see them. Still, he doubted the audience was interested much in internal tradesmanship between prisoners.

"Impressive, isn't it?" Sulashoun said. Daniel nodded, not wanting to reveal even more ignorance. He was lucky enough already that Sulashoun hadn't figured out who he was. "We do a great amount of business in mana crystals. They're the only thing Hell really produces—aside from entertainment, of course."

Daniel nodded in pretend understanding. Whatever mana crystals were, they were valuable. They must have something to do with magic. He imagined a place called the Crystal Mines might have one or two of those lying around.

Sulashoun led him to a door at the end of the counters and opened it for him. There were fewer demons in the back hallways, mostly undines. Sulashoun guided him to a private room and sat down with him, offering him some green sludge from a cooler set against the wall. Daniel waved it off.

He expected Sulashoun to finally ask what he wanted to trade, but when the demon remained quiet, Daniel decided to prompt him. "What are we waiting for?"

"For a guest such as yourself, my superior shall negotiate," Sulashoun said. "I request your patience."

"Sure, sure," Daniel said.

Almost as soon as he spoke the words, the door opened again. A dwarf—fat, even by their standards—waddled into the room. He plunged himself into the seat opposite Daniel, causing his beard to sit awkwardly over the table. He tucked it into his lap. "Sulashoun, why don't you..." the dwarf paused. "Human? Ah. That explains it."

"Might I ask your leave, so that I can continue..." Sulashoun trailed off.

"Yes, yes," the dwarf said, batting a hand at him. Sulashoun gave Daniel a half-bow, then left the room. The dwarf eyed Daniel up and down. "Can't say I've heard of you, and I try to keep track of humans. Where you from? Purgatory?"

"It doesn't matter," Daniel said. "I'm here to trade."

The dwarf slammed a fist on the table, making Daniel jump in his seat—but the demon bawled out a laugh. "See, this is why I like humans! Undines are great salesmen but sometimes you want to get to the point. Still, that's why Pinnacle stands at the top, we balance each other out!" The dwarf opened his hands. "What are you selling?"

"A weapon," Daniel said. "It can give you access to 25% of your magic for 5 minutes."

"Mmm. Mmhmm. 5 minutes?"

"Yes."

"And how many of these do you have?"

"Several," Daniel lied, "but I'm only selling one."

"I see. 5 minutes, huh? 5 minutes..." The dwarf ran his hand down his beard. His pudgy nose wiggled a bit as he considered. "Alright. I can do 5,000 points for one of them."

Daniel had no idea the actual cost of the thing, but even still, 5,000 points was far more than he was expecting. If he was being undercut—which he probably was—the actual value might be two or three times that price.

Daniel decided to gamble, doing his best to keep his voice steady. "5,000? I was hoping for at least 10,000."

"Ten? You must be out of your mind," the dwarf said. "Six. I can't imagine paying any higher."

"Better start dreaming, buddy. I'm not settling for less than 9,000 points."

"That's ridiculous," the dwarf said. "You're coming to us to trade, here. Tell you what. I like you, I like your style. 7,000."

"I can't go lower than eight," Daniel said. "I could get more if I auctioned the thing in public."

The dwarf scratched his chin. "Want to skip the rest of this part and split the difference at 7,500?"

"Done," Daniel said.

"Thank goodness," the dwarf said. "If it was an undine, you wouldn't get out of here until you were down to 5 point increments, I'll have you know."

Daniel cocked an eyebrow. "Glad I got a dwarf, then."

"Yeah, that makes two of us," the dwarf said. "Alright, you wait here. I have to visit our vault to withdraw the points directly, security reasons. Be back shortly." The dwarf stopped near the door. "By the way, are you here on behalf of a team from Purgatory, or—"

"It's an independent trade," Daniel said quickly.

"Ah. Understood. Back in a moment."

The door clumped shut as the dwarf went off to get the money. Daniel sighed and slackened back into his chair. He wouldn't be able to jump straight back to Purgatory, but his money worries were gone for the moment. He'd gotten away a lot better than he'd hoped, and he could avoid the mines altogether. There had to be a team out there willing to ignore the Order if it meant they had Daniel on their side. Maybe he could do some mercenary work, earn some cash working for different teams. Then it was back to Purgatory to fight Bathory again. Somehow.

He could go after other teams in Purgatory, first. Thanks to Beelzebub, his contractor magic would still absorb those he killed up there, so he could become more powerful, then challenge Bathory again. It was unlikely he'd get as lucky with the choice of arena, but hopefully by that time could overpower her. Their fight had been close, at times—close enough that he was willing to try again.

The biggest barrier was going to be arranging another duel. He wouldn't have the backing of another large team to justify the move, so he'd have to somehow force Bathory into another confrontation. If he could leverage his popularity as a human fighter and maintain his momentum, he could propel himself back up to Purgatory. PrisonWatch was always hungry for ratings—he could use that to pressure her into a grudge match.

As a path forward opened up in his mind, Daniel felt the weight come off his shoulders. His flickering flame of hope, about to be blown out, was now a light at the end of the tunnel. He took a breath and sat straighter. He could do this.

Daniel's face darkened. He *would* do this. And he would find out what happened to Jack. There was no way their whole time together was an act. Jack was a pretty terrible liar. If the Order was somehow involved, he'd take them to task—by force, if he had to.

If it really came down to it, Daniel had something even Bathory and Dracula couldn't reproduce. Unlike every other inmate, if Daniel killed someone in Purgatory, they stayed dead. His actions could end the farce permanently, rip away the security blanket that let them all keep at each other's throats without rest.

All he had to do was get back.

The door slammed open. Daniel turned, startled. Three trolls and a dwarf—the one he'd been speaking to—barreled into the room. The first troll punched Daniel in the back of the head hard enough to knock him out of his chair and onto the table. He rebounded and hit the floor hard.

"Put him on the wall! Don't let him use his armlet!"

Daniel was grabbed under the shoulders and pinned up high, high enough that his feet were dangling off the ground. Two trolls had him on either side; the third stood in front, club raised and ready to swing. The dwarf walked up to him and looked him up and down like a butcher eyeing a slab of meat.

"What the hell?!" Daniel shouted. He blinked blood out of his eyes from a weeping cut on his forehead. "I thought we had a deal!"

"You were banished from the Order of the Dragon and you want to trade with us? Not in this lifetime, you damn cave rat."

"The Order hates demons!" Daniel said.

"Yeah, Dracula doesn't make a secret about that," the dwarf said. "And they'd have no problem squashing us like a bug for associating ourselves with you. No human they send down comes back up, not one, not ever, and that's the way it is. There's no messing in human business unless you want to be split open like a rotten egg!"

"What? What are you talking about?!"

"And you shoulda known better," the dwarf said, rolling over Daniel's question. "Coming in here and acting like you're a little lost pixie that wants to make a trade? You insulting us? Trying to get us destroyed?"

"That's not what it was, I swear," Daniel said. "I'm not working with anyone else. I want to trade my item and leave. I won't tell anyone!"

"It's already on camera that you walked in here," the dwarf said. He raised his own armlet and pressed a few buttons. "Now you've got a choice to make. Either you hand over that item and we let you go, or we beat the hell out of you and send the recording to Rasputin for that bounty of his."

Daniel stared at him. "You people are full of crap. That mermaid gave me a bunch of lines about reputation, and now you're robbing me!?"

The dwarf gestured. The troll swung the club, slamming Daniel in the stomach. Daniel lurched and spat out air as something in him crunched. He coughed and spluttered as he tried to get his breath, but it wouldn't come. His lungs started burning.

Eventually, the healing magic went to work on him. The space around his midsection rippled, and suddenly, he could draw a breath. He sucked it in, then coughed as the rest of him healed itself back up. The other occupants of the room sat there, watching the process patiently while Daniel's abdomen returned to its proper shape.

"Let's try this again," the dwarf said. "The bounty for killing you, beating the hell out of you, or otherwise making your life difficult, is very high. Higher than what we'd be able to get even if we resold your weapon. So you hand that sucker over to us, and we let you go out the back door and that'll be the end of it. Then we get to tell Rasputin we robbed you, we get something out of it to make it worth our while, and you get to walk away in one piece, so we're all happy. Or, we beat you to death, right here and now." The dwarf moved closer, until he was staring right up at Daniel. "With all this magic healing you up, that'll take a while, don't you think?"

Daniel spat on him.

The dwarf wiped his face with his sleeve, then hacked a short laugh. "Straightforward as usual. I hope that was satisfying, cause you're gonna be in a lot of pain very shortly."

The club came in again, and as soon as the air left him, a punch from the dwarf caught him across the chin. Daniel's head snapped back the other way, and another blow caught him right in the throat. He could hear something delicate snap. He couldn't breathe.

The blows rained down on him. He couldn't move. They hit his stomach, beat on his chest. When they got bored with that, they took the club to his legs, bashing his knees in the wrong way.

Daniel screamed at that—tried to. It came out like garbled phlegm.

He convulsed, spat blood. It ran down his chin.

Another punch slammed into his jaw, and the world spun. A tooth fell out of his mouth. His head rang and buzzed. More fists caught him in the face, treating his head like a punching bag between their fists and the wall behind him.

He faded in and out; his attention would come back long enough to feel the hurt, and the ache, and then another strike would get him in the head, and it would all wash out again.

But eventually, the blows stopped.

His lungs strained to breathe. He throbbed all over. His eyes were swollen so much he could hardly see.

His legs cracked and reformed; it felt like someone rearranging nails inside his thighs and ankles. His jaw—which was disturbingly lopsided—shunted back in place. Teeth replaced themselves one by one, little daggers shooting through his gums. His ribs straightened one at a time, as if a hand reached into him and yanked them back where they belonged.

Air found its way to him again, but it was all spent on coughing. He coughed for what felt like minutes, until he could finally breathe properly. And with that, he could think straight again.

He wasn't sure what was worse—the beating, or the healing afterward, while he was still conscious to feel it all happen.

Daniel was finally able to open his eyes. Blood covered the floor, dotted the clothes of his assailants. His robes were stained with it. Bits and pieces—of him—were scattered on the floor. He recognized one of his teeth sitting on the table.

The dwarf was seated past that. He picked up the tooth, examined it, then flicked it at Daniel. It hit his clothes and *tacked* onto the floor.

"So, Daniel Fitzgerald," the dwarf said. It pulled a knife out of its robes, a long, nasty-looking thing with a hook on the opposite end of the hilt. "Are you gonna give us that item, or do we really have to go to work on you? Because what we just did to you probably wouldn't be enough for the terms of the bounty." The dwarf's gaze sat on him like a lead weight, and it had none of the mirth or good humor from before. The friendly merchant was gone, replaced by hard, stony ruthlessness. "I'd want to get some extra footage. Just to be sure."

Daniel shivered on the wall, still pinned up by the trolls. Their breath came heavy on him, snorted through tusk-lined mouths and smelling like compost.

He couldn't give up his weapon. It was his only lifeline. But how long were they going to keep him here? How long was this going to last? He would heal up again, sure—but the idea of getting beat up like that over and over turned into a dark lump in the pit of his stomach.

If he'd known how bad it would be, maybe he would've given it to them right off the bat.

The dwarf got up and came closer. Daniel flinched as he raised the knife. The dwarf stayed there, knife positioned to stab into his stomach. Daniel's mind flashed back to Bathory's wide-eyed grin.

"We both know you're gonna capitulate," the dwarf said. "I don't enjoy this any more than you do. So. Decision time." The dwarf extended his other hand. "Give over the orb, kid. Let's get this over with."

"No," Daniel said. His voice shook like a rusty wind chime as he forced the words out. "I won't. We made a deal!"

The dwarf heaved a defeated sigh. "Gotta be a tough guy. Gotta prove it to yourself, huh? But I have to say, I like your attitude. Most would've backed out right at the start. Most would be pissing their pants right now."

The dwarf jammed the knife into Daniel's thigh, all the way to the hilt. Daniel shouted as it went in; his leg spasmed, but they kept him forced up against the wall without budging. He grit his teeth; his breath rushed in and out as he tried to hold in the rising pain.

"I'm gonna give you one." The dwarf twisted the knife. "More." Then back the other way. "Chance."

Daniel screamed as the knife tore back and forward through his thigh. "Stop! Please! Stop, stop!"

"Alright." The dwarf released the handle. Daniel shuddered even at that tiny movement. "Well? What's it gonna be?" He waited until Daniel looked at him to continue. "I'm not gonna waste any more of my time on this. The next thing I do is I leave this room, and my boys here really start to work you over." His voice lowered. "And they're a lot less friendly than I am."

The trolls grinned at that. The one closest to him chuckled, sending another wave of putrid breath over Daniel's face. Its teeth were black, rotted nubs.

"Fine," Daniel said. "Fine."

"You made the right choice," the dwarf said. "Here." He reached up and tapped his armlet against Daniel's. "I've set the trade up. All you gotta do is press that confirm button right there." The dwarf tilted his head. "Let his other arm go."

Daniel glanced at his armlet. There was a popup hovering above it that had a simple Yes/No confirmation for the trade being offered to him. The terms were listed below that: one item, his power sphere, in exchange for nothing in return.

He hesitated. Maybe he could close the panel and activate the item itself before they could react. He envisioned the sequence of buttons he'd have to press to make it happen.

But if he messed up...

"Don't try it, kid," the dwarf said. "I've done this a hundred times. No one gets away with it. And then we have to make an example of you, and things get messy again."

Daniel looked back at the button. All he had to do was push yes, and it would be over.

But it wouldn't be over, not by a longshot. He'd be totally broke and stuck at the bottom of Hell. He'd have nothing left. He'd never make it home.

He'd never be annoyed by Felix again. He'd never see Aplington again, the stupid suburbs that he hated, the quiet houses with preened squares of grass, repeating itself over and over. He'd never see his school again, never hear Mark and Jensen nag at each other like a married couple.

He'd never see Rachel again. Even if he got back.

She wouldn't want this.

Daniel latched onto that thought like a man climbing onto a raft in stormy seas. Rachel wouldn't let him give up. She'd pull him up whether he liked it or not.

A moment of clarity hit him. These people had already lied to him. They reneged on the deal, tried to steal from him, beat him up—who was to say they'd keep their word, even if he gave them the orb? They might beat him anyway to earn good will from the Order—cash in on both the bounty, and their stolen goods.

There was another thing that stuck out to him. He was defeated by any measure—and yet, for some reason, they weren't stealing the one item they were entitled to from his inventory. Maybe they couldn't. Maybe there were different rules in the crypt, or some other exception Daniel didn't know about, but there was no reason to go through this whole thing if they could take it from him outright. For one reason or another, they needed his willing cooperation.

Daniel's lips firmed up. He reached over and mashed the button with his thumb.

The refusal alert flashed orange on both their armlets. The dwarf snorted. "I'll be back when my schedule frees up. Feel free to trade it to any of these fine fellows in the meantime, and we can put an end to this."

The door slammed shut behind him.

One of the orcs leaned in close, rotting teeth and fangs hovering in front of Daniel's face. "Big mistake, huuman."

"God, you're ugly," Daniel said.

The orc's fist smashed Daniel directly in the face, sending his head straight back into the wall behind him. For the first of what would be several times, Daniel blacked out.

Chapter 21
The Contractor Program

"Looks like you've hit a spot of trouble."

The voice threw Eleanor out of her doze and onto her feet. Her chair fell back with a thud onto the dirt floor. She whipped her head back and forward, taking in the walls of her cell as her heart pounded in her chest. "Who the—Xikanthus?"

"Just Xik, please," the spindly frog-man said. He was leaned up against the corner of the cell, as if he'd been settled in for a nap of his own. He tipped his hat to her. "Good evening."

Footsteps sounded down the hall. A guard—male, close-cropped hair, wearing a tabard—came into view. Eleanor froze, her brain scrambling for a reaction to being woken up and caught red-handed with someone her father was beginning to regard as an enemy.

The guard looked at her, not noticing the elephant in the room. "I heard a sound," he said. "Everything okay?"

Eleanor glanced at Xik—the frog had a smirk winding around his face—then at her fallen chair. "I dozed off," Eleanor said, hoping she sounded convincing. "Ended up startling myself."

The guard nodded. Before moving off, he glanced around the cell, but he didn't notice Xik—or couldn't. Eleanor stayed stock-still until his footsteps faded, then sighed away her tension. "Phew. Xik. Please don't scare me like that."

"I have to get my entertainment in somehow," he said. "So. Locked up by daddy?"

The word *daddy* didn't sound right coming out of his mouth, more creepy than mocking. "No thanks to you," she said. "You only seem to stick around long enough to get people into serious trouble."

"This time," Xik said, stepping away from the corner, "I've come to get you out of trouble. If you'd like."

"I don't see the point," Eleanor said. "My father would find me again."

"He knew you would be in Cleveland," Xik said. "All it took was a quick call to find out that was, in fact, where you were teleported. It wouldn't be so easy to track you down a second time—of that, I can make certain."

"Why are you here?" Eleanor asked suddenly. "Why are you helping me?"

"You're friends with Daniel," Xik said. "Isn't that enough?"

"No," Eleanor said, "it's not. What do you want from me, exactly?"

Xik considered her. "My plans have been thrown somewhat astray. As a result, I want to give you a choice."

"What choice?"

"The contractors are strong, but they're scattered. They have no organization, no experience with magic. Their powers are intuitive, but they don't have the kind of education, the training, that you have, and in the meantime they're being rounded up or killed."

"Killed?" Eleanor said. "We haven't been killing contractors except in self-defense."

"Other organizations are not as forgiving or lawful as your own," Xik said. "You know that."

"What are you getting at, exactly?"

"I want you to work for me. I know your father was grooming you for leadership. You have contacts with and are aware of magical organizations across the planet. Your experience and knowledge can be put to good use protecting the contractors until they're strong enough to protect themselves. You can guide them to their full potential."

Eleanor was taken aback. She went to her chair to buy herself time to think, picking it up and setting it straight. She sat down and brushed her clothes free of wrinkles. "You want me to lead...the contractors. The ones aside from Daniel?"

"Manage them, rather," Xik said. "But if they accept your leadership, so be it. That's between you and them."

"The last contractor I met aside from him tried to kill me," she said. "Jack Killiney."

"You have to admit, there were certain circumstances—"

"The point remains," Eleanor said firmly.

"I can't account for their individual behavior," Xik said, "but I think you'll find that most of them aren't as extreme as Jack. Particularly the man a few cells away from you."

Eleanor remembered him—he'd killed the Vorid assassin. She hadn't realized he'd been kept so close to her, but if his powers were sealed by his own set of bracers, he'd be harmless enough. For now.

"He was almost killed in the attack, earlier," Xik said. "Several other contractors scattered around the globe *were* killed, and with the magicians helping things along, humanity can't afford more losses. The Vorid will send more waves of assassins. They will attack in force again, soon."

"Why aren't you doing all this yourself?" Eleanor asked. "Why do you need me?"

"I'm busy with other matters," Xik said.

"What would those be, exactly?"

"Mostly," Xik said, "delaying the Vorid entry into your world as long as possible. Among other things." Xik stopped, rubbed his chin. "I'm not here, really." He put his hands out, gesturing to the ground around him. "Not physically. Rather, an image of myself is projected here. All the spells I cast are projected here, across dimensions. While this has its advantages, it takes a tremendous amount of energy to push anything across the boundaries between worlds and keep it in one piece. It's one area in which Vorid technology surpasses the Klide. My activities are limited by this cost. I have to spend my time and allotted resources very sparingly."

"Then so far," Eleanor said, "you've mostly left the contractors to their own devices, and you're delaying the Vorid?"

"As I tried to tell your father, they're preparing a major assault," Xik said. "It will begin shortly. The contractors have been additional boots on the ground, you might say, to shore up your gaps."

"What do you mean by an assault?"

"It's actually more of a distraction than an assault," Xik said. "While you're busy fending them off, they'll finish construction of a gateway that will allow a Vorid prince to come to Earth. He will be the spearhead in a true invasion of your universe. If that happens, humanity is finished."

"A prince?" Eleanor said. "Royalty? Someone we can reason with?"

"It's a Klide classification of battle potential," he said, "as close as I can translate it. Let me see...prince, grand duke...perhaps cardinal, in the religious sense? Warlord, general. All of those things, at once. It's approximately two tiers above the lord Daniel fended off in New York."

"Two...tiers?" Eleanor stared into space as she grappled with the concept. "I don't understand what such a creature could want from us. With that amount of power—" She stopped herself. "We're discussing beings that could wipe away the surface of the planet."

"Quite so," Xik said. "It won't be here to negotiate, but suffice to say, that would be the end of any meaningful human resistance. Of course, it wouldn't want to kill everything so dramatically, that would be a waste. Its goal is to absorb humanity as fuel for the Vorid war machine."

Eleanor's spine shivered at the idea of people being used as fuel. "How strong is this thing, exactly?"

Xik cocked his head in thought. "At that level, strength varies between individuals, but it could squash a Vorid lord as if it were an ant, were it displaced."

"Are you serious?"

"Yes," Xik said. "In battle, we've seen the Vorid cannibalize their lessers, so to speak, especially as punishment after repeated failures or losses. If someone cannot handle their power properly, then it is transferred to their superiors, where it can be put to better use."

"No, I mean—" Eleanor stopped again, caught between conflicting thoughts. "They routinely do this?"

"Many Vorid sacrifice themselves if they fail repeatedly, or feel it is appropriate," Xik said. "It's considered a matter of honor."

"But are you serious about how strong this being is? You aren't exaggerating to make your point?"

"I'm quite serious," Xik said. "That's the low end of their power. Earth isn't important enough to warrant more than that, thankfully. I suppose if lords are the warrior class of the Vorid, princes are, as I said, generals. Not exactly a leader, but higher ranking. Of course, generals have their own rankings and so forth."

Eleanor clenched her teeth. When the lord had taken them by surprise at Times Square, it had beaten back multiple fully transformed dragons, held off Daniel, and nearly cut down her father—by itself, all at the same time. And a prince could treat a lord like a bug.

There was no fighting that kind of existence.

"How do we make sure it can't come here?" Eleanor said.

"Simple," Xik said. "I'm delaying them as long as possible, but what we need, as a permanent solution, is a dimensional anchor." Eleanor, unfamiliar with the term, waved her hand for him to continue. Xik cleared his throat. "Essentially, the more power you try to move between worlds, the more costly the transportation becomes, in exponential fashion," he said. "This is why princes don't simply skip around the multiverse, crushing worlds with ease. It's also why the Vorid initiate with a slow, secretive buildup. Vastly more efficient in terms of energy collection. On an interdimensional scale, energy is the currency of economics, and of war. Material, physical resources are still important, but energy collection and distribution rules the day. Ultimately, any civilization has to take in more energy than it expends."

"So that's why you're projecting yourself here."

"Precisely," Xik said. "It would take tremendous energy to actually transport myself to Earth. The Vorid are bound by the same rules, even with their inventive means of breaking into other dimensions. Weaker Vorid come through at cheaper cost, then construct a gateway in this universe to ease the passage of mightier allies. The assault is just a distraction while they finish their work."

"What's this anchor that can put a stop to it?" Eleanor asked.

"Earth needs its power concentrated in one location—ideally, one individual. That individual will literally anchor reality down and interfere with interdimensional transport."

Eleanor shook her head. "I've never heard of this."

"How do I explain?" Xik said. He tapped at his chin. "Well...hmm. Imagine reality as a blanket, spread over a bed. Now imagine you drop a ten pound weight in the middle of the bed. What happens?"

"You get a wrinkled blanket," Eleanor said.

Xik nodded. "Those wrinkles make travel very tricky. Not impossible, but harder. The more weight added in one spot, or even several spots, the more wrinkles, and the greater the cost of transporting the prince to Earth."

"That's what the contractors are," Eleanor said, coming to the realization. "That's their purpose. Weights to wrinkle the blanket. But it only works if they get more powerful—if they're heavy enough, in other words."

"Exactly," Xik said. "I want to impose very challenging requirements on the Vorid gateway in order to buy time. Then we can mount a counterattack and destroy it before it's completed."

"Why haven't you told all of this to us already?" Eleanor said. "This is too important to ignore. Henry might have made a different choice if—"

"He already knows," Xik said.

"What?!"

"I told the leadership of humanity all this information months before the Vorid invaded," Xik said. "At first, they distrusted me, especially before the Vorid got here. But eventually they refused to listen altogether. They won't tolerate the solution that is the contractors."

"Does Daniel know all this?" Eleanor asked. "About the prince, the gateway? Do any of the contractors?"

"No," Xik said, "and that is by my design."

"Why wouldn't you tell them?"

"So that I could better judge their character," Xik said. "They understand the Vorid threat—all of them do, one way or another. It impacted them all. They know the stakes, but not so much the specifics." Xik nodded to himself. "I gave them power, gave them a goal, then stood back and let them work. I wanted to see who was most motivated, who could go the farthest. Who would use the powers for their own ends, and who would focus on culling the Vorid. Not only who could become the anchor for Earth, but who should be that anchor."

"Didn't that slow you down?" Eleanor said. "Why not pick one person and work with them?"

Xik folded his hands in front of himself, then sighed. "This is a complex issue. It involves the best way the Klide can help other worlds on a large scale. We've studied many methods carefully, in many instances, across many worlds. This is the best we've found." Eleanor nodded at him to continue. "The contractor system wasn't the first thing we tried," Xik said. "Not by far. Direct intervention was the first and most obvious method, but massive Klide support in the form of energy and advanced technology led to complacence in the long term. No one appreciates what they don't earn themselves. That's without mentioning the discord created by injecting a quiet, single-planet species with technology on a multiversal scale. You can't do that and expect stable social structures and traditions to keep up; they are by their nature resistant to change because they serve as backstops to chaos. Often the Vorid would wait until infighting weakened a world, after the Klide shifted focus, then swept in to clean up afterward. The Vorid don't always consume everything; they accept converts, and there were plenty of races willing to throw in with them for the promise of more than what the Klide could provide. That led to the waste of even more resources, resources we simply couldn't risk in world after world. The multiverse is huge, and while the Vorid consumed and regenerated with every conflict, growing larger and stronger, the Klide were weakened by repeated expenditures."

Eleanor was sitting back in her chair in the center of the cell. Her eyes were wide, but her focus was intent, her mind bent on absorbing all the details. "And this system, with the contractors becoming anchors," Eleanor said. "This is the next step?"

"It is one of several experimental methods designed to effectively stymie the Vorid more efficiently," Xik said. "We kept failing more often than not by doing what you suggested earlier, carefully grooming just one or a few contractors. The Vorid were able to identify and assassinate them, undoing our efforts. When we did succeed, we succeeded too well, creating dictatorships of power that twisted and sometimes destroyed the surviving peoples. The top surviving contractor, in a handful of worlds, betrayed us to the Vorid in exchange for personal power. What's the point in saving a world with those kinds of results?

"We discovered that we needed many determined warriors of equally firm character, capable of shouldering the burden of the future of their race," Xik said. He raised a finger. "That did not dovetail with the creation of martyrs, as we at first believed, but rather, people of mental toughness enough to survive the rigors of warfare and resist the temptations of power that followed. We couldn't seek to have only good people who do what is right; nor could we rely on those ruthless and cruel enough to win at any cost—they would just as easily sell out their own society. We needed people with skin in the game, as you humans would say, that had committed themselves to a cause that they wouldn't give up easily.

"The best way to develop such warriors was to allow them to struggle forward on their own with little interference, to sink or swim. It ferrets out those with the ability to do what is necessary, and no more, while at the same time solidifying enmity against the Vorid during the course of said struggle.

"There you have it," Xik said. "The nature of the contractor program. Highly experimental, highly successful—in most worlds. We need a larger sample size to implement it on larger scale." He looked at her, scanning her face. "I will make this simple," he said. "We're in a race. It's a race to destroy their gateway before they can complete it, but it's a race we have to win the right way. Otherwise, victory is only temporary."

"Wait," Eleanor said. "What's stopping the Vorid from building this gateway out in the middle of space where no one knows about it? Why invade in the first place before the prince arrives?"

"They hide it as best they can," Xik said, "but they need their special brand of magic for it to work, so they're forced to build it near enough sentient life as a result."

"For fuel," Eleanor said, spitting the words.

Xik nodded, not adding to her characterization. "Such locations are usually the main source of magic in any universe. They locate new worlds the same way—detection via magic. Luckily, that need is a double-edged sword which grants us a chance to counter their efforts."

Eleanor heaved out a sigh and ran her hands down her knees. Her eyes went past Xik, to the bars of her cell. She took it all in, the scale of the conflict, the weight of it all, sitting above her, ready to crash down on them.

Eventually, she looked back at him. "And my father knew about all of this?" she asked. "He's known about it this whole time."

"He has," Xik said. "In response to their inaction, I went my own way. And now..." Xik looked at her, big, red eyes blinking as they took her in. "I believe that your character is sufficient for this task. You ignored politics and chose to seek Daniel's family to fulfill a promise."

"You were testing me?" Eleanor asked.

"I need you to bring the contractors together," he said, avoiding her question. "Gather them under one banner—lead them yourself if you must—and fight back against the Vorid assault. We don't have Daniel right now, and one of them—or enough of them—have to become powerful enough to anchor down this reality and delay the prince."

Eleanor had trouble swallowing the lump in her throat. Her father knew. He knew, and he did nothing. He convinced himself it was lies, or they didn't need the contractors, or—or something. But Earth's leaders hadn't acted.

The prince was coming. Xik was delaying, but he couldn't hold on forever. Eleanor was annoyed that he had, in a way, manipulated her—but it wasn't cruel, really. He wanted to see what she was made of. And he had, at least temporarily, helped her avoid impending political marriage.

The contractors were fighting, but they probably weren't coordinated enough to combat the Vorid in a meaningful way. They didn't understand the fundamentals of magic like she did—they might not even be using all the strength they could. Xik was absolutely right—if they had a little direction and insight, they might be a lot stronger. Even Daniel, who was only able to learn a single physical sigil from Rachel, became that much more capable.

She was in a difficult position with the Ivory Dawn's leadership, internally, but she had an identity and clout that couldn't be ignored if she had the backing. She could be a face for the contractors. Capitalize on the videos that Daniel already released. Keep the good PR going, fight the Vorid, and stop the prince. Hell, she'd get out of marrying Matthew Aiken to boot—and when all was said and done, convincing Earth's leaders to release Daniel from prison was a real possibility.

All the variables pointed to one choice.

Eleanor looked up at Xik. He was still watching her, an expectant look on his face.

She wasn't quite sure she fully trusted him.

Everything lined up too perfectly. Everything was leading her along to agree with his strategy and do what he wanted. As much as she'd denied her father's paranoia, some of what he'd said held a small kernel of truth. But for the time being, she didn't have much choice but to give Xik the benefit of the doubt.

Eleanor stood out of her chair, and nodded. "I'm in. What should I do first?"

Xik grinned, then tossed her something. She almost fumbled, but came up with a small green stone. "What's this?" she asked. "It looks like the one you gave my father."

"That one was for communication," Xik said. "This one is the car keys."

"Keys to what?"

"A Klide ship. It can outrun anything else on the planet, I imagine. It has means to find contractors so you can gather them together, as well as instruments to detect dimensional fluctuations, such that you can predict and intercept Vorid attacks. But...there's a catch."

"What's the catch?" Eleanor said.

"Only contractors can use the stones, and fly the ship," Xik said.

"So if I want to get out of here," Eleanor said, "I have to follow your plan and take that man we captured with me."

"There's more to it than that." Xik stepped toward her. "I want you to become a contractor."

Eleanor's heart skipped a beat. "What?"

"Become," Xik said, "a contractor."

"I'm a mage," Eleanor said. "I thought we couldn't be contractors."

"You know," Xik said, "I never said that. Everyone seems to have assumed it based on whom I'm making contracts with."

"All according to plan, I'm sure," Eleanor muttered.

"I want you to show me that you're on my side, Eleanor," Xik said. "That you're against the Vorid before all else. Before your allegiance to the mages." Xik offered his hand.

Eleanor looked at it, then back at him. "Can I ask you one thing?"

"Of course."

"Are you intending to use me against my father?"

"No," Xik said. "I tried convincing your father in the first place. I'd much rather have Earth's forces as allies. Maybe where he ignored me, he'll instead listen to you."

"You realize," Eleanor said, "that if he doesn't listen to me—and signs point to no—then becoming a contractor sets me against him and every other mage on Earth."

"Unless you change their minds," Xik said. "But in the end, what's more important? What others think of you, or the lives you might save?"

"Did you ask Daniel the same question?" Eleanor asked. "When you made him this offer?"

"I didn't have to," Xik said.

Eleanor hesitated another second, then reached out and clasped his hand.

Xik smiled. "I honestly didn't expect you to accept that quickly."

"I've come this far already," Eleanor said. "And I'm not joining your side." She stared back at him. "I'm joining Daniel's—Rachel's side. Earth's side."

Xik's smile widened into an almost Cheshire Cat-like grin, stretching across his face and pulling his green skin taut around his cheeks.

Green fire erupted from their point of contact and rushed up Eleanor's arm. She flinched back, but the flames kept going, spreading over her body. The cell was as dark as before—the fire made no light. It didn't burn her. But she could feel it, crawling, creeping its way down across her chest, around her hips, and down her legs. She stared down at the stuff as it sat on her skin, an otherworldly ectoplasm that molded to her form.

There was a pause. Eleanor could feel something building. Something was shifting inside her, at the point in her inner world where her magic rested. A foundation had been laid.

And then the sigils appeared, glowing with a shock-red haze. There were numbers, symbols she hadn't seen before and didn't understand, connecting and interconnecting in ways that were beyond her. It all circled around her too fast for her to grasp, constructs and runes dancing in a choreographed laser light show. She was the focal point of the spell as it built up into a swirling ring that rotated around her, faster and faster—

Until it suddenly stopped.

The red light intensified, brightening as if there was a power surge, only it never cut out and the power kept surging. The cell was dyed pink-maroon, and then the colors changed, maroons becoming blue and pink becoming black, as if she was looking at a photonegative of the world around her.

The magic shuddered within her. Eleanor felt a bridge form inside herself, a connection that reached out to something. She touched it, briefly. It was energy—dense, endless energy, rippling in an expanse so large and tremendous that it threatened to swallow her up and disintegrate her very being. She shut her eyes and tried to pull back, tear herself away from being dissolved into nothingness.

Wind whipped her hair across her face. The sensation drew her back to herself, to reality—and the bad feeling, the sense of connection, was gone.

Eleanor opened her eyes. Xik stood there in front of her, unmoving, though the smile was gone from his face. "So," he said. "How do you feel?"

Eleanor sent her senses inward. She couldn't detect Xik's spell anymore. Whatever had changed, it was gone.

"It feels like nothing happened," she said.

"Good," Xik said. "That's normal."

"For a minute there," Eleanor said, "I felt…lost. What was that?"

"It's the reason I've resisted making trained magicians into contractors," Xik said. "It's riskier. Higher chance of failure."

"You're telling me this now?" Eleanor said.

"The details are a secret closely held by my race. That's already too much, especially for someone with the knowledge you have." He leaned his head toward the hallway. "I put the guards to sleep, but I'm needed elsewhere. Ask other contractors how to scry; they can teach you." Xik leaned back into the corner, and his body started to turn translucent, so she could see the wall faintly behind him.

"Wait," Eleanor said. "Where am I supposed to go? Where's the ship?"

"Outside, behind the trucks," Xik said. "They won't see it until you board. Be quick—that will break the illusion I cast over it." He was almost gone, now; she couldn't see his legs, and his torso was fading fast. "Oh! I nearly forgot."

A ghostly hand moved through the air. Eleanor's bracelets fell off. No alarm sounded. She rubbed her wrists, amazed at how he'd dealt with the enchantment that quickly.

When she looked up again, he was gone.

Eleanor peered into the hallway. It was quiet. She went up to the gate of her cell and pushed. It slowly creaked open.

She walked down the hall. The guard that checked on her earlier had collapsed on the ground at the first intersection. His head lolled to the side with a long snore.

Eleanor tiptoed past him, making it to the next cell. The old man was inside. He didn't have a chair, forcing him to sit hunched in a corner.

"Hey," Eleanor hissed. She put her face up to the bars. "Hey, wake up!"

The man glanced up—he wasn't sleeping. "Well, well, if it ain't the ice queen. Come to finally say thank you for me saving your life?"

"Xik came," she said. "He let me out. And I'm here to let you out, too."

"Our amphibian ally, huh?" The man was quick to his feet—faster than Eleanor would think for someone his age. He dusted his jeans and sauntered up to the bars of the cell, looking at her from beneath bushy eyebrows. "Why did you, of all people, have to be let out in the first place? Thought you were in charge."

"I can explain the fine details later," Eleanor said. "The short version is, I'm on your side. We need the contractors to beat the Vorid."

The man gave her the stink eye. "What brought about this sudden change of heart?"

"A lot of things," Eleanor said.

"At least tell me what Xik said."

"We don't have time for 20 questions."

"Then give me the short version," John said. "I'm not skipping out on federal custody for a pretty face, no matter what I said to chili pepper back then."

"Xik gave me a way to get out of here." Eleanor raised the green stone in her hand. "He left a ship outside for us, something that can fly us away. This stone can unlock it."

The man reached into his pocket. He brought out another green stone—almost identical to Eleanor's. No. Perfectly identical.

"It's funny," he said. "They patted me down good and thorough, but they didn't take this. Almost like they didn't notice."

"Maybe they couldn't," Eleanor said.

The man nodded. "Alright, little lady. Guess that'll have to be proof enough, and I'm bored to hell anyway. Let's book it."

Eleanor tested his cell door. Locked. She focused on her magic, welling up a tiny bit. A hint of water condensed inside the lock, and she formed it into ice, letting it weave into the shape of the tumbler inside. She gave it a mental twist, and the latch dropped free.

"Let's go."

The man eyed the door up and down, then went to follow her. "Neat trick. So what's your name, anyway? Yvonne? Melindra?"

"Eleanor Astor," she said, slightly annoyed.

"Heh. I knew it would be something good and fancy."

"Well, what's your name?"

"John Smith," he said.

"Sounds like something plain and boring," Eleanor said.

John chuckled. "Alright, that was deserved. So, what's the plan? I sure as hell want my gun back before we get outta here."

Eleanor peered around the next corner. "Looks like you might be in luck."

Ahead of them was the entrance to the prison block, marked by a small guard post. A steel fence that stretched to the ceiling walled off what looked like a stockroom. Eleanor could see a box with her bag inside and next to that, more boxes. Two guards near the door were slumped over; another guard, at the desk inside the fencing, was drooling on his magazine.

"Pays to have friends in high places," John whispered.

"Yeah. Come on." Eleanor magicked the side door to the room open, and they started poking through the containers. John found his gun, and its holster, in short order, proffering it excitedly before securing it at his waist. Eleanor grabbed her bag—which held a few books and her cell phone. Felix's tablet was gone.

"Damn," she hissed.

"Eleanor?" a small voice said. "Is that you?"

Eleanor and John spun; a sharp click resounded as he leveled his gun. Sitting in the corner was Felix Fitzgerald, the tablet tucked on his lap, open to a game of Candy Crush. His eyes went wide at the weapon.

John clicked the hammer down and put the gun away. "Jesus Christ. Just a kid." John's face screwed up. "A kid?"

"Not just any kid," Eleanor said. She rushed up to him and knelt down. "Felix, why are you here?" The obvious struck her a moment later. "Did Xik bring you?"

"Yeah-huh," he said. "Xik told me everything. I'm a contractor too, now, like Daniel!"

Eleanor's mouth fell open. John folded his arms. "You gotta be kiddin' me," he said. "Makin' a child into one of us? The hell is the frog playing at?"

"I'm supposed to go with you guys," Felix said, sounding a little miffed.

"This is absolutely..." Eleanor's words caught in her throat. "You can't come with us. You need to get back to your dad and stay there."

"No," Felix said. "I'm helping Daniel! I'm not sitting in a tent all day doing nothing!"

"You can eat dirt and crap daisies for all I care," John said, "but you keep your voice down!"

"Sorry," Felix said more quietly.

"What about your dad, Felix?" Eleanor said. "He needs your help, too."

"Xik said he'd explain everything to him," Felix said. "I want to help you guys. Won't that help Daniel?"

"What did Xik tell you, exactly?" Eleanor asked.

"A lot," Felix said. "But he said I could help Daniel if I became a contractor."

Eleanor gave John a look—he responded with a plaintiff shrug—and then she turned back to Felix. She was about to try admonishing him into obedience, but then her thoughts turned to her father. Felix was a smart boy, but he was, what—8, 9 years old at most? He would be discovered if he stayed in the camp. A child contractor, in the hands of the witches, the wu...even the Ivory Dawn would want to pry into Klide secrets.

It was not lost on Eleanor that Xik had put her in this situation intentionally. Maybe he wanted to ensure her loyalty.

"Eleanor," John said, "we need to figure this out and keep moving."

Eleanor bit back a few choice swear words—words she was rapidly becoming more accustomed to—and nodded. "You can come with us." Felix's face lit up. Eleanor lifted a finger. "But only if!" She wagged it at him. "If! You do exactly what I say, when I say it. Do you understand?"

Felix nodded up and down rapidly.

"This is not what I meant when I said figure this out," John said.

"Do you have a better idea?"

"This isn't a field trip, dammit!" John hissed. "We can't drag around a kid while we're busy keeping ourselves alive."

"We don't have a choice," Eleanor said. "If we leave him...the mages will find him, eventually. They'll turn him into a test subject."

John sighed through his teeth and rubbed the back of his head. "I don't know..."

"I'm not letting the mages have him." Eleanor lifted Felix to his feet. "You stay close. Do not leave my side. We're going to a ship that Xik left us."

"That sounds awesome," Felix said.

"It sounds insane," John muttered.

"I'm not leaving him here," Eleanor said. "He's not going to be on the front lines anywhere."

John rolled his shoulders. "Fine. Have it your way. But for the record, this is damn stupid." He crouched next to Felix. "Piggyback ride, kid. Let's go."

"I don't want one."

"We're probably gonna run at some point," John said, "and I'm not holding up for those stubby little legs of yours."

"I don't want to," Felix whined.

John looked back at Felix. "You get the hell on my back before I whip your ass and toss you over my shoulder!"

Felix put the tablet to sleep and climbed up on John's back. The old man grunted as he lifted Felix up into the air. "Stop choking me, dammit. Hands lower. That's it. Hold on tight."

"It's easier to hold on to your neck, though," Felix said.

John fixed Eleanor with an iron glare. "Can we get on with this before the pipsqueak here gives me a cluster headache or something?"

"I'm not a pipswhatever," Felix said.

"Men," Eleanor said, rolling her eyes. "Stay quiet, Felix."

"He's the one making noise," Felix said.

"Shut up, kid."

"Enough, both of you," Eleanor said. "Now come on."

They made their way past the guard post and down the last hallway. The front door was in sight; she could see from the lack of light that the sun had set. They sidled past another sleeping guard. Eleanor reached for the door handle.

The door opened before she could touch it. Tamara stood there, hand on the knob, paused in mid-stride. They stared at each other, each side taking in the other.

Eleanor was the first to react. She shoved her magic out and swept both hands in an arc, blasting Tamara back with a blunt crescent of ice. "Run!" she shouted.

Eleanor roughly remembered the layout of the camp from earlier in the day. The trucks weren't far, past the potable water tanks on the right. Floodlights lit most of the camp, letting the soldiers continue their work into the night. She ducked into the space between the tanks and the outer fence bordering the camp, where it was darker. John was right on her heels, arms wrapped tight around Felix's legs.

Purple bolts of energy erupted through the tank ahead of them. The pressurized water blasted out in a wave. Eleanor's clothes were drenched in an instant, but before she could be swept off her feet, her magic was already working. She froze up a wall of ice, sealing the tank and stopping the flow. She used the excess ice and sent it flying in the direction that Tamara's magic had come from, hoping to catch her off guard.

They reached the edge of the tanks; a stretch of open ground sat in front of them. The trucks were up ahead—they could see one parking itself now, in row with a dozen others.

Looming above the end of the dirt lot was what looked like an alien spaceship straight out of a movie. The craft was made of sleek, silvery-green steel. It towered three or four stories tall, but was still longer than it was high. The ship tapered forward in the front, then rounded off, like a blunt teardrop. The single visible opening in the craft was a tiny porthole about halfway up the hull; a long ramp extended from it, down to the ground.

Lights were flashing near the trucks. Eleanor could hear shouts and see shadows moving in the distance. She pulsed her magic out in a wave, trying to get a sense for how many people were converging on them. There were a lot—mostly soldiers—but other pulses of magic answered her, other mages doing the same thing as she. Luckily, none were close except for Tamara, and they'd left her a bit behind after the last exchange.

A huge, thundering pulse erupted on the other side of the camp. *That would be father.*

"There's too much ground to the ship," John said. "We'll get ourselves shot!"

"No we won't!" Eleanor said. She raised her hands and ripped at the tank next to her, as if summoning a beast from beyond. The water tore out through the steel under her control, and it swirled around them. She solidified it into a half-sphere of ice between themselves and the rest of the camp. "Let's go!"

They broke into a sprint. Almost immediately, a hail of bullets flew at them from a small squad of four soldiers. The bullets sparked and pinged off Eleanor's ice shield, damaging it but not penetrating.

Eleanor made a fist and punched it toward the soldiers. Bits of ice broke off the good side of the shield and flew at them.

Before it reached them, she opened her hand and turned her wrist. The ice shattered into a cloud of snow swirling around the heads of the guards, into the neckline of their clothes and under their helmets. They fell into a panic as they swatted at the mini-blizzard harassing them.

"Nice one!" John said.

"You can compliment me later, run faster!"

"I'm not as young as I used to be!" John said, roughly hoisting Felix higher as he drooped too low on his back.

"That hurt!" Felix said.

"Shut up, kid!"

They reached the end of the trucks and broke for the ship, reaching the gangway in a few seconds. They clanged their way up the metal, not breaking their sprint.

Eleanor held her shield until they were up to the belly of the vessel. The entrance was dark, unlit. Eleanor took the last few steps facing the other way, waiting until John and Felix were well past her before turning inside.

A charged-up blast of purple energy caught Eleanor in the back, shattering her weakened shield and striking her directly. She was thrown against the opposite wall and hit the deck, hard. She groaned as she rolled over, pushing her magic to battle against the residual effects of the spell. It dug at her like little electric knives buzzing around her spine.

Tamara climbed into the ship behind her. "Sorry, Miss Astor," she said, "but it had to be done!"

There was a sharp click. Tamara froze as a revolver was placed up against the side of her head. "I'm sorry, too," John said. "But like you said...had to be done."

"John." Eleanor pulled her torso off the ground. "Don't hurt her. She's just doing her job."

John stood there, revolver cocked and set against Tamara's temple. Tamara's purple bolts hovered at her fingertips, still, but at the ready. Eleanor was on the ground on the other side of the deck, slowly gathering her magic as she forced the rest of Tamara's stun spell out of her.

"Alright," John said. "Hey, kid." Felix—who at some point, had dropped back to his feet—looked at John. Without taking his eyes from Tamara, John reached into his pocket with his free hand and pulled out his green stone. "You got one of these?"

"Yeah," Felix said. His eyes darted between them.

"You go up over to the front of this ship and start her up," John said. "You can do that, right? Fly the ship?"

Felix looked between them, obviously a little uncertain.

"Do as he says, Felix," Eleanor said. Felix nodded, then ducked away, footsteps echoing on the tile floor.

And then they stood there, each one facing the others, tense as a high-wire bridge.

"So," John said, "how we gonna do this, chili pepper?"

"My name," she hissed, "is Tamara."

"Hi Tamara," he said. "My name's John. Why don't you put your magic bullets away, and we can talk."

"Why don't you drop your gun and we can talk?"

"Nah. I found out what happens when I do that already."

"You've stooped this low, Miss Astor?" Tamara said. "Turning traitor? Using children as a shield?"

"You have no idea what you're talking about," Eleanor said.

"I've seen enough."

"Do not presume to lecture the person that is currently keeping you alive," Eleanor growled.

"You're working with contractors!" Tamara shouted. "Contractors! We're food to them, Miss Astor. They'll kill us to make themselves more powerful, he'll do it as soon as you turn your back!"

Eleanor's eyes looked between John and Tamara. "If that's how he really felt about it," she said, "he would have shot you already. Or he would've shot me. Or he wouldn't have given up his gun after we fought the Vorid. You don't want to do this."

"They're using you," Tamara said. Her expression was torn between anger and fear. "Don't you see that? You're being manipulated!"

"I don't have time to explain everything going on right now," Eleanor said. "There's more to the situation that I've learned that the rest of the Dawn doesn't know. My father is withholding information. The whole high council is."

Tamara's eyes were welling up. Her magic vibrated dangerously; her emotions were pushing it out of her control, to the point where she might hurt herself. "We all look up to you," Tamara said. "You're supposed to lead us when your father's gone!"

Eleanor's faced clenched up. "Tamara. Please. You have to let me—"

Lights flooded on around them. Eleanor blinked at the sudden glare. She heard a loud *oof!*—and Tamara was on the ground.

"What did you do?!" Eleanor said, scrambling to her feet.

"Relax, freezer pop. I pistol whipped her." John flipped his gun around and holstered it tight. "She'll feel it in the morning, but she'll live. You mage-types are made of tough stuff." John looked around at the neat white tile that lined the inside of the ship. The gangway started closing up. "Huh. Didn't actually expect the kid to figure it out. Good timing."

The ship rocked heavily. Eleanor caught herself on the wall; John fell to his knees. "The hell was that?" he said.

"That would be my father!" Eleanor shouted. A blast of something striking the ship made the floor vibrate. Eleanor could feel the rising tide of magic as her father started to build up for his next, even larger spell. "We need to get out of here!"

"I'll watch her!" John scrambled over to Tamara on his hands and knees. "Get to the kid and get us off the ground!"

Eleanor ducked down the way Felix had gone, deeper into the ship. The hall ended at a small pedestal on the floor. Eleanor stepped up to it, wondering if there was a ladder or ramp that would take her elsewhere.

She felt a small but strong jolt of magic under her feet, and then she was flying up through the air. Tile and white lighting flickered by.

Before she could get her bearings, she was slowing down, then stopped, brought level with the next deck—and in front of her was what looked distinctly like a bridge. Ten chairs were arranged in front of her in two rows; five in the front, sunk down below screens and displays; four behind those, in front of another set of displays; then one larger chair in the center.

Ahead of the chairs was either a one-way window, or a huge display showing the outside. Eleanor could see the camp below the ship; dozens of soldiers and a few mages were gathering around them. The soldiers hadn't fired on them yet, but the mages were preparing spells.

Felix was sitting in the command chair. His green stone was floating above a pedestal in front of it. "Felix, I'm taking over."

"I can fly it!" he said plaintively. "It's telling me how to do it."

Eleanor pointed her finger to one of the smaller chairs. "Out! Now!"

Felix shrank back, then hopped out of the main chair. As Eleanor seated herself, her stone flew out of her pocket and over to the pedestal. The green haze of energy grew brighter as it joined Felix's.

"Okay," she said, settling into the chair. "How do we do this?"

An electronic voice echoed in her mind. *Sensors indicate hostile spells imminent. Aggressors are targeted. Eliminate?*

"No!" Eleanor shouted. "No!"

Secondary recommendation, the voice replied. Its tone was chipper, but neutral. *Evasive action and defensive shields.*

"Shields!" Eleanor said, unconfident in her ability to pilot them out of the way. "Use the shields!"

Shields online, charging. 45% power.

A green haze enveloped the viewport, then vanished. The soldiers outside shifted nervously—they must have seen it as well. "Pssh," Felix said. "I could have done that."

"Felix," Eleanor said, "you promised you would do what I told you to do."

"I guess..." Denied his chance at piloting an alien spaceship, Felix looked like he was regretting it.

"Do you want to help us, or not?" Eleanor said.

"Yeah," Felix said, more quietly. "Sorry. I didn't mean to be a jerk about it."

Eleanor instantly felt a wave of guilt. "You weren't a jerk," she said. "But this isn't like school, or TV. It's not for fun. We're fighting, and I'm in command. So when I tell you to do something, you have to do it—not for me, but for everyone. And we can talk about it later, if you want, but right then, you must listen to what I say. Do you understand?"

Felix nodded. "I'll listen better, I promise."

Incoming energy mass. Shields concentrated on predicted target area.

A small screen appeared in front of her, like a computer monitor hanging in midair. It showed the back end of the ship—and her father, standing beneath a massive rising tide of water. He'd ripped open every single one of the water tanks. The water gathered into a raging storm of ice and raw mana, concentrated into a point like a massive spear.

Threat level: moderate.

The spell slammed into the ship. They rocked forward; Felix shouted, stopping himself from falling by grabbing her armrest.

Eleanor thought she would fall out of her chair, but an opposing force pressed on her waist and shoulders, holding her against it until the ship settled back onto the ground. Eleanor heaved a breath, but then something else struck from the front. The ship leaned back the other way, listing dangerously far.

"Felix!" Eleanor shouted. "Get in a chair, now!"

Felix clambered up into one of the other chairs; as he did so, his arms and legs were steered into position for him, until he was neatly seated in place.

Outside the front viewport, the mages had pooled their efforts, each one sending up a ray of lightning. They met in midair and combined into a concentrated stream of plasma that blasted toward the front of the ship. The green shielding worked against it, rippling under the forces, but holding steady.

Shields 38%. Sustained attack will rapidly drain energy reserves. Recommendation: evasive action.

"No, no!" Eleanor said. "I need to talk to them. Let me talk to my father!"

External communication line opened, the ship told her. *Speak to talk.*

"Father, stop!" she shouted. "It's me! Eleanor!"

The spells outside shifted. The burning line of plasma stopped short, melding into a liquid ball of heat that hovered above the mages' heads. It rotated slowly, a building dynamo of power that could be unleashed again at any time, connected to each mage by a line of gently crackling lightning. Her father's twisting blizzard continued to gather strength, but he held it in place.

"Eleanor!" came her father's voice. "Get out of that thing, now!"

"No," Eleanor said.

"Eleanor. Caroline. Astor!" Henry shouted. Even inside the confines of the ship, Eleanor could feel his anger roar over her like a cold blast of air. His spell responded to his emotions, and the giant spear of ice grew larger, snapping into a three-pronged trident that bristled with frozen spines. "I am beginning to lose my patience with you! Leave the ship, or I'll carve you out of it!"

"You know about the Vorid Prince," Eleanor said. "You know what the contractors are supposed to do to stop it."

"What?" Henry's face screwed up in confusion. His spell paused with his thoughts, quieting somewhat.

"Anchoring this dimension to stop the Vorid from attacking with their prince," Eleanor said. "That's what the contractors are for. That's why we needed Daniel!"

"We have other methods," Henry said. "We don't need the contractors."

"So you admit it!" Eleanor said. Her voice cracked. "You knew! You knew about this all before!"

"Xik is lying to you!" Henry said. "He's trying to turn you against us!"

"Well he's done a damn fine job then, because it worked! I'm a contractor now, too! So if you want to banish them all to Hell you'll have to do the same to me!"

Henry's spell stopped entirely. The wind halted; the spear hovered there, nearly the size of the ship itself, but its power started leaking away. Bits of frost and ice broke off from below it and fell like snow.

"What?" he said. "What did you say?"

"You heard me," Eleanor said. "I'm one of them, now. Xik made me one. But before you blame him, he's not the one that turned you against me. You are!"

"Eleanor, you can't," he said. "You can't do this. Come out of the ship. Talk to me!"

"It's already done," Eleanor hissed. "You put the fate of our entire planet at risk because you kept everything important hidden, because you couldn't stand the idea of contractor magic. We could have ended this before it started. Millions of people died because you did nothing! Hundreds of millions!"

"It's more complicated than that," Henry said.

"I don't care!" Eleanor shouted. "I'm not going to let everyone be eaten away while I'm holed up safe in some damn bunker somewhere. If you won't do what's right, then I will!"

"I won't let that happen!" Henry shouted.

"Go ahead then," Eleanor said. "Attack the ship."

Henry gestured with his hand. His spell restarted, gathering the power that had drifted away in the interim and reinforcing his spear. The ball of plasma opposite beamed into the ship, putting the shield back under duress.

Shields 33%, the ship said. *Recommendation: evasive action.*

"Fine!" Eleanor spat, deciding to trust the ship, or the computer, or whatever it was. "Get us out of here!"

Autopilot engaged, the computer said. The next part was louder—both in her head, and voiced over the intercom. *Main engines online. Liftoff imminent. Brace for movement.*

The ship leapt off the ground. The ray of plasma rocketed into her father's spear, and it exploded beneath them in a storm of steam and energy. The ship vibrated, heaving upward. Eleanor's backside left her chair before she was pushed back down. The shields plummeted to 17% percent, but held again.

After the brief jump, they rocketed into the sky; Eleanor blinked, and the trucks were gone, vanished from sight. She was forced down into her seat as they accelerated. Felix was shouting something; Eleanor couldn't hear him. Her face felt like someone had grabbed her cheeks and pulled her skin back.

Inertial compensators online.

The weight on Eleanor's chest lifted; she sat out of her chair and smoothed her hair back, then looked out the window. The camp became a tiny beehive of vehicles and brown tents, then shrunk into a blurry patch on the plains between highways. The airship patrolling the camp, *Higher Power*, was turning to follow them, but it was sluggish compared to their speed, and it was left behind as a shrinking pinprick a few seconds later. Then she could see Cleveland, and the Great Lakes.

They were still going up.

Calculating stable orbital course, the voice said. *Compensating for planetary satellites...course calculated. Entering orbit.*

Eleanor felt a tiny shift as the ship shot forward in addition to up. They were so high that the spiraling view outside was making her dizzy. She had a white-knuckle grip on the arms of her chair.

A *whoosh* from behind got her attention; she glanced back. John had arrived. "Did we get out of there alright?"

"Where's Tamara?"

"In the brig," John said. "Some little robot came and told me it would keep her secured. I just sorta went with it."

Eleanor sighed. "I feel like I've been doing too much of that lately."

John looked up and stepped forward. He whistled. "Would you look at that. Are we...is that Earth?"

Eleanor looked toward the windows. Her eyes widened.

North America was laid out underneath them like a piece of map stretched out over a massive globe. A blue-white haze marked the edge of the atmosphere, and beyond that was a dark, endless black, dotted with pinpricks of light.

Felix leapt up from his seat and punched the air. "This is the coolest thing ever! Daniel is gonna be major jealous!"

"What the hell did I get myself into?" John said.

"You can say that again," Eleanor muttered. She glanced into the black. The demilitarization of space never applied to mages; there were plenty of satellite-based weapons, and many airships could join them in orbit. Hopefully their Klide ship could conceal itself.

They stayed where they were, taking in the view as Felix jumped up and down on the deck. He ran around the ramps, past the lower row of chairs, then up to the middeck, then up to the column, then back down again.

"Kid's an energizer bunny," John said. "So what's the plan, freezer pop?"

"Do you come up with nicknames for everyone?" Eleanor asked.

A smile ran over John's face, only to be chased away by his usual scowl. "Only the ones I like. Or the good-looking ones."

"Don't get carried away."

John shrugged. "Eh, guess you're a little young for me anyway. Besides, I'm looking for a missus, not a brain freeze."

Eleanor sighed. Just what she needed, another comedian. "Here's the plan. We figure out how this ship works. Then, we find other contractors, like Xik said. And then…we hunt Vorid." Her eyes narrowed. "But first things first."

"First things first?" John said. "What could be more important than any of that?"

"Getting ahead of the narrative," Eleanor said. "Never let a good crisis go to waste." She pulled her cell phone out. "Let's hope this ship has WiFi."

Chapter 22
End of the Line

"Still no?"

"He won't give it over, boss," another voice said. It was heavier, deeper. One of the trolls. "He won't give it."

Daniel tried to say something back. It came out as a mumbled nothing, too weak for the words to form properly. His mouth tasted like rust, and flakes of the stuff were stuck in his gums. Dried blood.

"We've got enough for Rasputin. We'll edit out what we need to. Grab him and follow me."

Daniel felt himself lifted up. He groaned as broken pieces of his body shifted where they shouldn't go. Something wet hit the ground as he was jostled out of the room.

The magic was working on him already; his vision was improving quickly. Spots faded in and out as his eyeballs readjusted themselves. They'd put out his eyes altogether at one point, stabbed right into his face. It hadn't hurt as much as some of the other stuff they did—probably because he went unconscious almost immediately, that time.

He couldn't feel his toes, or his legs. He wasn't sure they were still there. The rolling, ugly sensation developing near his knees told him that whatever he had suffered was being undone, again.

Daniel felt a brief sensation of weightlessness, and then he slammed into the ground. A wave of pain wracked through him—but it wasn't any worse than what he was already feeling. Another drop in the ocean. He laid there, waiting. There wasn't anything else he could do.

And then he healed enough for the sensations to return in full.

He could hear himself crying, whimpering as his legs reformed themselves. His mouth shifted back where it was supposed to be. Out of habit, he started putting effort into spitting—bits of teeth, blood, crusted and wet. He pulled himself onto his elbows, away from where he'd been thrown, dragging himself away. He avoided looking at his legs. He didn't want to see what they looked like.

Daniel managed to get his head up. The dwarf stood there with a hand on the door, the trolls behind him. "Lucky for you we need that room back at some point, it's one we've paid in advance to keep off PrisonWatch camera. No hard feelings."

They went back inside, and the door shut with them.

Daniel lay there as his legs finished healing. He could move his toes again. He worked his jaw back and forward. It felt normal—something it hadn't felt in a while. He worked up some saliva and spat again.

He stared at the shut door the whole time.

Daniel felt something grip him. It pulled him up to his feet and sent him charging forward. He slammed his fists against the door, beat on it over and over. "FUCK YOU!" he bellowed at the top of his lungs. "YOU HEAR ME!" He kicked it, causing it to rattle in the frame. "FUCK. YOU!"

Daniel's hands slid down. He slumped against the door. And then he breathed, trying to reign himself and all the emotion back in. He wiped his sleeve across his face to clean it, but only smeared the blood and tears across his skin.

The anger, the emotion, it didn't accomplish anything. It didn't work for him. But he hadn't been able to take those words from a guy that sat there and ordered him beat to death.

Maybe that's how it was, in Hell. Everyone healed back eventually, so that level of violence wasn't unusual. Maybe the dwarf was desensitized to it; maybe they all were. But when he remembered the smiles on the trolls as they slammed their fists into him, over and over, his mind turned away from that train of thought.

Daniel stumbled his way out of the alley and onto the street. The crowd hustled and bustled this way and that, oblivious to his plight, or that anything had happened to him at all. He shouldered his way in.

The people in front of him started parting to avoid touching him; they had the look of people that spotted a cockroach. At first, he didn't understand—until he realized he was still covered in his own blood. His robe was in tatters; he had no hood anymore, no sleeves; holes dotted the chest, and it was cut off above his knees. It was the least of his concerns.

He glanced down the street; there was an enforcer standing near the entrance of a building. Daniel made his way over. He stood next to the machine, but the sense of exhaustion overtook him, and he slid down against the wall and sat on the ground. He put his hands around his knees.

The crowd went by. People—demons—entered and left the building. He got a few curious glances and a lot of sneers, but no one cared to stop. He blended into the wall behind him, a bloody smear washed out in all the brown dirt.

The enforcer stood quiet and still next to him. Despite the creepy eight legs and the red slit that crossed its face, the robot gave Daniel a certain sense of security, like one of those blue emergency lightposts on college campuses. He wouldn't be assaulted at random.

He should have known better. He shouldn't have followed Sulashoun inside, away from the enforcers—but the place appeared perfectly legit. And just like that, they had him, totally helpless.

Daniel reached over to his armlet. His hand was shaking, unsteady. He opened his inventory.

Sitting inside was a small golden orb. 25% of his magic for 5 minutes. It was still his.

He wasn't sure if it was worth it. He glanced at his armlet. At least they didn't take the thing away from him altogether.

Though he supposed they needed him to accept the trade, so they had no motivation to do so.

He checked the clock. The whole date was written out; apparently it was year 2552, Harkensolm-17, whatever that meant. It didn't translate for him any further. More importantly, about two and a half hours had passed since his phone call with Rasputin. It was almost audit time.

The thought boggled his mind. He'd only been inside roughly 2 hours. It felt as if half his life happened before he entered the building, and the other half was him inside that room.

Daniel stared at the street. He could hear sounds in his mind. The sounds. When he could barely feel the hits, the cuts, he could still hear it all—crunching. Bending. Snapping. He could hear it even when his hearing was gone, hear it happen inside himself, the way things turned dull and loud when you plugged your ears and could hear your heartbeat.

Daniel took a breath. *Get it together,* he thought to himself. *Head in the game. The fat lady hasn't sung yet.*

His next destination was likely the Crystal Mines. He tried to find some information on the audit process, but the help menu was vague, saying that he'd be forcibly moved. What kind of force was involved and how exactly he'd be moved were not specified. Daniel tried to hop onto the demon internet to get information, but he had no connection, and there were no public hotspots in the crypt. The internet Jack had in his apartment wasn't any good to him separated by several miles of solid rock—or however far away he was.

Jack.

Daniel didn't know what to believe. Their friendship had become awkward; maybe it really was on the rocks. But Daniel still thought things could be salvaged. Even if they went their separate ways, Jack didn't hate him—not like he'd said at the end, before Daniel went into the arena.

He'd looked so haggard when he was talking. Upset. It couldn't be that he was upset at Daniel; something else had happened. The way he said the words, the way he brought up Rachel—all of it—didn't add up. Something was just plain wrong.

If things didn't add up on that end, it might not mean that Rasputin was lying. Maybe Jack had lied to Rasputin. Not that Daniel trusted Rasputin, or anyone else now, for that matter.

The only person he could trust down here was himself. He knew that from the start. But seeing Jack again, trying to find comfort in restoring their friendship, caused him to let his guard down.

Daniel gambled everything on beating Bathory his first try. She had an answer to everything he was able to pull out. Even when all the tricks were taken off the table, she'd beaten him to a pulp with her bare hands. He caught her off guard a few times, but she'd controlled most of the battle. He shivered when he remembered the look on her face, reveling in the blood—his blood. *That was messed up. Everything down here is messed up.*

Daniel's face darkened. Even if he made it back to Purgatory, would a rematch do him any good? He had to take down more demons up there—absorb their powers. Get stronger. With enough magic, he might be able to fight her, blast his way to victory.

But how long would that take? How long would it even take him to climb back up, without a team, without money, with a bounty on his head?

He rubbed his forehead. So much had happened at once that he couldn't make sense of it all. He didn't know who or what to believe. His thoughts were scattered across a dozen different events and people, across what had been inflicted on him.

He needed help. Daniel thought of the one person that might do him some good—a certain green skinned alien—and even as he reached into his pocket, he could feel a green stone. Daniel lifted it up, and squeezed it in his hand.

Nothing happened.

Part of him hadn't expected anything. He wasn't worth anything to Xik locked away in Hell. Another part of him hoped against hope the Klide could bail him out—but Daniel still remembered the contract's terms. If he got himself in trouble locally—even if it was because he was a contractor—the Klide didn't have to assume any responsibility.

It still stung. Xik was slimy, shifty, but he wasn't evil. He didn't seem pitiless. But when Daniel most needed him, he didn't answer.

The more Daniel thought about it, the more it all seemed like the world had arranged itself against him. His friend had sold him down the river. Xik was nowhere to be found. Even Beelzebub hadn't contacted him since they first spoke.

Maybe he was a lost cause. One more fallen soldier in a much bigger war, forgotten at the bottom of Hell.

Daniel's armlet flashed red. An alert warned him that he'd be subject to audit in 1 minute unless he paid his 10-point fee.

Without anything better to do, he waited out the clock, trying to stay inconspicuous. At this point, he didn't have a choice. Time to ride the bus into the station.

Almost immediately after the alert closed, the enforcer reached down for him. Daniel threw himself backward, avoiding the metallic hand. The enforcer looked at him with its glowing red slit-eyes. "Attention inmate. You are being audited. Do not resist removal."

Another enforcer down the road grabbed at a passerby who was trying to run. He wasn't as quick as Daniel, and the metallic hand snatched him around the waist. The troll screamed and scrambled to get free. Runes lit up on the enforcer's body, flashed white, and the troll was gone.

Daniel swallowed as the enforcer's hand came down. He tensed up as metal fingers closed around him. The grip was surprisingly gentle, and it didn't lift him into the air—probably because it didn't have to stop him escaping. The enforcer's lights lit up, signaling that it was charging power for the spell.

Daniel braced himself as the teleportation spell activated. Light flashed, burning his eyes even though they were closed, and he was gone.

****

Daniel's arrival in the Crystal Mines was less dramatic than the crypt—no slide, no enforcer waiting for him. Rather, it reminded him of Purgatory, somewhat scaled down; he stood on a flat stone dais. Unlike purgatory's bustling main square, the dais was in the middle of what appeared to be a field of snow. He lifted his head, and his eyes tracked up, and out.

Soaring cliffs of blue-violet crystal defined the skyline—not that there was a sky. The cliffs went up, up—until the light ran out, and he couldn't see any further. Lower down, the light bounced off the shining surfaces, allowing him to peer an incredible distance. It was as if he was looking up from the bottom of the Grand Canyon, but the canyon was made of violet-blue sapphires, and the sky was made of darkness.

Connecting either side were great soaring walkways and bridges, some made of stone, or crystal; a few were wood. He could see people—workers—traveling along tiny ledges, in and out of distant caves, small as ants below the titanic walls. Most looked like they were pulling or pushing cargo of some kind. Flickering blue lights dotted the pathways, giving it all a ghostly cerulean hue.

Below the heights of the work area was a snow-covered town, a hub for the nest of walkways and roads leading out and away into the caverns. Another road, beaten flat from the ice and snow around it, led from the town and to the platform on which Daniel stood.

"Robe!" someone called. "Nothing on his armlet."

"Take him."

Daniel turned—on his left was a half circle of demons, partly surrounding the dais. Before he could react, his arms were snatched from behind.

Daniel twisted away, but a blow caught him on the back of the head. He went slack, vision spinning in circles as his feet tried and failed to get purchase. He was dragged over the ice to where the group waited at a flat slab of rock.

"Try that again," a voice behind him said, "and I'll bash your skull in, you get me?"

"Pull his head up," another voice said.

Daniel felt a hand grab his hair and drag him upright. He blinked at his captors. There were demons of all kinds—devils, goblins, undines. One harpy. They were wrapped in warm furs or thick cotton clothing.

A smaller group of four demons knelt on the right. They all had the uniform brown robes of the crypt, and they were shivering in the snow—obviously not dressed well enough for the weather. There was a colored imprint next to each of them, as if someone threw food coloring dye across the snow. One splotch was purple; another was orange; two of the others were red.

A sound washed over them, reverberating through the walls of the cavern. Daniel cocked his ears as it echoed around them, then faded. It sounded almost mechanical, like the pieces of a giant machine locking into place far in the distance. None of the demons were surprised by it.

The goblin stepped forward and seized Daniel's chin, wrenching his gaze up. "This one looks bloodied up, don't he?"

Daniel got a foot under himself and kicked the bastard, forcing the warty hand off his skin. The goblin stumbled back a bit, coughed, and straightened. "Looks like we got a wild one here. Barna."

A blow slammed into the back of Daniel's head. The dizziness swam back stronger; his limbs felt loose, numb. "Les' go of me," he managed.

"And it's a *human*," the goblin said. He glanced at the undine.

"Not an illusion," that demon said. "Bonafide human." There was concerned mumbling from several people behind him.

"Any word about this?" the goblin asked.

Daniel tried to focus to talk his way through this, but his tongue just flapped uselessly. The hold on him kept his armlet wrenched above his head, well out of his easy reach. The harpy walked over to the goblin and bent to whisper something. The goblin nodded, then gestured to the stone table. "Get his arm taken care of. This one is a permanent guest."

Daniel was dragged over to the slab. He could feel a bit of the magic working on him, healing the injury on the back of his head, but he couldn't get his arms to move the way he wanted. As he was dragged closer to the slab, he could see colors—orange, purple, red again, staining the slab. Dried on it.

Daniel tried to struggle when he saw the machete drawn from inside the coat of one of the trolls holding him down. He threw his legs out, shifted side to side. A devil walked over and stabbed its needle-claws straight into Daniel's stomach.

He clenched up. Gasping sounds came from his throat.

Daniel's arm was pulled straight. They pinned it over the slab. The blade fell, and his arm fell to the ground, taking his armlet with it.

Daniel tried to scream, but the sounds couldn't get past the wound in his stomach. His body convulsed as the pain gnawed at him.

They threw him into the snow next to the others. The magic went to work on him, healing and rebuilding his arm from scratch. He shivered as he felt his skeleton cracking and shifting; his flesh itched as it crawled over that scaffold and reformed, tendons, muscle and eventually fresh skin.

Daniel's breathing steadied as the pain subsided. He glanced at his arm—reformed—and tried moving it. Good as new. As he tried to get to his feet, a blade slipped in front of his neck. "Sure you want to try that?" came a rough voice from behind him.

Daniel swallowed. His skin pressed up uncomfortably against the edge of the blade as his Adam's apple moved up, then back down.

He was in the middle of unknown territory at the bottom of Hell, and—as usual—surrounded by torturous psychopaths. One of whom had a hand on his shoulder and was threatening to cut his throat. Daniel stopped trying to stand and stayed where he was.

The troll bound his hands behind his back. Daniel glanced over, trying to see what they were doing with his former arm—and more importantly, his armlet. Behind the stone slab was a small crate holding a pile of the things; the goblin slid his armlet off the severed limb and into the crate, not bothering to check it or take his item out of it.

There was a red stain in the snow next to him, now. His blood. The other colors were from the demons that didn't have red blood.

A light flashed, and a new demon arrived where Daniel had been a short time before. "Robe!" one of the trolls called out.

The process repeated itself, and this time, Daniel watched as what had been done to him was done to another. The three demons moved with the coordinated precision of people that had repeated the same work many times over. In short order, the demon was kneeling with the rest of them, a shivering, bleeding hulk that slowly had its arm regrown by Hell's healing magic. His armlet was deposited with the others.

The distant sound came again—a heavy, metallic *ker-chunk* that Daniel could feel in his chest. A trickle of snow fell from a ledge high up on a cliff as the canyon walls shifted ever-so-slightly.

Daniel glanced at the demons near him. "What is that?" he whispered.

One of the other bound demons—a goblin—glanced back at him. "Gears," it said, in a low voice. "The Hell seal. It's below us."

"Stinking human," another demon muttered. "Don't know anything about anything."

"Human?" said another voice. The devil at the front of the group, who had been staring down at the snow, turned and looked back. His black pupils met Daniel, and he smiled that shark-toothed grin the red-skinned creatures all shared. "Well, well. I didn't think I'd be seeing you again. What luck."

Daniel didn't recognize him at first—they all looked similar to him—but the words clued him in. This was the same devil that he'd competed against in his first challenge in Hell, the one that tried to attack him right after they made it to Purgatory—Zelunix.

"Luck," Daniel said, looking at him, "is not the word I'd use right now."

"Really?" Zelunix tapped at his throat—the demon chuckle. "I feel like the luckiest demon in Hell." The tapping at his throat turned into a full-on series of slaps as he *laughed* harder; a dull, hollow noise that drifted over the group even as another demon was dragged over to be butchered. And as that demon was dismembered, he laughed louder still. The sound echoed off the ice and rock, like a finger flicking on a used-up tube of cardboard. Dull, empty.

Daniel stared out over the canyon. He didn't feel cold, even though the others were shivering.

He fully understood how bad things were, in that moment. He quietly appreciated it all from a distance, as if withdrawn from himself. He didn't even feel the slightest bit upset anymore.

He didn't feel anything at all.

Epilogue

Several miles north of the Astor manor in upstate New York, the Ivory Dawn had just finished final preparations to open a full portal to the demon world. It was one of five that were being constructed across the world, gateways to allow the demon army onto Earth.

The portal was constructed according to Beelzebub's specifications, a steel-and-stone archway with a 127 foot radius. The arch soared above the surrounding forest, a lone monolith in the middle of an isolated clearing. A huge ruby was perched at the pinnacle, large enough that, standing on the ground, Henry could clearly see the red gleam of sunlight filtering through the gem.

Despite the towering height, the arch was only a foot thick. The weight of the stone would have caused it to collapse if it wasn't supported by magic. It stood on two mighty foundation stones, each studded with mana crystals, mirror images of one another.

The site was chosen for very particular reasons—close to where they thought the Vorid would strike, but far enough away from the refugee camps for them to feel safe. They'd detected dimensional shifts near the lingering, silent fortress still floating above New York City. The Ivory Dawn had dug in most of their forces around it, as it was highly suspect as a launching point for another strike from the Vorid. The demons would shore up those defenses, allowing them to keep the Vorid pinned down away from the general population.

Henry would've preferred to build the thing at the North Pole, but the cost of teleporting in the materials would've become even more burdensome.

Unlike a summoning—in which a mage helped a specific demon create a physical projection of themselves on Earth—the portal would allow the demons to come in the flesh, bringing advanced magics and technology with them. There were plenty of spells capable of banishing projections, but there was no way to quickly rid themselves of the demons once they'd crossed through the portal. To say it was unusual to allow the demons to simply walk in on a scale like this was the understatement of a millennia. The week prior, the largest portal Henry had ever seen was fifteen feet tall, embedded deep in a top-secret, high-security facility underneath a nuclear missile silo in Nebraska and guarded day and night by their best men.

Henry toured the outside of the foundation, helping with the final checks. The other magicians gave him space, letting him work in peace. His eyes scanned the sigils carved in the stone as he checked and re-checked where they linked with those on the foundation and then focused in around the mana crystals. At times, he would approach, touch his hand against the stone, and test a small stream of mana, watching it flow through the runes; then, satisfied, step away to another portion.

Once the portal activated, the space would be permanently tied open; they wouldn't need to continually provide it with energy. There was, however, a second set of mana crystals, quietly buried under the foundation. Those could be used to untie the space and shut the portal, should they feel the need to do so.

That would only help, though, if they could keep control of it.

He glanced up to the sky, seeking comfort in what he knew was there. Three of their airships were present, patrolling in steady circles like dark thunderclouds. Two of the three were their oldest, and most powerful, traditional airships. The third was the experimental airship, the *IVD Methuselah 138*. They'd poured tremendous resources into it, having crossed a bristlecone pine with a sequoia to produce its living core. The child tree-core, while sterile, married the weight and strength of a redwood with the longevity and tenacity of the bristlecone. The nature of the tree itself was directly proportional to its potential in powering the airship's functions, both in and out of battle, and the Methuselah had proven a fantastic success. In particular, it was equipped with the state of the art technology allowing them to monitor for Vorid incursions.

The Vorid were not the only thing to be defended against. The demons were allies of the moment at best, and the war effort had set off a magical arms race across the globe. Even as the strongest factions positioned themselves to fight the Vorid, they wanted to remain at advantage when the fighting was over.

As Henry rounded the foundation for the fifth time, he realized he was stalling. The runes were fine; the sigils were perfect. He was merely hesitating on the trigger.

He heaved out a breath, and his expression firmed. Xik had stolen his daughter from him—and in so doing made his stance perfectly clear. This was a necessary evil, one they'd deal with after the Vorid. The Ivory Dawn weren't the only group taking on the risk of a portal, and for that, at least, they could count on their rivals to help.

Henry made his way back to the waiting mages. There were ten thousand men encamped around the portal—mostly mundane military—alongside five hundred of the Ivory Dawn, crowded against the tree line, ready to receive the enemy of their enemy. Gerald Aiken was at their head, looking at him expectantly. "It's ready," Henry said. "Activate the formation."

Gerald turned, raising his hands as a signal. Five magicians began to chant, leading a group of 50 mages in each segment of the formation. One of the chanters was Eleanor's betrothed, Matthew; traditionally, leading any formation was considered a position of honor, and Henry had no problem giving them a sense of appreciation that cost him nothing.

Those not chanting drew a sigil in the air, each a single link in the massive formation. Typically, mages would be responsible for maintaining four or five sigils in a formation, but this brooked no mistakes. The other 250 mages were the backup if something went wrong, ready to step in to support anyone who faltered or work together as a group to bring rampant energies back under control. Gerald stood behind his son, nodding in approval as Matthew picked his way through the enunciation of the words.

Their preparation proved unnecessary. The spell hummed along smoothly, frighteningly smoothly, without any of the nastiness or messy sacrifice one might imagine creating a portal to the demon world might entail. In fact, the spell was remarkable in how little resources it used—a detail that grew more frightening the longer one thought about it. Beelzebub was very old and possessed a tremendous amount of very dangerous knowledge—especially concerning spells that shouldn't be cast.

The foundation stones began to glow. The light increased in intensity as the spell built to completion, focused in on the mana crystals; they shone with various colors matching their affinity, some white, others blue, red, black, green. Henry watched, unblinking.

The foundation stones went dark, and the collected energy lanced up each side of the arch in a wave of multicolored lightning. The sigils carved into the stone lit up as the wave of energy crackled past. Upon reaching the top, the waves of energy struck the ruby from either side, discharging into the gem.

A beam of red light shot down from the ruby and into the ground, holding steady as a laser. The glowing sigils flashed from white to solid red, washing out the light of day until it seemed the entire forest was painted in blood. The ground vibrated under their feet. The magicians held steady, but the mundane soldiers shifted and stirred, casting worried looks at the trees and the archway.

The laser of red light rotated, spinning a single circle within the confines of the arch. It was that action which twisted space together, linking their location with a matching one in the demon capital city, Dis.

As the light turned, the view of the forest behind the arch vanished, replaced by a view into a facility comparable to a massive hangar. Squared-off legions of demon soldiers lined the interior of the building, organized by race—goblins, ogres, devils, undines, and grazul, to name a few. Hovering tanks and smaller support vehicles were present between the larger squares of infantry. What Henry suspected were small aircraft lined the outer walls of the hangar, no doubt to be wheeled in after the infantry.

As the red haze of the formation faded away, Henry had a better view of the front row. Standing near the portal's edge was a small collection of demons of various races, each decked in gleaming armor and medals—the leaders and generals. Henry stepped forward with his own contingent from the Ivory Dawn's high council, squaring his soldiers and mentally preparing himself to receive them. The first impression was going to be important. It was no secret that humanity had fallen behind the development of Beelzebub's empire—to what extent, they weren't quite sure—but Henry was determined to demonstrate that the Ivory Dawn would not be trifled with, if push came to shove.

A fully transformed dragon emerged from the shadows at the top of the hangar and swooped through the portal. It was massive, at least twice the size of any dragon Henry had ever seen, the tips of its wings nearly touching the sides of the archway. Its scales shimmered bright purple in the light.

It roared down at the mundane military. Some soldiers flinched or cringed away from the beast, but most stood firm, probably too awed by the proceedings to process the fear. The dragon snorted smoke in their direction, then took off above the trees, buzzing one of the airships. It hovered there a moment, craning a neck to get its bearings, before flying southeast—the direction of the city.

"Are they trying to scare us?" Matthew said. "They'll have to do better than cheap intimidation tactics."

Gerald shrugged. "We're asking them for help. A little showboating is expected."

"That was a test," Henry said. "We can't let it pass unchallenged."

"They'll accuse us of nitpicking inflexibility, no doubt," Gerald said.

"Better we're perceived as inflexible than weak."

"True enough."

The other demons walked through the portal. The view rippled slightly at their passing, as if they were emerging from a pool of water. Henry made for the demon in front—a devil, judging from the white horns protruding from his helmet and the black nails jutting from the ends of his gauntlets. The rest of him was covered head-to-toe in jet black armor, spiked and beveled enough that he looked like a soldier of death. He wore none of the decoration or medals like the other demons.

As they closed the gap, Henry saw that the armor was streaked through with gold in a few places. A brief magical scan—all he could do while still being polite—sent his senses practically vibrating.

"Henry," Gerald said, keeping his voice hushed.

"I know," Henry said. "Orichalcum."

"That much in one place is worth more than five New Yorks." Henry was very much aware, considering his family still owned a good portion of the city. "Nothing written about Asmodeus mentioned this armor."

Henry shook his head in agreement, but withheld further comment. They couldn't whisper amongst themselves all the way to their counterparts.

Both groups stopped several feet apart. The armored demon stepped in, leading with a hand. Henry took it. The black armor was as cold as it looked.

After they shook, the devil waved a hand; an orange sigil flashed over his group, then disappeared. Henry was able to catch enough to recognize it as a basic translation spell.

"I apologize," the devil said. The words creaked out from his helmet, reluctant, but in perfect English. "For the behavior of my general, Varnifax." He gestured up to the dragon, now a shrinking dot in the sky. "He tends to get...enthusiastic."

It didn't sound like the demon was happy about it, but Henry was pleasantly surprised for the public acknowledgement. "We were certainly a little surprised," Henry said, "but I won't be upset about someone enthusiastic to take on the Vorid."

"Give him time," the devil said. "He ages like sour milk."

Henry smiled at that. "I'm Henry Astor, leader of the Ivory Dawn. Welcome to Earth."

"I'm Asmodeus," the devil said, "commander of the military." Henry noted that Asmodeus did not need to specify which military. "Are we clear to move in our troops?"

"There's space allotted, we're ready when you are."

Asmodeus turned and signaled to the demons through the portal. The troops began their march forward. The incoming column of soldiers—though otherworldly—actually seemed to help the mundanes gather themselves, following the stunned aftermath of the magical lightshow and raging dragon. People usually did better when given something to do.

Henry gestured to the encampment in the trees, and Asmodeus fell into step beside him. Their respective generals and leaders began to introduce themselves in murmured conversation behind them. "What's the situation?" Asmodeus asked, his tone all business.

"The Vorid are located in New York City, about 35 miles southeast," Henry said. "This location is our main strategic headquarters and planned fallback point if we lose the city. We've determined that the Vorid likely plan to attack from New York; they seemed determined to make that their initial foothold in the United States. It has our highest population density, and we believe they'll take advantage of the equipment they've left behind. We haven't been able to co-opt it."

"I'll have my people take a look. Maybe we can make something of it."

"That would be appreciated."

"Beelzebub," Asmodeus said, "mentioned a need to extend your capability to detect dimensional shifts, especially on the ground." His helmet cocked back slightly so he could take in the airships. "I have additional sensors arranged for all five portals. We should be able to get that up and running within the day."

"Excellent," Henry said. "We're confident we have the worst threats walled off for the time being, but I'd rather be absolutely certain."

"How goes the contractor situation?" Asmodeus said.

"We've rounded up quite a few following them being recently targeted by the Vorid," Henry said, "but reports suggest there are 40 or so still at large in North America. As many as 300 worldwide."

"Xikanthus has been busy," Asmodeus said.

"Yes," Henry said, fighting to unclench his jaw. "He has at that."

As they approached the trees, the magicians made way, doing their best to avoiding staring. A few guards waved their hands, activating control mechanisms for formations embedded in the forest floor. The trees in front of them rose up on their roots and swam through the earth, parting to reveal a long hallway of boughs and branches with the military encampment at the other end. The trees pushed back until the forest was clear almost fifty feet across, wide enough for the incoming soldiers to pass with their vehicles.

They continued to talk as they walked, Henry outlining more details for Asmodeus. As they reached the encampment, Nickolas approached from one side before stopping to press his fist to his heart and bowing slightly. "President Astor—news from your daughter."

Gerald flinched slightly at that; Matthew's ears perked up. Henry made a show of sighing, then turned to Asmodeus. "Excuse me a moment. Family politics."

Asmodeus nodded. "Take your time. We can go over the rest later—plenty on our plates for now."

Henry left Gerald and the others to deal with the coordination of the troops while he joined Nickolas in his personal tent. They both cast spells to ensure privacy before Henry spoke. "Have you been able to track the ship?"

"No," Nickolas said. "I have bad news. We won't be able to keep her escape under wraps much longer, especially not from Gerald."

"What happened?" Henry said.

"She's posting videos," Nickolas said. "Online."

"She's doing what?!"

****

The core of Hell was a machine, but it was unlike anything Xik had seen in person.

Klide technology was, as a rule, strictly directed. It was a meeting of material and magic, driven by formations, calculations, and pre-planned programming—sometimes incredibly complex programming—but never acting with autonomy. Early experiments revealed the dangers of magical spells that could function without outside input. Artificial intelligence given magical authority was a recipe for disaster, and the Klide had outlawed it. The Vorid sometimes edged near such things with their biological constructs, but spawn, for example, lacked the ability or intelligence to develop further on their own.

This wasn't like those things.

The core was at the bottom of a canyon of ice and darkness, the walls of which stretched up farther than he could see. Massive gears loomed into the icy dark, rotating in a slow chain reaction. When the largest few shifted, the sound of the cogs striking home rolled down the canyon like thunder.

Those behemoths were connected to smaller gears, shafts, screws, and pistons, which linked into the intricate nuance of the machine inside the building. That inner portion, both outside and inside the structure proper, was a fractal division of what lay outside, halving in size with each repetition—16 times by Xik's count. Eventually, the gears and screws became a miniaturized version of their larger cousins, packed in by the hundreds around a rotating core.

The core was a clear cylinder, six inches tall and two wide. It housed a soft white light that shifted and bubbled like a ball of plasma. The nature of the light proved unknowable to him, even with his current level of resources. Perhaps a team of scientists with diagnostic equipment and a hefty energy budget would have better results, but Xik wasn't about to acquire any of that in the middle of an active Vorid attack. Every single piece of the machine was painstakingly carved with runes following the fractal pattern. On some pieces, the runes were so small that Xik needed a magnifying glass to properly study them. But that wasn't the most remarkable thing.

The most remarkable thing was that it all kept changing.

Periodically, the light in the core would pulse, sending a wave of energy out and over the machine. When the light washed over the gears, the runes would shift—sometimes just ever so slightly—with little pinpricks of magic that flickered with different colors. Those shifts would replicate themselves back up the machine, all the way to the huge diagrams dug into the largest gears. Sometimes the shifts happened in rapid succession, multiple times a minute. Sometimes there were entire days with no changes at all. No single pattern ever repeated itself.

He stood in front of the core, having personally witnessed another change a few minutes ago. He couldn't spend all his time down here, so he'd long since set up surveillance to track it. Even then, he'd only been able to reasonably follow a portion of the machine's workings.

Careful analysis forced him to conclude that it was a self-perpetuating spell with the ability to change itself. He wasn't sure if it was alive or not, but if it wasn't intelligent, then it might carry the possibility of becoming so in the future. There was no active intelligence guiding the spell, artificial or otherwise. Rather, it was as if the spell itself was alive, subsisting entirely on its own devices to accomplish a distant and inscrutable goal. In this, it was unique.

Xik wasn't entirely sure what it was for, but he was certain it wasn't built for the sake of the prison. He determined that the Hell seal was, in fact, maintained by the machine, but that seemed to occupy only a tiny part of its function, which was the same portion Xik spent most of his time studying.

Those studies revealed sigil patterns and calculations that bore a striking resemblance to Klide contractor magic. He focused his efforts there, looking for a way it could be manipulated, but there was nothing—no hints at verbal commands, gestures, or input sigils; no place to insert reagents;

not even a lever to pull. It was as if it was incapable of accepting outside input.

His efforts to free Daniel—and other contractors—had proved fruitless. Selectively prying them away from the seal would be like trying to remove a single thread from a tapestry in the middle of a thunderstorm while on a small fishing boat out at sea, with only his bare hands and a pair of pliers.

He'd quickly given up on the notion. He was here for another reason. His surveillance had caught a hint of something else—someone else. He'd been wanting to meet this person for some time, but she'd proved elusive, even for him.

And so he waited, standing on a walkway that wrapped around the front of the core, hoping that if he showed himself in the open, she would come to him.

He wasn't disappointed.

"What do you want, outsider?"

Xik turned. Standing a third of the way around the platform was a man with light purple skin, dressed in an unadorned brown robe, cinched at the waist by a roughspun rope. He was entirely bald. His arms were folded, and his forehead was layered with frown lines—lines being put to good use.

Xik noted his ears, in particular; they jutted sharp from his head, ending in a tapered point. *So this is an elf.*

"Allow me to introduce myself," Xik said. He swept his hat off his head and bowed. "Xikanthus Vol'mund Dovian pom'Nafalstra, at your service."

"I care neither for titles nor obsequious self-introductions," the elf said. "I'm only here to determine what you want and then ask you to leave. Promptly."

Xik blinked at his biting tone, but decided to take it in stride. He didn't want to put them off now that they'd finally reached out. *In a manner of speaking.* "I've been studying the spell here"—Xik tapped the railing that separated the platform from the whirring gears of the machine—"to try and find a way to free a few prisoners. It isn't going well. I was hoping to speak with its creator about the matter."

"The Lady is resting," the elf said. "She doesn't have time for slithering schemers such as yourself."

"Surely, if we work together," Xikanthus said, "we could figure out how to release you, and her, as well?"

"You needn't concern yourself with the prison, outsider," the elf said. "We have our own plans in place. We don't need your help."

"If that's so, then why is she resting? Perhaps overtaxed in attempting to enact those plans?"

The elf's eyes sharpened. He unfolded his arms; his body tensed like a jungle cat ready to pounce. Xik felt a sense of dread wash over him, an almost physical doom that pressed down on his shoulders.

Xik drew on his source to fend off the pressure and stood straight. For a moment, the elf's aura caused him to bend his knees.

"I only made a simple observation," Xik said.

"I've finished entertaining your speculations," the elf said. "This is your last chance to leave."

"Peace, Malachi," came a female voice from behind the elf.

The elf—Malachi—fell from his tensed stance. He folded his arms at his waist and bowed his head. "Forgive my temper, my Lady. The outsider insulted you."

"His ignorance is no offense to me," she said. She sounded soft as silk; her words drifted like snow. "I will speak with him. Alone."

Malachi closed his eyes in acknowledgement. "By your leave." He straightened, and—throwing one more glare at Xik—made his way around the platform and down a stair on the other side of the machine.

The Lady in question drifted out from the center of the construct, emerging from the gears like a ghost. Her hair and skin were bleached white, almost as white as her dress. Her bare feet alighted on the platform without sound. Her eyes met Xik's gaze; she had red eyes, and red lips, the only parts of her that held color.

"Here I am," she said simply.

"I have the honor of speaking with the prisoner of Hell?"

"We're all prisoners," she said. "Of one thing or another. You've come to tell me about the Vorid."

"You know of them," Xik stated, more than asked.

"I do," she said. "You want your contractors back. Those sealed here by the magicians."

"Do you know why I need them?"

"Yes," she said. "You need to continue to pit them against one another, against the magicians, the demons. You need to nourish the chaos from which you hope your weapons will emerge. You want Daniel to be one of those weapons. Beelzebub. My peers, here. Me." She looked away from him, toward the machine, examining the whirling gears. "You need enough stepping stones for someone to climb in order to stand taller than the Vorid."

"The people of your worlds have to be made strong enough to defend themselves," Xik said.

"And you have fomented conflict to that end," she said. "Those two boys were right to suspect you, but in his innocence, Daniel has failed to convert many of his suspicions to action." She faced him. "Now that you know what I know, what would you have with me?"

"I want to help Daniel, in particular," Xik said. "But I can't influence this spell without doing tremendous damage."

"I doubt you could harm it."

"Don't underestimate the Klide."

"Don't underestimate me," she said. "I have decided to incorporate Daniel into my plans. The Vorid are helping me, in a way. Time will tell if your greater strategy works out for you."

"Can't we come to a more particular sort of arrangement?" Xik asked.

"If you want to play politics, you are welcome to speak further with Beelzebub," she said. "I have already made my arrangements. If you want Daniel freed, then when the time is right, return here. It may not be necessary, but I want your hand at the ready alongside my peerage—just in case." She looked at him. "In exchange for that assistance, I will ensure that Daniel realizes his full potential. Isn't that what you really want? A weapon?"

"I thought I'd take a more direct route," Xik said, gesturing to the machine, "and figure out how to work this device. Put it to use against the Vorid. Try as I might, I haven't gotten very far on that front. There seems to be a missing component."

Xik swore he detected the barest hint of a smile at the edge of her lips. "Oh? And what might that be?"

"Some way to actually use the device. An activation mechanism."

"Perhaps it's best," she said, "that no one uses it."

"If now isn't the time for such things to be used," Xik said, "then when is?"

She waved a hand in front of her, palm down. "I will say no more on the matter. Will you aid us at the moment of need?"

Xik thought for a moment. "How will I know when I'm needed?"

"You'll know," she said. "When it's time, everyone in our worlds will hear my Longinus."

At her words, the largest gears shifted. The rolling drum of the cogs pounded down the canyon walls and into the building, reverberating inside the machine's housing. Xik cocked his head to listen; it echoed for half a minute until the sound finally faded.

When he looked back at the platform, she was gone.

I wonder if that's how they feel when I do it.

Xik scryed briefly, but he couldn't sense the presence of either her or the elf. Or any other *peers*, as she'd termed them.

As Xik began to shift himself elsewhere, he couldn't help but smile. Beelzebub was convinced that humans were weak, but they were full of all sorts of surprises.

Acknowledgements

Over five years later and we have come to the end of the sequel of the original Contractor. Rest assured I will not leave the story to languish again. Thank you, dedicated fans, for sticking through the long and silent doldrums. I will do my best not to disappoint you.

This book was, more than any other narrative I have ever put to paper, completely re-written. The first iteration was only a skeleton of the finished and much better final product. In that sense it was something I had never done before, in that the editing was lengthier and more difficult than the actual writing. For those transforming improvements both to this book and to my writing skills I have to thank again my returning editors and beta readers: my mother, my older sister Ashley, and my best of friends Scott.

I would also like to especially thank Gareth Otton for his amazing work on the cover art for Prisoner. He has since authored his own fiction series and I happily recommend you to his works both as a writer (http://gareth-otton.com/) and as a graphic designer (https://www.thechunkydesigner.com/).

About the Author

Andrew Stephen Ball is an indie author and pharmacist. He is a graduate of Rensselaer Polytechnic Institute and the Massachusetts College of Pharmacy and Health Sciences. He lives and works with his fiancé, a nurse, in New Hampshire. He's been a lifelong fantasy and science fiction enthusiast. He does not trust people who don't like chocolate.

White chocolate doesn't count.

Connect with me:

Stay updated on Andrew and The Contractors book series at his official Facebook Page:
https://www.facebook.com/pages/Andrew-S-Ball/1515164785382499

Professional Inquiries? Detailed feedback? Typos? Questions? Rants? Email me here:
andrew.s.ball01@gmail.com

Novels by Andrew S. Ball

The Contractors
Contractor
Prisoner
Untitled (2022)

####

Following is a short excerpt from the upcoming sequel to Prisoner:

####

Daniel's mind swam in a dim half-wakefulness.

The first thing he felt was how damn uncomfortable he was. His body ached at every point it touched the hardpacked dirt—the heel of his foot, his hip, shoulder, elbow, and on his head, above the temple. It ached like someone had taken a hammer and steadily tapped at those bits of him, all night long, not enough to wake him but plenty to ensure they were bruised and tender.

He shifted, slightly—and his foot struck someone else. He withdrew it, cringing back from the contact, but a grunt and a snore was all the feedback he received. He sighed, then relaxed, turning over in place to swap those contact points to the other side of his body. They ached almost as badly. He'd tossed plenty of times in his sleep.

At least he wasn't cold. Everyone else—sleeping head-to-toe, shoulder-to-shoulder on the dirt floor around him—seemed to be constantly shivering.

Daniel blinked his eyes a few times, giving his surroundings a bleary but cautious once-over. His immediate neighbor was, thankfully, an undine. He'd ended up beside a troll the day before, and the smell alone was enough to keep him up half the night. The smells were starting to fade, though. Three straight days of sweat, grime, piss, and body odor would murder anyone's sense of smell.

There were no blankets, no beds, no pillows, and no privacy. Well, except for the one corner, where the members of the gang assigned to his tunnel slept, but Daniel kept as far from them as possible. The rest of the place was a low-roofed, ice-walled shack with a hole dug in one corner for the ugly business. His tunnel mates at least had the decency to keep the number two buried under the scraps of ice and rock they could find, but the dried urine was, unfortunately, as pervasive as the snores.

Daniel closed his eyes to it all, trying for a few more scant snatches of sleep—something that came hard to him already, being a contractor—but he couldn't ignore his stomach. It gurgled, growled, clenched. It felt like he had a cramp in his abdomen, and the lingering sting of heartburn sat in his throat. He hadn't eaten in three days. His stomach had gone on strike from the lack of food, and, without a solid paycheck, settled on eating itself.

Only the slaver cabal—Mining Group 3—ate well down here, normal food brought down from higher levels of Hell. The gang members ate better, too, being not quite Group members but their unofficial muscle—simple fare like bread, soups that actually had spices, occasional bits of meat. The miners—slaves by any other name—got a bland, mushy gruel, if they were lucky enough to bring in enough of a haul to afford PrisonWatch's draconian price schemes. And if the gang didn't skim too much in exchange for avoiding a beating. And if the Mining Group's taxes didn't take what was left.

A cruel but practical mind might argue that well-fed slaves did a better job with less hassle, but the harsh conditions of the Crystal Mines didn't impact productivity. Or, maybe they did, and the Group just didn't care. Hell's magic kept you alive, with or without food, but it didn't take away the hunger. The hunger gnawed at them, all of them, and it was fiercer motivation than the sting of a whip.

That being said, whips applied liberally. Daniel had been whipped on his first day—well, not so much whipped at beaten with wooden rods. He'd been slow to wake up, not used to the schedule, but he felt he'd been picked on for being the new guy in his unit. It was a reminder to the rest that the hunger didn't have to be the end of it if they acted out.

Daniel didn't linger on the memory, because his mouth was watering at the thought of food, of eating something, anything. He swallowed down tasteless saliva as his thoughts drifted to the lasagna he'd made for himself and Jack. There'd been so much left, all wrapped in foil and tucked away in Jack's fridge. He'd suck Rasputin's dick for a bite of that lasagna.

A sharp whistle jolted him from his reverie and the demons around him from his sleep. He bolted upright, then scrambled to his feet, hopping in line with the others who were just as quick to get up. The demons pressed around him as they made for the entrance of the long sleeping quarters. The gang members were already at the doors, rods and truncheons in hand, shouting and swearing at the passing miners.

"Let's go, let's go! Like you give a damn!"

"Get those feet moving! PrisonWatch ain't keeping the tunnels open all day!"

"Come on, don't slow everyone down! Move it!"

"First one back with a crystal gets half fees today! Word comes straight from the Group!"

There were some murmurs at that, exchanged glances. Daniel felt his motivation draw as tight as a stone sliding down a steel blade. Half fees meant that, with the right mana crystal, you could get enough points to eat well for a week. In practice, you'd have to share with the gang. They could just beat you and take everything if you didn't. But all said, it was a lot better than not eating.

Daniel kept his head low as he went out the entrance. After the first day, he wanted to keep a low profile. He got shoved between a minotaur and the icy wall of the shack on the way out; he turned sideways to squeeze out onto the open path.

Daniel broke free of the press of bodies. Just as he was past the doors, a rod fell flat on his shoulder. Daniel froze.

"Hey there, human." Daniel's eyes followed the rod up to the blood-red hand holding it, then up to the devil that was grinning at him. His teeth were crowded into points like a shark; his face was flat, except for a twisted, ribbed patch of flesh where a nose should be. A huge, mottle-skinned orc stood at his shoulder, patting a truncheon in its open palm.

"Settling in alright?" the devil asked. "Any complaints about the accommodations?" Daniel shook his head. "Oh, that's good. Good. You seem quiet, though. I remember you saying something about ugly faces and ripped off noses a few days ago."

"Yeah, man," Daniel said. He edged back from the rod, letting it slide off his shoulder. "Those undines, ugly fish-faced jerks. Sardine smell. Yuck."

The devil let Daniel slide off for the first moment, then lifted the rod and jammed the tip at Daniel's face, catching his cheek. Daniel couldn't move back because of the rush of bodies behind him. The devil pushed the rod in, stretching his mouth into a lopsided smirk.

"Wow. What a joker. You oughta smile more." The devil pushed the rod harder, until Daniel's teeth were aching from it pressing into his face. "Come on. Smile."

"Kinda busy sucking on your pole," Daniel said, words muffled by the rod that was jammed in his face.

"The laughs just keep rolling with you. Keep 'em coming, I got all day."

Daniel, seeing an opening in the crowd, batted away the rod and ducked across the path. He pitched his voice, shrieking above the sound of footsteps and morning chatter. "I know you have a human fetish, but your tiny tool doesn't do anything for me! It could never work between us!"

The other demons—miners and gang members—that had been not-so-subtly watching the show burst into laughter. The orc bawled in big, heaving growls, patting its oversized belly. The devil snarled at the surrounding miners. "The hell are you all looking at? Get down there before I make you!" That cut off the laughter quickly. Daniel heard the devil's voice echoing over them. "You'll be back around later, human, and we'll see how hard you're laughing then!"

Daniel slowed his jog back to a steady trot when he saw the devil wasn't making any move to go after him. He'd moved back to the front of the pack, now, heading down the path out from the town and toward the cliffs, and their tunnel.

The devil's words rung in his ears. Daniel would return to the shack later that day—or whatever passed for time in this place, with no sun to tell. He had nowhere else to go. He'd probably pay for the smartass performance several times over.

But it was worth the price. He'd been beaten quite a few times since coming down to Hell. What was one more beating? He had to keep himself sane, somehow.

There was a darkness lingering in the back of his mind. Bitterness over how he'd fallen, a thirst for something with a sharper edge than simple justice—cold vengeance and punishing recompense. But below that shallow, moment-to-moment anger, there was something worse; a slinking, creeping despair, waiting to swallow him whole as soon as he let it.

With all else stripped away, at least he could still crack a joke. His pathetic attempts at humoring himself prodded at the darkness like a starving man poked a bear to steal a lick of honey. It was a fool's errand, his likely reward swift disembowelment, but it was the only game in town.

But despite the hunger, the pain in his joints, and the looming threat of an afternoon beating, Daniel had a skip in his step he'd lacked the past two days. He'd worked hard yesterday, and he was confident his efforts were going to pay off—just in time to get half off his taxes. Today—definitely, positively today—was going to be the day he brought home a mana crystal.

Printed in Great Britain
by Amazon